QUEEN OF THE DAMNED

THE COMPLETE COLLECTION

USA TODAY BESTSELLING AUTHOR

KEL CARPENTER

LUCIFER'S DAUGHTER

To my tribe, for putting up with me.

CHAPTER ONE

Hell must have frozen over.

That's it. The only possible excuse for why Kendall Clackson, our resident Bible fanatic, was strutting through my favorite diner on a Saturday morning. She usually saved her shenanigans for earlier in the week, on days I didn't have off. Coincidence? Not likely.

I froze in my spot and considered bailing, but that thought only lasted about half a second before her smug face made me stomp across the diner and settle into my usual booth.

Fuck it. I've done the same thing every day for the last ten years. I'm not changing now.

Swinging my legs into the booth, I didn't even pick up the menu as Little Miss Georgia Peach approached me with all her southern charm.

"Ruby! What a pleasure seein' you here, hun."

I turned fractionally and nodded once, hoping she would get the hint. If there was anything that Kendall didn't understand, it was how insufferable I found her exaggerated southern accent to be. We lived in Portland for devil's sake.

"I hope you weren't comin' here lookin' for Josh. He's playin' golf with some of the other men in our church. Bless him. Found his way to the Lord through me."

I could barely contain rolling my eyes. *Oh, yes. I'm sure he did. Just as soon as you gave him what I wouldn't.* I snorted to myself, but didn't say anything. Kendall made it her job to remind me, and everyone else, that he had left me for her and God.

"What's so funny? You know, Ruby, you should find a church. It might help with your"— she dropped her voice low—*"issues."* Several regulars threw us curious, and somewhat scathing glances. It was an unspoken rule with us Saturday folks that you kept to yourself and didn't start trouble. Like Kendall was currently doing.

"Issues?" I asked, pretending to be mildly surprised by her comment. I knew damn well what she meant. I had a bit of a temper, but in my defense, there's only so much you can do when you're half-demon.

I waved down Martha on the other side of the diner, and she took one look at Blondie before rolling her eyes. Yeah, this wasn't the first time this had happened, but clearly, *I'm* the one with issues.

"You know, your anger—"

"What can I get for you this morning, Ruby?" Martha asked, appearing beside Kendall and seeming not to notice her at all.

"Black coffee and four orders of bacon, please," I said, not bothering to look at the menu.

Martha chuckled under her breath. "I'm not even sure why I ask anymore," she muttered as she walked away.

Kendall resumed her preaching, knowing full well her advice was unwanted. "You know, Ruby, you really should lay off the fat if you ever want to find a nice Christian man."

Something like heat prickled inside me, but I clamped down on it hard. Kendall could pick at me all she wanted. I knew it wasn't actually me she was angry with. It was my cheating ex-boyfriend that wouldn't leave *me* alone, despite my repeated attempts to send him away. It wasn't unreasonable that she was pissed with him. It was unreasonable that she stalked *me* for it, and made *my* life hell. Particularly, when she was the one he had cheated on me with in the first place. Yet, somehow, she didn't see the irony in all of this.

"Hmmmm…let me think about that. Bacon or church? Bacon or church? Well, it's really a no brainer, Kendall. I'm atheist, so I think I better go with the bacon," I said, smirking at the way her mouth popped open. I did enjoy riling her up. What could I say? I have a penchant for trouble.

"Is that Satan talkin,' or just your jealousy, Ruby? You should've known that Josh would find his way to our Lord, with or without you."

This was too much. I couldn't hold back my laughter and I failed miserably when I tried to disguise it as a cough. "Kendall, I hate to be the bearer of bad news, but we split up because he fucked you in a broom closet, and unless 'God' is what you call your vagina nowadays, I think you're fooling yourself." I gave her my most mocking of smiles and made a shooing motion with my hand. Even beneath the orange of her spray tan, I could see her face reddening. She thought she could come here, in my sacred space, and offend me. Slander me and throw my break up out there for everyone to see. She thought it would embarrass me. What she failed to see was that I didn't care. Josh was someone to pass time with, and his dick got the better of him. As a half-succubus, it wasn't my nature to believe in love. Not when the "heart" could be swayed by a pretty face and a three minute fuck.

Kendall's anger seemed to intensify. She put on a saccharine smile as Martha came around the corner carrying my bacon and coffee, but I didn't miss the look in her eyes.

"Bless your heart," she sneered, turning on her heel. I breathed a sigh of relief, but it was a second too early. Her foot came out and caught Martha's black sneaker before I could say anything. Next thing I knew, heat flamed my chest as the coffee splashed across my maroon sweater. It wouldn't burn me, but she didn't know that.

Martha caught herself, but the damage was already done. My bacon lay on the table, soaking in a puddle of coffee that was dripping into my lap.

Her white apron and yellow shirt smeared with grease and coffee, Martha spluttered, "I'm so sorry about that, Ruby! Can I—"

"It's okay, Martha," I said, glaring at Kendall. The bitch had returned to her seat where three other Stepfords sat, each blonde and almost impossible to tell apart. They wore the same impossibly pleasant smiles with their impossibly perfect makeup. Kendall had strength in numbers and gave me a little wave for show as she took her seat.

I. Saw. Red.

Standing from my seat, I hastily helped Martha clean up the mess. She kept repeating to me: "She's not worth it, Ruby." Not that it mattered. Someone needed to teach Ms. Upstanding Citizen a lesson. This was the third time she'd tried to corner me this week, and while it was funny playing with her, what she just did was unacceptable. Not that I deserved any of this, but Martha certainly did not. She wasn't even involved. Kendall could fuck with me all she wanted, but dragging Martha into this and nearly hurting her crossed the line of bullshit I was willing to take. It was time for her to reap the consequences for being a shitty human being.

I placed a ten on the table and left the diner without another word. The door jingled as it swung shut behind me, and I turned my eyes on Kendall's baby blue Mustang.

A fit of glee came over me as my inner demon smiled. I went to my car and grabbed the baseball bat and a lighter I kept in the driver's side door.

Josh should have warned you what happens when you play with fire.

CHAPTER TWO

"You broke the windows and set her car on fire. It blew up. How do you deny that when we have twenty-eight—no, I'm sorry—twenty-nine witnesses that saw you?" The officer leaned back in his seat, rolling his eyes. The cops picked me up half an hour after I did it, and dragged me back to their cesspool of a police station. Joe-Schmo and I had been going back and forth for the last fifteen minutes as he attempted to persuade me to admit guilt and pay for Kendall's car. Not fucking happening. At least not without a fight.

"They could be lying." I shrugged, leaning back in my own chair and kicking my feet up on the table. My boots clunked against the metal top as bits of mud and grass fell off. They hadn't even bothered to handcuff me when I was arrested, but I wasn't exactly new to this. Me and Joe were on a first name basis. Practically.

"Get your damn shoes off the table, Morningstar," he scolded. Guess we're on a last name basis today. "This isn't a resort. You're in for a lot of fucking trouble if she decides to press charges." Joe swatted at my feet and I pulled them off the table, leaving dirty streaks across the reflective surface.

"I'm not afraid of Kendall. She got what was coming to her," I huffed, crossing my arms over my chest. Joe let out a sigh of exasperation and scratched his head.

"You're not making my job easy, Ruby," he said.

"Where's the fun in that?" I asked, giving him a wink. The man had a pretty average build for any American man over forty who spent a lot of time at his desk and interrogating low priority criminals. It was the same stereotypical build all the movies portrayed: tucked in shirt with a too small belt, neither hiding the spilling beer gut. With his less than impressive physique, developing widow's peak, and crooked nose from being broken one-time too many—Joe was one hundred percent human. He was also the only officer that didn't spend his entire interrogation undressing me with his eyes.

"We're not supposed to be having fun. You're supposed to admit to your crime and try to settle before she calls her lawyer. Why do you always make this difficult? Huh? What's the point when we both know you'll pay the fine?" A sharp knock at the door interrupted his questioning. The chair scraped the tile as Joe scooted back and got to his feet. I listened intently as the second officer leaned over and told him my bail had been paid, taking his leisure of watching me while I cocked an eyebrow and snorted. His tongue flicked out, licking his bottom lip.

Not a chance, buddy. I smirked to myself as Joe turned back to me, oblivious to the silent encounter I had with the pervy officer.

"You're in luck. Someone paid your bail," Joe said, giving a sad shake of his head. To his credit, he just doesn't know what to do with me. I was more than most humans could handle. We demons were fickle creatures.

"Looks like Moira did get my message after all," I said. Moira was half-banshee and she happened to be my best friend. She hadn't picked up when I called, but I knew she'd come through before I was in here too long. She always did.

"Uh-huh," Joe said, sticking his tongue in the side of his cheek like he had more to say. The officer who delivered the message pulled the door open for me to cross and exit. His body wasn't huge, but he was stocky, and he purposely gave me no space to step through. Taking a deep breath, I shuffled by, "accidentally" elbowing him in the gut as I went. The putrid stench of alcohol and body odor made me gag.

On the other side of the door, I walked down the hall and signed the release papers. Until Kendall officially pressed charges, there wasn't a lot that could be done. I knew she would. And I would have to pay her, because as fun as this was, I had no intentions of sitting in jail any longer than necessary. I had no regrets, though. The look on Kendall's face when she saw the flames was priceless. Pure fucking gold. Moira was going to love this.

I pushed the door open and waved goodbye to the boys in blue. Outside the air smelled fresh. Crisp. The scent of rain still hung in the air. I stretched languidly, the way a cat does after sitting for far too long. I needed to do something. Burn off the energy that never seemed to leave.

I turned to tell Moira as much, but my friend wasn't the one lounging against the side of the police station. A black-haired devil with smoldering eyes stood where she usually waited. His hair was a color so dark, his skin looked ashen. When his amber eyes flicked to mine, I was suddenly very aware of the coffee stains on my clothes.

Keep it together, Ruby. There was nothing human in his fluid grace as he pulled away from the wall and began stalking toward me. Demon. And not a weak one, by the looks of it.

"Who are you?" I asked, narrowing my eyes.

"I just bailed you out of jail. Is that any way to greet me?" His voice dripped with arrogance. Maybe it was the designer suit he wore, or maybe he was just as powerful as I suspected. Either way, I didn't like the tone in his voice.

"I don't know who you are, so unless you start talking, we're done here." I crossed my arms over my chest and stared him down. His lips fell into an easy smirk. I knew that look. That sarcastic smile meant to belittle and demean a girl, expecting me to feel intimidated.

The words *kiss my ass* were only a breath away.

"My name is Allistair." He took another step forward as he spoke; his voice smooth and melodic, dark and captivating. It was bewitching. It was what an incubus did when pulling in their prey.

"I don't appreciate you trying to persuade me. That's rude, you know." Even as I said it, he cocked his head and took a step closer.

"You sensed that? Here I thought I was being subtle," he purred. Something in me said I should run. Not because I thought he would hurt me, which he would, but because the air tasted like something foreign and heady. His scent clung to me; tendrils of power reaching to pull me closer. He was quite strong, and if he touched me…

I needed to get out of here.

There was a reason I avoided demon men like the plague. Anything and everything this side of the Columbia River were drawn to me by a force I couldn't control. With demon men, it was so much stronger, and they were never the types to just let me run.

Oh, no. They would chase, and even as fast as I was, they would catch up.

"What do you want?" I asked, and to my credit, my voice didn't shake. He looked me up and down and my face heated.

"I need you to come with me, Ruby." The way he said my name made my stomach clench.

"How do you know my name?" I asked, looking towards the street as a car screeched around the corner. Moira's beat up, old Camry hit the curb and came to a jarring stop.

"I'll tell you if you get a drink with me," he said. His eyes flicked to the car and narrowed as I inched towards it.

"I'm good. Thanks, though," I said to the amber-eyed stranger as I got in. Moira didn't say anything as we started to drive away.

I looked in the passenger side mirror to see if the demon was following, but he wasn't. Allistair, if that was his name, was standing right where I left him, clearly pissed off. He took a step in our direction, and even with a parking lot of distance, it made me shiver. Something told me this wasn't the last I would be seeing of him.

****ALLISTAIR****

It was like she felt nothing at all.

She certainly gave no indication she knew who I was.

I cursed under my breath and walked towards my car. The sleek, black Audi R8 was the only thing that had brought me joy in the nearly twenty-three years I waited to see her again.

But she didn't remember me.

The thought sent a spike of adrenaline to my system, but the feeling wasn't welcome. All it made me want to do was fuck, or fight. I ran a hand through my hair as I climbed into the car. There was no point waiting around for a girl that wasn't coming back.

I fired up the engine and sat as it purred to life. The steady rhythm usually calmed the instinct to chase a female. Ruby wasn't an ordinary she-demon though, and this wasn't about sex.

I mentally sought out the only one of the three that I thought could do this without fucking it up even more.

"Rysten."

I pulled out of the parking lot and turned onto the highway. I wasn't going back to the penthouse just to report how poorly that went. That I fucked up the one thing I was supposed to be able to do.

"How did it go, mate?"

Anger coiled around my pathetic excuse for a heart.

"Your turn." It was the only answer I could give him as I floored it onto the interstate. My fingers flexed against the steering wheel.

"You want to talk about it?"

I rolled my eyes. He's been spending far too much time with humans if he thought I would want to talk about that.

"Just do your job. I'll be back tomorrow." I weaved through cars as I exited the city, wanting nothing more than to turn around and go back to the girl.

But she had no idea who I was.

Or what she meant to me.

To all of us.

This was the way it was supposed to be, but I don't think any of us were prepared for what we would find when we came for her.

CHAPTER THREE

WHEN I ARRIVED at Blue Ruby Ink the next afternoon, Moira gave me a once over and shook her head, dark green hair falling forward. "You must be feeling paranoid," she said.

"Why do you say that?" I placed the two coffees and paper bag on the counter. She continued to stare at my shoulder where Bandit was perched, staring down at the case of belly button rings, rubbing his little paws together.

"You brought the trash panda," she smirked. Bandit jumped onto the glass case, his grabby hands already looking for the fastest way in. I tapped him on the shoulder and wiggled my finger back and forth. He took the hint and wrapped his arms around my neck, hanging there like the big baby he was.

"He's not a trash panda. He's a raccoon," I argued, putting an arm around him. Most people called me crazy for having a raccoon when the majority of pet owners had dogs or cats. Something normal. I didn't want a dog or a cat. I didn't really want any pets until one day I found a baby raccoon following me home from work. He's been with me the two years since—and better trained than most people's children. Apart from the occasional biting problem. But kids do that, too, right?

Moira shrugged and kicked out the barstool next to her. Blue Ruby Ink was the tattoo parlor we'd opened together right after she graduated college at Portland State. I handled tattoos and piercings while she handled all our bills, appointments, and balanced the books.

"So…you want to talk about what happened yesterday?" she asked, flipping through her planner. I settled back onto the barstool next to her and took a sip of my coffee. Strong and black, just the way I liked it.

"Not much to say. Kendall started some shit, so I set her car on fire." Even thinking about it had me smirking. I wasn't sorry I did it, even if I had to pay for a new car. She's had it coming for the last month or so, and it felt damn good to repay some of the hate.

"Not that. The guy in the parking lot."

I gave her a sideways look, but she kept her eyes on the planner. "Just some guy who paid my bail and wanted to take me out for a drink."

"The hell? Just some *guy* that *paid* your bail? What'd you say?" she prodded. Subtle, she was not.

"No, of course." I opened the paper bag and took a huge bite of my double chocolate chip muffin. Calorie counting was for suckers. You only live one life, may as well eat your way through it—least that was my take on it.

"Still staying away from men?"

"Can you blame me?"

She frowned at her planner. "No, but I worry about what will happen to you," she murmured. I opened my mouth to dispute that, right as the front door chimed.

"How can we help you?" she asked, still not looking up. Too bad for her because there was quite a bit to see.

"I have a consultation with Ruby," he said. I was pretty sure I was staring at a blonde Adonis because there was no possible way his face could be any more handsome. His full lips quirked up at me and I scrambled to stop my staring.

"Name?" Moira asked, flipping back and forth in her planner. I bit at the corner of my thumbnail and ran my hand along Bandit's fur in a nervous gesture.

"Rysten."

"I don't have a Rysten listed," she said, only then taking the time to look up. He would only see her glamor, beautifully neutral cedar skin that masked her true mint green color. I could see through it, watching her cheeks as they tinged pistachio: the tell-tale signs of a banshee's blush, but she didn't seem affected by his presence otherwise. Unlike me. My traitorous pasty white cheeks that turned red under the barest hint of sun, or in this case, blush.

"I'm certain I booked one. Can you check again?" he asked. His eyes never left me, and while he seemed polite and good-natured enough…so was the demon outside the police station.

Moira switched from her planner to the desktop, pulling up my schedule. In the top right corner, first appointment of the day, it said *Rysten*. She stared at the computer silently, blinking three times.

"That wasn't there yesterday," she said matter-o-factly.

"I can assure you that I booked in advance," he said. He sounded amused. With what, I didn't know.

"How far in advance?" she pressed. I sighed, getting up from my barstool to swing open the gate and escort him back to my office.

"Several months. I'll only be in town a short time," he continued, either not noticing her narrowed eyes and twitchy pen, or simply not caring. Moira took her schedules very seriously. She could be nonchalant about picking me up from jail or setting cars on fire, but fuck with her schedule and you'll be dealing with a screaming banshee. I was not willing to sacrifice my eardrums.

"Moira, it's fine. I can take him back and do a consultation. It will only be fifteen minutes," I said, trying to ease the tension. She hissed under her breath.

"It's not about the consultation." Turning to him, she snapped, "What brings you here when you won't be in town long?" I put my palm to my forehead and ran it down my face, sighing in my frustration. I wouldn't say that she's ordinarily sweet to people, because she definitely had some crazy in her, but she wasn't usually this aggressive. When she sniffed trouble, she was a demon through and through.

Rysten took one look at her and smiled, like she was a hissing kitten and not someone that could burst his eardrums in seconds. "I'm here for Ruby," he said, turning his dark emerald eyes on me. The intensity was startling. I took a step back. "Your tattoos are all the rage where I'm from. I knew I needed to check them out for myself," he amended, giving me a boyish grin.

"Right," I drawled out. The awkward silence hung for a moment before I motioned for him to follow me back. Moira opened her mouth to object, but I beat her to the punch. "It's fifteen minutes. Please, just let it go. I could use the extra cash to pay for Kendall's car."

She glared at me and crossed her arms. "Fine. If you're late for your next client, it's on you." I conceded with a nod and closed my office door behind me.

Alone with Rysten, I settled behind my desk and leaned back in my chair, crossing my hands in a steeple under my chin. "So, is this the part where you tell me why I have a demon in my office, asking for a tattoo you don't actually want?"

Across from me, Rysten blinked, his eyes sharpening. The glamor surrounding him pulsed for a moment, but settled back to its nearly undetectable state. He was good; I'll give him that. Nearly as good as Moira was at hiding her green skin. His body had the slightest sheen over it; not a physical glamor. A psychic one.

"Clever girl. What gave me away?" he asked, that lazy smile reappeared like it never left his face. He may look like he just walked off a beach, but that carefree façade wouldn't fool me. Demons were not easy-going creatures by nature. The fact that he glamored himself meant he had something to hide.

I quirked my lips up in a neutral smile. "I can't reveal all my cards, can I? I still don't know why you're here." I wasn't weak, but I was nothing exceptional. I'd yet to come into my powers, if I ever would, and without any real gifts to speak of, it tended to make other, stronger demons view you as prey. It didn't help that the only true power I had was the fact that anything and everything with a dick wanted me. Whether I wanted them or not. Best not to piss anyone off too much until I knew what I was dealing with.

"I already told you why I was here, love," he said kindly. I frowned and scratched behind Bandit's ears to busy my hands. "I'm here for you."

"I'd gathered that much. What I don't know is *why*."

"I'm afraid I can't tell you that just yet," Rysten replied apologetically. "I wanted to get to know you first. Before the others got involved." He rolled his eyes in a very human gesture of annoyance.

"Others?"

"I can't explain that either. They wish to do it together," he answered, shrugging off my attitude. He was infuriating. Yet another reason to stay away.

"Wait…does this have anything to do with the creeper waiting outside the police station last night?" I probably could have been less demanding about it, but it was too strange not to overlook the possibility.

Rysten snorted. "Allistair?" I nodded once. "I look forward to relaying that message to him." Damn it. They knew each other. This was not coincidence, but I didn't get the feeling it had anything to do with them looking to dominate me. Our kind were not subtle in their endeavors, and if that's what they wanted, I think this conversation would be going very differently.

Bandit purred against my chest, clutching me tighter. I glanced down to see his tail was swaying side to side. He was either happy…or agitated. I was hoping happy because dealing with a biting raccoon was not high on the list of shit I felt like dealing with today.

Rysten eyed him, wrinkling his nose, he said, "I have to ask. Why do you have a raccoon?"

I pursed my lips at the mild disgust in his voice. "Why does anyone have a pet?" I asked. It was rhetorical, but he cocked his head like he was seriously considering my question.

"I suppose companionship. It's the only real reason I could see anyone taking in a wild animal." It was both a thoughtful, and yet, a very typical demon outlook. We had the capacity to understand, but not to empathize with most things. My bond with Bandit was abnormal, but I just chalked it up to the half-human in me and left it at that. "He seems quite fond of you," Rysten noted.

"He is."

We locked eyes, a world of silent questions swimming before us. I really wanted to know what the hell he was doing here, but he seemed to be content just watching me and evading my question. "You're not what I expected," he said eventually. I tilted my head, raising an eyebrow. Before I could ask, there was a knock on my door.

"Your first client is here," Moira called. I tapped Bandit's shoulder signaling for him to jump down. He scurried across the floor and up the massive cat tower I kept in my office for when I brought him to work. Most people weren't too fond of raccoons, and he wasn't too fond of most people.

Rysten stood, and I walked around the desk to open the door. My hand stilled on the door knob as I faced him. I was prepared to ask him once again why he was here, maybe even add a little persuasion to the mix in hopes of getting a real answer, but something in his eyes had me frozen to the spot. My mouth went dry at the intensity I found: so very similar to the demon from last night, and yet different. Allistair had a roughness, and an air of danger that edged that dominance. I had no doubts that there was more to the incubus than the cold arrogance he exuded.

Rysten had a different feel. His power was offset with curiosity, like I was the enigma he couldn't figure out. His glamor was still in place; he'd yet to drop it once. There was a flux of something behind it; almost like a ripple of power that he was struggling to contain.

What kind of demon are you?

He reached forward, his fingers only inches from my face, and a knock at the door brought the moment to an abrupt halt.

His hand dropped to his side, a boyish smile lighting his face again as the tension dissipated. I opened the door and stepped through.

"I'll see you again soon, Ruby," he murmured. I turned around to say goodbye, but he was already gone. His words hung in the air, a promise that had my skin heating with anticipation.

I was so royally fucked, and I didn't even know why.

I don't know what I was expecting after Allistair passed the torch to me, but she wasn't it.

She was warier than I thought she'd be. Cynical. Sarcastic.

I could see why his nature would rub her the wrong way.

She was fiercely independent, that much was clear. She wasn't going to like being told what to do, and given that she had no idea who we were, this wasn't going to go as planned.

The girl I just met was not going to drop everything and come with us. She had a life; albeit an odd one given that she kept vermin as a pet.

Not to mention the receptionist.

The banshee was suspicious. She knew I hadn't booked that appointment. That was going to be problematic. I hooked a left on the corner and stopped inside the first coffee shop I found. Ordering a medium roast with two sugars, I then took a seat by the window and mentally reached out to Julian.

"We need to talk." He was not going to like this, but what were we going to do? Forcibly remove her? No. This needed to be handled with tact; something my brother didn't have.

"I'm meeting with Allistair. What is it?" he replied. I sincerely hoped Allistair had told him how the original meeting went down, or he might try to throttle me.

"I've met with Ruby. We need to have a dis—"

"What do you mean 'you've met with her'?"

Well. That answered that. Pouting fucker hadn't thought to notify him when things went south. *"Speak with Allistair. Come find me when you are done. I'm changing the plan."* I could sense a brief surge of anger before his mind pulled away.

I sipped at my coffee, savoring the bitter burn.

We had her. She was right here.

Except the moment she looked at me and called me on my glamor, I knew we were in trouble.

There was spark of the devil behind her eyes and she doesn't even realize it.

CHAPTER FOUR

THE AFTERNOON PASSED in a blur as I thought about Rysten's parting words: *soon*. That could mean a lot of things, and I was pretty sure our next encounter would not be alone. He mentioned that there were…*others*. Including the one I already met. The thought sent shivers running down my spine.

"Moira!" I called, and she poked her head around my office door. "My schedule is clear, yeah? I'm going to leave for the night. Feeling a little under the weather." It wasn't a complete lie. I really was feeling strange, just not of the sickly variety.

Moira narrowed her seafoam green eyes. "Wouldn't have anything to do with that guy from this morning, would it?" she asked.

Nosy banshee.

"Why would it have anything to do with him?" I asked, as good a non-answer as I could get. I didn't like lying to her, but I was in no position to handle an interrogation right now.

"You've been acting weird since he left."

Weird. That was one way to put it. I was freaked the fuck out. I had no idea what was going on, but I didn't want to bring it up to her. It was one thing for me to worry when Rysten, and probably Allistair, would show back up for devil knows what. It was an entirely different thing to be calming Moira in that process. She was possessive. She'd hunt them down if she thought they meant to do me harm.

No. Until I knew what they wanted, I wasn't involving her.

I lifted the corners of my mouth in a tired smile and went to retrieve Bandit from his hidey-hole in the cat tower. He practically sprang at me, locking his arms around my neck like a sloth in a tree. "Bandit's been feeling a bit antsy today. I thought getting him out of the house would help, but it's not." I shrugged and turned for the door, hoping that was enough to satisfy her. As far as non-lie-lies go, it was golden. Moira's eyes flicked to him and softened, just a little. Inwardly, I snickered. She could call him a trash panda all she wanted, but I knew the truth. He'd grown on her.

"Get him a can of sardines. He'll be fine," she said indifferently. Bandit started chittering at the mention of his favorite little fish. Damned raccoon. Food was always the number one priority. Now he'd be yapping in my ear the whole way home.

I grabbed my purse off the desk and headed out. "I'll see you at home. Don't forget to lock up." She shooed us out with a hard look and wave of her pen.

Outside, the cool October air hit me full force, my teeth chattering as my breath fogged white. Bandit curled tighter around me, swinging his tail around my neck like a scarf. Crossing my arms to keep warm, I clutched my purse tighter as I cut down the alleyway that led to the parking lot. The ominous Cimmerian skies were heavy with rain waiting to fall. I trudged on through the grey bleakness, jumping when a large rat scurried past me and into the sewer drain.

My breath came in hot, heavy bursts as I stopped. Paranoia was eating at the edge of my already frazzled mind. I took a hazard glance behind me, just to soothe my beating heart.

Click.

The wrong end of Glock 19 pressed against my forehead.

"Gimme your purse," he said. My attacker couldn't have been older than twenty. The hoodie he wore wasn't inconspicuous in the slightest. Black and white skulls covered the damn thing like they were meant to inflict fear, but how could anyone be afraid when he wore his nose ring like a cow? I couldn't stop the giggle that escaped my lips.

"You laughin'? What you laughin' at, bitch?" He waved his other hand around in some kind of gang symbol and it looked suspiciously like the sign for 'off the hook'. I couldn't even pretend it wasn't ridiculous if my life depended on it. Clearly.

"Hey! I said why the fuck you laughin'?" He raised his voice, moving the gun like he was going to slam the butt of it into my head.

Bandit didn't take kindly to most people, and he sure as hell didn't tolerate wannabe thugs attacking me. In the time it took to cock his hand back, my raccoon flung at him, landing on his face with his claws out and teeth snapping.

I grabbed the wrist of his hand that was holding the gun. No way was I going to let him start firing that thing blindly. He screamed while Bandit bit down on his nose.

"Motherfucker!" he cried.

Yeah, kid, you're a mother fucking idiot. I slammed my knee into his groin. As I stepped to the side, he fell forward, his hand losing its grip on the gun, dropping it to the ground.

"That's enough," I said to Bandit. Even hissing and spitting, he listened to me, detaching himself from the kid's face. With considerable force, I brought my elbow down on the base of his skull. He let out a muffled cry and collapsed on the ground, unconscious.

I squatted down and picked up the gun. Hopefully, that taught the kid a lesson in trying to rob people, but just in case, I was confiscating the weapon. He didn't need to be running around killing people in alleyways. If I was an unforgiving demon, he wouldn't be leaving this encounter alive.

I reached over and turned his head to the side. The punk had some pretty gnarly scratches that would need stitches, and his entire nose was gone. I glanced over at Bandit. Next to him lay the boy's chunk of nose, with the cow ring still in it.

Ouch. With one hand, I dug my phone out of my pocket and dialed 911.

"Operator. What's your emergency?" I rattled off the street location and left it at that. The cops would find him soon enough and take him to a hospital to get his nose reattached. I didn't want to feel any guilt over his injuries. I mean, he was going to rob me. I seriously doubt he would have killed me, but you never know.

I sighed, letting go of the blame as I turned to Bandit. His teeth were bared, still hissing at the unconscious boy. He didn't even notice me until I shuffled a foot or two closer, both hands held out, palms open.

"Come here, boy," I murmured. I made little *shh* sounds until he calmed enough to run up my arm and perch himself on my shoulder. The pricks of his claws stung a bit, but I ignored it as I rose to my feet.

I gathered my purse and stored the gun in my waistband, ready to go home and see this day to an end. As I turned to leave the alleyway, I saw that Rysten had made good on his promise. With him was Allistair and another male demon that radiated immense power, even from several yards away.

Shit.

"Hey, there…" I said awkwardly, trying to figure out how to go for the gun without being obvious. Unlike the kid that attacked me, I was smart enough to know when I was overpowered.

They started walking towards me and I panicked, grabbing for the gun.

I held it up, aiming at the three of them, not realizing how much space they'd crossed while I was pulling it out. Only three feet away from the barrel, they surrounded me in a semi-circle.

"Don't come any closer!" I said. My hands visibly shook, making the barrel wobble about unsteadily.

"We're not here to hurt you, Ruby," Rysten said. He held up his hands in a show of surrender, but I wasn't a fool. Any demon worth their salt didn't need their hands.

"Who are you and why the fuck are you following me?" I demanded, swinging the gun towards Allistair as he took a step closer. He looked much the same as yesterday, with his tailored suit and styled hair. But his eyes…he looked pissed from the moment I saw him. *Great. I'm going to be incubus dinner.*

"Ruby, it's time to calm down," Allistair said. His eyes glowed amber and a sudden ease spread through me. I lowered the head of the gun slowly, until it was pointed at his knee instead of between his eyes. "That's right, just calm down. It's all going to be alright." The drowsiness intensified, and it was only Bandit's hissing that brought back a modicum of clarity.

"Stop trying to persuade me, demon, or I will blow your fucking knee cap out," I threatened, knowing full well he could probably kill me before that ever came to pass.

"Allistair, back up. You're making her nervous," the third one said. I turned my eyes on him, only to be struck by the similarities he and Rysten shared. His hair was the lightest shade of blonde I'd ever seen; so blonde it could pass for white. They had the same dark green eyes and light skin, but where Rysten had this hot-boy-next-door thing, this guy had an edge of beauty that was intense. His cheek bones were sharper. His teeth, whiter. His skin didn't have a single imperfection, and the power that rolled off him was not something that wanted to be contained. Couldn't be contained. That insight was all it took for the barrel of the gun to go from Allistair to the unknown guy in front of me. Panic surged at the swell of power that threatened to consume me, making the air hard to breathe. Bandit trembled against my shoulder. His fear consumed me, feeding into my own.

Without realizing it, I pulled the trigger, shooting him right between the eyes.

He didn't even bat an eyelash as it popped right out of his head and clanged against the asphalt. The gun slipped from my fingers and I choked out the only words I could manage to process.

"Who are you?"

"The world knows me as Death, but you can call me Julian."

Holy. Shit. Devil have me, because I think my brain just short-circuited.

"Is this the part where you kill me?" I blurted. I couldn't stop the word vomit that came after. "Because if you do, please don't hurt Bandit. He's a good raccoon, really. My friend Moira says she doesn't like him, but she really does, and she would take care of him and everything—"

"We're not here to kill you, Ruby," Rysten said.

"What?" I asked, looking between the three faces. My eyes landed on the one I'd shot. *Julian.*

"We're here to protect you, Ruby, and right now, that means we need to get out of here," he said.

"So you can kidnap me," I stated bluntly. Allistair growled under his breath, making me jump back. Julian pinched the bridge of his nose and sighed. Sirens blared in the distance.

"No, because you called the police to help the worthless human," Julian said. I blinked, only then registering where he was going. "You don't want to be found here with your raccoon that tore his nose off, his gun in your hands, and him unconscious," he continued slowly, as though he was giving instructions to a child.

"Right," I drawled. I picked up the gun, flicked the safety on, and tucked it in my waistband. Rysten bent down and retrieved the bullet, putting it in his pocket.

"You okay, love?" he asked. I glared up at him, crossing my arms over my chest.

"Cut it out, Rysten. We need to get her home," Julian said. I turned my incredulity on him.

Take me home?

"I can take myself home just fine," I said stiffly.

"No."

No? Who the hell did he think he was?

I opened my mouth to argue and he stepped forward into my bubble of ill-conceived safety. Standing close to that cold persona, that raw power staring down at me, every word I had just dried up.

"You have two choices: I can either throw you over my shoulder and carry you to your home, or we can drive there. Your decision," he said.

Was he joking? No. Definitely not joking.

"Drive," I ground out. I think the ghost of a smirk crossed his lips as we left the alleyway.

JULIAN

She shot me.

And then she begged for the life of a raccoon.

I didn't know whether I should be amused or frustrated. Rysten wasn't wrong. She was not what I expected. We hid her for almost twenty-three years. From everyone. Including ourselves. It would be foolish to think that we know her, or even understand her, after we left her on earth with the humans.

Not a day went by that I did not look forward to finally coming for her.

But I didn't expect to mourn the loss of time.

We had only seen her briefly. She was only a babe, not even an hour old, before her mother took her. Now…

I couldn't deny it. She was all grown up.

I adjusted the rearview mirror in her direction and those brilliant blue eyes met mine. The center was so light, nearly white, but they fanned out into cobalt flames before fading to black. I don't know how she stayed hidden for so long when the dark look in her eyes screamed of trouble.

Ruby was not a little girl, and we'd never known her as one. She was a grown woman. No. She was a grown she-demon who had yet to go through the transition. That made her vulnerable. She could stare at me with bedroom eyes all she wanted. It was our divine duty to protect her. To guard her.

JULIAN

The others may get distracted, but I wouldn't.
Even if a single look from her had me hard.

CHAPTER FIVE

THE HEAVY SILENCE while I sat in the back of my own car was crushing me. Julian had insisted on driving. With one look, he made me hand over the keys to my 1995 VW bug…and then moved the seat for me to get in the back. It was probably for the best, given that Bandit was riding on my lap, but I wasn't going to tell them that.

At least they gave me a choice about who rode in the back with me. Not that it really saved me. Rysten was just as massive as the other two and had his thigh flush against mine. As if that wasn't enough to make me uncomfortable, he also hadn't taken his eyes off me. Julian had purposefully moved the rearview mirror to face me instead of the back window, and I felt his gaze on me as well. Maybe he just didn't have any kind of self-preservation like I did, given that a bullet to the head couldn't make him blink. If I wasn't blushing before, I definitely was now.

I couldn't believe that I shot him. And that he let me live.

"Are you going to tell me who the hell you people are?" I finally asked. Bandit's frustration was leaking through, and I was on edge. He didn't like all the strangers in the car with us anymore than I did.

"Soon." Julian said. "We'll explain it when we get to your house. Laran is almost there already."

"Wait, who's Laran?"

I probably should have been more freaked out that they knew where I lived, but given that Allistair got me out of jail before Moira could arrive, it really wasn't that surprising.

"ANOTHER HO—" Rysten began, until Julian glared at him. "You'll meet him soon enough. He's a friend."

Great. Another one. Well then. I guess that's all there was to it.

Settling back into my seat, I held Bandit closer, stroking his fur to ease him. Blood smudged my clothes where he rubbed his face and paws. I was happy it wasn't his, but I didn't want to think about where it had come from. I lived fifteen minutes from the parlor and it felt like it took twice the time to get there. When we pulled into my driveway, whatever shock I felt faded away at the sight of my sleazy ex-boyfriend.

The car rolled to a stop, but no one in my company made a move to get out. Julian and Allistair shared a look in front of me, like they were seriously considering keeping me in here. Uh…not happening.

Not at all surprising, Josh had the nerve to walk up and tap on the window. Allistair didn't respond. Instead, Rysten, the one I thought was the most easy-going of the three, said, "We should get rid of him."

"If you let me out, I will deal with it," I said. While the thought of 'getting rid of him' appealed to me as much as setting Kendall's car on fire, I was already in enough trouble with the police.

They shared another look, but it was only when Julian shrugged that both he and Allistair actually got out of the damn car. Allistair silently held the seat forward for me. It would've been a kind gesture, but he barely gave me room. Forced to graze his suit as I squeezed by, my libido went into fucking overdrive. Didn't even touch his skin. His *suit.* The scent of him filled my nostrils, sending tingles…

I was breathing heavy by the time I was standing on my own two feet outside the car, and it had nothing to do with physical exertion. I glared at him, an arrogant smirk on his face.

"Hi, Ruby," Josh said, pulling my attention away. I turned my eyes to him and what I saw was disappointing.

When I met him, he had this whole lost soul thing going on. He kept his hair long and was in a band. I never loved him, but he was a good person to pass the time with. Until Kendall got her claws into him. Looking at him now, it was like two different people. This Josh dressed in Polos and loafers. His hair was short and gelled back, and from five feet away, the cologne he wore was enough to make me want to gag.

"What do you want?" I asked. I could hear the fatigue in my voice. Truth be told, I was fucking exhausted after the adrenaline high I'd already had today. I didn't have the energy to waste on him.

"I wanted to talk…" he started slowly, giving a pointed look at the three guys who stood behind me. I didn't even need to look. There was tension radiating through the air. I could feel it.

"I have nothing to say to you." Bandit growled at him from his perch on my shoulder. Josh paled, but he didn't back away. I sighed. *Idiot boy.*

"That can't be true, Ruby. You blew up my girlfriend's car. I know you still care," Josh said, even going so far as to take a step towards me. I didn't want to step back, because it looked weak. But I was worried Bandit might actually attack him. He'd never liked Josh, and right now he was being very protective of me and wanted him gone.

"That's because your girlfriend's a bitch. Don't confuse the facts," I said dryly. Without warning or permission, a strong arm wrapped around my waist. I tensed, worried that my raccoon's anger was going to turn on the person who had just touched me, but it appeared that Bandit was dead set on wanting to get rid of Josh, and only Josh.

"Is this"— he stammered—"Is *this* why you won't return my calls?" He motioned to the beautiful trio of men, his eyes bulging out. I could see what was coming next. "You wouldn't even have sex with *me*, and you have—"

My eyes flashed. "I'm not answering your calls because you and I are no longer dating. We are not a thing. We aren't even friends. What I do now is none of your concern." I had to work to keep the growl out of my voice.

Yeah, I didn't have sex with him. I didn't have sex with anyone because it was never a conscious choice. I could pick any guy off the street and he would fuck me then and there if I wanted, thanks to dear old Mom. So, despite my nature, I didn't fuck anyone. And this was what I got for it.

The boy actually had the nerve to take another step towards me. "This isn't you, Ruby. I remember. I know you. You wouldn't be with these"—he broke off, searching for a word that would suffice to describe the three stunning demons that were unlike anything this earth could produce. Even in his sub-conscious human mind, something registered that they were more than men—"*people.*" Someone snorted behind me, and I was pretty sure which one, given that only one of them had a sense of humor from what I could tell. The laughing stopped short when Josh said, "Come back to me."

"Why on earth would you think I am ever coming back to you?" I scoffed. I probably would have laughed had the arm around my waist not tightened slightly as he let out the tiniest of growls. It was so low I almost didn't hear it, but it was there. I looked up to see Julian.

My heart skipped a beat as I swallowed hard. My throat was dry and scratchy, but there was something so protective and feral about the way he looked at Josh that just made a girl wonder what a little taste of that might be like. To have a demon like Julian's complete and utter attention…

Pure bliss? Or pure hell?

Somehow, I thought he might be a bit of both. They say pain is pleasure, if you know what you're doing.

Damnit, Ruby. You need to focus. Now isn't the time to be thinking like a sex-deprived maniac.

Josh cleared his throat, and I blinked. *Shit. Did he say something?* I glanced back at my stuffy ex with his posh ironed khakis.

"I made a mistake, Ruby. I'm sorry—"

"I gotta stop you right there. We both know you're going to go home after this, screw Kendall, and then come back another day to 'beg' for my forgiveness. So, can we just skip all the unnecessary bullshit, and move on like adults? Because I'm really getting tired of her taking out her issues with you"—I pointed a finger at his weak chest—"on me."

I had really hoped it would work this time. That being straight-forward would do the trick. Silly me, thinking that Josh could think with his brain and not his dick. He didn't consider the words for more than four seconds before inserting his foot in in his mouth. Again.

"Ruby. Please. Let's just talk this out. I miss you," he whined. *Damnit. Not the whining.*

My patience was already running thin and he just stomped on the last layer that was positioned between him and the brutally frigid truth that came pouring from my lips.

"Go home and lay in the fucking bed you made. You cheated on me.

I'm not coming back to you, and this is your last warning. Move on." The pissed off look in his eye would have been funny, but I knew he'd forget about it soon enough. Then he'd be right back here on my doorstep, begging for something he'll never have.

"I think it's in your best interest that you leave now, while you still can." The menace in this voice sent chills down my spine. I turned to the figure that came strolling up my driveway.

Holy. Hell. His hair was so dark, it looked black…but when the light from the streetlamps hit it, I saw flashes of pure, undiluted *red*. He was the tallest of the four, with fierce black eyes and a savageness about him that told people he was not one to be fucked with.

Josh took a single look at him and I thought he was going to piss himself. While they still scared the shit out of me, I'd shot one and they still haven't killed me. That's a pretty good reason to think they won't. Josh didn't have that courtesy, and if he continued to stay here running his mouth about our lack of a sex life, I might decide to say 'fuck it' and let Bandit at him.

"Don't make me call the police, Josh," I said, knowing it wouldn't get that far. He was an idiot and a cheater, but he didn't want trouble with the law.

After one particularly snobbish look around, he got in his car and drove off.

I couldn't contain the sigh of relief as his tires squealed around the corner of my street, but that relief was short-lived. Only then did I realize Julian's arm was still around my waist. I was becoming increasingly aware that I may have just traded one bad situation for another.

They haven't killed you yet, I reminded myself. May as well get it over with. I stepped away from Julian, putting space between me and the four demons that sucked the air from my lungs.

"So, is this where you finally tell me who you are and why you're following me?" They didn't look at each other, but each of their faces was set in grim determination.

"I am Pestilence," Rysten said.

No…

"I am Famine," Allistair followed.

Devil save me.

"I am Death," Julian continued in a cool tone.

It should have clicked with me sooner.

"My name is Laran, and I am War," the fourth and final one said.

They didn't continue because they didn't need to. I knew who they were. Every demon in both worlds knew who they were.

"You're the Four Horsemen," I whispered.

CHAPTER SIX

I WAS HAVING a hard time wrapping my head around the identity of the strangers sitting in my living room. Even with a hot cup of tea and ten minutes to digest, there were some things that life simply can't prepare you for. The Horsemen were one of those things.

They were four of the most powerful arch demons ever created, only usurped by one power and one power alone: the devil himself. Which begged the question: why were all four of his personal guard stalking me and not back in Hell where they belonged?

"So…" I started in a slow, weary voice, "did I do something? This isn't about Kendall's car, right? I mean, I feel like you would have mentioned it by now, but—"

"This isn't about the car," Allistair said. He watched me like a cat did a mouse. The feeling was unnerving, but it also made my stomach clench in all the ways that were not helpful right now. With his ankle propped on his knee and hand stretched over the back of the couch, I couldn't tell if the small space he'd left between himself and Rysten was an invitation or pure coincidence. I averted my eyes to look away, but found myself staring at Julian instead.

"We need you to come back to Hell with us," Julian said.

"Wait, what? No! Why?" I asked, skimming the others. He was kidding, right? He had to be joking. A half-breed like me wouldn't survive in Hell.

I'd be turned into some other stronger demon's plaything, and that's if I was lucky. My eyes landed on Rysten as I began shaking my head no. "Why?" I repeated, when no one gave me an answer.

"Because you're Lucifer's daughter," Laran said. Rysten cringed, but didn't deny it.

Allistair rolled his eyes. "Way to go, War. Why not just drop it on her even though we agreed—" I burst out laughing.

I laughed—no, I roared—so hard I was tearing up in the corners of my eyes. They thought—what? They thought *I* was Lucifer's *daughter*? Oh, this was rich! Beyond rich. I laughed while they stared at me in stunned silence. Oh-ho-ho, they were here because they thought I was important! They didn't kill me because they thought I was the devil's daughter. Well, the joke's on them! I'm just a half-breed succubus with an affinity for picking up trouble.

"Ruby…" Rysten trailed off. "Why are you laughing?"

"You think"— I cracked up again—"you think I'm the *devil's daughter*."

"You are," he frowned.

"No, Rysten. I'm half-human," I said kindly. I don't know who told the Horsemen I was the King of Hell's daughter, but whoever it was better be running. I doubted they would be pleased when they found out the truth.

"Who told you that?" Julian asked.

"The demon orphanage I grew up in. My mother dropped me off in Atlanta hours after I was born. Told them she wouldn't have a half-human baby, and that was that," I shrugged. The story was slightly uncomfortable for me, but I'd grown to accept it. Demons were either obsessive or apathetic; there wasn't a lot of in-between. If my birth mother thought I was a waste of genetic material, then that was her prob-lem. It wasn't my fault she screwed a human and got pregnant. That's why there were orphanages in the first place. For the unlucky offspring of demons that wanted nothing to do with their mistakes, but someone still had to teach us how to glamor ourselves from the humans. Hell forbid the rumors of our kind ever become more than just that. Then again, if Hell really gave a damn, they'd close the portals between the worlds and be done with it.

"Your mother. Was her name Lola Morningstar?" Julian asked. I nearly choked on my sip of tea and narrowed my gaze in his direction.

"You probably pulled that off my birth certificate," I said coolly.

"Or I knew her," he responded in jest. A hard, icy tone had entered his voice making me shiver.

"Right," I drawled. I didn't believe that story.

"She brought you here to hide you," he argued.

"Because I was Lucifer's child?" I asked. Snickered, really. Julian didn't seem to find it very funny.

"Yes, and some very powerful demons wanted to kill you for it. They still do," Laran interjected.

They truly believed this nonsense. That I was some miracle baby.

Lucifer has been around longer than any of us, and as far as anybody knows, he doesn't have any children. Some rumors say he can't. Others say he doesn't want to share his power. Either way, in the thousands of years he's been on this earth and in Hell, not once has anyone come forward saying they have his child.

I was not going to be the exception.

"Let's say that you're right. *I* am Satan's spawn. Lola hid me to keep me away from all the people I'm assuming have a bone to pick with him?" I paused, they nodded. "So, answer me this: even if I was, why do I need to go to Hell? Aren't I better off living my life here where no one knows I exist?"

They all seemed to share a glance.

"Have you ever heard the story of the Four Horsemen?" Laran asked.

"Of course. The Four Horsemen are the bringers of the apocalypse. It was a warning to those who wanted to upset the balance," I said. Everyone knew that. I would've had to have lived under a rock not to.

"Not quite," Allistair said. A slow sensual smile lit his lips, making my cheeks heat. "We were never bringers of the apocalypse. We were the ones created to prevent it. Funny how history never seems to get that little detail right." He smirked at me, and I bit the inside of my cheek to stave off the lustful thoughts he was sending my way. The devil damned incubus knew exactly what he was doing.

"If you're not the bringers of the apocalypse, then who is?" I asked, trying to distract myself from the fuck me vibes he was sending.

"A few thousand years ago, there was a demon named Ragnarok who was gifted with premonitions. He saw the end of the world, as we knew it." He paused, letting a heavy silence fill in the gaps. "Humans have forgotten him, but remembered his vision. Ragnarok. The end of times.

"He said that one day the Horsemen would fail, and Lucifer would fall, and that when he did, the flames of Hell would go out. If the flames go out, then the gates of Hell open, leaving no barrier to stop all that lives in Hell from coming to earth," Julian said. "No barrier, that is, except Lucifer's child."

This is not the same version I was told as a child...

"Ragnarok prophesied that Lucifer would sire a daughter, and that she, and she alone, would be able to control the flames and stop the apocalypse, but it would be up to us to find her and bring her back." Julian took a deep breath. "Ragnarok's prophecy came true, Ruby. Lucifer died three days ago."

"*Died?* What do you mean he *died?*" I spluttered. "He's the fucking devil! The King of Hell. How the fuck does he just die?" Julian didn't bat an eyelash at my outburst. I don't think much phased him, but Rysten and Allistair shared a strained look. Laran's hands tightened, almost imperceptibly, were I not watching for it.

"To answer your question, love, he didn't. But that's a story for another time," Rysten interjected.

What the hell does that even mean?

I narrowed my eyes at him, not liking that answer, but knowing full well I had to accept it. Because what can you do? When the Four Horsemen are calling the shots, not a damn thing.

"The news of his death will trickle in over the coming weeks, and anarchy will ensue until the flames go out and Hell, for want of a better phrase, freezes over." Julian sensed my restlessness and stilled it. His eyes swirled with unnamable emotions and such a startling intensity that I almost didn't hear the second half of his statement. "We need you, Ruby. More than you know."

Whatever touching moment that might have been, stopped abruptly as I processed what was just said. They were deluded for thinking I was the devil's child, but they were abso-fucking-lutely insane if they thought I had the power to keep Hell in check. I could barely control my raccoon. The only gifts I'd expressed were that of a latent succubus, and I'd yet to transition. There was no way, not on this earth or in Hell, that I was destined to prevent an apocalypse.

"Look, I don't know whether you knew Lola or not, or what she may have said, but I have to be honest with you—I'm not the girl you're looking for," I said in a rush, setting my steaming cup of earl grey on the end table as I got to my feet. I crossed my living room and opened the front door. "I think it's best you leave."

Laran, the closest to me and the only one standing, narrowed his eyes. *War.* That's what the world called him. I could see it. He took a step closer, and I didn't move.

On the one hand, I didn't want to back down. That would make me look weak, and then they might not leave. On the other hand, he was now a lot closer than I wanted and I was well aware of the effect I had on men.

He leaned forward, so close that his breath caressed the sensitive part of my ear. I shivered as he whispered, "This isn't over, little succubus. We aren't going anywhere. Not without you. Don't even think about running. I like to chase."

His lips grazed the very corners of my ear and my breath hissed between my teeth. A zap of lightning went through me, making my blood sizzle. *What was that?*

"That's enough, Laran," Julian snapped. He pulled back a few inches, and I held my breath. His eyes had gone pitch black, blotting out any spec of color or trace of white. The air tasted thick with tension as he watched me for a heavy moment.

He's sizing me up. Full-blooded demons, and those who transition, have a harder time controlling our dark urges. I've been told the power can be maddening, and in some cases, consuming.

"War," Julian said sternly. This time someone physically grabbed him and pushed him towards the door. Laran growled under his breath and cast me one last heated look before leaving. I swallowed hard as Julian and Allistair followed. Rysten paused on his way out.

"I can't imagine this is easy to handle, love, but we will be here to help you through it," he said. I imagine most she-demons would fall all over themselves to hear those words from one of the Horsemen, but none of them were told they were supposed to take over the underworld.

"Please just go," I said. Rysten nodded in understanding and followed the others out into the night. I closed the door behind them and leaned against it. My legs gave out under me as I slid to the floor and Bandit came running out of my bedroom, his pink elephant in tow, stopping on my thighs to hold out his treasured toy.

"I don't think that's going to solve my problems this time, boy," I sighed. He kept pushing it towards me. I took the damn thing and held it while he climbed up my chest and wrapped his arms around my neck.

"Don't worry. I'm not leaving you. They can think I'm destined to be *Queen of the Underworld* all they want. It doesn't change anything." I don't know how much time passed until I dragged myself to bed, stripping off my blood-smudged clothes as I went.

If Julian thought he could intimidate me into staying away from her, he was wrong. I'd waited just as long as the rest of them, and unlike Rysten, who went to her because Allistair called on him behind our backs, I stuck to the plan and didn't try to speak with her.

Until the plan changed.

I didn't mean to touch her.

I just couldn't think.

She was so close already, and she smelled *so good*. I've waited thousands of years to meet her, but the last twenty-three were the hardest.

The plan was to let Lola take her and not come back until it was time.

I waited. I paid my dues.

But she wanted nothing to do with us.

"Laran, you need to chill the fuck out, mate," Rysten snapped. I looked up at him and snarled, but the bastard didn't respond in kind. He rolled his eyes and continued sipping his wine, like he classy or some shit. Fucking mommy drink is what that was.

Humans were making him soft.

"She wants nothing to do with us. How can you be sitting there like a fucking—"

"You think I haven't noticed? What did you expect, War? That we could come in here and usher her away? She doesn't know who you are.

Who I am. She doesn't even know who *she is.* She only knows what earth has taught her."

I turned my back on him, towards the fire. Maybe I couldn't call the flames of Hell, but I could call on earth's fire and wreak havoc like the world has never known.

"Why does it feel like they took her from us?" I asked softly into the flames, but they held no answers for me this night.

"Because she created a life," Julian answered.

"This was what we wanted," Rysten continued.

"No," I said sharply. "This is what *you three* wanted. I wanted to keep her in Hell where—"

"Where she would have died with Lucifer," Julian interrupted.

I bit my tongue from the denial that threatened to come pouring out. He was right, but that didn't make this any easier.

"What are we supposed to do now?" I asked.

Silence spread between us, each lost to our own thoughts over the girl who was destined to be ours, but didn't know it.

Rysten was the first to speak. "We give her time and get to know her."

"I suggest we do this individually," Allistair proposed.

"So you can fuck her?" I asked. My words were harsh, but I meant it.

"I wasn't the one all over her tonight, War," he snapped back.

"You don't deny it."

"Enough," Julian declared. I turned away from the flames, toward my comrades. My brothers. We have stood together through everything. Fought and won for Hell itself. We have killed and laid destruction to so many in the name of the future. Of Ruby. Yet...this was different.

"Becoming her guards will be unlike any mission we have had before. It has already proven to have some challenges we hadn't predicted, and I think I can speak for all of us when I say we already feel a sense of entitlement to her," Julian said.

He wasn't wrong, and none of us corrected him.

"That being said, her well-being comes before anything we may want or feel. She's not comfortable with us yet, so we limit the time spent with her as a unit. At least until word from Hell reaches here. We can't postpone the inevitable. She must come with us, but we can give her time to adjust."

My gaze darted to Rysten. The fucker was practically smirking to himself at Julian's decree. He'd spent more time on earth than any of us over the last two decades, and while we all knew why, no one ever thought it might make a difference. We assumed she would want to come with us. That she would be happy to leave earth behind. We didn't take into account that she would grow up, have her own life, and become a woman in her own right, with sinful curves and a sultry mouth.

We didn't take *her* into account.

Just the idea of her.

All of us, but Rysten. The fucker was probably real happy right now, but he wasn't the only one with cards up his sleeve.

I am War, and no one plays better games than me.

CHAPTER SEVEN

GROGGY AND EXHAUSTED, I woke to Moira screaming down the house. Not literally, but she may as well have been. I rolled over in bed and groaned. Bandit chittered about, jumping from his hammock hanging over my head and onto the floor. He paced wildly back and forth, scratching at the door.

"Ugh…why me?" I moaned, unwrapping myself from my sheets. I'd slept like the dead last night and woken up in a sheen of perspiration. I was going to need a shower before I went into the shop today.

Throwing open my bedroom door, I dragged my mostly naked ass into the living room. "What in the devil's name are you screaming about?" I asked, walking around the corner.

Rysten stood in the doorway with an extremely pissed off Moira. My best friend turned to respond, but lost the words once she saw me standing there in my underwear. I let out a frustrated growl and turned on my heel, ignoring the stark intensity that entered Rysten's expression. I wasn't a prude by any means, and took nudity in a pretty casual manner. Until you threw men into the mix. Bastards got a look of something they liked and never left me alone.

I dug through the never-folded pile of clean laundry sitting on the corner of my bed. At the very bottom was my black bathrobe. It was simple and cotton, definitely nothing sexy, and it would do the trick. I pulled on the robe and tied the sash at my waist as I walked back into the living room.

"Why is this asshole on our doorstep?" Moira demanded, like I was the one at fault.

"You think if I knew that I would've come around in my underwear?" I snapped back. She tilted her head to the side, narrowing her eyes as she considered that little detail for a moment before turning her anger back to him.

"What are you doing here, *boy*?" she asked him, not at all hiding her disdain at his presence. I nearly choked on the laugh that threatened to come out. Moira didn't know that Rysten was Pestilence. She didn't know he was a demon at all.

"I'm here to take Ruby to work," he said, not hiding his smirk.

"No, you're not," Moira answered for me.

"Hey," I protested. "I can answer for myself." Moira narrowed her eyes at me. *What's gotten into her lately?*

"Do you *want* him to take you to work?" she asked pointedly.

"Of course she does," Rysten responded before I could get a word in. I swung my glare in his direction. "Don't you, love?"

"No, I can't say that I do," I said hotly, stuffing my tongue in my cheek. I had mixed feelings where he and the others were concerned. It was my nature to want to play with fire, and four sexy and unbelievably powerful demons were just that. But. They also wanted to cart me off to Hell where I would probably die a terrible death once they realized they'd made a mistake.

"Now, love, I know this isn't easy on you, but—"

Rysten was still speaking when Moira slammed the door in his face.

"Why is he following you, Ruby?" she asked me, turning her back on the door. Rysten had gone quiet, but not for a second did I think he was actually gone. Not if they really believed what they told me, and given their behavior, I had no reason to think otherwise.

My eyes strayed to Moira and I gave her a non-committal shrug. "You know how men are."

"I do," she said narrowing her eyes. "But he's not human, is he?"

Well, shit. Maybe she did know a thing or two.

"No," I said grimly. "He's not."

She nodded like that's what she expected. "Have you slept with him yet?"

"No. I haven't slept with any of them," I snapped, realizing a second too late that I just gave away more information than intended. *Shit.*

"Them?" she asked, raising an eyebrow. I rolled my eyes, letting out a sigh of exasperation. There was no way she was going to let it go now that I let that one slip. Great job, Ruby.

"You remember the guy who bailed me out of jail?" She nodded slowly. "Well, he and Rysten work together with two other guys. The four of them came here for me because they have some crazy, delusional idea that I'm someone important. So, they think they need to protect me."

"Well, who do they think you are?" she asked, her voice filled with skepticism.

"Lucifer's daughter."

Silence ensued as we stared at each other until she burst out laughing. I waited for her to get her giggles out, and then she said, "That's a good one, but why are they really here?"

I stared blankly until her smile fell as the truth behind my words set in.

"They really believe you're the king's child?" she asked, like it only then occurred to her I might be telling the truth.

"It gets better," I said stiffly, and the whole story came pouring out of me. I collapsed on the sofa, all hope of making it into the shop early dissipated as I told her about the Horsemen and how they wanted to drag me back to Hell now that Lucifer died, all so I could somehow prevent the apocalypse from happening.

"Wow. I don't know what to say." Her voice was punctured by shock and disbelief.

"That makes two of us."

"What are you going to do?"

"I don't know, honestly. They wouldn't believe me when I told them they have the wrong person, but I have no intention of going to Hell just to prove them wrong." I picked at a piece of lint on my bath robe while Moira studied me.

"Are you sure…"

"Am I sure what?"

"Are you sure there's no way they may be right?"

I gaped at her, not even willing to entertain that thought. "Do you hear yourself right now? How is this even a question for you? You've known me most of your life. Have I ever come across as anything other than part-succubus?" My heart warbled in my chest while I spluttered the words.

"No," she exhaled. "But that doesn't mean you're not. There's always that chance your other half just hasn't manifested yet—"

"Do you really think that if Lucifer had a child, they wouldn't manifest before twenty-two?" I deadpanned.

Even she couldn't deny that. "Okay, so assuming you're not. What are you going to do about the Horsemen?" she asked as Bandit jumped onto the back of the couch and stuck his head through the blinds. Between the gap, I could see Rysten standing in the yard talking to someone on the phone.

"The way I see it, there isn't much I can do. They're going to follow me either way, and at least any other demons who think I'm Lucifer's daughter might leave me alone while they're around. I mean, they're bound to get the hint eventually, right?" I said throwing my arm over my face.

Moira shifted in her seat. "Hmm…possibly. They're demons, though, and when they take a liking to you…"

"That's an *if*, not a *when*," I pointed out, more for my own peace of mind than anything. I was happy with my life here. I didn't want anything to change, but they made it clear they weren't leaving me alone, even if I wanted them to.

BANDIT PERCHED ON MY SHOULDER, munching on a carrot, as I walked out the front door. I'd been planning on leaving him at home today, but every time I reached for the doorknob, he tried to claw his way up my legs to come with me. Needy. I knew if I left him home, he'd tear everything to shreds just to get back at me. He was vindictive that way.

Rysten stood in my driveway, leaning against my car. His sand colored hair hung in his eyes and he had his arms crossed over his chest.

"I take it you four aren't leaving me alone anytime soon?" I asked as I approached the car. Rysten shook his head, the dark twinkle in his eye making my stomach do little summer saults.

"No can-do, love. You're stuck with us now that we've found you," he said, opening my driver's side door.

"You're not going to try to take my keys again, are you?" I asked warily.

He snorted. "I'm not Julian. Unlike Death, I realize that you're independent enough to chafe if we try to do everything for you," he said, a knowing twinkle in his eye. I swallowed hard and pretended not to notice the subtle brush of heat against my skin.

"Damn straight, I am." I stepped around him and climbed in. The passenger side door opened, Rysten taking Bandit's seat. He growled under his breath at his usual space being occupied by this stranger, but he settled in the back of the car as I pulled out of the driveway.

"Your friend. She's not very fond of me, is she?" he asked. It was an abrupt change of subject. But given Moira's reaction to him on two occasions, I wasn't surprised he was curious.

"No. She's not very fond of most men who won't leave me alone," I said honestly.

"But I'm not a man," he pointed out.

"You're male and you've been stalking me. Close enough," I said with a roll of my eyes.

He chuckled under his breath, a dark and delicious sound. "It's good she's so protective of you," he said. "Even without being full-blooded succubus, I can feel the draw. A lesser demon would be hopeless to resist you." I swallowed hard, a question I shouldn't ask playing on the tip of my tongue. "You'll really be something when you come into your powers."

"*If* I come into my powers," I corrected. That earned another chuckle out of him.

"Oh, you will, love. Of that, I am certain." He sounded awfully confident for someone who was going to be hellaciously disappointed. I glanced sideways, but there wasn't a hint of the power or darkness I heard creeping into his voice. His glamor rippled when our eyes locked, and I quickly averted mine to the road.

"Why do you wear a glamor when the others don't?" I asked.

"Because the others are idiots in some regards," he said smugly.

"What do you mean?"

"What was your first thought when you met Allistair?" he asked. I thought of the brooding incubus. I'd known what he was from yards away, as much from the look in his eye to the way he moved. There was a raw power that radiated from him.

"He was"— I struggled to find a description that wasn't embarrassing, like sex-on-a-stick. That probably wouldn't earn me any points here —"intense."

Rysten nodded. "What about Julian?"

"Well, I shot him, so…"

"Exactly. And had you not met Laran when trying to get rid of your admirer"—his nose wrinkled in distaste–"you would have felt the same."

"That's one word for Josh."

"He's not worthy," Rysten said. Something about that response bothered me. It was almost territorial in a way, somehow implying *he* was worthy. I pulled into the parking lot behind the parlor and cut the engine.

Rysten brushed his thumb across his bottom lip, and I bit the inside of my cheek. While he was the most approachable of the Horsemen, he was still a demon, and a very powerful one at that.

"You still haven't answered my question," I said.

The corners of his lips turned up as he leaned forward. "Haven't I, love?"

My gaze went from his lips to his face, where his eyes gave away that very faint inkling of the darkness I sensed in him.

Realization dawned on me. "Because you think I'll let you get close to me just because you can make yourself seem more human."

His answering smile had me both pissed off and turned on. He leaned in, only inches from my face, and murmured, "That's what you're doing, isn't it?" His breath caressed my skin, drawing at the seductress within. I clamped down hard on my urges, fighting the lust unfolding inside me.

"No," I snapped, pulling back. "It's not."

I practically spun in my seat and wrenched the door open, jumping from the car to get as much space between us as possible. How could I have been stupid enough to ignore the obvious? I was more frustrated with myself than I was with him.

Bandit perched himself on the edge of the driver's seat and jumped towards me, wrapping his paws around neck. I put one arm underneath to support his weight and used the other to grip the car door.

Rysten tilted his head to the side as his glamor settled now that I wasn't so close. A boyish smile appeared on his lips as he said, "It's going to happen whether you like it or not, Ruby. You're ours to protect, and we take care of what's ours."

I slammed the car door and strode away from him as the reality of what it meant to have the Four Horsemen after me truly set in. This was going to be a long week. They would protect me from anything they saw as a threat because of who they thought I was.

But who would protect me from them?

CHAPTER EIGHT

I WAS JUST CLOSING shop for the weekend when the bell on the front door rang. I peeked my head around the corner and groaned when I saw who was standing there. It was none other than my lousy ex holding the sad makings of another apology in the form of a bouquet.

Why me?

"What are you doing here?" I asked. Bandit took one look at Josh and let out a growl. He held his head up higher at the sight of my raccoon. His posture couldn't have been straighter if someone shoved a pine tree up his ass.

"I came here to apologize for Sunday night." He motioned to the flowers in his hand. "I brought you daffodils. They're supposed to stand for forgiveness and new beginnings."

It took all my self-control not to gag. "I'm good. Thanks."

"Please, Ruby." *Devil save me, not the whining again.* I didn't have the patience for it today. I knew that it wasn't the loss of me that had him obsessing over our split. I knew it was the dormant succubus within. He had cheated on me claiming it was because I wouldn't sleep with him, but he also came groveling back every few days. It was exhausting. But sleeping with someone that didn't really give two shits about me, and had no choice, felt a little too much like rape. This is what I get for having *morals*.

"Please what?" I said, throwing my hands up in exasperation. "We broke up, Josh. I don't know what to say."

"That you'll forgive me and give me another chance—"

I held my hand up to stop him. "No. We are never, ever getting back together." I cringed as soon as the words were out, knowing I sounded like a bad Taylor Swift song.

"Is it because of those guys I saw with you? You have a"—he struggled with words for a moment, anger clouting his brain—"a *harem* now? Is that it?"

A harem? Now that's a thought. I was equally intrigued by the idea as I was pissed off by his attitude, given that he had absolutely zero reason to feel any sense of entitlement towards me. After all, his actions were what brought an abrupt end to our relationship, but with all the whining he was doing, I couldn't say I was sorry to see it end. At least I didn't have to feel bad about being bitchy this time.

"They have nothing to do with what happened between us, Josh. *You* are the one who cheated on *me*." I was beginning to sound like a broken record. This conversation was getting old, and fast.

"You wouldn't have sex with me! I waited months for you! Now you're sleeping with, what—three, four guys? But I'm willing to forgive you for your transgressions, if you can look past my small lapse in judgement."

Wow. I didn't even know how to respond. Unfortunately for him, he chose to be a total dick at the exact moment Laran was walking up. The door opened behind him, and he took one look over his shoulder and paled.

"I don't need your forgiveness because I don't want to be with you. Leave me alone," I said, hoping that Laran's presence would be enough to get him to go away.

Josh swallowed hard and uttered, "This isn't over. I will win you back." Delusional wasn't a strong enough word.

"Actually, you won't," Laran said darkly. "Stay away from Ruby, *boy*. My patience has an expiration, much like your life span." The menace in his voice wasn't soft or cunning. It was bold, and edged with a danger that just seemed to radiate from Laran. I'd only spoken with him briefly, less than the other three, and he scared the crap out of me. Josh would probably piss his pants if they kept this up.

"Are you threatening me?" Josh demanded. His face turned pink as he spluttered out his indignation.

"Yes." Laran stepped out of the way of the door, a not-so-subtle hint that it was time for him to leave.

Once again, Josh let out a string of curses, but did indeed storm off. The shop door slammed behind him, leaving me and Laran alone.

"Are all your exes this crazy?" he asked me. I guess at this point it was the closest we could get to small talk.

"Mostly," I responded. The ghost of a smirk crossed his lips, gone before I could tell if it was real.

"I guess that means I have my work cut out for me." He strode towards me like he owned the earth we walked on. Unapologetically and unequivocally male. My mouth dried as he neared me, but I didn't back away. The last thing I needed these demons thinking was that they could bulldoze me around.

"What are you doing here?" I asked, fidgeting with the corner of my sleeve. Strangely enough, Bandit stayed quiet as he approached me. Unlike Josh, whom he had always disliked, he didn't seem to care one way or the other if Laran was near me. I wasn't sure if I should find that comforting, or worrisome.

"It's my turn," he said proudly.

"Your turn?"

"To spend time with you," he clarified. I frowned. *They were taking turns on who—*

"Who says I want to spend time with you?" I didn't particularly care for being told what to do or who I would spend time with.

"Would you rather Allistair or Julian?"

"Um…" My non-answer must have been answer enough.

He smirked and held out his hand. "Come. I promise not to bite. *This time.*"

This time? I licked my bottom lip at the promise in those words. I wasn't supposed to be attracted to them, or at the very least, not playing out my fantasies, but I couldn't help but wonder what Laran might taste like. Just a bite. He was a full-grown male demon, well into his prime, and the things he could teach me…

My wishful thinking stopped as memories knocked me back to reality. It'd been a long, long while since I got laid, thanks to what happened last time. Seeing as I had no immediate plans to fix that, I just accepted that I was damned if I did, and damned if I didn't.

Taking a deep breath, I said, "Fine, but I need to drop Bandit off at home first. He doesn't like people, and humans are prejudice dicks."

Laran gave me a savage grin. "Who said anything about humans?"

I wasn't sure if I should be excited or concerned at the prospect of whatever the Horseman of War had planned. The demonic glint in his eye should have been all the warning I needed.

HALF AN HOUR after dropping Bandit at home, we pulled of the highway. A 'Keep Out' sign sat just before the bend in the road that turned and revealed this run-down lot in the middle of nowhere. The bits and pieces of trash scattered about would have made it look like any other abandoned lot you find, had conifers not towered over the make-shift building, keeping it hidden from unwanted eyes. It looked like a great location for a horror movie. In front of a rickety shed made of plywood was a moderate plot of compacted dirt, currently being used as a parking lot for the few cars parked outside. Spray-painted lines marked the spots where cars were supposed to park, not that it seemed the drivers paid that any mind. The slightly bent brambles and flattened grass were the only indication that an unmarked road existed just off the highway that led here. There was just something too convenient about that, and it didn't sit right with me.

I suddenly felt like we were about to walk into the middle of some shady shit.

"Where are we?" I asked as we got out of the car. An upside-down pentagram hung from the top of the lopsided door, the only indication about what might await me inside.

"I thought I'd take you on a little field trip. Get you away from all the heaviness of this past week," he replied without hesitation. I faltered mid-step, tripping over a rock because I was too busy looking at him. My arms flailed as I started to fall towards the ground, but Laran caught me by the elbow. Swift. Firm. He pulled me back so I didn't fall flat on my face, or through the uneven door.

"That's oddly considerate for a demon. The Horseman of War, no less," I murmured. Laran stepped closer and bent down, his lips grazing my jaw.

"Haven't you heard the saying, *all is fair in lust and war?*" he whispered. I shivered at the brush of his lips against that sensitive place just beneath my ear.

"I'm pretty sure the saying is *love and war*," I responded dryly. His lips curved up against my skin, leaving a trail of heat in their path.

"I like my version better," he rumbled. His very demeanor called to me, dark and seductive. Like a moth to a flame. But a moth didn't realize it was going to get burned. I was smart enough to know, and part of me wanted it. A small sadistic side of me was drawn to these men—to all men—and it had nothing to do with love, or war.

I swallowed hard, shoving my inner she-demon back. She was going to get me into trouble if she had her way.

Laran chuckled as I stepped away from him, but didn't release his hold on my elbow. His fingers were distracting, but I didn't complain as he pushed open the lopsided door and escorted me into what was, for all intents and purposes, a dive-bar. For demons.

All eyes turned on us and I froze.

Why the fuck would he take me to a bar for demons in the middle of nowhere? He may as well have offered me up to them on a silver platter and said bon appétit.

"What are we doing here, Laran?" I hissed through gritted teeth. I moved to shrug off his grip, but he held me tighter.

"Relax, Ruby. They don't know who I am. Anyone who looks at me will just see a glamor of a male demon they won't want to fuck with, and by extension, you." I stared up at him, my gaze slowly falling to the hand possessively wrapped around my arm. He was…laying a claim on me. A warning to anyone thinking they might want a new plaything. He was letting them know I am not on the market.

I let loose a shaky breath as he moved us further into the bar. The scent of smoke and citrus drifted over me and my muscles relaxed instantly. I inhaled deeply, the softest of sighs escaping my lips as the tension left me altogether.

"Feeling better?" Laran asked. His lips twitched in an amused smirk.

"Much," I answered through the haze that was beginning to cloud over. The corners of my vison softened, but the world never seemed so bright.

So…tempting. My inner seductress smiled at the crowded bar as I walked away from Laran and squeezed my way in between two mischievous looking males.

"I'll have a Black Russian on the rocks. Make it a double." My voice came out sultry. The succubus was out to play.

LARAN*

She disappeared.

One minute she was standing next to me, sexy little smile lighting up her face, and the next minute she was gone. Someone was going to fucking pay for this, and it wouldn't be pretty.

A barely-tempered fury pounded in my chest as I scanned the gambling tables. Imps of every shape and size, banshees of all colors, a Chupacabra here and there, even a few shades littered the crowd, but no Ruby. Her amaryllis and lavender scent filled the air, mixing with the pungent smoke of burning white lotus. White lotus: the drug of choice for most demons, and a far kinder version of the black lotus that was known for its…undesirable effects.

I left the gambling tables and searched the bar where I picked up the briefest hint of her. She was close, and yet, as I searched the entirety of the bar, I couldn't find her anywhere. *How the fuck did I lose her? The only person in the world I was created to protect?*

This shit was unbelievable.

The itching inside me that something had gone terribly wrong sped up as I barreled toward the stairs. If I found her in one of these back rooms tied up like—I couldn't even finish that thought. If she was up here, someone was going to die. I squared my jaw and kicked open the first door I saw.

A sallow-cheeked she-demon looked up at me and let out a purr while the male behind her continued pounding into her flesh. She was bent over a desk that had seen better days. Her feral grin and crooked finger she used to try to beckon me forward was not appetizing in the slightest. There was only one person I felt like slamming my cock into and it wasn't the drugged-out whore before me. I didn't bother with closing the door as I moved on to the following rooms. They were all much the same: she-demons with one or two males, and no Ruby.

I ran a hand through my hair as I paced the balcony overlooking the bar.

Where the fuck was she?

Nearly half an hour had passed since we walked into The Black Brothers and there was still no sign of her. Much longer and I was going to need to scour the grounds to see if someone snuck her out. I would have thought she would put up enough of a fight, but I didn't get the vibe she was used to smoking white lotus, and the room itself was a hefty dose that left even the stronger demons slightly delirious.

She's young. She hasn't transitioned. What the fuck was I thinking bringing her here?

I took one last round of the bar before my patience ran out. She was here somewhere. I could smell it, but someone was glamoring her.

"Allistair, I need you to get your ass down to Black Brother's. Ruby's missing."

Under any other circumstances, I would chew my own arm off before I called on one of the other Horsemen. Glamors weren't my specialty, though, and there was no way I was calling on Julian for this. People always thought I was the biggest, baddest fucker around, but that's only because they'd never seen Death in action. Truth be told, you were already a goner if you saw him lift a finger in a fight. His particular brand of subtly was not needed for this, and Rysten had already pissed me off too much this week. I didn't know what state Ruby would be in when we found her, but I would rather place my pride on Allistair's help than the doom-and-gloom twins.

"How the fuck did you lose her?" His response took longer than I'd hoped, given who we were talking about.

"Someone fucking glamored her and is hiding her underneath my nose. I need you to sniff the fucker out," I snapped back.

"I'm on my way." Thank the fucking devil for that. I needed him here yesterday.

I didn't want to check the clock, but I knew the time was racking up. I gripped the railing, not noticing that I'd burned most of it away before I began to stumble over the edge. I pushed a gail of wind up from the floor below, and it hoisted me back onto the upper platform as parts of the broken railing fell on the poker table below. So much for keeping my cool.

I could burn the building down. Tear through it with a twister unlike any other. Flood it with rain that would drown half of the demons in this room. Even decimate it with an earthquake that would level all of Portland.

But Ruby was in here somewhere, and I needed to get my shit together until I found her.

Allistair came striding through the door in record time. Famine must have been staring at himself in the mirror when I reached out, given how quickly he got here. I was halfway down the stairs when his eyes locked on something. I hoped to Satan it was Ruby, because if it wasn't, I would level the Black Brothers to the fucking ground.

"Laran," Allistair said. The surrounding demons gave a wide berth when they realized who my friend was. I dropped my own glamor and the bar went silent. All except for one.

Allistair snapped his fingers, and disintegrated her glamor. Across the bar at the very first table I checked, was Ruby.

She was sitting on an imp's lap, letting out breathy little gasps.

Air tunneled through the bar at my beck and call, winking out the fire that burned the lotus leaves. The imp's hands crept tighter around her, pulling her supple skin closer to his body. The look on her face was dazed and confused.

He *dared* to conceal a claimed she-demon?

I saw red, and it was war.

CHAPTER NINE

T{\scriptsize HE} M{\scriptsize ALE} on my left turned to me and said, "Strong drink. What's your name, dollface?"

I gave him an appraising look. Neatly kept dark hair framed a handsome face. His eyes were wicked red and his teeth unnaturally white. He had a mischievous look about him, and I instantly put together that he was an imp. One of the most common demons in these parts, but also the ones a succubus would least want to tango with, if she were thinking clearly. I most certainly, was not.

A full-blooded imp has some impressive powers to any lesser demon, but lesser I was not. Even a half-breed like me would be a prize in a place like this. Our skin was the most potent aphrodisiac on the planet, ten times more so to other demons.

It was why I'd always stayed away. For fear of what someone skilled in persuasion, or Hell forbid, blood magic, could do.

But for the first time in my existence, I did not feel afraid. On the contrary, his enigmatic persona was drawing me in, and he hadn't said more than six words. Either he was more skilled with persuasion than even I could have guessed, in which case I was already fucked, or I was a glutton for punishment. Given how he exuded confidence like some men wore their desperation, I was inclined to believe it was a bit of both.

How lucky for me.

I eyed the black edges of a brand that were simultaneously peeking out of his collar and the cuff on his wrist. The ink was white, not the traditional black. Somewhere in the back of my mind, that meant something. So did the edges of what appeared to be flowers petals, but for the life of me, I couldn't seem to hold onto that thought, that concern, for more than a moment before I relaxed back into a state of forgetfulness. My heart rate slowed to a steady thump, falling in line with the rhythmic beat of a song only I could hear. I smiled coyly to the imp as the bartender slid my drink to me and said, "It's on the house."

I turned my pretty little smile on the bartender and he gave me a wink as I accepted the Black Russian and walked away from the bar. The imp would follow. I was sure of it. For a brief moment, I wondered where Laran went, but as I approached the table where the smoke was coming from, I seemed to no longer care.

All thoughts of Laran, the Horsemen, and even thoughts of myself vanished as I stood over the crowded gambling table. Dice and cards were flying everywhere, but the slow burning pot in the center made it hard to tear my gaze away.

"You want dealt in, poppet?" someone called out from the other side of the table. I shook my head.

"Can I watch?" I heard the soft, velvety purr in my voice. The males at the table looked up at me, and the scraping of a chair made me turn. The imp from the bar had pulled up a seat, and the others moved to make room for him. He lithely sat down in the chair, his knees parted as he leaned back and beckoned me.

"If you're sitting on my lap, you can," he growled. My stomach tightened at the challenge in his voice. I strode up to him and threw my head back, finishing my Black Russian in one swallow. I slammed the cup on table and turned my body around to perch on his knees. The imp took my invitation for what it was and placed a hand on my waist. Something like obsession took me as I focused on the funny looking leaves in the pot. The edges curled slowly, burning bright. I watched them, in a state of suspended euphoria that didn't seem to have a beginning or end. It just was, and I existed within it.

The imp flexed his fingers, the claw tips biting into my skin just beneath the sweater. I let out a sigh and shifted back. Closer to the demon. To heat. His arm wound around my waist, and I parted my legs so he could pull me back. Flush against him, I could hardly contain the moan building in my throat. Devil have me, I wanted him. I wanted all of them. I wanted to feel something heavy and hard between my legs, placating the need that drove me.

The imp's other hand clamped down on my knee that was pinned between his legs. Hot and heavy, his breath made my flesh break out in goosebumps as he whispered, "What do you want, dollface?"

I squirmed restlessly on his lap as his hand unsheathed its claws and slowly started the ascent up my leg, dipping into the jagged rips in my dark jeans. A sigh escaped my lips as the hand around my waist tightened, and his fingers slipped under my shirt. The brush of his claws made me ache and my back arched—

"Get your fucking hands off of her."

The hands on my body froze and I let out a hiss. That was not part of the deal. I turned my hooded eyes up to the demon that dared interrupt us, but was not prepared to see Laran and Allistair standing there.

Laran's face was a mask of frozen fury. I shivered leaning back into the demon whose lap I was currently sitting on. He didn't feel so hot anymore, and the ache I was feeling was on the cusp of pleasure and pain.

"Famine. War, I'm sorry. I didn't realize who you—"

"Ruby. Come," Allistair commanded. My eyes swiveled from the glowering demon threatening to explode, to the demon striding towards me with a voice that my made my stomach jerk. He reached out with both hands and plucked me from the imp's lap, locking one arm under my knees and supporting my back with the other. I squirmed in his grip, but Allistair held tight.

"Save your words, imp. You glamored her and tried to separate us after I placed my claim." Laran's voice boomed, shaking the tables enough that glass rattled against the countertops of the bar and shattered as it fell to the earth. In my delirious state, I couldn't process what was happening, or why. I just felt the need that drove me. I leaned into Allistair and inhaled deeply. Smoke filled my lungs, making me burn at my very core; a raging inferno that would not be denied.

"I'm taking her home, Laran. Make sure you clean up your mess."

Laran grunted in response and Allistair began moving. We crossed through the bar, moving faster and farther from the smoke with every second. I watched over Allistair's shoulder as we crossed the threshold, the embers on the smoking leaves expiring, and then we were gone.

One moment we were outside the bar, standing in the parking lot, and the next we were in an oddly familiar bathroom. Home, I recognized, as he opened the bathroom door connected to my bedroom. My queen-sized bed loomed in front of us and all I could hear, all I could feel, was the heat radiating through him. I turned my face towards his, biting my lip when I saw the fevered intensity. His eyes were not just amber. They were molten gold. He was angry, but I couldn't register why.

Only that I knew I wanted to take it away.

As my back hit the bed, and Allistair started to pull away, I fisted his shirt in my hand, holding him there.

"Stay." It was a single word: a command, a request, a plea, but it reverberated across the room and over his skin. I bit my lip again as his eyes dilated and darkened. He leaned forward, drawn in by the effect I had on him as I pushed my need through the air, through his clothes, over his skin, and into him.

"Ruby," he growled. The pain in his voice echoed the burning between my legs. I tugged him closer, grabbing his shirt with both fists and pulling. The buttons popped and ripped open when he stopped only inches away. I let out a growl and reached again, tearing through the undershirt. The moment our skin came into contact, an intense current of electricity shocked me, only it didn't hurt. But the burning beneath my skin didn't subside. A lust like I'd never known owned me.

"I need you," I whispered. The craving shook my body so hard, I was trembling. Allistair hovered over me, looking me up and down as I cocked my head, the succubus inside of me knowing just how to play the man before me.

"It's the drugs," he growled, the muscles in his arms flexing as he held himself inches away from me.

"I don't care. It hurts," I mewled. Allistair's eyes flashed and he took a tight breath before a resolution seemed to settle over him. He moved back to step away as I quickly sat forward to stop him. He wrapped his hands around my wrists, holding me at arm's length, but making no move to let me go. Gently, he pushed me until my back touched the bed and released my arms with a strained kind of control.

"I'm going to make it go away, Ruby, but you have to do what I tell you," he murmured. I nodded as he removed his suit jacket and ripped shirts. I gripped the sheets as I drank in his very scent, waiting for him. Admiring the shape of him, the ripples of his muscle, the contours of his abdomen traveling below the line of his belt…he settled on his knees in front of me and motioned for me to sit up again. I hated being told what to do, but the throbbing ache between my legs was not going anywhere.

Slowly, he hooked his fingers under the corners of my sweater and pulled it off. The crisp air hit my flesh and I let out a gasp. He placed a single finger against my lips, instructing me to keep quiet. Knowing it was rebellious, I opened my mouth and bit his finger as he let out a sharp hiss. Without warning, I was on my back, legs dangling over the edge of the bed, my jeans ripped off. I tried to sit up, but he forced me to my side, pinning both arms above my head as he lay next to me.

"Let me—"

"Shhh…" he whispered in the hollow of my ear. His other hand gripped my hip and began caressing my skin, teasing me as he moved his hand up my body.

"I'm not going to have sex with you, Ruby. Not tonight. You will barely remember, and I want you to remember the first time I make you scream." He squeezed my hardened nipples through the soft cotton of my bra. Pulling down the cup, he freed my breast to the chilled air and locked his deft fingers around my taught peak, rolling his thumb to send a sharp pleasure shooting through me. I let out a low moan as his lips brushed over my neck, and a throaty growl escaped as he bit me hard, sending shocks through my body.

"I'm not even going to kiss you," he continued. He moved his hand from my breast and trailed it down, grazing lightly over my ribs and settling on the apex of my thighs, cupping me over my cotton underwear.

"But I will take care you. I'm going to take the hurt away, Ruby, but no more," he whispered against my bare shoulder as his fingers rubbed over my sex. My head lolled as I arched into him.

"Please," I moaned. Allistair bit into me harder, and I let out a sharp yelp. It broke the skin, but it felt so good. I pushed against his hands, but he wasn't having it.

"I am going to let you go. And you will do as I say if you want your release. Is that understood?"

I whined in answer.

"Promise me, Ruby. Say you'll be good and you'll do as you are told."

Every part of me aching for his touch, I nodded and breathed out, "I promise. Just…please."

Allistair pulled away from me, his commanding presence dictating my every move so that I could have the one thing I wanted. He told me to sit up. I sat. He told me to move to the center of the bed. I moved. He told me to lay down on my side. I did as I was told. Allistair climbed in beside me and pressed my back to his front, positioning his arm underneath the curve in my side to wind it around my waist and shackle both my arms simultaneously. I writhed in the constriction.

"Shhh…you promised you would be good." He slipped his free hand down my hip and into my panties. I opened my legs as far as being spooned against him would allow me, and he took the invitation. He parted my folds with his fingers, grazing my clit just enough to make me buck. Impatient, I ground back into his hips, driven by the feel of his cock against my backside. He was impossibly hard, and yet, he wouldn't have me. I grit my teeth as I rubbed against him.

He hissed, and his fingers stopped.

Something dark and ugly unfurled in my chest, but I kept it in and stopped all movement. His fingers continued. I tried to keep my moans from escaping as he slipped a single finger inside of me, the slickness of my desires coating him. My body was begging for more, but he was drawing this out.

I shifted again, grinding against him. Again, he stopped.

"I'm not going to fuck you, Ruby. You take what I give, or you get nothing at all," he growled. Power lashed out from him, for just a moment, but it forced me to be still. The moment I stopped, he slipped two fingers inside of me, gliding them back and forth, pressing his palm into the swollen, sensitive nub. I arched my hips, trying to move against his fingers. Feel them deeper. Faster. Allistair's grip didn't give my body a single inch of room to chase my own pleasure the way I wanted. He kept at a slow torturous assault, letting an intense ache build inside of me that only he could relieve.

"More," I whispered, but I didn't dare rock back into him. Not when I was so close. I was so fucking close. He would reward me…

The force of his palm against my clit, rubbing it in rhythmic circles, faster… his fingers sweeping, plunging deep inside me…the pressure building, twitching, and burning as his speed increased…

"Come for me, Ruby," Allistair commanded. He left a trail of suckling kisses down my neck as I found my release. Stars exploded behind my eyes, so violent and so sudden that I couldn't scream. Waves of pleasure crashed through my body as I poured. I couldn't do anything but ride it out as I shuddered, his fingers never ceasing, working me all the way.

The moment my orgasm stopped, he pulled his hand away and clarity started to fill my mind. I twisted, trying to turn towards him, but his hard, unyielding body kept me trapped how he wanted me.

"Sleep," he whispered. The sound of his heart beating was the last thing I heard before the world faded black and sleep overcame.

****Allistair****

I DIDN'T KNOW if I was a Devil damned saint, or the worst fucking piece of shit in her life right now. No, I couldn't be the worst. Laran now held that title, thanks to his little excursion tonight. A low growl slipped from my throat before I could cut it off. Even in her sleep, she arched into me. Wanting something I very much planned to give her.

Soon. Just not tonight.

She wouldn't remember everything the white lotus brought on, but she would remember enough. I was not taking advantage of her when she was high. That would be fucking despicable, even for me.

My cock twitched as she moved closer, completely unaware of the effect she had on me. Well, not completely. She thought she was keeping her distance this past week. Ignoring me as best she could. What she didn't realize was that I could see that glint of need in her eyes every time she looked at me. I could feel it, as sharp and painful as I felt my own.

The only difference was that I wouldn't make her suffer because of Laran's fuck up. Even if it made it harder for me to stay away and keep my hands off of her. Julian's rules could go fuck themselves.

He could spout honor and duty as much as he wanted, but I knew the truth.

He wanted her just as bad as the rest of us. He just wouldn't give in.

I wasn't nearly as selfless, or stupid. It's what kept me here, in her bed. When I knew I should have left. She was a temptation; not quite forbidden, but entirely unexpected. When Lucifer brought us forth from the flames and gave us our purpose, I never imagined that I would want to fuck her like I do now.

I was supposed to protect her from men like me. Like Laran. Like Rysten. Especially Julian.

She wasn't a child though, and I never knew the child she was. The babe I saw all those years ago was gone. A week ago, I thought I hated myself for it because I missed out on knowing her. What I really hated was that I wanted her. If I'd been here when she was a child, that would have never come to pass. I wouldn't be in her bed right now, contemplating all the ways I was going to fuck her.

There was no going back now, not when her lips had my mind painting pictures of her on her knees. Putting her smart mouth to much better use.

Her dark blue hair slid across my chest as she twisted around in her sleep. So beautiful. So unique. She thought that we had the wrong girl, but never before have I met someone with hair the color of the flames. Not even Lucifer. I slid my hand through the slippery strands, mesmerized by the color change. The blue was dark enough to pass for black, until the light reflected the most stunning of azures.

"Where is she?" Laran's presence brushed against my mind, uninvited.

"She's at home. What do you want?" I replied tersely, brushing my fingers across the curve of her neck. The skin was so soft. Supple. A breathy little moan escaped her lips.

"I'm going to stop by and check on her. Can you tell Jul—"

"There's no need. I'm here with her." I sent back, focusing on the girl before me. They would call me away soon, but I didn't want to move. Not yet. Not when tomorrow was already coming.

"Why are you still with her?" There was a challenge in his tone. I frowned in annoyance, running my hand over the curve of her hip.

"Because she was so fucking high on white lotus, she may have hunted down the first man on the street to sate her if I hadn't made her go to sleep," I snapped back. There was no need to mention what happened before she went to sleep. Not even I would have been strong enough to calm her had I not given her what she needed first. She was the strongest succubus I had encountered pre-transition. The oldest, too. She was using powers she shouldn't have before the

change, and starving herself while she did it, no less. I don't know what went down in her past, but something happened that made her hesitant with men. Male demons even more so. Her body was begging to be touched and fulfilled, but her mind wanted no part of it.

Not consciously anyway.

"Meet me back home. Rysten is on his way to watch her." A sudden flash of anger boiled within me at his blatant attempt to get me away from her. He even went so far as to call in Rysten, who he hadn't bothered with at the bar. The fucker needed to remember it was his carelessness that caused this, and I had just as much right to her as he did.

"Feeling a bit heavy-handed, War?" I mentally growled back, sending my displeasure along with it. Ruby winced against me, pushing back. Her mind lashed out with power like an iron lifted right out of flame. It speared through my shields without effort, and took a sharp stab at the innermost part of myself. Attacking, where no demon had ever held the power to before. I recoiled from her, catching myself as I toppled out of her bed.

Had she felt my displeasure? Had that made her lash out? Or was it something more?

Even more curious, was where that power came from when she'd never given a hint of it before. I knew that something lurked inside her, as it had her father. I was almost certain that was not it, but something else entirely.

I watched her for a moment longer, the blood in my veins calling me back to her bed. As much as I didn't want to, I needed to get back and report what just happened.

It appeared our girl had more to her than meets the eye.

CHAPTER TEN

THE BIRDS WERE CHIRPING. The bees were buzzing. It was Saturday morning, and I didn't have work. The pounding in my head served as a reminder for the bad choices I made the night before. Like letting Laran take me to a demon bar, and getting felt up on some creepy imp's lap. Oh, and let's not forget how I finished the night off by throwing myself at Allistair.

Yeah. Last night was a shit show by anyone's standards.

I wanted to yell at Laran and blame him for putting me in the situation to begin with, but he didn't really make me go. He didn't make me high. I'm also equally sure he didn't make me seduce Allistair. All of which meant that as much as I wanted someone to blame, this was all on me, and it fucking sucked.

Being a demon and having lowered inhibitions wasn't always fun, compared to what people might think. At the end of the day, or really, the next morning, we still had to wake up and deal with the consequences.

"I'll have four orders of bacon and a cup of coffee. Thanks, Martha."

Yep. My consequences were me hiding in Martha's Diner and treating myself to bacon while I sat at my usual booth and stewed about the bad life choices I'd made. I liked to pretend it was a pre-reward for when I chose to do the right thing next time, but honestly, it was just another Saturday morning, and that meant this booth was the only place my ass would be.

The jingle of the bell on the front door pulled me from my inner rambling. *Please don't be Kendall.* I was not in the mood to deal with her shit today. By the time my head swiveled around to check the door, the shift in power that was seeping through the room left little guesswork about who it was.

Golden eyes bore into mine and the sinking feeling in my stomach became an anchor tugging me to the linoleum floor. I wanted to evaporate on the spot, but not even disappearing would save me from the embarrassment of last night. I straightened my spine and kept my head high.

"I went by your shop, but you're closed on Saturdays," he stated. He wasn't loud, but he projected enough that I heard him from across the diner. Devil damn him. Between Allistair and Kendall, the Saturday crowd would not be happy with me. I chose to ignore him, but I knew he wouldn't go away. "What kind of tattoo artist are you? That doesn't make a lot sense."

"It's the one day I have off, and it has been that way since I started taking care of myself. Now, if you'll excuse me…" I let me voice trail off, making it abundantly clear that I wanted him to leave. Silly me, thinking one of the Horsemen knew how to take a hint.

"Rather limiting, don't you think?" he continued, crossing the diner in smooth, measured steps. I growled under my breath, but shoved down the urge to throw a salt shaker at his head.

"If someone wants a tattoo, they can come in the other six days of the week. I'm not staying open until two in the fucking morning on a Saturday for drunk rejects to stumble in and get something they'll regret in the morning. That's not how I run my business, and it's a great way to tarnish your name." I leaned back in the booth and crossed my arms over my chest.

"If you say so," he said when he reached the table. He placed a hand on my shoulder and I slapped it away instantly, like he was an annoying fly and not someone whose every movement I was keenly aware of.

"What do you want?" I snapped at him. Allistair grinned at me, like he knew *exactly* where my thoughts had been going.

"You," he said bluntly without having the decency to keep his voice down. The fucking audacity. I swallowed hard, pleased that the vixen inside me was stomped on by a sizzling anger racing through me. I opened my mouth to tell him off, but he put a finger to my lips in the most publicly sexual way possible. "Now, now, Ruby. No need to make a scene. It is my turn after all."

I considered biting him just to prove a point, but the coughing behind him and the smell of bacon brought me to a halt. Allistair stepped aside and took the seat across from me as Martha sat down my pile of bacon and a cup of steaming black coffee.

"There a problem here, Ruby?" Martha asked. Her sharp brown eyes cut towards Allistair. It wouldn't have been the first time some jackass wouldn't leave me alone. If only Allistair was a stalker. He wasn't though, and even if Martha threw him out, I know he would just find me later. Better now in a public setting where he couldn't try any funny business.

"I'm good, Martha. Thanks," I said. She watched him for a moment longer before turning to me.

"If you need anything, just holler. Ol' Ben keeps a baseball bat in the back just for the persistent ones." I choked on my sip of coffee, silently waving her off. She threw Allistair one last look of disdain before leaving us.

"The old woman thinks you need protection from me," Allistair noted as I took a swig of my coffee.

"Do I?"

Allistair's eyes flickered with something akin to amusement, but that wasn't all that was lurking there. The onyx flecks swirled around the iris; mesmerizing, but deadly. Allistair was the Horsemen of Famine, and as far as I could tell, the strongest incubus I'd ever come across. He said he was here to protect me, but my hazy memories from the night before didn't lend to that. There was a darkness in his eyes, something so sharp and painful, but in the most pleasurable of ways. A predator. I had no desire to be his prey.

"You have nothing to fear from me. I make no guarantees for the rest of this world, but I would never harm you," Allistair said.

"Because you think I'm Lucifer's daughter?"

Allistair narrowed his eyes and replied, "You are his daughter. I have no doubt about that." His smug voice and cold arrogance was off-putting. I pursed my lips, taking another sip of coffee.

"My birth certificate is hardly proof," I scoffed. I'd always hated having the last name Morningstar, but in a world full of humans, most people didn't know how odd it was to be a demon named after the king himself. Not once in my almost twenty-three years have I ever questioned there being more to it, and given my lackluster abilities, I wasn't about to start.

"Your birth certificate is just what we used to track you. We didn't need it to prove who you were. We know who you are. We've always known. We were there the day you were born. We were there when Lola smuggled you out of Hell. Rysten's the one that made your birth certificate while Lucifer placed his mark on you. You grew up invisible because we needed you to." The controlled passion that lay beneath that smooth, honey-like voice silenced me. I didn't know how to reply, because I didn't know if he was telling the truth. He sounded like he was sincere, but I wasn't dumb enough to trust my instincts. Demons lie. They cheat. His abilities alone could probably make me believe the sky was yellow if I gave him the chance. There was also a hole in his story…

"I don't have a mark."

Allistair's eyes dropped to my chest and back up. If I didn't know any better, I'd say he was checking me out. I opened my mouth to tell him where his eyes belong—

"Ruby!"

Fuck me. I knew that voice. It belonged to the only person in Portland that could make me cringe out of both pity and annoyance.

"Kendall," I muttered under my breath, rolling my eyes. I took a long drink of my coffee, hoping she would see I was with someone and leave. Unfortunately, that was not the case.

"What are you doin' here? You should be banned from comin' here after what you did to my car," she sneered as she stomped toward our table.

"I don't know what you're talking about," I feigned innocently as I schooled my face into a bored expression. Her brown eyes sparkled with hatred until they turned to the person sitting across from me. I didn't know if it was because Allistair exuded sex appeal, or if she really couldn't stand to see any man near me, but her eyes roamed over his designer suit and dark hair, turning more lustful and jealous by the second. *Oh, boy. Here we go.*

"Who might you be?" she inquired, waiting for his name. There was a subtle coax to her voice that I think was meant to be alluring, but instead made her sound desperate. Allistair tore his eyes from my face to give her a dismissive glance.

"I'm a friend of Ruby's," he said coldly. I wasn't sure whether I was supposed to do a little clapping dance in my head, or be concerned by the venomous glare she turned back to me.

"I'd be careful keepin' company with a girl that has her *record*. She's goin' to find herself in such trouble one day that even the Lord can't save her from it," Kendall said. Her words were meant to be chilling, but her implied threat didn't worry me.

"You can't save someone that's already damned," I muttered under my breath.

"Are you admittin' your indiscretions?" Kendall said tersely.

"Only if you admit yours." She blanched on the spot and I cocked an eyebrow.

"I don't know what you're talkin' about," she said stiffly. I munched obnoxiously on a piece of bacon because I knew it annoyed her.

"Isn't that my line?" I shot back, hiding my grin behind the lip of my coffee cup. She narrowed her eyes, smoothing over her yellow dress. Always so prim and proper in front of people.

"I have no idea what Josh ever saw in you," she said snidely.

"Self-respect and pure fucking awesomeness," I deadpanned. Kendall's mouth set in a firm line, and while it was mildly amusing to push her buttons, I wanted her to leave.

"My lawyer will be in touch," she said grimly. She started to turn away when Allistair thrust out his hand. She froze mid-turn and glanced back.

"Be sure to give him my card. I'll be representing her from now on," Allistair said in a voice devoid of any warmth. I was a bit shell-shocked myself, given that I didn't think he was a real lawyer, or would be suitable representing me for a damn parking ticket, much less arson. I wasn't going to say that in front of her, though.

Her perfectly manicured nails, extending like claws as she took the card and turned those hateful eyes on me.

"I'd be careful who you sleep aroun' with for favors, Ruby. By the looks of him, I think you've bitten off more than you can chew," she said with a cunning smile.

"Thanks for the concern, but I think I'll be just fine. A little whipping never hurt anybody," I snapped. The words were out of my mouth before I could think about it.

Kendall's face flamed red as she turned and marched out of the diner muttering "*Satanists*" under her breath. The diner went oddly quiet as the other customers pretended to be absorbed by the daily news or a speck of lint on their shirts. Even up at the counter, Martha was taking her time ringing up orders, albeit with a grin on her face. I drained the rest of my coffee as Allistair let out a chuckle under his breath.

"You know, I'm not one for whipping, but I'm sure Julian would be happy to oblige if you—"

"Stop talking."

"Is there something else you would rather do?" he asked, the wicked glint in his eyes making my stomach clench.

"Not with you."

"That's not what you were saying last night," he mused. I pinned him with a hard glare even though I felt dirty inside. Dirty because I liked what I remembered. I liked it a lot, but neither of us were in our right minds when we did it.

"That won't happen again. You can thank Laran and the Black Brothers for that one," I muttered.

Allistair watched me for another moment. "Perhaps. But we have an eternity together, and I look forward to every minute of it once you realize that." His words sent shivers down my spine, both good and bad.

I should have heeded my own warning about playing with fire.

CHAPTER ELEVEN

THE SHARP KNOCK on my office door made me jump. My head smacked against the hanging overhead lamp and I cursed under my breath. Things were crazy since the Horsemen had shown up, and Bandit wasn't with me today, making me instinctively edgy. I set aside the drawing I was working on and called, "Come in."

A wave of green hair fell through my office door as Moira pushed past it and closed the door behind her. Her dark green eyes scanned me, her forest colored brows drawn together in what appeared to be worry, but I couldn't feel it. My empath gifts only extended so far, and while I could usually guess when Bandit got up in arms about something, Moira was more complicated than that.

"Something wrong?" I asked, motioning to the chair in front of my desk. She ignored my offer and walked around to my side. Pushing the papers into a pile, she slid back onto my desk, letting her legs dangle a few inches from the ground.

"I'm worried about you."

"Okay," I drawled out, taking a loose breath. "Is this about the Horsemen?"

"Possibly," Moira said, biting her lip. She glanced at me, looking up and down like she was searching for something. I was the same Ruby I've always been: ripped up jeans and unbrushed hair, pulled back to hide my general laziness. "I just feel like there's something you're not telling me. Did something happen with them?"

I let out a sigh, considering my answer. Apart from last Friday, when Laran took me to a bar that gave me some kind of demonic high, not much had happened. Sure, the guys were still following me everywhere, showing up at the oddest of times, but I was beginning to settle into a routine with it. Typically, Rysten came first, then Laran, followed by Allistair. I'd only seen Julian a handful of times; unlike the other three, who were giving me subtly stronger fuck-me-vibes with every day that passed. I wasn't sure how much of their spending time with me was for my actual protection, and how much was them attempting to sink their claws into me.

Moira coughed, and I blinked once. *Shit.*

"So," she said with narrowed eyes, "there is something that happened, isn't there?"

I leaned back in my chair and kicked my feet up beside her on the thick glass surface. I tilted my head back in my chair, relaxing my spine as I stared up at the ceiling, counting the flecks of dust.

"Not something specific, per se. It's just been a long few days."

"The Horsemen are getting possessive."

Well that wasn't what I expected to come out of her mouth. She hadn't been around us all that much, and I hadn't mentioned it. I cracked my knuckles absentmindedly while I asked, "What makes you say that?"

I couldn't see her face, but I suspected she was giving me a look along the lines of *are you kidding me?* She huffed under her breath and I smirked just a little, waiting for her answer.

"Josh came by the house before you got home yesterday, as per his usual Sunday groveling routine. I tried to chase him off, but Laran showed up. I think Josh just about shit bricks when Laran told him that you're theirs and he'll feed him to the hounds of Hell if he comes near you again."

I facepalmed as I let out a heavy sigh. *Feed him to Hell hounds? Very creative.*

"Well, that sounds unpleasant," I said lamely. Moira didn't reply. I raised my head from the back of my chair to see her watching me. She was not amused.

"They've taken a liking to you, Ruby."

"You don't know that for certain…" My words fell short when she gave me the look. The Moira look. She wasn't buying it. I let out the most unflattering of noises, somewhere between a sigh and a groan, as I slouched back into my chair.

"Yes, I do."

"Admitting it doesn't change anything. It just makes the current situation even more messed up," I muttered, throwing an arm over my eyes.

"Maybe it's just because they think they need to protect you; maybe it's more. On the bright side, if it is a passing obsession, they should get over it eventually—" She stopped mid-sentence and examined me carefully. "I'm not helping, am I?"

I didn't want to be rude. It wasn't her fault her own anxiety was leaking over into me and made my slightly cautious brain light up like a police siren telling me I should run like hell. I'd been taking on others' emotions long enough, I knew how to tell the difference between what I was feeling and what they unintentionally pushed on me. With Moira, it just seemed that I was more in tune and struggled on where to draw the line.

"Not really. I know you mean well, but the best I can do is to just roll with it for now. It's not like I have a lot of choice in getting them to leave me alone. Besides," I said, placing a gentle hand on her knee, "they really aren't that bad. Julian is a bit standoffish, and Allistair likes to push my buttons. Laran's pretty cool when he's not being all 'War smash', and Rysten is—" Her soft smile went sour and she swatted my hand away.

"Don't do that! You know I don't like it when you mess with my emotions. It's weird," she said. I raised an eyebrow. "It's weird if I try to help you feel better, but it's not weird when you make people's eardrums explode?" I asked, fighting a grin. She nodded without a trace of humor. "Whatever." I rolled my eyes and stood to gather my things.

"I actually came to tell you Rysten's here. I just wanted to talk with you before you left. You can tell him, and the rest of his cohort, that I'm taking you out this Friday, and no, they're not invited." I slung my bag over my shoulder and grabbed my keys.

"It's my birthday. Shouldn't I be the one that says who's invited?" I asked absentmindedly. I already knew the answer. It was Moira I was talking to, and normal people logic wouldn't work here. She was just as possessive as the Horsemen and didn't give a single fuck.

"Nope, they've been hogging you since they showed up, and you only turn twenty-three once. I've made plans for us. They can find someone else to stalk for the night," she said as she hopped off my desk and opened the door. I followed her out into the lobby where Rysten was standing off to the side, both eyebrows raised as he watched us approach.

"It took you that long to tell her I'm here?"

She bristled instantly, and he grinned like a fool. Out of all the Horsemen, he was the only one that truly seemed to take pleasure in tormenting her. Not that she was all that innocent either.

"It makes sense that you're Pestilence. You're more of a pest than the other three," Moira responded icily. It wasn't even very funny, but the venom with which she said it made Rysten let out a dark chuckle.

"I've heard that one a time or two. You might want to get some new jokes, banshee," he said holding his hand out for me. I ignored the invitation and proceeded towards the door.

"I'll see you tonight," I called over my shoulder without waiting for a reply. The chill in the autumn air hit me full force and swept the strands of my messy bun away from my face. The sky was a dull shade of black that matched the city cement, but the wind howled as it sent dead leaves tunneling down the alleys of Portland.

"What's on the evening agenda today, love?" Rysten asked, strolling up beside me, his footsteps silent as the grave.

"I'm tired. I think I'm going to go home and watch *How to Get Away with Murder* with Bandit," I said.

Rysten frowned. "You're a demon. I don't think it's that difficult figuring out how to get away with murder, but if you need someone taken care of, I can do it for you…" His voice started to trail off as I let out the first true laugh I'd had this past week. I had to put a hand against my car to steady myself as water pricked my eyes.

"I don't need someone killed, Rysten." I said hoarsely.

"But you said—"

"It's a TV show about these law students that—" I stopped at the first hint of a smirk on his lips. He leaned forward and whispered, "Gotcha."

I groaned under my breath and opened the driver's side door. That dickwad. He knew exactly what I was talking about. I slammed the door and started the engine, taking my foot off the brake right as the passenger side door opened and Rysten got in beside me.

"Don't be mad, love. You said you were tired. I thought you could use a laugh," he coaxed me, batting his eyelashes.

"Uh huh," I grumbled under my breath. The words were sweet as sugar, but I didn't believe the sincerity I heard there.

"I'll have you know that Viola Davis is one of my favorite actresses," he continued. I rolled my eyes as I pulled out onto the main street.

"How do you even know who she is? I thought you spent all your time in Hell until Lucifer"— I searched for an adequate word that didn't sound dickish, given that they thought he was my father. They'd guarded him for thousands of years, and I had no idea how their relationship had been with the King of Hell—"uh…died. I mean, isn't that your entire job?"

Rysten went quiet for a moment, and I thought he wasn't going to answer. "While we did serve in guarding him, he was not who we were created for. When you came along, it was like we finally saw the purpose for our existence. We were supposed to stay in Hell so that no one knew Lola smuggled you out, but instead, we ended up taking turns coming to earth. We didn't know where you were, and we weren't supposed to look until the time came. Being here on earth, though, we were closer to you than in Hell —" He stopped abruptly, like he'd said more than he intended.

My knuckles turned white against the red fur that lined the steering wheel.

Bit by bit, the pieces were falling into place about the Horsemen, and while I didn't know where attraction played into all of this, I was pretty sure I just figured out the possessiveness. If they were created for Lucifer's daughter, whoever she is, it made sense for them to feel so attached.

"So, you spent your time here watching TV, and that's how you discovered Viola?" I turned the subject right back to what we were supposed to be making small talk about. I didn't want to think about the real heir of Hell, or ruin Rysten's mood by pointing out for the hundredth time that I'm not her.

"Yeah, sometimes. I spent a lot of time going to concerts around the world, meeting people, learning about humans. I knew that you'd be raised like one, and the others were too daft to think that when this happened, it might be scary for you. I wanted to be the one you got close to." He smiled a little, not quite his brazen confidence I was getting used to, but something more genuine. We didn't say anything else for the rest of the drive home.

As I killed the engine, I couldn't help the words from popping out of my mouth. "You want to come inside and watch TV with me?"

Rysten grinned. "You sure the green one will be okay with that?"

"Moira will live. She's already staked her claim on Friday night. We're going out and she said none of you are invited," I replied, throwing my door open. I was pleasantly surprised that Josh wasn't waiting on my driveway when I got home. Maybe Laran really did scare the shit out of him. The thought brought me an obscene amount of glee.

"I can't say I'm terribly surprised. She heard me on the phone with Laran before she went back to get you. He wanted us to take you out for your birthday," Rysten sighed. I thought back to Moira's adamant insistence. Yeah, she was sneaky enough to pull that. Not that I was shocked or upset about it. For the most part, I only saw one or two Horsemen at a time. The four of them together were overwhelming, and I was more than happy to avoid that a bit longer.

I trudged up to the front door and Bandit peeked his head through the blinds. I smiled as I swung the door open and got mauled with his hugs. He jumped from the corner of the couch onto my chest, wrapping his arms around my neck.

"I missed you, too," I murmured, flicking the light on. I tossed my bag on one of the couches and carried him into the kitchen. Pulling out a Tupperware of cooked chicken, I proceeded to heat it in the microwave and feed Bandit his dinner.

While he was eating, I excused myself back to my room and changed into yoga pants. As I pulled the dark red sweater over my head, I noticed something strange in the mirror. Between my breasts were two little black dots. I moved closer, running my fingers over them. They weren't large or bumpy, but they were placed in a straight line. I frowned.

What the hell is it?

A sharp knock on my bedroom door startled me. "You okay, Ruby?"

I rolled my eyes, already somewhat regretting inviting him inside. I dropped my sweater and turned away from the mirror. I'd deal with it later when I didn't have prying eyes watching my every move. I slipped into the hallway and closed my bedroom door behind me, not realizing how close Rysten was until a breath of warm air brushed the back of my neck. My skin broke out in goosebumps. I spun around, trying to keep a modicum of distance between us, but it was hopeless in the narrow hallway.

Rysten's dark green eyes stared down at me. Intense and mischievous. My mouth went dry and I swallowed hard.

"See something you like?" he rumbled. There was a challenge in his voice that had me imagining how soft his hair would feel tousled in my fingers, his head... I blinked, pushing the thoughts aside.

"Yep"— my eyes slid right past him just as he began to grin—"my couch."

Rysten clutched his chest. "You wound me."

I snorted and squeezed by him, holding my breath so I didn't inhale his scent. It was unlikely he'd smell like post-gym body odor, because that would be way too convenient, wouldn't it? I settled in the corner of my oversized sectional couch, the grey microsuede upholstery welcoming me to lean back. I stretched across the couch for the remote, and Rysten sat cozy, flush against me. Of course. Out of all the spaces he could sit, he would pick the only one that is literally right next to me.

I didn't say anything as I pulled up the TV guide and turned on the fifth episode of season one, but just as I leaned back, Rysten put his arm across the back of the couch. I glanced sideways out of the corner of my eye, and the devilish grin I found on his face made me bite my cheek.

I crossed my arms over my chest as the show started. My thick sweater made it so we weren't touching, but a pleasant warmth radiated from him. Unlike Allistair's presence, that caused a scorching heat and spurned a need in me, Rysten's was a comfortable steadiness that made me ache. It was delicious and frustrating at the same time.

After forty-five minutes of sitting still as a rock, I shifted to try to get more comfortable—and farther away. Rysten chose that moment to scoot even closer, pinning me between him and the couch as I sat crisscrossed beside him.

I bit my lip hard and gasped when I tasted blood. The tangy scent of ichor and something else caught me off guard.

"You alright?" Rysten asked. I turned my head a fraction of the way towards him and nodded, not trusting my mouth to work.

"You're bleeding." His eyes dropped to my lower lip as I freed it from my teeth. He raised his other hand and ran the pad of his thumb across my lower lip. A burning started in my chest, hot and scorching, as it spread throughout my limbs. Adrenaline spiked my system as he drew his hand away, a single drop of dark blue blood staining it. He brought his thumb to his lips, and his tongue flicked out, licking the single drop away.

I don't know why the hell that turned me on so much. Maybe it wasn't the act. Maybe it was the look in his eyes; the way he watched me while he did it.

Frozen in my spot, I could do little more than watch as he reached out again and ran his thumb across my lower lip. I found myself leaning into him as he slid his cool fingers along my jaw.

I shivered as his warm breath hit the sensitive part of my ear. His lips brushed against me, barely making contact, as he whispered, "Tell me when to stop."

Heat pooled low in my stomach, but my brain didn't seem to be working. I unraveled beneath the curve of his lips as he trailed them down my jaw. The last thing I saw as my eyes fell closed was his expression: hungry, but vulnerable. A moment passed, suspended there as our breath mingled. That scent that I couldn't define filled the air around me; intoxicating as I breathed it in.

It was wrong. I knew it was wrong, because nothing this good was ever right. It was rare that I found someone who so fully captured my attention as he and the Horsemen did. I was a damn fool for caving, and I almost pulled away. Until he said, "You're everything I didn't know I wanted."

His lips met mine, smooth and sweet, but the gentleness didn't stay for long. He shifted his arm from the back of the couch to wrap around me as I uncrossed my legs and turned into him. His fingers tangled into my hair, cupping the back of my head, pulling me closer as his tongue parted the seam of my lips. Coaxing me. Claiming me. I reached out, fisting his shirt, pulling him closer than I'd dared to with anyone in such a long time, the other night notwithstanding. That was because I was high. This was exhilarating and frightening, but the air crackled with a tension that couldn't be denied.

I kissed him like my life depended on it, but that was nothing compared to the way his lips destroyed me. Fuck living. He kissed me like he was dying. Like this was the first and last kiss we'd ever have—and maybe it was. But he was doing an awfully good job at branding it into my memory.

He broke the kiss just when I realized I needed air or I'd faint, but his lips didn't leave me. He kissed his way back up my jaw, and left stinging bites all down my neck. I arched into the little dose of pain, silently urging him on. Pushing him to give me more. He pulled the crook of my sweater to the side, exposing my shoulder so that he could taste every inch of me. He left a string of reddened skin, slight purple teeth marks to the very edge of my shoulder before making his way back. A low moan escaped my lips as his teeth scraped the sensitive part of my neck, just beneath my ear.

His hands moved to my hips as I straddled his lap and ground myself into the hard bulge beneath me. The breath hissed between his lips, and he bit down on my earlobe.

"What do you want?" he asked. My hands seemed to move on their own accord as they slipped beneath the edge of his shirt. He bit my earlobe again, a touch more pressure. I let out another breathy moan as he said, "What. Do. You. Want? Tell me. Soon enough, I won't be able to stop."

His breath was cold against my burning skin.

I scrambled to get off his lap as fast as I could, but he didn't let go.

"Let go of me," I said. I bit the inside of my cheek to stop from moaning as his hand slipped underneath my shirt. The circles he drew against my lower back with his thumb sent an inferno blazing through my self-control, but I held strong.

"Why?" he murmured, leaning into me.

"Because we can't do this."

"Give me one reason why, and I'll let you go," he whispered, his face against my neck, his words against my skin. I'd avoided this conversation for the last week, and again at the diner when Allistair confronted me. Trapped with Rysten between my legs, I had to speak up now, or whatever happened next was on me.

"Tell me *why* you want me," I said. Rysten ran his lips along the edge of my collarbone, and his non-answer was point enough. "You don't even know, do you? That's the problem. You have no choice *but* to want me, and I can't screw someone who has no choice in the matter."

Rysten froze beneath me, but did not release his hold. I became painfully aware of the slow, steady thrum of my own heartbeat as it reverberated beneath my skin. Rysten slowly pulled back.

"Ruby, have you been torturing yourself this entire time thinking that we could only possibly want you because we have no choice?" he asked, a smile playing on the corners of his lips. I didn't find this funny in the slightest.

"I've never met a man where that's not the case," I replied tersely. He slipped his entire hand underneath my sweater and flattened it against my back.

"We've already had this conversation before. I'm not a man."

"Man. Demon. You are still male. You're all the same where I'm concerned. I've had women come onto me before, so it's not gender specific, really. My point is that if I sleep with you, it won't be your choice, and that's kind of rapey, if you ask me."

Rysten didn't hold back from laughing at me. I pushed his chest trying to wiggle my way off him, but he wasn't letting up any more than he was before. His laugh trailed off into a heavy silence, the air between us stretched taut with pressure.

"Ruby, love, I can't believe we're having this conversation right now, but if we need to have it for you to feel comfortable, then we'll have it. I want *you*. And not because it's my job, or because you're a succubus. You think I can't see past the draw of a succubus? That the allure captures me and renders me unable to make my own decisions? Yes, I want you because the very smell of your skin makes me hard. Every time you bite your lip, I imagine what you taste like; what it feels like to bite that very same lip and hear you moan. But those are not the reasons *why*. Those are simply *wants*." He paused, letting out a strained breath. "You have a fire in you that I have not seen in anyone in a very long time. A wildness about you. I told you once already: you are not what I thought you'd be. But now that I know you, I don't know how I could possibly imagine you any different. You are everything that we could have ever wanted you to be, and so much more. When I am with you, I realize how lucky we are that no one ever swept you off your feet, because I don't think that any of us would have let them live if they had."

My mouth popped open. I didn't know what to say to that. His eyes were dark and lustful, but he didn't seem to have the crazed obsession I was used to seeing. He'd be fumbling a lot more if he did, and he sure as hell couldn't string his thoughts together so well.

"How do you know you're not being affected without realizing it?" I asked.

"You do realize who you're talking to? You know what I am. I'd make for a poor Horsemen if I didn't have the knowledge or strength to fight off desire. And not even you, Hell's heir, are strong enough to make me do anything against my will. That's why we were created: to be the only equals that could protect and balance you."

Aside for the being Hell's heir part, he had a point. The legends never told what *kind* of demons they were, only what you would find if you ever crossed them. I couldn't argue his logic that my few latent powers weren't nearly enough to force his hand.

Then the door opened. And Moira walked in. Her eyes wavered between Rysten and me, and she let out a dramatic sigh.

"I see why you're beginning to think they're not so bad," she commented. My face burned as a blush crept across my cheeks. I scrambled back, and this time Rysten let me go. Moira cocked an eyebrow and nodded towards him. "Time to go, pest," she said unapologetically.

Rysten didn't argue. He simply stood and said, "I'll see you tomorrow, Ruby. Get some rest."

I watched him disappear outside my front door and I turned towards a rather pissed off Moira. She didn't say anything as she walked back to her room. Her silence spoke louder than any words she could have chosen.

CHAPTER TWELVE

Four days had passed, and Moira hadn't said shit. The morning after she saw me with Rysten, I had woken up to her continuing on like everything was normal. Except it wasn't. In the time since, not once had she bitched about the Horsemen. Hadn't engaged in her usual antics with Rysten. She was acting normal…but that wasn't 'normal Moira,' and it was driving me fucking nuts. At least our plans were still on for tonight. I closed shop early in the hopes of trying to talk with her without the Horsemen showing up, but she was particularly good at avoiding me when she wanted to.

Standing in the shower, I glowered into the plume of steam that wrapped around me. The water was turned up as hot as I could get it, and it still wasn't hot enough. Flipping the nozzle off, I used the other hand to wring my hair out. Strands of wet, dark hair clung to my fingers, reflecting indigo in the light.

The bathroom door thudded twice as Moira called out, "We need to leave in half an hour if we're going to make it there before the switch."

The switch? I frowned, wrapping the purple towel around me. She made it sound like we were going to a prison. I crossed the cold tile floors, slick with condensation. The door knob was slippery in my grasp as I turned the handle and asked, "What do you mean 'make it there before the switch'?"

Moira smiled, and I saw a little bit of the stunning banshee underneath the glittering pale eyeshadow. "You'll just have to see, now won't you?" she said, turning on her heel. The black baby doll dress she wore swished just past her ass, her legs barely protected by black floral tights. Her mint colored skin practically glowed beneath the sheer fabric. It's such a shame the humans couldn't see her in her full glory. She would be wearing a glamor tonight, just as she always did, and that beautiful green would disappear.

At least we weren't prison crashing. Not even Moira would get all dressed up for that. Looks like we were going partying at an unknown indoor location, given that it wasn't even thirty degrees outside and she liked the cold about as much as I did.

I closed the bathroom door and got to work on my hair, blow drying it into soft billowing waves that really showed off the stunning blues. I applied only the bare essentials in makeup and moved on to my outfit when Moira came back in.

"Why are you still wearing a bathrobe?" She swung open my closet door without waiting for a reply. It took less than a minute before she was ripping things off the hangers and tossing them at me. "Put these on. We gotta go."

I disrobed and dressed in the skinny jeans and the crop top she gave me, making a mental note to grab a jacket before we left. Moira grabbed my shoulders and turned me towards the metal framed mirror. A branch of iron thorns surrounded my scantily clad body. Moira had chosen well; the crop showed off my curves while still flattering my tall frame.

"I think you should—"

I zoned out as something caught my eye. The number of dots seated on my sternum had increased. Previously, there were two sitting across from each other. There was now a third that sat an inch lower on the right side.

"Ruby, are you even listening to me?" she snapped, pulling me from my thoughts.

"Yeah," I said, rubbing my chest where the dots were.

"Excellent," she said gleefully, smacking her nude lips together, a pair of spiked black heels in her hand. I took one look at the shoes and groaned. "What are you waiting for? Hurry up!"

I could do little more than comply. At least she was acting like herself.

Within the next two minutes, we were out the door and on our way, hooker heels and all. Bandit kept grabbing at my leg wanting to come with, but I knew he wouldn't be welcome in whatever public shindig Moira planned on taking us to. In the end, all it took was can of sardines and he was content to let me go.

Fifteen minutes later, and almost two car accidents, thanks to Moira's driving, we pulled up outside Pandora's Box, the hottest and most exclusive nightclub in town. I'd only ever heard rumors about what went on inside, usually from my clients. How Moira was going to pull this one off was beyond me.

Outside, the club was sleek and void of any windows or doors, apart from the front entrance that currently had a line wrapped around the block. Moira pulled up to the curb, and the valet that approached us gave her a questioning purse of his lips.

She hopped out of the car and handed him the keys, ignoring his mutterings about how he wasn't sure if we were in the right place. I couldn't blame him. Her ten-year old Camry didn't really fit the bill with one taillight out and a dent on the front bumper. True to form, Moira didn't give two shits. She passed him a fifty and said, "Keep the change."

The valet, pleased with his tip, changed his attitude as I clambered out of the car. With the damn heels, I was well over six feet tall. Moira was wearing some impressive shoes as well, and that made our height difference almost minimal. I glanced between her and the line, because I didn't know about her feet, but mine were not going to put up with standing in line for three hours just to be turned away at the door.

As if she'd read my mind, Moira linked our arms and leaned in. "Relax. I have connections," she muttered as she led us up to the front of the line. A bouncer took one look at us, and just when I thought he was going to turn us away, his face lit up in a warm smile.

"Hey, Moira, this the friend you were telling me about?"

Moira nodded demurely, but even in the low light coming from the sign above, I could see a faint blush creep across her cheeks. Bouncer boy flashed his dimples again and unclipped the rope, ushering us through.

We hadn't even crossed the threshold when I leaned in to ask, "So, what did you have to do to pull this off?"

Moira's smile only increased as we took our first steps into the dazzling lights that were Pandora's Box. "You don't want to know," she said and smirked at me. She's right; I didn't.

Still linked arm in arm, we walked toward the bar. Purple and blue lights danced across the crowd of bodies on a dance floor that was packed so tight, I didn't think even Moira could slip between them. Rhythmic dance music pulsed through the air, the vibrations thrumming against my skin, luring me with its hypnotic melody.

The bartender turned towards us, his gold bow-tie shimmering in the light. Moira flashed him a come-hither look as she crooked her finger and beckoned him closer. I rolled my eyes as he asked, "What can I get for you ladies?"

"Dirty martini," Moira rattled off, looking over at me expectantly.

An odd feeling crept through my veins. I couldn't place what caused it, but I didn't like it.

"Ruby! What drink?"

"I'm not sure…" I muttered. I took a quick glance around the room, but there wasn't a demon in sight. We'd been out drinking hundreds of times, and nothing ever happened. So why was I feeling paranoid suddenly? *Because drugs and an imp with grabby hands in the middle of butt-fuck nowhere…*

"It's your birthday," she said crossly. "I did not suck tha—"

"Birthday girl, eh?" the bartender said, cutting her off mid-rant. He gave me a lopsided smile and said, "I've got something for you. On the house."

"Alright," I agreed. Moira and I settled in at the bar and I took another sweeping glance of the club. There was just so much to look at: the dancers, the lounge, the winding staircase that led up to darkened hallways with unmarked doors, hiding secrets of their own. All bathed in shifting violet light.

"What do you think's up there?" I asked her.

"No clue." She shrugged, turning back to the counter as the bartender came with our drinks. Moira took a sip of her martini and let out a little sigh of happiness while I stared at the swirling concoction before me. It was pale white with just the faintest hint of blue whorls. I took a daring sip.

"Oh," I murmured, blinking. It was good! Really good. It reminded me of a piña-colada, but somehow tangy and less sweet.

"You like it?" she asked. I nodded as a steady warmth built in my chest. I felt lighter, but not out-of-my-mind-sexed-up like I was at the demon bar. I finished my drink within minutes and ordered another.

"Ruby?" I turned in my seat, just as someone put their hand on the small my back. I knew that voice, and it definitely didn't belong in a club with me.

"Josh?" The steady buzz building inside me made my lips loose. "How'd you get in here?"

"I know a guy," he said smugly. His hand still hadn't moved. He was getting cozy as he placed himself between me and the empty barstool. I frowned.

"Stop touching me," I said. The bartender chose that moment to appear with my drink and I smiled gratefully. Josh dropped his hand from my back, but didn't move away from me otherwise.

"I just—I need to talk to you, Ruby. Me and you, without your…bodyguards."

I took a long sip of my drink. *Bodyguards…that sounds about right.*

"Josh"— my voice was obnoxiously loud, even by my standards—"how many times do I have to tell you that—"

"You don't get it, Ruby!"

I swallowed hard, considering his once bright blue eyes, now blood-shot…but there was something else there. It didn't look human. *What is wrong with him?*

"I can't stop thinking about you. I know you're having a hard time forgiving me, but please hear me out," he pleaded. I took another swig of my drink, prepared to cut all pretenses of civility from my voice.

"Leave. Her. Alone," Moira said in a voice like death. "Stop following her. Stop showing up at our house to talk to her. If I see you come around one more time, I'm getting Rysten to come take care of your ass and make you disappear. You hear me, Josh? Go. Away." Moira jumped to my defense with a fierceness I couldn't have predicted, and what's more, she even brought Rysten into it. I turned to my best friend, temporarily stunned, but her glowing green eyes were focused on Josh.

"You just don't get it!" he said, louder than before. "I can't eat! I can't sleep! I can't think about anything but Ruby!"

Devil fucking take him already. This was getting old.

His obsession was getting worse, and I wasn't even around him enough to fuel it. Without warning, he placed another hand on my back, rubbing it in fevered, rhythmic circles. His need to touch me, to be *with* me, was getting out of control. I swung around in my chair and bared my teeth, the little bit of power I did have rose to the surface and made my hair crackle.

"Don't fucking touch me. You're crazy. Obsessed. And you know what? You and Kendall deserve each other." Any normal person would have let me go by now, but he wasn't normal anymore. This wasn't normal. He was close enough to me that I could feel the hard on in his pants, and the way it twitched every time I spoke told me all I needed to know.

This is why succubi cut and run.

Humans were weak. I hadn't even slept with him. Yet, he was just as crazy as the one I did sleep with at sixteen. The very memory made me shiver, but the fear turned to anger as more heat flooded my system.

Moira placed a hand on my shoulder, forcing me to swivel back towards her. She grabbed both shoulders and looked me in the eye.

"He's not worth it, Ruby. We've been down this road before," she said quietly. It was the subtlest of words that she could use to talk about what happened nearly seven years ago. "It's your birthday, and I won't let this loser ruin it. Okay?"

I nodded, and behind me, Josh let out the coldest, most deranged of laughs. In a club that was bursting with music and bodies, it was lost on all but us.

"You're mine, Ruby." That was the last thing he said before I felt his angry presence disappear in the crowd. Moira's mouth was pressed in a thin line, but we both ignored him until he was gone.

"Thank you," I whispered.

"For what?" she asked, tilting her head.

"For always being there."

She eased her grip on my shoulders and slid her arms around me. "I'll always be here. Even when you don't tell me things," she murmured into my shoulder. A shred of guilt ran through me as I hazily recalled the last few days.

"I'm sorry about that. I'm just…confused when it comes to them. I don't even know how I feel about it myself—"

"I'm not getting after you, Ruby. You're allowed to keep things to your-self, but I worry about you because of shit like Josh happening. The Horsemen don't seem like that. I trust you know what you're getting your-self into. Just let me know before I try to cock block someone and blow out their eardrums, eh?" I must not be the only one that was feeling the burn, because Moira was starting to slur her words a little.

"You're drunk. The Moira I know never forgives this easily."

Moira pulled away, a demonic glint in her eye. "It's your birthday. Call this an exception. I'm not nearly drunk enough, and neither are you. Finish that," she motioned to the half-full mystery drink. "Hey, bartender! Bring us some shots for the birthday girl!"

I tipped back the remainder of the cloudy sweetness.

Bottoms up.

CHAPTER THIRTEEN

WE ONLY MADE it through two rounds of shots before we went stumbling drunk onto the dance floor. Devil knows how I made it in the heels I was wearing, but I did. The techno beat of the music kept me going as one song blended into the other. Around me, the room seemed to be gaining more energy as the club continued to fill with people. The lights dropped into a darker hue as the music became louder.

"I'll be right back!" I yelled to Moira.

She turned her head fractionally and shouted, "What?"

"Bathroom," I said back, trying to mouth the word so she could read my lips.

"Need me to come with you?" she mouthed in return, laughing and pointing to herself and then to me.

I shook my head no, waving her off as I began weaving through the crowd. The surrounding people pushed and pulled, swaying with the music like one living thing. I stumbled off the dance floor and caught myself on the stair railing that led to the next level.

The bouncer next to it smiled at me. He was the same one from outside, but it was only then that I realized I recognized him from somewhere.

"Have we met before?" I asked. He said something, but I couldn't hear his response. The words came out distorted. They didn't blend with the music; they warped around it. I needed to find the bathroom. Maybe some cold water would help me. It was difficult to communicate that I needed the toilets, but he seemed to know what I was asking.

He pointed upstairs and said, "Your boyfriend's up there waiting for you."

I must have heard that wrong. I didn't have a boyfriend. Maybe he said bathroom?

He unclipped the rope and ushered me through. I was halfway up the stairs when I started to get dizzy. A sudden need to lie down hit me and gripping the rail was the only thing that kept me upright. I eased my way up the rest of the stairs and stumbled down the hallway.

My legs didn't want to cooperate. I lost my footing and fell towards a door. Strong arms caught me, pulling me back.

"Thank you," I slurred. One of the hands that caught me reached forward and opened the door. I stumbled in, my eyes having trouble adjusting to the low light. Hot breath fanned my skin as someone's lips began trailing down my neck.

Behind me the door gave a harsh audible click.

"Wha—" I started to protest, but the world tilted as the stranger pushed me onto something flat and hard. My face smacked into the surface and sent pain shooting through me. Sharp and cruel. I whimpered as the stranger started turning my body over, my back against the cold surface beneath.

Even in the dim light with inebriation setting in, I recognized the man pulling my legs apart.

"J-joshhh…wh-why are—"

"You wouldn't listen to me, Ruby," he said harshly. His voice sounded far away as my consciousness began to retreat. I wanted to move my legs to kick him, but I no longer had control. My entire body had gone numb.

"This is your fault. You think I want to do this?" My legs hanging limp over the edge, he placed himself between them. His hands wrapped around the back of my thighs, pulling me closer. I wanted to scream, but I couldn't form words anymore. I couldn't do anything.

"I can't get you out of my mind, but you won't come back to me. I hurt for you so much, Ruby. Not even Kendall can soothe it anymore. It must be you." He continued speaking, muttering to himself. A blind panic set into me. I knew what was about to go down, but I couldn't put the words to it. I couldn't stop it.

Josh's hands continued groping me, reaching beneath my top. His sweaty palms wrapped around my breasts, and terror seized me. He was seriously going to do this.

"You wouldn't let me touch these when we were together. You were such a prude. Not anymore, though, are you, Ruby?" Squeezing my breasts, his face in my neck, I could feel his pathetic excuse for a cock pushing against me. Pins and needles prickled my skin as I tried to cry out for someone. Anyone. I screamed and screamed, but I was locked in a nightmare where no one could hear me.

Josh's fumbling movements worsened the more he touched me. My skin did that to people. I was such a fool for even wanting someone to pass the time with. I was lonely and starving. For attention. For sex. For everything. I was a fucking demon deprived of all that I needed, so I played with fire and now I was going to burn.

Burn.

I was burning inside.

"You're mine, and I will have you." Josh pulled back, fumbling to undo his pants. I couldn't see the movements, I couldn't move my head, but I could hear every notch of his zipper, and every rustle of clothing as his pants dropped to the floor.

It was so similar to before. It was scary.

Except this time, I didn't have Moira to save me.

Josh's filthy hands wrapped around my waist, pulling me closer as he rubbed himself against me. It was savage and disgusting. His hands clumsily tugged at my shirt, pulling it off, my head lolling as he jerked the fabric over and tossed it aside. I could feel everything and nothing, and I couldn't escape. I was no longer me. My consciousness retreated further, searching for safety in some dark corner of my mind.

The girl on the table was pinned and helpless, but not so far away—I was burning with hatred. Burning like I never had before.

As his mouth wrapped around my nipple, I stopped screaming for help, and started screaming for death.

His death.

I wanted him to bleed for this.

I was going to hurt him.

Hell, when I came to, I was going to kill him.

It was that simple thought that unlocked something inside of me. Something I'd never known was there. For the first time, lying on a table, drugged and unable to move, I saw a glimpse of something…not of this world.

Something dark.

Deadly.

And as his hands unbuttoned my pants, that something cracked its eye open.

Something reached into my chest and yanked my heart out.

At least that's what it felt like.

Out of nowhere, a pure undiluted terror seized me. It demanded my attention; all of it, as the searing pain crawled inside me. I grasped at my chest as I fell back into the sofa. My wine slipped from my hand, spilling across the pale furniture, staining it a deep burgundy. The pain eased for a moment, and I looked up around the room. Julian gripped the island counter hard enough that the quartz crumbled beneath his fingers.

"What the fuck was that?" Laran yelled down the hallway. He emerged holding a hand to his chest, his eyes glowing red.

"I have no idea, but I'm going to assume we all felt the same thing?" Julian replied tersely. The words were hardly out of his mouth when it started again. Worse than it was before. The pain that ripped through me burned. Only when the scorching heat died down, did my vision clear enough to see the world around me.

Laran's knees must have buckled, because he'd fallen to the floor. Allistair was collapsed sideways into the wall, his glass of scotch seeping onto the carpet in an amber pool. Even my brother, the strongest of us Horsemen, was leaning onto the counter for support. A vein in his temple bulged; the only indication Death would ever give he was in pain.

"Who could possibly attack all four of us?" I breathed.

Silence enveloped us as another wave of heat tore through my chest. This surge tasted of fury, not just pain. The psychic power bypassed my shields like they were nothing, igniting a torture I had never known.

As it waned, I realized a small piece of the essence was familiar. It was wild…

The truth and the horror hit me at once.

"Ruby."

All it took was her name to spur us into action.

I had no idea how she'd done it. How she could possibly be hiding so much power? Allistair had said he felt it…but in that moment, I didn't care. All I cared about was finding her and ending whoever was hurting her—if there was even anything left of them.

We were the Horsemen, and we were immortal. She had brought the four strongest beings that roamed any world, outside of herself, to their knees. It was very plausible that whoever hurt her was already dead.

"We need to find her now," Laran said.

I shadow walked out of the room and onto the streets of Portland. They would catch up if they hadn't already. Right now, Ruby was the most important thing. I made it three steps down the street, before another wave of uncontainable rage washed through me. It was crippling, and I stumbled, but I would not stop. I would not fail her.

I used the pain and the rage and the terror to fuel my hunt. They would lead me to her.

I had no idea where she was, or how to reach her, but somehow, her power guided me.

Like a string connecting the two of us, it wrapped around me, pulling me towards ground zero.

I came around another corner and stopped immediately at a door. I could feel it in my bones. She was here. This was it. I was standing at a club called Pandora's Box.

I pushed through the line of people to the front, punching the guard that dared block my way. They were not my concern. Inside, it smelled of liquor and sweat. The humans danced, if you could call it that, grinding on one another in sync with the music.

The lights above shifted and moved as I dove into the crowd, pushing the humans out of the way as I went. I ripped through the dance floor and scanned the bar. Ruby wasn't here, but I could feel her close. Her pain was more pronounced now. Her terror more defined.

Images flashed through my mind.

My blood ran cold.

Lured by the invisible line, I found myself at the base of the stairs. Not a single bouncer tried to stop me. They were more preoccupied with the humans that had started collapsing one by one. Ruby's power tainted the air, and I had no doubt she was the cause.

I raced up the stairs after War and Death; Famine at my heels. The world slowed down to one single purpose, and that was getting to Ruby. I was so focused on reaching her, that when Julian kicked the door open, I was unprepared for the rage that took me as I stared at the bare ass of her ex as he was removing the jeans from her limp legs.

He'd drugged her. He'd molested her. Now he was about to rape her.

I lost all sense of rational and let my fury consume him.

CHAPTER FOURTEEN

THE DOOR BURST open and light danced across the ceiling.

Josh halted in his fevered attempt at removing my pants, and the brief interruption ripped my consciousness away from the inner beast. But the damage was done. I now knew she was there, deep inside of me. Sleeping in a cage, waiting for the door to open. My vision swam as voices began to file in.

My head had cleared enough I could make them out.

"I told you what would happen if you came near her again." Fire blazed to life overhead, and a face appeared before me.

Dark sage eyes and white blonde hair. Julian's hard profile stared down at me. His expression unreadable. He reached a hand out, his fingertips barely touching my forehead as he brushed my hair aside.

An icy wave ran through me. Cold. Brutal. It was the kind of cold that hurt so much it blistered. Every inch of my skin prickled against his touch, absorbing unspeakable pain. When it finally started to ebb, I found myself clinging to it and wanting more.

"Can you hear me, Ruby?" he asked softly.

I tried to nod my head, and to my surprise, it actually moved. I swallowed hard, tears pricking my eyes. "Y-yes," I rasped.

Slowly, but surely, the numbness began fading from my body as I came to. Enough so that I could make out Josh's screaming.

I struggled to sit up, and Julian put a hand out to hold me down.

"You don't want to see this."

"…have to," I whispered.

Something unspoken passed between us. Maybe it was the moment. Maybe it was the remnants of whatever drugs Josh gave me. I don't know, but in that moment, Julian understood me as my eyes met his.

He didn't say anything as he slipped an arm around my naked back and helped me into a sitting position. I realized why he didn't want me to see it, but I felt nothing as I watched the scene play out before me.

Josh was kneeled before Rysten, his mouth gaping open in a now silent scream. The glamor that always surrounded Rysten was nonexistent. A wave of power that smelled distinctly of rot and decay filled the room as he held Josh's face between his hands.

His eyes bled from their sockets as Rysten extracted the only sort of revenge I would ever get to see. I don't think he could have stopped, even if I asked him.

Rysten leaned forward and whispered something in his ear that I couldn't hear. Over his shoulder, Josh's bleeding eyes met mine. Even dying, he looked at me hungrily. I grit my teeth together and said the only thing that could bring me peace.

"Kill him."

My words were a whisper upon his grave. The moment they left my lips, his eyes exploded, and his heart gave out.

I'd never been one to revel in death, but after being stalked, drugged, and defiled, let's just say it does something to your soul. I stared at his corpse, but there was no guilt. No kindness. No remorse.

I wanted him dead because he tried to take from me the very thing that I never wanted to take from anybody: the power to choose.

And if the Horsemen hadn't come, he'd be raping me on a conference room table at this very moment. The truth of that thought hurt more than any physical pain.

But this wasn't the time to process shit.

Not here, in a room where his corpse was still warm, and I was half-naked only being held up by Julian's arm. No. Not here.

Allistair came forward to lift my arms while Julian put my shirt back on me.

I should have worn a bra.

"Listen to me, Ruby," Allistair said. He repeated my name three times before stepping in my field of vision and forcing my attention. "We're going to clean this up. It'll be like it never happened. No one will know where he went, but that human will never hurt you again."

Like it never happened. Those words played over and over in my mind.

"Moira said the same thing," I murmured. Images of a night not so different than this played out before me. About a boy and a girl who played a game, and caught fire.

"What are you talking about?" Allistair asked gently. My thoughts began spinning wildly out of control.

"I never wanted him to lose his mind. I just couldn't stop myself," I whispered.

I could still remember the color of his hair. So yellow; kissed by the sun. He was barely a man when we met.

"Ruby, this isn't your fault. What happened here—"

"He hurt me, too. And I made him pay." My words were so soft. So quiet. Four pairs of eyes turned on me.

"She's in shock, and she's hurting. I'm going to take her home. Get this cleaned up. All of it," Julian commanded. He leaned down and put his other arm beneath my legs. As he carried me out of the conference room, I looked over his shoulder.

Laran held out a hand, and Josh's body went up in flames. Across from him, bathed in the firelight, Rysten's eyes found me. He didn't say anything, but something in the way he watched me made me think he knew what I was talking about. Then again, maybe I was just seeing shadows in the eyes of one killer to another.

No one questioned Julian as he carried me out of Pandora's Box. I had to wonder what kind of security they had here if they just let men carry barely conscious women out the front door. I guess that was humans for you. They were as fucked up and flawed as we demons were. They just turned a blind eye to their own nefariousness.

Outside of the club, the wind picked up and the temperature dropped. I huddled against Julian as he walked farther from the club and turned down an alley. The midnight skies were a welcome sight after what seemed like a trip down the rabbit hole. I breathed a sigh of relief, but it was too soon.

"Going somewhere, mate?"

Glancing over Julian's shoulder, I looked at the entrance to the alleyway behind us.

Devil save us.

It was the imp from the dive-bar, and he brought friends.

CHAPTER FIFTEEN

"SINCE WHEN DO the Horsemen get involved with human affairs?" the imp called. Wind barreled down the alley and I clung to Julian as he turned towards it. Overhead, a dark cloud covered the moon. Thunder roared as a light drizzle broke out.

"What we do doesn't concern you, imp," Julian sneered. He and Allistair had that cold-arrogance-thing down pat. I didn't feel the need to tremble with Allistair, because he was just condescending towards humans no matter what. Julian was different. There was a chill that followed, like death dancing on the wind.

"Actually," the imp grinned, "it does, since your mate killed half my men and took my eye as a warning." He stepped into the light of the single lamp that hung over a door in the alley.

One eye was glowing red, just as I remembered it. The other was an empty socket, horribly scarred by what looked like knife marks…Laran literally cut his eye out. All for touching me.

On any other day, that thought might make me a bit queasy. Today, I could not bring myself to feel much of anything, except the small bit of self-preservation I still had that wanted to get the fuck away from here.

This was the part where Julian was supposed to say he had nothing to do with it, and let bygones be bygones.

"You touched a she-demon he laid his claim on," Julian replied.

I froze. *What the actual fuck? That's not what you were supposed to say*!

Apparently, the imp thought so as well, because an evil smile that promised very bad things slipped onto his face.

"The very she-demon you're holding now, if memory serves me," the imp commented, his eye dropping from Julian to me. I regarded him warily, wishing no part in this. It was too little, too late.

"She is under our protection. Anyone that thinks to harm her will die a very slow and painful death by my hand. Don't try to cross me, imp. If you thought War's punishment was hard, you will find that Death is much more permanent." Julian's words were brittle. He sounded confident, but I could sense the worry pulsing through him. He may be able to hide it from them, but I knew the truth, and it didn't bode well for me.

"Protection? Your she-demon glamored herself from him and was practically begging to be fucked. I might still oblige when we're finished with you." His gaze roamed over me, far too heated for my liking. "Although, I am curious as to what one single girl could do to provoke the protection of the Four Horsemen. I've been hearing some rumors out of Hell. Interesting rumors. Kind of make a demon wonder…"

Julian bristled against the imp's accusations. He wasn't alone.

"She isn't your concern, though, is she?" Julian asked. I don't know if the imp could tell how hard he was trying to divert their attention, but I sure as hell could. He wasn't panicking by any means, but worry was going head to head with his urge to kill them where they stood.

I was just hoping he would find a way to get us out of here.

"It's because of her your mate did this to me," he said as he pointed at his eye. "I'll think of a suitable punishment when we're done here. If she is who I think she is, my master will be very interested. Perhaps enough to earn me a promotion, after I use her to lure out the other three." I gripped the collar of Julian's jacket to hide my trembling.

The imp whistled as he backed away and the demons in his liege started toward us. Off to the side, one in particular caught my attention.

The bouncer from the club.

I opened my mouth, but before I could say anything, someone lunged. Julian kicked them out of the way and took another one down, but there was no way he was going to win this fight if was holding me.

"Put me down," I said as he dodged a punch.

"Not happening," he grumbled. That was before some of them pulled out knives. He had six demons in front of him, not including one-eye and the pussies that stood watching. Probably trying to make sure I don't escape.

My voice was barely a whisper. "Damn it, Julian. I'm dead weight. I can barely hold onto you. Put me down, or we're both dead." It only took one swipe of a knife and him getting stabbed in the arm for him to listen. Without turning away from our attackers, he swung me behind him.

"Run to the end." I took two steps before dizziness began to overtake me. Damn drugs were still in my system. I managed another two steps before I fell sideways into the wall and collapsed to the ground, dragged down by the heaviness I still couldn't shake.

Dirt smeared my face and hands, and I took a trembling breath. My teeth chattered in the cold and rain. Thank the Devil I couldn't get pneumonia. Then again, maybe a sickness induced death would be kinder than whatever the imp had planned.

Julian was fending quite well for himself, given the bodies that were piling up around him, but there was one problem: the imp had thought ahead and brought scores of demons. For every body that dropped, there was another one waiting to take its place.

Even so, Julian let out an animalistic roar, plunging his hand through a demon's chest, pulling out its still beating heart. My mouth popped open, and in that exact moment, his eyes met mine.

I wish I could say that time stood still, but it was quite the opposite. He had made that one fatal mistake: he took his eyes off the fight.

I saw it coming, but there was nothing I could say to stop it.

A demon wrapped a cord around his neck.

Another gutted him. Again. And again. And again.

Another bashed his knees in with a crow bar.

I watched in horror. I couldn't look away as they surrounded him. They had overpowered him so completely, I couldn't see anything of Julian at all. It was only then that the imp came out of the shadows. He took slow, steady steps toward me. The bouncer from the club fell in line with him.

My heart pounded as I tried to scramble back, stumbling as I searched for false security in the shadows. The imp gave me a lazy smile as he squatted down in front of me.

"Hello, dollface." I glared up at him. "Now, now. No need to be so hateful. We were getting along rather well at our last meeting, before your friends did this." He turned his face so that I was staring into the empty eye socket. "Fortunately for you, I need that face to be pretty in case I'm wrong and my master doesn't want you. Can't sell you off with a missing eye, can I? That's why I have my friend here."

His ink colored hair blew with the wind, water dampening it and causing the ends to stick to his forehead, converging around that terrible scar. He snapped his fingers once, and the bouncer stepped in front of him, blocking my vision. The bouncer glanced back and forth between me and the imp. It didn't take a genius to see he was nervous. Clearly not nervous enough, if he was going along with whatever the red-eyed shit had planned.

"What do you want?" I said in a raspy voice. The imp smiled, and it would have looked genuine, if not for the violent sounds echoing behind him. I didn't dare to look that way, fearing what I might see.

"You can talk. Color me impressed. The drugs he gave the kid should have knocked you out cold," he said.

My heart skipped a beat.

"You gave him that?" I asked, recalling the out-of-body experience. If that's what it did to a demon…that shit would kill a human at its most potent.

"No, I had my mate here do that. He was going to give them to you, but then your boyfriend showed up and had no problem using them himself. Said he didn't care what it took to have you." The imp let out a callous laugh. The scars distorting his once handsome face.

"How'd you even find me?" I breathed in a grated whisper. I just needed to keep them talking until the others arrived. My chances of surviving this night were decreasing with every minute that passed.

"Wasn't that hard, dollface. All my men saw you last Friday in my bar. I gave them all a hefty dose of what was left of my stash after War came through. Told them if they saw you, use it, and call me." Well, that answered that question. At least Moira was safe from all this. Small comfort, as it was.

The ground shook as something let out a terrifying roar. I'd never heard anything so primal or powerful in all my life. Around us, the dead rose up and began attacking the demons still living. It was unlike anything I'd ever seen, but I knew without a doubt who caused it.

"Julian," I whispered.

He was a necromancer. No. He was *the* necromancer. As if the Horsemen of Death wasn't scary enough.

The imp made a motion with his hand, and the bouncer walked forward. Sharp pains pricked the tips of my fingers as I tried to scramble away from him. He reached out and back-handed me across the face.

I didn't even register the pain as my body hit the pavement. My mouth tasted of copper and grit. I turned just in time to see him reach for me again and I spat in his face. Blue blood, mucus and bits of gravel hit his cheek.

"You little bitch," he said. He reached out and tried to grab me, but I planted my foot in his sternum. It was a feeble attempt; my legs had no strength. He let out a growl and threw my leg to the side, pinning me to the asphalt.

Panic ate at me as his hand wrapped around my jaw and squeezed. He reached in his back pocket and pulled out a small baggie. Using his teeth, he ripped the top open and grinned down at me.

"You see these?" he asked me. I didn't dare open my mouth. "I gave your boyfriend two, and you still can't walk. What do you think another two will do?"

I sure as hell wasn't about to find out.

He tightened his grip on my jaw, pressing his fingers in to try to get me to open. I strained against his hold, thrashing as best as I could. He squeezed harder.

The blood in my mouth flowed and the first trickle of pain finally hit me.

Followed by anger.

I scratched and clawed at his arms, but he only squeezed tighter. My jaw popped, and a sudden, sharp pain filled me. I gasped.

Before I could stop him, he dumped the contents of the baggie straight into my mouth and closed my jaw shut. The pills fizzled within seconds.

It was only a matter of time.

Terror and adrenaline swept through me at the prospect of being taken. My heart pounded harder and faster, and my palms sweat. The rain pelted my face as the thunder roared.

And then the burning started.

A conflagration that couldn't be controlled, a raging inferno tore through my chest. It was icy and hot and electric and grounding all at the same time. It was everything I've ever felt, and nothing at all.

It was a fire so hot, it felt cold.

And somewhere, deep inside me, a door opened.

The beast, my beast, took one look outside of her prison walls, and decided she wasn't going to be confined again.

I screamed against the pain that ripped through me, swallowing the mixture of blood and drugs as I did. The demon that sat on top of me gave me a cruel smile as he moved to hold my arms down. The beast within surged forward, and my screaming came to an abrupt halt. His hands turned black as coal. He jumped away from me, but it was already too late. A devil wearing my face smiled up at him.

CHAPTER SIXTEEN

"No," he whispered, backing away.

The fire in his veins wouldn't abate. Not until it consumed him.

The darkness spread up his arms, throughout his chest, and to every unseen nook and cranny. I cocked my head to the side as he began clawing at himself. He tore at his clothes, his hair, tearing his very skin in a desperate attempt to escape the fire that took him.

And I felt all of it. His clawing. His tearing. His burning flesh and melting skin.

It was awful. Horrific.

My beast didn't care.

He opened his mouth, maybe to shout or to scream, but no sound came out. It was the kind of pain, so raw, so intense… it was almost unimaginable. He was in his own personal hell and I felt every moment of it as he died.

Pleasure and pain coiled inside of me as I sat back and let the beast have her way.

Blue light shined behind his eyes as the skin around his face turned black and charred, mirroring the rest of him.

First his hands stopped moving. Then his arms. His legs. When the fire behind his eyes winked out, and all that was left were pits black as sin, I knew he was dead.

A single wind swept down the alleyway, and the husk of the once living bouncer disintegrated into ash. The only hint as to what happened to him was a single blue ember, and then it winked out of existence.

The beast looked to the imp that was backing down the alley. He had thought he could challenge Death, but the site of me scared him? My beast smiled, and it wasn't kind.

She shifted my body onto its knees, like we were going to make a move for him, and the imp took off running. He bolted like the coward he was, leaving the rest of the men he led here to die. She turned her eyes to the alleyway before us, where the dead bodies that had risen were dropping like flies, their purpose fulfilled now that the once living had joined them in the afterlife.

A hand plunged through the chest of a demon, spraying blood across the already navy tainted cement. The body fell to the ground, and standing there among the chaos, was Julian.

He shook his once blond hair and blue flung from it in droplets. Rain dribbled down his undamaged body. His shirt was torn, exposing lean, unblemished muscle. Blood soaked his pants, his own and theirs. But despite what they'd done in an attempt to kill him, he was perfect. Whole. Only a single cut ran from his brow to his chin, but in the time that we took to stare at one another, that, too, had healed.

Death. He truly was Death.

Could he even be killed?

I wasn't certain, but his flawless unmarked body, free of scars, made me wonder.

"Ruby?" he asked quietly. Hesitant. I wondered what he saw that made him tread so carefully.

"They hurt her." The voice that came out of my mouth was cold. Flat.

Julian nodded his head and held his bloody hands up in surrender. "I know, and I'm sorry I couldn't stop them all sooner. Thank you for taking care of her," he said softly.

The beast didn't respond as he walked towards us. His steps were small; measured and careful. He tread like he was walking on glass. Only when he was standing before us did she speak again.

"They've hurt her before, but I could not save her last time. She does not wish to leave this world, and yet…"— the cold voice trailed off —"if they hurt her again, I will burn it to the ground." There was the softest menace in her voice. The promise of unspeakable horror. A true apocalypse brought forth from our hands. She would make Sodom and Gomorrah look like child's play, brought forth from a benevolent God, because she would wipe the earth clean of all humankind.

It would be the most brutal healing and genocide the earth has ever seen.

And she—*I*—had the power to do it.

Julian didn't flinch. He didn't give any indication that he was afraid. Feeling his emotions filtering through, there was wariness and some residual pain, but not fear. The beast appreciated that. She could respect that.

Julian crouched on one knee before us, but he made no move to touch. He was smart for that. "I will do better, but right now, I'd like to talk to Ruby." He didn't phrase it as a question. He wasn't asking permission. He was telling her that it was time to recede.

The beast wasn't keen on that idea. She had been locked away for a very long time. So long, she didn't even know who put her in her prison.

"How do I know that I will not be caged again?" she asked. It wasn't child-like or inquisitive. The voice was lifeless, but there was an icy undercurrent that held a rage of its own. Julian stared at us for a long moment and spoke with absolute authority.

"Because I will kill any who try."

The beast liked that. She liked that very much.

I reached out to coax her back, and this time she agreed to recede, knowing that she would not be imprisoned again.

"Take care of her." Her parting words.

An invisible force shoved me into my own body again. A whimpered moan escaped my lips as the weariness of the night weighed on me. The gravel that pricked at my knees hurt, sharper than it should. The dizziness in my head was all too familiar after the first time being drugged. My consciousness was already beginning to wane.

"Ruby," Julian said as he breathed a sigh of relief. "Are you okay?"

"Force…drugs…want…h-home," I slurred. The effects were already coming back. I probably had moments before the paralysis and out-of-body experience returned, but this time, I wouldn't be alone. The beast was there, waiting through it with me.

Julian didn't hesitate as he picked me up and strolled down the alley.

I looked over his shoulder at the scene behind us. Dead bodies lay in heaps on the alley floor. Their arms and legs were bent at odd angles. Some had gaping holes in their chest cavities, others were decapitated.

Julian truly was a monster.

But then again, maybe I was, too.

Ashes blowing in the wind, the last thing I saw before we stepped into the shadows and it all went black.

The endless darkness only lasted a second before he was carrying me through my front yard. He can shadow walk. Now I knew how they got around so easily. The thought was only of passing interest when I realized Moira's car wasn't there.

The driveway was dark, but Julian navigated just fine as he ascended the porch. "Where's your spare key?" he asked. My head lolled against his shoulder.

"Don't…one," I mumbled. He didn't say anything, didn't sigh in annoyance. He simply moved to hold me with one arm. There was a sharp crunching sound, that I assumed was him breaking the lock, and then the door opened.

The blood curdling screech that awaited us stirred me from the drugged-out haze settling in. Julian let out a curse as something flew at him full force before settling on my chest. We weren't even through the doorway completely, but Bandit was here and waiting.

"Hey…bub-by," I slurred. My raccoon wrapped his arms around my neck and purred louder than I'd ever heard him. Maybe that was just the drugs.

Julian kicked the door shut behind him and flipped the light on as he moved into the house. My living room disappeared as he rounded the corner to my room. He laid me down in bed, pulling the covers around me. I was already far enough gone that my arms and legs were useless, and the feeling of helplessness crept in. The beast inside me twitched, pacing uneasily. She didn't like this anymore than I did, but sometimes there was truly nothing you could do except wait it out.

"What can I do?" Julian asked, his voice tense. Strained.

"Lights," I murmured. Bandit snuggled closer to my chest, and right then it was the only thing that kept me sane. That kept the panic at bay.

"What else? What do you need? How do I fix this?" he asked. I could hear the desperation in his voice, but his emotions were lost on me. I couldn't feel them. I couldn't feel much of anything, except the contentment coming from Bandit.

"Can't…" I croaked. "M-m-moira. W-w-wa-want Mmm—" I strained against the pressing weight sitting on my chest, but I hoped he got the message. Eyes heavy and fluttering, I stared at the ceiling. I started to drift across the universe. Time itself was transcended as the violet and blue lights of the club swirled around me again.

I became lost in a world of memories and nightmares. People's faces, men's faces, passed me by as I waded through. Then came Josh, and the imp, and the bouncer, and Danny…as they all bled together into one. I saw the faces of times gone by, and they slipped through my fingers like smoke, always eluding me.

But then the faces changed. And the lights grew bright. And when the smoked settled, all that remained was fire. The flames were black and shades of blue as they danced through my dreams.

They were the flames I've dreamed of ever since I was a little girl. They were the flames of Hell. The only thing in this world that could outright kill a demon—outside of Death himself. I suppose that should be strange, but I was a demon dreaming of things that little demon girls do. Flames and fire and ash. They gave off no smoke, but they destroyed everything they touched.

It was within those flames that a beast led me, hand-in-hand, to a new place.

Where the pain couldn't reach me, and the demons couldn't find me, and people on earth could no longer hurt me.

Because I was one with the flame.

One with the fire that burned inside my soul.

****JULIAN****

I didn't know how to help her. I didn't know what to say that could make this better, or make up for the pain that I couldn't save her from. The human drugged her with black lotus, and then molested her. He would have raped her, had she not called out. It was the hurt she projected in a cry for help that led us there. That let us save her. I don't think she even realized she had done it. But if Ruby was as strong as I think she was…we weren't the only ones that felt it.

If my instincts proved right, demons would be coming for her from all corners of the earth. Some would want favor. Some would seek to control her. Others would simply wish to kill her in a bid to open the gates of Hell.

I thought we had more time. I'd hoped we could get to know her better. I'd wanted her to come to it on her own, but time was running out. Even if her psychic assault didn't reach another soul past the four of us, we had a bigger problem.

The beast had awoken, and with it would come the transition. Maybe not tonight, or tomorrow, or even next week, but it would come. And we needed to be ready when it did.

Lucifer had created us to be able to handle the beast. To ground her when she could not ground herself. If we were to have any hope of being able to do that, we needed her to trust us.

Trust isn't earned lightly, and it takes time. More time than we had. If she really was on the verge of the transition, we didn't have more than a month. And that was a generous estimate.

The front door flew open, and a tiny green-haired banshee stormed around the corner. The girl didn't even look to me, her eyes frantic as they sought a single person. I moved aside for her, hoping she could do what I and the others could not.

She ripped off her heels fiercely and climbed into bed next to Ruby. Her slender green arms wrapped around Ruby's slightly wider shoulders. She began murmuring things under her breath, but I closed the door. The things said between two people that close were not meant for others to hear. Certainly not after a night like tonight.

I walked back down the hall and into the living room where the other three waited. Rysten was seated on the couch, staring with a vacantness that was telling. Allistair faced the window, his back to us and his posture stiff. Unyielding. Laran paced before the door and the wind blew harder outside. The moon had been eclipsed by dark clouds as heavy rain came down. The forecast hadn't called for rain this night, which meant it was War.

"Is it taken care of?" I asked.

Laran nodded. "The bodies have been burned; the ashes scattered. No one will know what happened. They never existed as far as this world is concerned." He was the most solemn I'd seen him since the Ring Wars.

"And the human?" I asked. If I didn't have Ruby's needs to be concerned with, I'd be calling him back from the veil right this moment to make him pay ten times over. Twenty. I could make him relive his death a hundred times.

But it would never be enough for what he did to her, and she didn't need to know *that* particular aspect of my power just yet.

"I've erased every trace of him online. Social media. Bank accounts. Vendor accounts. Birth certificate. Social security. It's gone. All of it. But unless any of us suddenly learned how to take people's memories…it will be impossible to erase his memory from her life completely." Rysten blew out a harsh breath. "Humans will remember him, but there is no evidence that his disappearance could be linked to her."

I nodded once, but it was Famine that spoke. "That's the best we can hope for, unless we plan to kill everyone he ever knew." I considered the validity of that statement. Weighing the good and the bad, the domino effect that would have.

"The imp with one eye escaped. We need to prioritize hunting him down before he becomes a problem," I replied. Laran nodded, but he wasn't as enthusiastic as he usually was about the prospect of hunting. I couldn't blame him; not when failure sat like a stone upon our backs.

"There's more…say it" Rysten prompted. I turned to my brother. The darkness I knew well still hadn't left his eyes. Killing the human wasn't enough. Many were going to die tonight when this conversation was over.

"The beast has awoken. One of the demons got to her, and she burned him alive from the inside out," I replied. Rysten nodded. He must have sensed it the same as I had.

"She's stronger than she realizes. I don't know how she's repressed her powers this long, but I don't think it's a coincidence she hasn't gone through the transition yet. Something happened to her, and I'm not talking about tonight," Rysten said.

Silence spread between the four of us, the air thick with things unsaid.

We saved our apologies, our hurt, our sorrows, because they were not meant for each other. It was not each other we failed, but Ruby. If Rysten was right, it was possible we failed long before we even came for her.

If something happened in her past to cause her to suppress the transition, it was enough to make me question if we were right sending her to this world in the first place.

To a world where monsters and men were the same thing.

CHAPTER SEVENTEEN

I woke up toasty warm, and panic immediately replaced the calm a deep sleep had given me. My eyes flew open, expecting flames and a burning house, but no such sight awaited me.

My room was dimly lit, cast in a warm yellow glow. On one side of me, Bandit was sprawled on his back, his head pillowed by my arm that he had drooled all over. On the other side was Moira, still wearing her dress from the night before. Her arm was slung across my bare waist, wrapped protectively around me.

Then the memories from last night came flooding back.

The club. The drugs. Josh. The imp. The bouncer. The fire.

My beast.

I didn't even need to check that it was true, because she was still there. Right in the back of my mind, watching me and waiting for the moment she was needed.

I swallowed hard, and my throat protested loudly. It was as parched as the desert. I moved to shimmy out from beneath Moira and Bandit, but she tightened her hold on me, and my best friend looked up.

All it took was one look from her and tears formed in the corners of my eyes.

"Oh, honey…" she whispered and held me tighter.

"How much do you know?" I rasped.

"Not much. Allistair came and found me last night. Told me some bad shit went down and you were drugged," she murmured against my shoulder.

"Did he really say that?" I asked.

"That some bad shit went down?" she asked. I nodded. "No. I'm paraphrasing. He used more adulty words, but I kind of lost my shit because I knew something was up before he found me. You didn't come back. I was looking everywhere for you. They brought me home and I saw you lying in bed—" She stopped and hugged me tighter.

"I killed someone, Moira," I whispered.

She didn't even hesitate. "They probably deserved it."

I choked back the sob that threatened to escape me. Whether from shock or gratitude, I didn't know. What I did know was that Moira was the best fucking friend that I could ever ask for.

"You don't have to talk about it. Just tell me where, and I can bury the body. No one will ever know." Wet tears streamed down my face as I hugged her tighter. The dryness in my throat stung as I tried to swallow the lump that formed.

Devil knows what I did to deserve her.

"He's already gone," I whispered.

"What do you mean?"

I took a deep breath. I was prepared to tell her everything, but not yet.

"Can I take a shower first? I feel disgusting, and after—" I didn't even have to finish. Moira unwound herself from me and jumped out of bed. Her makeup smeared across her face, and black tear marks trailed from her eyes to her chin.

"You don't have to explain yourself. I'm going to go start some tea and make a pot of coffee. I'll be in the living room when you're done." She smiled weakly and left me to my own devices. I was probably supposed to cry then. It would have made sense.

Cry for myself. Cry because I killed someone. Hell. Maybe if I were another girl, I would have cried for the man I killed.

They were rapists and killers, and I wouldn't cry for that.

They didn't deserve my tears.

I inhaled through my nose and gently removed my arm from underneath Bandit. He rolled over onto my pillow and left a trail of slobber behind. At least some things never change.

The transition from laying down to standing was harder. My head began pounding, and the room swayed. I took it slow, gripping the headboard as I went. When my feet touched the floor, it took a minute to adjust before standing. Oddly enough, the shift to standing wasn't terrible. My legs felt weak, wobbly. I suppose that getting drugged twice in one night will do that to you.

I made a promise to myself right there: no more bars. Me and Moira could get drunk at home if we wanted, but I wasn't stepping foot in another fucking bar as long as I lived.

My first steps towards the bathroom were slow and shaky, but they were steadier by the time I reached the door. I gripped the handle tightly, ignoring the mirror as I entered. I didn't want to see myself like this. That might actually break me.

I crossed the cool tile floors, staring at my feet as I went. My mind was numb. My body acted without thought. The throbbing in my throat stung, but the grime against my skin was worse. I was dirty in a way that even water couldn't clean, but that wouldn't stop me from trying.

My skin reeked of sweat and alcohol.

I stepped into the shower, still clothed, and flipped it on. Even the memory of where Josh's fingers and mouth had been made me want to scream. Not in pain, but in fury.

I tore at the shirt plastered to my chest, shredding the fabric until it no longer clung to my skin, littering the floor of my shower in scraps and pieces. The rest of my clothes followed. I would burn what was left of them before the day was over.

I scrubbed the shampoo into my hair, washing away the sweat, dirt, and ash that coated me. I emptied the body wash onto myself as I tried to scratch my skin clean with the loofah.

My hair smelled of lavender, and my skin was red and raw, but it wasn't clean enough. Inside me, the beast paced. She didn't like this. She thought it was pointless. She'd rather be out there burning the world down. I ignored her as I let out the one and only scream I would allow myself.

After this, what's done is done. I would give myself these few minutes. Not to cry. Not to anguish over the demons that died, or my would-have-been rapist.

I screamed because I could.

Because it happened.

Because I was violated.

Because words could not describe what I felt, but the animalistic roar was as close as I could get.

When my voice broke and my ears rang, the back of my throat raw and tasting of blood, I finally heaved a sigh of relief and let go of the sponge. I turned the water off and stepped out of the shower, feeling lighter than before. I dried my skin with a clean towel and wrapped it around my waist. While brushing my teeth, something caught my eye in the mirror and the toothbrush fell from my fingers.

Five points now adorned my sternum. Black lines connected them. A circle ran around the edges. And the realization of what I was staring at made the beast within me purr.

After twenty-three years of believing I was half-demon, an upside-down pentagram formed between my breasts.

I had a brand. Which meant I would transition.

That brand was Lucifer's mark.

I tore my eyes away from the mark on my chest and brushed my teeth as quickly as possible. I didn't want to look at it. Not today. Today, I would be Ruby. Just Ruby. The tattoo artist who had a pet raccoon and a crazy best friend.

Today, I would eat a bucket of Rocky Road ice cream. I would drink two pots of earl grey, and spend the entire day laying on my sofa watching Viola Davis and her team of wannabe lawyers. I would wear pajamas and make Moira braid my hair because I was too lazy to do it.

Today, I was the half-succubus from Portland, who attracted more trouble than even the Horsemen of Hell knew what to do with.

Tomorrow, I would be Lucifer's daughter.

The demon destined to be the next ruler of Hell.

But today, I was just Ruby.

To be continued…

WICKED GAMES

CHAPTER ONE

*T*HE STIFLING HEAT *smothered my skin as fire licked at the earth around me. I padded across the endless wasteland, my arms stretched wide before me. The beast smiled down at the world on fire as blue flames spread across the land.*

She enjoyed watching the humans run. The way they panted, hard and heavy, as they attempted to flee. How they would pause and look back, their faces blanching the moment they realized their feet couldn't carry them fast enough. That her rage—my rage—would consume them before they could take another step.

"Ruby!" The scream ripped me from sleep.

My eyes flew open and Moira was the first thing I saw, the glow of flickering blue flames dancing on her face as it burned all around us. Claws pricked at my upper chest as Bandit scrambled in a wild panic to climb on top of me. "Ruby!"

She straddled me, shaking me with a fervor as she let loose a scream that could wake the dead. Our front window shattered instantly.

Shit. This wasn't the wastelands. It was my home, and Moira and Bandit had braved the flames to save it. I inhaled sharply, terror seizing my heart for them—what I could do to them—as I tried to calm the inferno. I focused on the connection and tried to force them to die out. But they only fanned higher as I panicked about my apparent lack of control.

Inside me, the beast frowned at the scene before us and snarled at

Moira and Bandit for stupidly putting themselves at risk. It only took a single look from her and the fire dissipated immediately.

Well then.

"Moira," I croaked. Her scream cut off the moment the flames dispersed, leaving a thin glittering black residue that I could only assume was ash. A cold wind blew through the window, stirring up the blinds enough to let a crack of sunlight slip through and illuminate more of the scene before me.

My naked body shivered against the barren concrete where a couch and carpet used to be. My living room wasn't much more than charred remains with four walls. Piles of black dust littered the cement foundation, drifting across the room as a harsh gust of wind whipped through it. Bandit wrapped his arms around me tightly and Moira's naked body clung to mine as she gripped me in a desperate embrace. Where she had been clothed was now nothing more than a fine film of black against her pale green skin. Where everything else had been consumed, my best friend and raccoon had been spared.

"I'm sorry. I didn't mean to—" My shaky apology was interrupted by a pounding on our front door.

"One second!" Moira yelled. The loud whapping on the door ceased.

"Ruby?" Laran called. His voice drifted through the broken window with ease.

"I'm here. Just give us a second," I replied. He let out an impatient harrumph, but didn't push it. Moira jumped to her feet, pulling me up with her. The fine powdery ash covered us both, shining like granules of onyx in the low light coming from the kitchen. The large sectional couch I had been sleeping on was completely gone, as was most of the room. The fire seemed to have spread all the way to the edge of the kitchen and hallway before the beast had finally put it out.

"You really are Lucifer's kid," Moira murmured. Her seafoam green eyes had flicked to the brand in the center of my sternum.

"So it appears," I muttered back. The upside-down pentagram sat snuggly between my breasts, a thick ring of black circling it. She reached out with light green fingers to brush the brand just as another fist pounded on the door.

I felt like I jumped two feet in the air and Moira threw a harsh glare over her shoulder towards the pounding. It wouldn't hold up against Laran's fists forever.

"Come on, let's put on some clothes and greet your males before they have a conniption." She wasn't wrong, but it felt weird hearing it out loud. *My males.* Like I owned them or something. The beast perked her head up and agreed with great vigor. They were *ours.*

I turned and walked down the hallway and into my bedroom with Bandit hot on my heels. The sweet scent of Amaryllis filled the air, but it couldn't mask the stench of charred fibers and musky raccoon. I reached over blindly to flip on the light as a massive thud sounded in my living room. I popped my head outside the bedroom.

A plume of soot and debris swirled, thick enough I couldn't make out anything but a wall of what looked like black glitter. The particles danced for a moment before descending slowly.

Laran took a sweeping glance of the room, his brow furrowing more as his gaze swept up the hallway and stopped on me.

"What happened here?" he roared. I swallowed hard, but I, nor the beast inside, was going to answer to someone who had the audacity to break the door down like an uncivilized animal after I had just told him to wait. I closed my bedroom door sharply and threw my black bathrobe on in record time. I was just tying the knot around my waist when my door creaked open.

"I would have let you in had you waited another minute for me to dress," I said sharply. My words fell on deaf ears.

"Why is there glass outside your house? What happened to the window? Why does—"

The slamming of a door cut him off abruptly. He turned to face the she-demon behind him. Moira slipped around his hulking frame and came to stand beside me. Her own bathrobe was white and sheer, definitely sexier than anything I owned. Demons in general were very lax about clothes. I doubt she even noticed how great it made her legs look, even as black dust smudged the robe.

"Do you just storm into other people's houses without invitation all the time? Or is this bad behavior just you attempting to prove your domi-nance?" Moira snapped at him. His face darkened as he took a step forward, towering over us.

"That's not the question at hand, banshee," he rumbled. I wanted to facepalm myself for the pissing contest going on between the two of them.

"She could have burned down all but a single cupboard and that would still be the question. You Horsemen need to learn to respect—" He silenced her with a wave of his hand. Her jaw snapped shut as if by force.

"Hey!" I protested, whacking him in the arm with my hand. Laran raised an eyebrow at me. I didn't know whether it was surprise that I hit him, or a dare to make him stop. Either way, I didn't have to think on it long before Moira's mouth was magically unsealed.

"No talking, or I'll do it again," he said to her. If he had been talking to any other demon, they might have heeded his warning. Moira was anything but. Really, she was just bat-shit crazy.

"I'd be careful who you piss off, Laran. There's an awful lot of ghosts that like to hang around you. It would be a shame if I let slip what some of them tell me…" Her voice was sweet as sugar, but her words were nothing but a bluff. Moira never gained the ability to see the dead. As a half-banshee, she was left with very few talents outside her sonic scream. Not that Laran knew that. He gave her a leery glare that hardened the longer she smiled.

"You wouldn't dare."

"Try me," she goaded. It's a good thing I only needed a day to mope and recover. Their bickering was already driving me nuts. It was like Moira was constitutionally incapable of not picking a fight with the Horsemen about anything that involved me. If it wasn't respect, then it was stalking, or possessiveness, and she even went so far as tell them they couldn't be allowed inside because of their gender. I can't remember what day she told them that we were lesbians having hot lesbian sex and no dicks were invited. Seeing as Rysten and Allistair both knew that wasn't true…I just chose not to get into it.

"Someone want to explain to me why the living room was burned down?"

The question came from down the hall. My beast started licking her lips the moment Julian came around the corner. He looked the same as he did the night the demons came for us. His blonde hair so light it could be white, laid perfectly to one side. His skin was unmarked. Pale and without blemish. Everything about him was radiant, but his glow wasn't warm or kind. It was like an endless winter: ethereal in its beauty, but unforgiving if lost in its depths.

This was the first time I'd seen him since my drug-induced coma two nights ago. It was the first time I'd seen any of them, but for some reason, it was Julian that made me think of that night. How the lights reflected off his hair making it look violet and eerie as he carried me out. A heat crept across my skin as a faint blush stained my cheeks. After everything that happened, that was *not* what I should be feeling when I looked back at how that night played out.

"You okay?" Moira asked, returning to my side in an instant. She sent both of them a withering glare as she snaked an arm around my waist. Behind them, boots crunched on glass as someone let out a low whistle. I could only assume the other Horsemen had shown up, thankfully before I made myself look like an idiot. I was a half-succubus, not some blushing school girl that fawned over a pretty face. Julian saved me because it was his job. I would do well not to confuse the facts.

I nodded my head to silence the blood pounding in my ears and muttered, "I'm fine."

Moira didn't argue, but her arm tightened imperceptibly.

For devil's sake.

I wasn't a helpless child. I mean, I did just start a fire in my sleep. The overprotectiveness on everyone's account was more than a bit annoying, given that almost everyone who tried or had hurt me was dead. The thought was both depressing and comforting at the same time.

I shrugged off Moira's arm and pulled at the sleeves of my bathrobe. Yesterday, I was Ruby. I ate an entire tub of ice cream and drank a pound of tea. I laid on my couch curled up in a snuggie, binge watching Netflix like I hadn't just killed someone.

Today, I woke up to my best friend screaming because I almost burned our house down.

As much as I hated to admit it, I needed to find a way to bridge that gap in my mind, because the pentagram on my chest wasn't going anywhere.

And neither were the Horsemen.

CHAPTER TWO

I wish I had time to process and wrap my head around what it means to become Lucifer's daughter practically overnight. But the Four Horsemen were already standing in my room, waiting for some kind of an answer.

Unfortunately, all I had was, "Well, I kind of had an accident."

No one laughed.

Tough crowd.

"What kind of accident?" Rysten asked, pushing forward. Laran huffed, but stepped out of the doorway to let him through.

"I started a fire in the living room. I didn't realize what was happening until Moira and Bandit woke me up…" My voice trailed off as Bandit scaled the rope ladder I had made for him and flung himself into his hammock. He let out the most dramatic of sighs, like even my retelling it was too much work for him to think about. I cracked a brief smile at him, happy for the reprieve from all the strangeness of this morning.

"What were you doing when the fire started?" Rysten continued.

"Sleeping," I said. My eyes flicked back to him, only then noticing that he wasn't wearing his glamor. I chose not to comment even though the beast grinned like a fool. She preferred seeing them for what they were, not the human that Rysten could almost pose himself to be.

I didn't know if I agreed with her or not just yet, given that my thoughts were occupied by more important things. Like my lack of a living room. And that it was my fault. Not to mention that I think I was hallucinating because Bandit was wiggling his eyebrows at me... he's a raccoon...did they really even have eyebrows?

"Just sleeping?" Rysten asked slowly, his eyes squinting just a smidge. His only tell that he was worried.

"Yes."

He and Julian exchanged looks. Behind them, Allistair's gaze was frozen to my chest, but not like he was ogling. I looked down at myself to see the black fabric had parted enough between my breasts to reveal the top half of the brand that claimed my skin.

Shit.

I hastily pulled the robe tighter around my body and crossed my arms over my chest.

"When did the mark appear?" Allistair asked quietly.

"I don't really know. Sometime between getting ready Friday evening and waking up yesterday morning." I swallowed hard, looking away. I don't know why I was so uptight about it. Maybe it was because I still haven't adjusted. Maybe it was because my brand sat seductively between my breasts. Either way, I didn't feel like discussing it or how it came about. I definitely didn't want anyone asking to see it.

"And less than thirty-six hours later you started a fire in your sleep." He didn't phrase it like a question, so I chose not to answer. "What were you dreaming about?"

I blanched, recalling those final moments before Moira woke me. Fire raged in a world consumed by flame. A world I ruled. Well...the beast and me.

I'd never had a dream quite like it before, and I wasn't keen on sharing it just yet. Given that they hadn't been pushing my return to Hell, I didn't want for them to have any reason to start again. I may be Lucifer's daughter, but I wasn't ready for that.

Not yet.

"Umm..." I drawled, extending it out like I was thinking. I scratched my chin and cocked my head. "I don't remember exactly. I woke up to Moira screaming her head off and realized the house was on fire." I shrugged, biting on my lower lip. If Allistair thought I was lying, he didn't say anything, but his eyes darkened.

"Who put the fire out?" he asked slowly. The question had a simple enough and self-explanatory answer, but the way he said it made me hesitate. Was this a test?

"I did," I replied.

"Why do you sound unsure about that?" he countered smoothly. His line of questioning was odd. Belittling, I'd say, if he didn't use that buttery soft voice of his that made me fidget uncomfortably.

"Why are you questioning me like I did something wrong?" I snapped back, stuffing my hands in my armpits to hide the shaking.

I mean, I *did* do something wrong. I set my living room on fire, but he didn't need to make me feel like a criminal about it.

"I didn't mean to upset you, Ruby. You're progressing faster than we thought you would and I'm trying to figure out how much control you have and how much is...the other one..."

The other one.

My beast.

I guess Julian did know what lurked in my eyes that night, and he must have told the others. Then again, it was around the same time the full pentagram showed up, and it was too much of a coincidence for them not to be related. Maybe the beast was as much from Lucifer as the brand on my chest. Given what I knew before that night, I had to think as much.

Someone trapped the beast and didn't want it found.

Not even by me.

"How do you know about her?" I asked him warily. Julian chose that moment to step forward reservedly. If I didn't know better, I'd have thought he was afraid of me. He didn't stink of fear. I would have felt that bleeding over into me, but the cold calm that exuded from him was gentle. Soothing, even.

"She is the reason we were created. The reason you can control the flames. Right now, she's probably agitated and feeling impatient with us for asking questions. We just need to know how much control you have, and how much she can control you. You're still new at this and we don't expect you to be perfect, but if you're in danger of transitioning soon, we can't let you out of our sight. Do you understand?" He loomed over me; dark, but not as imposing as he'd once been. Inside me, the beast smirked because she was the reason why. She liked the power she lorded over them. She liked it a lot. Almost as much as the smell of his skin and the...

I withdrew my thoughts away from her, only then realizing how close she was to the surface. She wasn't being malevolent or forcing her way for control, she simply liked them and wanted to be closer to them. She didn't care if it was me or her that got us there.

I ignored her entirely and focused on what they were asking from me.

"I'm in control, but this morning I couldn't put out the flames on my own. I panicked when Moira woke me up because I thought I had hurt her. The beast put them out once we realized what was happening." I looked away, hoping it would make her stop pushing me to go to them. She was somewhat agitated and impatient, just as Julian had guessed. Just not for the same reasons.

"Allistair's right. You are progressing faster than anticipated," Julian said, his eyes flicking back to meet Rysten's. He nodded. "We need to reevaluate the living arrangements until you're ready to return to Hell."

My mouth popped open.

That wasn't what I expected.

I glanced between the four of them, dumbfounded and shocked, but I didn't even need to say anything before Moira went off.

"Reevaluate living arrangements? Who do you think you are?" she snarled, lunging forward to stand in front of me. Devil save her.

"Her protectors. Unlike you, we were created to help her diffuse the power and stay in control. If she's having trouble, then one of us needs to be nearby. Especially when she's sleeping, if that's when she's having the most trouble," Laran rumbled. He was taller than Julian, and almost as menacing as he glared down at Moira. My best friend didn't shrivel like a frail little flower, as most who faced the Horsemen would. She returned his glare unafraid and entirely sure of her place in my world.

"You sure this is about helping her?" Moira challenged, a feral grin gracing her lips. Rysten chuckled under his breath, and Julian threw a warning glare at Laran.

"You're not helping the situation, War," Julian said stiffly.

"The banshee doesn't understand her place," he growled back.

"*My* place? What about *your* place—"

"My place is by her side," he snapped back at her.

"Do you know how many men, demons and human, have told me that over the years?" Moira sneered. Okay then. Time to deescalate the situation before Laran tries to silence her or she blows his eardrums.

"Guys. You are both being ridiculous. The sooner you both are quiet, the sooner I get to take a shower, so shut it." Moira pursed her lips and stepped aside. Laran didn't say anything, but the tick in his jaw was telling. He was being quiet because I asked it, but the moment Moira went off again it was going to be a throw down in my bedroom.

"Originally, I thought you had longer before the transition. Now, I'm not sure. I would be more comfortable if you moved in with us in the meantime—with the banshee, if you insist," Julian added quickly as the expression on Moira's face soured.

Move in with them? Did he realize how crazy that sounded?

"You can't be serious," I said, trying to brush it off. I would have laughed at him like I did when he said I was the devil's daughter, but I'd already been proven wrong once. If that was possible, I suppose anything was. Even Julian and the Horsemen getting such a crazy idea as to want me to move in.

"I'm quite serious," Julian replied stiffly.

I could tell my reaction displeased him by the tension in his eyes, but he wasn't arguing. Not yet at least. Rysten took one look between Julian and me, perhaps sensing his brother's thinning patience now that I declined their offer. Devil knows I could feel it.

"Look, love, you don't have a living room. The insulation in the floor is ruined and it's November. In Oregon. At the moment, we won't make you do anything you don't want to, but please understand you're only putting off the inevitable," Rysten said softly. I met his jade colored eyes and softened inside. Even with his power pulsing through the room and not hidden behind a glamor, this was Rysten. The same Rysten that came to earth and learned to be more human for me. The one that tried to give me a choice, even when the other Horsemen were being ruled by their dicks and exuded nothing but pure arrogance.

"You know how crazy this sounds, right?" I asked him softly. His lips quirked up in an almost human grin, reminiscent of the boyish smile I thought he had. His real smile was more animalistic; less refined. But it was still him.

"I know, but you must understand: we're demons, Ruby. We don't think like humans do. If you were anyone else, we would take you without asking. We'd probably be halfway to Hell already. You were raised by humans, and so we're trying. For you."

Rysten was the only one of them that had mastered pretty words that could make a girl swoon, and my ability to feel the emotions of those around me told me he meant every one of them.

I bit my lip, letting the pain scatter the heat that was beginning to spread through me. The beast perked her head up and eyed Rysten thoughtfully. The words meant little to her. She was not one to be swayed by emotion. She didn't care for much outside me and mine, but in that moment, Rysten held her interest as she eyed him with something akin to want. Possession.

"Mine," she insisted. My lips thinned as I pushed her aside. So not happening right now. She hissed at me, but didn't make a serious lunge for power, thankfully.

"I appreciate you giving me the choice, but I need to think on it," I said. The beast downright sulked at my non-committal answer. She could get the fuck over it. As sweet as Rysten could be, moving in with them, however temporary, was not something I needed to decide on before coffee.

I shooed them all out before anyone could try to change my mind or give the beast reason enough to surface. She was already pacing impatiently, and I knew if she came forward, they wouldn't leave without me in tow.

That knowledge alone had the possessive bitch downright gleeful that even if I didn't go now, eventually she was going to get her way.

I hoped that with coffee I could disagree with her, but there were some things that even caffeine couldn't change. The Horsemen's bond with me was one of them.

CHAPTER THREE

Black particles glittered like ground up stardust as they swirled down the bathroom drain. The ash was all that remained of my living room and everything it held. I couldn't tell one spec from another, whether it was my beloved couch, the first piece of furniture I bought, or the threadbare blanket that Moira wove me when we were fifteen—I would never know. Because it was all gone.

It was only a room and they were only possessions, but they were a good portion of the only things I'd ever owned. The house itself we were still paying off, and while the money we made running Blue Ruby Ink was good…it wasn't good enough to fund these kinds of repairs amidst everything else. Not exactly like we could file a claim with insurance for starting a fire with magical blue flames while I was sleeping. I didn't need some fire investigators poking around here. No. We'd have to do this ourselves.

Worry nagged at me as I finished my shower, but there was no point. What would worrying do? Not a damn thing. I shook the heaviness that tried to descend upon me as I wrung out my hair and dried off. The towel was hardly enough to keep the bite away from the bitter cold as I opened the bathroom door. It was chillier in here than I remembered, but not cold enough for me to think much of it. I dressed quickly, donning long johns under my jeans and two thick shirts to go with my sweatshirt.

From up in his hammock, Bandit watched me curiously. I could have sworn he cocked an eyebrow at my choice of clothing.

"What? You expect me to freeze my ass off? We don't all have fur to keep us warm, you know," I said, putting my hands on my hips. He let out a chittering noise and jumped to the bed. I crossed the room in a few quiet strides, my bare feet losing feeling against the cold carpet fibers. I lifted Bandit from the bed and held him to my chest. He wasn't so keen on being cuddled like a baby right now and opted for scurrying up my front. He wrapped himself around my shoulders and neck like a poufy scarf.

"Uh uh. Not happening," Moira's voice carried from the door. I turned towards her as she crossed her arms and leaned against the frame. "Trash panda's not coming with."

I shot her a look of annoyance, burying my fingers in his fur.

"Why not? I bring him into work all the time," I said defensively.

"Because we're not going into Blue Ruby today. Fuck all, we're going to Voodoo Doughnut. He may like you a lot, but last I checked, vermin aren't allowed inside." She picked at an invisible piece of lint on her jacket. The puffy black material was sleek enough I didn't think even the plumes of ash in our living room would stick to it.

"What do you mean we're not going—"

"I took the liberty of rescheduling your Sunday appointments," she said. Her face was blank. Neutral as could be. I wasn't fooled; guilt and worry swirled inside her just below the surface. They were eating at her protective instincts, enough so that I bit off my retort about her rescheduling without asking, and simply said, "Okay."

She blinked once and cleared the surprise from her face in record time while I grabbed my boots and heavy wool socks. Bandit wasn't happy that he wasn't coming with, but in the end, a breakfast of rewarmed tilapia was enough to placate him.

The drive to Voodoo Doughnut was swift, made faster by Moira's *skilled* driving. It takes a special kind of person to put a Camry on two wheels and not bat an eyelash. Some days I wondered if she even noticed things like stop signs and traffic lights. Or maybe she did and simply thought they were mere suggestions as opposed to actual rules. Knowing her, it was entirely possible.

Pulling up outside, the parking lot was mostly empty. Only two cars and the van unloading were present. The Pepto-Bismol pink bricks of Portland's most notorious doughnut shop were a more welcome sight than I'd realized. After eating nothing more than ice cream for over twenty-four hours, something solid would be good, even if it was more sugar. My stomach rumbled in agreement.

The shadow man from the sign above the door stared down at me as we approached the building. His eyes looked oddly real for the black abyss they were supposed to be. I frowned, but didn't comment as we walked inside, the tiled black and white floors gleaming at us in welcome. The scent of fresh doughnuts made my mouth water.

The girl at the counter smiled up at us and waved. Her hair shined white at the roots and darkened to a neon purple at the ends of her pigtails. She wore a tight t-shirt with the shop name that stopped short of her low-cut jeans, exposing her midriff and the edges of a white tattoo around her left hip bone.

"Hi there, what can I get for you ladies?" she asked. It was right about the moment we reached the counter that I noticed how pointed her teeth were. She took a breath, looking back and forth between the two of us, and her smile widened. "Apologies for the mistake," she corrected in a purr. I glanced down at the nails that were tapping against the glass counter. Wicked sharp and painted in a gleaming royal purple. "It's rare that I find two she-demons in this area. Not to mention unclaimed." Her eyes appraised us with interest.

"This isn't marked territory, is it?" Moira asked sharply, her eyes focused with an intensity that would have made a weaker demon subservient. The unknown did not lower her gaze, which made Moira's question even more pressing. For unclaimed demons to walk into another's territory, particularly a half-demon like Moira…the scenarios ranged from bad to worse.

And it was that thought alone that had the beast leaping forward.

I lunged to maintain hold, only barely beating her to it as the she-demon watched me with mercury-colored eyes. They were the most exquisite shade of silver I'd ever seen, and it threw me for a loop at identifying what kind of demon she might be.

The beast in me shifted restlessly and the unknown demon smiled.

"Relax. This area is not yet claimed. I was sent here by my master because of some…disputes going on in the area," she said with a toothy grin. It was a smile that was almost impish, but somehow darker.

"Disputes?" I asked tightly. I wasn't aware that there were clans this far north. Demons hated the cold. The imp from the Black Brothers was an outlier. At least I thought he was. Me and Moira didn't exactly stay on the up and up of the demon world here on earth. We had a hard enough time making it with the humans, so we left demons and their politics behind by the time we were seventeen. We set out to forge our own way, for a time. But it seems the demon world wasn't letting go. Not now that I had a fucking pentagram branded on my chest.

There was no hiding forever, but this was exactly why I was in no hurry to leave.

The unknown she-demon clicked her tongue, dragging it across her jagged teeth. I waited for a smear of blue blood to show, but she didn't cut herself.

"Dead demons turned up outside a night club a few days back. Or at least their ashes did. Wouldn't know anything about that, would you?" she asked slowly. I pulled my eyes from her seductively threatening tongue. I was used to drawing everything male my way, but somehow, I always felt awkward when females came looking. They were never as mindless as the men, but ever as persistent. It made me have both a certain appreciation and fair amount of wariness with all demons. After all, all it took was a brand to be claimed.

"Nope," I drawled out. "Haven't heard anything about that," I replied slowly. My heartbeat slowed to a crawl as persuasion tried to leech its way into my voice. As tempting as it was, she was bound to realize something was off if she even caught the smallest inkling of it. I was better off lying through my teeth for the time being.

The she-demon seemed to consider this, leveling me with a falsely positive stare. There was amusement hidden there, in the depths of her eyes. And something darker.

"Good to know," she said softly and clapped her hands together. The noise startled me, and I jumped back from the counter. She let out a husky laugh and started motioning to the doughnuts that were spinning around in the glass case to my left. Moira put a hand against my shoulder and made like she was trying to see around me. Her fingers dug into my skin, pumping into me her strength. Calm. I eased against her while she selected her doughnut and the unknown she-demon turned to me. Her eyes betrayed nothing. Whatever darkness was there had vanished.

"And you?" she asked. I didn't even need to think about what I was getting. I got the same thing every time.

"Triple chocolate penetration for me," I said. She smirked as she reached for the extra chocolatey doughnut. I licked my lips when a voice me made me freeze.

"Excellent choice, little succubus." Allistair's power wafted through the air. His strength was like a fog, and it pushed through every cell of my being the closer he came. It invaded my mind with dirty thoughts and constricting around my core without my permission, sharpening the need that already enslaved my body most days and nights.

I took a tight breath and turned my head only a fraction towards him. His eyes were dark, but not with need. *What the—*

I followed his stare from me to the she-demon behind the counter who was ringing up Moira. She hadn't appeared to have seen him yet, but there was no way she couldn't have heard him. The sinister little smile on her lips made me boil with contempt.

Contempt?

No, that can't be right. There's no possible—reasonable—explanation for why I may want to rip her throat out…except for the look she gave Allistair the moment Moira turned away from the counter. Her eyes brightened with an unnatural shimmer as she waved to him.

Unable to stop myself, I let out a growl. It was soft. Silent to human ears. Yet it dripped with a rage that was completely foreign to me. The beast was pushing against my hold. She wanted to tear the demon's throat out for looking at someone that was *hers*.

"Ruby?" Moira asked. Her voice sounded far away even though she was right next to me. I couldn't answer her while the beast and I were locked in a silent battle of wills. I couldn't even look at her, because the beast demanded that we watch this other she-demon before she tried anything.

The silver-eyed demon turned her gaze from Allistair to me, and another growl escaped my lips.

"Ruby," the darkest of desires called out to me. Passion made flesh. Pure masculinity given sound. Both the beast and I were powerless to resist it. We turned as one, drawn to the voice that dared taunt us. Tempt us.

"Look at me, Ruby."

A single tantalizing finger hooked under my chin, drawing my eyes upward, only to be pulled into amber depths so vivid they looked like molten gold. The beast nearly purred as I leaned into the touch. Allistair's lips parted, breathing a taste of warmth across my face that caressed my skin.

For a moment, I was transfixed in an in-between state of reality where only Allistair and I existed. Until the door behind him opened and a group of blushing girls walked in, entirely unaware of what we were or the sticky situation they could so easily have placed themselves in, had his presence not calmed the beast enough to retreat.

I bit my lip and turned for the door, not looking over my shoulder once at the purple-haired demon we were leaving behind.

"What happened in there, Ruby?" Moira asked, coming up on my side. The slap of the cold made me stuff my hands in my armpits while we walked. My hunger for food all but forgotten as my best friend took a hulking bite out of her doughnut. Bavarian cream dribbled down her chin from the very aptly named Cock and Balls. The phallus shaped doughnut was her absolute favorite, and more than likely the source of the chuckle behind us.

"She started to lose control of the beast," Allistair said almost cheerfully.

"Why do you sound so excited about that?" I snapped at him. I don't even know how he found us, or why he was here, but given how the Horsemen always turned up at the most inconvenient of times, I didn't question it.

"I'm amused, little succubus," he said softly in my ear, "because she is possessive enough of me to fight you. It makes me wonder what twisted little thoughts you have hiding in that mind of yours, and all the things I can do to figure them out." I shivered and trudged forward, blaming it on the cold. He's lucky Moira didn't hear him. There would be a throw down in the parking lot.

"Keep dreaming, incubus. You forget that Moira was there as well," I said over my shoulder. The grin fell from his lips as he considered what I said, failing to notice what I didn't say. His eyes shifting between me and my best friend as we climbed in the car.

Moira thrust the pink box at me while she maneuvered the car with one hand and annihilated her doughnut with the other. Half the cock and one of the balls were already gone and it hadn't been a minute since we'd set foot outside the store. I shook my head at her and barely contained my grin at the frown that graced Allistair's lips while he watched us pull out of the parking lot.

I shifted my eyes away from him to the sign over Voodoo Doughnut. There in the middle was the shadow man, with his gleaming black eyes. Moira turned the corner sharply and floored it onto the road. Out of the corner of my eye, just far enough that I could still see, I could have sworn the shadow man winked.

But that's not possible. It must have been a trick of the light.

****ALLISTAIR****

The beast was raging inside of her.

She didn't think I saw it. The way it looked out through her eyes with a challenge. She was the ultimate predator, and it made her highly possessive of anyone she deemed as hers. While the banshee may fall in that category, I was not stupid. She wants me, and her beast already thinks it owns me. It's only a matter of time until she comes around.

My would-be queen, just ripe for the taking.

But I'm getting ahead of myself here.

I needed to break through those walls and let her see that Rysten isn't the only one with a heart. However pathetic an excuse for one mine may be. I was an incubus, and the only one of us four that could understand what she was going through. At least from a sexual deprivation level.

She was brimming with power, so much so that her body was trying to find outlets, to siphon it off—and it was being made infinitely worse by how much she was starving herself.

Not that she was going to let any of us fix that in the short term.

First, I needed to find a way to patch up her mind from the damage the human caused.

Then I will devour her and show her what someone truly worthy can offer.

CHAPTER FOUR

WE SPENT the afternoon cleaning ash out of every nook and cranny of our house. Well, Moira did. I was on dustpan duty and in charge of disposing it in our metal trash can out back. I probably made thirty trips outside that afternoon and ignored the shadows as they crept around my house.

The Horsemen were there, just beyond my line of sight. I couldn't see them, but I could *feel* them. Their essence called me; to more than just me. It called to the thing pacing restlessly inside. My beast didn't understand, couldn't fathom, why I bothered with cleaning the house when we could be with them. When we *should* be with them.

She couldn't understand my human emotions, when we were not human. Not even a drop. That I was raised with humans was unimportant to her. She saw my need for independence and space as cumbersome. Inconvenient. Irrational even. My desire for time to adjust was laudable in her mind, but given that I knew exactly why she pushed me and what she wanted, I wasn't inclined to listen. Not to a sociopathic entity that had very few true emotions of her own outside of desire and rage.

She goaded me. Poked. Prodded. Did anything and everything she could to try and force my hand as the sky bled from blue to black. I didn't give even an inch, because she would take a mile.

Sleep was unachievable that night. Not with my body wound so tight that I ended up staring at the ceiling for the better part of the early

November morning. Bandit curled around one side of me and I could sense Moira's presence only a room away. Peace of mind never came. Just a restless and dazed drifting where time crawled at an agonizing pace. I must have blinked a thousand times because somewhere along the way, the night had passed, and morning was here.

Soft light gleamed through the cracks in my curtains, illuminating my room with the soft grey glow of the cloudy sky. Despite the outward appearance of serenity, the beast still paced within me. Not at rest, even after a night of forcing myself to stay in bed with the hopes of finding peace. Oh no, she was not the least bit put off or worn down. If anything, she was more irritable. Her frustration leaked into me and the blood in my veins sizzled with life. Right at that moment, in my sleep-deprived, pre-caffeinated haze, I realized I wasn't planning on sitting around or cleaning for another day.

I needed to get out. Do something. Otherwise the damn beast was going to drive me crazy, or even worse, straight to the Horsemen's beds.

I jumped up and began digging through my closet, cursing under my breath at how cold it had gotten. Frigid enough that when I hunched over to dig through my pile of clean laundry, my breath frosted, turning into smoky white puffs in front of me. My lips thinned as I pulled on a pair of jeans over the long johns I wore to bed. The rips in the front of them showed the dark grey material beneath, giving me at least some kind of protection from the chill. I pulled on a t-shirt and two sweatshirts to finish myself off. It was going to be cold as balls outside, but I wanted short sleeves if I was going into Blue Ruby today. I never liked to tattoo in long sleeves. They felt constricting. Tight. Particularly in some of the awkward positions I have to get into to work.

Just as I finished lacing up my boots, Moira appeared in the doorway of my room, steaming cup of coffee in hand.

"Going somewhere?" she asked. Her tone was testing, not quite bossy, but the displeasure was there. She crossed her skinny green arms over her chest and cocked her head.

"Yep. I have four clients today, two of which I had to reschedule with last week. Not to mention whoever else rescheduled yesterday," I replied, equally as terse. From his hammock in the corner, Bandit flung himself at me, wrapping his arms around my neck. He let out the most pathetic mewling noises ever, and I'm pretty sure they were all for effect.

"Are you sure? Even the trash panda is worried about you. Maybe it's better you stay home for another day," she said as Bandit let out another screech in my ear. His tiny paws grabbed at me as his claws dug into the back of my neck.

"I've already stayed home for two days. I broke my tradition of going to Martha's every Saturday, and I have never missed one in ten years. I'm not staying locked in the house anymore. You and Bandit can get over it. We still have bills to pay and a tattoo parlor to run," I said resolutely. The raccoon hanging around my neck literally started quivering and bawled like a fucking baby.

For fuck's sake.

A knock, or pounding rather, interrupted us. Bandit shut his trap and climbed on my shoulder, switching modes from whining little shit to vigilante protector. I shook my head and muttered,

"Unbelievable..."

Moira followed behind me as I approached the front door. I put my hand to the lock as I stared through the little peephole. Never in my life had I bothered to check before opening the door. Until now. I guess being drugged, molested, and then almost kidnapped would do that to you.

"Ruby, I know you're there, love. Why don't you open the door for me?" Rysten called. His dark green eyes stared at the hole in the door. His sandy blonde curls, Miami Beach t-shirt, and trendy jacket were so misleading for what lurked beneath his glamor. His dark powers weren't what made me lock the doors, as formidable as they were.

Silently, I cracked it open.

"There you are. I've been worried. Allistair told us you had a little problem yesterday with keeping the beast at bay. I thought I might come spend the day with you," he said gently. His hand was more insistent than his words as he pushed the door open further. Just wide enough to see Bandit bolstered to my shoulder, and Moira standing next to me with her arms crossed over her chest. "That one"—he motioned to Moira and his jaw ticked—"sent me away last night when I tried to check in on you."

"Me?" Moira gasped innocently, looking from side to side before placing a hand to her chest. She opened her mouth in pretend shock. Rysten threw a glare in her direction and she dropped the façade, cackling even though she was only doing what I asked her. But who was I to ruin her fun?

"Well, as you can see, I'm taken care of and I'm actually running a bit late for work…" My voice trailed off as the other three Horsemen stepped into view from the side of the house, where I could only assume they were hiding.

"I can take you to work," he said. His voice was falsely cheerful. Hopeful.

"Or we all can," Laran cut in, placing his hand on Rysten's shoulder in such a way that would have been supportive, even brotherly, if he weren't squeezing the crap out of him. Yeah, subtlety wasn't War's strong suit.

"There's not enough room," I said. Laran had the audacity to cut his eyes towards my VW bug and actually consider it. Even when a frown graced his lips, he didn't yield.

"We could—"

I held up a hand to stop him. To both my surprise and pleasure, he stopped talking. The beast purred.

"I know you guys mean well, but I need you to give me time to think about things. Okay?" I asked. Next to me, Moira muttered, "Some space wouldn't hurt either."

Both men cut her harsh looks and I let out an exasperated sigh. My nerves were just too frayed to put up with the bickering today. Sleep deprivation wasn't treating me kind and the snarling beast inside me was royally pissed.

"Can I have a minute, Moira?" She gave me a cool look that promised this wasn't over as she strode away, her bathrobe stirring in the breeze.

The four watched me reproachfully, their faces unreadable, but all emotions splayed open for me to see. It was a spectrum that ranged from an ever-present controlled rage, to the throbbing intensity of desire that invaded every cell of my body, making the hairs on my arms stand on end.

"Look guys, I'm heading into work. Without you. Any of you. I need the day to just try to pretend that everything is okay. That it's *normal*. Do you understand?" I asked slowly. A flash of pain shone in Rysten's eyes, but he smiled nonetheless.

"Of course, love. If that's what you need," he replied. Laran opened his mouth to disagree and Allistair grasped his shoulder.

"Let's go for a walk, War," Allistair said briskly. His golden eyes flashed to mine, and then they were gone, leaving only Rysten and Julian on my doorstep. The resemblance between them was striking, but it was only skin deep. When you really looked at them, there couldn't be two people more different.

Rysten was kind, easy to laugh and quick to smile. He was the hottie-next-door you always dreamed about. The guy that has his pick of girls but marries his high school sweetheart and settles for life. The kind that every girl wants to date, and every guy is friends with, and across it all, you just can't help but love him. He's the sweet guy. The good guy…but Julian was entirely different.

He didn't strike me as the type of bad boy that roamed from woman to woman. He was more reserved than that. More guarded. There was this air to him that had an edge of something stronger, harder than steel. Colder than ice. Darker than even death. Julian wasn't a bad boy or the boy next door. He was the kind that lived in the darkness. That fostered it. Nurtured it. The kind of man that mothers warn their daughters about. The kind that no matter how smart a girl you are, no woman could possibly say no to.

He was the kind that may not leave a string of hearts in his wake, but when he did find someone…

Heaven and Hell will not be able to separate them. Not even God herself.

My cheeks warmed and I silently cursed my pasty cheeks.

"Ruby?" The question brought my comparing them to a grinding halt. I drew my eyes away from Julian's lips, the lips I had been staring at so intently and not realized it.

"Yes?" I asked, slightly breathless.

"Everything alright, love?" Rysten asked slowly. Their eyes were focused on me with an intensity both sinfully delicious and unnerving at the same time. Lucky for me, I was pretty sure my thoughts were my own. Unlike me, I didn't think they could read emotions. Except maybe Allistair…

"Yep," I drawled out. "I'm just tired and still processing everything. Let me have today to get back in the swing of things…" I trailed off at the look the brothers were sharing. It was unreadable, but undeniably there. "Is there something you have to say?" I snapped. The up and downs between me and the beast were giving me whiplash. One moment I was turned on and the next I was agitated. Maybe it was me coping. Maybe it was the transition. But it was probably just the Horsemen.

Rysten approached me. Unlike Laran, who had no issue crowding my space, or Allistair, who wore a wicked sneer as he tempted me, Rysten simply stopped short and took my hand in his. Bandit grumbled under his breath but settled back on my shoulder, the closest that he ever comes to accepting anyone outside of me and Moira.

"I can only imagine how hard this is right now." Rysten's words sounded tight with an unnamable emotion that I didn't want to feel. I wondered if it was his inability to truly empathize, or sympathy at the situation their arrival had put me in. "But you need to have a guard around you at all times now, love. We can wait to talk about the changes coming, but please don't ask us to leave. We can't. Not when one of the demons who attacked you still roams free."

I sighed deeply, running my free hand over my face. I didn't like it. I didn't like any of this. I planned to keep pushing back until there was no other choice, but maybe for today having one of them with me wouldn't be the worst thing in the world. The beast was restless and called for blood, and I didn't want to give her a chance to spill it. As much as I hated to admit it, they soothed her.

Keeping her calm was just as important as keeping bloodthirsty imps away. My control over her, even if it was barely, was the only reason they were still giving me choices and letting me decide things for myself.

"Fine, *one of you* can come with me today, but this doesn't mean I'm moving in or agreeing to being watched twenty-four-seven. It just means I don't feel like arguing today. Got it?" Rysten nodded, a smirk playing on the corners of his lips. Beside him, Julian's expression turned cold, his emotions laced with something almost like…jealousy?

I raised my eyes to his, the question almost playing on my lips. I didn't feel it was my place to ask, but before I could decide, he turned sharply and strode towards the shade of a large conifer.

"Keep an eye on her. One of the other's will switch in this afternoon, if she'll let us." His voice was icy. Curt. The long-sleeve shirt he wore bunched around his shoulders where the muscles contracted, taut with tension. He didn't spare a glance over his shoulder as he strode into the shadows and disappeared like he was never here at all.

RYSTEN

He had no reason to be pissed at me.

He knew exactly how this was going to go down the moment all four of us laid eyes on her. She's not just an infatuation, and she never will be. He was daft for continuing to hold her at arm's length while expecting the rest of us to do so as well.

We weren't just her guardians anymore, even though she herself did not want to see it.

Her beast chose us.

I knew the moment I saw her standing at the door, crossing her arms over her chest like she could cover the truth. She's formed an attachment, to each of us, and the beast accepted it.

Not that it would have ever accepted anyone else. Humans were not even worth that predator's attention and other male-demons would not be able to handle it, or her.

She was more her father's daughter than she realized, and Lola would have been proud.

I've never met a she-demon that I felt truly possessive over. It's difficult when you know that the one you were created for may come along at any point, but never in my wildest dreams did I imagine that very she-demon would be the one to draw out the darkness.

To goad it. Rile it up.

And make me want to slaughter any male outside of us who dared get close to her.

CHAPTER FIVE

The bell jingled on the front door of Blue Ruby Ink.

"We're closed for lunch right now," I said without looking up. Rysten and Moira had left only minutes ago to find lunch for us while I completed the revisions to the design a client requested.

"We need to have a little chat, you an' I."

The thick southern drawl was unmistakable.

As was the blonde haired, blue-eyed beauty behind it.

"What do you want, Kendall?" My words were terse; laced with a hint of the beast I could not hide. I was going to need to make this little meeting short, or risk her upsetting the dark entity that disliked everything she represented.

"Josh is missin'," she started, her voice quivering a fraction as she said it.

I set the pencil down and slid the design aside, placing it in a seal-tight envelope to protect it from Moira's klutziness and any *accidental* spills that Kendall was prone to.

"I'm not certain why you're coming to me with this. We broke up over six weeks ago," I said lightly. Her glistening eyes hardened at my dismissive tone, but not for one second did I believe she was here for anything good.

"I *know* he was still seein' you, Ruby. And now he's up an' disappeared. I haven't heard from him since Friday…" She swallowed hard, fighting her wasted tears. Part of me wanted to tell her to keep her tears; save them for someone worthy. Someone who wouldn't be with her while still pining for his ex like a dog in heat. The rest of me knew not to believe any show she put on.

"Well, I haven't seen him. So I don't know what to—"

"Don't lie to me!" she snapped. I blinked in surprise but didn't react otherwise as Kendall smoothed her bubblegum pink dress. "I'm givin' you the chance to confess your sins an' tell me where he is." Angry tears burst through causing her black mascara to streak down her cheeks. She didn't outright cry or sob, but the venom that filled her eyes was telling.

"I don't know what you're talking about."

I didn't even miss a beat in my response because I'd planned for this moment since I woke up from that nightmare at Pandora's Box. Kendall was nearly as obsessive as he was, and I knew that as much as the Horsemen assured me it would be like he never existed, this wouldn't go away.

Sure, they could cover up his death, but they couldn't cover up his life. He wasn't a demon. He was human. A weak-willed human that lost his mind from a desire I caused but didn't know how to undo.

I couldn't bring myself to feel bad, not when his very name awoke memories of that night. Nightmares of lying on a conference table, drugged out of my mind and unable to move while he dry humped my body and molested me.

He would have raped me if the Horsemen hadn't shown, and so I would not feel guilty.

Not for him.

Kendall dabbed at her eyes and cheeks with a handkerchief, erasing the evidence of tears. A cruel smile stole her lips as she reached inside her purse and withdrew a single sheet of paper.

She crossed the space between us and extended her hand.

Devil save me.

It was a photo. Of Josh and me. At the bar in Pandora's Box.

This couldn't have been taken more than an hour before he tried to rape me.

Before he groped me, and undressed me, and—I was going to be sick.

Blood roared in my veins as I toppled sideways from the chair. The onslaught to my system hit me fast and sudden as I tried to heave up food that wasn't there. My stomach rolled as the world went sideways and my connection to the outside severed.

I'd never had a panic attack in my life, despite all the bad things that had happened.

Whatever the experience, I took them and then locked it away where they were never found again. I took those memories, even as they were happening, and stored them in a box. Placed inside a vault where I would lock it away, never to see the light of day again.

That was how it worked. How I coped.

I didn't have panic or anxiety. I lived my life, accepting that it happened but forgetting a little more every day.

Until I couldn't.

"What in the name of—" Kendall started screaming. I went from hearing nothing, being trapped in a bubble of my own creation, to being yanked back into a reality where the picture in her hand made me sick to my stomach.

He's dead. He can no longer harm you.

I swallowed hard, taking in deep breaths as the door to the shop slammed open.

I didn't have to look to know that Moira and Rysten had returned. Their combined emotions were like jumper cables to my heart. The fear receded as the cold fury of an entity that very much wanted to burn her alive took its place.

I was still in control, but hanging on by a thread.

"Kendall, I don't know what the fuck you are doing here, but if you don't walk out right now, you're leaving in a body bag. You hear me?" Moira didn't scream. She didn't shout. Hell, she didn't even raise her voice. She let the calm chill of her words settle over us and wrap around Kendall, using the quiet to speak her intentions louder than the words themselves.

"Th-thi-this isn't over! I know what happened! I know the *truth!*" she screamed and then she was gone.

The truth? She didn't know that. I doubt any of them knew the whole truth as to what happened that night. I knew the truth, because I'd seen it before.

Josh's case was not specific to him. It was the same story for most males that crossed my path. I'd accepted that and learned to live with it a long time ago. Or so I thought.

Moira hugged me and whispered promises of revenge. She meant to soothe me. To calm me.

Right there in the place I chose to leave my mark on this world, I decided that this would not break me. Kendall said this wasn't over, and I would be ready when she returned. Ready to let the lies run from my lips.

Even if I cared nothing for Josh, it was not the truth that mattered here. Only what Kendall saw as the truth, and for all his affections and obsessive thoughts—I was still the one, even in death, paying the price.

CHAPTER SIX

Moira and I didn't speak on it as the day went on, but I could sense her worried glances. Both what she directed at me as well as the ones shared with Rysten. I locked myself in my office after my last client left and didn't come out, even when she knocked and told me she was leaving. I didn't feel like seeing anyone.

Alone with nothing but my own thoughts, I chewed at the corner of my thumbnail and flipped through my files for designs to work on. It wasn't much, but it was something.

The first design I completed was done in pencil. A simple black and white drawing of a rose for a mother who lost her daughter as a baby. The second was a tempest, quite literally, done in the most brilliant of blues and yellows. The sky was clad with lightning and the clouds rolled so effortlessly they could have been real. This one was for an older woman who had once been a sailor. She told me of the skies and the sea, and how they tried to claim her life again and again. She endured, much like the mother had when her daughter died. That old woman had cancer now, but she wanted a sleeve on her right arm as a reminder of what she's been through. An aid, to weather the storm.

It was beautiful. One of my best pieces, and I hadn't even shown her yet. I smiled, running the tip of my finger around the heavy Aegean clouds dusted with traces of lapis blue. The words replayed over and over in my mind: *an aid to weather the storm.*

People had faced far worse things than I and lived to smile again. To fight again. Hell, I usually was not one to be thrown so far off track from myself that a picture could blindside me like it had. So what had changed?

Was it me? Was it the Horsemen? I know I didn't care for Josh enough that it was his actions that stirred me. I'd been down that path before, with devils and demons that were stronger than him. Was that it? That he was weak, and yet he'd bested me? But could you even call that besting when he had to drug me to do it?

My mind was a place of colors and secrets, of paradigms and lies. I did not hurt easily, but little things made me snap. I didn't consider myself a liar, but my entire existence was one fat fucking lie. I was created to be a ruler, and not just any ruler. The ruler of Hell.

Queen of the Underworld.

But a fucking picture brought me to my knees. There was something so right about that, and yet so cruel. After all, I wasn't the one who died that night. I'm just the one that has to live with everyone else's mistakes. The one that got drugged, not once, but twice—thanks to the imp that Laran pissed off for touching me. Of course, he wouldn't have been touching me if we hadn't gone there in the first place. Could I actually blame him for taking me there? No. Not as much as I could blame Josh for his actions. I didn't regret his death, and I still don't. But that doesn't mean I'm unaffected either.

Seeing that, doing that, it fucks with your head, and this wasn't the first time it's happened. It's just the first time it's happened with the Horsemen. What about next time? What happens when we go to Hell? I'd woefully turned a blind eye to the demon world because I didn't want to see it, but now it's here and it can't be denied.

Fuck it all.

I jumped up from my desk and stored the artwork away where it couldn't be ruined from spilt coffee or takeout tacos. I grabbed my purse and washed my hands, cleaning away the remaining residue from the colored pencils. The water bled blue and yellow, turning a sickly shade of green. I wasn't one to believe in omens. That was a different kind of demon, but the color didn't sit well with me.

The shop was quiet when I locked up and the sun was long asleep. An obsidian sky stared back at me as I stepped out from the light of Blue Ruby Ink.

Calm brushed against my skin and the beast settled for the first time today. It was not a natural calm; not something I gave myself, but a gift from another.

"I take it that it's your turn?" I asked softly. Allistair stepped out of the shadows. The sharpness of his high cheekbones was particularly prominent tonight against his alabaster skin. During the day, he was devastatingly handsome, but at night…he was somehow more. The light in his eyes shined brighter, and the lushness of his dark curls just begged to be touched. At night, Allistair was the most beautiful creature I'd ever seen.

The corners of his mouth turned up into a knowing smile.

"Let's go for a ride," he replied. On most nights, I probably would have protested, given where I ended up last time I let a Horseman take me somewhere without telling me.

But Allistair wasn't Laran, and I was a different kind of Ruby now.

He extended his hand, and all I could think about was an *aid to weather the storm*. I didn't know who I was right now. I was Ruby. I was Lucifer's Daughter. I was a monster. I was…living the best I could in our messed-up world and doing the best I can.

But sometimes, you just gotta let a devil take the wheel.

I DIDN'T ASK him where we were going as the lights streaked by like shooting stars. Allistair had the nicest car I'd ever ridden in. Black leather, heated seats, and a cup of tea waiting in the cup holder. I wrapped my hands around the steaming cup, trying to leech its warmth away as I took a small sip.

Earl Grey with a hint of honey and a splash of milk.

Perfect.

I let out a small sigh. This calm was fabricated from him. Instinctually, I knew that.

In reality, I didn't care where we went as long as it didn't end.

"How's the tea?" he asked.

Small talk. It was such a very human thing to do. I didn't know whether I should be thankful or annoyed that he was bothering at all.

"It's perfect," I replied without turning his way. It was easier not to focus on anything. The lights were brilliant and beautiful, carrying with them all my melancholy as they passed by.

"Excellent," he said. I smiled, just the briefest lift of my lips at the pride in his voice. I'd been wondering if Rysten told him how I liked my tea as a way to cheer me, but maybe Allistair paid attention more than I realized.

The car descended into silence for another moment. This one longer than the first, so long in fact, that the lights were becoming fewer and fewer. We were leaving the city.

The thought both had me intrigued and mildly nervous, but I kept quiet because if he were smuggling me away somewhere for any length of time, I knew the other three would be here, too.

"You know," Allistair said, breaking the silence, "I know what you're going through. Right now." I tensed, and his hand slipped from the steering wheel as he reached across and took my hand from my lap. "You don't have to say anything. I don't expect you to. I'd just like you to listen."

And I did. The blood in my veins heated at his very touch. It wasn't a sexual touch, nor was it fraught with his own messy emotions. Instead it was... kind. Reassuring. He wasn't holding my hand like a possessive prick, but instead to offer the only kind of comfort that I was always deprived of.

And then he said the last thing I ever expected him to say.

"In all my time, both in this world and ours, I have only ever fallen in love once." Even in the dark cab of the car I could sense his eyes watching me. "As someone raised among humans, you might find it surprising that it only ever happened once," he continued. "But as a woman who is half-succubus, I think you can understand.

"I have lived for thousands and thousands of years, watching women do anything in the name of what they call love. I have seen women kill themselves, their lovers, even other women they thought were a threat... just to get to me.

"In the beginning, I struggled with the blame and where it lay when I realized there was little I could do to stop them. Eventually the guilt faded, replaced by anger at the women for being so stupid. For not seeing what I thought was obvious. For not seeing the *love* wasn't real—or so I thought at the time." That almost pulled a scoff from my lips, had I not been so speechless at his confession. He was Famine, one of the Four Horsemen... and still just a male at heart. Except unlike the men of earth, demons were not confined by gender roles and stereotypes. We saw ourselves as we were and did not apologize for it. In some ways that made us, him, better than the people of earth.

I kept my thoughts to myself as he continued.

"And then eventually I did fall in love with someone. A female that was forbidden in every way, but I could not stop myself. I was as caught up in it as the foolish women who'd chased me for centuries. Until I wasn't."

"What?" The question popped from my lips before I could stop myself. Allistair smiled, but there was nothing kind about it. If his hand weren't wrapped around mine, I would be scared shitless at the hateful smile he wore.

"The falling out is unimportant. The moral of the story was that the female and I split up, and we went our separate ways. She is the only one I have ever been able to do that with and it not end in bloodshed. Do you know why that is?"

I shook my head and the car came rolling to a stop. I didn't recognize where we were, only that the headlights stared off into an abyss where only the night sky reigned.

"Because they were beneath me. I was created to be strong enough to rival you, to ground you when it was needed. Women, she-demons, they were not strong enough to combat that. They were beneath me. Just because we wear the same form does not change that. I cannot apologize for being what I was created to be, any more than a hellhound can apologize for being loyal."

I was starting to see exactly where he was going, and as someone raised among humans… I didn't know where I fell with it.

"I can't be some mindless person that just walks around killing people. That's not me, that's—" I stopped myself short from admitting those dark desires aloud.

"The beast?" he asked softly.

I bit my lip, nodding my reply.

"You were created to be the ultimate predator. The one that can keep our kind in line." He said it so simply; like that's all there was to it.

"And what if I don't want to be?" I asked.

"Don't want to be the beast, or don't want to be a succubus?" he countered, another smile playing on his lips.

"Both." He actually had the nerve to laugh.

"I don't think it's that you don't want to be them. I think it's your misconceptions of who you are and who you think you need to be. I think you're apologizing for existing, because you think that without you, things would have been different for all the men that crossed your path."

Devil save me. He was either brilliant, or a much better manipulator than I gave him credit for. I was pretty sure I was fucked either way.

"And what would you have me do?"

"Stop apologizing. Be who you are and be unashamed. I know that you want to. I can see it in your eyes. This world has done nothing for you, and yet you bleed for it. Why? You don't feel bad for the pig when you eat the bacon. Why do you feel bad for the man that hurt you?"

I shook my head. "It's not Josh I feel bad for." His hand tightened around mine briefly before he pulled away.

"Come with me."

We opened our doors and welcomed the night as an icy breeze ran over me. My ponytail whipped away from my face, a slave to the current that caught it. I walked around the front of the car, taking in deep breaths of air. It tasted different out here. Cleaner. Crisper. My boots crunched on the frosted grass as I followed the headlights to the edge of the ravine.

I gasped as I looked down. At that same moment, the lights clicked off.

Darkness sprang from the shadows, bathing me in night. I didn't move an inch as I took in the view from hundreds of feet above. I couldn't make out the surface below us, where the rock face ended, and the dark lake began. I wouldn't have known it was water at all, if not for the two moons. One up in the sky and the other down below it, settled on the horizon. The ripples in the water scattered the light of the stars, fragmenting the vision of space around us.

"I've never seen anything quite like it," I whispered.

In a void where sound is violent, a whisper became a shout.

"I thought you might like it. Our kind have a longing for beautiful things," he murmured. Strong fingers settled against my lower back, and even through three layers of clothing, my skin flamed. "We also seek out thrills and out of this world experiences," he continued.

The heat was joined by a prickling sensation. A warning?

"Do you trust me?" he asked, his lips grazed my ear and there was nothing friendly about this touch.

My breath stalled in my throat as my mouth hung open. Allistair moved behind me as he nipped my earlobe, the heat of his breathe tingling against my skin. I throbbed to life in the flip of a switch, instantly feeling the aching throb between my legs.

"Do you trust me?" he repeated.

Did I trust him? Here? Now? That was a hefty request. His fingers fisted in the fabric of my sweatshirt, bunching it around my back.

If I was going to make bad choices, I may as well enjoy them.

"Yes," I whispered.

"Keep your eyes open," he replied.

And then he pushed me.

CHAPTER SEVEN

I FELL through the stars waiting for the moment I would hit the water and die.

It's a strange thing being this close to death. Oddly freeing in a sense, as the inevitable washed over me. I probably had no more than a hundred feet left to drop, and while I could be asking myself all sorts of questions like, "How could he do this?" or "Why me?" The only thing I actually found myself hoping for was that Moira and Bandit would take care of each other.

The water rose up faster and the freeing feeling in my chest constricted. Wasn't there a saying that death was easy and life was hard? I was going to find out. Lucifer's daughter or not, I doubted a fall from several hundred feet was survivable.

Well, this is it. Your famous last words were trusting the guy that pushed you.

I hope Moira gives him hell.

My own reflection rose up to greet me, and I waited for the impact.

And waited.

And—

My body slammed into someone else. The impact rattled my bones, but their strength held me firm, an arm cradled under my leg and another cradled against my back. I hadn't died. I blinked and my head swiveled around. The midnight sky was the same, but there was a ridge just like the one I'd been pushed from…I frowned and swung my head back to see if the car was where I remembered it. This was just too weird. My vision was blocked by whoever's body I clung to. I followed the rise and fall of his chest up to the curve of his neck and stark cheekbones. All the way to the amber eyes that stared back.

All thoughts of dying aside, my fury clawed its way forward to greet him.

"You motherfucking bastard! How dare you push me off a—"

"You're not dead, are you?" he asked.

"No! But that's not the—"

"And you're not hurt at all, right?"

"Well no, but I'm pissed you even thought—"

"Then what are you mad about?" I could almost believe he was genuinely unaware that this was fucked up. Almost. If he hadn't been smirking down at me. He was every bit the prick I thought he was.

"Fuck you," I spat.

Allistair let out a dark chuckle. "Is that an open invitation?"

I let out an inhuman growl and bunched up my fists.

"Put me down," I snapped. Allistair swung me onto my feet but kept his arm around me. I pushed at him and tried to step away, but my legs failed me. The world tilted on its axis as vertigo hit me. "Wow," I croaked. The second my vision cleared, and my legs were my own again, I turned on Allistair. He grinned down at me, not manically, but still clearly out of his mind.

I took a swing at his face.

"Ow, man! What the fuck are you made of?" I swore angrily, shaking my hand out. Fingers dug into my right hip, holding me in place. If he were human, he'd be bruised and on the floor, just like the punk that tried to rob me. But Allistair wasn't human. Hell, he wasn't even a demon, really. He was something more.

"Did you just punch me?" he asked, working his jaw out.

"Did you just push me off a fucking cliff?" I replied. His clutch on my hip tightened and I lay my hand over his, gliding up his forearm and scraping my nails down.

Before he pushed me, before the out-of-body experience, before I thought I was about to die, I had been aroused. His presence was enough, but his touch ignited something in me every time. Then when, I didn't die,

I was pissed. I wanted to hurt him. Now I just wanted him. Somehow it seems we've come full circle. My emotions swirled together in a dangerous and promising tempest within me, just waiting to be unleashed.

"Just when I think I have you figured out, you go and surprise me again," he murmured, letting his other hand drop from his face and resting it on the other side of my hip. My mouth went dry as all the insults and curses in the world left me. "It's rather refreshing, you know," he continued, leaning back to sit on the hood of his car. His hands were slowly drawing me closer. I stepped into the space between his legs and pressed my icy hands onto the curvature of his chest. In the pale moonlight, his eyes darkened from amber to bronze, drawing me in deeper.

My inner beast purred. She liked this exchange. And she wanted more.

Never breaking eye contact, I leaned into him, running my tongue over my lips, my intentions clear. The hands at my waist slipped beneath the thick material of my many layers. Hot but cold, his fingers brushed the outline of my hip bones, along the edge of my pants.

Feeling almost out of control, my body jerked towards him knowing he could give me more of what I craved so deeply. I could never before be with a man in this capacity. The world of possibility left me wanting, and more than a little needy.

"So responsive," he said huskily. His breath fanned my face as a sigh escaped my lips; his hand splayed across my back, beneath my shirt, moving to pull me in and close the space between us. I slid my hands up over his shoulders to rest at the base of his neck. My fingers brushed against stray curls of obsidian hair and tightened around the soft locks.

Allistair let out a low groan and captured my mouth with his.

His lips were not hesitant or sweet as they sought out mine and devoured me wholly. Allistair was not the kind of man to be gentle in his endeavors. Like me, there was something inside him that fed on the need and sexuality in weaker beings, and it was a downright high to taste something equal. One of his hands shifted from the grip on my back to the fabric of my bra. His dexterous fingers, skilled in seeking what they wanted, squeezed sharply, freeing my breasts.

My mouth opened more as I moaned into his mouth and he kissed me deeper, his tongue searching. He tasted of want, rich scotch, and something entirely his own. I clung to him, meeting his controlled ravaging with a fierceness that I could not contain. My fingers fisted in his hair, pulling hard, and the breath hissed between his lips, his mouth breaking from mine.

"Be careful, little succubus. My control only goes so far. I've yet to feed since I met you," he whispered against my skin. His warning had the opposite effect, only increasing my desire for him. I leaned forward, taking his bottom lip in my mouth and scraping it lightly with my teeth, sucking while I pulled away slowly.

He reached beneath the loose bra cup, palming my breast, grazing the taut peak and teasing me. Cool fingers grasped my nipple, tugging it just enough to bring me to the edge of pleasure and pain. The sensation shot straight between my legs as an ache began to build. I bit his lip as payment.

He cursed sharply and drew away. His tongue flicked out, tasting his blood on his lips. I stared at him, cocking my eyebrow, daring him to respond.

"You're savage in your desires," he said. I couldn't read his tone, but there was a wickedness to his smile. Surprise, challenge, amusement: he was making a mental note for what he would have in store for me later. His eyes didn't leave mine as he reached down and clamped his hand over the apex between my thighs. I rocked my hips into him while he watched me with dark and hungry eyes.

Right here, right now, I wasn't Ruby, and I wasn't the beast. I was a sexual being consumed by a burning need that ached within me every single day, never sated, apart from the weak relief I could find with my own hand beneath the covers late at night.

I relished the pressure of his palm over my jeans, using three fingers to rub me back and forth along the seam, the fabric blocking contact but allowing the sensation to build me up. I matched his rhythm, rubbing myself against him. Allistair would give, but I had to play by *his* rules. That was my job in this game. To take what I was given. To do as I was told. But I couldn't help myself. I ground harder against his hand, wanting more.

His hand stopped and a growl started in my chest.

"Careful. I didn't bring you out here to fuck you, but I won't leave you like this so close to transition," he groaned. I gave his hair a sharp tug and he pinned me with a glare. "You have to behave if you want it. I'm hard and fucking starving. For me to feed without fucking, I need concentration. Something I won't have if you continue biting and pulling my hair. Can you be good?" His words held the promise of what I wanted most right now. I loosened my grip on him and nodded.

He gave me a dark smile as the hand on my breast tightened again and I breathed a low moan in pleasure and relief. I'd been here before. I knew what he wanted, and I wanted to give it. The look he rewarded me with almost had me climaxing on the spot.

Allistair pulled his hand from between my thighs and made a turning motion in the air, silently telling me to turn around . I froze and cocked an eyebrow, but I did as I was told, ignoring the smirk on his lips just before he disappeared from view. I was faced with the night sky as he pulled my body back against his.

With one hand he brushed my hair to the side, while his lips grazed my skin and bit into the pulse on my neck. My breath hitched in my throat, but I didn't move. I didn't dare grind my ass onto his rock-hard cock that was flush against it.

"Mmmm, I like you this way," he murmured. I opened my mouth to reply, but one of his hands slipped underneath my shirt and flicked open the button on my jeans. My heart ricocheted in my chest.

He slowly unzipped the fly on my pants, taking his merry time. The only thing that made it bearable were the faint kisses he was leaving along my neck. His cool lips on my burning skin was a trail of straight ecstasy. He nibbled as he went, alternating sharp bites and sucking at patches of my bare flesh. I would never be this patient or play this game with anyone else. With Allistair it came naturally. I *wanted* to do as I was told; to please him. I wanted him to please me.

He tugged my jeans down a few inches and my excitement spiked. His fingers slipped inside my jeans and rubbed my clit through my panties. I couldn't help it when my body jerked in response, my ass pushing against his cock. He nipped my neck in warning and I quickly regained control. My head lolled to the side, begging for more.

"Good girl," he praised. I moaned as he pushed my panties aside, his skillful fingers entering my slick folds. I cried into the night as I tried to keep still, to play our game, my leg twitching with anticipation, my body screaming for him to make me come. Allistair hummed his approval against my neck as he massaged his fingers in deeper. The palm of his hand resting over my clit, rubbing me while he brought me closer.

"Please!" It was a guttural, useless cry. He wouldn't give me my release until he was good and ready.

"Where are my fingers? I want to hear you say it."

What...?

Through clenched teeth, I growled at him in frustration. "No..."

"I want you to tell me. I want you to say it."

Focusing on the pleasure, clenching my jaw, I was determined not to say the words.

He slowed his hand and desperation flooded me. "Where are my fingers, Ruby?" he repeated firmly, pushing in deeper as he pressed against my g-spot, sending a shock through my limbs as he sped up inside me.

"Your fingers...are in...my pussy," I managed to breathe out as my climax built further, not wanting him to stop.

"And what do you want?"

"I want you to make me come. Please make me come. Please..."

"Hmmm," he murmured. "I like the way you beg. Maybe another night we can see how many sweet sounds I can draw from those lips. I still plan on making you scream."

I kept as still as I could while the ache pulled at me, his pressure deepened, and his rhythm increased. I could feel my entire body twitching on the brink of release.

For some women, his controlling nature would have been a turn off. Hell, I didn't understand why it did the things it did to me. Usually I was wanted to throttle him, but for some reason, my anger was lost when his fingers were buried inside me and I did and said things I didn't understand.

"Say my name when you come," he demanded.

I didn't have the power to tell him he was a bastard as my orgasm hit me. My head tilted back as I clenched around his fingers and I gave up being good for the reckless abandon of riding it out. "Allistair!" I choked. My hands wrapped around his thighs on either side of me, clawing at the material of his slacks, pressing myself closer to him. Feeling him against me, riding and grinding in time with his fingers as continued to sweep inside me. A wave of euphoria pounded though my muscles, still spasming around his fingers. Amongst it all, there was this faint twinge inside of me as something fanned the flames and made my pleasure last longer than ever before.

Is he feeding? I wasn't sure. I'd never been with an incubus, so I didn't know what to expect, but the intense heat that flooded me was more than welcome.

I wanted more.

I pressed back against his hard length, sliding my ass up and down, reaching around for the buckle on Allistair's slacks. His sharp intake of breath made the beast purr. I pulled at his belt, but he froze instantly. He pulled away from me and pushed me out of the confines of his arms.

"I—" I swallowed the statement in my throat. I turned to look at him, speechless at his sudden and icy rejection. I fumbled as I tugged my jeans back up and hastily buttoned them.

"It's okay. You caught me off guard. I've never had—never mind. The point is it's not happening tonight." Allistair didn't normally have jarred speech, but maybe I was having more of an effect on him than I'd realized. He pulled away from the car in a fluid motion and approached me gingerly. This hot and cold attitude was getting on my last nerve. What was it he said about apologizing for things?

Oh, yeah. *Don't.*

If he wanted to be a dick, then I was just fine getting off while he got none. I crossed my arms over my chest as he raised a hand to my face and brushed his thumb over my lips. To my credit, I didn't lean into him for once.

"I didn't mean to—"

"Save it. You're still not forgiven for pushing me off a cliff." With my head clear and my body relaxed, I pushed his hand away and strode back to the car. We didn't speak as we both got in and he started the engine. The dashboard lit up, reflecting the time. It was a little past two in the morning, and I was devil knows where with him. I scowled at the expanse before us as he pulled away.

"So why did you bring me out here, huh?" I asked as he pulled onto the interstate.

"I wanted to show you where I go to relax when my burdens get too heavy from time to time. I thought you would appreciate it." His knuckles tightened against the steering wheel, but he kept his voice level when he spoke.

"You pushed me off a fucking cliff. I thought I was going to die—"

"And how did that feel?"

"I—I don't know," I stammered. "That's not the fucking point!"

"That's exactly the point," he replied. I eyed him cautiously. This was some kind of game, I could feel it. He was fucking with my mind, but I'd yet to see how.

"You wanted me to think I would die?" I asked in a shaky breath.

"I wanted you to find yourself, even if only for a moment. The cliff I pushed you off is where an entrance to Hell used to be. It was closed centuries ago. With the portal no longer active, it acts like a feedback loop. You can jump as many times as you like, and it will always spit you back out. I took you there because it's where I go when I'm faced with tough choices. It's an instinctual response to thinking you are going to die. You realize what matters, and it's the most freeing thing I have ever felt in my existence."

Freeing. Isn't that the word I used while I fell?

His words were sincere, despite the way he went about it. Suddenly the conversation in the car and his actions made sense. Not in a normal way. In the fucked-up way that only demons could ever seem to think is something close to logic.

"And after that?" I asked, my cheeks heated but the darkness made me brave.

"Was because I wanted to, and I take what I want. I didn't plan that, if that's what you're asking."

"You say you take what you want…" My voice trailed off. I was unsure how to go about asking this question.

"Yes?"

"Do you want me because you have to?" I asked. He bristled at my questioning.

"We are equals, Ruby. I don't want you because I don't have another choice. I want you because I just do. It's really as simple as that. Don't over-think it," he replied.

"But what about you being a Horseman? You're not the only one that wants me. Is that because—"

"No, it's not. Our duty as the Horsemen does not impose some kind of supernatural bond on us to make us want anything. Whatever the others *feel*"—he said it like the word was dirty—"it doesn't come out of a place of duty. We simply want what we want, and right now you have all of our attention." I couldn't tell if this pleased him or if it was bothersome. The same way the dark hid me, it also hid him. I fell silent and leaned against the doorframe as a thought came to me, unbidden and savage as my desires.

What if I wanted all of them?

Now *that* was a wicked thought.

Almost as wicked as the answering smile from the beast within.

****ALLISTAIR****

I couldn't predict her even if I tried, and believe me, I have.

One moment she is perfectly submissive, making sweet little moans. I loved the sounds that came out of that mouth. Perhaps a little too much. The next minute she fucking bites me and it becomes increasingly difficult not to bend her over the hood of my car. I've started to dream of the latter nightly.

She doesn't know how desirable she is. She doesn't know that I crave her filthy mouth for more than sucking my cock, but one day and one day soon—she will.

She almost fed tonight after I took from her. I could feel it. That tentative soul of hers reaching for mine and I don't even think she realized it. If I hadn't pushed her away, she would have fed and it would have triggered the transition instantly, and neither of us were ready for that. As much as I would love to be the only one to take her through the transition, the timing was all wrong.

We had no way of knowing which half of her would surface, or if both would come forward. Ruby the succubus was one thing…pre-transition she was much stronger than she realized. And that was the better outcome. If the beast surfaced out here in the woods, I would have no way of containing it. Our little foreplay would have turned into a very real game

175

of cat and mouse, possibly ending with her burning down the entire fucking forest.

And still…I almost didn't stop her.

The beast yearns to claim its first mate and she's holding it back. There is almost nothing more that I want, except to keep her safe. That includes from herself.

No matter. She is close. So very close, and when the time comes…

I will be at her side as one of her claimed mates, and nothing in either world will stop me.

CHAPTER EIGHT

A couple of days passed where no one said anything. Allistair didn't
comment about our time in the car. Moira didn't comment on how late I
was getting home. Rysten didn't ask what changed, or why I went back to
normal. Laran didn't comment on how I sent them away, but then Rysten
still got to go with me. And Julian…he pretended that there was nothing
there when he looked at me, but I could sense a growing attraction fighting
his darker emotions every day. I never mentioned the jealousy in his eyes
when the others would pick me up, because he never made a move. It
wasn't my business to intrude on his private thoughts just because I could
read his feelings.

Every day, one of them would ask me if I'd made up my mind about
moving. Despite lack of insulation in my house, I always gave non-
committal answers. Part of me was tempted, but my independence was
holding me back, and for now they accepted that. So it was good enough
for me.

I was just finishing up shading on my client's shoulder when I heard the
door jingle.

"I'll be there in a moment," I called, setting down the tattoo machine.
After three sessions and over eighteen hours, this client's upper back was
finished. A beautifully articulate pocket watch was the centerpiece were it
all started. I drew the design from his grandfather's pocket watch that was

given to him as a child. From there, a pattern of gears and spiral coils developed around it, branching over his shoulder and around his upper arm.

This client was a watchmaker's grandson who had gone on to be a mechanic. I incorporated his love of cars and wrenches and the end result was breathtaking. These were my favorite kind of projects because they were ones that held meaning. I priced myself in such a way that I tried to deter young kids that were looking for their girlfriend's name on their chest or the latest trend in that dated an era. They were easy work, but they weren't fulfilling. Not like this.

"Let me get a mirror," I said to him. The middle-aged man grunted in response. I walked to the other side of the small cubicle and grasped one of my middle-sized mirrors. I held it up at an angle to the man's back so that the reflection in the small one was displayed on the full-length mirror in front of him.

"It's perfect," he said. Moisture gathered in the corners of his eyes, but I pretended not to notice. I went through the motions of bandaging it up while I rattled off the instructions for care. He tipped me generously and thanked me for my work.

As I escorted him around the side awning that separated us from the front lobby, my lungs constricted in my chest. A man with mousy brown hair and flat blue eyes waited for me. I smiled tentatively at him as I gave my client his aftercare sheet and watched him leave.

"Hello, John. It's been a while," I said, leaning against the counter to give off the idea that I was relaxed. When really, I was anything but.

John was Josh's best friend. He was every bit as logical and straightforward as Josh had been…before everything happened.

John nodded and took a deep, exhausted breath. The bags beneath his eyes told me why he was here.

"It's good to see you, Ruby. You look…well." His eyes were carefully trained on my face. I wasn't sure if his words were meant to be sarcastic or kind.

"I am well. What can I do for you today?" I asked, cutting straight to the point. He blew out another breath that I almost thought was a sigh of relief. Maybe it was disappointment. I kept to myself and didn't read into his emotions. That's what always got me in trouble in the first place: the desire to fix them.

I knew why he was here, and there was no fixing this. I only had lies meant to buy me time.

"Josh is missing," he started. Unlike Kendall, there wasn't the conflict of dealing with the crying-girlfriend-but-also-a-sadistic bitch routine. John was just John. He was a simple man that acted without all the ulterior motives.

"I heard."

"Look I—I know you probably don't care. He cheated on you, and you broke up. Then he got obsessed and started acting all crazy—I mean, I'm sorry, Ruby. I'm sorry for all the shit he did. I told him it was wrong, but he didn't care. He just lost it…but he's missing now." He swallowed hard and it pulled at my heart strings. "You have no reason to care. You're probably thrilled, and I wouldn't blame you. Not after the things he's told me, but you gotta understand that deep down, he's not a bad person. He's just…human."

Human. Somehow it always comes back to that. I didn't blame John for what Josh did any more than I blamed myself. They were all the same. As if the admittance of flaws was inherently a human trait and an excuse for being a monster.

I wasn't angry with John, but I think I was finally starting to get what Allistair meant.

They were human, and I was not.

With my heartstrings pulled taut, I cut them away. Severing myself, not from humanity per se, but from all notions of being something I'm not.

"I don't know what to tell you, John. I get that you're his friend, but he did some really bad shit. I don't know where he's at, and I don't want to know. I just wish that everyone would leave me out of it and let me heal." My words were half-truths and full-lies, but they did the trick. John nodded in understanding and started backing away to leave.

"Of course. I'm sorry, I shouldn't have come. I just—" He stopped and took a deep breath. Grief etched every line of him, and Josh had only been missing six days. That fucker didn't deserve a friend like John. He didn't deserve to be missed. I told myself that when I ordered Rysten to kill him and I would continue to until the day I died.

John stopped at the door and turned back.

"I'm sorry for everything. I feel like I should warn you: Kendall is saying a lot of things right now. She's got pictures and videos; god knows what else. I don't know what happened, or if it even has anything to do with you. I hope for your sake it doesn't." That was the last he said to me before he walked out my door.

I waited until I saw his car drive away before I made any move to leave. With Moira off for the afternoon, staying home to deal with the window, and none of the guys lurking in plain sight, I could never be too careful.

I bundled up in two sweatshirts before grabbing my purse to brave the cold. Today the skies were a mix of cerulean and arctic blue: colors so vivid and striking when placed in a cloudless sky. It was the first day this week that rain, slush, or sleet wasn't coming down on us. I was going to make the most of it.

I locked up shop and traveled a few blocks down. The wind howled as it funneled down alleyways carrying dead leaves and bits of loose grit. The painted shops and side streets were one of my favorite sights in all of Portland. Antique stores, old books, art galleries, and more. On the streets in front of them, musicians dotted the block, playing a range of instruments —usually with such skill that they put big name musicians to shame. Further proof that success is not always equated by talent or capability.

At the end of the block, food trucks sat around the perimeter of a square, packed so close together that some of them didn't even have room to fit a person in between. The smell of fried fish, gyros, eggrolls, and tacos filled my nostrils as I inhaled deeply, my mouth watering as I waded through the dense crowds of people to a truck on the other side of the square.

Someone was just walking away from the counter when I walked up to my favorite Thai food truck in town. The woman taking orders smiled down at me.

"It's been awhile. What have you been up to?" she asked me.

"Same ole', same ole'. Business is booming. Makes it hard to get away from the shop," I shrugged. The lie fell easily from my lips and she nodded in understanding.

"Will today be your usual, then?"

"Yes, please." I paid in cash and went to stand on the other side of the sidewalk while I waited for my food. People of every age and ethnicity continued to pass by. Today was a particularly busy day given the number of people out and about with their kids. Across the street there was a park made for sitting. Most people took their food there on days like today when the weather was nice. Parents let their children run around and chase the pigeons. Men and women out for a run would take their dogs through and stop for a short break. Even college students congregated around the concrete steps, books splayed open and headphones on.

An itch ran across the back of my neck. Something about this picture wasn't right. The kids, the parents, the dogs, the people: they were all fine. I couldn't tell what it was, but something just struck me as odd. It was almost like…

It was almost like I was being watched.

"Ruby!" The girl at the counter called out. Just as I moved, I finally noticed it in the periphery of my vision.

At a distance, it was hard to tell. They wore non-descript clothing and a black hoodie. Underneath that hood, I could have sworn I saw an eye watching me.

Red as a ruby.

I grabbed my food and ran back to my spot to see if I could get a better look.

Whoever it was, they were already gone.

CHAPTER NINE

I left the shop earlier than usual on Friday, making sure to lock the door and check my surroundings as I went. No one had shown up since Allistair dropped me off and I wanted to get home while it was still light out. I was feeling paranoid after my sighting yesterday and the beast was back to shifting restlessly.

Perched on my shoulder, Bandit clung to me as best he could through my many layers of clothing. The cold was bone-deep and the wind was brutal. Above me a storm was brewing, staining the skies an ominous shade of Cimmerian. The forecast on my phone called for snow, but if the ground wasn't cold enough, it would be slush by morning. I mentally made a note to wear rain boots to Martha's tomorrow as I got in my car.

The engine cranked up groggily, but faithfully stayed running once it was on. My car liked the cold about as much as I did. I flipped on the heater and pointed to the dog bed I put in the passenger seat. Bandit dived from my shoulder to the plush bed. He curled into himself, purring when the heater finally warmed up. I rolled my eyes and pulled out of the parking lot.

I stopped at Little Big Burger and got dinner through the drive-thru. I proceeded to spend the rest of the ride home trying to keep Bandit away from my food. Damn raccoon didn't care that I was driving or that it was *my* food. No, he wanted my fucking truffle fries something fierce.

I gave him one and snatched the bag away, ignoring the chitters of protest he gave me whilst cramming bites of fried goodness down his throat as fast as he could. You would think I was going to steal the single fry I gave him by the looks he gave me.

"Unappreciative trash panda," I grumbled to myself as I pulled in the driveway. I swung my car door open and Bandit jumped through it, racing up to the front door with half a French fry hanging out of his mouth.

It only took him three seconds to start screeching because I wasn't fast enough to his liking. I cursed under my breath as I approached the front door, guarding my dinner from the likes of him. I knew this little game. As soon as I opened the door, he'd make a move for my food, damn near tripping me and harassing me until I dropped it.

Not this time, furball.

I turned the key and swung the door open, wrapping both arms around my bag of food like a linebacker with a football. Bandit scurried inside to escape the cold and I followed.

"Interesting decorating you have here."

The food tumbled from my hands and Bandit let out a screech as he scurried up to stand on my shoulder.

"What are you doing in my house?" I asked, a sliver of the beast inside peeked out at the she-demon from Voodoo Doughnut. She was almost the same as I remembered her. Pointed teeth. Painted claws. White hair with pigtails that looked like they were dipped in purple.

"I'm paying you a visit because we need to talk…*without* your body-guards present." She gave me a cheeky smile and the beast surged forward.

"Speak." My voice turned cold as Death. Stark as Famine. Rageful as War. Unforgiving as Pestilence. The unknown she-demon cocked her head, a flicker of fear entered her heart. It was only an ember, but an ember was all the beast needed.

"Do you remember when we met, and I asked you about the demons who died outside the club?" she asked slowly. The beast did not reply and I continued to stare at her stone-faced. "I am searching for the rogue demon that caused their deaths. He belonged to my master. That same demon is following you."

She stared at me, waiting for some kind of reply. She was dealing with the wrong Ruby if that's what she wanted, and she went about it in the worst way. The beast cared for very few, and even then, it wasn't out of some notion of love. It was possession and desire. With all others, there was only one type of feeling that could even be considered an emotion, and that was rage.

"Do you have a point you wish to make?" the beast asked. The she-demon did not appear to harbor ill will, but she broke into our house. That was reason enough to not recede until she leaves.

"I would like to work with you to lure the rogue out," she said, not sounding nearly as confident as when I'd walked in.

"Not interested."

"What do you mean, *not interested?*" she asked. Her white brows drew together as she glared at me. I didn't want to be involved. The Horsemen would figure out how to deal with the imp, or she would beat them to it. It didn't particularly matter to me, so long as he stayed out of my life.

"I do not trust you. There is something you are not saying. Leave now, or die," the beast snarled at her. The she-demon turned ashen and pursed her lips.

"You'll regret this. I have information," she said quietly. The beast didn't give two fucks. I reached my hand out and snapped my fingers. Blue fire came to life.

Holy shit.

I started to panic a little bit and attempted to surge forward and put the fire out. She was firmly in control and had no intentions of stopping until the other demon left.

"All things come with a price. I'm not willing to pay for spoken half-truths that will likely find me dead. Leave." The final word was an order from the beast, but a plea from me. I wanted her gone before my other entity decided to burn the rest of my fucking house down along with her.

She took one look at me, snapped her mouth shut, and walked right out my front door.

We watched her through the newly installed window as she turned her face skyward. The clouds opened and rain began to pour down in heavy sheets. She stood there for what seemed like forever.

And then she disappeared.

The fire in my hand extinguished as I got shoved back into my own body. The beast receded quietly and did not argue for the rest of the evening. I cleaned up my dinner from off the concrete. By the time she left, it was already cold. All that remained of it now was the grease smudges left on my barren floor.

Thirty minutes passed where I debated leaving to go get more food, and a space heater while I was at it. I had my mind made up when someone knocked on the door. I grabbed the baseball bat out of my closet and went to answer it.

"Who is it?" I called.

"Your favorite Horsemen," Rysten called back. There was a thud outside my door. "I brought company and food," he continued. I put my eye to the peephole and grinned at what I saw. Rysten had a hand to the door frame, relaxed as could be. Next to him, Julian stood, stoic and aloof. He held a paper bag in one hand and eyed his brother warily. I put the bat behind the door and swung it open, plastering a smile on my face.

"There you are, love," Rysten smiled warmly. He moved in front of Julian and led me through my own living room and into the kitchen, leaving his brother and the food at the door in the pouring rain.

"You mentioned food." I turned to eye the paper bag as Julian came striding into the kitchen. He wore his impassive mask well, but displeasure radiated from him in waves.

"Your house is freezing," Julian commented while he unloaded the bag.

"It's a little bit better with the window replaced," I said lightly.

"And the living room insulation?" he asked. A bit more forceful than asked really. Not quite a demand, but his underlying point was clear.

"Moira met with them yesterday. We were going to discuss our options over the weekend," I replied stiffly.

"If you moved in with us you wouldn't need to worry about it," he continued. I narrowed my eyes at him and stuffed my tongue in my cheek. Before they arrived, I had been debating on texting one of them to tell them what happened with the she-demon from Voodoo Doughnut. Now I wasn't so sure, given that Julian would just use it in his arsenal of reasons why I should become dependent on the Horsemen, and then just skip out on life and fast forward to becoming the destined queen he so desperately wanted me to be.

Rysten ran a gentle hand down my arm and motioned to the rickety table before us. "Why don't we eat, and we can discuss you moving in later?" he suggested. Julian's jaw did that tick thing it does when he's angry, but we all took our seats and pretended that the tension wasn't palpable.

Rysten reached forward and started removing tops from dishes. My mouth watered instantly as the scent of Shrimp Pad Thai fell over me. "Is that what I think it is?" I asked, reaching for the tasty dish.

"Shrimp Pad Thai, number five, from E-San," Rysten smirked. It reminded me of the smile Allistair had when I told him the tea was perfect.

"You're the best," I crooned between mouthfuls of steaming noodles. As soon as the words were out of my mouth, whatever storm was brewing within Julian became infinitely worse.

All four of the Horsemen have the problem of wearing their power too loosely. I have grown to realize that is partially because they can't help it. In the same way that my beast fights me, their power is simply too much to be easily contained. The fact that Rysten attempted to for my sake was sweet, and it was honestly somewhat frightening that he could even accomplish it. The other part of them, I believe, is that they have done it for so long that I don't think they notice it.

Unlike me, who was new to this whole power dynamic, they have been around for thousands of years. They've never had any reason to contain it.

The problem was that it bleeds into me and colors my own perceptions. Much like it was doing right now.

I clamped my mouth shut to keep from saying anything, but the damage was done. My good mood had gone sour. I placed a lid on my dinner and pushed it away. My elbows rested on the table as my hands fell together in a steeple. They both set down their forks and regarded me curiously.

"Something wrong, love?" Rysten asked. The shuddering in my heart intensified. Blood roared in my ears.

"Do we need to talk?" The question was aimed at Julian as a not-too-subtle hint for him to either say his piece or calm the fuck down.

"Have you been outside this afternoon?" Julian responded. Was he purposely evading my question? He can't be so stupid as to not see what I was getting at. Maybe him changing the topic was his way of saying he'd cut the shit out.

"I came home right after work." They locked eyes, and it didn't take a mind reader to tell that they were engaged in a silent conversation. "Did something happen?" I asked slowly. Rysten sighed and turned away from his brother. He reached behind him, into his back pocket, and withdrew a folded-up piece of paper.

"What's this?" I asked. Rysten handed it over to me silently.

"Open it," Julian said.

I ran my fingers over the fraying edges and slowly unfurled the single sheet of paper. Dread formed in my gut when there was nothing left but the final unfolding and my fingers stilled.

What could possibly be in here that would make them both so melancholic?

Only one way to find out.

I opened the paper.

And instantly understood.

In large, bolded black letters: ***Justice for Josh***.

Accompanied by a picture of his face.

But that wasn't all.

My face. And the picture she showed me several days ago. That picture had a date and time stamp and a website claiming to have more information underneath.

She all but said I outright did it.

Whatever *it* was.

My fingers brushed over the creases in the paper, committing them to memory. I didn't say anything while I allowed myself time to process this. Eventually I muttered, "Where did you find this?"

"She has them up all across town," Rysten replied softly. I didn't want to see the pity in his eyes, but it was too late. Just as much as blame and self-loathing existed in Julian's. Maybe I had misread Julian. Maybe not. Right now, it didn't matter either way.

"Am I going to be arrested?" I asked, the thought should have scared me more than it did.

"No. Allistair has already taken the liberty to speak with the police on your behalf. You have an alibi, and because these pictures were illegally obtained, they aren't admissible in court." Rysten knew just the thing to say. He was so sweet. So kind.

Maybe that's why it was what he didn't say that I heard the loudest.

I won't be arrested, but there is going to be blood to pay for this.

"How did she even get this picture?" I continued. Ask questions. Get answers. That's all I needed to do right now. Just one step at a time.

"We don't know yet. I've currently got a program running to hack into the club's security system and see who accessed this video tape," Rysten said.

Again I nodded, because nodding was better than crying. Nodding was at least doing something. It meant I was at least trying to get answers and keep my life together.

Crying meant I was falling apart, but these people... these *humans*—they weren't worth falling apart for. Josh was dead. The damage was done. Yet somehow, it always came back to me paying the price.

There is always a price. Isn't that what the beast said?

Was this my price for getting even? For choosing to end my own suffering? For making the choice to not be a victim, but instead a survivor?

Whatever heartstrings I had left had been severed when John came to me. All that was left was the shallow beat of my own heart, the strength of my own limbs, and the fortitude of my mind to continue forward.

To survive.

My fingers wrapped around the paper, crushing it into a ball. My beast called upon the fire in my veins, and blue flames sprung to life. The paper blazed a brilliant cobalt blue, and then it was gone, leaving nothing but obsidian ashes behind. I rose from my seat and dumped the handful of ash in the garbage, washed my hands, and took my seat back at the rickety table I bought from Goodwill three years ago.

I reached across the surface and unclasped the plastic top. The scent of Shrimp Pad Thai was no longer as appetizing, but I didn't care. I was going to eat every damn bite.

Because for the second time that week, I made the choice to not let this define me. The choice that it will not break me. The choice to not be afraid.

I know who I am, and Kendall can paint this however the fuck she wants.

I was done caring.

CHAPTER TEN

I was ripped from a dead sleep by Moira's ring tone, "Fergilicious."

"What?" I croaked. My mouth tasted like dragon's breath.

"Don't come into the shop today."

I bolted upright. "Why? What happened?" I asked, kicking my feet out of bed. I flipped the speaker phone on and set my phone on the nightstand while I dressed in a hurry.

"Kendall happened. I'm being serious, Ruby. Don't come in. You don't need to deal with this shit," she sighed into the speaker. Moira didn't wait for a reply. The line went dead.

Fuck that. I was not sitting at home and making her deal with everyone like I was some fragile flower. I was Ruby Morningstar, damnit, but today the world could call me karma.

I brushed my teeth and fed Bandit in record time before running out the door, only stopping to see if my shoes matched after I was in the car. My fingers shook as I gripped the steering wheel.

I took a deep breath. *You can do this.*

I was pulling out of the driveway within three minutes of the phone call. Halfway there I felt like I was getting stopped by what seemed like every red light in the fricken city.

"For fuck's sake, change already," I growled. My complaining didn't make it go any faster. After another ten agonizing minutes in my car, I was finally pulling into the lot behind Blue Ruby Ink. Despite the cold, my palms were sweating as I pulled the key from the ignition. I thrust the door open and raced down the alley, not stopping to catch my breath for one second. My heart pounded in my chest as I ran towards my store, stopping short when it came into view.

I wasn't sure what I expected to find, but a mob of protestors was not it.

Fifty or sixty people were gathered out front, screaming terrible things at Moira as she attempted to rip all the flyers away from the glass wall. These weren't just a few flyers either. They lined every inch of the front of my store, stuck to the glass by rain. More sat at her feet, forming piles of mush at least half a foot tall. The crowd screamed nasty things at her. Called her a murderer and whore.

And right there in the middle of it, was Kendall.

Her white blonde hair was damp from the misting rain. She was dressed as the proper lady with her dress and sheer hose, despite the freezing temperatures. From this angle, I couldn't see her face, but I could imagine the smug smirk on her lips. Or maybe it was the crying girlfriend that showed up today.

I didn't care.

Beside her stood a woman with a microphone. Not a megaphone.

That's odd. Why would she have a microphone? Unless…

A man stood a couple yards back with a massive video camera mounted on his shoulder. A news reporter. She was fucking interviewing with a news reporter, telling the world how I killed Josh. Or kidnapped him. Or tortured him.

Honestly, after everything both of them have put me through, I wish I'd tortured him a bit longer. I wish that I had been the one to burn him alive. If I was going to be blamed for it, I may as well have committed the crime.

Despite all, that wasn't what broke me.

It was when a someone threw a rock.

They didn't throw it at my store. Oh, no.

They threw it at Moira.

It was like the diner again, on the day that started it all.

Except this was a thousand times worse. This time it wasn't just my rage. It was the beast's rage I channeled as well.

"They must die. Nobody hurts what's mine," she seethed.

"No. We won't kill them. That's too easy. I have a better idea," I told her. My feet were sure and steady as I approached the rallying mob. I completely walked around it and right up to Moira. I threw the door open, feeling the crowd behind me start into a frenzy when they realized I had arrived. My best friend looked at me with tears in her eyes.

"I'm sorry," she whispered. I pulled her with me inside and locked the door behind us.

They have no idea who they're messing with.

If I was a different kind of demon, I would kill them all and be done with it. That was what my dark entity wanted after all.

But I wasn't a different kind of demon.

I was Ruby Morningstar.

And they would not break me.

I guided Moira into my office and motioned for her to take a seat in my chair. She wobbled sideways and all but fell into it as the shock set in. In the other room, I grabbed a bottle of water and brought it back to my office, uncapping it and setting it on the desk in front of her.

"Drink it," I told her as I got down on my knees. Behind my desk I kept a safe. Most people would think that was where the money was, given that I was paid in cash quite often. Actually, it was where I kept a list of things in case of emergencies. One such emergency was in case we were ever robbed. I kept the money in an account that Moira managed, but the robbers didn't know that. Like I'd keep that kind of cash around.

"What are you doing?"

"What I should have done the first time she crossed me." Moira didn't say anything when I placed the gas mask over my head and grabbed a small tank from the safe. I slung it over my shoulder and hauled myself to my feet. I placed the taser in Moira's lap and closed the office door firmly behind me.

"I'm going to need your help for this to work," I whispered.

"Make them pay."

I unlocked the door and stepped outside. People were already backing away, but not Kendall. Her back was to me, still interviewing on camera. She wouldn't know what was coming until it was too late. I smiled faintly beneath the mask as I set the tank down a few feet from the door. Two or three broke away from the crowd in a vain attempt at running.

The beast and I laughed together, because we didn't need a switch or a trigger.

We were the trigger.

My eyes flicked over to the container, no bigger than a loaf of bread.

And then it exploded.

My ears rang with the start of a bad Archer joke about tinnitus. Just like the beast told me, she set it on fire, but no more. She was giving me the chance to take my pound of flesh in the way I wanted to, and for that, I thanked her.

Dust and debris mixed with the particles of chloroform as the light mist carried them far and wide. One by one the rioters dropped like the dead. Falling flat on their faces. It was a terrible sight. Bad in a way that was almost beautiful. I stood amongst them with my gas mask on, rain dampening my sweatshirt, my aged converse sneakers soaked to my ankles from the puddles I ran through in the alley.

It was a monumental moment for me as I stood in this place in-between. Me versus the world. Isn't that the way it's always been though? I was born a demon with two sides and raised a human to hate both of them. Oh, how the world loved irony.

I waited in the rain for every single person in the lot to drop. The cameraman was the last to go, and I looked forward to watching the footage as bodies dropped around, standing against them like the murderer I was.

If I wanted them dead, they would be. It was as simple as that.

No amount of explaining would ever earn back my reputation. Not after this. I acknowledged that as I walked forward, ignoring the squelch of my feet in the water clogged shoes and squishy socks. Leaning down, I turned the recorder off and removed the media card. Bringing my foot down on top of the machine as I did.

Honestly, my foot did very little, but it made me feel better.

I pocketed the card and turned to Kendall.

Her blonde hair was splayed across the dirty concrete. The ends were stained black and her clothes were speckled with mud, but she was otherwise unharmed.

I took a deep breath through my nose, inhaling the dust and mildew that clung to the mask. This was it. The moment I made my mark.

"They hurt Moira," the beast reminded me. That was all she needed to say for me the grab the girl's feet and start dragging her inside.

It was going to be a long day, and I was just getting started.

~

THE SKIES LET OPEN SOMETIME that afternoon, releasing a downpour that caused anything further than three feet away to fade into the nothingness. It was nice, having a small piece of quiet while I worked. I suspected it would not be the same after today, but I could worry about that tomorrow.

For now, I was out for revenge.

And I'd come to collect.

Moira sat beside me on her favorite barstool, biting her nails as she watched.

"There's no going back. You know that, right?" she asked me for the seventeenth time. I nodded my head, as I brought the tip of the of the tattoo machine to Kendall's face.

She had spent nearly two months torturing me for something that wasn't my fault. Most people would say I should be the bigger person. I shouldn't respond. Just call the cops and let them deal with it.

Here's the thing about that.

People like Kendall, they don't care about the rules any more than I do. Her family has the police in their pocket. She's been playing this game with me for long enough now that I realized she had no intention of getting me arrested. If I were arrested, then suddenly all of it goes away. She no longer has someone to blame, and without someone to throw under the bus, how could she possibly continue to play the victim?

The simple answer is, she can't.

She needs me. She couldn't continue to harass me, to start riots, try to pin a death or disappearance on me that she knows nothing about if I suddenly didn't exist. Because if she did know something about it, she wouldn't be here right now. She would have torn every flyer down herself if she knew what actually happened to him, because no one, not even her, would risk her own skin if she realized the things the Horsemen would do to people who hurt me.

Josh got what he deserved.

And now Kendall would, too.

I was going to give her everything she ever wanted. I was going to make her face so unrecognizable between the carefully shaded wrinkles and artificially added unibrow, that people would give her the pity and attention she craved for years to come. She would be the beautiful twenty-something young woman that lost her face in a wicked game.

A game of truths and lies.

A game she should have played better.

A game that I wasn't going to lose.

Not this time.

The creases around her eyes now formed crow's feet, even when she was at rest. Her cheeks were weak and sallow, age spots dotting her face. Her brows were constructed of a blend of white, blond, and browns, meant to not only match but to make sure that even if she had laser surgery to remove it—she would never fully be free. Not until her skin was truly old and wrinkled.

Josh may have died by Rysten's hand, but the world would do well to remember that there are some punishments worse than death. As a demon that grew up among humans, I've studied them long enough to know their weakness, understand what makes them tick, and ultimately—destroy them.

Except I didn't want to burn the world to the ground.

I just wanted to get even.

I placed the machine on the table beside us and dabbed at the fresh ink. Kendall's once youthful face now looked like that of a ninety-year-old woman with a unibrow and wispy chin hairs to match. She would do her damnedest to remove it when she woke and saw what I'd done.

I applied bandages to her face as gently as I would any other client. I even took the liberty of having Moira break into her car so she had a dry place to sleep while the chloroform wore off.

How kind of me.

"Can you help me move her?" I asked my green-skinned best friend. Moira's shaking stopped shortly after I dragged the body in, and the suspicious over-calculating banshee demeanor was slowly setting back in.

"I can't really say no. We've already come this far," she sighed dramatically. "Just so we're on the same page: you're the crazy one. I may scream and shit, but I've never done anyth—"

"She overstepped today, and now I'm making sure that she never even thinks about it again. Call me crazy. Call me spiteful. I don't care. I am what I am, and I'm not apologizing anymore." I shrugged my shoulders and leaned back against the low back of my chair. My back let out a series of successive cracks and I groaned in relief.

Warm arms wrapped around my shoulders, drawing me into a tight hug. I tried to open my eyes, but the mass of dark green hair blocked my vision.

"I'm proud of you," Moira said against my hair. Her voice was muffled and raw, with what I suspected were tears that she was trying to hold back. "Now let's go move this bitch before she wakes up."

I cracked a smile for the first time in days. Despite it all, I'd done exactly what I said I would. I didn't break. I didn't crawl. I rose up to the challenge and I'm pretty sure I just beat her at her own game.

Moira and I pulled apart, and I pretended not to notice the moisture in her eyes while she subtly wiped it away. "You know, I kind of hate you for making me cry," she muttered. I chuckled under my breath.

"Is that your way of saying you want the arms?" I mused, rolling the tray that held all my equipment out of the way.

"And risk her flipping out and biting me if she wakes up? No thanks." Moira walked to the end of the cubicle and grabbed Kendall by the ankles. She didn't stir.

"Ready?" I asked, taking both wrists.

"Ready." We heaved her off the table and started the slow trek towards the front door. She was surprisingly heavy for someone so slim. It couldn't possibly be because she had anything upstairs. Must have been the boobs.

We finagled our way around the front door without dropping her, although I did *accidentally* bang her head a time or two on the way out.

Her car was a good fifty yards away, which was fine and dandy if not for the rain. Fortunately, I planned for that and had removed my sweatshirt to wrap around her face. Hopefully she wouldn't suffocate in the ninety seconds it took us to cross the parking lot.

Wind and water hit me simultaneously, and my chattering teeth turned into an all-out symphony. Rain drenched my thin t-shirt, putting the world's hardest nipples on display for anyone that drove by. Luckily, no one did. I'm sure they wouldn't have even noticed my freezing tits when we were swinging a body back and forth as we made our way to Kendall's car.

I held both her wrists in one hand and yanked the driver's side door open, kicking it wide so that Moira could put her feet in first. I wasn't sure if it was a blessing that this wasn't the first time we'd done something like this, or a sign that we needed to find better, less illegal hobbies.

Wrapping a slick hand around one of her slim shoulders, I shoved the rest of her body in the car and positioned her head upright before removing my sweatshirt. Her eyes were still closed and the bandages still dry. My sweatshirt, on the other hand, was a different story. I didn't even try to fit the slopping material over me. I was more likely to freeze inside it than without it.

"We good here?" Moira yelled over the rain.

"One last thing," I yelled back and pushed the wet strands of my hair away from my face. Moira cocked an eyebrow, and I pulled out the metallic silver sharpie in my back pocket.

"What are…" Her voice trailed off as I leaned inside the cab of the car and wrote a message on her steering wheel. "Oh."

"Oh indeed," I smirked while I capped the marker. Moira slammed the car door shut and let out a wicked cackle.

"You know, Ruby, sometimes I think we were made for each other." She threw an arm around my waist, tugging me close. I slipped my bare arm around her shoulders and strolled back to Blue Ruby Ink through the rain without a care in the world.

It was nice being me some days, and other days it wasn't.

But I make the most of it by choosing to be happy as I weathered the storm.

CHAPTER ELEVEN

I SENT Moira off to run an errand and I closed shop soon after. Now I sat huddled in my driveway, dreading the thirty feet I would have to walk from the warm confines of my car all the way to the living room where I was ninety percent certain that it was below forty degrees inside.

Not that it could get fixed anytime soon, given the numbers Moira was quoted at. We made decent money at Blue Ruby. Not an outstanding amount, but enough to live and go out for drinks once a week…up until Pandora's Box. After today, I wasn't so sure that would be the case anymore.

I'd taken the preventive measures to avoid any trouble with the law by calling in a favor to a friend of mine that was a cop. Really, he owed me one hell of a favor, so I figured this would be where I cashed in my chips. He won't be able to keep me out of the woods forever, but he could at least buy me some time before they came knocking with questions. Still, the damage Kendall did to my reputation was already done. I had set off a tank of gas and knocked people out.

Yeah, business was bound to be booming. Not.

I loved my house dearly, and everything it stood for. At twenty-years old, I purchased it with money I was making from doing tattoos. That may not seem like much to everyone, but it was everything to me. It was proof that I, Ruby Morningstar, a girl that barely scraped by in high school, could still succeed. I didn't take the traditional route and go to college. I supported Moira by putting a roof over our heads while she did.

My life was changing. A lot faster than I wanted it to.

And I wasn't so sure where the house, the shop, or even I fit into it.

Something needed to give if I was going to get through this.

With numb fingers and a heavy heart, I reached across the passenger seat and pulled my phone from my purse. I scrolled through the contacts and hit call.

It rang once.

"Ruby? Are you okay? Where are you?" Oh man, Julian sounded pissed. Maybe I should have called Rysten instead.

"Yeah, I'm fine. Listen I—"

"Where are you? I'm at your shop. There's a horde of humans outside that are waking up and appear to be having some memory problems. No one seems to know why they're here."

"They're—I—I'll explain everything when you get here," I sighed. "I called to let you know I'm at home, packing up my stuff. Moira and I are going to move in this week."

"Would that have anything to do with what looks like the remains of a bomb that I cleaned up before anybody saw it?"

Well shit. I knew there was something I was forgetting.

"I plead the fifth."

"Mhmm. Pack up. I'm sending Laran over," he replied. The line went dead.

I scowled at the rain outside as I stored my phone and began the slippery walk up the steps. The rain pelted me relentlessly, not giving a shit that I was already soaked to the bone and freezing. The elements were uncontrollable and unforgiving that way.

When I reached the top of the aged wood steps, I noticed that something wasn't quite right. The front door was open just a crack. Like someone had closed it in a hurry, by the latch didn't stick. I wouldn't have noticed at all, if it hadn't slightly moved with every whipping gust wind.

A month ago, I probably wouldn't have thought anything of it.

Today, I realized that Moira's car wasn't home.

Someone had either been in my house or was still there.

My heart thumped in my chest as fight or flight kicked in. It wasn't really a question for me, to run or go inside, because I had reached the max on my bullshit meter for the day, and I'd hit that about six hours ago.

I squared my shoulders, took two steps forward and brought my foot up, kicking the center of the door. It didn't resist in the slightest as my foot and the wind carried it hard and fast into the wall behind it, slamming with a thud.

My badassery was short lived.

In my haste to get to Moira this morning, I put on the worst possible shoes for dealing with rain and slippery steps. I lost my balance and went sprawling as my feet went up and I went down. My ass compacted hard with the porch, pain spiking through me.

No. No, this was not how this was supposed to go, damnit.

I landed in a tangle of my own limbs with a bruised ass and bruised ego.

"Well, well. Look what the rain brought in."

I squinted through the haze to see two demons staring down at me. They wore cruel smiles; a stark contrast to the otherworldly beauty they had. Like many of demon-kind, it was a harsh loveliness that straddled the edge of horrifying and magnificent.

"Who are you? And why are you in my house?" My voice had just the right amount of uncertainty and distress. I played the part of a mouse well, and part of that was because I truly was terrified. Sweat coated my skin and my limbs shook from exhaustion. I took heavy, labored breaths while my lungs screamed in anguish.

Inside me, something else writhed, but I held her back.

"Look how she talks. So brave for a child," the female noted. Her teeth shone black like cut onyx. Great. Not only are they the condescending types, I'm pretty sure those pointed teeth could do some serious damage.

"Don't antagonize the poor thing, Lydia. Let's just get it inside and do the job," the man sighed. *Do the job? What the fuck was that supposed to mean.*

The chick named Lydia bent and wrapped a claw-tipped hand around my bicep. I frowned, kicking my foot underneath hers. She tried to catch herself from toppling forward, but I swiped a hand across her chest, throwing her to the ground next to me. I flipped my own body across hers, straddling her chest to pin her to the ground, slamming my forearm into her jugular.

"You little bitch," she choked out. I pressed down tighter.

"Who are you?" I shouted.

She smiled coldly and dread formed in my belly. Strong arms grabbed me by the shoulders and tore me away from her. I struggled with the male as he hauled me back into my own house, fighting my own rising panic. I needed to stay calm so I could trick them into giving me answers and not accidentally unleash the beast. That would just end in bloodshed, and quite possibly me burning down a section of Portland.

I'd rather not give the police anymore reasons to arrest me or land myself on the FBI most wanted list.

The man's grip on me didn't ease until he'd hauled me all the way into the house. The female came in after us and closed my front door behind her.

"Savage little beastie. You surprised me there. I'm going to enjoy this one, Ryku," she grinned maliciously. I gave her my best apathetic look and she cackled.

"Just do the job so we can get paid," the man behind me said.

"And if I want to drag it out?" she said in the sappiest voice, pouting her full lips while she stared at him with a sensual longing.

What the actual fuck?

"I don't know, Lydia…something's just not right here. She doesn't feel like the others." His English was almost perfect, but there was a hint of something foreign in it. I just couldn't put my finger on what…

"Oh? Then what does she feel like?" Lydia said and crossed her arms across her chest. The dark fabric hugged her curves perfectly, and the gesture lifted her breasts in a way that could *almost* be played off as nonchalant.

"I don't know. She smells like a succubus, but there's something else. I've never encountered it before. It just *feels* old. Like ancient magic." I cocked my head slightly as the pieces started clicking together. The woman eyed me suspiciously and I knew instantly that look had nothing to do with their job, and everything to do with my nasty little habit of drawing men to me.

"Well then. Why don't we cut her open and see? The imp said he'd pay us double if we made it hurt." Her words were impassive, but her eyes held a sneer. She reached the holster at her waist and pulled out a knife. This wasn't just any knife. The handle was well-used and worn. If I hadn't seen the flash of the blade, I would've thought it was just another hitman job.

But I'd never heard of one that used an obsidian blade with glowing cobalt runes.

Oh no. These weren't just your run of the mill hitmen.

They weren't even demons.

"You're demon hunters," I whispered.

Every one of us had heard the whispers. Demon hunters. Magic harvesters. We knew they weren't a myth. I never dreamed of actually running into one.

"In the flesh," she replied. The woman smiled, lifting her ceremonial blade to twirl it on her palm.

"Sent here to kill me," I continued, swallowing hard. The beast glared at me, silently urging me to fucking hurry up with my questioning. She did not like the look of that knife. Can't say I disagreed.

"The imp paid quite a nice price up front," she grinned.

Yeah, I bet he did.

"Lydia…" the man behind me growled. He was getting impatient. I liked impatient. It made people foolish. Rash. I smiled up at her from my place on the floor. I was outnumbered and without weapons. My knees ached and my arms still trembled, but I was not afraid.

"Did you ever stop to think why he sent you instead of coming himself?" I asked her. It was only in that moment that the gears seemed to turn.

She narrowed her eyes and took a step forward. At that moment, a bloodcurdling scream came from down the hall.

Oh no. Please don't let that be what I think it is.

She raised the knife in defense as Bandit came running down the hallway.

"NO!" I screamed.

Time slowed down. I couldn't focus. I couldn't think. Yet I saw every single thing that was happening. It was sensory overload.

A gun shot rang through the air and my newly fixed window shattered into a million pieces. My reflection glared back at me in fragments of my face.

One moment my eyes were blue. The next they were black.

I didn't even register the change as the beast pushed forward. Only the desire to save Bandit fueled me as he charged fearlessly at this bitch to save my life.

"You should have listened to your partner," my entity snarled.

Admiral blue and navy flames leapt to life at her feet, curling inward, licking at her flesh. Inside, I flinched from the gruesome sight as the fire burned brighter and her skin turned to ash, but the beast looked on without a care in the world. Black craggy creases appeared, spreading up her legs to her torso, then the arm holding the knife, and beyond. Those vicious cracks splintered and widened as liquid sapphire glowed from inside them. Her magic blade fell from dead fingers and clattered against the ground as her body erupted in a plume of crystalline ash.

Bandit launched himself at the ash statue the moment it exploded. He landed halfway across the room, hacking like a maniac while I whirled on the man behind me.

Except… he was already dead.

A bullet wound right between his eyes. How that ended up there, I had no idea. Only that it probably had something to do with the window shattering. Someone shot him, but they didn't stick around for the finale.

The beast took this in within a matter of seconds. Listening for any hint of a beating heart in his chest, even though half his brains and blood were splattered across my living room wall. When no sound came but our own beating heart and Bandit's coughing, she turned to the window in search of whoever fired the gun.

Whoever they were, they were long gone.

The only hint of an answer was the glint of silver too far in the distance.

CHAPTER TWELVE

My living room door flew open and the beast turned with a hand raised to kill.

"Ruby," Laran breathed a sigh of relief when he saw me standing among the remains. It wasn't his Ruby that stared back at him, and after Julian's promise to keep me safe, she wasn't pleased with any of them.

Laran made it six and half feet through the door before his steps fell short. Bandit came up beside him and began tugging on his jeans. He did that when he wanted to be picked up. Was that because he liked him? Or was it because he saw what Laran hadn't noticed? He paid no attention to my raccoon as his eyes fell on me, or my beast, rather. Her intense gaze locked on him like a cat with a mouse.

"So tell me, War. How many Horsemen does it take to protect one girl?"

There was no mistaking it. She was *pissed*.

The only thing that was saving him was that she considered him hers. We all were in some form or fashion. With Moira and Bandit, it was my love for them that gave her a sense of duty. She protected them for me.

With Laran and the Horsemen, it was something more akin to desire and possession. She owned them, because they were hers. They always have been. They always will be. They were created for us. They were the only males that stood a chance, and the closest thing to a mate we would ever find. Except we had four of them.

"What happened here?" he asked. His tone wasn't subservient, and she couldn't decide whether she liked that or not. It was angrier than Julian had dared get with her, and he was Death. What could War possibly possess that made him feel invincible?

She smiled.

"The answer is none because that's how many of you are around when she needs you," the entity sneered. Laran clenched and unclenched his fists.

Please, please don't get in a slugging match with War. I prayed, but not to god. Oh no, she would not hear these prayers spoken by the daughter of the devil.

She was just as spiteful as him in that way.

I prayed to myself, because here on earth, now that Satan was dead… my beast was the only thing that might possibly listen.

"I didn't know she was in danger. I would have—"

"You would have what? Hurried? Ran faster? Not been so lax in the first place?" The blood rushed in my veins as my heart slowed. Steady, like war drums. My body was gearing up for a fight, but it wasn't me in charge. She had complete and utter control.

She took three steps toward him, closing the distance, desire fueling some of this exchange. It seemed we had little control when it came to them. I equally wanted to kiss them and throttle them most days. She had similar thoughts, if not more detailed.

"I will not apologize because words mean nothing. Only actions." A declaration, but not touted as such. He spoke them softly, but there was nothing gentle about War. Only stark truths that could bite as much as they could heal.

The beast liked him for that. She found the truth refreshing, but not enough to forgive.

"Make it up to me," she demanded.

His dark eyes changed, the color altering from onyx to a shade of deep burgundy wine. The hands at his sides went limp as she closed the last foot between us and rested a delicate palm against his chest. Through the thin material of his shirt, a heart thundered.

"Ruby…" He murmured my name like a prayer. Maybe it was a plea. I was not the one he had to appease, much as he might wish it.

"Did I stutter? Make it up to *me*." The Siberian winter held more warmth than the voice that came out of my mouth. Laran did not shiver or balk. Nor did he hide from her command.

He stayed still as stone when she wrapped my hand around his shirt, twisting the fabric to pull him closer. She could sense the conflict he felt within. A storm brewed with such intensity. A need, want, and desperation to be burned by her. By me. He was not like Julian who tried to cover his wants, nor was he like Allistair who pushed me persistently. He was hot and passionate, and his feelings were as muddled and needy as my own.

His lips loomed before us, and she did not hesitate.

My mouth crashed into his. Hot and fierce. She wrapped my hand around his neck, maintaining an iron grip while my lips parted his. Heat swept through my system like a monsoon, relentless in the things it made me feel while doing desire's bidding.

Laran gripped my waist as he hoisted me from the ground. My legs instinctually wrapped around his waist, his cock pressing into me. He carried me with an assuredness and every step rubbed against my swollen clit. I ground against his bulge while his hands slid from my waist to cupping my ass, digging his fingertips into my skin.

A purr escaped my throat, dark and needy as the beast met him head on and without hesitation. I…I was not in control, yet I felt every movement. Every scrape of my jeans against my clit. Every thrust of his tongue as he tried to consume me as much as the beast tried to consume him. For all intents and purposes, it was me, but without the reservations.

I reveled in it, knowing that my mind would be torn with indecision if it were really me in control. This was so much more freeing in many ways, and the beast knew that.

My back hit something hard and solid, but Laran plowed through, a thud reverberating as the door came crashing down. In this moment, I didn't care what we destroyed. I didn't care as we slammed onto the bed. He started to pull back, and I ripped the shirt from his chest.

A growl rumbled in his throat as he bit my lip. Hard. Copper and sweetness spread between our lips. He broke the kiss right when I gasped, taking in a breath of chilled air. His hands slipped beneath my damp sweatshirt and skimmed my ribs as he pulled it over my head, taking the shirt I wore with it.

I arched my back into his touch. He was so different than Allistair and his need to dominate. Or Rysten, who was sweet and sought to please me. Not even Julian, who's very essence held a pain that made me want more.

Laran wanted me to burn and to burn with me.

I loosened my hold around his waist, letting my legs drop to either side of him and dangling my feet over the edges. He skimmed his lips over my half-naked body, letting the chill air slap my sensitive skin. Without asking what I wanted or needed, he began tugging at my boots, and made quick work of pulling away my socks and layers of pants. He tugged them free with a growl, and the beast smiled and sat up to watch him.

Bared before him in only my panties and bra, Laran got on his knees. With my legs hanging over the edge of the bed, we were eye level as he reached around and unhooked my bra with a swift flick of his thumb. The straps slid loose over my shoulders, the cups falling away from my breasts to the floor beneath us.

He wrapped a well-muscled arm around my waist and pulled me to him. His bare chest brushing mine as he consumed me in another passionate kiss. He pulled away to trail his kiss down my neck, taking his sweet time to leave bites as he went.

I wasn't sure what it was with all of them and biting, but I didn't want it to stop.

I moaned inwardly, but the beast made not a sound. He dipped his head lower and took my nipple between his teeth. Pleasure shot straight between my thighs and I ground against him, arching my back to give him better access. He let out a groan of approval and continued his descent while the beast leaned back on her elbows and watched.

Laran's perfect physique was speckled with scars, dark and light. The skin did not warp or edge at an odd angle; it was blissfully smooth, but the stories of his past marked him. Much the same as the red brand that peeked out over his jeans. From this angle, it looked like some kind of knot made of fire, but my attention wavered as he trailed his nose down my chest, over my stomach, and to the triangle of cotton between my thighs.

He breathed in my smell and kissed my sex through the thin material that separated us. I was drowning in sensation, unable to do anything, but not wanting it to stop.

She ground my feet into the edge of the bed, lifting my hips for him to make her intentions clear.

He growled, blowing a wave of heat through my panties and straight to the most sensitive part of my body. My hips bucked once, outside both her and my control.

"Tell me she wants this," he groaned against my inner thigh. My breath hissed between my teeth as the beast stared down at him.

"She and I are the same: two sides of one coin."

"That is not what I asked," he growled as he bit into my thigh. He gripped my panties tightly and ripped them, exposing my puckered flesh, ripe with arousal.

"Please us both and you'll find out," she said, swaying my hips before him.

Indecision weighed on him as he watched the beast flout my body. *Our body.* She wasn't human, and she truly would not give an inch if Laran didn't please her. Maybe he saw that, or maybe his own need was consuming him.

Parting my folds, he blew once over my clit before locking his teeth around it and sucking sharply. The beast purred, fisting his hair in my hand. He shifted lower, moving his hands to my thighs, grabbing me roughly. He spread my legs wider and leaned forward to brush his nose over my skin.

"You smell like you were made for me," he murmured. The beast cocked an eyebrow at him, waiting impatiently for more. Laran growled and twisted his head to the side, sucking on the flesh of my inner thigh. The beast didn't make a sound as my heart hammered in my chest. Laran nipped at the skin with his teeth, trailing down the inside of my thigh, a moan escaping from her lips.

"You're teasing me, War," the beast breathed, her voice unsteady. There was a huskiness in my voice—her voice—that let him know just how much this affected her.

Laran's fingers pressed into my legs as he brought those nips back up my thigh and licked my wet and waiting flesh. He thrust his tongue inside of me without warning, pushing my thighs down onto the bed, exposing my cunt.

My back arched as pleasure drove me to rock against him, pushing my hips more with every thrust and flick of his tongue. Slipping two fingers inside me while he nipped my clit with his teeth, gliding them back and forth as I tightened and fluttered around him. As my body began to shake, he pulled back his hand, sliding his arms beneath me to hold my hips steady and pull me closer to his mouth. My climax built, my body uncontrollably curling forward as she locked my legs behind his arms, shifting my hands from his hair to both shoulders.

Only a moment before it happened I realized what she was going to do, but it was already too late. Laran pulled back only a hairsbreadth, when a burning started in my palms and tore through both our bodies like a wildfire.

The aching pressure and searing pain swirled together, triggering my orgasm as Laran took my clit in his mouth, sucking hard. The beast receded instantly, pushing me forward to scream in ecstasy while my body writhed, pouring pleasure onto the bed beneath us.

The release was long and mind-shattering. I was still gasping for breath when it stopped, shaking from a bone-deep exertion that didn't make sense. I unhooked my legs from his arms and tried to shift back, but Laran grabbed both legs and pinned them down as he rose to kneel over me. His eyes blazed with a scorching heat that would have turned me on again, had I not seen what now adorned the top of his shoulders.

"Laran, I—"

"Did you want me?" he interrupted. The sincerity in his voice shook me.

"Yes, but—"

"Then don't apologize," he replied.

"What?" I asked, my voice edging with hysteria.

"I know this seems like a big deal to you—"

"It's a massive fucking deal. Look at you!" I snapped.

Whatever desires and things we wanted to say would remain unspoken as we both jumped up when a door slammed at the other end of the house and Julian roared, "What happened here?"

For devil's sake…

I wiggled my way out from beneath Laran in record time, slipping my robe on right as Julian stormed around the corner. He stopped short of the broken door that littered my floor in pieces. I crossed my arms over my chest and stared at the ceiling while silence spread between us.

I didn't look, because I didn't have to. Julian's emotions turned from concerned and desperate to shock laced with anger. The polite thing to do would have been to ignore what happened between Laran and I, let me get dressed, maybe even ask about the dead bodies or blown window.

Is that what he did?

Oh no.

Instead, he said, "Why is War branded with your mark?"

Jealousy did not look nice on anyone, human or demon.

But damn I was good at inciting it.

LARAN

She branded me.

Twin pentagrams now adorned my shoulders, identical to the one between her breasts. Except these were not black, but blue. They glimmered faintly in the evening glow coming from her window. Swirling. Moving in a way that brands normally did not.

I touched the tips of my fingers to them, but the skin was unmarred.

Old magic.

Even older than I.

I swept my gaze across to her, wanting nothing more than to reach out. She gave me the greatest gift that could be bestowed on me. The highest honor.

I was the first mate.

And she felt guilty about it.

Possessiveness and territorialism pounded through me, wanting to pummel Death into the fucking ground for what he was doing. The fucker was jealous it wasn't him. It just as easily could have been if he didn't have a stick up his ass and would just talk to her.

He didn't need to make her feel guilty about it.

I took a step closer and her sapphire eyes flared with heat.

That's it, baby. Come to me.

My mind reached out tentatively, trying to brush against her fragile psyche. She'd yet to display any form of telepathy, but I wish she had.

Oh, I wish she had. The things I was going to do to her once I had the chance…once I got Julian the fuck out of here.

"War!" Julian shouted. It reverberated through my very bones, yet none of us had spoken a single word. I cut my eyes to him.

"What the fuck are you doing? Can't you see I'm in the middle of—"

"She hasn't transitioned yet, you fool!" He never shouted. Never raised his voice. In the eons of our existence, I could think of only a handful of times.

It was the tone of his voice that had ice racing through my veins.

She hadn't entered the transition. Not even after branding me had she entered the transition, but oh, she smelled like it. Time was not on our side, and I just made the situation infinitely more complicated and likely to blow.

Because there was no way I was going to be able to stay away now.

It was hard enough not to run to her and fall to my knees.

To give her everything she deserved.

I was claimed and owned as the first mate of the next queen, and I couldn't even act on it.

Fuck me.

CHAPTER THIRTEEN

"WELL…SHE was not very happy with you all for leaving me unprotected, and we had a little problem with getting her to comply…"

The beast huffed inside of me, purring like a fucking kitten after what she'd done.

Yeah. Little problem didn't even touch the tip of the iceberg on this one.

"The beast." Julian's jaw did that thing again where it ticked. "She branded him?" he asked.

I nodded guiltily.

Julian said nothing as he glanced between us, schooling his face into a neutral expression. Somehow, I didn't think Laran was buying his show any more than I did, but whatever. He was the one that would barely look at me most of the time, pretending he was uninterested. It wasn't my job to figure his shit out. I wouldn't feel guilty. If I had anyone I needed to feel guilty towards, it was Laran. He was the one I'd branded.

"Well. I suppose we should talk about what happened that led up to *this*." He motioned between me and Laran, a pile of clothes, torn panties and a ripped shirt, at our feet. I bit off my retort about how none of this was happening before they showed up. There wasn't a lot of point. Blaming people got us nowhere.

"Where would you like to start? With the mob I found outside of my

shop this morning, or how I was attacked this afternoon when I got home?"
I crossed my arms and gave Julian my best neutral expression. His brows
bunched up slightly as a small amount of surprise leaked through.

"Start at the mob," he replied.

"Please," Laran added. I gave him a tight-lipped smile and Julian rolled
his eyes.

How very human of you, Death.

I gave them a brief rundown of the morning, skimming over what I
tattooed on Kendall's face and moving onto the attack. Both Laran and
Julian stayed relatively quiet, apart from the occasional outburst of 'why did
you do that, Ruby' or 'I can't believe you put your life in danger, Ruby'. By
the end of it, they both were watching me with troubled expressions.

"The transition is looming near. Laran should have known better
than to—"

"Oh piss off, Death. I'm not in the mood and it's none of your fucking
business." With that, Laran stormed out of my bedroom.

"Are you sure about that?" Julian responded, his voice no louder than a
whisper.

Oh for devil's sake, can't we all just get along—

A banshee scream reverberated through the house, shattering the
window in my bedroom. I clapped both hands over my ears and pushed my
way past Julian and into the hallway where Bandit was screaming bloody
murder along with her.

"Moira!" I shouted, but she couldn't hear me over her own scream. I
shoved into Laran hard, jostling him enough that I caught sight of her on
the other side of him. Her eyes flashed to mine and the screaming died in
her throat instantly.

Bandit ran toward me and started scratching at my bare legs. I reached
down and scooped him up, cradling him to my chest. The ringing in my
ears didn't abate, even after she ran and nearly tackled me to the floor.
Laran placed a firm hand against my lower back, holding all three of us up
as she threw her arms around me.

"I'm so sorry, Ruby. I just saw the dead bodies and lost my shit. I
thought something might have happened to you, but I hadn't felt anything
and that just made it worse and—"

"Shh…" I whispered. Her fawning over me, while kind, wasn't helping.
That damn screech of hers was going to make me hard of hearing one of

these days. Not to mention poor Bandit was going to need a visit to Dr. Lummus to make sure she didn't cause any real damage. Oh, he was going to *love* that. She fed him tuna while I rubbed his belly to keep him calm enough for her to be able to give him a simple physical. And when he needed shots? Ha. I was dragging Moira's ass with me for this one.

"What the hell happened here?" she asked, pulling back to glance at the body and pile of ash behind her.

"I was attacked by hunters," I murmured, moving around her. I walked several feet across the cold concrete floors. The footsteps echoed in the absence of furniture, aiding the howling wind outside. I leaned down and picked up the ceremonial blade buried in the ash pile.

"Is that what I think it is?" Moira squeaked. I glanced up at her and took a deep breath. She held her arms crossed over her chest, her forest green hairs stood on end. *Goosebumps.* I blew the glittering ashes off the blade and the runes lit up.

"That depends on how much you believe in ghost stories," I murmured. "I've heard rumors of assassins for hire that can take more than just a life." Moira's eyes never left the knife as I turned it over in my hands.

"Demon hunters?" Moira whispered.

I nodded solemnly.

"Who would hire someone—"

"The imp," Julian answered gravely before the question left her mouth. She stopped short, her face turning a shade deeper.

"He needs to be dealt with," she demanded. She balled her hands into fists. Guilt and outrage battled within her, but in the end, only a creeping helplessness and fierce need to protect me remained.

"He will be," Laran vowed. A gust of wind swept through, carrying the ashes out of the busted window. He knelt to exam the body: the man shot between the eyes. Julian moved out of the shadows, his eyes sweeping across the dead assassin with nothing short of a clipped fury and cold cruelty.

"You said they looked alike?" Julian asked. I nodded. "That's unfortunate," he murmured to himself. Julian narrowed his eyes on the body, running his fingers across his jaw. He brushed his thumb across his bottom lip but didn't seem to notice. His full attention was on the dead before us.

"Why is that unfortunate?" I breathed, barely wanting to ask.

"Because they were not human, nor were they demons. The dead body before me is Seelie, and your savior knew that." I took a daring step towards the body. In life, his skin was the color of lead. In death, it had darkened to slate; weathered and ashen, like a corpse much older than this one was. His wide eyes were the darkest crystalline white, but held no vitality to them.

Moira's eyes seemed to ask the question that hung in the air.

How?

"Iron," I murmured. "The bullet they used must have been made of iron." The Fae were as ancient as us demons, and while I had never come across one—we all knew the tales. Or at least the whispers of them. The she-demons that ran the orphanages I've lived in were never fond of the stories. They were banned. Written off as legends meant to scare demons and humans alike.

You don't get through this world as a weaker demon and not listen to those whispers. You never knew what they might say; never knew what information could make a difference in your survival.

The Fae, specifically the Seelie, were rumored to be hunters of all demon-kind. Dark and unyielding in their pursuits, they fought in the name of the first Seelie—Eve.

Yes, *that* Eve.

As it so happened, Eve wasn't the first woman on earth. She was one of two sisters, and there was no Adam. He came much later down the line after Lucifer fell and the worlds were cleaved in two. What was once Eden, became Hell. Her sister, Lilith, remained immortal, beautiful, and more importantly—she got Lucifer. For a time, anyway. Clearly, if I was here, he'd taken up other lovers. As one might imagine, Eve wasn't too happy with her half of the deal. She got stuck with Adam, earth, and mortality. Eve's mission was to bear as many children as she could whilst wiping the world of the unholy divine.

Difficult to hunt demons when you're a mortal. Hence the babies.

"Iron bullets are not something the everyday person carries about. Not even demons." In the back of my mind, something tugged at my memory, but the thought would not surface and make itself clear.

"Whoever saved her knew of the Fae," Laran said gruffly, turning the man's face side to side.

"Indeed," Julian replied. Something unspoken went between them as they locked eyes, no longer than a moment. Maybe I was observant, but I was getting better at reading them. At seeing what was coming next. "Rysten and Allistair are coming to pick you up and take you back to our apartment. Laran is remaining with me to continue to assess the threat and clean up the damage. One way or another, you will be safe until it is time for you to take the throne."

Take the throne.

My stomach squeezed in painful, taut knots.

Again, the question ran through my mind, unbidden, but sharp as it was true. *If I am not safe here in Portland, what safety could Hell possibly grant me?*

The beast in me snarled at the implications of that statement. She didn't think we should worry for safety. The world should quiver in fear at her wrath.

"How original," I thought dryly.

"Fear is for the weak. It will kill you faster than anything," she hissed back at me.

"A healthy dose of fear means I've considered my options," I pointed out, too pertinent for her liking.

"It means you hesitated."

"Without it, we would not know who sent the Seelie after me."

"With it, you could die."

I grit my teeth, pursing my lips. My jaw was beginning to ache from the tension. Bandit clung tighter to me, letting out a pathetic mewling noise that I'm pretty sure was him complaining he was cold. *Get in line, buddy.*

"Ruby," Moira said hesitantly as she approached me. "I know we didn't want to move in with them, but today was shit. First Kendall and the shop, now this—I mean, I just had the living room window replaced. We can't afford renovations, all our windows are broken, the heat bill is going to be insane this month. I just…" She trailed off as her lips rolled together in a tight frown. Several dark strands of hair slipped free of her ponytail and blew in the wind. "It's not safe for you to be away from them anymore," she whispered.

"I know," I said. Her hands were smaller than mine, with short stubby fingers. It made it easy for me to wrap my awkwardly long hand around hers. They shook from the cold and the declining adrenaline rush.

"It's not safe for you to be here—in Portland. Ruby, I think it's time we…" Her voice broke off as she struggled for the first time to give words to what I'd known since the day the pentagram showed up on my chest.

"I know. That's why I already told Julian that we're moving in with them. We'll need to figure out what we're going to do about Blue Ruby and selling the house, but after today, I think we both know my time here is… limited." I paused, swallowing the lump in my throat. "I'm not ready to go to Hell. It would probably chew me up and spit me back out, but right now, I'm not seeing a lot of other options."

I so wasn't ready for this. Any of it. I don't get that luxury since I inherited not only Lucifer's kingdom, but a swath of enemies as well.

"We'll figure it out," Moira said. I shook my head sadly.

"I'm so sorry you got dragged into this mess. I'll find a way to make it right. We can set you up somewhere nice, and I'll come back to visit—"

Moira threw her arms around my neck, hugging me close. "I've invested twelve years of my life into you. You think I would let you run off to Hell alone to become queen? I want a return on my investment!" she declared. The worry that held me thawed against the course laugh that broke through my lips.

It had been a long day, and there will be many more to come. My friend could hold the cops off, but only for so long. My house was wrecked; my reputation going up in flames behind it. I branded Laran, even though I'd yet to hit the transition. The imp was still out there, hunting me, as the Horsemen hunted him.

Some days happiness is not easy; it is a choice.

Despite it all—I chose to smile.

JULIAN

The moment my brother picked her up and took her back to the apartment, I reanimated the Seelie and questioned him.

Not that I expected much of anything beyond what Ruby said.

"I asked who sent you," I demanded for the third and final time. I
wanted to push the matter and force it, but souls struggle to linger more
than an hour. As it was, the Seelie was twitching uncontrollably, fighting to
break free of my control.

"I told-d you-u-u," the body rasped. "W-we were paid-d. I n-n-never
sssaw the facccce." The body started gnashing its teeth together. If I forced
him to stay, I'd be dealing with a zombie. While that punishment would be
fitting, I needed to conserve my strength for something else.

"And you were told to make sure she knew it was an imp that sent her?"
I forced the soul to stay with us long enough to nod confirmation, at least as
much as the dead could. Releasing it was akin to dropping the leash on a
dog. It slipped through the body and into the air as a vague outline of the
Seelie he had been. The ghost winked at me and I sent it back to the void,
letting War incinerate the thing's body.

"Seems odd that whoever hired him would want her to know the imp
did it if they were sent to kill her," Laran said over the crackling flames.

"Unless they didn't expect her to die."

"Maybe they just wanted to scare her," Laran suggested.

"Perhaps. What I can't understand is how they would take a job *from* a demon and not kill them instead?" Something seemed off about this attempt. It was both too poorly thought out, and too convenient for it to be what we were seeing. There was more to it, but what more was hard to tell.

"I'll get Rysten on it. See if he can find anything," Laran said. We stood in silence while I waited for the flames to wink out of existence before I stalked across the room and punched him in the face.

"Was that for her being attacked, or for me being claimed the first mate?" War cracked his neck back into place and spat a glob of blood.

"You're a fucking idiot for putting her at risk," I snapped, having to reign it back in so we didn't accidentally level her house.

"Ahh. You're pissed because she branded me, and you think it should have been you." He didn't shout. Why would he when he was claimed as the first mate? He wasn't wrong about why I was angry, but I punched him because he put her in danger.

"Our duty is to protect her. She's now even closer to the transition, and if anything triggers her before we find the imp—or whoever sent these two —all of us will be put in a vulnerable position. Think about how long most demons need for it. Now realize who we're talking about." His eyes flashed, but he said nothing. As he shouldn't. He fucked up big time here.

"She could be stuck in it for *weeks*. That is *weeks* of appeasing the beast. *Weeks* of trading off which one of us will be with her while the others guard. And that's if she only wants one at a time. We have no idea how large her appetite will be given that she is half-succubus."

Oh, but I dreamed.

In the beginning, I could tell myself that she did not affect me. That I was only her guardian and that's all I will ever be. I could blame her bedroom eyes on her succubus nature. I would tell myself her sinful curves and sultry mouth affected all of us this way.

It meant nothing.

Then the beast emerged.

It was not as easy now that she smelled like she was fucking made for me.

I wanted her with a desire so sharp it was painful.

That's exactly why I couldn't have her.

CHAPTER FOURTEEN

YOU KNOW that feeling when you have a million and one things to do, you're standing in line at the grocery store, and the cashier is just blabbering away why she takes her time to ring up a gallon of milk and bag of powdered donuts? That's a bit how today felt. Six clients called and cancelled their appointments. Another ten I had to schedule throughout the week to finish up with. What was left of my house was getting appraised in three days and put on the market—we had to have our shit out by Friday. Blue Ruby was being closed down and the lot sold off. And ever since I had branded him, Laran was strutting around like the prized stallion he thought he was.

I wasn't handling any of this. No, I was avoiding it like the fucking plague while I focused on finishing coloring the pepperoni in my current client's sleeve. At the time, I thought it was an amusing request, albeit odd, to have all her favorite foods tattooed on her. I should have realized then how weird this chick was. She's been running her mouth incessantly for the last hour about macaroni and cheese—a staple food that she had requested I make the base of this design.

I was just finishing up the slice that wrapped around her forearm when the bell on the shop door jingled. I glanced over at Rysten, standing guard next to my cubicle. We'd told mac'n'cheese lady he was shadowing me, and she didn't question further. You wouldn't even have realized he was there if it weren't for the occasional looks the client gave him while licking her lips.

"Can you go check on th—" My words cut off at the sound of approaching footsteps. Too heavy to be Moira, too fast to be a client. Rysten wasn't alarmed. He did little more than let an easy smile slip onto his face as Allistair rounded the corner.

"I need a word with you," he demanded. His eyes swept over the situation, but he didn't seem to particularly care I was in the middle of a session. Fire burned in his eyes, a quiet rage that no doubt had something to do with me. I glanced over at my ogling client to see her mouth was just kind of hanging open.

I rolled my eyes. "Let's break for five minutes. Feel free to get up and move around, but don't touch your arm or brush it against anything." Her head snapped up like she just realized she had been staring and nodded sheepishly. I turned to follow Allistair out and both men held smug grins on their faces. I cocked an eyebrow, walking past and *accidentally* brushing up against them both as I went.

I left the office door open behind me and crossed to the other side of my desk before Allistair entered. The door clicked shut softly and I swallowed hard. Taunting him in the hallway didn't seem like such a good idea anymore. Funny that.

I clasped both hands behind my back so he couldn't see me fiddling with them. Why was he here anyway? If this was about Laran…*Shit.*

Allistair didn't seem like the jealous type. But neither had Rysten until Laran apparently started walking around shirtless this morning in their apartment. I got to hear all about that already. Living with them was going to be a real pain in my ass.

"When were you going to tell me?" His voice was soft as velvet, but it was woven into a noose. I shifted uneasily side to side, debating on calling Rysten in.

"It's not like I *meant* to do it…" Wrong. Wrong way to start this conversation.

Allistair's eyes hardened. "How in Satan's name do you mean to tell me—"

"Hey!" I snapped at the tone in his voice. My own temper rose to match. "You said yourself the lot of you want me. It's none of your damn business what goes on when I'm with the others. Hell, if I want all of you—then I'll have you."

Allistair's mouth dropped open and he fell silent. A thrill of victory ran through me, making me brave. I crossed my arms over my chest, letting my smugness permeate the air. Not that it lasted long. Allistair's shock wore off rather quickly and those sinful lips curved into a knowing smile. My own smirk slipped from my face as my lips dropped into a neutral expression.

"What are you talking about, Ruby?" His lips caressed my name. So wicked. Heat pooled inside me, making me stand straighter. Just the way he said my name made my pussy clench. I pressed my thighs together and his eyes flicked down at the movement, his smile growing into a wolfish grin as he took a step closer.

"I…" The words caught in my throat as he took another step towards me, maneuvering himself around the desk.

"You what?" he murmured and took another step, putting him inside my bubble of safety. My bubble of clarity. I couldn't think with him, or any of them, this close. I took a step back and he pursued. Faster than I could react, he grabbed my hips and planted my ass on the desk. His hands gripped me tight, but not painful. Not yet anyways. He used one knee to knock my legs apart and push his way between them.

"I—" I broke off, snapping my mouth shut. I didn't appreciate being manhandled into giving him what he wanted…and yet, with him, I did. I bit my lip hard and swift to clear my mind. "Why don't you tell me what you're doing here. I have a client I need to get back to, and I doubt you are going to fuck me here on my desk."

He dipped his fingers under the hem of my shirt, toying with the skin.

"Be careful with that mouth of yours. I haven't fed in a week, and I can think of *much* better uses for it," he whispered. Cool lips brushed against mine and I moaned against him.

Motherfucker.

"Now, now. Is that anyway to talk to me?" he sniggered. I froze.

Shit. I didn't think I actually said it…

"Fuck off. Either tell me what you came here for or let me finish up this client," I snarled back at him. Allistair took a step back at the same moment the beast lunged forward and wrapped my hand around his shirt, holding him eye level just long enough to utter, *"Mine."*

Devil fuck her. She slipped back just as fast she came, leaving me to handle Allistair's probing stare.

"She's possessive," he commented.

"So it appears," I replied dryly.

"If she is, then you are, little succubus."

"I branded Laran." The words popped out of me and there was no taking them back. Allistair blanched, schooling his face into an unreadable expression. I didn't need his body language to know the truth. He stood far too close to hide it, and with my own guilt already twisting inside of me, I didn't want any part of him influencing me, too.

I pushed him to move and he stepped aside, giving me just enough room to close my legs and slide off the desk. I avoided his gaze as I stepped away from him, straightening my spine.

"What are you here for?" I repeated, crossing my arms over my chest.

"To scold you for how unbelievably stupid your stunt with Kendall was," he replied briskly.

"There's no proof," I muttered like a sullen child.

"No proof? Did you really just fucking say that?" His voice rose with the cold arrogance he seemed to pride himself on. Only I knew his secret. It was all a façade.

"I took the video. Broke the recorder. There's no proof the court can hold me to," I said in my snootiest and most obnoxious voice possible.

"You tattooed her whole fucking face, Ruby. You left a *message*. What was it? 'Now your outside matches your inside?' The only thing saving you is my money and reputation—what are you doing?"

I bent over to unlock the safe where I kept my goodies, angling my body so Allistair couldn't see inside. If he was going to have a conniption about Kendall, he sure as hell wasn't going to like what I kept in there.

"One moment." I reached down and plucked the paper I needed, locking the safe back up again before standing to face Allistair.

"What is that?" he asked suspiciously, motioning to the paper in my hand.

"A signed waiver so she can't press charges." I couldn't hide the smugness from my voice.

"You forged her signature," he deadpanned, ripping the paper from my hands to examine it.

"She ruined my reputation, tormented me about Josh for months, and you know what? I didn't care. It was getting old, but I never gave a damn for anyone's opinion but my own and I'm not about to start." I met his gaze with nothing but honesty. "She crossed a line when someone in that mob threw a rock at Moira. I may lose my license. I may get fined. They may even try to put me in jail, but I've already lost this life, and I'll be long gone before the court acts. But Kendall"— I paused, my eyes dropping to the scattered designs across my desk—"she will never be able to forget this. She will never outrun her past. She can try to have it removed. She will be in so much pain and it will never truly be gone; I made sure of that. Every single day of her fucking life she will see the face I gave her when she looks in the mirror. I've killed people and come to think that it was too easy a punishment. Making that person live with the consequences…that's justice."

Allistair did not speak. We said nothing to each other for a very long moment, long enough those five minutes were most definitely up. We simply stared.

It was not a staring contest in the sense that he was waiting for me to break and look away, but in that he was searching for something in me and I think he found it.

I think we both did.

"Consider the legal side of things handled. We still need to discuss what you want to do with the house and Blue Ruby, but I will try to make the transition as smooth as possible." He turned on his heel and made to leave. "And Ruby?" He paused with his hand on the knob.

"Yes?" I asked. A single word never felt so exhausting.

"Your father would have been proud."

I opened my mouth, but fell short of finding any kind of intelligible response to that. Allistair didn't wait for one and the door clicked shut behind him.

Given that my father was the devil, I wasn't sure if that was a compliment or an insult. Knowing Allistair, it was probably a bit of both, and I was best not to dwell on it too much.

I still had to survive the week. And it was only Tuesday.

She's so close and yet so far.

Julian is trying to keep us at a distance ever since she branded War. That fucker has been sporting it about, how he was *chosen* first. Of course, now that it's happened once, she's even more careful, holding me at arm's length because she's scared it will happen again.

I blamed him.

What none of them know is how close her and I have come to that, but I put her first and stopped it from happening. War is an idiot if he doesn't realize that he's fucking lucky Julian showed up and stopped them. We can't afford for her to enter the transition right now. Not with the imp out there sending the fucking Seelie her way.

I don't even know how she managed to brand him without entering it. Not only is it unheard of, but it lends more credence to Pestilence's theory. Something happened, and like her feeding, she is holding off.

The problem is that eventually something will happen again, and she will blow.

We're handling a hair trigger that could go off at any moment, over anything.

But at least she thought to forge the girl's signature before I went and paid off the cops and the judge. Funny how little the law was enforced when money was flowing.

I had to praise the forethought she used, and I meant what I said.

Her father would have been proud. She will make a great queen.

Fair and ruthless. I couldn't ask for more in a she-demon that will one day rule.

Which is exactly why I will be standing at her side.

Rysten is hell-bent on being claimed next, but not if I have anything to say about it.

CHAPTER FIFTEEN

WE HURRIED down the well-lit street, our shoes softly slapping against the wet pavement. A subtle mist permeated the air, making the freezing temperatures downright icy. I shoved my hands in my armpits and ambled towards my favorite restaurant, The Alley Cat. Next to me, Rysten let out a soft laugh.

"You won't be laughing when your balls freeze and you can't make any little pests," Moira snapped, storming ahead of me. I smiled at her back as she tugged her hood tighter and shoved past the drunken group of college kids. A chorus of, 'Hey! Watch it!' followed her as one of the boys fell over sideways into a trash can.

Talk about getting wasted. I sniggered at my own pun.

Moira didn't spare them a single glance as she plowed on, diving into a side alley. I followed after her, ignoring the shouts behind us. They may yell, but no one would dare cause trouble with Rysten standing beside me. Easygoing nature aside, he had a strict no bullshit policy where I was concerned. Only Moira and Bandit were exempt.

It was reassuring, but also a bit patronizing. He was at least considerate in his duties, unlike the other three, who were all their own unique forms of overbearing. Rysten made it feel more like the three of us were just getting dinner. The reality was it was me and Moira, and he had to come along because I can't go anywhere alone. Not anymore.

I treaded carefully across the cobbled street. It wasn't pavement like most of Portland, but instead a layer of rocks imbedded on top of a cement finish. The stones were smooth and slick in the misting weather. Rysten saddled up to me, gently cupping my arm at the elbow to help me keep my balance.

"Thanks," I breathed, pulling my arm away as soon as we reached the steps. Rysten didn't say anything, but I could feel the pleasant warmth that radiated from him. Did he know his hand was like a hot iron against my skin? Could he feel the way my body reacted underneath three layers of clothes?

I shook my head to clear away those thoughts as I gripped the wrought iron railing and ascended the steps. Inside, Moira waved an arm in our direction, beckoning us toward a booth in the back.

"*This* is your favorite restaurant?" Rysten asked skeptically, his eyes swinging from the very plain wooden booths that lined the space to the moving tables that traversed the room. Each one oversaw an aspect in pizza making: dough boy, the sauce guy, toppings, and finally to the oven where it baked into delicious goodness that waitresses would then serve out. The moving tables shifted and turned without managing to hit each other as they created pizza so heavenly, the owner must have been an Italian grandmother in his past life. I smiled fondly at the young man spinning dough high in the air before tossing it onto the next table.

"Yep, and the main event hasn't even started," Moira answered gleefully, a low chuckle escaping her lips. Rysten gave me a sideways glance as I slid into the booth next to her and shrugged innocently.

"Main event?"

"You'll see."

She and I shared a smirk at the scowl on Rysten's face. For once it was *us* who was in on the joke. Oh, how the tables have turned. Quite literally, as the dough boy moved his station in front of us.

"What'll it be this evenin,' ladies and gent?" he asked in a strong New York accent.

"Two large house specials and a pitcher of whatever seasonal draft you're carrying," Moira answered for all of us. His hands were already kneading the dough.

"Got some ID on ya?" he asked. I blanched. Did Rysten even have an ID? I mean, he made my birth certificate and all when I was a child, but what about now? I fumbled with my mini-backpack, giving him a sideways glance out of the corner of my eye. He flipped open his wallet and flashed it at the dough boy who nodded while I dug out my own ID.

"Alrighty then, food will be up shortly," the boy said with a wink in Moira's and my direction. He moved the cart to another table, and in the process, sent the pizza dough spinning onto the sauce cart while calling out our order. You had to admire the organized chaos that The Alley Cat thrived in. When I was thirteen, I wanted to work here. Then I hit puberty and well…c'est la vie. That's what happens when you're half-succubus. A secluded job was my only prospect after that.

"I didn't know you had an ID." I eyed the wallet he was quickly closing.

"There's a lot you don't know about me, love." He winked as he slid it in his back pocket. "How do you expect us to get around on earth without the documentation humans are so fond of?"

"Well," I drawled. "I kind of assumed you operated around the law and just came and went as you pleased." Our conversation paused when a young woman came up carrying a pitcher in one hand and three frosty mugs in the other. She poured our glasses one at a time and left the remaining half pitcher on the table without a word.

"As nice as that would be"—he paused to take a swig of the frothy ale —"we can't do *everything* around the law. Allistair couldn't handle your legal trouble if not for the fabricated scores on the bar that made him a certified lawyer."

Instead of replying, I took a drink of the seasonal draft. Rich and malty, the pleasant notes of vanilla finished with a hint of peppermint as a faint warmth built in my chest.

Much better.

"Should I be concerned about this case with Kendall?" I asked in all seriousness. If Allistair never took the bar…I guess it was safe to assume he probably never went to college either.

"Concerned? Really, love? We started the firm some hundred years ago. If anyone can get you out of your legal troubles, it's him." Rysten assured me, using his hands to gesture. I wasn't the only one the alcohol was loosening up tonight.

"When you say *the firm*"—Moira cut in—"do you mean that all of you own it?"

"Yes, but Allistair handles the actual lawyer business. Don't tell him I said this, but I think he gets a power trip from it. Certainly wouldn't surprise me," he scoffed. I snorted and choked on a bit of my beer. Moira clapped me on the back harder than necessary, all the while eyeing Rysten with interest.

"Why do you say that?" she asked.

"That he gets a power trip from it?" She nodded and Rysten let out a dark chuckle. "Because Famine and my brother have been at odds for control for a very long time. Him being the lawyer meant he was providing for Ruby, and Julian wasn't. I suspect that's half the reason he does it without complaint." He took another long drink of his beer, draining the mug. Moira was more than happy to pour him another one.

She's so thoughtful that way.

The nosy banshee was well aware of what was making his lips loose— and for once, it wasn't me. Right then, a waitress came carrying two ginor- mous pizzas, and when I say ginormous, I mean literally two feet in diame- ter. They barely fit on the table around the pitcher and mugs. Rysten drained his again, refilled it, and topped mine off before handing the girl the empty pitcher. We all echoed our thanks as she retreated, looking slightly skeptical we could eat it all. She didn't know the appetite banshees have. They're notorious for eating ungodly amounts of food, and judging by the size of Rysten, I had a feeling she wasn't the only one.

"So, if Allistair is the only one doing lawyer business, what do the rest of you lazy fucks do?" Moira asked, pulling a square off the tray and biting in while it was still piping hot. She let out a freakishly loud moan and the next table over threw us dirty looks. I held up my hands, like I had no part in it—not that it mattered when Moira flipped them off. The woman picked up her toddler and covered the boy's eyes while the baby clapped.

It almost reminded me of Bandit.

"Really?" I asked her. Moira flipped me off, too, shrugging her slender shoulders. For fuck's sake, let's at least *pretend* to be grown ass adults.

"Well, us lazy fucks, as you so nicely put it, do all of the work outside of the courtroom." Rysten replied, watching me with amusement as I dug into the pizza. I folded it like a sandwich before plopping it into my mouth.

"Such as?" I asked around a mouthful of food. Moira sniggered, arching an eyebrow. I glared back as I swallowed the rest of the slice whole and grinned like a motherfucking champ.

Succubus without a gag reflex for the win.

"Nothing all that terribly interesting," he said vaguely.

"You forged my birth certificate and I'm willing to bet you're the one that forged Allistair's bar results," I replied, much soberer than he was in that moment. His hand halted mid-bite, and his sage colored eyes flicked up to mine. Bingo. "So that's your thing? You forge stuff? Documents?"

His lips twitched as a grin fought its way through. "Amongst other things."

"Hmm." I took another slice of pizza, savoring the zesty tomato sauce and hot red peppers. With the winter beer and warm atmosphere, I was right at home here.

"What about Laran? What's he do?" Moira asked, drawing our attention back to her. She'd only been silent because she was too busy eating. Half of the pizza before her was already gone.

"War isn't really one for politics or computers…" Rysten trailed off, picking up his beer right at that moment. The smirk of his lips told me he clearly found that amusing.

"Figures. He's probably the one that beats people up in alleys," Moira shrugged.

Rysten choked on his beer and put the mug down with enough force to muster a thunk from the impact.

Well, well, now…if that isn't interesting.

"That's what he does, isn't it? He beats people up?" I asked him.

"Not so much anymore," Rysten supplied.

"Anymore?"

"Should I be scared to ask what Julian does?" Moira piped up with too much enthusiasm. Rysten threw her a glare as if to say, *don't you dare.*

"Look, love, we built ourselves a name on mostly honest work. We had a few mobsters back in the early days, a drug lord here and there to keep the money flowing. What do you expect though? We're not exactly guardian angels." With that, he drained the last of his mug and helped me finish off our pizza.

Nothing like a last supper before we leave town for you to figure out who you're moving in with. Although, if I'm being honest, it's wasn't all that surprising. They dealt with the Josh scenario too efficiently for it to be the first time. I mean, they're the Four Horsemen—and I burn people alive. It's not like I have any room to judge.

"Ladies and gents, boys and girls, now is the time we've all been waitin' for." The charismatic voice of the young dough boy drew my attention to the center of the room where workers were clearing away tables. He stood on a lone chair, overlooking the lot of us. He wore a Cheshire smile like the grandest of kings. How fitting for what came next.

"These two lovely young ladies will be coming around with pails of spoiled compost for sale. Five dollars a bucket, to crown the fool!" He clapped his hands and a young girl appeared, probably no more than sixteen, pushing a cart loaded with old vegetables and fruits. The eggs always made for a particularly fun show.

"How many?" the girl asked, blushing at the sight of Rysten.

"We'll take four," Moira said, drawing her attention away from the male across from us. The girl pulled the empty trays from our table and moved the buckets while Moira counted out her cash.

"You got a five?" she asked me and I reached for my wallet.

"I've got it," Rysten said, waving us off. He handed the girl a fifty, told her to keep the change, and gave her a wink. The girl's porcelain skin blushed a deep shade of scarlet while she murmured her thanks and moved to the next table.

"How dashing," Moira muttered. I snorted in agreement.

"So what are we going to do with all of this"—his nose wrinkled in disgust—"garbage."

"You'll see," I replied cryptically. Moira cackled, and a tenor of her banshee rang through, making the buckets warble. I clapped a hand over her mouth as her eyes grew wide.

"Did that just…" she said around my hand. I pulled it back for her to speak freely.

"Yep." I took a sweeping glance around the restaurant, but no one noticed. No one apart from Rysten, who watched us silently with his brows drawn together, a slight pucker formed between them as he ran his fingers over his jaw.

"Interesting…" he murmured. I opened my mouth to ask him what he was talking about, but the dough boy chose that moment to get started.

"Alrighty, listen up!" the young man projected, his voice gravitating over us as he called the room to silence. "It's time for the main event. The one night a month that we come together to crown the King of Fools. This. Is. Bad Poetry Night!"

The room let out a thunderous applause as people slammed the buckets of slop up and down. Moira and I let out a woot, pumping our fists in the air. Rysten stared at us like crazy women.

"This is what you dragged us out here for?" he whispered in disbelief. I shushed him with a wave of my hand as the boy—now known as the marshal since bad poetry night was well underway—called up the first volunteer.

"State your name and poison, if you wish to be the King of Fools!" the marshal called out, stepping down from the chair. His coffee colored hair reflected the soft lights coming from the ceiling, and his chocolate eyes sparkled with mischief, making him look younger than before.

"I'm Standing Willow," said the man that walked forward. His rainbow beanie slouched sideways, only covering half of his long, greasy hair. He wore a baggy t-shirt with a peace sign on it that did nothing for his thin frame, and his gypsy pants bunched at the waist, poofing out around his legs and cuffing at the ankles. I was also pretty sure I owned that same pair of Chacos he had on, except I only wore them when it was *above* freezing.

"Welcome, Standing Willow," the marshal said. His lips twitched like he was having trouble saying that in all seriousness. The beanie man took up his spot on the chair, clearing his throat obnoxiously before starting.

"Shall I compare thee to a summer's day?" the man started.

"Boooo!" Moira yelled. Rysten turned, stricken, which for a drunk demon, was quite amusing.

"Shhh!" he scolded her. "Can you keep your voice down? That's quite rude."

No sooner than he said it did a chorus of boos rain down from around the room. I wasn't sure if I should be amused or feel bad for the guy. On one hand, the idea was to bring the worst poetry to the table, so maybe he was making a joke of dear old Shakespeare. On the other hand, he looked the type that might take this to heart.

"Thou art more lovely—" And that ended right there as Moira arched around me to throw half of a tomato at him. It flew all ten feet, straight and true, right into his mouth. His eyes went wide and he looked down his nose, mortified at the chunk of tomato half hanging out of his mouth.

The marshal stepped up and circled around the beanie man. "First pie hole of the night. What's he going to do?"

The guy doubled over and threw up, spewing not only the tomato, but a good portion of his dinner. He toppled sideways out of the chair where his friends who put him up to this were waiting. They caught him, smiling through their tear-stained eyes, clearly laughing so hard they cried. He righted himself and looked around, pink tinging his cheeks. Standing Willow, it seemed, did not realize what kind of poetry night this would be.

As a cleaning crew came to mop up the mess, the marshal turned to the crowd and shouted, "Disqualified!"

Moira and I smacked our hands on the table, drumming along with the rest of the patrons while another fool came forward.

"So let me get this straight," Rysten said, talking over the noise. "You come here to listen to people recite bad poetry and throw food at them? Isn't that a bit…demeaning?"

My heart fluttered as it had little spasms in my chest. He didn't completely understand the purpose, but his sentiment was in a good place. Better than one might expect for the Horsemen of Pestilence. But I didn't get the chance to explain to him.

"I told you we should have brought Laran instead," Moira muttered just loud enough for him to hear. Rysten froze for about half a second, narrowing his eyes at her. She arched an eyebrow and motioned to the bucket sitting in front of him. The second fool had just finished her performance and the crowd was going nuts. Meanwhile, Moira was giving Rysten a test.

One it appeared, he was not going to fail.

He grabbed a bell pepper off the top as I leaned over, whispering to Moira, "You're a cunt. You know that?"

She sniggered as Rysten pelted the girl with the pepper to the head and she swayed in the chair. Her hand reached out to grasp the wooden back as she righted herself and pumped a fist in the air. The crowd went wild, throwing all kinds of spoiled goods, but she held firm and proceeded to the next round.

"Wait—so they *want* you to throw food at them?" he asked dubiously.

"Yep," I said, shaking my head while Moira laughed like a fool. A dark glimmer entered his eye, but that was all he said about it for the next few contestants. One at a time, more chairs were accumulated, and bad poets were tested. Some brought snark, others used humor, and only a few dared use something as overdone as Shakespeare. This wasn't the place or the crowd for it really. The ones who were simply booed and had nothing thrown at them were eliminated. Of the others, only those who could remain on the chair withstood. Not that we made that an easy task. Moira had quite a knack for throwing shit. I probably would, too, if my first foster home had been like hers.

The marshal stepped up and waved his hand in the most ridiculous fashion. Really, I think they picked the kid for this job because he acted the part and the crowd loved it.

"Last call for contenders in this month's bid to be the King of Fools," the young man broadcasted. All around the room people looked to their right and left to see if anyone wanted to join the ranks of the three fools that had ascended to the next round.

"I will."

I turned sharply, my mouth falling open. Rysten rose out of the booth and strutted towards the marshal with unmistakable swagger. His tall stature towered over the marshal, who looked up at him uneasily. Like somehow he knew there was something about this man that he should be very, very afraid of.

"What's your name…fool?" the marshal asked bravely.

"Rysten."

Moira grasped my arm while he made his way to the chair, and I was questioning if it was going to break under him. It's not like they gave them sturdy chairs.

"I can't believe he did it. The pest has balls after all," Moira snickered.

"You keep poking him and he's going to snap."

"I'm counting on it." She licked her lips watching him with narrowed eyes. A hint of something ugly ran through my chest, almost akin to jealousy. The word my beast liked to say most frequently danced on my lips. *Mine.*

Moira cut her eyes at me, cocking her head.

Oops. I think that slipped out.

"Yours, huh?" she asked, her eyes shining with mirth. "Took you long enough."

I opened my mouth, but she shushed me as Rysten began to speak.

"Rubies are red, your eyes are blue. Your soul is like fire, I want to burn, too."

Did he just—

Oh yes, he did.

My heart thundered in my chest, beating wildly with the force of hurricane winds. The world slowed as we locked eyes and the tiniest of smiles found its way to my lips. I don't know what it was that suddenly had me so turned on. Maybe it was the look he was giving me, that dark gleam that showed me there was so much more to him than I knew. Maybe it was the deafening silence that spoke louder than the words themselves…

Or maybe, it was the way that he withstood and did not look away from me, even as Moira threw an eggplant at his dick.

He took the hit with about as much grace as could be expected. His lips twitched in a grimace, but he held firm, standing taller than any of the other fools around him. Even as Moira literally drained an entire bucket, just on him.

She was my best friend, and as lovely, brilliant, and loyal as she was— she acted like a fucking child with the Horsemen, arguing over me day and night. She ordered them around enough, I sometimes wondered if maybe it was her destiny to rule, given how adept she was at telling people what to do.

"Alright, ladies and gents, feast your eyes upon the fools. As they prepare to recite it out, to win your favor! Let's begin."

Recite it out? Really? He couldn't come up with anything better than that? Lame.

He turned to the first girl who withstood getting hit in the head with Rysten's bell pepper, and she preceded to recite some nonsense about a llama and a desert. It was bad, but not funny, and while people booed her, they did not throw anything. She was eliminated.

Next came a stout girl with a Scottish accent that sounded like Hiccup's mom from *How to Train Your Dragon*. She cleared her throat once and said, "Skinny went to take a bath, he never told a soul. Forgot to put the stopper in and slipped straight down the hole."

I let out a small chuckle, but the real amusement was when two small children squealed in delight. People started pelting the woman with food, just to get a reaction out of the kids. She watched them with so much amusement that she didn't see the stale bread Moira chucked her way. And just like that, she came toppling down. Another one eliminated.

They should really make people sign a waiver for this sort of thing.

The next fool stood on a chair closest to me. His baby blue eyes seemed to bounce shrewdly between me and Rysten. A sour feeling churned in my stomach when he smiled. Moira stiffened, wrapping an arm around my shoulder protectively. It was like she instinctively knew what was wrong as the boy opened his mouth.

"Roses are red, ready to pluck, I'll pick you up at eight thirty, be ready to…" He left his poem open ended, puckering his lips at me slightly as he smiled. The room once again erupted in boos as they pelted him with food. Moira made a point of trying to knock him off with a couple well-aimed grape tomatoes for the eyes. Bastard held on tight and winked at me while he was at it.

My lips thinned into a neutral grimace as I looked to Rysten. My heart stilled in my chest at the way he eyed the human on the other chair. The guy's face went stricken as a sheen of sweat broke out across his skin. He opened his mouth to say something, but instead, all that came out was the loudest fart I have ever heard in my life. The room went silent and Moira threw a tomato, hitting him square in the face. He toppled off the chair and caught himself with his back towards me. I then realized it wasn't a fart.

Those were shit stains spreading across the seat of his pants.

And the smell…

"I think I'm going to be sick," I told Moira, pinching my nose. The guy looked around as people sat wide-eyed, shaking with silent laughter, pointing fingers in his direction. His eyes skipped over them and he took off straight for the bathroom. Not even looking back when the marshal choked out, "Eliminated! Aye—can we get some air freshener up in here?"

Workers scuttled out from the corners of the restaurant where they'd hid among the crowd to laugh and cheer with us. Several people started sweeping up the food off the ground, and the girl who had brought around the buckets of vegetation earlier came forward with a crown in hand.

A paper crown to be specific, like the ones you get at Burger King.

"I crown thee, Rysten, King of Fools! At least until next month," the dough boy-marshal declared. We pounded our empty buckets on the table as Rysten accepted his crown with grace, or with as much grace as one could while being coated in a variety of rotten and spoiled food.

With the main event over, people started filing out, but Rysten didn't seem to be in any kind of a hurry as he sauntered over to us with way too much arrogance for someone covered in tomato juice. Behind him, out of the corner of my eye, I saw a glimmer of red. An eye that was watching me from the massive crowd departing. I peered around him, wanting to get a better look. But in a blink, it was gone.

Must have been another trick of my imagination. The beer getting to me, making me paranoid.

"King of Fools, eh?" Moira said as we slid out of our booth.

"Every queen needs a king," Rysten murmured, opening his wallet to lay down a hundred-dollar bill. Moira didn't comment as she stepped ahead, getting ready to wade into the night. Rysten followed behind and I watched for a moment, smiling to myself.

"Why have one when you can have four?" I whispered, trailing after them.

RYSTEN

Why have only one, you say?

Ruby, love, I think you've figured it out.

She may have branded War first, but I would be the second. If Julian was intent on ignoring not only his reactions towards her, but her feelings for him, who was I to get in the way?

In the meantime, her beast is pacing. Relentless. It is looking to claim its second mate.

That will be me.

I couldn't stop myself from exploiting the human. He was making her uncomfortable. A good potential mate would not allow that, but humans don't work that way. Particularly Ruby. She would have been upset if I killed him. My blood pushed for it. I only didn't because he wasn't a potential mate. Should another male try and enter the equation while she's so vulnerable…it would go very poorly for them.

I settled for sickness. All it took was allowing the bacteria in his gut to fester and grow.

He would never know it was I who caused it.

Now that Ruby knows what she wants, I have no qualms with pursuing her. And trying to get War in check while I'm at it. She hasn't transitioned. I don't know how. We have already passed the deadline I assumed she wouldn't meet, but she displayed powers that are unheard of for a demon pre-transition.

We needed to find the imp, and quickly, before something triggered her.

Time was running out. She can't hold off forever.

CHAPTER SIXTEEN

I FLIPPED the sign on the front door. It was such a small act, just another chore at the end of every day that I had to do while closing. But this time was different.

This time was the last time. Blue Ruby Ink was officially closed, and I didn't know how to feel about that. We were one of the newest, but most successful tattoo parlors in Portland. I created this business with Moira and raised it from the ground up. There was quite literally sweat, blood, and tears put into this place and now…it was over.

I already missed it because of the simplicity this life held for me. Here I was Ruby: a half-succubus whose life revolved around my clients, keeping my head down, and eating at Martha's every Saturday.

It was a nice life. Simple.

But I had this predetermined destiny and nothing I ever did was going to stop it.

It didn't matter that I didn't know about it. It didn't matter how hard I tried to avoid it, tried to resist. I could have been doing any number of things, and it would have ended this way, Kendall or no Kendall.

I guess it was a bit like damned if I do, damned if I don't.

Hell was going to take me either way. I suppose leaving in the next few weeks when it was my choice (and I was still breathing) was probably the smart way to go.

At least that's what I told myself as I dragged my feet back to my office.

There wasn't any point in bemoaning the events that led me here. That would help no one. It would just be a lot simpler if I knew what exactly I was moving towards when all of this settled. Would we just go to Hell and bam—I'm queen? I wondered if I would sit at a desk much like this, ordering people about. Somehow, I didn't think it was going to work like that. Call it a hunch, but the guys were being particularly cagey anytime I asked. That sounded awfully boring anyways, but it's not like there's anyone else up for the job. Except maybe Moira.

At least I'll have her and Bandit. I wasn't quite sure what my ferocious little raccoon would do in Hell, but I wasn't leaving without him, so I guess we were all going to find out. Would that make him a Hellcoon now? I had no idea, but Rysten assured me he would be fine. The portals for Hell transported much more than just demons in and out, and while I'm sure he meant for that to be comforting…all it did was bring me nightmares about what I would find when we eventually got there.

Three knocks at the door made me jump. I turned back just as Moira popped her head in. She took one look at me and her brows drew together, her lips pursing before tightening into a slight frown. "Why are you in here wallowing?"

"I'm not wallowing," I snapped. She arched a perfect eyebrow, slipping through the door and closing it softly behind her.

"Yes, you are."

"Moira—"

"Ruby Morningstar, I have lived with you for twelve years. I know when you're happy. I know when you're upset. I know when something is wrong, and right now, I *know* you are wallowing. Don't deny it. I know it." Moira crossed her arms over her chest, waiting for me to cave.

"I'm not wallowing, Moira. I'm thinking. You know that thing sane people do when making huge life choices?" I quipped back. She didn't seem to find it funny.

"Well, stop it. It's not like we're leaving anytime soon. We only just got the house on the market and we've still got to deal with getting this place cleaned out." She looked around my office like she somehow found it lacking. I lived in organized chaos. Sue me.

"I know it's not the end, and I know we're not leaving yet…" I took a deep breath, looking up at the specks of dust on my ceiling that I've counted a thousand times before. "It's all just moving too fast for my comfort." I shrugged, pulling on my long sleeves awkwardly while I waited for Moira to throw her head back and laugh at me.

"You would be crazy if it wasn't, but that doesn't mean I'm going to tell you not to do it. You've been attacked more times than I'm okay with and as much as I find the Horsemen obnoxious, I know they'll keep you safe." I blinked when she wrapped her arms around my shoulders and pulled me close. She smelled like fresh laundry and a hint of mint. It was a scent I knew well.

"That's surprisingly sappy for you," I muttered into her hair.

"Tell anyone and I'll deny it," she huffed back.

Someone knocked on my door twice before opening it without permission.

"Excuse you," Moira snapped. "We could have been having hot lesbian sex in here and—"

"I know she's straight, banshee," Laran smirked.

"You don't know that," Moira replied testily.

"Yes, I do." His self-assured expression and subtle reminder about his brand made my cheeks heat. He gave me a wink and held the door open, motioning for us to go through. "Still want to go by the house before we head back to the apartment?"

"Yeah, I need to pick up a few things. Bandit's been going stir crazy at night without his pink elephant." Next to me, Moira grumbled in agreement. He's been keeping us up half the damn night trying to crawl under the blankets and nip at my feet for ignoring him. Bastard drew blood last night. Yeah. Now that I think about it, he'll probably do just fine in Hell.

"Is the banshee coming?" Laran asked.

"The banshee has a name, you know," I replied. He didn't even attempt to look reproachful or sorry. I think he was still a bit salty about Moira ringing him out two weeks ago for pounding down my door. Not that she was really making it any better.

"I'm going to stay and pack up some more," Moira said, waving off the invitation.

"You sure?" I asked.

"Yeah, I'll swing by the house afterwards to load up my car with more boxes and meet you back at the apartment," she said, practically pushing me through the door. I kissed her cheek and headed out with Laran.

Today's skies were a cloudless blue, but the day was already nearing sunset. Across the city, the blue darkened to indigo and violet where the sun was barely touching the horizon. Without the cloud coverage, the air was even more frigid, and my teeth started chattering in seconds.

"Cold?" Laran asked, tugging my hand out of the jacket pocket. I didn't complain. His hand was toasty warm, abnormally so.

"How are you not?" I asked, eyeing our linked hands.

"I'm an elemental. We don't experience cold the way the rest of demon-kind do," he rumbled. If only he knew what that deep throaty sound did to me...

Focus, Ruby. Focus.

"You're an elemental?" He nodded. "I didn't know that." He nodded again.

"We keep our powers to ourselves for the most part. If the enemy does not know the extent of what we can do, they err on the side of caution. They are more likely to make very stupid mistakes, much like the imp did with you," he said. I didn't want to think about the imp right now. Not after all the possible sightings I've had these past two weeks. Thinking too much...it made me wonder why he hasn't tried anything. What he was planning. Our kind were not the type to forgive and forget, but instead of saying that, I steered our conversation in a different direction.

"So what elements do you have affinities for? I know about the fire... but I'm guessing that's not the only one." I thought back to the night Josh died and the way Laran had set fire to his body. I shivered again, and not because of the cold. I wasn't afraid of Laran, not anymore at least. We were both capable of truly terrible things.

"I have control over all of the natural elements and their forms."

"Really? How much control?" I asked. I quickly wished I hadn't. Wind swept across the skies, howling like a hound. Clouds rolled in where there previously had been none. Electricity crackled through the air as a single bolt of lightning struck not five feet in front of us.

I stopped dead in my tracks, standing frozen in the middle of the parking lot. My heart pounded in my chest and my eyes went wide as I stole a glance in Laran's direction.

He didn't just have enough control to burn a body.

He could control the very atmosphere.

That type of power was...immeasurable.

If he could summon a storm in seconds, what could he do when he really got angry?

"You can cause natural disasters. That's why you're War," I murmured. The words suspended between us as the pressure dropped. Closing in around us, pulling us together, like magnets. His eyes flashed from black to the darkest of reds. Not brilliant like a rose or a ruby, but still glinting with danger and secrets.

"I have great control over all of them, but I align myself with fire. Maybe that is why I am drawn to you as well." Be still, my beating heart. Laran was not really a sweet talker, but that made his words all the more endearing.

"You Horsemen are much more forward than human men. I'm not sure if I should find it refreshing or concerning," I whispered back. He squeezed my hand gently, but with enough strength to make my skin tingle.

"That's because we're not men. We're demons, and heir to Hell or not —we take what we want. You branded me, Ruby Morningstar. There's no getting rid of me now." His words were a scorching fire against my skin. Words that I reveled in. There was just one thing…

"Do not mistake that brand for love. The beast is possessive. You may like it now, but if you were to be with someone else…" I let my voice trail off as my eyes dropped to his lips. "I can't say for certain, but there is a strong chance I might burn them alive."

"The only reason the human lived as long as he did was because you did not return his affections. Rest assured, Ruby, this brand does not go one way. You may own me, but the only reason I have not branded you is because you share a room with the banshee. For now."

Holy shit.

How the hell could his words turn me on so much when they also kind of scared the shit out of me? Don't get me wrong, I wanted to fuck him seven ways to Sunday.

But branding each other? The beast pushed and shoved, trying to claw her way forward. She wanted that. With all of them.

I wasn't sure if I was ready for that kind of commitment, but I guess I should have thought about that and had a conversation with the bitch inside me before she went and branded him.

Fuck me.

"We should probably get in the car before I do something reckless,"

Laran whispered. I bit the inside of my cheek to stop myself from leaning forward…

Nope. Nope. Get yourself together, Ruby. Stay strong.

Instead of lunging forward to kiss him, biting his lip, and breaking whatever self-control he held, I rolled back on the balls of my feet and said, "Yeah, we probably should."

I couldn't help but notice the clouds that scattered while I drove to my house in silence. It was a comfortable silence. Not awkward really. I had Laran wait in the living room since he refused to wait in the car while I grabbed the couple of things I needed out of my bedroom: Bandit's pink elephant and hammock, another week's worth of clothes, and the Amaryllis flower I kept in my room. Just because. It would be nice to have a touch of home.

We were in and out in less than fifteen minutes and pulling into the parking garage under their apartment building in another thirty. Would have been half that if not for the traffic.

Laran held the flower pot in one hand and the pink elephant in another as we made our way across the garage. Our footsteps echoed in the silence. The lot was rather empty, but it catered to one of the most expensive high-rises in Portland. The few cars that were down here put my VW to shame. The cheapest one was worth a hundred grand, easily. There weren't tattoo artists living here, that's for damn sure.

"Your firm must make good money for you guys to afford this place," I said as I pushed the button.

"Hmm?" he asked.

"Your firm? Rysten mentioned it the other night," I said absentmind-edly as we got in the elevator.

"He told you about Cocks Brothers?" He turned an access key as my hand stilled on the button marked PH. I pressed it once and glanced at him sideways as the doors closed.

"*Cocks* Brothers?" I asked and he stared at me in question. I tossed my head back and roared. "You named yourselves *Cocks* Brothers?"

"Not that kind of cocks," he said defensively. Like I was the one with my mind in the gutter. "Caux. C-a-u-x."

"Like that's any better," I scoffed.

"Allistair's the one that picked it," he grumbled. That got another chuckle out of me.

"Why does that not surprise me?" I said as the doors dinged and slid open.

I took one step outside the elevator when I stopped and stared in awe at the scene playing out before me. Rysten was in the kitchen, desperately trying to protect something. Food. Baked chicken, by the smell of it. Wearing oven mitts, he held a pair of tongs in one hand and a large baking pan that was still giving off little wafts of heat in the other.

That wasn't the part that caught my attention. Not really.

It was that he was holding the pan away from the counter and snapping the tongs as if they were a weapon, trying to deter a certain raccoon standing on the worktop.

"Off! Off with you. No food for the vermin," Rysten scolded, jabbing the tongs in Bandit's direction. Bandit hunched back on his feet and let out a hiss, swiping one of his paws towards the chicken in an attempt to grab it.

Satan save me.

"What are you doing?" I asked them. Both Rysten and Bandit froze mid-fight and slowly their heads turned towards me. Laran stepped out of the elevator beside me and started laughing his ass off.

"What are you laughing at?" Rysten demanded.

"Both of you."

"He's trying to steal all of the fucking food. What do you expect me to do?" Rysten asked. Bandit made a chittering sound, slowly turning around and walking across the counter.

"He's a raccoon, Rysten. What do you expect? Have you been feeding him and giving him plenty of water like I asked you?" I motioned with my hand for Bandit to come to me and he jumped down and ran.

"Yes, I've done everything you asked. He's worse than a bloody hellhound when you're gone," Rysten said. He slowly started to put the chicken back on the counter, watching Bandit like a hawk, expecting him to turn around and make a go for it. I can't say I blamed him. Bandit's done it before.

"Now, Bandit, bud, we've really got to work on your house manners with…" My words left me as I watched him go to Laran and tug on his jeans. Not mine. *Laran's.*

He waited for a whole three seconds as Laran leaned down and offered him his pink elephant. Bandit ignored the elephant and scurried up his arm to perch on his shoulder. Laran stood back up, putting the elephant in the crook of his other arm and scratched Bandit behind the ears.

"What?" Laran asked me.

"Nothing," I said quickly, hurrying into the living room. I've never seen Bandit act that way towards anyone outside of me. Not even Moira. The most he's ever done is tolerate a select few and their presence. That Laran seemed to be growing on him…it gave me hope.

I crossed through the living room, and for the first time, it didn't feel quite so sterile and harsh. Black hairs clung to the expensive white fabric: tale tell signs of Bandit's romping about. As pristine as the white walls, marble floors, and all white furniture color scheme was—I preferred a more lived in look myself.

I walked down the hallway to the left of the fireplace, going to my and Moira's temporary room, sandwiched between Rysten's and Julian's. Inside we had boxes lined against the back-wall of the things we wanted to take with us. Apparently, you can bring possessions to Hell. It just took some finagling to get through all the red tape so the portal keepers would allow it. Who knew?

Perk of having the Horsemen, I suppose.

I tossed my duffel bag on my faded black comforter. Moira's lime green alarm clock read five thirty in bright white numbers. I wondered what time she'd be rolling in. She said she was packing, and that meant she was cleaning as she went, and that by itself could keep her there until seven tonight, but at least she would miss traffic.

"Dinner's ready," Rysten said behind me. I turned and gave him a small smile.

"Lead the way."

When we got back into the kitchen, Laran was leaning on the counter feeding Bandit pieces of chicken off his plate. I smirked at my raccoon, shaking my head.

"Must you feed him from the table?" Rysten asked, whipping us up two plates. Laran ignored him while Rysten set them on the bar and pulled out the middle chair for me.

"Laying it on a little thick, aren't you?" Laran said without looking our way. I choked on a snort and Rysten glared at him, taking his seat on the other side of me.

We ate our dinner in relative silence, since any time either of them tried to speak with me it devolved into slights of hand and petty slurs. At least the food was great. Baked chicken, roasted potatoes, and green beans. I ate two plates before I had to put my dish in the sink and accept surrender.

We migrated towards the couch where the stalemate continued. Laran sat on my left and Rysten on my right, while Bandit ran off with his pink elephant. Probably burrowing it in my sheets for me to find later.

"What do you want to watch on TV?" Rysten asked, flipping through Netflix.

"We could start season two of *How to Get Away with Murder.*"

"Alright."

He pressed play and the intro started rolling. Not ten minutes into it, a quiet tension started building between the three of us. I peeked a glance at Rysten, but his eyes were firmly on the TV. When I looked over at Laran, he had his elbow propped up with his chin in the palm of his hand.

Well, maybe it was just me then. I folded my hands in my lap and tried to force my attention on the TV. Nope. Still wasn't working. I only made it another ten minutes before I started fidgeting and shifted in my seat. I brought both feet up and tucked my knees under my chin, wrapping my arms around my legs.

There. Maybe that will fix it. Then I am touching absolutely no one.

Five minutes later…

Ten minutes later…

Fifteen minutes later…

The show was almost to the end and I had no fucking idea what was even going on. Somewhere along the way, both Rysten and Laran had scooted closer. They both were such sneaky bastards about it that I didn't notice.

Ah hell. I stood up from my seat and walked into the kitchen. Under the counter on the far right, they had a wine cooler Rysten had so nicely pointed out. I was going to make use of it.

"What are you doing?" Rysten asked.

"She's clearly pouring herself a glass of wine," Laran mocked. The damn bickering, while funny at times, was beginning to get on my nerves.

"Who said anything about a glass?" I muttered to myself, pulling out a nice bottle of Chardonnay and popping the seal. I dug through three drawers before I found the wine opener.

"Ah-ha," I said under my breath. Popping the cork, I inhaled the sweet scent. I took a small sip straight from the bottle and moaned in delight.

"Enjoying yourself over there?" Laran called. I waved them off and took a much larger gulp. The full-bodied white wine washed over me like an old friend. The zest of fruit and unmistakable sweetness paired with a hint of vanilla was simply excellent.

I wasn't a wine snob, but I could pretend, eh?

"So, what did I miss?" I asked, strolling up around the couch during the credit scene. They eyed me with varying levels of amusement as I clutched the bottle in one hand and plopped down between them. If they were going to test my limits, I could sure as hell return the favor. Especially with my trusty friend here.

"Nothing much. I don't understand what the point of this show is," Laran grumbled.

"What's not to understand? You got Viola Davis over here as our badass lawyer. She's followed around by her team of wannabe lawyers. Meanwhile, they've all killed someone or fucked someone they shouldn't have and need to cover it up. Hence, *How to Get Away with Murder*. It's a high production soap. Don't think too hard." I stopped to take another drink of the Chardonnay. It was quite good.

"And this is what humans spend all their time doing?" he asked incredulously.

"Pretty much, yeah," I said. He held out his hand for the bottle of wine and I debated telling him to get his own. Then again, technically, this was his and I was the one mooching. So there is that. I passed the bottle over. "If you drink it all, you have to go get me another one."

He drank about a third of the bottle in two large gulps. Prick.

Rysten clicked start on the next episode as Laran passed the bottle back. I shifted to lean my head against his shoulder as I kicked my legs up and swung them over Rysten's lap.

The beast purred, much preferring this arrangement. After a moment of brief shock and silence, they settled in. Laran angled his body so that my head fell on his chest while he wrapped an arm around my waist. The sound of his heartbeat lulled me into a temporary calm while Rysten massaged my feet.

Just for this alone I could keep them around. Rysten can cook. Laran gets along with Bandit. Both seem to have a decent idea of what cuddling looks like. Although, if it weren't for there being three of us, I suspect we'd be doing much more interesting things right now than pretending to watch a TV show.

I finished off the bottle of wine only fifteen minutes in, not that it was really me drinking the whole bottle when Laran kept stealing sips and grimacing. He struck me as more of an ale kind of guy. You know, the kind of guy that stands there shirtless while he throws axes and drinks a stein of beer. But who was I to tell a man what to drink?

We watched another episode or two, finally settling into some sort of temporary peace. I knew the jibes were there just under the surface when every now and then a character would say or do something that had Laran either rolling his eyes or scowling while he muttered how utterly stupid they were. Rysten simply smirked and we would share a private glance. He understood the show and what I liked about it. He got me in that way, and it was something that I knew I was going to be eternally grateful for as time went on. Outside Moira, he was the only one.

Moira…

What time was it? And why wasn't she home?

Something wasn't right here.

As the end credits rolled across the screen for the third episode in a row, I moved my legs off Rysten and onto the marble floor. "I need to use the bathroom," I told them. Not a lie, but it wasn't the whole truth. Laran's arm slipped from my waist as I stood up off the couch and padded down the hall into the side bathroom. In one hand, I still clutched the empty wine bottle as I reached for my cell phone with the other.

It was nearly eight thirty.

And I had no new messages.

Paranoia and panic vied for control as I typed out a message to Moira. It was just a quick, 'Are you ok?' And then I sat down to use the bathroom. I washed my hands in the pretty stone sink and swiped my empty Chardonnay bottle off the floor. *Why did I carry this in here?*

My phone buzzed. It was Moira. She sent a picture.

I swiped left, half expecting a dumb gif revolving around yoga or *Rick and Morty*.

But what I saw…it was my worst nightmare.

Time rolled to a stop. My heart skipped a beat and adrenaline flooded my system as I took in all the details. Moira's bedroom. Her rumpled bedspread. The blue shimmering liquid that matted part of her forest green hair to her face.

Forest green. Her glamor was down.

THE DAZED LOOK in her eyes. She was alive, but she was strung out.

My phone rang to "Fergilicious." It was a ringtone I knew well.

I swiped right and brought the receiver to my ear.

Praying I was wrong.

Knowing I wasn't.

"Did you get my picture, dollface?" I'd heard this voice before.

I was dumb enough to believe it would stay in my nightmares.

"Yes." My voice was stiff, but steady. I don't know how, but I was thankful it was. Moira wouldn't want me to beg.

"Excellent."

"What do you want?" I asked him. It wasn't a plea, but it was close. I would get on my hands and knees and fucking crawl if that's what he asked.

But he wouldn't.

That wasn't enough for him. Not after that night. After Julian.

"I've given her too much black lotus it seems. You have twenty minutes to come home before she receives a second dose. This one will be fatal. If you tell anyone, I will put a bullet in her brain and be gone before they can catch me."

The bottle slipped from my fingers and shattered on the marble floor as I thought of her dying. Flicks of pain and slices of fire licked at my skin where the glass edges cut me. I didn't give a single damn.

"Time is ticking, Lucifer's daughter."

The phone went dead at the same moment the bathroom door came off the hinges.

Laran and Rysten took in everything from the shattered bottle to my terror-stricken expression. I had two choices: lie through my teeth and run off to be a hero, possibly dying while I was at it...or I could tell them the truth and send the full might of the Four Horsemen to kill him and save her.

"He has Moira," I choked. "He took her."

I knew how these manipulation games worked. He wanted me to ask myself too many questions.

Would he really know whether I told them or not?

Would he actually kill her if I did?

The answer was yes and no.

He would kill her, but he had no fucking way of knowing if I told the Horsemen. He was a single demon. Not an omnipotent entity.

He wouldn't know until it was too late.

Deep down in my heart of hearts, a funeral march was beginning.

He took Moira.

How? I did not know. I could only assume he cornered her somehow and forced those terrible drugs into her.

The hopelessness. The desperation. It all came down on me like a tidal wave intent on holding me under, but I would not succumb. Not yet.

"Ruby, I need you to tell me how you know that?" Laran asked. I held up the phone screen and his face changed color. "She's been drugged."

"He called after he sent this. I have twenty minutes to get home before he gives her a second dose that will kill her. If he sees you coming, he said he will shoot her in the head and be gone before we can catch him." This time my voice shook. Was it despair that had me? Or was it death?

"We're going to get her back, I promise—"

"Don't make promises you can't keep."

"Ruby—"

I pushed past him into the hallway where Allistair and Julian had just arrived. How had they gotten here so fast? You know what—it didn't matter.

"Don't! You know as well as I do he has no intention of letting her live. Whether I go or not." I spat the words like a vile poison and started tugging my boots on over my bloodied feet.

"You're right," Julian said putting a hand on my shoulder. I brushed it off and stormed towards the door, but Allistair grabbed me by the wrist and pulled me back.

"Which is exactly why you aren't going," Allistair supplied.

"What?" I looked between their faces, searching for any indication of why they would possibly do this. "What do you mean *I'm not going?*" I demanded, my voice rising an octave.

"Calm down, love. Think about this—"

"Don't fucking tell me to calm down!" I snapped. "Moira is not just my best friend. She's my family. If there's even a chance she's going to die, I need to be there." The flames in the fireplace turned blue, bathing us in an unnatural light. Allistair didn't release me, and the Horsemen didn't yield.

"If you go, then our priorities will be to keep you safe. If you love her, then you will stay here while we—" I raised my hand for silence.

"While you go and fight?" I supplied. The bitterness in my tone couldn't be faked, but neither could the hardness in his eyes. He wasn't yielding. Nor would Allistair. Nor Rysten. Not even Laran…although he looked like he understood.

"Yes."

I shook my head, not believing this. I was supposed to be queen. To rule one day. I couldn't even get them to let me go after one single fucking demon that *they* couldn't seem to track down. I did the responsible thing and told them. I wasn't keeping secrets.

And yet…I was beginning to wonder if this was only the beginning of the bars that being Hell's heir would create. To one day rule was to be a prisoner…

And if Moira died…

"Well, let me tell you this, *Death*." I spat his name like it was poison. "I will die if she dies. So you better give everything you have to save her. I don't care what you have to do. I don't care who you have to kill. You understand? I don't care. But if you don't bring her back alive, then don't come back at all, because there will be no one here waiting when you return." It was not the beast speaking, but the Queen. The would-be queen. Never in my life had I made demands of people, but this time… nothing was too great a price for Moira. *Nothing.*

They all watched me with stunned faces as I shook off Allistair and took my seat at the bar. Bandit came running down the hallway and leapt onto my lap, curling protectively around me.

Just like that, they were talking around me again, but no one dared ask my opinion.

I was just the precious fucking heir. Too powerful to be risked.

What a crock of bullshit.

My phone vibrated again and my stomach plummeted.

Please don't tell me he knows...

But it wasn't Moira who texted me.

It was an unknown number. I frowned, hiding the phone behind Bandit as I opened the message.

'You're late for work.'

I stared at the four little words. Late for work? Blue Ruby was closed. I had no clients, and devil knows none of them would say—

Slowly, I typed out, *'Who is this?'*

The reply was instant: *'A friend.'*

A friend, huh? I could message back and forth all day to try to weasel the identity out of them, but Moira doesn't have a day. She doesn't even have half an hour.

I watched the four demons in front of me as they talked strategy on how they would enter the house. Talked about who was needed, and who would stay. For my protection, of course.

You know what? Fuck them.

'Is my friend at work?'

I waited for the reply. The guys were now speaking in hushed tones between themselves, and I knew it was almost time.

My phone vibrated again.

'Yes.'

Shit. If that meant what I thought it did...

'Thank you.'

I clicked the lock button as the Horsemen broke apart and turned to me. It's been less than five minutes and already so much had changed. We now stood on two sides: me with secrets, and them in the dark.

I had no idea what would await them at home, but my gut told me it wasn't pretty.

"Three of us are going, one will stay behind. Decide," Julian said. If this was a test to see who I cared for most, then they were all fools.

I glanced between them weighing my options, a plan already forming in my mind. I swallowed hard hoping he wouldn't hate me when this was over. Praying I didn't read him wrong.

"Laran stays."

Julian's expression gave away nothing, and while Allistair was mildly jealous, he knew it wouldn't be him I chose. The only one who really took it to heart was Rysten.

The problem with Rysten is he cared for me too much for this. For what I needed.

Laran aligned with fire. With risks. With passion. With fury.

If anyone would listen, he would. If he didn't...I would cross that bridge when I came to it.

"I'm sorry," Rysten said. He looked like he meant it. I said nothing; not even a goodbye as he and Julian walked into the shadows and disappeared.

"Stay safe, little succubus," Allistair murmured. He turned and walked straight through an obscenely large mirror. I thought they had so many because he was vain, but a mirror walker made just as much sense. I filed that information away for later.

My phone buzzed one last time, but I didn't dare check it with Laran watching me so closely. He crossed the living room with sure and steady steps. Coming to stand between my legs as I remained perched on my barstool.

"You didn't choose me because you care more about me or to spite the other three."

"No, I didn't."

He nodded, stuffing his tongue in his cheek.

"Why did you choose me, Ruby?" He didn't say it hard or brash. It was honest; more resigned. Open.

"Because you're War. Because you're smart and you can think about your enemy if you stop thinking about me. So far, none of you have stopped thinking about *me*. Can you honestly tell me that you think this enemy would be so stupid as to tell me where my best friend is at, and even risk me telling you?" I was taking a major gamble here, but he'd yet to shut me down. I waited for a moment while he struggled with his own internal debate.

Eventually he said, "No."

"What would you do?" I asked, trying desperately not to keep checking the time. I needed him to believe me. To believe this. To see that I was smarter and better and stronger than they believed.

To trust me enough to not try to stop me.

He cocked his head for a moment, and for the first time I saw the wheels really turning. "I would set a trap and then I would move her, anticipating that you would tell us. That way, if you didn't, you were eliminated, and if you did, we were. Either way, someone dies. Then I would kill Moira and disappear into the night…" His lips parted as he stared at me. Was it shock? Or was it suspicion? Either way, we were running out of time. "She's not at your house. But you already knew that."

"I also don't think he waited to give her a lethal dose of black lotus. Moira is not a full-demon, Laran, and if he did, she is dying." I was breaking inside. My palms were sweating. My pulse was sprinting. I could barely think, and I didn't dare feel.

"You're right. She's not the real target."

"It isn't me either. It's you. You destroyed him for touching me. Julian killed whatever demons he had left. None of this was ever about me, and it only is now because he knows I'm the way to get to you." He did not flinch or look away, despite the hurt I knew that caused him. He blamed himself for that night so much more than I did, but I would not pull punches where the truth was concerned. Not when Moira's life was at stake. I refused.

"If anything happens to you, I will never forgive myself," he said, but I could see I was wearing him down.

"If anything happens to Moira, I will not be the Ruby you know. I will not give a damn if Hell freezes over and the apocalypse comes." Every word was like an ice pick against his armor. I pounded relentlessly at the bond he and the others had, asking him to do the unthinkable and turn against them. "I'm not asking you to kill me, Laran. I'm asking you to trust me. I am not defenseless and I'm tired of being treated like I am. I get that the world is dangerous, but how do you expect me to ever rule Hell if you do not let me make my own decisions? Moira is dying, and if we don't save her, then you will only have yourselves to blame if I become the beast that you are so hell-bent on having me learn to control."

His jaw tightened and I knew I hit a low blow, but we were out of time. It was now or never.

"Don't make me regret this," he growled.

Oh thank fuck. Now I just hoped we made it in time.

"We need to get to my shop. I think he's holding her…" I started for the elevator door when a swirling vortex of flame appeared before me.

"You can *pyroport*?" I asked, staring into what very well could be a portal to Hell. You'd never know until you crossed it.

"Aye," he breathed, linking my hand in his. "We're only going to have a fraction of a second before he realizes we're there. Your job is to handle Moira. Do not engage with him unless you're forced. We don't know how many will be there. Do you understand?"

I nodded, staring into the flames. Not so long ago, I was afraid of men and demons. I went out of my way to avoid them and keep my head down for the most part. Sure, I played with fire on occasion, but I always knew I was going to get burned.

For the first time in my life, I was willingly staring into the face of danger and I could truthfully say I was unafraid of it. Fire bathed my face, but I stared back at it ready for what I would find.

I was a friend of death, and a queen of demons, and a slayer of men.

I was a girl on fire, and the flames only answered to me.

****JULIAN****

She hated me.

More than any of the others, she hated me. But we couldn't let her go.

She didn't have a firm grasp on her abilities. Ruby was just as likely to kill the banshee as she was to save her, particularly this close to the transition.

She was a keg of gun powder waiting for a single spark.

When she goes off…

I hung my head because it didn't matter what happened tonight. I had failed her. She was my queen, and I made her my prisoner.

But I simply couldn't do it. Even if Moira dies and Ruby never forgives me…at least she's alive.

"It'll be okay, mate. She'll get over it." Rysten clapped me on the back. I bared my teeth and shook him off.

"No, brother, she won't. She'll forgive you because you're as bad as the fucking humans. But I don't think she'll forgive me," I mentally spat at him. We'd shadow walked to a house down the street from hers and clung to the darkness as we skipped down the row.

It was unnaturally quiet, like the calm before the storm. The pressure in the air was charged for a fight as we stepped into her front yard.

The shattered windows were boarded up, but no light peaked through. Not a single sign of life.

"Can you hear anything?" I asked Rysten. He paused and cocked his head.

"No heartbeat. Only her alarm clock ticking," he replied. I grit my teeth, clenching me jaw.

I was to go in first, through the front door, while Rysten entered the back, and Allistair kept watch outside.

"Allistair."

"I'm in place." he responded instantly. We could not see him, but that was the idea.

If we couldn't see him, neither could anyone else.

"I'm going in," I told them both. Rysten stepped back into the shadows, repositioning himself beside the back door.

"Three."

I crossed the yard in four bounds.

"Two."

I jumped onto the porch, landing about as light and soundless as a gunshot.

"One."

My boot connected with the door, kicking it clean off the hinges. I stormed into the house headed for the bedroom when I heard something.

"Julian! Julian, it's not an alarm clock, it's a—"

"Bomb," I finished.

Bam!

My skin shriveled and died as the layers were torn to shreds, fire burning and ravaging. Tendons and ligaments stretched and snapped as the impact shattered every bone in my body. I didn't have time to cry out or register the pain. Waiting for my body to repair itself, I focused on my remaining consciousness as my body was ripped apart at the seams. I could hear the echoed voices of my brothers in arms.

"He's down, and I can't reach War."

"What do you mean? Where the fuck is Ruby?"

"This whole thing was a trap. Where the fuck are they?"

I faded into the void where all souls go to cross over. If I were anything less than Death, I would be dead, but I was more than a human or a demon.

I was a god.

Immortal.

Filled with a wrath so cold, it burned.

He planted a bomb meant for Ruby.

Someone was going to pay in blood.

I flexed my fingers and opened my eyes.

The only thing more permanent and guaranteed than my immortality was how quickly I would end his life once I found him.

CHAPTER EIGHTEEN

WE STEPPED through the portal together and appeared inside my office. In only a fraction of a second, the portal was closed, but to our dismay—my office door was not.

From this angle, all you could see was the wall of the cubicle, and while it was silent, we were not alone. A slow clapping began. I looked to the doorway, but the sound wasn't coming from there. Nor was it behind us. The clapping echoed around and within, and from above, but below. It was everywhere, and that's when I knew I was in trouble.

I turned for Laran, but he was nowhere to be seen. It was like he disappeared.

But that can't be true.

Can it?

"I'm so happy you decided to show up, dollface. I didn't think you would figure it out, but pleasant surprises are *always* welcome." The demons voice echoed through my mind.

That couldn't be right. There wasn't an echo in here. This didn't make sense.

I took a hesitant step towards the door and maniacal laughter ensued.

Somehow his voice was blocking everything out. I could hear nothing but him, despite being certain Laran was still with me. He would never abandon me…but I couldn't see him.

Where had he gone?

I took another three steps towards the door when the room turned upside down. The floor was now the ceiling, but I was still standing on the floor. I turned in circles, when a touch ghosted against my back. I jumped and turned, but no one was there.

"Looking for me?" I whirled around to see the imp standing right behind me.

He wore a suit that fit well, and I instantly deemed it pretentious enough that Allistair would wear it. The jacket was navy blue with a white button up. Personally, I think it clashed with his eyes—

He doesn't have two eyes. He only has one.

So why were two watching me?

This made no sense. But then, that was the only part that made sense.

"This isn't real," I whispered. He smiled, and it was almost kind. Almost handsome.

"Very smart, dollface. My mother was not an imp, but a nightmare. She gave me some very useful gifts for making people pliant. Let's see how strong your mind is, shall we?" The smile dropped from his face as the ground dropped out from beneath me. I fell into free fall and appeared in a room that I wished I had forgotten.

My legs dangled uselessly at the end of the conference table. I struggled to move, to scream, to yell. No one came. Not as Josh dry humped my body or licked my breasts. Not as he undid my jeans and slowly started tugging them down.

Any second now…

Josh whipped them free from my legs. When this happened, I was able to retreat into my mind. That was not an option this time. I was stuck in my worst nightmare. Unable to wake up. Nowhere to flee.

Oh God, don't do this. Don't let this happen. What the fuck did I do to deserve…

Nothing. I did nothing to deserve this.

The first inkling of heat touched me, but it wasn't enough to break free.

It's not real. It's not real. It's not real. I chanted to myself over and over again. Maybe the guys wouldn't come, and maybe I was trapped inside some kind of nightmare, but that didn't make it real.

Just because I had to relive it didn't give it power over me.

As soon as the thought occurred to me, the memory shattered like glass. Breaking apart into a kaleidoscope of images that made up my history.

I fell deeper into the shards of my past and recoiled in horror when I landed.

Josh was terrible. I wished him dead. But this…

This was the real start of it all.

His name was Danny, and he was my first love. At least I thought he was.

We met here in Portland. He was reassigned to the orphanage I lived at. I was fifteen when we first met. Barely more than child, and definitely not a woman. We became fast friends, him and I. Even Moira liked him, which was a first. She literally liked no one but me.

And no one else since.

We knew each other six months before we went on our first date. He took me to Olive Garden. I spilled soup on myself, and because I was too self-conscious to go to the movies after that, we went back to the house and stargazed on the trampoline instead.

Six more months passed, but Danny changed…he grew more demanding in how much time I spent with him. He became insufferable after we had sex. He didn't like that I spent so much time with Moira and tried to get rid of her.

Of course, it was that night I revisited in this nightmare.

My footsteps creaked as I closed the door and crawled into bed. Moira was already out cold for the night. It was unusual, given she had trouble sleeping.

I pulled the thin blanket up over my chest and found myself lulled to sleep faster than normal. I woke, what felt like only minutes later, but when I did, I realized I was not alone.

I opened my mouth to scream as a rag was shoved in it, blocking my cry, constricting my airway. Horror racked my body as I realized who was in bed with me, and what he was doing.

He only used a mild sleeping sedative, thinking that would be enough. He didn't realize the fight I would put up when he got into bed.

Then again, I'm not sure that he was in his sane mind that night, or the months leading up to it.

I lashed out with everything I had, and I mean everything. My body was not strong enough to fight him and get away. I did not know about the beast. I did not have access to fire.

But I had something else.

I latched onto his mind and shredded it like paper.

It was the only thing I could do. I didn't see another way. Hell, I didn't even know I could do it…until I did.

I was so terrified, so hurt, so broken, that I lashed out and drove him mad. Of course, when he realized that I was causing it, he tried to pull away. He tried to run.

He didn't even make it three steps before he collapsed.

I wasn't going to let him get away.

He started babbling about how my touch drove him mad. He didn't consider what my mind could do.

But I was born with a unique ability so terrifying, I forced myself to forget it.

To forget what I did to him.

To forget what I am.

I didn't just shred his mind. I ripped apart his soul, and I didn't even need to touch him to do it.

Moira had awoken. She told me that I called to her. That I needed her. That he was hurting me.

She found him screaming and bashed his head in with a paperweight, leaving him bleeding, his eyes as wide and vacant as a doll.

She found me curled up in a ball. When she hugged me, it hurt less. When she helped me get rid of the body, she made it go away. When she cleaned the blood stain off the wood floors, she became my anchor.

I was drowning in the pain of that night and what I'd done. Because I remembered all of it now. Someone ripped the blinders from my eyes and made me remember what happened.

Remember that I killed his soul.

That Moira broke his body.

And we became sisters tied together by blood.

Once upon a time this memory had the power to break me.

So I forgot it.

Now, I remembered.

And the demon that had forced me to relive this underestimated how much I'd healed since then.

How much stronger I had become.

I couldn't find my flames in here, in this nightmare he created.

But he gave me an even deadlier weapon. And he couldn't take it back.

Mentally I reached out, searching for the very real essence that was all around me. Instinctively, he shied away. Running from the power. He only just realized his mistake.

I knew the moment he withdrew from my mind, because I found myself on my knees before him as he backed away towards the door.

A single eye stared back at me and I smiled, dark and lovely.

"You should have killed us when you had the chance," I said, but I did not give him another one.

He opened his mouth prepared to scream, but the time for screaming was over.

I ripped into him, rage fueling an immeasurable force, devouring his very soul.

Fire sprang to life at my beck and call, breaking his body apart until it was nothing more than glittering ash, dancing in the flames.

I waded through the fire, to the room beyond where I could hear Moira's heartbeat slowing as the drugs took effect in her veins. He was liar and I was killer, but I refused to let Moira be the consequence.

I refused to let her die.

"Ruby!"

I did not turn to the voice as I approached the chair where the demon strapped her down. It was a chair I knew well. I'd tattooed countless people in it.

Flames licked at the ropes, breaking them apart. Her unconscious body slumped over and I lunged forward to catch her. The beast slipping into place. She cradled my best friend as we picked her up and sank to the floor. Flames brushed over Moira's skin, but it did not burn or char.

Moira was immune to my flames.

"You're going to hurt her. I need Ruby back," Laran called, appearing above us. He was a sight to behold, bathed in a world of only fire. Like Moira, the flames did not seek to harm him.

"She is dying. I will save her because she is our tether. Ours to protect," the beast said in that same lifeless voice. She used my hands to cradle Moira's head with such care.

Moira's skin was so pale that it didn't even look green, only a sickly ash color that pained me to see on her. Her entire body was limp. The heartbeat in her chest fighting to keep pumping despite the drugs weighing it down.

This was Moira.

My Moira.

And she was going to live one way or another.

A brilliant blue light poured from my hands and into her temples. The fire worked quickly as it raced through her blood, burning the chemicals that threatened her life.

Maybe it was a blessing she was asleep for this because this kind of cleansing would not be easy. It was one thing to be immune to the flames, and another to be burned from the inside out. Still, the beast continued to pour fire into her veins until she started to scream.

If she was strong enough to scream, then she was strong enough to live. Then, and only then, did the fire die out. I saw Moira's eyes staring up into mine. No longer green, but cobalt blue marked with an upside-down pentagram that ran through her pupil and ringed in black.

"I marked you," I whispered.

And then I fainted.

****LARAN****

She consumed the world in fire.

The flames of Hell raged at her beck and call, incinerating everything she loved and held dear. Enslaved by her fury, and there was no possible way she could control them.

I was locked in my worst nightmare, so sure she was going to die. So sure that I had made the greatest mistake of my existence.

Then the scene shattered, and before me was not just Ruby or her beast, but an avenging goddess.

She struck him dead with a force from her mind that could not, and would not, be contained.

It was a force unlike any other, and for the first time, I wondered which half of her was stronger. The succubus girl that risked everything for her friend, or the beast that let flames loose upon this world.

I did not know, but this was going to change everything.

She was no longer just Lucifer's daughter, Hell's heir, or even a queen to-be.

She was my mate.

"Ruby!" I yelled, chasing after her through the flames. They did not burn me, but I could thank Lucifer for that. The banshee would not have the same immunity. If she killed her like this…it would break her. I did not doubt, not even for a second, that she meant what she said.

If the banshee died, she would not be the same, and both worlds would crumble.

I dived through the fire, unprepared for what I saw.

Ruby sat on her knees holding a half-demon who should not be alive.

No, not Ruby. The beast.

Her eyes were black as sin, void of any emotion.

Only pure obsidian gemstones that belonged to the creature who branded me.

"You're going to hurt her. I need Ruby back," I called. At first, I didn't think she heard me. How could she above the roaring of the flames?

But then she spoke.

"She is dying. I will save her because she is our tether. Ours to protect."

She is our tether…

How did we not see this? The bansh—Moira wasn't just a friend or family. She was Ruby's *familiar*.

This was the reason Ruby could hold off the transition. The reason we had no idea how strong she was. The reason Moira could withstand the flames…was because Ruby physically could not hurt her in any capacity.

Moira had taken on the role of the Horsemen and funneled the power because we had not been here. We just never realized it.

We had completely and utterly failed her before this night.

I fell to my knees before her, keeping my mouth shut.

The signs were all there and we never saw it.

Maybe it was time to watch and listen.

The beast laid her hands on the banshee's face. The smaller girl's normally spring colored skin was sickly and pale. Ruby had been right about that, too. The imp never waited, but I was not dumb or optimistic enough to think he would.

Blue fire spread from her fingertips, flaring to life beneath Moira's skin. It spread like plumes of smoke, lighting up every inch of her body until she glowed so bright that it physically hurt to watch, but I would not look away.

The banshee let out a scream as her eyes flew open. The flames receded instantly.

"I marked you," Ruby whispered.

I threw my arms out and caught her as she fainted.

Blue Ruby Ink was gone. Standing amongst the piles of ash were the Horsemen.

Watching Ruby and Moira with the same grim realization as I.

The world would come for both of them, and if anything happened to Moira…

Ruby would burn anything and everything to the ground.

Our job just got infinitely more complicated.

CHAPTER NINETEEN

I woke to the faint whisper of wind as it brushed across my face. Cool.
Gentle. I blinked once, taking in the darkness. After floating through a
suspended void, I couldn't really call my room at the apartment darkness.
Moonlight bathed the boxes aligned on the far wall and shimmering white
drapes stirred from a gentle breeze. Someone left the door open to the
balcony.

My legs were stiff and unwieldy as I slid them over the black bed sheets
and onto the soft carpet. I crinkled my toes, wrapping them around the
fibers beneath.

How long was out? How long had passed?

Reaching for my robe sprawled across the comforter, I shrugged it on. I
glanced back to the bed where Moira slept soundly. With her eyes closed, I
could pretend that it didn't happen. She looked much the same as normal,
apart from Bandit being wrapped around her. He clung to her shirt with
one paw and wrapped the other around his pink elephant. His face was
pushed up over her flat stomach, using her like a pillow. He definitely
drooled on her enough for one.

I smiled because they were safe. Inside, my heart was heavy with what
would come in the morning. Was Laran alright? Were the others? Someone
had to have brought us back here. Those were questions for the morning.

My legs protested as I rose from the bed and took shaky steps across the bedroom to the open doors. The flames of Hell were not nearly as physically exhausting as my other ability.

Soul-shredding, was it?

Something along those lines. I could ask Moira in the morning.

I reached out and grasped my hand around the edge of one of the balcony doors, using it to stabilize me while I crossed over the threshold and out into the night. My toes tingled against the cold stone. I wrapped my arms around myself, drawing the bathrobe tight. Not that it did much in this weather.

Twenty-three stories up in the dead of night...the view was breathtaking. Skyscrapers towered high around the city, but none so tall from where I was at. They lit up in shades of gold, blue, and green against a dark, starless sky. I truly felt small.

I drew in a deep breath, knowing I was not alone.

I knew she was there in the shadows where I could not see.

She'd been following me for some time now, after all.

"You know, some thought I was crazy for wanting to leave the south and live here. They called me a child because I saw the picture on a post card once and made it my mission to move. Far enough north to hide from most of demon-kind, but in a city of marvels so that I always had inspiration." My voice was hardly a whisper on the wind, but I knew she heard me.

"It's a great view. I'll give you that," she said quietly. The wind carried her words to my ears, as I gripped the stone ledge of the balcony.

"Why did you help me?" I asked, still not looking her way. She wouldn't kill me. If she wanted to do that, she would have let Moira die.

"Which time?" she replied.

The pressure shifted as her presence drew closer. I could sense brutal power and pain coming from it, but also...resistance. Where my own inner light was blue, this light was distinctly darker. A shade of indigo.

Startled, I realized that was her soul.

This was going to take some getting used to...

"You told me where to find her. How did you know I would listen?"

"I didn't, but I suspected."

"You suspected?"

"You knew someone was looking out for you, but in the end, it was your choice," she said.

"And the Seelie?" I continued, still staring at the skyline. I was going to learn to treasure these sights because they would be gone from my life very soon.

"I wish I could say it was out of the goodness of my heart, but it wasn't." She breathed out a very tired sigh. "You're the next ruler of Hell, and that makes you a very powerful person. A threat to my master. I was sent to take out the rogue demon, and to watch you, even kill you if I had the chance."

So the legions of Hell had arrived. The Horsemen weren't kidding.

Powerful people wanted me dead, and now, they knew where to find me.

"But you didn't," I said, drawing my eyes away from the view. She stood no more than three feet from me, almost exactly as I remembered her; the exception was a dark cloak, obscuring most of her body. Her snow-white hair reflected silver in the moonlight. She had it pulled back in a braid, the purple ends hidden from sight. The darkness made her mercury colored eyes more vivid and striking.

"No," she whispered. "I didn't."

"Why? I kicked you out of my house. I threatened you. You didn't even have to do it yourself, and I probably would have died…but you saved me. Why?" We stared at each other suspended in time. The wind did not move, nor did the sky. Not a single living being stirred, even those only feet from us.

"Because I was watching when the mob came to your shop and I saw what you did when they threw rocks at your family. I watched you, and I saw good. I saw a future for Hell that wouldn't be marked by blood wars and senseless killing." She averted her eyes to the heavens, but there would be no God that looked down on us this night. An assassin and a killer. Two demons entering something unholy and yet divine. "You have not been around long enough to see the things I have. The horrors our kind must either become or endure. You are not like the rest of us, not completely. You, Lucifer's daughter, can change the future of Hell. But more importantly to me—you can change my future."

A loose strand of white and purple hair slipped free from her braid, blowing in the wind. I wasn't sure if I should be thankful for what she did, anxious about the supposed future she saw, or concerned because now we had gotten to the heart of the matter.

"You want something from me."

"Yes," she replied. "Not right now, but later. Call it a favor for investing in your future."

"And yours," I said tersely. Her eyes narrowed as she watched me, debating if she made the right choice trusting me. I didn't fault her for it, just as I didn't fault her for expecting something in return. That was just how the world was; an exchanging of goods and favors. It's how empires were built, and queens were made.

I would do right to remember that.

People always said the road to Hell was paved with good intentions, but no one's intentions are ever actually good. We all are a little selfish. More than a little for most of us. I couldn't trust someone who walks with good intentions, but I could bargain with someone who had honest ones. The path to living wouldn't come without a price. This was hers.

"I owe you, and should I actually live long enough to rule—whatever that entails—well, you know how to find me." She relaxed just a fraction before whipping out one claw-tipped hand and swiping at me. I jumped back, hitting my back against the stone balcony, and my weak legs wobbled from over-exhaustion.

"What was that—"

I watched as she dragged the same claw across her own skin, my blood mixing with hers. A sizzling sensation spread across my left breast where she'd cut me. I pulled the fabric aside, to see a very thin but already cauterized scar.

"Blood magic," I whispered. I didn't dare say more.

"Consider it insurance that you make good on your word," she replied.

I swallowed hard and nodded. There was no point challenging something that can't be undone.

The she-demon turned away and I knew our meeting was coming to an end.

"Wait," I called. She paused and tilted her chin to the side.

"The text messages you sent me—they were written in code. Why?"

She smiled, like she was pleased with me. Certainly not surprised. "We are being watched, you and I. There are more coming."

"Who's watching?" I asked. There was no point in asking who was coming. The Horsemen had already warned me of this. Demons. From all over the world. The demon from the Black Brothers had known who I was, and I would bet my life savings he made sure the rest of the world knew it, too.

"I can't say."

"Is it your master?"

Again, she smiled. I was starting to get the hang of this. She could intervene, but only so far. I had to work for the answers I needed.

"There are powerful people in play. Trust no one, not even me, if you want to live long enough to see yourself on the throne. Evil doesn't just hide in the shadows." Her parting words made me shiver, and in the blink of an eye, she was gone.

I didn't bother searching up and down for her. She would turn up again when she wanted to be found, and not a minute before.

The first rays of a new dawn broke the cusp of the skyline as I returned to bed, only then realizing that I didn't even know her name.

CHAPTER TWENTY

It was all over the news the next morning. A fire burned down the entire strip Blue Ruby Ink was in. The kitchen on the other side of us had a wood oven. Press said someone didn't shut the chamber and the fire spread. The restaurant's furnace cracked and fire shot down the lines of the building, leveling everything in its path.

It was a freak accident, but luckily not a tragedy.

No one died. No one human, anyways.

I tugged my hood forward as I stood across the street from my old life. Blue Ruby Ink was gone. My house was gone. Ashes blew in the wind and mixed with the rain, coating the street before me in a black glittery sludge. Cold seeped through my thin jacket, burning my lungs with every breath, giving me the clarity to look at the scene before me and see it for what it was.

The last nail in the old me's coffin.

Was it fitting my fire would be the thing that took the place I loved away from me? It was certainly ironic. My life goes up in ashes, and from it I rise again.

That sounds nice, right? Motivational? Inspirational?

"What are you thinking about?" Moira asked. I tore my eyes away from the dreary, fucked up mess before me.

"That I'm tired of running from whatever comes next," I said. She grinned up at me, and the pentagrams in her cobalt eyes swirled like smoke.

"I guess that makes two of us. Do you want to ask the lazy fucks if they want a ride to Martha's, or make them work for their forgiveness?"

I grinned back at her, happy to see that at least some things don't change.

"I should probably offer. Try to smooth things over with them," I said begrudgingly. We walked a few yards down the sidewalk where Rysten and Julian waited. They'd tried to give me space since I woke up, but I didn't know if it was for me, or for them.

I suppose only time would tell how long it took to repair the trust on both sides. Moira would have died. So I didn't regret or even apologize for what I did. No matter how many I'm-sorry, but-please-never-do-that-again hugs Rysten tried to give me, or broken stares that Julian thought I didn't see. They could be sorry all they wanted, but it wouldn't make a damn difference. I wasn't changing, and if they thought I was going to let them make all my choices for me after we left…they had another thing coming.

"Would you like to ride with us? I want to get breakfast at Martha's before we leave," I asked them.

"That would be nice. Thank you, love," Rysten said, offering me his arm as I linked mine through it. I looked at Julian as I held out my other hand. He froze for a moment, until I turned it over and opened it. "You can drive."

Julian looked at the keys and a wiry smile came to his lips. He took them from me and strode ahead. A little more umph in his step. It would take time for us to fix this between us, but olive branches went a long way at bridging the gap.

"I call shot gun!" Moira said, stomping right after him. Yes, some things never change.

"I'm not sure what to think of this," Rysten muttered.

"Think of what?" I asked.

"You branded War *and* the banshee before me," he said. "And here I thought I was your favorite."

I chuckled under my breath as we sidled up to the car.

"I was saving Moira's life. You can't exactly be jealous about that," I said, fighting the smile that Rysten still seemed to be able to pull out of me. Even after all this.

"Just promise me something," he whispered in my ear.

"Mmmm?" I leaned in, grinning into the crook of his shoulder.

"I'm next," he growled. If my lady parts didn't just light up…I shivered into the soft caress of his lips. Oh yes, the beast was more than happy to make him next.

Filthy slut.

"Ahem," Moira coughed. I caught her arched eyebrow over Rysten's shoulder and started to pull away.

"Earn it," I whispered back to him. He chuckled under his breath and let me go. We drove to the diner in relative silence, or at least as much silence as could be expected when Moira was in the car and giving Julian driving tips.

Meanwhile, my mind wandered.

We had to leave Portland for obvious reasons and couldn't go to Hell just yet. Allistair would stay behind and get my home and business insurance settled, and then begin the process of getting all my shit moved across worlds. What was left of it, anyways.

Not to mention the questions being asked about the convenience of both my house and my tattoo parlor blowing up the same night. No allegations had been brought to the table, but Allistair would sort them out.

At the end of the day, it was mostly a ruse. He was sticking around to keep his ear to the ground. Trouble was coming, and I would be long gone by the end of the hour.

But I did want my things.

They still hadn't told us where we were going yet. All I got this morning were vague answers about Laran getting everything 'squared away.'

We pulled into Martha's Diner and my eyes pricked with moisture as I got out of the car. The door jingled the same as it always did when we walked in and we took my usual table. Kendall and her cronies were nowhere to be found and I suspected she wouldn't be for a good long while.

I slid into the booth and Rysten followed suit, with Julian and Moira taking a seat across from us.

"What will it be for you this morning, Ruby?" Martha asked, coming to us from behind the counter. She smiled without reservation. Good, she hadn't heard the news. That will make at least this goodbye easier.

"Four plates of bacon and black coffee."

"I don't know why I even ask."

It was the same conversation we had for ten years. I was going to miss the ease, but even now, it no longer felt quite so simple. When breakfast was over, it would be time for me to go.

"It's going to be okay, love," Rysten leaned in and whispered as everyone placed their order. That was all any of us said that even hinted at what's to come. The rest of breakfast was filled with Rysten's dry wit, typically at Julian's expense, while Moira and I laughed along.

When Martha brought the check out and wished me a happy Saturday, I smiled and wished her one as well. She would never know what happened to me, and I couldn't tell her. No one could know we were leaving, but I suppose the tip I left her would probably be a hint. I was the last to walk out of the diner and would not be there when she noticed that I had left my life savings and car keys on the table.

Granted, it wasn't much, but they were all I had to give to the woman that watched me from afar these past years and gave me a safe place to go. Eventually she would see the news, but maybe now she would know I was alright.

As we walked down an alley, the clouds opened, casting down a single ray of sunshine. I thought it was odd...then I realized what it was spotlighting. Or who, rather.

"Hi there, stranger," I called.

Laran saddled up to my side, Bandit riding perched on his shoulder.

"Alright, you've been holding out on us long enough. Where are we going?" Moira demanded, putting her hands on her hips. Apparently, I was the only one that believed in any kind of common courtesy around here.

"What is this about me holding out on you?" he asked me, completely ignoring Moira. She narrowed her eyes at him and I could practically see the wheels turning.

"Do I need to scream to—"

Before I could speak, a portal of fire appeared before me and someone pushed me through. I screamed for all of two seconds before landing with a thump on something soft.

What the fuck did he—

"MOTHERFUCKKKKKEEEEEEERRRRRR!"

Thunk!

I rolled over in the bed to see Moira sitting next to me, wide-eyed and pissed off.

"That asshole just pushed me through a portal," she cursed.

"Yes, well. Rest assured, we thought it was quite amusing," Rysten said, stepping out of the shadows.

"Allistair told me how much you loved being pushed off things," Laran laughed, appearing through a ring of fire.

"I might actually kill you," I spat, leaping from the bed to tackle him. Bandit jumped from his shoulder to protect himself and started making this awful choking sound. If I didn't know any better, I would say he was fucking *laughing*.

"Now, Ruby, are you sure you want to do that? Look outside," Rysten said right as I barreled into Laran, and to my credit, slammed him into a wall.

What the—

"Did that actually just happen?" Moira screeched. "Like, she really just *body slammed* War—"

"Ruby, love. Why don't you come here for a second?" Rysten asked, his pleasant tone coated in concern.

I stood still, shocked, both hands pressed on Laran's chest, trying to discern why my head was *so* hot.

I mean, it was burning.

I could barely even think—

"War, are you physically able to move?" Julian asked behind me. His voice was cool and calculated, emanating power.

Laran tensed against my hands, but didn't move a single inch. I pushed against him, harder this time. A crack ran through the house as he fell through the wall, landing in a heap of drywall and dust on the other side.

"Well that answers that," Julian noted.

"What the fuck just happened?" I asked, snapping out of it and pulling away.

"Well, love. It appears that you're entering the transition. You won't have more than forty-eight hours before it goes into full effect," Rysten said calmly. He approached me with his hands raised in surrender.

"Why are you acting like that?" I shouted, storming out of the room even though I had no idea where the fuck I was. Laran just pushed me through a damned portal and then—

I closed my eyes and cursed, taking in deep breaths.

In the background, I could hear the guys debating back and forth.

Something about Julian needing to man up and my impeccable timing. I opened my eyes and blinked. The emotions cleared just long enough for me to take in my surroundings. The fuzzy white carpet and black leather furniture. The startling glass wall in front of me, reflecting sunshine off the dust particles in the air.

The cityscape that every single demon child on the North American continent is taught to recognize.

New Orleans.

The city of the dead.

Also known as Hell's gates.

Fuck me.

To be continued…

A DAY IN THE LIFE OF BANDIT
THIS IS AN EXCLUSIVE SHORT STORY TOLD FROM RYSTEN'S POINT OF VIEW THAT TAKES PLACE DURING WICKED GAMES

I *really* didn't like the damned trash panda.

Yet, somehow, I was always the one that ended up watching him.

"Now be good, Bandit. Rysten is going to babysit for the day." Ruby embraced the mask-faced vermin for the third time that morning and he let out a little wail. Her shoulders sagged, and she gave him a rueful look before turning to me.

"You sure you got this?" she asked. Her hair was pulled up in some kind of messy knot, but the long strands of sapphire slipped through and framed her face.

I gave her an easy smile and lied through my teeth. "Of course, love. Everything will be fine."

No. It wouldn't be fine. My day was going to be a fucking waste of time, but I wouldn't tell her that. Even if the thought of babysitting the striped rat made me want to fester a plague of Ebola and watch a room full of humans die. Slowly.

She kissed me on the corner of the mouth and turned to leave. Behind her, the banshee rolled her eyes and started jamming the penthouse elevator button for the doors to close the very second Ruby stepped in. Either Ruby didn't notice, or she pretended not to. The doors slid shut and for the third time that week, I was left alone with Bandit. The raccoon let out a huff and waddled off to start rubbing his black fur and disgusting musky scent all over the white furniture.

I ignored him and left him to it. I'd learned this week that telling him to stop only made it worse. The thing had an uncanny way of knowing how to get under my skin.

I retreated to my office to check on the program I had running to sweep the cameras across Portland for signs of the imp. He'd disappeared like smoke in the night and getting a trace on him was proving to be more difficult than we'd thought. So far, every time he'd turned up, the trail ran cold. It was strange the way he disappeared, but we would catch him eventually.

We always did.

I sank into the cool leather seat and zoned in on the program, fiddling with it to see what could be improved. I couldn't have been working more than ten minutes when a loud crash came from the kitchen.

"Bloody hell…" I pushed the chair away from the desk and stalked down the hallway to see what the raccoon had gotten into.

Every single cabinet in the kitchen had been opened and the dishes pushed out. Broken pieces of glass and porcelain covered the counters and floors. Metal pots and pans lay discarded on their sides, and at the very back of the room, standing on top of the fridge, was the fucking raccoon.

"Now, listen here, mate. You really don't want to—" I lifted my hands and slowly made towards him like he was rabid.

What did the blasted thing do?

He shoved at the half-empty bottles of red wine, knocking them over. They fell through the air and landed with a smash, red liquid spraying the marble flooring and white cabinets.

Bandit lifted his head and started clapping, an evil glint in his eye.

I stopped and took a deep breath, running a hand through my hair. Ruby would never forgive me if I killed the little asshole. Or dropped him in the Siberian winter.

"You're lucky she loves you," I hissed.

The raccoon didn't reply, only jumped down and skipped across the counters before launching himself into the living room where he disappeared down the hallway.

Yes, Ruby would be vexed if the little rat died, but I would be fucking elated.

Alas, that's not how the world worked. Not the human world anyway. People apparently *liked* these fucking animals, or at least Ruby did.

I took a frustrated breath and started cleaning the kitchen. Sweeping up the broken shit was easy enough. Cleaning up the wine and little splinters of glass? Less so. Still, I scrubbed and bleached every inch of that kitchen until it shone again. After filling and tying off the second trash bag, I hefted both over my shoulder and debated between shadow walking and taking the elevator. It was only a short lift down and I didn't want to attract unwanted attention to myself should someone be in the garage.

But the vermin...

Could I leave him here on his own? I knew humans had strange rules about leaving children home alone, and the thing was only two years-old according to Ruby…but taking him with would be a massive headache. Besides, Ruby left him home all the time. It couldn't be that bad if she did it, right?

Maybe if I hurry…

With a sharp glance down the hall to where Bandit had disappeared, I pressed the button for the elevator and stepped inside. The apartment was all but silent when the doors slid shut. That should have been my first inclination that the striped rat was up to something.

I made the trip down to the garbage bin and back in less than three minutes. Really, there was no way he should be able to get up to anything in so little time… At least, that's what I told myself as I shifted uneasily waiting for the damn door to open. The elevator pinged, and I braced myself for the worst.

The living room was quiet and nothing *appeared* broken or ruined. I walked forward, carefully inspecting the furniture and rugs as I went. His fur was everywhere, but he hadn't pissed while I was gone or knocked anything over again. Maybe he really was done for the morning.

I brushed off the sense of unease as I went back to my office and the door was open. *He opened the fucking door.*

All of the monitors were black. Mostly. Some of them had lines of color: purple, blue, and red. The scent of raccoon piss hit me with a pungent vengeance. I stopped and crouched down to check the multiple computer cases on the ground. As I'd suspected, the cords were unplugged or chewed through, and one of the larger cases had a puddle of piss beneath it.

I let out a low growl and turned for the door.

"Bandit!" I yelled. "Bandit when I find you—"

CRASH!

I stood there, and for the first time in my immortal existence, I wondered how stay-at-home mothers did it. How did they not end up killing their children? After this, I had the utmost respect for anyone that chose to spend time with kids or pets. They were both germy and disgusting and protected by laws that I would have broken in the case of Bandit—were Ruby not a factor.

Staring at all my ruined gear, I couldn't find it in me to give a shit what he had just broken. I was already going to need to order thousands of dollars in electronics to replace the shit he had literally pissed on—not to mention all the broken plates in the kitchen and the rare bottle of wine I had gifted to Ruby. Despite all of that, it was the time wasted that pissed me off. I'd have to start over hacking into the city's cameras to look for the imp, and starting over means we are not tracking him now. While replacing the wine wouldn't be terribly difficult, that particular bottle was quite old and one of her favorites. Finding another from that batch wouldn't be easy to run down. Then there's the matter of cleaning out all of the broken equipment and getting the stench of piss out of the carpet.

I sighed.

Nope. I couldn't find the fucks to give.

That's it. We were leaving.

I didn't care where we went or what we did, but at least if he broke something outside of the apartment, I wouldn't have to replace it. And if he went missing…well, that was an added bonus. I'd get Ruby a puppy once we settled in Hell. Women liked puppies, right? Nice animals. Docile. No grabby hands to climb with.

Now that gave me an idea. I knew exactly where I would take him for the day.

"Bandit! Oh, Bandit! We're going on an adventure," I called out to the raccoon as I came around the corner. He stood beside one of Allistair's many mirrors—this mirror now lay in a thousand shattered pieces.

I ignored the urge to throttle him and instead went for my shoes. We had a field trip to go on.

I slipped my foot inside the first sneaker and froze.

"What the—?" I tugged the shoe off and lifted it, leaning in to take a whiff.

Disgusting. Absolutely disgusting.

I peeled the sock off that was now covered in raccoon feces and tossed both it and the ruined shoes in the trash.

Our excursion was on temporary hold.

First, I needed to find new shoes that he hadn't already taken a dump in —then we were going out. Somewhere that he could be the feral animal he was without me having to care.

The dog park.

*

As it turns out, raccoons don't care for wearing a leash. Who would have thought? Bandit sat on the compacted dirt beside me, hissing and spitting as he tried to forcibly remove the collar from his neck, but the dog park had rules. No collar. No entrance.

I pulled on the leash to get him to cut it out, but all the little bugger did was turn and hiss at me. A young woman walked by wearing a tracksuit and sneakers, her eyes were hidden behind dark sunglasses, but the firm tug of her lips as she pulled her golden retriever quite forcefully around us was telling. Two men walked by, one of them holding a puppy that was wriggling to get out of his arms to try and come see Bandit. Both owners stopped and stared at the raccoon for a second, then me. After thirty seconds of holding their stare, they turned and walked right back out of the gate, muttering about feral animals being diseased.

"Now, now. The other owners are giving you funny looks. Stop that."

He did not stop.

A pack of three dogs were playing off to the side of Bandit. One great big black animal wrestled with a smaller russet brown one. They were a tangle of saliva and teeth that had me grimacing. The third stood off to the side barking. I couldn't tell why. Maybe it didn't like to be left out? Bandit let out a growl towards the noisy animal and all three turned his way. The one barking froze and slowly approached the hissing raccoon. Bandit drew himself back and bared his teeth, his coarse hairs standing on end.

It probably should have occurred to me that allowing another creature in his zone while he was angry wasn't a good idea, but I didn't particularly care. I was so ready for this day to be over and hand him back to Ruby.

The hesitant dog approached and whined, its tail wagging uncertainly. I don't speak dog, but I think he wanted to play with Bandit. Unfortunately, Bandit liked to play with no one.

The raccoon turned and lunged. It was only my quick hand tugging on the leash that kept him from killing the damn thing. The dog let out a surprised yelp and backed away, its tail between its legs. Its owner seemed more preoccupied by the cell phone in his hand than the crying fur mass at his feet. I shook my head, but at least it was one less person giving me weird looks.

"How are you going to make friends acting like that?" I asked him.

Bandit returned to clawing at the collar and gave me a death stare.

Maybe this wasn't the greatest idea. I had a feeling I would need to start checking my shoes regularly.

A ringer beeped as my cell phone started vibrating.

"Rysten," I answered.

"Hey," Ruby paused, and the sound went dead for a moment before she was back. "So, I might have forgotten that Bandit had a vet appointment scheduled for today."

"Okay." Inside I was slowly shriveling up and dying. A vet appointment? With the trash panda?

Nope. Not happening. No fucking way—

"I'm kind of running late with a client. I was hoping you could take him and I could meet you there…"

Her voice trailed off, like my silence had clued her into how I might feel about this. I lowered the phone for a second to let out a heavy sigh. "I could call and ask Laran, if it's too much of a—"

Any resistance I felt flew out the window. "Nope, I'd love to help."

Fuck me. Did I really just say that?

Yeah. I did.

"Are you sure? I know Bandit hasn't been the easiest for you…" she started, and while the concern in her voice was nice, there was no way in Hell I was handing this task off to Laran. He was already branded as the first mate *and* the raccoon liked him. I needed to earn some brownie points here if I was going to catch up.

"It's no problem at all, love. Just let me know when and where."

Right as I finished speaking, two other dogs approached Bandit, growling. He stopped tugging at the collar and paused for a heartbeat, then launched at the animals, swiping viscously. The owners ran up, yelling at me and Bandit as they pulled their animals away, sending both me and the raccoon filthy looks while muttering under their breaths about dog parks being for dogs.

"Is that barking in the background?" Ruby asked.

"Nope. No barking," I said, only half-paying attention as I pulled Bandit away from taking a snap at someone. The asshole turned and sunk his teeth into my leg. I groaned inwardly as I grabbed him by the scruff and attempted to pull him away from my calf. He bit down harder.

"Strange. I could have sworn—"

"Hey, love, if you text me that info, that'd be great. I'm a little bit busy right now."

My voice was smooth and easy. There was no way she could tell how hard I was lying without her empathic abilities to help her. Even when I was currently glaring down at a certain furry creature that insisted on taking a chunk out of me.

His teeth stung like a bitch. This "little biting problem," as Ruby liked to call it, was really getting out of hand.

"Sure thing. The appointment is in half an hour. I'll send the address right now." The sound of her voice took me to my happy place, and for a moment, I could pretend her 'pet' wasn't trying to eat me.

"Thanks, love. I'll see you shortly."

"You too."

The line went dead, and I pocketed my phone before returning my attention to Bandit. He glared at me stubbornly, like it was my fault he was angry. It probably was, but I'd tried. He hadn't made any effort at all. Fucker.

"Let go of my leg," I demanded. He chomped down harder. "Damnit, let go of me, you vermin—"

"Excuse me," a shrill voice said. A woman was hovering beside me. I couldn't tell her age through the pound of make-up caked on her face, but she appeared to have overdone the Botox as well. She looked like the kind of woman that would put plastic over her couch cushions and spend a fortune on fine china she'd never use.

"Yes?" I asked, letting the annoyance bleed through.

"This is a dog park." The woman straightened her designer handbag, self-importance oozing from her.

I rolled my eyes. "Really? I hadn't noticed all the dogs," I said.

Her polite smile turned brittle. "*That's* not a dog."

I nodded like I was listening.

"And I'm not a human. Do you have a point? Because I'm a little busy here." I kicked out my leg for emphasis. I decided she looked like a Barbara.

"Excuse me?" she asked, utterly shocked by my lack of manners. Tough shit.

There was only one she-demon I bothered with the theatrics for and this lady and the puffy white ball in her arms weren't it.

"Bandit, I would really appreciate you letting go right about now." I turned my attention back to the raccoon at hand. Or leg, as the case may be. He stopped gnawing and looked straight at me. Then he flicked the leash.

Message received.

"If I take the leash off, do you promise to stop biting me so we can go to the vet?"

Wild animals can't speak English, or so I assumed. But still I tried to reason with it—he seemed to respond better when I didn't just assume what the asshole wanted.

A nod.

Too bad it turned out the vermin could lie. As soon as I undid the leash, he released me and rapidly turned to spring at Barbara. She wheeled away, her expression a mix of fear and outrage. Maybe she was worried about getting rabies?

I shrugged to myself as I grabbed him in midair by the scruff of his neck and carried him towards the car. Bandit attempted to claw and bite me, but his efforts were wasted since his portly stomach prevented him from reaching out too far.

How am I going to get him back in the cat carrier now that he's a hissing, spitting ball of fur?

The answer: carefully.

*

"Hello?" I called out, slowly opening the front door.

There had only been one car outside, but the faded sign that read *Exotic Pet Whisperer* meant this was the correct place. Not that I would ever call a trash-eating mongrel 'exotic,' but I wasn't about to question Ruby's choice of vet.

A bang sounded in the back and the door directly in front of me opened. With it came the stench of sickness and wet dog. A disgusting, if not expected combination. Out stepped a frazzled woman who appeared to be in her mid-twenties, her curly brown hair pulled back tightly and her large circle-shaped glasses seeming almost comical.

"Are you Dr. Lummus?" I stepped up past the empty front desk that had seen better days. Her receptionist should really dust around here.

"I am," she replied. Her voice lilted unnaturally, and I instantly disliked it. "How can I help you?"

"My..." I paused. What was the correct word to describe who Ruby was? Queen? Future mate? No...those all seemed barbaric for what they liked to call each other. "...partner asked me to bring in her raccoon for a checkup. She said she made an appointment."

The vet paused for a second before smiling. "That's right. I completely forgot about it, what with lunch break and all..."

"It's four in the afternoon." *How astute, Rysten.* I was being a bit of an ass, but something felt off here.

"We vets keep odd hours," the woman replied without blinking. I nodded slowly and approached her with Bandit's cat soft carrier. The furry rat hissed as we got closer, but since he liked no one but Ruby and Laran, I assumed his behavior was a given.

"Where would you like us?" I asked, noting the shelves of animal food lining the walls. Mis-grouped cans were hastily placed together. I'd never had a pet before, and so I'd never needed to go to a vet, but this one didn't seem to have its shit together. Ruby was a bit eccentric though, so I guess her choice wasn't that surprising.

"We can just step into the back room here." Dr. Lummus opened the door and ushered us through. The exam space had a simple table, two chairs, and a counter with assorted jars and a weighing scale on it. She motioned for me to place the kennel down on the table and take a seat. Bandit swiped a paw at the netted side with his claw extended, tearing a hole in the fabric.

"Fucking racoon," I swore as I moved to stop him.

Bandit wasn't slow though, despite the pot belly. He clawed his way out of the carrier, screaming his head off and destroying it in the process. He then scrabbled across the table, *away* from the vet.

Dr. Lummus reached for him, but the bugger leapt off the table and onto my lap, climbing his way up my chest to my shoulder where he perched there like a fucking bird, growling at her.

"You've treated him before, haven't you?" I asked, trying and failing to forcibly remove him from my shoulder. He hooked his talons in tighter, piercing the skin beneath my white cotton shirt. Speckles of dark blue blood bloomed on the material, ruining the ivory fabric.

I glanced back at the vet, who hadn't answered my question and paused in my raccoon-extraction.

Her brown eyes were large and wide, the pupils dilated, as she stared at the blood on my shirt. The pupils themselves morphed into narrow slits. My mouth fell ajar as her nose grew, turning into a long snout, her skin becoming ashen and moist. The woman's body began stretching as she grew taller. The sound of tearing fabric echoed through the room as she grew, and instead of a young woman, there was now what looked like an eight-foot-tall albino crocodile standing on two legs, glaring with reptilian eyes.

Skinwalker.

Fuck. Fuck. Fuckity fuck.

No wonder the damn raccoon didn't want to go near it. That thing *ate* people, and it was probably planning on eating us—along with the vet, if it hadn't already. After all, I doubted that Ruby would take her vermin to a carnivorous people eating monster for a checkup.

The skinwalker focused on us with its slitted eyes. The color around the pupils had changed from brown to an angry yellow.

"Now hold up here—" I started. The monster threw back its head and laughed, a deep and haunting sound. Behind the guffaw, a scream tore through the room. Its stomach bulged, moving as whatever had been its lunch started thrashing.

"Mmmm," the skinwalker murmured. "Tasty, tasty."

A flat gray tongue snaked out of his mouth as the skinwalker continued to stare at the tiny blots of blood on my shirt. Bandit let out a growl and bared his teeth, but the demon didn't even notice the warning sound.

"Get me out of here!" someone screamed. It had come from *inside* the demon. The voice sounded high. Feminine.

Shit.

I *could* cause a massive bacterial growth that would kill the damn thing in under a minute, but whoever was trapped in there—probably Dr. Lummus—would die too.

I looked to the ceiling and kicked myself internally.

The other Horsemen were right. I am hanging around humans too much.

"Dr. Lummus?" I called out. Mentally I chanted, *please don't be her.* Then I can just kill this thing without pissing off Ruby.

"Yes! It's me! Help! Please get me out of—"

The skinwalker jutted its head back, wrenching its mouth open, it made a gagging sound, followed by a pungent smell of cat piss, barf, and rotten eggs.

"Oh, that's disgusting." I pinched my nose with two fingers.

Grabbing hold of the raccoon, I dove out of the chair and bumped into the one beside it as the body-snatching bastard lurched forward and spewed an oily yellow substance at me. It splashed half the wall and the chair I'd just been sharing with Bandit.

I felt like I was going to be sick and I was the devil-damned Horseman of Pestilence. Nothing in either world compared to the stench their acidic venom put off. It and the flames of Hell were one of the few things that could kills demons outright. After eons of death, decay, rot, and plagues, you'd think it wouldn't bother me. Just one more 'human' thing the guys would give me shit for. Ugh, but that smell...

The chair melted, the acid-like substance eating through the floor as well as half the wall, opening a window into a second exam room and earth below. I glanced between the yellowish guck on the ground and the skinwalker that was backing away from its own acidic venom.

I leaned over and grasped the half of the other chair that hadn't melted yet. Gripping the sturdy metal leg, I snapped it off from the base and tossed the rest of the chair into the steadily growing pile of dissolved wall.

Wielding the metal leg in one hand, I swung it like a bat, smashing the skinwalker in the jaw. Its massive, footlong mouth snapped with a bone-crunching sound and it shrieked in pain. It recovered quickly and leapt forward. I dodged, Bandit clinging to my shoulder precariously and screaming as my back hit the still-intact segment of wall.

The skinwalker ran for us and I side-stepped, wincing as the demon smacked into the wall and bounced off. I reached around behind me, feeling for a door handle, but there was nothing except smooth plaster. Fuck. A light switch jabbed into my back and I got a wicked idea.

Skinwalkers had two things in their favor: the most corrosive acid spit known to any creature, and a hulking size that gave them great strength and durability.

Know what they didn't have?

Good eyesight.

I flipped the switch and shadow walked through the darkness, falling into the grey behind me and coming out on the other side of the room behind the demon.

"First rule of picking a fight—make sure you can win."

I swung the metal leg a second time and cracked him on the head. He didn't even have time to react as his brains splattered the remaining wall. As it started to collapse, I lunged forward, catching it just before it landed in its own acid. Pulling it through the shadow realm with just a slight redirection and small amount of power, I let the body drop inside the lobby, where the floor was solid and smelled a lot better.

Given that the vet building was kind of dingy, that wasn't really saying something.

I couldn't hear any screams from Dr. Lummus as I flipped the carcass over. Striking just above where its stomach bulged, I stabbed through the thick layer of skin and pulled the sharp edge of the chair leg downward. It cut through the hide about as easily as a plastic knife through a watermelon rind, but with persistence, there was a hole big enough for the doctor's head to pop out.

Blood and mucus smeared across her face and hands as she pushed her shoulders through the opening and wriggled her way out. I turned the skinwalker on its side so gravity would help her the last bit of the way. She hit the linoleum floor with a wet thud and body juices from the skinwalker poured out behind her.

"Are you alright?" she asked. "You look like you're going to be sick."

"You're covered in all of that *stuff*. Shouldn't I be saying that to you?" I responded, a bit incredulous.

Bandit jumped off my shoulder and approached the woman, sniffing the air cautiously. I went to pull him back away from the woman whose smell was nauseating, and the raccoon smacked me away. Clearly I was chopped liver now that the brat didn't have to fear for his life. Ungrateful shit.

"Well, it's not ideal. Can't say it's the first time a skinwalker has swallowed me. I always date the wrong guys." She shook her head and scratched Bandit behind the ear, leaving a smear of grossness. The raccoon purred, all but forgetting how I'd just saved his furry little hide.

"You mean to tell me you *dated* this guy?"

"And his brother," she replied happily enough. I shook my head and did a double take of her. Now that I could see her, she was clearly a demon, but not full. Succubus, if the lilt in her voice was to be believed. She had nothing on Ruby, but it explained why my blue-haired firecracker would come to her. A fellow succubus would be less likely to feel the draw and wouldn't put up with bullshit. Given how well she was taking her dead boyfriend trying to eat her, I'd say she was going to be just fine.

"Something tells me you don't have a lot of luck with our kind," I muttered.

Dr. Lummus smiled. "No, I can't say that I do." She let out a raucous laugh. "Let me take a quick shower in the back and I can give Bandit his exam. Ruby mentioned something about Moira and being worried about tinnitus."

I snorted. If anyone was going to end up with tinnitus, it would be me.

"That would be lovely, thank you." I backed away from the dead skinwalker pretending nonchalance. The smell was getting to my stomach.

"No problem, it's the least I can do." She stood and turned for the hallway that must lead to this supposed shower. "And Rysten," she paused, waiting for me to look up. "If the smell is too much, there's a trashcan behind the desk. We keep it for the interns with weak stomachs."

The smile she gave while covered in guts was unnerving.

*

The sun was setting on Portland when we walked out of the office. Dr. Lummus held Bandit in one arm — and a can of sardines that she apparently kept for when he came in — in the other hand. The fat lard was purring like a cat while she rubbed his belly and fed him smelly fish, all the while giving me dirty looks like I was the reason his day had been so terribly stressful. The one time she'd tried to hand him over to me, he let out a stinky fart and scrabbled to get away, lifting his tail to show me his asshole while he was at it.

A car door shut just behind me. "I'm so sorry I'm late," Ruby called across the parking lot.

Dr. Lummus flashed her a smile and a sardine-filled wave, no mention of the dead body in her office.

"It's no trouble at all. I was just telling Rysten that Bandit's looking great and his hearing doesn't seem to have suffered at all from Moira." She winked at Ruby as she handed over the raccoon. His baby act with Dr. Lummus was nothing compared to the show he put on for Ruby. I bit my tongue.

"Oh, awesome. I was worried about how he would do for his check up without me. Was he good?"

"Better than he's ever been. I think he's a little fonder of Rysten than he was of your last guy," she snickered.

I doubted that she knew Josh was dead, but Ruby paled for a second before allowing a nervous laugh. Hatred of the human that had hurt her stirred the darkness inside of me, but my rage wasn't for the vet and so I stowed it away, wearing as much a mask as the one that Dr. Lummus wore for Ruby.

"Yes, well that's good to hear. Rysten's a little more…permanent than the last one." She gave me a small smile and my heart thudded.

"Aw, good for you," the doctor told her. "I have a few things I need to clean up before heading home for the evening, so I'll leave you to it." She shook my hand and waved at Ruby, stepping back inside her clinic like it was just another day at work. Hell, for her it might have been. All the better Ruby not know.

"How was Bandit for you today?" she asked, her voice hopeful. She was trying so hard to make it all work that I smiled and nodded.

"He was great, love. We still on for dinner tonight?" I asked her, smoothly deflecting from the demon in her arms. There were hellbeasts that I would rather watch more than that thing.

"Definitely, let me just drop Bandit at the penthouse and we can pick up Moira from the shop on the way." I kissed her on the cheek and watched her turn for the car.

Dinner with the banshee was not my preference, but I'd take it.

After the day I'd had, I'd take just about anything that didn't involve the trash panda. Something told me that Hell wasn't going to know what hit it when we got there, because Ruby and Bandit were nothing but trouble.

As Ruby unlocked her car, the raccoon looked at me over her shoulder with too much awareness to be just a dumb animal off the street—and then he winked at me.

That fucker. I didn't know how to interpret raccoon, but that couldn't be good. There was definitely something going on with him, but that was a problem for another day.

I had a dinner to go to, and a she-demon to impress.

The End.

INFERNAL DESIRES

CHAPTER ONE

I was on fire.

At least it felt that way as I turned from the wall of glass that left all of New Orleans on display. The city of the dead. We were at Hell's motherfucking gates, and what happens?

I started the transition.

How long did Rysten say I had before it fully set in? Forty-eight hours? And then what?

I shivered and it sure as hell wasn't because I was cold. I was half-succubus and half…the beast. Pre-transition, I burned down Blue Ruby Ink. I branded Laran *and* Moira. I shredded the nightmare imp's soul. And I've nearly fucked all of the Horsemen but one.

So…what would I do during the transition? Would it even be me—or would it be the beast?

I sighed roughly, running a sweaty hand through my hair.

This was all assuming I didn't spontaneously combust into flames by then.

"Everything alright, love?" Rysten asked, pulling me back to reality. I blinked away the haziness to see him standing in the doorway.

"You said I have forty-eight hours. What happens then?" I asked, my throat already dry and scratchy. I took another step toward him and stopped abruptly when I felt a shift in the air. It was almost undetectable. His eyes dilated and he shut them, inhaling deeply.

And when he opened his eyes, it wasn't the Rysten I knew and cared for.

I blinked as a mist formed around him. Individual flecks of white formed on his skin. Gathering and condensing as they slowly built, it fell around him like snow…or ash. Oddly beautiful. Terrifyingly strange.

"Are you seeing this…" my words trailed off as he took another shuddering breath. He let out a groan.

"So sweet," he murmured.

I frowned, narrowing my eyes. The mist shifted and swirled around him, twisting and pulsing in sync with something. *His heart.*

"What happens then?" Those three little words came out far more seductive than I thought possible. I took a step closer and Rysten's eyes darkened from green to nearly black, but not with rage. With…

"Either your succubus nature or the beast will take over. Possibly both." His tongue darted out, licking his bottom lip. The heat inside me climbed ever higher. Pretty soon I was going to be at risk of passing out. Maybe that was for the best, considering the look Rysten was giving me.

"And then?" I asked hoarsely, my voice no more than a whisper. He smiled, but there was nothing boyish or cute about it. A feral look had entered his eye, that of a predator with only one purpose.

"You will need to feed." He took three steps towards me before my brain realized what he was doing. The haze was already starting to descend again. The pulsing heat inside, guiding me towards it. Towards him.

"What are you doing?" I whispered through chapped lips. My legs shook the closer he came, and I wasn't sure if it was exertion or need. Even in his scary as fuck state, I was incapable of feeling truly afraid. He wouldn't hurt me.

Rysten crossed the distance between us with measured steps. By the time he was standing before me, his eyes were completely black. Not a trace of any color in sight.

I bit my lip, simultaneously fighting the urge to lean into him and to faint. Rysten made my choice easy, reaching out and wrapping a strong arm completely around my waist. He gripped my hip, claw-tipped fingers biting into the skin just beneath my thick sweater. I let out a low moan and breathed deeply.

His scent hit me like a freight train and I wrapped both my hands in the material of his shirt. Rysten took that as all the invitation he needed. He reached up with his other hand and buried it in my hair, using his hold to guide my head back. My body turned to Jell-O at his touch as the burning inside me grew out of control, seeking some sort of release.

He brought his lips to mine and every thought vanished.

I simply couldn't think, couldn't feel anything beyond his lips as they melded to mine. He kissed me with such passion that I was blindsided by lust. Consumed by it.

Enough so that I didn't think twice when he dropped one arm from my waist to my ass and hoisted me up. I wrapped my legs around him without needing to be told. The hard bulge in his pants rubbed against me, causing a frenzy to set in.

I placed my hands on his shoulders, relishing in the hard, corded muscle I found there. My fingers teased his collar, dipping inside his shirt before my impatience got the better of me. My fingers wrapped around the thick fabric and pulled. Buttons popped as I ripped his shirt down the middle. My hands flattened over the smooth skin of his chest. He growled in approval, making my stomach flutter. Inside, the flames fanned hotter.

My back touched cool glass, clearing my head just enough to know this wasn't normal. I may be a bit horny more often than I liked to admit, but I didn't usually jump someone's bones in two seconds flat. I pulled back from our kiss to breathe and ask him what the hell was going on. Rysten used that brief half a second to grind into me, trailing a delicious row of kisses and bites down my neck.

My head lolled back, resting against the glass while arching my back to give him better access to *everything*, because in that moment nothing else mattered. Only the burning within and between us that kept me in a hazy reality where the only thing that made sense was his skin on mine.

"What the—"

The sudden interruption was loud enough to register but not enough to permeate the blazing heat that gripped me. One moment I was pressed against the glass, and the next I was on my hands and knees.

A savage snarl escaped my lips as I looked up at the two Horsemen that restrained Rysten, his pitch black demon eyes locked on mine.

"You're a fucking idiot," War snapped at him. He moved to put Rysten in a headlock and Death let him. I let out a warning growl of my own as outrage took hold of me and acted. It didn't even occur to me that the beast was goading me into it until after I shoved Julian out of the way and bitch-slapped Laran.

I stopped dead in my tracks as the haze cleared again and dread formed in my stomach. Laran stood stock-still, gaping at me as he dropped Rysten like a lead weight. Whatever trance-like lust seemed to have fallen over him snapped the moment he hit the ground. His eyes cleared, turning back to a vivid dark green as the ivory mist around him evaporated.

I shook my head, trying to make sense of the craziness.

"Ruby, love, I am *so* sorry—" His apology broke off when Laran kicked him in the head.

"Hey!" I snapped at Laran, the spiraling rage that started this all leapt to the forefront again. "What the hell, Laran?" My fists clenched on their own accord, but I kept myself from taking a swing.

"Ruby," Julian said in a deceptively soft tone, "do you realize your hands are on fire?"

I dared a glance at my hands to see that blue fire did indeed consume them. The tendrils skated up my arms, as high as my elbows, but didn't burn.

I swallowed hard again and grit my teeth, willing the fire to go out.

Of course, it wasn't that simple.

At first, nothing happened. It didn't shrink, but it also didn't grow. In some ways, I called that a win. After all, almost every time I've used the flames, someone has either died or a building burned down. So in some ways, nothing happening was an improvement.

Until my clothes caught.

"For fuck's sake," I groaned, turning to the beast inside me. She extinguished the flames without making me ask, but I didn't miss the vicious smile that followed. The beast knew what was going on here. That very soon I would have little to no control.

In a matter of days there would be no one to truly stand between the beast and the world.

No one except the Horsemen, that is.

I guess it's a good thing this was what they were created for, because looking after me is turning out to be a full-time job.

CHAPTER TWO

I STEPPED around Laran with a huff, striding down the hallway. Moira stood in the doorway, bent over at the waist, laughing so hard she swayed sideways and bumped into me. I rolled my eyes and grabbed her arm, hauling her into the bedroom behind me before slamming the door shut. It wouldn't keep the Horsemen away forever, but it might give me a few minutes reprieve.

The door pounded behind me.

"For the love of—" I cracked the door, but Julian was the one I least expected to find.

"Ruby, I know this must be—"

"Five minutes. Can I have five fucking minutes to myself?" I snapped. Julian didn't flinch, and he didn't leave.

"With the transition starting in—"

"Rysten said I had forty-eight hours. I'm asking for five minutes." Refusing to back down, I held his gaze before it turned glacial and impassive.

"Fine." The muscle in his jaw ticked. I moved to shut the door, but he caught it with his hand. "If I hear anything—"

"Five. Minutes," I repeated, pushing against the door. It didn't budge until he pulled away, giving me a tight nod as he did.

The door clicked shut and I turned, leaning back and resting my head against it. Staring at the ceiling, I finally got the nerve to say, "What am I going to do?"

"Same thing you always do," Moira said. I rocked my body forward, pushing off the door. My gaze dropped to my best friend as I cocked an eyebrow in her direction, silently asking what that was. She pursed her lips and said one word. "Survive."

Bandit walked over to me and tugged my jeans. I leaned over and scooped him up in my arms, walking over to sit on the white feather comforter. Moira joined us, sprawling out beside me.

"I'm scared," I whispered into his fur. He purred, nuzzling against me.

"Of course you are," she scoffed. "I'd be worried if you weren't." Moira arched up to tuck both her arms behind her head like she didn't have a care in the world. She did, but it was only my empathic abilities and years of watching her that told me so. "But you have me," she continued, very self-important-like. "And the trash panda *and* the Horsemen. At least part of them, when they're not trying to fuck you." She snickered and Bandit let out this god-awful rasping sound. I splayed a hand over my forehead, swiping it down my face, letting out an exasperated sigh.

"That's what I'm worried about," I muttered. "What if the Horsemen can't stop me? What if—" I paused, steeling myself to tell her the truth. To say my next words. "What if the beast emerges and I end up killing everyone in New Orleans?"

Moira seemed to ruminate on her response, sucking the air between her teeth before replying, "I don't think it will come to that."

I squinted at the ceiling, tilting my head. "How do you figure that?"

"Two reasons. The first is that all four of those lazy fuckers have a raging hard-on for you. I thought Julian was going to bend your ass over and fuck you there when you started growling at them all come-hither-like on your hands and knees," she chuckled again.

"I did not—"

"Oh yes you did," she smirked, wagging her finger. "Save the modesty for someone else. You've been my best friend for over ten years. I know what you're like when you get horny and can't fuck. Hello, welcome to the past five years."

I rolled my eyes, arching to grab the pillow from underneath me to chuck it at her face. She caught it without missing a beat.

"The second reason," she said with exaggerated slowness, "is because you're a succubus that's been starving for over five years. Something tells me your transition is going to be one hell of show." She grinned, the blue pentagrams in her eyes swirling around mischievously.

"Please tell me you are not planning to watch—"

"Fuck no." She made a gagging noise that descended into giggles. "I love you, Rubes, but you're like my sister. Your transition is one porno I am not interested in watching. If I want to get it on, Bourbon Street isn't far."

Bourbon Street. The one place on this continent that you could throw a rock blindfolded and be more likely to hit a demon than a human. Only three blocks from Hell's Gates, it was practically overrun with our kind. Which meant it wasn't safe for me or for her, not with those glowing blue-branded eyes.

She wore the Devil's mark, and if her glamour slipped for even a second, it was all over. The world would know that a new soul carried that name.

"Please tell me you're not planning on going down to Bourbon Street with everything that's going on…" I said. She inclined her head and wariness permeated the air. "Moira, you can't be serious." She let out a sigh.

"I wouldn't say planning is the right word. More like *considering* my options," she defended. "It's not like anyone is going to cross over until you transition. Once you fully hit it, that could be weeks. It would be a shame for me to miss out on the chance before we left earth…"

I know she didn't mean for it to come across like she was guilt-tripping me, but her subtle reminder pulled at my heartstrings. Both because this is entirely on me, and because I almost lost her once. Despite that, she chose to follow me, and not just to the ends of this world, but to another world entirely.

I sat up, ignoring Bandit's protests as I moved him aside and embraced her, wrapping my arms around her petite frame. "I'm not going to tell you what you can and can't do. I just worry about you," I whispered into her dark green hair. She smelled like mint and spring.

"I know." She wrapped her arms around my waist, holding me tight against her. "It's the same for me. I've never worried about anyone or anything in my life until you, and I'm not even getting some," she grumbled. "Which is why I'm *thinking* about it, but my mind isn't made up. You know I'd never do anything that puts you in danger."

"It's not me I'm worried about."

A knock at the door interrupted us and I growled under my breath. Moira clutched me tighter, shaking with silent laughter as the door swung open.

"Ruby, love, I hate to break this up, but Allistair will be here shortly and we need to talk about how you want to do this."

I could only assume he meant go through the transition, to which I didn't have an answer. Still, I unclasped myself from Moira and followed him back out into the living room.

He took a seat in the lone armchair across the room, shooting me an apologetic look. I briefly wondered if his distance was because of our unexplainable make-out session earlier, or the shattered trust we'd yet to mend from Moira's kidnapping. Judging by Julian's turned back as he faced the glass wall, arms clasped behind him, I could only guess it was some of both.

I took a step towards Laran who sat on the black leather loveseat, freezing when his eyes swept up—hot, heated, and cautious. It was that last one that gave me pause.

"Is something wrong here?" I asked, my voice coming out a bit sharper than I intended, a hint of the beast inside me creeping through. She was not happy with him. Neither of us understood why he, out of any of them, would be wary with us.

He was branded.

He was *ours*.

A heavy fog formed around him, seemingly coming from nowhere. Red as human blood, frothing and foaming as it poured outward from him. I blinked, narrowing my eyes as I cocked my head.

"I asked you a question, Laran." It was not my voice that came out, this was sultry and smooth. Layered with seduction and fire, the words seemed to settle over him. His eyes went wholly black, blotting out any trace of white. My lips parted as heat circled through me, shooting up my veins to that aching place in my core. A pounding started in my head.

I took another step towards him, only mildly aware of the outside voices speaking words that didn't matter. Laran clenched his hands as if trying to restrain himself. From what, I didn't know, but the pounding urged me closer, pushing me towards him.

I moved to stand directly between his legs, reaching forward through the fog—

Strong hands wrapped around my waist, yanking me back, pulling me away from him. From my—

"Snap out of it, Ruby," a voice, rough and thick with desire, whispered in my ear. I stepped back into something solid. My lips parted on their own accord, tasting the air around me. Lust and heat. Darkness and shadows. Cold so chilling that it ignited a burning desire going down my lungs, straight to that place between my thighs.

The body behind me stayed still as the dead, neither pulling me closer nor releasing me to the world. Like he was having trouble making up his mind. I reached my arms up and around behind me, gripping his shoulders. My fingers trailed across his taut muscles, sweeping up the bare skin of his neck, and twining around short locks of hair that I knew would be white. I gave a sharp tug, smiling as a growl escaped his composure.

The hands at my waist tightened, almost painfully so, but he did not budge.

"Do not test me," Death whispered in my ear. His lips were chilled as they brushed down the nape of my neck and up again. He inhaled deeply and I shuddered in delight. "Hell's heir, you may be, but no one courts Death unless they wish to *submit.*"

My control was already hanging on by a very thin thread. The image that swept through my mind of him dominating me snapped it entirely. The beast pushed forward and ground my hips back into the hard erection that pressed against me.

The breath hissed between his teeth.

"Death, you may be, but you will kneel all the same," my beast replied. Her version of kneel looked nothing like what most imagined. She didn't just want his submission. She wanted his adoration, his devotion, his very fucking soul.

Her idea of Death kneeling ended with his face between my thighs and my mark branded on his fucking cock.

Oh man, I was so utterly screwed.

But I couldn't bring myself to stop it.

Heat burned through me like a building inferno. Pounding. Beating. Pushing me towards something that I didn't fully understand. I pushed back, running my ass over the length of him—

Crack!

I blinked. Not that I was opposed to pain, but I found it rather unexpected. My vision cleared, and it was not Death or any of the Horsemen standing in front of me, but Moira.

She arched one dark green eyebrow, her arms folded over her chest smugly.

"I know you are horny as fuck right now, but there is a time and place, and it is not in front of my not-so-virgin eyes. Get it together, Rubes."

My beast blinked at her.

"Did you just slap me?" the beast asked, frowning in confusion. Moira didn't back down.

"Yes. You're a thirsty bitch. I get it. But I need you to hold yourself together just a little bit longer." The beast looked at her, tilting my head, the pounding in my veins easing for just a moment. "For me. Can you do it for me?" she asked quietly. Not pleading, because Moira never begged. Instead, she was demanding of the beast what no one else in this room could.

Because they were not our tether. The one who kept us together when all else failed.

And for her, we would do anything.

The beast reached out with our hand and swept a stray lock of her dark green hair aside. Intimate, but not sexual in any way.

"For you, who has protected her always. Be warned: very soon I will not be able to stop." Our head rose as she locked eyes with Laran who sat several feet behind Moira, watching me intensely, his gaze dark. "I will claim *all* my mates before we return home."

With that she receded, leaving me clammy and confused.

I didn't even have time to register the voice behind me before the bright spots in my vision exploded. The world went white as sleep found me, but the fire inside did not abate.

Not even sleep could save me from my infernal torment…or desires.

JULIAN

She had me. She had me, and she *knew* it.

Whereas Ruby and I had danced around her growing attraction to me and the painfully addictive things I felt for her, the beast would not. We'd been chosen, created, to be her protectors, but the beast wanted more.

It wanted all of us. All of me.

She wanted to own every aspect of me. My soul.

At least that creature cared not for whether there was some semblance of a heart left in me, beyond the useless beating thing in my chest. I wouldn't fail her in that regard. She may have been raised human, but the girl in my arms was fire and ash through and through.

Her skin glowed like the embers of a budding flame. Hotter than a star and deadlier than anything this world could imagine, the power she kept within her was rarely present, apart from when she slept. In this state, I could feel her need clawing at me, getting beneath my skin, even more pronounced than when she taunted me.

I cradled her body close to my chest, pretending not to be affected by the way she wrapped her arms around my neck, clinging to me even in sleep. I breathed in the scent of her. The way it called to me.

"We need to move her," Laran said.

I couldn't admit it to them. The way I felt. I couldn't admit it to Ruby herself, even though I knew it pained her for me to deny us both. I wanted her unlike anything or anyone that came before her.

And much as I tried to stay away, for the sake of us all, I was rapidly approaching my breaking point.

"She will need to feed when she wakes," Allistair began. I growled under my breath at the mere thought of it because I wouldn't be the one to do it. "Do you have something to say, Death?"

I held her closer by a fraction of an inch.

Did I have a problem?

I did.

I was far too conflicted about this. If I was doing my damn job, I would hand her over and let it be done. I would refuse her advances. I would deny the mating bond that she's offering.

I would keep her safe and not get distracted. Not dream about the color her skin would turn after meeting my belt, or fantasize the ways she might moan for me.

I would know that the only way this could end, is up in flames.

And yet…I couldn't walk away.

Neither could I admit any of it aloud.

Instead of answering, I walked away, carrying the sleeping she-demon in my arms.

"Hey," the banshee screeched behind me. "What do you think you're doing? Where are you going?"

"Keeping her safe."

It was the only answer I could give. I didn't want to think about what Allistair would do to her. With her. My own possessiveness did not lend to sharing, and if I took her through her first feed…I would brand every inch of her skin.

But Ruby wouldn't want that, and I couldn't stop myself.

Something slammed into my back and crumpled. Not a person, but an object. I turned slightly to see shards of broken glass. A lamp. And the banshee who threw it.

"You don't get to just remove her without answers. I asked you what you were doing, because if you idiots aren't smart, all you'll do is piss her off and if you think I'm bad, you ain't seen nothing yet!" Her words strayed toward a southern twang the more she got worked up.

"Calm yourself," I replied coldly. "The transition is messing with her mind. She will be unable to think logically until she feeds. I'm moving her to a private room that is warded heavily enough for her to do so and not be a danger to the city."

The banshee paused. She didn't trust us, and it was somewhat admirable that she distrusted anyone with her best friend. She truly was a proper familiar. Possessive. Slightly irrational. Distrusting of anyone else's intentions, but entirely loyal to the one who bound her.

It was the only reason she was standing after throwing a lamp at me.

"She's not going to like this."

"The alternative is we wait for her to wake and give her a choice, at which point she will either agree to it, or the far more likely option, her anger will again spiral and I will not be able to put her to sleep." Allistair chose to step forward and interject with a more diplomatic understanding of the scenario. "Ruby is the strongest succubus I have seen pre-transition and she is scared to go through it. That is going to make it very difficult on her already. If she burns the city down in a rage, that will only make her more volatile and unstable. This is the best solution."

Her eyes scanned Ruby, softening as she watched her with a weary expression. She didn't like this, but she was out of her depth. We were the Horsemen, and this was what we were meant to do. Familiar or not, the responsibility of ensuring Ruby transitioned safely was on the four of us.

With a nod from the banshee, I turned my back on them and hoped that we were enough.

That we could do just what we'd told her we would, because if not…it wouldn't just be the banshee's anger we would have to answer to.

CHAPTER THREE

Shadows danced in the candlelight when I came to. I laid there for a moment, in that strange in-between state where I was awake but not fully, staring at the shades of black and grey as they swayed from side to side. There was something so peaceful about it, but that didn't resonate with me. Not this time. Not with my body wound tight as a spring, coiled and waiting for release.

Where am I?

I rolled over, pausing midway. Lantern-like orbs hung from the ceiling, emitting a soft glow. Tiny, twinkling lights blinked in and out of existence—absorbing me with their simple beauty. I leaned up, reaching for one with an outstretched hand.

"How are you feeling?"

I jumped. The voice that spoke was low, rich, adding an ember of seduction to the peace and tranquility. I followed it to the end of the bed where Allistair sat watching me in the silence. My hand dropped to my lap and I pushed the crimson sheets away, trying to ignore the soft texture between my fingers and the way it brushed my thighs.

My bare thighs.

I blinked.

"Where did my jeans go?" My throat was dry as the Sahara and my words came out in a rasp. I swallowed hard, over the thickness that was building. It was suffocating, and in the sweltering heat that continued to plague me, downright delirious.

"You burned them," he replied. That voice sent a shiver down my spine. "Moira dressed you while you slept. She thought you might feel most at home in…minimal clothing." His eyes roved over the pale flesh of my legs, past the plain black boyshort underwear, and up my very fitted shirt. My arms broke out in goosebumps and I clasped them across my chest, hoping he couldn't see my taut nipples through the thin material.

The predatory flash of his eyes and upturn of his lips said it all.

"Where is Moira? And why are you here? I thought you were dealing with—"

"Moira is out. Pestilence took her down to Bourbon Street to try and enjoy herself. We told her if your familiar is stressed, it will make the transition harder. I thought you would appreciate the small lie so that she would not be here feeling all of what happens next." He took a deep breath and stood to remove his suit jacket. "As for me, I would think that's quite obvious. You can't last more than a few moments without trying to feed and I am the only incubus among us. We are going to…rectify this situation."

What the actual fuck?

I jumped up from the bed, but my legs got tangled in the sheets. I slipped on the cool stone floor, only catching myself *after* I landed on my ass. Legs splayed and arms bracing me, my position was utterly compromising from where Allistair stood. I jerked my head, flicking my long blue locks out of the way so I could glare at him properly.

"Rectify? You're not rectifying shit, asshole," I snapped, trying to crawl backwards, away from his probing gaze. Well over six feet tall and standing not five feet away, he could have ogled my breasts that were spilling out of my low cut tank top, but he didn't.

He kept those golden eyes on mine and lifted one eyebrow in question.

"We're back to this?" he asked lightly. Indignation swept through, but I didn't respond. Too scared of the words that might come out. "I see," he murmured lightly as he undid his cuffs links. "Well, why don't you tell me what you want?" he continued conversationally as he began to unbutton his shirt.

I swallowed hard, but the words didn't come.

Need and want were beating at me like a fucking battering ram, but I didn't want to give in. Not like this. Not when he—

"You knocked me out," I breathed, my anger and need going head-to-head.

What was wrong with me?

"I did what I had to," he said matter-of-factly. "War had this room specially prepared for your transition, and with you coming into it so quickly, we thought it best to move you early. Try to take the bite off before things get underway."

I grit my teeth, snapping my legs shut as I moved to stand. Of course Allistair was there. Offering his hand like the perfect gentlemen. I slapped him away, grimacing when he stumbled back several feet.

Fucking strength.

Fucking transition.

Fucking Horsemen thinking they could decide what's best for me.

And Moira? Had she really gone along with this?

Sweat trickled down my back as the fever climbed to all new heights. I was going to die from dehydration before anyone stuck their dick anywhere.

"Ruby, I know that it's difficult for you to be rational right now, but I need you to trust me," Allistair crooned. It took him no time at all to recover and approach me again, using his lovely voice in an attempt to subdue me.

Bastard thought pretty words would fix it? Think again.

He wasn't the first of our kind I'd had to deal with.

"Trust you?" I breathed harshly. "You knocked me out against my will and brought me devil knows where"—I waved my hand around the room, only then noticing the assortment of *instruments* on the far wall—"without my permission. I don't have to do anything you motherfucki—"

"Let me take the edge off so we can discuss this somewhat rationally," Allistair interrupted. The button-up shirt he wore slipped from his shoulders, falling to the ground haphazardly. It probably cost more than my mortgage, but he didn't give a damn. His gaze remained on me as he padded forward, barefoot and now shirtless, wearing only black slacks and cool arrogance.

I glowered at him and turned to look for a door in far corner of the room, making every attempt to step around Allistair. He grabbed my hand before I could make it two feet, snapping me back to him like a ball attached to a string. I hit his chest with a thump.

Anger. Desire. Betrayal. Want. Fear. Need.

They swirled together like the winds of an incoming storm. My desperation heightened as the beast inside me thrashed with rage. I didn't understand what was going on. I couldn't process it.

Couldn't process anything.

Moira had left me with them to—to—fuck them.

Brand them.

Submit to them.

Transition with them.

I couldn't understand it. Wouldn't understand it.

They had not earned the right to be the demons that brought me over. In fact, they had taken that choice from me. Assuming they could push the issue. Push me.

"I have no desire to push you or take your choice away, Ruby, but if someone doesn't take the edge off, you will hit the transition in a very bad place, even more confused than you are now. If that is what you wish, then I will take a seat right over there." He motioned to a large overstuffed armchair on the other side of the room. Beside it was a rack of restraining equipment. Collars, leather and metal bindings, varying lengths of leash with clips on the end—all hung from the pegs on the wall. "And I will remain until you tell me otherwise. However, I don't think that's what you really want."

Once again, my insides liquefied just being in close proximity to him. This back and forth within was giving me whiplash, making me all the more desperate to find my way back to sanity. If only the burning would cease…

Long elegant fingers trailed up and down my sides in a motion that should have been soothing, but wasn't. My skin had become hypersensitive in the time I slept. His fingers would have only been the barest of a brush before, but now funneled fire and heat into my veins and through every essence of my being.

"Will it stop?" I breathed, pressing my hands against the contoured planes of his chest. My breath was coming in short, fast bursts and he was barely touching me. Maybe this wasn't the worst idea…

"Stop? No," he replied, straight to the point. "Lessen? Yes. You should have a short reprieve where you can think about this with a clearer head." His heart shuddered beneath my palm, but the stroke of his thumb around the underside of my breast was steady.

Control. Allistair was very much in control.

Me? Not so much.

I slid my hands up his chest, running my fingertips along the edges of scars that had long since faded. A heady swelter built inside me, making my legs sway. I reached my hands around the back of his neck and gripped the firm muscle, digging my nails into despicably soft hair. Why couldn't it feel like a porcupine? That would make this so much easier. Of course the incubus had to have hair more luscious than mine.

"No sex. I'm clearly not thinking right." I gripped him tighter, but his head didn't move an inch. I guess that newfound strength was as unreliable as my fire. "You teach me to feed and that's it. You hear me?" My words would have sounded a lot bolder were I not panting from the feel of him pressed against me.

"I think you will find that feeding can be quite addictive," Allistair mused as he slipped his fingertips under my shirt, teasing the soft flesh. I gasped, and he chuckled.

Prick.

"Answer the question."

I wasn't willing to close my eyes and give myself into this without his word. Maybe I shouldn't be so trusting, given we were demons and all, but he was Famine. One of the Four Horsemen. There was no law I could hold him to, no promise I could make him keep. No matter how this went down, I had to trust that he meant what he said, because at the end of it, he was the only one that could hold himself to it.

"No sex *this time*. You have my word," Allistair replied. His lips twisted into an arrogant smirk as his hands continued their light ministrations. I groaned, both in frustration and desire. Satan damn him. He was going to be my undoing and we were barely even started.

You know what, though? Two could play at that.

I drew him in and Allistair leaned closer, allowing me better access as I brushed my lips across his jaw. His hands paused around my waist and I wriggled my hips a little, pushing my lower stomach against him. His erection twitched and the breath hissed between his lips.

"What are you doing, little succubus?" he breathed. I paused, noting the dangerously low tone of his voice. Like maybe I had pushed him too far, but the beast inside didn't think this was anywhere near far enough.

I moved my hands to either side of his shoulders and pushed.

His body yielded, stumbling back onto the bed and falling softly onto those blood red sheets. I didn't wait for his shock to wear off as I straddled his lap. The beast hummed a nod of approval as I wrapped my arms around him and ground my hips into the hard erection beneath me.

The fever-induced delirium blotted out all sense of rationality. I quickly forgot the point I was making and instead sought something infinitely more primal.

Release.

Allistair was the first to move, sweeping up to kiss me so hard our teeth clanked. A normal person might have stopped to think that this bestial urge came out of nowhere once again, but as his tongue parted the seam of my lips, all resistance flew out of my mind.

I groaned. This man kissed like a God. I always thought myself a good kisser, but Allistair wasn't like the sloppy boyfriends I'd had the last few years. He pried me apart with such expert precision I didn't realize I'd finally relaxed and was losing myself in him until I was already gone. Those skillfully long fingers wrapped around my wrists. He drew my arms behind my back where he switched his grip and held both wrists in one hand.

I struggled against him, testing my own strength. Once again, it was gone, leaving me a not very reluctant prisoner to an incubus with a free hand and many more lifetimes' worth of practice.

"Much better," he purred.

I shuddered at the way his voice floated over my skin. I'd underestimated him. He wasn't just some jo-schmo incubus off the street. He was pure seduction. Raw desire. His skin itself was a powerful enough aphrodisiac to make even the strongest woman lose her mind.

All this time I'd been worried about taking his choice away when he could have so easily taken mine. My body trembled with uncontrollable desire.

"What are you doing to me?" I muttered as his free hand slipped underneath the back of my thigh, pulling my arms tighter, my back arching as I was pulled up onto my knees. Fingers skated over my skin with feather light touches. He cupped my ass, squeezing it like he couldn't help himself as his hips rolled up, barely skimming me. My lips parted in a low moan as sensation wrapped around me, and I wouldn't let go.

Devil save me. I was going to need to feel a whole hell of a lot more to get my release, but at this rate I would be begging for him to just fucking do it.

"Allistair." I bit his bottom lip in warning and sucked. He tasted of blood and scotch, a spiced tang that could make me high. He groaned, and my traitorous body tried to inch closer even as he tightened his hold, eliminating any wiggle room I might have had.

"So savage, little succubus. Is it pain that you're craving?"

"Are you going to show me how to feed, or keep being a twatwaffle—"

His hand slipped between us and rubbed through the material of my boyshorts. My eyes rolled back in my head as my hips followed his command.

"I asked you a question, Ruby. No need to be rude."

His voice lulled me deeper into the desperate haze, my fever inching higher with every point of contact between us. The sound of him. The smell of him. The feel of him. All of it sent me spiraling into a version of me that I had never known. I was passion. I was desire. I was burning.

"I need an answer. Is it pain you are craving, or will you submit to me while I teach you how to feed?"

His torturous fingers slid further between my legs, hooking a single one through the thin strip of cotton. It brushed across my bare skin, feeling the dampness there as his did it.

"I submit to no one," I groaned.

"Ruby," he said in warning. "I'm losing my fucking mind right now wanting to be inside you. We both need to feed, and you asked me not to screw you six ways to Hell. Which means you have two options"—he paused to rub the back of his finger against my entrance and my hips gently swayed with him—"You either submit to me, or I bring Julian in here and you *will* submit to him. What's it going to be?"

The beast inside me wanted them all. At the same time.

She was a filthy slut that way.

I wasn't sure I would survive them both at once. Let alone four.

But the thought did have its merits…

I groaned as Allistair rubbed back and forth, teasing.

"I don't need pain right now," I bit out. Allistair smirked, but he wasn't letting me off so easily.

"Then what will you do?" he asked softly.

We were back to this. Of course, we were fucking back to this.

"I'll…" He arched an eyebrow. Daring me to say it. It was almost enough to rile the beast, but that wasn't what I wanted right now. "I'll do as you *ask*," I said eventually.

For a moment I thought he was going to keep pushing until he heard what he wanted, but even Allistair was not patient enough for that. He crooked his finger and tore the fabric of my panties straight down the middle in one swift motion.

"Very well," he said with a bite in his tone as he bared me to the air. "You are going to come. Hard. And when you do, I am going to feed on your sexual energy. It's going to feel like a tug, but do not worry. We've done this before."

Without warning, he plunged two fingers inside of me and I cried out in shock. He didn't miss a beat as he started pumping them in and out, slowly building a rhythm. My blood sizzled with the scorching desire that flooded me.

A thick cloud of smoke began to form around him, shimmering like molten gold. His thumb pressed against my clit and the smoke drifted outward, molding around us. Shaping us. It fanned my skin, making the hairs tingle with energy. I shuddered against his fingers and they didn't relent.

"More," I breathed as I tried to writhe on his lap, but Allistair didn't give an inch. My back arched with my arms securely behind me and his grip kept me pushed up onto my knees as I tried to take all that he would give. Allistair hummed in approval, leaning down to press his mouth to my right nipple.

"You know the rules."

Sucking it hard, he whorled his tongue around the peak, inching me higher and higher as his fingering slowed. His thumb made lazy circles around my sensitive nub, giving me enough pressure to drive me crazy, but never tip over the edge.

I growled at him and the bastard bit me. My aching core constricted, desperately reaching for my release, and I let out a groan in frustration that bordered on a cry.

"Say my name when you come."

Possessive bastard.

"Yes," he snapped. "I am."

I didn't even have time to reply before he left a trail of suckling kisses across my chest. He nipped at my other nipple and sucked it sharply, twisting his fingers simultaneously.

"Allistair!" I shouted. My body convulsed around him, tightening on his fingers where they still pushed greedily inside me as he took all of my pleasure and then some. Just when I thought the high would drop, there was that tug, suspending me in bliss. I ignited and the room itself shook with me.

All too soon the suspended orgasm ceased, leaving me wiped and yet… as Allistair released my arms and allowed me to drop on his lap, the coarse material of his slacks rubbed me where his hard cock strained beneath it. I pushed into him, enjoying the deep groan that I didn't so much as hear, but felt.

He wanted me. *So why was he denying himself?*

Allistair reached down and grasped me by the hips, lifting me off him with ease and leaning over to place me on the floor in front of him.

"What are you—"

"Get on your knees." I blinked at the tone in his voice. It was deeper than usual. Huskier. Almost more…*desperate.*

I sat back on the cold floor, in-between his spread legs.

My heart hammered against my chest as I stared up at him from below. I'd never considered myself submissive in any way, but this side of him intrigued me. The side where I could almost feel him coming…unhinged. He wore his arrogance with a swagger that few could manage, but beneath it I sensed a desperation. His control was more for himself than for me.

"Will this do?" I asked softly.

"Yes."

I wanted to shudder as the gold dust around us pressed against my skin, tingling everywhere it touched. I swiped my tongue out over my bottom lip, tasting his blood mixed with something potent. Something…delicious.

"What you are tasting is called kama. It's the sexual energy that feeds our kind." His words hazily made their way into my brain as the curling gold particles pulled me to him. Urging me to come closer. Take more.

"Kama…" I muttered. "Like Kama Sutra?"

Allistair chuckled. "The very same."

I lifted a hand toward him, letting it hover only inches away. The shiny yellow substance coated my fingers and brought them to my face to examine. It really did look like gold dust. Tentatively, I raised my forefinger to my lips and licked the gold powder off. An insatiable urge hit me and I wrapped my lips around that finger, groaning deeply while I sucked it dry.

"Enough," Allistair snapped, drawing my attention back to him. I stared up, biting my forefinger softly. His pupils dilated and a low growl started in his chest. "It's not polite to toy with others of your kind, little succubus."

There was that edge to his voice that I remembered. The crisp cut of words sharp enough to sting flesh, but made a girl crave more.

"You're the one that keeps turning me down, Famine."

It wasn't entirely me that let that slip out. The beast was very, very close to the surface and through his own need I wasn't sure Allistair saw it. His nostrils flared and his pupils continued to grow. Darker. Fuller. Until there was not a speck of white in his eyes. He looked at me like every bit the Horseman he was. A monster to both worlds.

But so was I, and he did not scare us.

"Unbutton my slacks."

I stared, slack-jawed for a minute at the forwardness of his request. Wasn't I the one that had been goading this for weeks? Playing with him. Taunting him. I laid the law for no sex, but I needed to feed and he needed to fuck. That much was clear.

If me sucking my finger made him almost come unhinged…the beast pushed forward and blotted out the last of my hesitations.

I reached out, placing both my hands on his inner thighs, gripping him so I could shuffle forward. He groaned as my hands swept up, running over the tight muscles of his legs, slowly inching towards the hard bulge in his pants. He twitched when my palm slipped over him and I rubbed his hard length up and down twice.

"Unbutton my slacks," he repeated.

I pinched the zipper between two fingers and dragged it down with exaggerated slowness. Normally, I would have a snappy reply in hand, but it wasn't so easy when I was breathing in all this gold dust. His…kama. The damn dust made my brain go foggy, making it harder to hold onto thoughts and words when all I wanted to do was screw him. We even had a bed and everything…nope. Nope. I shook my head.

Suck. Not fuck. Got it, Ruby?

When the zipper was halfway down, I paused, and my lips parted as his erection forced it down the rest of the way.

"Commando?" I asked, my voice wasn't as light as I would have liked it to be. There was too much tension. Too much emotion swirling in my chest. Too much aching between my own legs.

Too much of the beast coming out.

Still, he didn't acknowledge it.

"I like to be prepared," he shrugged, but when I trailed a single finger along his length, I didn't miss the way his body tensed beneath me. I leaned forward, using my tongue to follow the same path as my finger.

He shuddered, and a single glistening drop formed on his tip. I was going to enjoy this very much.

I closed my lips around his swollen head, tasting his saltiness, careful to keep my teeth sheathed. Allistair groaned encouragingly and I took him in. His tip touched the back of my throat, making me gag once, coating my mouth in saliva.

He wrapped a hand around my hair and guided me forward. I went down, taking him deeper.

"Fucking hell, woman—you're going to kill me," he growled.

Allistair was not small by any means, but fuck, if he was any bigger I couldn't take him to the base. As it was, my eyes stung as tears began to form, but this power over him…this sense of what I could do to him—take from him—even while being at his mercy…

It was thrilling. Exhilarating.

It was…I breathed in through my nose and was unprepared for the sudden assault on my senses. I could only describe it as the most sensational experience of my life, where I existed everywhere and nowhere simultaneously. My body tingled with power, energy, kama—I pulled back, letting my tongue sweep across his underside and whorl around the tip. Allistair twitched in my mouth, and to my shock, the aching spot between my thighs throbbed hard.

I lifted my gaze to him, eyes flashing with accusation. While it was my mouth he was taking, his kama made it feel like more. A small smile played on his lips as he watched me.

"Feels much better than you thought it would, doesn't it?"

My only response was dropping my left hand as I began rubbing myself.

"When I come, my kama will start pouring out. You're going to need to breathe it in, Ruby. Envision yourself pulling as much as you can inside you," he said through gritted teeth. I sure as hell didn't need the encouragement. This was fucking great.

The beast thought so too, but I was so far gone I didn't notice.

I sucked hard on him, whirling my tongue over the tip one last time before Allistair gripped my hair tighter. As he guided me down, he thrust up once, forcing me back to his base in one go. My eyes burned with tears and my core felt hotter than the flames of Hell as he thrust himself down my throat. I rubbed myself in fevered circles, rapidly approaching my own climax with him.

Oh fuck yes.

I moaned around him, swallowing once more and he came undone. His come hit the back of my throat as he took several shallow thrusts, and then…*kama*.

As he said, it poured out of him and into me. Seemingly knowing what to do, I breathed in, trying to focus on that as I brushed over my clit and came apart. My fingers went lower, dipping two inside of me, riding out my own climax while taking as much as I could from him.

Spots burst behind my eyes, bright flashes of white against the blackness that took me for a few seconds. When my vision slowly came back, and my body stopped throbbing, I realized I still had my lips wrapped around Allistair and he had yet to *let* me move.

I started to pull away but had two palms flat against both sides of my head. Holding me there.

Control freak.

"*Mine*," a presence growled back.

The possessiveness of it pushed at the beast's control and she snapped. High on kama and brimming with power, she shot forward. In the mere blink of an eye, she took all control and laid her hand flat against his lower abdomen. Allistair moved to readjust, but she gripped the base of him with the other hand, swallowing around the half-hardened cock in her mouth as it twitched. Allistair dug his hands into her hair, but I don't think he realized which Ruby he was playing with, not until she pulled on the tiniest seed of flame and poured in on his stomach. The burning slowly started to build. Certainly long enough he should have known what was going on, but he didn't stop it.

Why didn't he stop it?

Panic started to build within me, but the beast kept a firm claim on control. I'd made it perfectly clear in her mind that he was an acceptable mate. We were both on the same page, which meant he was hers to claim.

Allistair had to have known this. Had to have somehow realized, and yet his dick hardened, and he held both sides of my face with a fervor. The beast looked up at him with coy eyes, and there was no doubt in my mind. He knew, and he arched into her touch.

The burning in her palm intensified as the magic hit a boiling point. The breath hissed between his teeth as she branded our mark onto him. He let out a harsh groan, pulling her in…pulling her closer…

She pulled back. Her right hand curled where she was branding him, and her left stroked him with powerful thrusts. I would have been scared shitless that I'd accidentally rip his dick off with the strength running in my veins, but the beast wasn't worried. She used her considerable strength to bring him right to the brink of climax again. Her tongue licked at his head, but just before he could thrust up, she released him and leaned away.

Allistair reached for her, not giving a damn about the blazing blue pentagram that shifted on the "V" of his hips.

He slid one hand into the curve of my neck to guide my jaw, wrapping the other roughly in my hair. I would have let this go on. I knew that in my heart of hearts. I would have sucked him off again, and quite possibly let him take it further.

I would have let him shatter me, as I very well suspected he would have —promises be damned—had a door not just been thrown open.

I blinked and Allistair paused for a fraction of a second. He didn't ease up on me, but he also didn't pull me closer.

"I felt the ward straining…" Julian's voice trailed off at the sight of me, basically nude, face flushed, and lips parted to take the erect cock not six inches from my face. "She's fed," Julian surmised. The raw cold that emanated from him sapped the heat right out of me, and with it the beast left too.

I pulled out of Allistair's grasp, my strength once again temporarily overriding his. My thighs slapped the smooth marble as I toppled sideways, coughing hoarsely. Allistair growled under his breath and Julian stayed at the entry point, arms crossed over his chest. Without a handle and only smooth cream paint, the doorway I hadn't previously realized was a doorway blended in with the rest of the wall. But clear as day, he stared at me with hard green eyes, unreadable if I were only looking at what my eyes saw. Desire and wariness were the bulk of his feelings, outside the small spark of envy he was still trying to temper.

"See something you want?" I snapped at him, feeling insanely irritable over the jealousy that continued to eat at him. The jealousy that he was choosing to ignore like a fucking child and not a grown male. It just made this whole thing even more complicated and difficult for me to wrap my head around.

"What are you talking about?" he asked, but it wasn't in the flirtatious way Allistair liked to do things. Julian was honestly still trying to play this game. To act like if we both ignored it, that it would magically go away.

"Never mind," I coughed leaning back against the wall. Allistair at least had the decency to get up and fetch me a drink. Meanwhile, Julian stood there, his smoldering gaze eating through any and all pretenses of what was really going on here. I rolled my eyes and accepted the glass of amber liquid Allistair offered to me.

"Wha-what is th-this?" I choked out, tipping it back.

"Two-hundred-year old scotch."

I spluttered for a second and then swallowed it down before coughing even harder than I already was.

"What the actual hell? Why on earth do you think scotch is appropriate when someone's coughing—"

"Why would I not share my scotch with my *mate*?" There was a twinkle in his eye as he said it and it confirmed my suspicions. Allistair genuinely wanted to be claimed. Just as Laran had, and just as Rysten still wanted.

But Julian was another story.

He was willfully blind and the kind of jealousy he felt for them would only get worse if it continued. We were supposed to be together forever. Literally until the end of time because they were my protectors. At best, this was going to make our relationship difficult if he kept it up. The beast wanted him. She wanted all of them, but forever was a long fucking time to deal with this nonsense.

I averted my eyes from Allistair and said to no one in particular, "I want a bath. I want to see Moira. Then I want to talk. In that order."

Julian's jaw twitched, but otherwise he didn't let his annoyance show.

"Any other demands?" Allistair snapped, turning standoffish.

I knew it hurt his feelings on some level. That while he had wanted this —I hadn't seriously thought about it, but my wishy-washy attitude on the subject was a little too late now that the beast went and made another life changing decision. Julian's presence only served to remind me I needed to think—because as soon as I entered the transition it was all over. That much I was painfully clear on.

"Yeah, actually"—I pointed to the half-full bottle of scotch Allistair was holding—"I want the rest of that. I think I'm going to need it."

****ALLISTAIR****

I could rip his dick off and shove it down his throat until he choked on it.

Unfortunately, Death could not die, and I had more class than that.

Watching Ruby flee from the room with my scotch in hand was one of the harder things I've had to endure. There were many types of bonds and brands, but the mating bond and branding was a special sort engagement. For me to be branded and claimed as the second mate was what I wanted, but for her to act that way after doing so…stung.

My fingertips traced the edges of the dark blue pentagram. Julian coughed from the doorway, his pointed way of saying to put a shirt on because he's a jealous bastard and can't handle it.

"Is there something you needed, Death? Or do you just enjoy being a masochist?" His glare turned brutal as winter in the Arctic circle.

"Don't fucking start with me, Famine."

I cocked an eyebrow. "Don't start with you? You interrupted us about *the wards*—that we both know would have held through the first feed." His eyes flashed, and he looked away. *Yeah, I'm aware of how well enforced they are.* "Admit it, Julian. You're being a bastard because you don't want to share, but you don't want to make a move."

"You don't know what you're talking about—"

"I can read your fucking emotions. Cut the shit. I know why you're here. Care to tell me how long you stood outside before interrupting?"

I adjusted my slacks despite the extremely uncomfortable case of blue balls I had thanks to the she-demon who ran out on me because of this prick. I'd never had a girl leave my bed before. Or one that could walk properly after we were done, for that matter. Then again, Julian had never dared cockblock me.

"Long enough," he replied.

His way of saying he never left. Some would have been enraged by that, perhaps Julian himself, given the shame he felt, but I couldn't afford that luxury. Not when we all had too much riding on us—Ruby especially —to let their unresolved issues fester into a hard resentment.

As much as it pained me to cover her brand, this was not a normal engagement and would require more tact than any of them had. I found the dress shirt I'd discarded on the floor and put it back on, being sure to button it up properly and put on my cuff links before I turned back to him.

"Did you hear my offer to her when she started to resist?" I asked him. Again, he gave a non-committal mutter under his breath. I took that as a yes. "Because if you did," I paused, "you should know that the possibility... intrigues her."

Julian tensed, and it was that stillness of a predator, even more lethal than I, that told me how affected he was by her.

"I don't share," he said eventually. I shook my head as he turned to leave.

"You don't get a choice."

Julian rounded on me. "You know why I'm staying away. Why I *have* to stay away."

I did, but I didn't think his reasons were good enough. Much as I would have liked to keep her for myself, I could share if it meant keeping some part of her. I could let her be a Queen with four consorts, so long as it was only us.

But Julian couldn't.

"There are bigger monsters than you in this world now, and one of them has chosen you as its mate. You cannot walk away because of duty, and yet you won't give her what she wants. You think you can't share?" I let out a dark chuckle and his eyes flashed in warning. "Imagine the next eternity of watching this while you play the sad, pathetic time of her transition over and over again in your head, asking yourself why you made the most idiotic decision of your existence." I paused when his head bobbed and fists clenched. If he was this close to losing it, then her transition should go about as well as the beast's tantrums. "I cannot make a decision for you, and frankly I don't know why I'm forcing this conversation when less of you means more time with her for me. You need to get your head out of your ass where she is concerned. You will never have any part of her and will ruin any feelings she may hold for you if you keep acting like an adolescent boy and continue to run away from the reality of our situation. Mate with her or don't, but don't make her feel like shit in the meantime. She has too much on her plate already to deal with your self-pitying attitude."

There had only been a hand full of times in our existence that I had to save Julian from himself. As I walked through the mirror and left him to think alone, I wondered if I would look back one day and realize this was one of times. If me pushing him would be the thing he needed to finally work past his own demons, or if the very thoughts themselves would be too much for him to handle and would ultimately consume him.

CHAPTER FOUR

JULIAN MAY HAVE ROLLED his eyes, but I got the rest of the scotch.

Half an hour later, sitting in the Jacuzzi tub, I couldn't be bothered to give a shit about much of anything as I drained the last bit of the bottle and set it aside. The jets worked away at the tension in my shoulders, and for the first time in the last sixteen hours I felt like some semblance of my usual self. A pounding head from interesting life choices and drinking a crap ton of booze beat out lighting shit on fire and throwing myself at the Horsemen any day.

There was a knock at the door before it swung open.

"You know, you can't keep hiding out in here forever."

Moira's voice drifted over me as she walked into the bathroom, barefoot but dressed like she just got back from clubbing. She wore a little black dress and onyx stud earrings that reflected in the dim light. Her dark green hair was pulled back into a massive ballerina bun, not a single hair out of place. It made her blue eyes pop and the pentagrams swirled. The devil's mark—my mark—forever branded on her.

"I'm not hiding," I lied. "I just don't feel well."

Moira gave me a no-nonsense kind of look and I groaned leaning back to rest my head on Bandit since he chose to sprawl out on the edge of the bathtub behind me. He purred, curling his tail around my neck. I absent-mindedly reached back to scratch him behind the ear.

"Of course you don't feel well. You're entering the transition. I'd be shocked if you did." She came to sit behind me, her footsteps almost silent against the stone floor. "Every time you're around one of them, you either want to fuck 'em or kill 'em, and funny as it is…that's not you. It's the hormones, or whatever you want to call it." I felt her hands in my hair as she undid the messy knot I'd pulled it in and began working through the tangles.

"I'm frustrated they feel they can tell me what to do and decide what's best for me, and given the complicated relationships at the moment, I don't think that's unreasonable," I grumbled. Moira gently massaged my scalp, her steady warmth and contentment bleeding into me.

"They are…trying. This isn't exactly the most conventional situation. You're a hell of a lot more powerful than they expected, and your moods are all over the place. Sorry, but it's true," she added when I opened my mouth to object. "Plus, the beast has already made it clear she intends to claim them. Not to mention the whole familiar thing, which we haven't even gotten a chance to talk about." I opened my mouth to apologize and she tugged a little on my hair. "Don't even think about apologizing. There's enough crap going on. It can wait until we have a chance to breathe. Seriously. I've been your familiar for years if the Horsemen are right. You branding me just makes it official."

I don't know how I ended up so lucky to have a best friend like her. For as crazy as she may be, she was the rock I needed when the world went to shit. A tear pricked my left eye, and I wiped it away before it had the chance to fall.

"Are you upset that I branded you?" I asked quietly, increasingly aware of the sound of water dripping from the faucet and three heartbeats filling the huge space.

"Hell no. Why on earth would you think that?" She didn't even have to think about her answer.

"Because I know how you feel about branding in general and I don't want you to think this means I own you or some shit. I'm not that kind of demon." I swallowed hard. "I didn't mean to…I just wanted to save you." Moira released my hair and came around to sit on the side of the tub.

"You don't need to apologize for this, Ruby," she said and motioned to her eyes. "I know what kind of demon you are, and I know you didn't brand me out of some fucked up possessive complex. You saved my life, and the way I see it is Hell is going to be a lot safer with your mark on me. No one fucks with a demon carrying the devil's pentagram. People will think twice before trying something." I reached over and took her hand, squeezing it gently. She wrapped both of hers around mine and squeezed back. "The Horsemen are also fucking livid because they were supposed to be your familiars. I like that being one means they can't just take you from me. They and everyone else knows where the score is now."

I chuckled under my breath. Of course she would see it that way.

"We're a package deal," I agreed.

"Yup. You, me, and the trash panda," Moira snickered. Bandit grumbled and tucked his tail tighter around me.

"Raccoon," I corrected her.

"He *literally* ate trash before you took him in. You can't even argue he's like a less domesticated cat. He ate trash—"

Another knock at the door and it cracked open.

"Everything okay in here, love?" Rysten called.

"We'll be out in a minute," I said. Moira rolled her eyes as the door slammed shut. "How was Bourbon Street with him?"

She groaned. "It's hard to have fun when you're being babysat by someone who doesn't want to be there. I swear, he spent the whole time pouting because you were back here, and he didn't want to be on 'Moira duty'. What the fuck is that anyways?"

"Well, I'm sorry you couldn't get laid," I chuckled, not feeling all that sorry. I'm sure she'd have a plethora of demons lining up at her door in Hell, where I hoped she would be safer.

"Speaking of getting laid"—she paused and raised an eyebrow —"what's the deal? I could tell you were having some *issues* earlier. Is it the whole branding thing? What's going on there?"

Oh man.

I wasn't sure I wanted to have this conversation, but I was running out of time where choice would even be an option. Pulling my head up from Bandit, I slowly scooted forward so I could get out of the tub. The warm air fanned my wet skin, making my head feel fuzzy.

"It's complicated. I do want them. All of them, but we've got some issues to sort out. I don't want them making choices for me."

That was putting it mildly. We had several big problems to sort through, but I wasn't sure how much I felt like going through it all in my very limited time with Moira. I released her hand to step out of the tub and my toes curled into the shaggy white rug beneath me.

"Me being pissed with Allistair when I woke up could have been avoided if they'd told me, 'hey, you need to feed' versus knocking me out and putting me in a room with him. That really wasn't cool, and while I do feel better, that doesn't excuse that it was a shitty thing to do." I reached over for a fluffy white towel and dried myself off.

"I don't know if you can tell, but to the rest of us you haven't been thinking that clearly. You gotta remember that, and this is coming from me. You know I'd shove my foot up any of their asses if I thought they were doing something they shouldn't be, but as it is, you started a fire in the living room. A fire no one but you can control." She paused to press her lips together in a troubled smile. "I didn't think what Allistair did was all that smart. I told them it would probably piss you off more, but I also get why they did it… the bigger thing here is I'm trying to make sure this is what you want, because you already claimed that fuckface, War, and pretty boy, Famine. Pest is champing at the bit to be next. So if you don't want this…"

She left her prompt in the air, but we both knew what she meant. If I don't want this, it's a little fucking late. Brands can't be undone.

Wish someone would have gone and told the beast that before she pulled this.

I shook my head turning to the opaque white counter where a pair of yoga pants and my favorite tank top undershirt sat waiting for me. In Oregon, it had been too cold to wear anything sleeveless this time of year, but down in New Orleans and its sticky Louisiana heat, the humidity stayed year-round.

I dressed slowly, taking my sweet time while I tried to sort through my thoughts. Already the fuzziness was starting up again. I didn't give myself an hour before I was delirious.

"My life was already changing faster than I was comfortable with. Now I'm starting the transition to becoming immortal with two mates, but the beast wants more." I pressed my hands together, twisting my fingers around. "It's not the sex that gets me here. It's my lack of control in branding them. I didn't mean to brand Laran. I sure as fuck wasn't planning on branding Allistair. The beast did that shit, and now they're both my mates even though we haven't consummated it. She wants all of them and I have no way of stopping myself from tying them to me in every way." I paused, finally feeling like I was getting to the crux of the matter. "But what if they don't want that? I mean—I *know* Rysten does, but Julian? He's made it pretty clear he doesn't want to go further, even though he's greener than you. He should get the right to choose that, just like Allistair and Laran should have… but I'm afraid if they don't want me, the beast isn't going to let *any* of them choose someone else either…"

I let out a heavy sigh, my shoulders folding in. I cared about the guys. All of them. I really did, but would I feel that way in hundred years? What about a thousand? I already had Laran and Allistair to worry about. Having this talk with them wasn't going to be nearly as easy as it was with Moira. Having it with all four of them? The idea of it made my head spin.

I leaned my hip against the counter and rubbed my temples. I guess this is what it means to have demon problems and commitment issues, but what could you expect out of someone who couldn't give a guy a blowjob without them going nuts?

"Okay, first, Julian is fighting a losing battle. We all know this. Hell, even the trash panda knows it—" She broke off to frown as Bandit let a chittering kind of…*laugh*. Almost like he was chuckling. "Point is, he'll get over it. Second, have you met the four of them? Are we talking about the same Horsemen?" Moira asked, crossing her arms over her chest. I scrunched my eyebrows together, confused as to where she was going. "Because those four have been fucking crazy about you ever since they showed up."

"That doesn't mean they wanted to spend forever with me, Moira." Bandit walked over and tugged on my pants, signaling for me to pick him up. "Or that I wanted to spend forever with them," I added as I gathered him in my arms.

"You're spending forever with them whether you fuck them or not," she pointed out, tapping her foot almost impatiently.

"Yeah, and I'd rather the beast not try to rip anyone's balls off because they decided they didn't want to be with me anymore, or with me to begin with," I snapped, impatient as hell back. Her own moodiness at my hesitation was bleeding over into me.

"But if you can't stop it, then it's going to happen either way." She lifted both eyebrows and pursed her lips, making her point. "And have you stopped to even ask them how they feel instead of just assuming? I mean, for devil's sake, Ruby, their entire existence is wrapped around you. In their eyes you could have hung the fucking moon, babe."

"Didn't we already have this talk about diving into things without about thinking it?" I asked in almost whine. Bandit held onto me tighter and used one paw to stroke my cheek. Moira rolled her eyes.

"Yes. We did, and we came to the conclusion that you're the fucking Queen of Hell whether you like it or not. This is no different, Ruby." She marched right up to me and grabbed me by my chin, pulling me down to her level. "You've got four insanely hot guys that that beast of yours chose and sitting here in denial isn't going to change that," she said in a calming voice. "Now you can she-demon up just like you've done with everything else in your life, or you can sit in here being pouty and drinking scotch. What's it going to be?"

My lips pressed together as I glanced over at the empty bottle.

I knew this. I knew before we even talked what I needed to do. I just didn't want to admit it.

But that's the thing: I either keep up with the program, or one of these times the problem will get ahead of me. I wasn't going to let that happen.

I was Ruby Morningstar, for devil's sake.

I'd found out I was Lucifer's daughter and survived multiple assassination attempts. I'd lived through abuse and came out stronger. I'd learned I had more gifts than I ever thought possible, and now—I was going to transition like a motherfucking boss.

Hopefully. Because it's not like this job came with a training manual.

And I was running out of options.

CHAPTER FIVE

The sun was peeking over the horizon when I stepped into the living room. An inch-thick glass wall was all that separated me from the wonders and dangers of New Orleans. Out there, somewhere, was the portal to Hell, but at the moment I had greater things to worry about. They came in the form of four dangerously seductive demons, who all happened to be waiting for me.

"You seem to be feeling better," Allistair smirked from across the room. He sat shirtless, leaving the blue brand across his abdomen on display. His arm sprawled across the back of the long leather couch where a vacant seat was waiting between him and Rysten.

Damn him. He was no better than Laran. They both got far too much enjoyment out of this for the wrong reasons. On one hand, it made me want to throttle them. On the other…maybe Julian could use the prodding to make him sort through his shit…

"I am, thanks for asking," I said, displaying a smirk of my own and crossing my arms over my chest. Instead of taking the waiting seat between them, or the one beside Laran, I veered straight for the single armchair. Bandit leapt on top of it, poising himself where he could simultaneously watch them and be petted.

"We need to discuss your transition," Julian said, turning away from the cityscape. "Or more pertinently, how you would like to go about it." Both his arms were clasped behind his back. He wore dark pants and a fitted long sleeve shirt, despite the New Orleans heat—then again, maybe it was just me burning up given how high the air conditioner was jacked. His jaw tensed, waiting for my answer. The picture of utter control.

"Ummm…" I drawled out. "I don't know. Considering no one ever thought I would transition, I didn't pay all that much attention to the house mothers at the orphanage…" My voice trailed off at the look he and Rysten were sharing. Allistair sighed deeply, and even Laran looked a bit uncomfortable.

"You have no idea what the transition entails?" Julian asked slowly.

I shook my head. "Not really. Theoretically, I know that I might gain some cool powers and I'll stop aging, as for how…" I shrugged. "Like I said, I never thought I would."

The room seemed to let out an audible sigh of frustration. Clearly the Horsemen had expected more than that. Expected more of me. It's not like I signed up for this job, though. I had no idea until they showed up on my doorstep to drop the news. The awkward silence made me tense and I looked away as Moira came to sit on the other arm of my wide chair, throwing her arm around me. She smelled a bit like sweat and booze. Great.

"It might be a bit easier, love, if we started with your questions and worked from there," Rysten suggested. His lips quirked up in an encouraging smile.

"Well…" I started when Moira decided to cut in.

"Let's start with you Four Hobos."

Did she really just call them that? Yep. Yes, she did.

"Her beast wants to claim all of you. Is there going to be any issues here? Because she's all caught up on not wanting to take anyone's choice away—"

"I think that's enough, Moira," I cut in. My eyes narrowed at her as she shrugged her slim shoulders.

"I'm tired. It's six in the fricken' morning and we're holding an intervention. Someone had to break the ice."

And you clearly appointed yourself in charge of that.

I think I went indigo from head to toe with the way the four of them were watching me. I moved my hands to my lap and twiddled my thumbs; behind me, Moira let out a groan.

"Is that what she really thinks?"

The words drifted through my mind. Sudden and without preamble. *Where had that come from?*

I frowned.

"I would have branded her an hour ago if she was concerned where I stood."

Okay. I *know* that wasn't me. Something weird was going on here.

"Ruby, love, you are aware that harems are quite common in Hell, aren't you?" Rysten asked, the first to break the silence as far as I could tell.

"Yeah," I said. "But you guys aren't normal demons. It's not unreasonable to think that each of you might want your own harems one day…" I trailed off, feeling sheepish under the look Laran was giving me.

"She really doesn't see herself the way we do."

I perked my head up, trying to figure out where the voice came from, but no one spoke. This was getting kind of awkward…

"Being chosen by the beast is the greatest honor we could receive—" Rysten started kindly.

"I don't give a damn about honor, Rysten. I need to know what you guys want. Each of you." I swallowed hard and looked at each of their faces. Julian: stoic. Rysten: thoughtful. Allistair: flirtatiously seductive. Laran: intense, as always. He sat shirtless, twin pentagrams already branded on his shoulders.

"I'm sorry I branded you. Both of you"—I cut my eyes between him and Allistair—"without talking first. I never would have—"

Laran moved, rising to his feet. The low-slung jeans on his hips did naughty things to me, but it was his imposing stare that kept me transfixed as he crossed the living room. He came to kneel before me and rested his large hands over mine. Bandit inched forward, rubbing himself against Laran and let out a purr.

"Never apologize for branding me. I would not have it any other way. You are my mate, Ruby Morningstar. Now and forever." The sincerity of his words made my blood rush. A slow, steady tempo building in my head. My heart. My body. It thrummed with power. *Heat.*

"Laying it on a little thick there, War?" another voice whispered unceremoniously.

Laran's teeth clenched oh so slightly, but they did. Could he hear it too?

"Ruby, you must understand that it is not our place, nor anyone's, to brand you first. Just as no other but you would be able to brand us. That is how things work in our world," Allistair inserted, lazily watching the scene between me and Laran.

His feelings felt different, though. While not jealous, he was…possessive. Not so dark or dangerous as the way I felt it from Julian, but I got the distinct impression he wanted to be doing very bad things with me right now. Maybe it was better he wasn't on his knees expressing his undying devotion like Laran.

"You are Lucifer's daughter. For us to claim you before you and the beast choose us…it would be presumptuous, at best, and a deadly insult, at worst. Think about what the beast would do if another male were to claim you now. Would she allow it?" he asked me already knowing the answer.

Outside of them? No. No, neither of us would. I shook my head.

"Precisely," he sighed. "We have not claimed you because we're waiting to be chosen. Not because we want a harem of our own. I think I speak for us *all* when I say that," Allistair continued pointedly. I didn't miss the sly glance he shot at Julian whose true emotions were hidden behind an impenetrable mask.

"You already know how I feel, love. If not for it being your first feed, I would have gladly taken Allistair's place," Rysten added.

The warm fuzzy feeling in me spread. The beast appreciated their devotion, but she was still a bit irked by Julian's lack of response. The way she saw it, she chose him, and he was pushing against her dominance as a mate. I wish I could back away slowly with both hands raised, but that's not exactly possible when two beings occupied one body.

"Her first feed?" Moira interrupted, pulling me back from the perilously close edge I hadn't realized I'd approached. The beast was trying to lure me back so she could come forward again.

"The first time a succubus or incubus feed, we need more kama," Allistair explained. "Our own kind produces more than another demon, and demons produce more than humans. Ruby could have fed from one of them the first time, but they would have been severely depleted." He cocked an eyebrow at me, and I pursed my lips. Was that admiration on his face? Pride?

"Or died. Given how she fed she may have actually killed one of them, but fuck that would have been some way to die. Her mouth wrapped around my cock was—"

Two fingers grasped my chin, pulling me forward. I turned my head and met Laran's insistent stare.

"We were created to be your equals. For us, that meant that no other female would be ours. Even if you did not claim us, we would never have our own harems. That's not how we were made," he said in complete and utter seriousness. That was War for you. Not a man of many words, but the few he said were profound. At least to me.

"That doesn't mean you *have* to choose this…or that all of you want it," I finished, turning my eyes to the only one who had yet to speak. The one I currently couldn't read. The real core of this problem. "Do you?"

Julian stared at me with the most beautiful eyes I'd ever seen. They were a shade of green so deep and vibrant that I could try for a hundred years and still wouldn't get the color just right. But for all their beauty, they were incredibly cold. Like death…

"I want to keep you safe," Julian said evenly.

"That's not what I asked."

His words were a chip to my heart, but I wouldn't show it. They gave me every other part of themselves freely. I would not demand this from them. From him. The beast be damned. I would not tie him to me if he didn't want that.

Even if the other three did. Even if this would cause issues for years to come.

For centuries. I still wouldn't do it.

I wouldn't take his choice away.

"He's a fucking idiot—"

"Can't he pull his head out of his ass for two fucking seconds—"

"He's not fooling any—"

I pulled away sharply, breaking Laran's grip on my chin to shake my head.

What was going on? No one's lips were moving. No one was speaking. Was I going crazy?

Was I hearing voices?

"Ruby, babe…" Moira said, sliding away from the arm of the chair.

Panic flooded me at the loss of contact. I hadn't realized how much she was holding me together. How much her exhausted state of calm was keeping the burning at rest. My hand whipped out, faster than lightning. I wrapped my fingers around hers, pulling her to her knees before me with a flick of my wrist.

She hit the ground about as gracefully as could be expected, shoving Laran on her way down.

"What's up? Talk to me, Rubes," Moira murmured, raising a small green hand to my cheek. She hadn't called me that in years, and now three times in one day?

Embers flared inside of me. They drifted through my veins, catching fire where they went, and I was helpless against it. Hopeless to stop myself as power surged within me.

So far, every gift I had developed was deadly.

The flames of Hell.

Soul shredding.

Feeding.

What would be next? What personal hell would fate cook up to test me?

How much could I take before I broke apart at the seams?

How hot could I burn before the world caught fire with me?

I wasn't sure, but the sweltering fever that was coming on again didn't leave me all that confident.

"So…*hot…*" I breathed, the words shaking as I said them.

The room seemed to look almost…glassy? Like when you stood outside on a day that was hot as hell and stared into the distance. The way it almost smeared together as the sun cooked the very earth.

But we were inside. In December.

Which meant…

"Can you hear me, Ruby?" Moira asked, a tenor of worry in her voice.

I don't know when or how, but suddenly everyone was there. Allistair was at my left. Rysten at my right. Laran kneeled beside Moira, and Julian stood right in front, assessing the situation with a clinical gaze if I ever saw one.

"The transition is speeding up," he murmured.

"Do we move her—"

What's going on?

"She's heating the room, Julian—"

Where are these voices coming from?

"Something's coming—"

What's coming? Why isn't anyone answering me?

"She's starting to lose it—"

I clasped my hands over my ears and let out a choked cry.

"What is she doing?"

Can't they hear me?

"Do you think it's—"

"Stop!" I shouted. A wave of power flashed through the room and the glass warbled. Fire ignited at my fingertips where I held Moira's hand, but she held tight as it inched up my bare arms.

"Rubes, I need you to talk to me…" Moira trailed off as I raised my head and pulled her to me. Acting without thinking, I did the only thing that felt right in that moment.

I kissed her.

Never in my life had I felt anything sexual toward Moira, and this was no different. But a sudden burning desire to lay one on her filled me with a compulsion I couldn't control. I coaxed her lips apart with ease and breathed, exhaling the swirling tempest out of my chest and into her. I didn't understand what was going on. Why the power within was trying to claw its way out of me into anything. Into her.

Her lips pressed closed with a finality and I pulled away.

What the—

Of course, that's when she screamed—and I don't just mean any normal banshee scream. This was the sound of raw, undiluted pain.

And the very foundation itself trembled.

"Moira!" I cried, reaching out to her again. I didn't understand what had possessed me to do that, but the moment our skin made contact, the screaming died instantly, like someone cut her vocal cords.

She collapsed inward, her dark green hair spilling across my lap. I brushed my hand over her, my fingers snagging on something warm.

"What the—" I broke off as I turned her head.

Two tiny flaming horns poked out of her head, black and blue swirls coming together and solidifying in seconds, like the flames had frozen and been given form. They couldn't have been larger than two inches, but they were hard as stone and wicked sharp.

"Horns," Rysten whispered.

"And wings," Allistair added dryly.

I turned my gaze to the massive pair of flaming blue wings, slumped over like the girl whose back they were attached to. Veins of cobalt and indigo colored the strands of fire. Sections of dark flame moved through them, seemingly shifting and turning while still maintaining shape.

But her wings…they did not solidify.

They burned.

I reached out, brushing my hands over the hot strands, but felt no heat.

"How is this possible?" I whispered, fighting to regain control of the situation. Moira had wings—and horns—although the latter wasn't terribly surprising. I always knew she had them, but now the rest of the world could see it too.

"It's hard to say," Allistair murmured. "But if I had to guess, you might have inherited more abilities from Lola than we initially thought. Your mother could imbue objects with magic."

"Imbue with magic?" I asked, fighting the bristling that was running down my spine and the beast's cool gaze. That bitch knew what was going to happen to Moira. She knew, and she didn't give a damn.

If anything, she waited, sulking in the back of my mind until the pressure became too much. She allowed the power that had been lying dormant in me to unleash suddenly and violently, knowing how I would react because she knew me better than anyone. Even myself.

I wanted to hate her, but hating the entity that lives within me wouldn't help anyone. We're a package deal. Even if she branded all of them without asking, just to further her own selfish desires. Cunt.

"Imbuing is using your own power to alter something, or in your case, someone. Lola used to create weapons that could do things I have never seen. You pushed Moira through the entire transition in seconds. She won't be just a half-demon anymore…" I brushed my hand over her forehead, Allistair's voice falling short at what we saw.

"Is that what I think it is?" I didn't want to ask, but I had to. I was terrified at what it meant, because I'd only heard of a mark like this once.

"The horned helmet never lies," Julian replied.

A horned helmet with two black wings.

A brand. Moira had a brand.

But not just any brand.

"She's a legion," Rysten said in disbelief. "You've got to be kidding me."

Suddenly the beast's smugness made a lot more sense. We didn't just give her horns and wings of flame. We'd made her damn near untouchable, because a legion bore the mark of Cain.

Yet another thing that humans fudged across time. I guess that's what happens when immortal beings come to a mortal planet and conquer. Eve was sent here as punishment by her sister, Lilith and Lilith's lover, big daddy Lucifer. She had turned on them in the war between immortals at the dawn of time. The whys and hows have never been clear, partly because Eve started to lose her mind once on earth. She fucked anything and everything that could walk, sometimes killing the men in the process. Across all of that, she had only ever bore three sons. Seth, who disappeared and was never heard from again. Abel, who died. And Cain, who killed him.

The bible leaves out that Eve had commanded him to do it. She claimed to have had a vision of a horned helmet with black wings, and should one of her children offer up a worthy sacrifice, they would be gifted with this mark.

Only Cain was willing to listen and find out.

Since then, the mark had shown up again only a handful of times across history. It was legendary, because it was real. Cain had gone on to slay many demons. After impregnating as many women as possible, he ventured to Hell. He was the first and only Seelie to do so.

He also never came back out.

The mark of Cain appeared only in exceptional circumstances to those truly willing to do anything and everything for a goal. A purpose. Cain was the only Fae known to bear it, but there were whispers of children marked by blood or rune magic in an attempt to see if it held. If it could be recreated. It was said that any who bore this mark returned pain sevenfold.

I didn't know if that was true.

But what I did know was that for all intents and purposes, my best friend and familiar just got a hell of a lot harder to kill.

Unfortunately, I was the one that did this to her because whatever powers I had were running rampantly out of control. Judging by the Horsemen's pained expressions, they had already come to that conclusion.

"It was an accident."

I seemed to be saying that a lot nowadays. Despite having the Four Horsemen, Bandit, and Moira at my side—I couldn't seem to stay out of trouble. Or stop setting shit on fire.

And judging by the beast's shit-eating grin, she wasn't about to stop anytime soon.

On the contrary, she was just getting started.

CHAPTER SIX

I ASKED to see Moira for the hundredth time.

For the hundredth time, they said no.

"She's fine, love. Let her sleep it off," Rysten said.

I grumbled in response, leaning against the bed and ignoring the wall of instruments that had been taunting me for the last twelve hours. Shortly after Moira collapsed, they moved me back to my warded room, no matter how many times I protested. Eventually, Julian ordered War to move me whether I liked it or not.

Laran threw me over his shoulder and dropped my ass on the bed and he and Rysten had been watching over me since.

What they didn't realize was that the beast was pissed with them for it.

And so very close to the surface.

Julian had riled our anger, and very soon he was going to pay the consequences for that.

"Careful, Pestilence. She almost persuaded you that time."

Had I? I hadn't noticed?

It didn't take long being stuck in here with them to realize the voices I was hearing were not voices at all, but thoughts. Their thoughts.

"She's growing stronger. This bloody room is hotter than the fourth providence."

So it wasn't just me. That's nice. If they wanted to be assholes and lock me in here, at least they were sweating it out too.

"She has fire in her veins. I expected nothing less."

How was it that War's internal voice could make me shiver? My cheeks warmed and I turned away, but not fast enough.

"Something wrong, love?" Rysten asked. He stood by the door, trying his best to look at ease and not like a guard. He failed.

"Nothing, I just—"

"Ruby, you're a terrible liar."

Oh crap. I could come clean that I'd been hearing their thoughts, and let's be honest, they were bound to find out soon enough. But it was nice having insight into the things they wouldn't normally tell me. For all I knew they had a way to turn it off, and I'd rather hear them than sit in silence like they thought I had been doing.

"Um—well—you see—"

Rysten lifted his eyebrows, a grin forming on his lips. Still, I don't know what persuaded me to say what I did next.

"I have to take a shit."

I couldn't believe I had just said that.

Just when I was going to retract my statement, my beast mentally shoved hard, not vying for control, but throwing me off-kilter long enough that by the time I looked up, Rysten had a tinge of pink on his cheeks.

"Oh, I see…" he trailed off, looking to Laran for help.

War sat in the lone armchair on the other side of the room because he was trying to keep his hands off me. Apparently, I smelled good.

"Should I let her go to the bathroom?" Rysten asked silently.

"If she has to shit, then she has to shit," Laran shrugged.

"Maybe I should ask Julian…"

Really? Now that irked the hell out of me. He didn't know I didn't actually need the bathroom, but he was going to ask Julian if I could go?

I bent, clasping my stomach. My motions were more guided by the beast than I wanted to admit. "I really gotta go, Rysten," I groaned. His decision wavered. "Unless you want me to shit on the floor…"

Rysten stepped into a shadow and disappeared. The next moment the door cracked open and he waved me forward.

"For the record, love, that's disgusting. Next time just say you need to go."

Isn't that what I started with? May as well make use of the opportunity…

As soon as I crossed through the ward, I knew something was up, but it wasn't until I closed the bathroom door behind me that I knew what.

"I'm right outside the door if you need me," Rysten called. I loudly grunted my response as I placed my hands on the bathroom sink.

A shudder ran through me.

What was that?

I stilled, pressing a hand to my chest. Nothing.

I breathed a heavy sigh and moved to use the bathroom.

Instantly, my stomach twisted in hard knots as a second shudder ran through me. I cried out once, leaning against the counter for support.

I had never been one to suffer from extreme cramps. Even my time of month was mild compared to Moira. But this was something else. I'd never felt a pain that wrapped around your insides and pulled like it was trying to tear apart every muscle.

I gasped in mouthfuls of air, but the reprieve didn't last long. A splicing sensation ripped through me, running straight from the apex of my thighs to the brand on my chest. It left a searing pain trailed by pleasure as it rammed into my sternum.

The pentagram pulsed. Once. Twice. Like a tidal wave it gathered its strength, building deep inside me, pulling from every essence of my being.

Laran had said I had fire in my veins. He wasn't wrong.

Those very veins lit up beneath my skin, casting me in an eerie light blue inside the semi-dark bathroom. My brand pulsed faster beneath my shirt, the outline showing up through the thin cotton tank top. I brushed my fingers against the fabric where it connected with my skin, and the brand flashed brighter. It began spinning beneath my shirt and an awful gut-wrenching feeling filled me.

This was it.

My shirt caught fire, erupting in a brilliant blaze that disintegrated not even a moment later. Heat engulfed me as I stumbled back from the bathroom counter. Head pounding. Heart beating. My knees hit the floor with a bang as flashing lights danced before my eyes.

Black. White. *Blue.*

The flames of Hell.

Banging.

I could hear banging in the distance as the Horsemen called to me.

It was too late for that. Too late for me.

Wrapped in a cocoon of flame and fire and ash, my conscience wavered.

I could feel it, my power approaching this crest as the tidal wave within swept through me. It built so far, so fast, that when the beast took my hand, I was glad. She could control it. She could get us through this when I couldn't.

Because there was no way I could possibly control what was coming.

Moira was just the beginning, and there was a hell of a lot more inside me where that came from. I saw a vision: a flaming girl with a crown of charred bones, sitting above a blackened city.

The Horsemen thought they could control me. They thought they were ready for me.

They thought wrong.

This was a pivotal moment where I could decide what part of me took control in transition.

But we both knew who I would choose when it came down to it.

We both knew what was coming.

My beast and I stepped into the flames of my soul together. We felt the immense power that lay there.

Power beyond what this world knew.

It didn't belong here.

We didn't belong here.

And in that moment, the future of both worlds was hanging by a single thread.

Because when it snapped, I would never be the same again.

"I will do what must be done," she whispered to me.

I believed her.

Maybe that was my first mistake. Maybe the fire and the heat had really gotten to me.

Or maybe it was what needed to be done for me to survive.

For Hell to survive.

Either way I would never know, because I wrapped my arms around her and the thread ignited.

And then we fell.

Fell into the flaming pits of my own self, where I would rise again.

Not as the half-breed I always thought myself to be.

But as the queen I must become.

When my eyes opened, they were not blue, but black.

I had hit the transition.

The bathroom door blew open. With her head bowed she could not see who, but she knew. She always knew. The beast was so much cleverer than they gave her credit for.

They thought her wild and savage, but they failed to see how much she loved her games.

She raised her head to the Four Horsemen. Her mates.

Though one of them had yet to see it.

No matter.

They stared at her with a challenge and she smiled wickedly.

It was time to play.

RYSTEN

Power erupted like a shock wave through the apartment. Dread didn't have time to fill me, because I knew. I knew what was coming.

My fists smashed against the door as I tried to break it down, to tear it off its hinges. Soon that banging was not just me, but Laran as well. A second wave swept through, stronger than the first, and then we heard the screaming.

The transition was not kind. It was not enjoyable. For something that was mortal to become immortal, your own body would turn on itself. Your mind would go mad.

Ruby talked about burning before, but for someone as strong as her? I don't know how she would overcome it. Power comes with a price, and for the strongest of us, we pay the most.

My transition had been unbearable. I'd rotted from the inside out so long that I grew to resent the power of Pestilence. Julian's transition had killed him. Except Death can't die, and so he lived and died, again and again, until it passed.

But Ruby? She was more than death or destruction, and judging by her screams, she was burning.

"Open the door, love!" I called out.

It was hopeless. Somehow, some way, she had sealed the bathroom.

Where my strength alone should have removed the door with one hit, it stayed firm, not a single mark made.

She had to have imbued the entire fucking bathroom so no one could enter.

I doubt she even realized it.

A third shockwave ripped through the building.

"The wards aren't going to hold her."

"There is a plan B if they don't," Allistair replied.

He didn't sound anymore thrilled about that plan than I had been. A cabin in the middle of a remote Tennessee forest. Then when she burned something down, there would hopefully be no people.

A single tendril of fear wrapped around me. Not fear for myself, but fear for what that would do to her should the wards fail. Should *we* fail. The insanity will set in and our only hope will be that it is Ruby to reason with, and not the beast.

I shuddered. If that creature were subject to the power within her while the bite of transition warped their reality…

Hell have mercy on us all.

I sent one last thundering punch into the door and the wood finally gave. A quick kick and it blew off the hinges, releasing a wave of power that even I had not predicted. The wards buckled instantly.

Fire obscured everything from view and then it died out. Nothing had burned. Nothing and no one, but the still and silent girl, crouched on her knees. Her long blue hair covered much of her naked body, but not all. Blue ivy-like vines crawled across her skin, moving and shifting like the brands she'd placed on others. It seems the transition had given her a second mark. Unheard of, but not surprising.

We waited for her to make a move.

To scream in pain.

To lash out.

Dread formed in the silence. Dread and fear.

She lifted her face and I was right to be afraid.

The wards had failed, and the beast stared back at me.

CHAPTER SEVEN

Rysten was the first to move, taking a single step through the door. He watched her with caution. Like she was a wild animal.

And maybe she was, but it was too late for his caution now.

Or his pretty words.

"Why don't we go back to the room, love…" His voice trailed off when she started laughing. It began as a low husky sound. Not quite as cold as she had been in the past, but the callousness was still there.

"Do you really believe that will work on me now?" she asked him, a very self-assured smirk applied itself to her lips.

If they didn't know it yet, they were in deep shit.

"I assumed you wished to claim your next mate," Rysten said carefully. He didn't declare himself it, but he insinuated.

"There lies the problem," the beast said. She brought her arms up over her head, cracking several joints in her body. She arched into the stretch, completely and utterly naked, only covered by a thin film of black. "You make too many assumptions. Just because she is young does not mean she cannot make choices for herself, yet you only listen when I am here."

Oh shit. I knew where this was going, but for once…I didn't really disagree.

"We do not mean to make decisions for her—"

"War," she interrupted like Rysten wasn't speaking at all. From the doorway, Laran straightened a little, but did not approach. "Do you wish to come with me, or join your brothers?"

She sounded almost bored in how she asked it, but I don't think the tone was fooling anyone. She was giving him a choice, while telling them she was leaving.

"Join my brothers?" he asked slowly. He was much better about teetering the line of respect.

"For the hunt," she supplied. He stayed still as stone, watching her with a troubled gaze.

"Don't make me do this, Ruby," his thoughts pleaded. He still didn't know we could hear.

"And you, Famine? Would you wish to join me?" the beast continued, giving nothing away.

"She intends to run," our other mate projected.

They thought they could stop her. She found this amusing.

Almost as much as the tick in Julian's jaw. At this rate, he would crack a tooth if he continued to clench so hard.

"Very well," she said after several seconds passed. "I'll be on my way, then."

A hidden smile crossed her lips as she took her first step forward and Rysten dived.

In the blink of an eye, she slammed the palm of her hand into his sternum and he went flying—straight into the mirror.

Silence filled the air until the other three registered what had just happened.

They exchanged uneasy glances, as if deciding who would try next.

Of course, with their size, the three of them couldn't all enter the bathroom and expect to fight. And while they may be born and bred warriors, the beast wasn't above playing dirty.

Allistair stepped forward and smiled, but there was nothing gentle in it.

"Little succubus," he murmured, "do you wish to play?" His voice brushed against her skin, but she wouldn't be thrown by his persuasion so easily. No matter the promise it held.

"Very much so, my golden one," she purred back, smirking with more than feminine sexuality. Allistair raised a hand, palm open, as if to offer an olive branch. She cocked her head and laughed a dark sound. "But I think we have different games in mind."

He lunged for her at the same moment she ducked. Spinning, she skated just beneath his grasp and landed a kick at his back. Allistair, too, went flying. He crashed into the bathtub, his head banging the porcelain as he did. A crack appeared and a chunk of it fell, but he looked unharmed.

The beast smirked down at him, feeling the last two enter the bathroom while she did. She couldn't see them, but she felt them. Their power. Their emotions. Their very essence called out to us. To her. She turned with a well-aimed punch to the jugular, only to hit the palm of Laran's hand. He wrapped his fingers around her fist.

"Don't make me do this, Ruby," he said, trying to pull her in. Claimed mate or not, he would try to stop her. What they all failed to see was that that's why we were in this position to begin with. I gave, and gave, and gave. I did what was asked of me. I walked away from my old life.

But I would not walk into my new one as a prisoner.

Rysten made the first move when he tried to physically subdue her.

She had washed her hands of whatever happened next, long before the first punch was thrown.

Using power I hadn't known I possessed, the beast looked up at him and leaned forward. Taking a light breath, she exhaled slowly, forming a small "O" with her lips.

Blue smoke saturated the space around him and he inhaled upon reflex, not realizing his mistake until it was too late.

"Kneel," she commanded.

And Laran—the Horseman of War—one of the most powerful beings on this world and the next—fell to his knees before his queen.

He released her hand as if compelled by whatever spell she put on him and lowered his head in respect. She gave him a glance that no one would see. It was as close to affection as this creature could possibly get.

"You did not wish to harm me, War. I will not punish that," she murmured, just a hairsbreadth above a whisper. Laran groaned but did not move. She had full control over his actions. For how long, I wasn't sure, but I had a feeling we were going to find out.

"Please don't maim any of them. They're rather pretty how they are," I told her. The beast let out a cold laugh.

"I have no intentions of hurting that which is mine," she replied.

"Ours," I corrected.

She shrugged. To her, the semantics didn't matter. We were two beings in one body; some things were bound to be a bit difficult.

Only one now stood between her and the door.

The only one who had yet to speak.

But his silence spoke more than words could.

"Do you think you can stop me, Death, where your brothers could not?" she asked him.

He stood tall and impenetrable. His clearly defined muscles stretching beneath the thin cotton shirt. The fitted black lounge pants really accentuated his assets.

While I admired his physical traits, the beast appraised him with cool, calculating eyes. Out of all the Horsemen, he would be the hardest to get past.

Not only was he the strongest, Death was the most resistant, fighting his own attraction and the inevitable claiming.

The thought alone infuriated her, but she kept that fire close. Contained.

"Why?" he demanded, not answering the question. "Why are you doing this?"

He should have known better. His bare feet padded across the marble floors, staying just out of her reach. Circling her, but not attacking.

The beast cocked her head and watched him closely.

Trailing him where he walked was an almost invisible silver mist. It clung to his pores, brushing against his skin, filling the air with something not sweet...but sharp. Painful.

Kama.

He was giving off kama.

Did he even realize it? Did he know that he was provoking her?

They liked to talk like we were the ultimate predator. Yet, they seemed to have such a blatant disregard for these things. I was a succubus and the beast, in full transition. I wanted sex and blood and all things unholy.

But her? There was only one thing she wanted more.

She had waited twenty-three years to be let out of her cage and she had patience in spades because of it.

"I am a queen," the beast replied. "But you four seem to have forgotten that along the way. I do not exist to be put in a cage because you have deemed me too powerful. You were created to *balance* me, were you not?"

He didn't answer, but his unreadable features were slowly cracking under pressure. He liked to pull his emotions inward and bury them. To wear a mask as cold as the marble beneath her feet.

But even marble could break.

"How would you like to be put in cage? Locked in a room and told what to do? Because that's exactly what you did to us." She motioned to her own naked body.

"That was not the intent," Julian said slowly through clenched teeth.

"Intent matters not," she replied. Another fissure appeared in his armor, his emotions leaking through. He was not afraid of us. Of her. But he did feel other things.

Anger. So much anger. Unlike us, who felt fire in our belly. His wrath was cold. Desolate. All-consuming.

And right now, she was the cause of it. He wanted nothing more than to tie her up and show her what a monster he was. To lock her away from both worlds, prophecies be damned. Earth and Hell be damned. He wanted to show her what a true mate could bring and make her forget about all the humans that ever thought they could keep her. To purge them from her memory. To let her feel the bite of his teeth and the crack of a—

A barrier slammed into me, closing me off from his emotions. Julian tilted his head to the side and examined her closely.

"Ruby isn't fighting you," he murmured, more to himself than anything. "Why isn't she fighting you?"

Could he feel me in his mind? Could he sense that the beast did not hold me prisoner in my own?

She cocked her head and smiled. "There is much to be done before we return home. She knows that."

He narrowed his emerald eyes, the anger within him seeping through.

He didn't understand. None of them would. It was up to us.

I would transition and claim my mates, but the beast knew things I didn't. She could teach me things they couldn't. Make me stronger. We shared this body, and for once, our interests overlapped, even if the reasoning wasn't exactly the same.

"It's the transition. Ruby wouldn't run," Julian replied. "She knows she's safer—"

"Stop telling me what is safe!" I snapped mentally. Julian blanched like I'd struck him, and the beast smiled.

"You see, Death, I am not the only one that is tired of this. You chafe against the inevitable. You impose where it is not your duty. We want a partner. A mate. Not a bodyguard."

Without preamble, she bolted through the door, faster than Death could stop her, but not so fast that he couldn't react. She made it to the living room before he appeared in front of her, walking out of the shadows.

"There's nowhere to go and you cannot teleport," he said. Like that would stop her. Had he learned nothing? "Stop this, Ruby—"

"Why?" the beast asked, her voice turning cold. "So you can chain me up? Lock me away?" she asked mockingly, and his face darkened. He took three large steps toward us, his presence filling up the space. In his chest was a tempest of emotions, so strong, so thick that I could drown in them if not careful.

Still, she let him closer. Close enough his shirt brushed against her bare breasts. They pebbled against the friction and the ever-insistent fire burned. She looked up at him with a challenge because we weren't the only ones that had shit to work on here.

Julian stared down at her, silver particles falling from his skin. She leaned forward and inhaled deeply, a frenzy starting in her chest. His pupils dilated. Another fissure in his carefully composed mask exposed as his hard cock pressed into her belly. Her lips brushed up the hard contour of his jaw, the stubble doing deliciously wicked things to my imagination.

A growl started in his chest as he reached out and grasped her hips, pulling her closer. His control was so very close to snapping. She had every intention of letting him unravel so that we would have to put him back together. "You want me, Death?" her breath whispered across his skin, promising what was to come. "Come and get me."

The words had hardly left her lips when his hands tightened. Just as with Laran, she breathed out a heavy blue fog that he foolishly inhaled.

His hands went slack as if by command and she easily stepped out of them.

"That's a nifty trick," I said.

"I'll teach you how to do it. How to do everything, once I take care of them."

The other three Horsemen had recovered and spread themselves around the living room. Slowly closing in around her.

They muttered words in a language neither of us understood. First

Laran. Then Allistair. Followed by Rysten. And Julian had regained his composure. A thread snapped around them as the four moved closer.

Binding. They were trying to *bind* her.

I wasn't sure how that possible, given what they were. None of them possessed powers to bind someone. Allistair could make me want to fuck him till I died. Laran could kill me using every element known to man. Rysten could inflict any disease on me. Julian could hold me, my spirit, between here and the veil, never allowing peace.

But none of them could bind me.

It shouldn't be possible, and yet, that is what they were about to do.

Laran withdrew a blade and sliced open his palm. Power that was not my own crackled through the air. He passed the blade to Allistair. She looked up at him with destruction in her eyes. Allistair was her second mate, but they had barely spoken on it because of the circumstances in which it came about. I could tell not by his eyes, but by his emotions, that he didn't want to do this. He didn't want to force some kind of binding on me.

But when the beast looked at him, she was not forgiving or understanding.

He sighed under his breath in frustration, but at least had the balls to look at her as he brought the knife down. Blue blood splattered the carpet and the air popped around her, almost like a vacuum. She could hear nothing but them and their whispers as it slowly rose to a chant.

Rysten took the knife next, his eyes speaking an apology that his mouth would not say. She stared back at him defiantly and he cringed as he slashed his hand. Blood swirled, moving to form a circle around her. All it took was one and the binding would be complete.

She moved to knock the knife away and hit an invisible barrier.

I grimaced, but she was not perturbed. The beast had an ace up her sleeve that no one, not even I, had realized.

She felt for his presence and called to him.

They could not stop her. No one could.

Not when she had her familiar*s*.

From down the hall a wild screech rang out as twenty pounds of fur and fury launched itself towards us. Bandit had been waiting and answer the call, he did.

He leapt through the barrier that was meant for her, and she leaned down for him to scurry up her arm.

She summoned a circle of flame around them and forced it outwards. The two magics clashed together at the edge of the circle and the fire swayed. They were strong. Strong enough that without Bandit she might not have been able to do it.

His claws pricked her skin, the sharp pain filling her with a sociopathic sort of calm.

She ground her nails in the palms of her hands and the sweltering heat within us snapped, sending a pulsing wave of fire at their circle.

The blood incinerated, and the binding broke as the flames of Hell consumed it all. The Horsemen were thrown from where they stood by the immense power that erupted from within her.

She stepped out of the blood circle and I made note of the magic they had used.

Magic that I had only seen once before.

Magic that demons could not use.

My attention focused on the scene before me as she looked over her shoulder and blew them a kiss. Blue flames burned at their clothes, but the Horsemen were unharmed, albeit furious as they watched her.

None more so than Death.

"If you want us, then you will earn us."

She turned back to the wall of glass and took off at a run.

It exploded on impact and melted before it could cut her skin. The wall of glass that had kept us in was ultimately the weakest point, allowing us our freedom.

Stark naked, she jumped from the third story of the apartment building and landed with a victory cry from Bandit.

Without a glance back at what we'd left behind, the beast and Bandit walked into the shadows of New Orleans and she whispered into the dead of night, "Let the games begin."

****LARAN****

Shattered glass and black ash. The fleeting scent of amaryllis and old magic. Ruby hadn't just left us. She'd destroyed us. She and the beast.

It gave me a choice, to stay or to go. I chose wrong.

At the time, I didn't think she would get further than ten feet. That one of us would catch her.

But no one did, and now she was smoke in the wind.

Burnt carpet and the tang of blood filled the air in her stead. It was all that remained of our failed attempt to not only catch Ruby, but to contain her as well.

"We have to go after her," Death growled.

"No fucking kidding," Allistair spat.

They were angry. They should be. I should be…and yet, I wasn't.

As a claimed mate to the daughter of the devil, I was privy to some things. Brief flashes of emotion. A sense of knowing. Our bond was only half formed with a fraction of her own magic placed beneath my skin. Nothing near the amount Moira should feel as her familiar, but a small sliver of that wild magic lay there. Pulling me. Prodding me.

Even from far away I could sense the panic inside of her. The turbulent emotions were more reminiscent of a firestorm, as opposed to the pure lust a succubus should feel in transition. She was upset, and something told me we were the ones who caused it.

I sighed deeply, walking to the edge. Glass crunched beneath my bare feet as I looked out over New Orleans, but the dark city kept its secrets and hid my transitioning mate.

We had to find her. They weren't wrong.

But we had to make it right.

I turned away from the glass and walked through the house. The other Horsemen did not follow me. I was not their concern, not now, not ever.

A single unmarked door sat at the end of a hallway.

I did not delay.

The metal of the handle was hot, but not as heated as the room inside. Nothing was ablaze, apart from the wings of a sleeping girl. She lay on her back with her flaming wings spread limply across the bed. Arms strewn across her chest and head lying at an angle, the pinched expression of her face did not make me think she was having happy dreams.

I looked to the ceiling knowing that once I did this, it was done. There was no going back. I was waking a sleeping monster, quite literally, who may be as powerful as me for all we knew.

But she was my mate's familiar, and if anyone could bring her back to us, it was this girl and only her.

"Moira," I said her name once and that was all it took. The banshee's eyes flew wide open. Glazed and unfocused, she stared at the ceiling for a moment.

"What have you done?"

CHAPTER EIGHT

I DON'T KNOW what in Satan's name I was thinking giving her control, but it's not like there was much I could do about it now. With my out of control magic and never-ending fever, we were safer with her in charge. As odd as that may sound. She at least knew how to control the flames. That was more than could be said for me. Last time I tried, the best I could manage was *not* spreading the fire and my track record wasn't exactly stellar.

Bandit let out a chittering noise, drawing my attention to them because she was heading into a pretty shady part of town. Covered by nothing more than a thin film of obsidian ash, the beast strutted forth with a self-assured confidence, paying no mind to those on the street who passed her.

"Where are you going?" I probably should have asked that before now, but I guess it was better late than never.

"I'm hungry." Umm…there was two ways to construe that and I wasn't very comfortable with either. *"I expended a lot of energy breaking the binding."*

The binding they shouldn't have been able to create as demons. Best not to forget that. Only the Unseelie had blood magic, and while the Horsemen weren't any old demons, they weren't Fae either. Something wasn't adding up here.

"How were they able to cast that in the first place?" I wondered.

"I don't know." Her body did not react, but I sensed her displeasure. Not with me, but with the unknown. With the things that neither of us knew or

understood because of the roles we'd played for twenty-three years. Her, the prisoner waiting to be released. Me, the ignorant half-demon that didn't want to believe the truth when it bailed me out of jail. Neither roles left us well-equipped for what we would become. Good thing I was a quick study and she could simply use brute force.

She rounded a corner, ignoring the damp air that embraced her like a lover. It may have been December, but we weren't in Oregon any more. Here you didn't just drink your water. You inhaled it. And judging by the thick clouds looming in the night sky, tonight was going to pour. The wispy base of the clouds lit in shades of purple and pink from light pollution, casting a glow over the crescent city. Meanwhile, soft music drifted from somewhere in the distance. Calling to us.

The beast lifted her head and parted her lips, inhaling the stray gust of wind that broke through the heavy atmosphere. Scents of sweat and blood filled her nostrils, along with something else…the barest hint of kama.

"Dinner," she surmised, following the wind. It led in the same direction as the music.

"I'm not fucking anyone but the four males we left back there, so if that's your great plan—" I started to protest.

"We're not fucking anyone," the beast replied. She didn't give any further explanation as to what we were doing, but as long as I was in the backseat, I guess the best I could do was watch.

She strolled through the brightly lit streets with purpose, tracking that infinitesimal fleck of kama. Several men hooted and hollered, women too, but she paid them no mind. As Allistair would say, they were beneath her attention.

The beast purred at the thought of him. Not because she missed him. Oh no. She was more fucked up than that. She purred at the fact that they were probably going out of their minds trying to find us, because she wanted them to earn their spot. It was going to be a fun game of cat and mouse as they tried to catch us, and she repeatedly slipped through their fingers.

They wouldn't catch her and keep her until they got smarter and learned we would go where we pleased. That we wouldn't be locked away.

We could hold our own in every way and they needed to fucking realize that.

She laughed as she came to a halt in front of a door. Outside, two men

—no, two demons—stood with their arms over their chests. A line wrapped around the block, consisting of both humans and demons. Internally I frowned, until I realized the only people they were turning away at the door were humans.

She glanced up, a smirk coming over her lips at the name of the club.

The Lotus.

This sounded like a bad idea if I ever heard one.

"Are you sure you know what you're doing here?"

Instead of answering me, she walked up to the front of the line and took a slow breath. This was indeed the place. Kama flowed into our lungs, both sating the succubus side and luring her deeper. My thoughts scattered, slipping through my grasp as I tried to cling to a reason for why we shouldn't enter.

Not that the beast cared whether I did or didn't have a reason. She walked forward to stand at the rope, and both the bouncers, as well as most of the line, took notice. Hard not to when there's a naked girl covered in glittery black shit.

I really hoped she chose to find us some clothes soon, because the two large blokes looked like they might eat me.

"What do we have here—"

"Move," the beast cut him off. There was such darkness in her tone. An inkling as to what they would find if they disobeyed.

The larger of the two demons peered down at her, his glamor non-existent to her eyes. Bright red skin and a tail. He was a rare form of monster, exceptionally useful for guarding things, but not the smartest of demons. The rubrum were born with skin the color of bone, but as they proved their battle prowess and bathed in their enemies' blood, it gradually turned red or blue, absorbing the pigment. Judging by his skin at this unknown hour in the night, I'd say he was middle of the way.

That his skin was red and not blue like demons' blood spoke volumes as to what most of his kills were. The beast did not shy away.

The rubrum was not who answered her, though, but instead an imp with hard features and a vicious smile. He didn't know that we had history with his kind, and that if he didn't watch himself, he'd end up Bar-B-Que. Or raccoon food. It was a toss-up at this point.

"That's not how it works, little lady."

Why was it that males loved to use pet names? I sighed internally, and the beast cocked her head.

"You will move, one way or another."

With that, she held up her hand where both humans and demons could see and snapped her fingers. A small blue flame appeared, spreading to her fingertips. She took a step forward and the imp took a step back. That made her smile.

The humans started running.

The demons in line had the good sense to either back away slowly or stay still, lowering their gaze in a sign of submission.

"Whoa…we didn't mean—"

"I know what you meant."

Bandit's claws pricked at her arms as he arched forward and let out a growl. Clearly, he wasn't a fan of the demon either.

Fortunately for them, that was the moment the imp decided to make this easy. He unclipped the rope and stepped aside, lowering his head slightly. The beast walked forward and unflinchingly gazed up at the rubrum who was still trying to decide whether he should attempt to take us on. The imp elbowed him in the side and flicked his eyes down, trying to give the other bouncer the hint.

She waited, her eyes staring past the black irises of the lesser demon, straight into the fiery pits of his soul.

Broken loves and stinging losses filled the empty void in front of us where the rubrum stood. His soul was marked by pain that was used in an attempt to make him pliant.

Abuse. He suffered from extreme abuse at the hands of other demons. The beast took this in, staring at the angry red light from within his chest. While my own internal light was a bright blue that flickered like flames, his was dark. Dangerous. The rubrum were a loyal lot, but someone had hurt this one inexplicably.

I don't know what possessed her to do what she did next. That's not true. I knew it was me. What I didn't know was that I possessed any power over her. However, it seemed that our body was always at odds in trying to balance us, and neither one was completely in control.

Either way, I acted on instinct, just like I had with Moira. Leaning forward, I pushed the beast to place her hand on his chest, driven by an urge I didn't understand and had no hope of controlling.

Her fire-tipped fingers splayed across the cheap material, burning straight through his tight t-shirt. The rubrum did not scream or lift a hand against her. He was better trained than that. His muscles clenched tightly as the fire licked at his chest. She pushed the heat inward to burn at the festering wounds around his soul. It hurt more in the moment as the fire burned away the dead and dying parts. I could sense his pain, feel it, searing through his chest. He thought he was being splayed open before the world, but really, the demons around us had no idea.

Fire was destructive. Deadly. But if used right, fire could heal. As the most brutal form of cleansing, it had the power to wipe clean the stains. Our fire ate through the diseased parts of his soul that held him down, cauterizing wounds that were slowly killing him.

He burned in an inferno that others couldn't see.

And then it was done.

The beast pulled away, not bothering to avert her eyes from the charred handprint she left on his chest. But there was no pentagram like there had been with the others she'd claimed. The beast was careful to heal, but not to bond in any way.

Which was good. The Horsemen might've killed him if they thought otherwise.

The beast stepped away and turned for the door, even more depleted than when she'd walked up. Internally, she was grumbling something about me being allowed to make requests. It wasn't her I was really listening to.

"Hey—hey—" A warm hand wrapped around her arm. She turned slowly, her dark gaze falling on him like the chill of death. The rubrum had the good sense to drop his hand. An almost sheepish look crossed his face as he sank to both knees before her. "You…you healed me. How can I repay you?"

The beast stared on impassively. "You have nothing I desire."

The rubrum frowned, running his hand across his five o'clock shadow. "Nothing?"

His brows inched up as she repeated, "Nothing."

I didn't get the impression he was used to other demons not wanting anything from him. That's how it was with most of our kind.

"That won't do," he mumbled, his tail shifting back and forth as he frowned to himself, thinking in silence. "Surely there's something I can give…" He trailed off, almost like he was distraught. I hadn't met any rubrum before, but he definitely wasn't panning out like the stereotypes.

The beast cocked her head, pursing her lips. "What do they call you?" she asked.

"What do they call you? Really? This is the twenty-first century. No one talks like that," I sniped at her. She didn't reply.

"The name's Eugene McGee. My friends call me Gene," the rubrum answered, almost chipper. That was…unexpected.

"I need to replenish and then I need a guide. Do you think you could handle that, Eugene McGee?" she asked him in her heartless voice. I wanted to bang my head against the wall, but it would do no good. Whatever power I momentarily took from her to heal him was already gone and she was firmly in control with a plan that was batshit crazy on a good day.

"They're going to go insane looking for us. You know that, right?" I asked her. The beast smiled outwardly as Eugene McGee got to his feet to escort her in, ignoring the annoying imp who couldn't stop gawking.

"I'm planning on it," she replied as she stepped into the strip club.

When they finally caught up, she had every intention of going with them, but that didn't mean she was going to make it easy. She'd waited a long time for this, and she was going to make the most of it.

MOIRA

"You did *what*?" I snapped at them, momentarily transfixed as the words left my mouth…like a ripple on a lake, the tenor pushed outwards and towards the walls.

The room strained beneath the tension. I blinked.

"Moira, we need your help right now—"

I tilted my head. His voice also gave off waves, but these were flexible, not hard or unyielding as mine were. I reached out to touch the almost invisible bending of light and sound.

The wave parted, and a dual echo filled my ears.

Strange…

"You were saying," I murmured. Again, a ripple filled the air. Like the sun in a desert, the longer I stared at the distant wall in front of me, the more the ripples continued. They hit the walls in front of me, flattening with a ping against the hard surface.

"The beast is free in New Orleans—"

The almost invisible bending lines followed the direction of his voice. I pushed them backwards wanting to shove them down his throat at the obscenity of that statement.

And guess what?

They did.

The taut tendrils snapped and raced back inside of him. Laran—tall, broad, and strong as he was—clutched his throat in pain.

I smiled cruelly.

"You lost her?" I asked, this time focusing on War and not the power coursing in my veins, or the way the air practically sang.

There was sound in *everything*.

And I had power over sound.

"We didn't lose her," he ground out with a rough growl. I gave him a non-amused look and pushed those waves back inside of him. Harder.

The asshole choked, and I didn't feel the least bit bad.

I couldn't remember much before sleeping. Ruby had been having one of her Debbie downer moments and I told her to get over herself. Fuck them, brand them, and be done with it.

We didn't have time for anything else.

Clearly, she had deviated a bit from that, somewhere along the way.

"You're awake?"

The sound came from a different dumbass. I whipped my head around, relinquishing whatever hold I had over the ripples that caused Laran pain.

"Obviously." My voice cut through the air like a scythe. Sharper than any blade, and it was well below a scream or a shout.

I was quite surprised when a crack split the air as it ran through the wall beside him. I arched an eyebrow, because that was just too fucking convenient to be anything but me. But I was just a banshee, and a half-breed at that…

But the wall had cracked.

And Laran had choked.

And Rysten was pale as a sheet.

"I'm assuming he told you then?" He flicked his eyes to Laran. Not quite angry, but also not kind. He hadn't wanted me awakened.

Awakened…

Why did that sound so—I reached for my chest gasping for a tight breath, because I remembered. I remembered *everything*. The burning. The tear. The ripping in my back as my muscles were torn apart. The scorch as the flames ran through my blood, filling every nook and cranny with a volatile magic. It filled my very being, mixing with everything that I am.

It fused with me. Molded to me. Changed me.

The feeling of a knife carving into my forehead sent a fresh wave of anxiety as I rode the memory, lost in a flashback.

There was a heavy aching in my back where a weight that shouldn't be there sat like a log. I reached out to brush the sweat from my forehead and pull the tangled hairs away from my face. My hand snagged on something sharp.

I pulled away. Blood. A thin line of blue blood ran down a cut in my palm. I frowned at the trickle of sapphire, and then I reached again.

Horns.

I had fucking *horns*.

Should I have been upset? Because an almost gleeful feeling began to fill me.

I turned and caught a glimpse of something large and blue and made of...*flame*.

Wings.

Those were *wings*. And they were attached to my back.

I had wings. I had horns. I was seeing waves in the air—and controlling them, for that matter.

But most of all, there was an incessant tugging in my chest. An invisible line that led from me straight to my blue-haired best friend. I'd felt attached to her before. She was my family after all, and apparently, I was her familiar. This was something different, though, and a sneaking suspicion sat on the edge of my mind. I grasped for it, trying to piece every bit of information that I held. Like smoke, it slipped through my grasp, but I wouldn't give up so easily.

Something wasn't right here.

"What am I?"

Rysten blanched. Laran sighed.

They were feeling nervous now? Shy all of a sudden, *after* they woke me up? I didn't wait for them to start rambling. I pushed my way out of the door and walked down the hallway, passing both Julian and Allistair as I turned for the bathroom—and stopped dead in my tracks.

Black ashes. Broken glass. A mirror splintered into a million pieces.

There, in all the shards, was my reflection refracted a thousand different ways. I leaned over, aware of the silence as I picked up a single fragment of mirror and looked at myself.

A horned helmet atop two black wings.

The mark of Cain.

And it was branded on my forehead.

Well, well, well. It seems that somehow, in some way, I had transitioned.

"Alright pony boys, it's time you start talking and tell me how the fuck I became a legion." Pestilence choked on a cough.

"And then, we're going to figure out how to get Ruby back."

CHAPTER NINE

THE DAYS BLURRED as we traveled from one club to the next, feeding on the kama in the atmosphere. True to her word, we didn't screw a single person —but as the days went by, I was itching to. We were still very much in transition, and while she seemed to be able to control it, the brief moments I had peeked through only resulted in…small catastrophes…or miracles. It really depended on how you looked at it.

Eugene McGee was the only demon whose soul I healed, but he was far from the only odd case of magical output. On the first night in the Lotus, she ended up so high that I slipped in momentarily and ended up turning Bandit's hair blue. Not that he seemed to mind being ringed in black and blue. If I didn't know any better, I'd say he thought he looked rather stylish. He certainly seemed to be flaunting himself more, but that may just have been the steady diet of fresh fish Eugene was bringing him. The rubrum seemed to feel that he owed me a life debt, and no request the beast made, no matter how outlandish, swayed him to thinking otherwise. He'd decided our well-being was of the utmost importance, and while I could almost find it sweet at times—the hero worship didn't sit well with me. Not to mention how the Horsemen would react when they did catch up.

Red lights pulsed through the club, lighting up the stage and casting the strippers in a dark glow. The Devil's Dancers was packed tonight, filled with naked demons of both sexes, catering to all tastes. The kama that the audience was putting off was keeping us fed and alert. Her body tingled against the colored particles that pressed against her skin, slowly slipping beneath it. It kept us calm, but the need for sex was beginning to heighten, and the beast wasn't happy the Horsemen hadn't gotten their shit together yet. I mean, how hard could it be for them to find a blue-haired she-demon dressed in a stripper's get-up? In New Orleans? The answer was it was like finding a needle in a haystack.

She leaned back, crossing her legs where the thigh-highs stopped. She'd asked Eugene to bring her clothes at some point and he came back with an itty bitty dress, complete with thigh-highs and hooker heals. While it garnered more attention than necessary, it also made it easy to get into the demon clubs he brought us to. Everyone was dressed kind of sleazy and it was often difficult to distinguish the strippers from the guests.

The beast looked on, ignoring the sweltering fever that made her body slick with sweat. Her skin clung to the vinyl chair, uncomfortably so. Not that anyone could tell when they saw her. Where the heat had driven me to violent extremes, she was able to take it all in stride.

Her stare was unflinching as she examined the crowd before her. Demons were fickle creatures. One moment they could be partaking in an orgy without a care as to who watched them. The next they could be ripping each other's throats out while still balls deep in one another. It was a gut-wrenching sight, filled with savageness and primal instinct. Humans called us evil. I could see where that notion came from. We were not of this world. Me. The beast. Any demon or Fae. We didn't come from here.

We didn't belong here.

That was a thought that seemed to be running through my head more and more as of late. Maybe it was because of the fire in my veins, or the quite literal desire to start burning shit. Maybe it was because I was beginning to harden further to the world, sinking deeper into the monster I was becoming. Or maybe the more I looked, the more savageness appealed to me in a way that human conventions never did.

While I'd run from the demons on earth before, I was never really normal. I never blended perfectly with the humans. The slew of stalker exes and my mile-long rap sheet were proof of that. I was only ever biding time.

Similar to how the beast was now.

"I'm not biding my time," she grumbled. Her moods were already crappy enough. This game wasn't making them better.

"You're waiting for the Horsemen to find us," I snorted.

She grimaced outwardly while Bandit stretched out on her lap. He wore a tiny cone-shaped party hat attached by a stretchy string. Where he got it, neither of us knew, only that he insisted on wearing it.

"I'm letting them learn an important lesson," she replied. I suppose that was one way to look at it. *"One that you agreed with,"* she continued.

Now it was my turn to grumble inwardly. That put a smirk on her lips.

"Yes…no…I don't know. You haven't exactly put us in an easy situation and it's not like we're doing much." I muttered the last bit. Not like that kept it from her. She knew every thought and feeling I had, as much as I knew hers in return. So when the strange combination of humor and annoyance swirled in her chest, I found myself dreading what would come next.

"You're bored," she said pointedly.

No. Maybe…I tried to squelch down any reaction and it only served to intensify her emotions more.

"I was pissed at them in the beginning, but I got over it," I started, mentally fumbling when I could feel her growing agitation. The truth was that I was mad. Now I wasn't, and we were in a city crawling with demons, with no back-up if and when shit went sideways—apart from Bandit. While my raccoon was awesome…he wasn't from Hell. He didn't have powers. He just knew how to bite the shit out of someone while I started burning things up.

"You're being emotional about this," she replied coldly.

Emotional? The beast wanted to talk to me about being emotional?

"Says the person who is running all over the city in some fucked up game of hide-and-seek because they got a bit controlling after we threw Laran through a wall," I quipped back at her. She seemed to consider this for a moment, slowly stroking her fingers through Bandit's thick fur while watching an orgy taking place in front of us.

"You agreed," she settled on eventually. I sighed, wanting to shake my head at her, but I wasn't in control.

"Yes, and I don't regret that. I'm just saying we could be doing more than sitting around and waiting to get abducted…again."

The beast snorted. Yup. Actually snorted. I wouldn't have believed it if

I hadn't known with absolute certainty. Just like that, her anger was gone, replaced by mild amusement and weary agreement.

She arched forward, and a smacking sound filled the air as the vinyl that had been sticking to her back released. Sweat clung to her skin like a layer of clothing, insulating the heat within. The burning was beginning to get out of control, but the beast hadn't cracked. She wouldn't. While the sweat may be annoying, she was a creature of the flames confined by a mortal body. Soon to be more. The heat within didn't just come from her. It *was* her.

So, suffer I would, and I counted my lucky stars she was taking the brunt of it instead of me.

She hauled herself out of the armchair, waving down Eugene with a single look. He caught her watchful eye and nodded, pushing his way through the orgy to come to her.

"Ruby, what is it?" he asked, a slight frown forming.

He'd been nothing but attentive to her every demand since we'd healed his soul. I wonder if he realized exactly who he was dealing with, or if he just didn't care. I was leaning towards ignorance given the lack of fear, but that could just be because she saved him, and he thinks he's safe.

No one was safe. Not unless you wore her brand.

"I'm bored. Find me somewhere more interesting."

To Eugene's credit, he kept his face neutral and didn't balk at the unreasonableness behind her request. We both knew why she was bored.

She didn't want to be in a dingy bar watching other demons fuck.

She wanted to be fucking *our* mates. Of course, getting her to admit that was like getting Bandit to eat brussels sprouts. Not fucking happening.

"There's a—"

A scream rang through the air, cutting him off. Her muscles tensed. That wasn't just any scream. It was a banshee's scream.

Adrenaline surged within her as she searched for the source. Bodies pressed in around her. Their slick skin brushing against hers as she pushed her way through the crowd, quickly growing impatient. While most people possessed a sense of fight or flight, the beast only contained one mode and limited emotions, extreme as they might be.

She elbowed a male demon in the stomach that stepped too close for our liking, letting out a threatening snarl. Another bout of screams erupted to her right. Her head whipped around, and her muscles trembled as she took in the scene before her.

The banshee wasn't Moira. Thankfully.

They all might have died if it was.

While she shared her scream and dark green locks, their faces looked nothing alike. Moira burned like the fire inside me. This she-demon was completely and utterly terrified of the two males that had her trapped. Blood leaked from both their ears, dripping down their shoulders. Despite the damage she'd inflicted on them, one stood at her back, using his arms to cage her while he painfully squeezed her bare breasts. The other stood in front, flush against her body, playing with something between them…

Thick and dangerous, rage wrapped around our chest when we saw the shredded panties in his hand.

The banshee let out a raspy scream. Her voice broke as the demons around us watched with lust in their eyes. She writhed in their arms, throwing her head back in an attempt to smash her attacker's nose. He dodged last second, leaning forward to bite her neck in warning.

The beast didn't hesitate where all other demons did. She walked forward with vengeance in her eyes and fire at her command.

"Help me!" the girl cried, meeting our eyes over his shoulder. Up close, the tears running down her face were making an awful mess of her make-up, but without all the gunk on her face, she looked young.

The beast's face remained impassive as she reached out, wrapping a burning hand around the male's shoulder. He let out a roar, throwing his weight back in an attempt to break her grip. She wasn't having any of it.

The beast turned her finger's claw-like, digging into his leather skin. He groaned in pain as she shredded through the muscle and tendons, crushing him straight to the bone.

"You like to gang rape unprotected demons?" she asked him. At some point the club had quieted so only labored breathing and "Sweet Dreams" could be heard. "Because I like to hurt those that deserve it." She wrenched him down to eye level using the unnatural strength I never could get under control. "Do you deserve it?"

He gave a grunt of pain and black spikes popped out of his skin. Chupacabra.

"Listen, bitch, I don't know what—"

She slapped him so hard his neck cracked.

"Wrong answer."

That blow would have killed a human, but instead it left his head hanging at an odd angle as his body rapidly tried to heal itself. She threw him ten feet, his back snapping as he hit the stage at a bad angle. One of his spikes shot from his skin, aiming for her chest. She caught it in one hand and turned, slamming it into the remaining rapist's shoulder. His arms convulsed around the small banshee as the poison instantly started to spread.

"You…you…" His words faded as his veins turned black beneath his paper white skin. His eyes rolled to the back of his head as he stumbled, his legs now struggling to hold him. The young banshee looked between us, unsure if she had traded one danger for another.

The beast turned her eyes back on the chupacabra. His pain turned to rage as he looked away from his friend's steadily weakening form and back to the beast.

He didn't use words before he came at her, moving faster than she expected with his body broken. Still, that didn't stop her. He swiped an arm in her direction—letting loose three spikes. She acted without hesitation, summoning a wall of hellfire to extinguish the poisonous spikes before they could touch her.

That was when the screaming started. Not from the banshee beside her, but the monsters standing on the sidelines. Not many things could kill a demon flat out, but the flames of Hell were one of them.

Quickly tiring of the games, she strode forward through the fire, relishing how it licked at her skin. The chupacabra didn't run. He didn't fight. He simply watched the fire behind her, knowing that if she wished him dead, there was nothing he could do to stop her.

"Who are you?" he whispered, swallowing hard as she approached him. She grasped his naked cock as it hung limp between his thighs like a broken toy.

"Evil's executioner."

There was a wicked glint in her eye as she castrated him by fire. He was curled into a ball of agony when she moved onto the demon lying comatose from the poisonous spike she had impaled him with. He didn't even have time to beg before his appendage was removed by flame.

And then it was finished. Well, Bandit ran up and pissed on him for good measure, but the damage was done.

All she was left with was the wide-eyed she-demon she'd saved, Eugene McGee's troubled expression, and a roomful of demons that fell to their knees. They were bowing…to their queen.

The banshee blinked twice before dropping onto her knees. This didn't sit right with me, but the beast didn't seem to care. At the very least, they were showing the respect she felt she deserved.

Selfish cunt.

Of course, before she could say anything to the lot of them, two very familiar faces stepped out of the shadows.

Rysten…and Julian.

They'd come for her. For us.

Finally.

Unfortunately, this little turn of events had her blood pumping. The beast rather liked taking a more proactive role in getting scumbags off the street. Doling out punishments as she saw fit. If they had come not ten minutes earlier, she might have gone.

But now… now she had plans. Ideas.

If the Horsemen couldn't catch her, she had every intention of following them through. She let out a whistle and Bandit scurried across the stone floor, leaping halfway up her body and climbing the rest of the way. He perched on her shoulder, growling at them on principle. They weren't Laran. This didn't surprise me.

"Ruby," Julian growled under his breath. The look he gave her…it made me shiver. If he caught her, there was no way he was letting her go. Over his dead body, and considering I was pretty sure he couldn't die…

"Death," the beast purred with the voice of a siren. The vein in his temple bulged as he took her in, skimpy dress and all.

"Come now, love. We've won the game. Time to go." Rysten prowled in the shadows of the room, jumping from spot to spot, slowly getting closer to her. She threw her head back and let out a wicked laugh.

"You've found me, Pestilence, but you've yet to win."

She turned to Eugene McGee and nodded once. He took two steps. Rysten needed three.

But they were already gone, falling through the floor beneath them.

My arms wrapped around air. Hot. Sweaty. But ultimately empty air.

I stopped where I stood and looked down at the spot where the beast and some rubrum had been. A sinking sensation in my gut said I'd fucked up. Not only had I been the one to release her from the wards and lose her the first time, I'd also been the one to deviate from the plan and fail a second time.

"Where is she?" Julian roared.

I didn't flinch against the brutal thrust of power that swept through the room, searching for the missing she-demon. If they had been invisible, he would have found her, but the beast and the rubrum were not here. That almighty power that Julian released turned fraught and chaotic with the sharp bite of cold.

Demons hated the cold, but Julian embraced it.

I grit my teeth against his rage and kept a tight leash on my own power. If I let loose the sickness that ate away inside of me, the room of demons would die a very painful death and Julian would take it as challenge with the state he was in. All of our existence he'd been not just the strongest, but the most rational. Ever since we'd found Ruby, his controlling nature and tortured mind had begun to unravel. The beast walking out seemed to have brought out the worst in both of them, and while I had every intention of killing that rubrum with her when I found them—losing my temper would not be a wise idea.

So, I did what I was best at.

I dropped my arms and settled all of the darkness deep inside me where my brother couldn't see it. I would go hunting when he was asleep to get it out of my system. I turned my face, hiding the emotions I had a more difficult time keeping from him. In his primal state, he wouldn't even notice I was doing it. Ruby was the first who ever had.

"She's gone, Julian. I went too early and she ran before Moira could even attempt to calm her down." Honesty. It worked best for him in situations like this.

"She can't just be gone," he hissed.

The darker side of his magic clung to him more and more as the years went by, making him more like the beast than he ever would admit.

"We need to get the banshee and track her down before she goes too far." That was my only reply before I turned my thoughts to Allistair. Before I could reach out to him, something smashed against my face. I turned and spat blood across the club floor. It mixed with the blood the beast had painted this place in, and the urge to kill someone filled me again. Harder to control this time, when I recognized my attacker.

"What the fuck was that?" Laran bellowed.

I popped my unhinged jaw back into place and gave him a level stare.

"I saw an opportunity and I took it—" He hit me again.

I coughed hoarsely, spewing droplets of blood across the damn place. On the other side of me, Julian didn't say a fucking word, leaving me to deal with the anger of War alone. Maybe he wanted to hit me too, so this was him giving me a chance to at least fight back. I wouldn't.

"Listen, mate," I paused to rip out a tooth that was half hanging on by a chunk of gum. The new one was already pushing through. "I fucked up, but—"

His fist slammed into my face a third time, and I roared back in response. That tight hold I kept on myself strained for a moment, as my power itched to unleash an even worse fate on the hotheaded asshole. Pain like broken teeth and missing limbs were often easier for people to handle than a wasting sickness that ate them alive from within. I saw it every day with humans, and we demons—we were no different.

It took me a moment to recover from that one, staring at the shiny concrete floor, my face a mass of broken bone and flesh was healing rapidly. When I could move my lips I said, "Do not hit me again."

It would be the only warning. He had the right to be pissed, and I would even grant him the first punch for breaking the plan and trying to talk to her myself. I thought I could fix what I had done. I was wrong, but I would only grant him so much before he got a taste of the rot that lurked within.

"You broke formation. Moira was moving in, and *you* spooked her."

His fists were a pain that I could take. It was his words that cut me because I already knew it was my fault. That my actions blew the chance we had.

"Moira can still track her," I said. Like she'd done a dozen times already, just for the beast to cause some kind of havoc and disappear before we even saw her.

"Actually…" a fourth voice interjected. Allistair stepped out from behind the stage. Moira wasn't with him. "She can't. After you blew the plan, the banshee decided that she was better off doing the job on her own."

Fire and ice clashed as both Julian and Laran turned hostile.

"She said that?" Laran demanded.

"I believe her words were, *if I want it done right, I should do it myself.*"

"You let her leave." Julian's words were hardly more than a growl. His own sanity was beginning to fray at the edges.

"I attempted to persuade her to stay and she somehow redirected it. By the time I could break my own persuasion, she had decided flying was the best way to leave without me being able to follow."

Fuck.

This just kept going from bad to worse. I knew the banshee was not thrilled with us, but I didn't exactly expect her to follow through on her threats. Son of a bitch. If the beast gets both of her familiars, and is left unchecked, New Orleans will burn.

"There has to be another way to find her," I said. "Something— someone that can track her—"

"We need more than just to be able to track her." There was a dark note in Julian's tone.

"We won't be able to bind her if she has both of her familiars," Allistair said.

"More than a binding," Julian answered.

"Are you suggesting—" Allistair started, and there was a heavy warning in his voice. A flicker of unease, because what Julian wanted to do to her... not even I would be willing to face her ire when she found out. Ruby would forgive a lot, but this? Julian was too far gone.

"I am."

He was going to get our girl back, no matter the cost.

CHAPTER TEN

H ER ASS SMACKED onto the cold, hard ground and Bandit let out a mewling sound. Techno music blared in the background, adding to the disorienting stars exploding in front of her. She growled, waiting for the world to stop spinning before attempting to sit up. Pulling herself to an upright position, she ignored her protesting muscles. We were still mortal after all, and that wasn't a short fall. Bandit clung to her chest, wrapping his arms tightly around her neck like he was hanging on for dear life. He probably was.

The ceiling had to be a good twelve feet or more above us. She glanced around the room, taking note of the pool table to our side and sheer number of…men. Human men. Many of which seemed to have better dance moves than me.

After observing the shadowed corners, she quickly got to her feet, turning to look for Eugene. He stood a few feet behind her, cloaked by glamor to look like a beautiful dark-skinned man with long, luscious hair. I wanted to ask why he chose that particular look, but the beast didn't give a shit. She just wanted a way out of here.

"C'mon. I know a back door." He jerked his head to the hallway cloaked in shadow. While it was the ideal place for Rysten or Julian to grab her, it was less obvious than the front door. They turned and headed for the dark hallway, ignoring the catcalls some of the men made as she walked by.

"Hey, sweet thang," someone rumbled behind her. She turned her head, hand curled inward just itching to have another castrating session—something I didn't agree with down here unless someone made a move. But the dimpled man wasn't looking at her...

Eugene flushed a purple hue beneath his glamor, tipped his chin and kept on walking.

At the end of the corridor, a metal door opened up into an alley with a screech, slamming shut behind her with an audible click.

Outside, the night was chilly, pleasantly so. She trailed after Eugene, ignoring his odd behavior as they made their way through the darker parts of New Orleans that tourists didn't go to. Here you only walked around outside if you were brave, stupid, or a demon. Those labels weren't mutually exclusive.

After stumbling on the uneven pavement for what seemed like the umpteenth time that night, the beast paused and tore off the seven-inch hooker heels we'd been wearing for days. I was already tall, and while I wouldn't consider myself uncoordinated, I didn't exactly wear heels if I had *any* other choice, and that was in the best possible conditions. Certainly not on these terribly maintained streets. The beast must have shared that sentiment since she ripped them off her feet and chucked them down an alley. Eugene paused at the end of the street and didn't comment when she caught up. It was smart of him. Good survival instincts.

We walked another five minutes in the stifling silence before a creeping feeling had the hairs along the back of our neck prickling. She stopped walking.

"Everything alright?" Eugene asked, concern edging his voice.

The beast watched him for a hard moment before turning her gaze to the decrepit buildings. Nothing *looked* out of the ordinary, but still she stared a few seconds longer at the darkest of the shadows.

A distinct feeling of unease filled us, and the urge to run.

But there was nothing there.

She turned to continue walking when she saw it.

The thing moved like darkness, absorbing all light that it touched. Its eyes were the color of lava, red and angry. Molten with rage. Animalistic fury.

My mind formed what her mouth would not.

Hellhound.

The thing raised its head, snarling a breath across the twenty meters that separated us. It smelled like fire and ash. Death and decay.

But did the beast run?

No, she fucking didn't.

She stared at it like an equal, not even willing to lower her eyes. Bandit arched his back and let out a hiss, like that was going to scare the damn thing off. I could have sworn the hellhound tilted its head and let out a low growl. A sharp whistle cut through the air, and the hound sat back on its haunches. Each of its four legs alone had to be ten feet tall. The head was the size of my old VW bug, with a pointed snout and ears that sat straight up like a Doberman.

"Eugene!" a man called out of the shadows. "Well, if it isn't Eugene McGee."

No, not a man: a demon. For the second time in my life, I saw a rubrum. Tall and imposing. He stood a good eight feet tall with skin so dark it looked purple. Humans weren't the only thing he had slayed, and his soul didn't reek of pain.

"Creag Le Dan Bia," Eugene answered in return.

The beast turned, taking in the way his mouth twisted at the sight of the other rubrum. The light in his chest turned from a soft kind of pink to a dark red. His breathing hitched, and his muscles tightened.

"What did I tell you would happen if I ever saw your worthless hide in my territory again, *boy*?" Eugene blanched, and the beast's brows furrowed.

"That I'd be dog food," Eugene replied. The other rubrum threw his head back and let out a raucous laugh. Behind him, two other demons stepped out of the shadows.

"And yet, you're dumb enough to show your face here again after what you did?" the larger male egged him on, casually crossing the distance between us and them.

"We're just passing through," Eugene said, but his voice lacked conviction. He knew no matter what he said, these assholes weren't leaving. Not with him in one piece. It had me curious to know what happened here, but there were more pressing matters at hand. Like us not dying.

"We?" Creag asked. "You're telling me this lovely specimen is with you?" His eyes turned to us and there was a dark glint, filled with lust and violence. His shirtless chest puffed up a little bit as he took a step towards us, the bulge in his jeans growing.

Oh hell-to-the-fucking-no.

"You better know how to get us out of this," I told the beast.

"He won't touch us."

Of that, she was completely sure. It did little for my confidence in her when the big ass hell dog turned his eyes to us again. He sniffed the air, and I had a feeling Eugene might become dog chow if we didn't find a way out of here fast.

"Leave her out of this," Eugene spat. At the mention of me, he came forward and tried to put himself between Creag and the beast. She rolled her eyes at the overdramatic nature of it all.

"I don't think the female is much impressed by you," the purple rubrum mused. "Maybe she needs a real demon to show her a good time—"

"Why is it," the beast began, "that males always think with the head between their legs and not with the one on their shoulders?"

Eugene didn't react, but the other male stiffened. Only when they were feet apart could I tell that the purple rubrum was a good six inches taller. Great.

"Feisty, that one," Creag said. "I like it when they fight back. Makes their flesh taste all the sweeter after they're chained to my bed."

Holy fuck. This dude was nuts. Totally whacko.

I mean, don't get me wrong. Being chained to a bed had my imagination running to all kinds of places…so long as it was with one of my mates.

But this dude got his kicks from violence and torture.

Well, little did he know the beast also liked those things.

Just probably not in the same scenarios he imagined.

"Get out of here, Ruby," Eugene said. His tone was pleading, but he should have known by now that the beast tolerated commands from no one. "Creag, your fight is with me, not—"

"You both talk too much."

The beast whipped her head in the direction where the voice came from.

Moira stepped out of the shadows, her beautiful blue wings tucked in tight behind her. She was dressed in dark leggings and a ripped tank top made to accommodate her new form. Her boots weren't the most practical of choices. They had a three-inch heel, albeit chunky. My best friend's swagger was undeniable, but even the beast could feel her hidden anxiety.

"Getting she-demons to fight your battles for you now, Eugene?" big-ugly said. The beast chafed at his arrogance. She was going to knock him down a foot or three.

"Hey, asshole," Moira called out as she strode forward. She ran a hand through her hair, pulling it back tight so that even in the low lamplight, you could see the mark there. The mark of Cain. "I'm not just any she-demon, fuckface. I'm the devil-damned legion, and you are going to regret messing with the Queen of Hell's errand boy."

Oh no. She did *not* just introduce herself as…fucking hell.

Only Moira would go off touting her new title and mine. Oh, we were going to have words when I got my body back. Me and her, and the beast, and the Horsemen, and even Bandit for good measure, given that the little asshole was growling at the hell monster like he would stand a chance.

Creag Le Dan Bia turned his eyes to her, and what I saw there…it was enough to set the beast off. Envy. Lust. Greed. Violence. He took every inch of my best friend in like she was a feast to be enjoyed.

"Turn and leave now, or your life is forfeit," the beast growled, and it was his only warning.

The large male looked between Moira, the beast, and Eugene, calculating his next move. He lifted his hands in surrender and slowly backed away, one step at a time.

"I hadn't realized who I was dealing with," Creag said.

This rubrum was smarter than Eugene. Maybe that's why he set the beast on edge. Or maybe, it's because she saw a flash of metal as Creag turned to leave. His large arm reached around his back and grasped the handle of what I could only presume was some kind of knife. He twisted as he pulled the blade from its sheath at his back and turned to throw it straight for Eugene—but Eugene beat him to punch.

A dagger protruded from Creag's chest as his skin cracked, very similar to when I killed someone from the inside out using the flames. Except the light appearing in those crevices was not blue, but red. He screamed in anguish, falling to his knees and the dagger stuck in his chest began to glow.

The beast watched, not feeling all that inclined to intervene when his body exploded and ash rained down on them. At the same moment, a flash of red appeared where Eugene was standing, and then he was gone.

"How the fu—"

"Le Dan Bia will be hearing about this," one of the two remaining demons said. He snapped his fingers and the hellhound let out a cry of pain, its collar suddenly extending spikes into its neck. The two henchmen backed into the shadows as the hellhound reluctantly melded into the night. His molten eyes seemed to give off hurt and sorrow, not all that dissimilar to Eugene when we'd first met him.

"You care to explain what the hell just happened?" Moira demanded, crossing her arms over her chest. The beast ignored her question, instead choosing to answer with a question of her own.

"How did you find me?"

"I'm resourceful," Moira replied. The beast was not amused.

"How did you find me?" she repeated.

Moira rolled her eyes. "I'm your familiar and now I'm a full-blown demon. Seems one of my badass powers is knowing where your ass is at all times."

So, she could track me. That was good to know.

"Why are you here?"

"To join you. Obviously," she answered with the same bored expression and flippant attitude despite the scene before us. The beast eyed her for a moment.

"Are the Horsemen following you?"

Moira grinned savagely. "Why? Do you want them to?"

Her prodding wasn't doing anything for her chances here. Especially when Bandit doubled over on the beast's shoulder, making a deep, choking sound. Seriously…was he laughing? I wondered if he was going to fall off, but he sprawled his body around the back of her neck and sighed his annoyance with her.

After watching Bandit's little display, Moira rolled her eyes again and said, "Doubtful, but possible. Those four have a rather one-track mind, and they are much more concerned with getting you back." This pleased the beast. "Although you wouldn't know it with how shit they are at doing it," Moira muttered at the end.

"I assume you helped them find me at The Devil's Dancers," the beast continued, although most of her attention was focused on the scene before her. A glowing dagger Eugene had thrown. A demon that was killed instantly. A body, and a missing person. But what to make of it?

"Yes, but again, the feckless foursome suck at their job. I ditched them to find you."

The beast nodded. "Do they know you're with me?" she asked and walked forward to where the knife lay. The blade couldn't have been longer than a foot and the handle was some sort of dark material, covered in glowing red marks and wrapped tightly in place.

"By now? Probably. Without me as their guide, it's doubtful they'll find us anytime soon, though." That was what she wanted to know.

"So, who was the red bloke and why did they want to kill him?" Moira asked, coming to stand beside her as the beast crouched down to better examine the knife.

"His name was Eugene McGee. I don't know why they wished to kill him."

We didn't know, but if Le Dan Bia was after him…

They were the biggest clan on the North American continent. Tasked with maintaining and guarding the portal, they ran this town and everyone in it. Eugene must have pissed them off somehow, but now one of their own was dead, and Moira and I were part of it.

Fuck…

"Do you know where he went?" she asked.

The beast didn't want to answer. No. Not a fucking clue. We didn't know much of anything about this or what went down here tonight, and what we saw…it didn't make sense.

"We should call the Horsemen in," Moira said.

The beast let out a growl. The last thing we needed was them thinking we couldn't handle our own problems. They'd just lock us up again.

"Ruby—"

"I am not Ruby," the beast snarled. She didn't correct Eugene because he needed something to call her. Moira knew better. Our tether, she may be, but that didn't excuse her from the beast's rage.

"Fine. Beast—bitch—cuntmorphon—whatever you want to be called. I say we grab the dagger and—"

Moira reached down and grabbed the handle.

Bandit let out a screech.

Then the world exploded in color.

ALLISTAIR

We were treading on thin ice. In our haste to reclaim her, we lost her again
—and this time we didn't have one of her familiars handy to track her
down.

No matter. We had someone better.

Sin may not be able to instantly find our girl like a familiar could, but
she also wouldn't step out on us at the first failure, and as much as I wanted
to flay Rysten for going against the plan—someone had to keep us together.
Over four thousand years and we'd never had a true division amongst
ourselves. As much as I wanted my mate back, perhaps we needed this.

I glanced over at Julian. The necromancer spoke in a low voice with his
back turned, the volatile cold inside of him seeping into New Orleans itself.
We needed to find Ruby, but I had to wonder if perhaps my little she-
demon wasn't so far gone. Wonder if the beast had known that her leaving
would be the thing that would finally spur Julian to make a decision.

He wanted her back as much as the rest of us, if not more.

And in the end, it would make all the difference. We were united now,
in our search, our cause, and our reasoning.

Julian hung up the phone and leaned against the granite countertop of
the apartment. The beast had trashed a good portion of the first one in her
escape. Fortunately, we'd bought the entire building. Relocating to the floor
below had only taken a matter of minutes.

"What did she have to say?" I asked him, angling the glass of scotch in my hand. It refracted a face behind me as a woman stepped out of nothing.

She smiled at me in the reflection.

"Hello, Sinumpa," I said cordially.

We had a complicated history. Made more so by her mother. As some of the longest living immortals in both worlds, you ended up running into each other once every hundred years or so.

"Long time no see, Allistair," she replied with a Cheshire smile. Her white hair swayed gently in the air conditioning. The ends were still purple, much like the last time I'd seen her.

"I much prefer this look on you," I said. Our banter always came easily, even if seeing her was anything but.

"Last I saw, you had your eyes on the child you're supposed to be protecting." Her voice lashed at me like a whip, but it missed its mark.

"Ruby is not a child. She's your Queen." Her smirk didn't falter at my reply as she wiggled an eyebrow.

"When you've lived as long as us, most things in the world are children. *Your mate* will only live to be the true Queen if she survives the Six Sins. You should know that."

So, she did know Ruby and I were at least partially mated. Good. That would make this easier, although I didn't appreciate her reminder about the Sins because I was painfully aware of it already. It was yet another reason to make sure her bonds with each of us were cemented before we arrived in Hell. Without them, the Sins might actually break her.

"That's why we need your assistance," Julian broke in. Impatient. He paced back and forth, his hands clenching and unclenching. I knew that Sin saw this in a matter of moments by the way her grin turned vicious.

He was unhinged, and that provided her with an opportunity.

She always was her mother's daughter.

"What you need is enough magic to bind and contain the most powerful she-demon to ever transition. Do not attempt to insult or lowball me, Death. The cost for this will be steep."

I knew what he was going to say before the words left his mouth. It was the only reason I had held off on telling any of them, especially him, that I already knew she was in town. A tangle with Sin was never cheap, and one never came away unscathed.

"Anything for her. I'll pay it."

I looked away. It was never good when you let another immortal know the single piece to use against you, and Julian was making no attempt to hide it in his desperation. He wanted our girl back.

We all did.

And that's why none of us stopped him.

"Excellent. Let's get started."

CHAPTER ELEVEN

The air sucked in around us and popped like a bubble.

Where before there had been only darkness, night, and the red glow, now there was only light. Brilliant. Blinding. It filled her vision so fully that there was no darkness. No shadow. No Moira. Only her and the all-consuming power that couldn't simply be described as light. It tasted of wild magic. It smelled like heavy perfume and rain. It brushed over her skin, searching for something.

And then it dissipated. Breaking apart in a shower of sparks, the image shattered, revealing just where she was.

It was a room of some kind, but her vision was disoriented. Off. After seeing only what I could describe as true white, this shroud of darkness was hard to make out. Candles littered the room. From the chandelier above her, to the side tables across the room, to the ones sitting on top of a stack of books, all the way to the ones dotting the circle drawn on the floor below her. Beside her, Moira was sprawled out and moaning. Her eyes were squeezed shut and her brows furrowed. Pain. She was in a lot of pain.

Bandit scrambled to his feet, very much alert as the beast turned to the two figures.

"What is this?" she snarled, her gaze narrowing on Eugene McGee as he stood beside a tall, grey-skinned male with obsidian hair that changed colors like oil in the light. He wore dark fighting leathers, making the silver of his eyes and red glowing brand stand out.

Wait a minute—*shit.*

The blazing red marks on his forehead weren't brands. They were runes.

The etchings on the knife were runes.

Devil-fucking-damnit.

The beast growled under her breath.

This guy wasn't a demon, and fucking Eugene McGee—what had just happened? Red blotted out all reason within her as she let out a roar, breathing fire in an attempt to set the Fae man aflame from across the room. Blue flames spewed from her mouth and ran into an invisible barrier, flattening against it in a wall of black and blue.

Her mouth snapped shut sharply. This was bad. Very bad.

Maybe Moira was right that we should have gone to the Horsemen—

"*No,*" the beast growled at me.

"Are you done now?" the Seelie asked with an air of annoyance. His accent was foreign, but I couldn't place it.

"Why have you brought me here?" the beast demanded, keeping her eyes on the Fae.

"I didn't bring you anywhere, *child,*" the Seelie said distastefully. "*Your* familiar grabbed a weapon that did not belong to her. She's lucky that Gene told me you were not the ones to attack him, or *her* life would have been forfeit."

"You're working with demon hunters," the beast said to Eugene. An almost sheepish blush crept across his cheeks for the second time that night.

"I'm sorry, Ruby. I should have warned you about—"

"The thing inside that girl does not want explanations, my dear." He reached out and rested a hand on the rubrum's shoulder almost affectionately. "And you," he turned back to the beast. "It is unwise to make assumptions on things you know so little about, daughter of Hell."

She narrowed her eyes at him, not liking his tone, or the fact that he knew who we were.

"Oh yes, I know who you are, girl. Most of New Orleans does after the way you've been parading about, mid-transition, leaking ancient magic into the world." I wanted to cop a snide remark at the beast, but it really wasn't the time for that. She was already raging. "*But,* as much as it pains me, I mean you no harm. You healed my lover from his wounds and stood your ground with Le Dan Bia."

"And the binding?" the beast said pointedly, motioning to the red line surrounding her and Moira.

"A necessary precaution for any who try to steal a Fae blade. It's one of the few things in this world that can kill a demon outright. Can't have it go missing, now can I?" he said rhetorically. Still, he didn't drop the barrier.

"I wasn't trying to steal it," Moira rasped from the dirty concrete floor. She sucked in a noisy breath and sat up to cough hoarsely.

Somehow, the blade that brought us here had gone missing after Moira grabbed it and was left sprawled out without an explanation. I didn't trust the Seelie, whether Eugene did or not. But I did respect his power.

"Yes, well, I didn't know that until Eugene took the time to explain it, just before I let the air within the binding crush you." He said it without remorse, much as the beast would have. It was a certain kind of jadedness and I wondered how someone like him could be with someone as naïve as Eugene.

"Enough," the beast commanded. "You know who we are. Now release us."

"Well, you see, I can't do that just yet…" the Seelie trailed off at the deadly glare the beast gave him.

"Donnach," Eugene groaned. "Please don't do this. This isn't her fight."

"Someone has to deal with them, Gene. If not her, then who? Who else has the power to do that outside my own people?" Donnach replied with an undercurrent of anger. Eugene deflated, running a hand over his smooth, bald head.

"I don't like this," the rubrum said.

Donnach's features softened for a fraction of a moment.

"I know, but you know better than anyone what they will do to Morvaen if she remains. I cannot allow that, and she is the only way to prevent a war."

Both Donnach the Seelie and Eugene the rubrum turned to watch the beast. She had one arm tucked under her breast and the other sitting on top of it, bent at the elbow so that she could stroke her bottom lip with the pad of her thumb. Bandit had gone silent during this exchange, as if he could sense the significance of what was happening. Moira had stopped coughing and rose to her feet on wobbly knees, but was very proudly holding her head high and wings partway open.

The Fae sighed, and then he began.

"Know that if I had another option, I would go with it before asking your kind for anything."

If that was meant to make this better, he fell short.

Moira rolled her eyes at him. "Get on with it."

He smiled thinly, razor sharp to the edge of cruelty…but there was something else. Something *old*… This Seelie looked fairly young. Certainly no older than his mid-thirties, and yet…something didn't feel quite right. His eyes spoke of battles gone by. Of bloodshed and brutality.

There was more to him than her eyes were seeing.

"Very well"—he paused to take a breath—"several of my kind are trapped in an underground fighting ring hosted by Le Dan Bia. I'm assuming you know who they are?"

"We care not," came the beast's reply.

The Fae man gave her a withering look.

"You're supposed to be the next Queen, and you don't care that your people have overstepped their bounds on the planet *my kind* were sentenced to?" he spoke quietly, but his question was bold.

"That was before my time," the beast replied. She shrugged her shoulders and reached around to pet Bandit.

"Yet, you are the heir now."

They stared at each other for a solid minute, neither wanting to crack or yield in any way.

"We did not agree to this. You transported us here against our will, and now you try to manipulate me into solving your problems for you. Find somcone else," the beast declared.

Internally I blanched, but the beast watched him without a single fuck to give. They weren't hers. Why would she care?

I sighed. I shouldn't care. I really shouldn't…but I shuddered to think of the fighting rings I had heard of growing up. Of the fighting ring Moira had been subjected to as a child before she was transferred to Portland.

When she'd arrived, her body was bruised and broken. There was a wicked cut on her head that had been haphazardly sewn together. She walked with a limp for six months, and that was after she was able to walk again.

She was a child, barely able to protect herself, and our own kind had thought to use her as entertainment. To beat and break her. She was a demon and they did that to her. What would they do to non-demons? To Fae? To Seelie?

"It doesn't matter," the beast said.

"It does. If we stand around and do nothing, we are no better than them."

"Save your feelings for our mates. We're not doing it."

She was trying to shut me down. Outwardly, the beast turned a quarter of an inch to glance at Moira out of the corner of her eye. My best friend was quiet, and awfully pale. She still remembered those dark times.

The beast was fire and flame, but the wrath that filled me was sharp. Crackling.

I should have let the beast continue fighting and try to rip him to shreds, but I couldn't let this go. Not yet. Not when the anger I felt with her was beginning to break through the carefully structured wall that kept me at bay and her in charge.

"This is not our problem," the beast snarled. *"We don't negotiate with terrorists."*

Did she really just say that?

"You don't even know what that means! We're supposed to rule these people. This is every bit our problem," I snapped back.

"Why us? Why not him?" the beast finally said through gritted teeth. She was struggling to contain me when I wasn't willing to go along with her plans so easily.

"Eugene used to belong to Le Dan Bia and will be killed on sight—as you saw—before they allow him to step inside their territory. You two, however"—he motioned between the beast and Moira—"they would not realize the danger until it was too late. While young and untrained, you are pure of soul with nearly limitless potential." He walked forward, cocking his head to the side while he watched them both. While clearly shaken, Moira stared back at him with an inner strength that spoke volumes of her person.

"You want us to enter Le Dan Bia's territory, infiltrate their bait ring, and release members of *your* people—putting both of ourselves at risk, for what? So that you don't have to do the dirty work?" Moira spat the words like poison, her anger harsh and cold.

"That's not what I said," the Seelie responded, clearly growing more impatient by the moment. "Any demon can enter their territory without suspicion because they are the portal keepers. Getting into the 'bait ring,' as you call it, would take little effort. I would portal you out of here, directly on their doorstep. The reason I am coming to you"—he motioned to the beast—"is because if I send my people in there, it will result in an all-out war that very well may spread beyond New Orleans. As a new ruler, that is not what I imagine you would want."

That bastard.

He knew what buttons to press and where. The beast, she didn't give many fucks about much of anything. Our familiars? Yes. Our mates? Also, yes. Past that, there were only two things she cared about. One: my safety —we shared a body, so that was a given. The second was our crown.

And a war that spread beyond New Orleans? That most certainly was an issue for the latter.

"We have no reason to trust you," Moira countered. She wasn't wrong, and the beast agreed with her. I did too, for that matter, but apparently, I was the only one seeing reason here, or at least trying to.

Donnach clicked his tongue in annoyance. "She is a young queen asserting herself to her people while doing me a favor," he said sharply. "It prevents a war *this time*, one that I don't think she would like to start her rule fighting. Not while she has many enemies within your own kind. While you may not have a reason to trust me, she also doesn't have one to distrust me. Have I attempted to harm either of you, or the creature, even once?"

The beast glanced at Bandit who stood tall on her shoulder, his teeth bared at the Seelie. His eyes, once black, were now blue like mine and the swirling pentagrams turned like smoke within them—the same as Moira. I'd done it on accident, but like Moira, he remained altered somehow in ways I still hadn't figured out.

"Is declining your offer an option?" the beast asked bluntly.

"I will not take away your ability to choose." He narrowed his eyes. "If you wish to do nothing, I would let you leave and that would be it. However, we will not leave them there to be ripped apart by the beasts of Hell." His voice sounded sincere, but cold. I wished that I could think him a liar. It would have made the situation easier. I wouldn't have felt like they were my responsibility. Like it was me who should fix this. After all, I'd only just stepped into this role. It's not like I was raised to do this.

But I was born to. And the moment Lucifer died, everything began to unravel.

My life. My identity. My powers. The future of not only earth, but Hell itself.

They would continue to unravel until I pulled my big girl panties up and stopped being a pussy.

I wasn't a defenseless half-breed. I could take on demons three times my size. I could escape all four of the Horsemen and outwit them when needed. I had Bandit and Moira at my side, and the beast containing the deadly power inside me. She'd said she was evil's executioner. Maybe she should live up to it.

"I don't trust this," the beast told me.

"You don't have to. But clearly if he can bind us then he could probably do a lot more. He's not wrong about Le Dan Bia. They're a problem, and our names are already on the list thanks to Moira."

The beast stood immobile for what seemed like hours as she considered what to do, but it was really only minutes. Like me, she was coming to the conclusion that we should do this, or at least that we should consider doing this. The Seelie wasn't wrong that by knowingly letting them go after the clan to free their own, we were risking war. As a newly appointed ruler with powerful enemies and a wide opposition, that really wasn't something we could afford. The beast didn't care for politics, but in this she could at least see a glimmer of reason.

We may have left looking for a good time, but it seemed that trouble was always fast to find us. A war with the Seelie was not something we could afford, which meant it was time to step up.

She didn't trust this. Not one bit. But I wasn't yielding to her unless she gave me a damn good reason.

"Don't tell me you're seriously considering this," Moira said. "We can find another way to deal with it. We can send the Horsemen. We can—"

"We do not run from threats, Moira."

My best friend stopped and swallowed hard. She took a minute to stare at the wall across the room, her eyes glazing over as she considered her own reasons. Eventually, she said, "You are powerful, and you are right to not run. But you don't know the evil that lives in places like that. I worry about you—about Ruby—if you choose to go down there."

The beast considered this and with a heavy sigh and deep reluctance, she lowered the barrier that kept me in, protecting me from my own magic. The transition of pushing me forward was sudden and violent, but she sat close to the surface, ready to take it back after I said my piece.

Silently, I thanked her.

"I worry too," I said. Moira's head shot up, her eyes blinking rapidly.

"It's you!" she breathed, throwing her arms around me.

"It's always me," I chuckled and hugged her back. "But I can't stay. The beast is in control because I need her to be. At least until my powers are no longer a danger. She's doing this because I want her—I need her to. We can't allow demons like the ones who attacked Eugene to continue. That's not the kind of Queen I want to be, now or ever."

Moira stepped back and took both my hands in hers. She held them tightly and let loose a steady breath.

"I left the Horsemen and came to find you because I was worried she was going to get you killed. Now I know that it's in fact *both* of you playing off of each other's thought processes that leads you to such awful decisions. I honestly don't know what you'd do without me," she said and gripped my hands so tight the skin around her fingers turned pink.

"You don't have to come with me, you know."

"You're even crazier if you think I'm leaving you to face that alone."

I smiled sadly at her as the beast impatiently waited for me to finish up. "I'll be me again before you know it," I whispered, and with that, I settled into the back of my mind. The beast dropped Moira's hands and settled her hands on her hips as she lifted her gaze to the Fae.

"Double cross us and I will kill him myself." She jutted her chin towards Eugene, who swallowed thickly.

"My dear, if I lied, you wouldn't know it until you stood on the other side of the veil." His words were slippery sweet, but truthful. The Seelie raised his hand and the barrier between us lowered until the light coming from the binding fizzled out.

He lifted his slate colored hand across the space. There was a resolution there, in his eyes. A tautness to his face, a pallor to his skin. This Fae called Donnach was ready and would do anything to bring his people home.

Even make a deal with the devil.

****JULIAN****

We were born to blood magic. Created with the ability to use it sparingly so that we could combine our strengths. So that we could do the job.

But fate had played out in a very different way. Instead of Ruby bonding with us as familiars to protect her, she and the beast chose us as mates. In our place, she picked familiars from two of what should have been the weakest creatures that would ever walk into Hell. Fate threw us another wrench, in that where their bodies were not strong, their will was. The banshee and the raccoon had a fierceness about them that made them as suited for the job as me. They protected her and Ruby fed on that inner strength within them. It bolstered her where we could not and made her stronger than even us.

If my blood wasn't pounding so hard with aggression and rage, I might have been impressed. Instead, it made me desperate.

I could admit it. So much so that I could make a bargain with Sin.

That I could owe her a favor and enter a blood oath just to get Ruby back.

She wanted a mate that would put her first. Someone that wouldn't just protect, but would own her heart and soul. I would show her what kind of mate I could be.

What kind of mate I *would* be.

She provoked me again and again and again.

Now I was going to make sure she couldn't run. Make sure that she was mine.

Even if I had to tie our very souls together to do it.

Sin cut into my skin again and used the blood to trace her markings. Even after so many years, I never understood the magic she used. How she was able to blend two impossible things. I suspected, much like the other Horsemen did. But we were smart enough to keep our mouths shut in our interactions with her.

"Think of her. Focus on her brand."

She cut down my chest, splitting the bone in two. Most could not survive undergoing this kind of sacrifice. But blood magic had a balance. To receive, you must give a worthy offering.

I wished to own my little Morningstar. To remove her will. To enslave her body.

To do so, I had to give that and more.

Sin plunged her hand into my chest cavity and grasped my still beating heart. I did not allow my mental image to stray for even a second as she pulled it free from my chest.

A dark mass formed around the organ in her hand as the magic accepted its offering. It devoured my heart, attacking the flesh and blood with inky black tendrils. The magic consumed it whole and then shot downward, returning my heart and filling the void in my chest cavity as my skin closed itself back together. Sin's magic was violent and turbulent as it swept through me, searching for the demon I wished to bond with. Searching for the brand.

I knew the moment it found it.

The moment the blood formed her brand on my chest.

Because in that same moment, I felt the beat of her heart as it pulled me toward her. The magic begged me to fulfill its purpose to the point of pain. The breath hissed between my teeth, but I accepted it. I accepted this pain, because the moment I touched her skin, she wouldn't be free of me and the beast would no longer be in charge.

I was taking her through the transition whether she liked it or not, and there wasn't a fucking thing that she could do about it.

CHAPTER TWELVE

HE FLICKED his fingers and sparks shot from the tips. The beast eyed the Seelie warily, but he'd dropped the barrier. He'd explained what was to come. He'd sworn on rune magic to do us no harm except in defense, and he hadn't made the beast swear the same.

I wasn't sure if it was stupidity, arrogance, or something else entirely.

I'd never seen someone work so fast. His fingers flew through the motions, as if playing piano in the air. Red, swirly shit appeared everywhere he touched. The glowing marks didn't make much sense to me, but after a few seconds of nothing happening, I felt it.

He stopped, lowering his hands. There was a massive whoosh like we'd stepped into a vacuum and the marks shone brighter, becoming more intense as they moved to converge. The air crackled with power as the magic formed an incandescent orb. The sheer force that radiated from it unsettled the beast. The thing sucked in all the magic from the air, pulling physical objects toward it. A couple of books came flying out of their piles and ended up being absorbed in the damn thing as it nearly tripled in size before exploding outward. A portal six-feet in diameter snapped into place.

On one side stood the beast, Moira, Bandit, Eugene, and the Seelie. On the other, separated only by a thin film of red magic—a dark street leading towards a shadowed alley.

In truth, I didn't understand a lot about how their magic worked. I'd only heard snippets here and there growing up, but to my understanding, runes—or brands as I knew them—held power. Power the Seelie could tap, just as the Unseelie used blood. They were old magic. Older than any demons I knew of, including the Horsemen. I kept those thoughts to myself as the beast walked forward, toeing the edge of the portal.

The entrance to the underground fighting ring.

"If this is a set-up, *harvester,* you will be sorry," the beast warned. Although he had sworn up and down not all Seelie were out to kill our kind, the beast was less forgiving and more irritated with him than I.

"Duly noted, *child,*" he replied, putting just enough sneer into his voice that the beast's fingers twitched with the desire to backhand him.

Without any formal goodbye or even a glance at Eugene, the beast stepped through the portal. For a moment, her movements were sluggish as the magic strained against her skin, simulating the feeling of moving through water. With a pop, it broke, and she crossed over, stepping onto dry pavement. Bandit shook himself like a wet dog and began grooming his paws while the beast waited for Moira.

She didn't take long. Coughing and spluttering, she stumbled through the portal, her right wing smacking into Bandit. He let out a cry of dismay and jumped to the ground. He ran at her and bit her pinky finger, jumping away before she could swat at him.

"Ow! Little asshole, what the fuck is wrong with—"

"Come." The beast leaned over and he hauled himself up onto her shoulder again as she strode into the night. Moira let out a slew of curses behind them but followed after.

Above them, the skies looked tumultuous. Thick clouds blotted out every star, reflecting back the lights of the city in a red haze that lit the midnight streets of New Orleans.

She walked down the broken sidewalk, stepping around the chunks of concrete and smashed beer bottles. She didn't even cringe as the tiny shards of glass cut her feet. In front of her, the alley loomed. Tall. Imposing. With the red haze in the sky, she should have been able to see down it. An umbrella of dark magic and midnight covered it entirely, hiding away what lay below—unless you knew it was there.

Together they made their way forward, stepping through the veiled murkiness. Her foot felt something smooth. Another, but this one was lower. Stairs. They were going down stairs. She continued, taking the lead as they descended further, and the path slimmed. She still couldn't see anything apart from the glow from Moira's wings, but she could feel it. Feel the dark magic around her. Feel Bandit as he clung to her, quietly mewling with displeasure. The beast ran a hand through his fur, soothing him, and my raccoon purred.

At the very bottom, they stopped, and Moira lifted a quivering hand to knock twice. The sound reverberated through her bones, echoing up the stairway.

"Are you certain you can handle this?" the beast asked softly into the dark night.

"Too late to turn back now," Moira grunted. Her heart was hammering so loud even we heard it.

The door swung open, and a tall male zeroed in on Moira, assessing her with interest before turning his predatory eyes on us. The beast stared back without emotion, impassive as always. Time for that moment of truth. Did the Seelie deceive us? Or was it really going to be just that simple?

The yellow-eyed chupacabra stepped back and held the door open, silently letting us pass. From behind him, music thrummed with a steady beat and a mix of alcohol, sweat, and blood wafted in the air, luring the beast into the underground shithole with the promise of violence and booze. Can't say I faulted her thinking as she roughly shoved past him, lightly casting him aside with a push of her hand as he tried to crowd toward her. I doubt he even noticed the exotic pull my body held over him. All the better that she tossed his ass around to snap him out of it. We weren't here for sex. If that's what she wanted, we had four mates just dying to get a location on us.

The beast walked into the bar like a guy with a big dick in the locker room. You know the type. She strutted in as if she owned the place and heads turned.

Behind her, Moira's chest had gone into overdrive. Fear. Anger. Hurt. *Pain.* She wasn't handling this. She wasn't coping. Her distress made the beast hesitate, and Bandit dug his claws into her. Blue blood dripped down her shoulder as a painful clarity cut through her mind, allowing her to separate our emotions and Moira's. Several male demons, imps by the looks of them, decide to try coming up to us. Bandit bared his teeth at them and let out a hiss, even when they switched to approaching Moira who was only just starting to break through her own paralyzing fear.

The beast grabbed her by the wrist and pulled her forward, ignoring the curious onlookers. This was a bad idea. Really, quite awful actually. Why did I think bringing Moira here was a good idea to begin with?

I didn't. I listened to the word of a hunter and let my own judgement be colored by a sob story. I wanted to protect my crown and stand up for what's right. But look where it got us.

The beast shook her head at my doubts and second-guessing. We had come this far, and she was going to do what *we* set out to do.

The concrete flooring was discolored. Stained in shades of brown and blue.

Blood. It was stained with blood.

To her left, the floor dropped off with nothing but a pathetically weak rail to prevent people from going over the edge and into the hell below. Blood and dirt smeared the walls down there and something let out a terrible screech of pain. Bandit instantly began growling. This place even made him nervous. He didn't like being here, so out in the open like. It made him…uneasy.

And all I could think about was that Moira had told us. She'd warned us of the kind of evil that lurks in places like this. In clans like Le Dan Bia.

We didn't want to listen.

But we were here now, and despite the paralyzing fear within her and the anxiety Bandit was now giving off, both her and the beast had every intention of showing them that we won't tolerate this.

The place itself stank of piss and death. How anyone could keep a child down here…yeah, the beast was going to knock some heads in before we left. She wasn't going to be complacent with this kind of behavior. Neither of us would.

She continued towards the bar in the back, well away from the pit and fighting that went on below. She walked right up to it like she wasn't dragging Moira behind her, and slapped her hand on the sticky surface, ignoring the pungent odor around us. The male behind the bar turned as he finished lighting a joint. Instantly, the scent of white lotus hit us, sharpening the need in our core. The beast grimaced, eyes flicking to the burning end as it exploded in his face. He jumped back, moving to drop it, but it had already disintegrated into nothing more than black dust.

His dark eyes flicked from the wasted lump of ash in his hand to our face, growing angrier by the second. Fangs slid into place and he lunged to grab our hand. The beast moved faster. Releasing Moira, she grabbed a half empty beer bottle from the demon standing two feet over—and smashed it on his skull. Stale beer spilled over the shade that thought to hurt her, splattering her own form. Bandit leapt at him, attaching himself with great vigor to the demon's face. He stumbled back, hitting the wall before regaining his senses.

He moved to grab Bandit and she let out a shrill whistle. My raccoon disengaged, tearing one of the barman's eyeballs out as he jumped away. The painful scream rivaled that of the creature in the pit below, and Bandit only barely avoided the swipe of a clawed hand as he landed on the bar in a hissing pile of fur. The beast held out her arm and he climbed up, reaffirming his place as he glared at the now one-eyed demon.

I hoped she knew what she was doing, because the last time we left a one-eyed demon hanging around, he tried to kill me, and almost killed Moira. The beast laughed, cold and callous, as she sent his body up in flames.

The demons around us jumped back, only now realizing the predator that walked in their midst. She held the broken neck of the beer bottle in one hand as a makeshift weapon and a globe of fire in the other.

"We were supposed to come in under the radar," I glowered at her.

"This place reeks of perversion. They must be taught a lesson."

Devil-damnit. Every fucking time I thought she had the right idea going, she turned around and pulled something like this. Every fucking time.

"You better keep Moira and Bandit safe," I snapped at her, not wanting to distract her too much.

"I always do," she replied, seemingly unperturbed by my frustration.

Crazy psycho bitch.

She almost grinned at that comment. Of course she would. Only crazy people found it amusing to be called so.

"Who are you, and what are you doing here?" the demon from the door said as he walked to the front of the crowd, no longer as appraising as he'd been.

Good. That will make this easier—wait a minute—was that her thinking? Or was it me?

Oh fucking hell. This whole sharing a body thing was really screwing with me.

"Who I am, matters not. I've come for the Seelie you stole."

"It's her!"

For fuck's sake. Could we not catch a break here?

"That's Lucifer's spawn and the legion."

Moira stiffened and blinked. She lifted her head, and when she looked at them she saw shadows. I didn't need to ask to know what they represented to her. What this place represented to her. I had come to peace with my past, but Moira never had.

She had never needed to, until now.

"Interesting," the chupacabra from the door said. "You kill Creag Le Dan Bia and then return for the hunters. I can't see any daughter of Lucifer being a Seelie sympathizer." The demon looked at her for a long moment, and then he looked to the others in the room. "What do you have to say about that, lads?" It was only then that she noticed the vicious grin on his lips. "Do we have ourselves a fake?"

Several of them regarded the fire she held in one hand, but clearly it didn't scare them enough. She'd taken on demons twice her size the last week when standing up for the weak and abused, but a hundred demons? Maybe more? Even I wasn't sure she could handle that many. That we hadn't grown overconfident in ourselves and only just realized the hole we dug. While some feared the power she held, others seemed completely unperturbed by the fact she'd killed one of their own with little thought.

Savages.

I had thought it, but Moira said it. She spat the word from her mouth like venom and snapped her wings open in all their glory.

"Savages, you say," he mused, smiling with very pointed teeth. "Darling, you haven't seen savage if this scares you." He lifted a hand and snapped his fingers.

Three demons came forward in a bid to grab us and the beast let out a growl.

"Touch her and you're fucking dead."

She stilled.

We knew that voice.

That cold whisper of *Death.*

"Oh thank fuck," Moira breathed.

The beast swung her head around looking for the source, but she saw nothing except unfamiliar faces. Then the brand on our chest began to burn—and I mean *burn.* It sizzled with a sharp all-consuming pain that almost felt like pleasure as it spread throughout her body. The three demons paused, also looking for the source of the threatening voice—only to come up dry.

They took another three steps toward me before coming to a violent halt. One by one, their skin blackened from the inside out. The whites of their eyes turned blue before exploding.

I'd seen that happen only once before. Most shades were not skilled enough to do that much damage to someone's system. However, Pestilence was not most shades.

He'd killed Josh with as little effort. These three assholes were nothing —and while it likely wouldn't kill them—they wouldn't be able to heal from this kind of damage for hours.

That meant hours writhing in agony.

I rather liked that thought, even if another lance of red hot pain was shooting through our body. The beast blinked, just as confused as I about what was going on—and the next thing I knew, it wasn't her staring out of my eyes—but me.

What in Satan's name—

I didn't even have the time to finish my thoughts before someone grabbed me from behind. To my credit, the beast was not the only one that had some cool moves. Armed with a broken beer neck, I let my adrenaline take over as I twisted to the side and slashed out.

Cold blue ichor hit my face as I severed the demon's carotid artery.

The only problem was that this was not just any demon.

It was Death. He'd found me.

And right now, he looked pissed as hell that I tried to kill him. Again.

All bravery left me as I turned to run—but Julian was smarter than that. He wasn't letting anyone get me out of here this time.

Julian grabbed my hips roughly, slinging me over his shoulder. I didn't even register him moving before we stepped into the shadows and all sounds of the brawl taking place behind me receded.

The beast had wanted to court Death. She liked playing games.

Once again, I somehow got stuck paying the price because the bitch got her wish.

Me.

Him.

And if the sudden change in temperature was any indication, nowhere to go for miles.

LARAN

Where were they?

Rysten and Allistair were sweeping the city while I made my way through the underground, but it seemed that every sign of Moira and Bandit was gone. I held out the bag of cookies I'd brought with me, just for the furry creature.

"Bandit! Bandit!" I called his name, shaking the bag. Usually he would come to me instead of the other Horsemen, but this time he was nowhere to be seen. The underground of Le Dan Bia was all but empty apart from me. I let out a frustrated breath and didn't bother wasting my time calling for the banshee. She would start screaming eventually and all of New Orleans would know where to find her, but the raccoon was not as simple.

"Have you found anything?" Allistair's presence brushed against my mind for a moment. Worry edged at him as well.

"Nothing," I answered, leaning against the bar. Most of the demons that had been here were either knocked out cold or dead. Their bodies littered the floor. Fuckers deserved it after trying to harm Ruby and Moira. I'd always hated Le Dan Bia. They were always straining at Satan's leash and out of the seven portal keepers, their clan always had the most reports against them. We'd be doing the world a favor wiping them from existence, but I knew this was far from the whole of the clan. Once some of the ones who weren't dead healed, they would wake and try to come for us with a

vengeance. It was the only reason the three of us were wasting our time scouring the city for Moira and Bandit. We needed them out of the equation while Ruby transitioned. Somewhere they would not be in harm's way. That was difficult to do when you can't find them.

Still, I kept searching and I would continue until I found them.

We just had to hope for our sake—and Ruby's—that it wasn't too late when I did.

CHAPTER THIRTEEN

Trees, dirt, and the sound of howling wind told me we weren't in New Orleans proper anymore. The ground below was dark, too dark to make out much beyond the forest floor. Leaves crunched as he began walking, not stopping to put me down. His breathing was quick, harsh.

"Hey! What are you doing—" I snapped, kicking at him. He reached up and swatted my ass. Another flare of pain ignited in my chest where my brand pulsed. My hips bucked against his hand—that he hadn't removed. He squeezed tightly through the little black number I wore, a growl starting deep in his chest. I smacked my hands against his own backside, my interest perking up at the hard muscle I found there. Once again, the strength I could sometimes display was gone—leaving me weak to Julian's manhandling.

"I would not keep fighting me if I were you, Ruby," he said quietly.

It was only then that I homed in on the dangerous emotions swirling in his chest. They were no longer closed off like the last time I saw him when the beast handily took out the four of them. Now he was wide open, a mix of anger and fear and a need so sharp it was painful.

I'd known he was jealous because he wanted me as the others did, but I'd never realized how much. Just how deep it ran.

I'd once said if he wanted a woman that not even Heaven or Hell could separate them. Little did I know then how true that was.

"What are you going to do to me, Julian?" I asked, my voice more than a little unsteady. I blamed it on the blood running to my head from being held upside down this long.

"What do you think I should do to you, Ruby?" he asked in return.

Devil fuck me. The things his voice did to me. Another spasm of pain ran through me, straight to the apex of my thighs. I let out a desperate mewling sound and Julian stiffened. His hand trailed over the back of my thighs, singeing my sensitive skin with fire. I squirmed, trying to get out of his hold, but he held tight, never giving me an inch.

"Stop fucking with me, Julian. You're being an ass," I snapped in a heated frustration. A sharp jolt went through me as his hand came down hard on my ass.

Did he just spank me…?

"Yes, I did. And I'm going to do a lot more than that if you keep testing me."

There we go again with that nifty mind-speak thing, except he could hear mine apparently. I grumbled under my breath and deflated a little bit. His hand flattened against me, gently rubbing over my now blazing ass.

I wanted to send another string of curses at him, but this felt good. In a strange, fucked-up kind of way. Pain can be pleasure after all, if administered correctly. He slipped his fingers just beneath my dress, into the thin panties. I squirmed again, not quite comfortable with how intimate this felt given I couldn't see him or move. His fingers expertly slid over one cheek and down the center, entering my heated skin.

"Do you know how you smell to me?" Julian asked quietly.

He slipped two fingers into my wet folds, pressing down to hit my G-spot as he pushed them in and out. I let out a low moan, turned on so much by his aggressive nature. He could be as cold as he fucking wanted as long as his fingers kept doing what they were doing.

"Did you know that your very scent changed the night the beast came forward because you had subconsciously chosen me as a potential mate?"

No. I didn't know that, but I also didn't really care. He pressed down, rubbing in circles. Slow. He was going excruciatingly slow.

What the hell was wrong with him?

Fire lanced through me, very real this time as my frustration grew. I smiled wickedly at the smell of burning cloth.

Julian removed his fingers and slapped my ass.

"Don't fucking try it."

I growled at him and slapped his ass back. It's not like I could fucking control it. I was in the middle of the transition and he was fucking playing with me, going on about how I smell when I just wanted him to fuck me.

"You'll be fucked when I decide to fuck you," Julian snapped.

What the—

Did I say that out loud?

"No, but your mind is wide open—and before you think it—no, I don't give a shit that you can't control it either."

Ass.

That got me another slap on my backside.

Bastard. I arched my back and brought my elbow up and around, contacting with the back of his skull. Julian let out a groan, his grip slipping, and I swiftly kicked him in the jewels.

Had these fuckers learned nothing? The beast and I shook our heads in annoyance as breath whooshed from his lips. I toppled sideways, my back hitting the hard ground beneath me. I groaned as sticks punctured my skin uncomfortably, and then jumped to my feet.

I took off into the trees without waiting to see him follow. Part of me knew I wouldn't get very far. It was pitch black outside. The entire place was nothing but shadow—which meant this was his element. Still, the rest of me was annoyed with him for this manhandling bullshit. He could have just taken me how I wanted, but instead he throws me over his shoulder and acts like an asshat. I wasn't inclined to make a single part of this easy for him after the last week.

I ran blindly into the woods, not daring to look behind even as he shouted at me.

"You do not want to play this game with me, Ruby! It's only going to make it worse when I do get you. You played with Death, and it's time to pay up."

Too late, motherfucker. You should have thought about that before—

Agh!

My feet snagged on a root sending me face first into the forest floor.

"Devil-damned—motherfucking—cunt-kissing—asshole—" My string of curses was cut off sharply by my body being flipped over against my will.

I stared up at Julian's pale form standing over me. Even in the dark I could see his eyes blazing with fury.

"I told you not to run," he glowered.

I stared back, all smartass retorts drying up on my tongue. He was shirtless—why was he shirtless? Didn't he know that a girl can't think straight with all those perfectly defined abs just waiting to be licked—

A smirk tugged at his lips.

Shit! I was doing that mind thing again. I just knew it. Julian held out his hand for me to take it. Part of me wanted to, but the rest of me knew not to be swayed but such a simple gesture. His rage and desire were eating him alive from the inside out, bleeding into me.

I slapped his hand away and moved to stand, only to find myself lifted and my back slammed against a tree. I gasped, trying to feel my way up from down. I only knew it was a tree because of the rough bark scraping at my back. Julian was gripping my hips way tighter than necessary, and there was no getting out of it this time.

"Wrap your legs around my waist," he commanded.

"Fuck you," I spat.

Did I really mean that? I don't know. His emotions were out of control, which was sending mine out of control.

"Ruby, do not fucking push me right now—"

And what do I do?

I slap him.

Full on bitch-slap to the face, and apparently my seriously not reliable super-strength had come back because his face whipped around as the crack echoed into the night.

Whatever burning fury he felt before was nothing to what would come next.

Slowly, so slowly that my anxiety inched up another ten notches, he turned his head back toward me and I saw it: the awful turbulence of emotions in his eyes. The emotions that he didn't know how to hide from me any longer. Just as I couldn't seem to keep my thoughts from him.

I sensed it in him. The shift. So sudden and swift. He lowered one hand to my bare thigh, hoisting it up around his waist, followed by the other. His cock twitched against me as he rubbed me through the thin material of my panties with the hard friction of his jeans. Even though it went against everything inside of me, I moaned, my back arching off the tree as the desire clashed hot and hard against the burning anger inside me.

"Do you hate me?"

I don't know what possessed me to say it. Probably the tornado of emotions running through me, angry and unforgiving. That's how it felt inside.

But his—his felt like a volcano, the pressure boiling and just waiting to erupt.

Still, the moment the words left my lips, Julian paused and the look he gave me…it was broken. So broken.

And that's when I knew.

"I wish I did. It would make my job so much easier," he whispered. His breath was cool as the arctic when it fanned my face. He reached up and brushed a stray lock of blue hair away from my face. "I can't hate you, Ruby. Not even when you—" He broke off, swallowing hard. There it was again, that vulnerability he covered with fury. "Not even when you ran from us. You let the beast in, and you ran from us. We had no idea where you were. We couldn't find you—and when we did, you were with that— that *male*." His voice came to a stop, his eyes darkening once more and it all made sense. He slipped his hand down the side of my face, his fingers applying pressure to my throat as he held me there.

"You think I…" I paused, watching the anger in his gaze fizzle up again like a darkness he couldn't shake. "I healed Eugene's soul. That is why he was with me. You should know by now that I'm not interested in anyone else, Julian." My voice was soft. A reprimand, but gentle. Kind, if not for the slight growl at the end. The beast wanted to throttle him for being a territorial idiot.

His hold on my throat loosened as he swept his thumb across my jawline almost…tenderly.

"You can't see him again," Julian insisted. Completely irrational, as always.

"You can't tell me who I can and can't see," I replied.

I didn't care to see him again, but it was the principle. They needed to learn this and learn it now. I was not taking orders from them. If we were equals, then damnit, they needed to treat me like it.

Julian dropped his hand from my throat, sliding it down to rest over my chest.

"I don't like other males near you."

Really, Sherlock? I couldn't have guessed. Julian's lips thinned as he stared at me. Yeah, he heard it. I didn't give a shit.

"Eugene is gay, Julian. You're being unreasonable."

He blinked. "I still don't like it."

I brought my hand up to smack myself in the forehead. Were we really doing this?

"I don't like a lot of things, but you don't see me being a dick about it. Maybe instead of being an ass, you should give me a reason to stick around and not feel the need to leave, then I won't be running into other demons."

Julian seemed to consider this before he asked, "What kind of reason?"

He leaned forward, his breath grazed just below my ear, sending a wave of chills over me. I groaned. His lips pressed against my throat as he brushed them up and down.

"What kind of reason, Ruby?"

Oh fucking hell. His mood swings were giving me whiplash.

"You could stop being a jealous prick and make a move if you want to be with me."

Why had I just phrased it that way? Great mood killer, Ruby. You and your socially awkward mouth.

"And spanking my ass doesn't count," I added.

Julian didn't even seem perturbed by me calling him on it. On the other hand, he seemed a lot more at ease once I cleared away his fears of Eugene —although I wasn't apologizing for running. Not over my dead body.

"I rather like spanking your ass," he replied, his erection digging into me.

He slid his hand back to my throat and tightened it. It wasn't enough to choke, but the possessiveness that lay beneath it was clear.

And you know what? I liked it.

In fact, I kind of loved it.

But I wasn't letting him off that easy.

"And I like not being treated like a child."

For some reason, I felt like I needed to push this because as soon as the clothes came off, I would be a goner. And they were coming off. Very soon. That much I was sure of.

Another lance of pain slashed through my chest, stronger this time. Fire tore through the forest as I cried out in an excruciating pain that was tinged with the briefest of pleasures.

I didn't understand what was going on. I'd gone days in transition without this happening. What had changed? What had—

Guilt.

It bled through from the only other living creature around me as Julian held me tighter, rocking his hips into mine. The contact made it better, more bearable, even as the fire grew out of control and began to incinerate our clothes.

If I thought I was out of control before, that was nothing compared to this.

"What did you do?" I moaned, knowing that he was somehow at fault. Julian swallowed hard as he ran his hands up and down my bare flesh. It made the pain better, but this time it wasn't completely abating.

"I'm…I'm sorry, Ruby. I didn't know what to do—" his voice broke off as a scream built in my chest. His touch helped, but it wasn't enough. Whatever he had done was making the transition a thousand times worse.

I thrashed against him as images filled my mind. Images of him and the others. Images of blood being spilled. Images and snapshots of what he did.

That fucker.

He'd *bound* me. Truly bound me. Except he didn't bind me in a circle. Oh no, he didn't have the power for that once I had left, so he did the next best thing.

He bound me to *him*. As long as I was in the transition, my body needed his. Begging for his touch to the point of pain if I didn't fulfill it.

He wanted to make sure I didn't run again, and he bound us together so that I couldn't.

"You motherfucking, cock-sucking, son of a—"

His mouth descended on mine, hard and insistent. I stayed frozen to the spot at first, not wanting to give in despite what my body and heart so desperately desired, but that's the thing about this bond. It made him a drug to me—

The thought was snatched away before I could see it and I growled at him. Julian knew that he couldn't hide now. Not after what he'd done.

I leaned into him, wrapping my arms around his neck. I clasped my hands flat over the back of his neck, pulling him to me before I dove into his mind.

His kiss turned rough—savage—as he pushed me back into the already burning tree. Our clothes were all but ash at this point, and his bare erection was hard against my skin as it slid over me without entering.

He groaned, his nails biting into my thighs as I nipped at his bottom lip.

"What's the rest of it, Julian?" I asked breathlessly, slipping a hand to cup his jaw, leaving the other on the back of his neck. "There was more to what you did, and you took the memory away before I could see it. What are you still trying to keep from me?"

Ignoring me, he sank his teeth into my shoulder, and it wasn't just an act of passion. He wanted to mark me. To make me his. He trailed his lips up my jaw and down my throat.

"What did you fucking do, Julian?" I asked one last time.

I really didn't want to test how well I could go through his mind. It felt like an invasion of privacy, but if he wouldn't tell me, I would do it. After all, he was the one who took my choice away and used fucking blood magic to bind my body to his. Not that I didn't want it long before he did so, but the act itself was still dancing on the hairsbreadth edge of right and wrong.

Julian growled as I fisted his hair and writhed against him. He rocked into me as kama started pouring out from him. It filled the air around me and I breathed it in, relishing the crisp cut that tore through my throbbing core.

Damn him, he was addictive.

The tree behind me cracked and I began to topple backwards as the massive oak no longer supported our weight, but instead of hitting the forest floor, my back hit something soft and I could feel the smooth sheets and comforter beneath me.

The room was black as pitch and my flames had stopped burning at some point. I moved to pull back, but Julian gripped me tightly, biting into my other shoulder.

"What the fuck—"

My body shuddered as his hardness rubbed against the sensitive bundle of nerves that left me moaning. There was pleasure in pain if done right. Wasn't that what I always had said?

How right I was.

"We had to find you, so I did the only thing I could do," he whispered against my neck and then the scene opened up again.

He knelt in a dark room, and a girl—a girl I recognized—stood before him. Her white blonde hair barely shifted as she leaned forward and cut his skin. Then she used his blood to draw the runes. The runes that would pull me to him.

So that I would feel what he feels. So that once he touched me, I would crave him for the remainder of the transition. So that I couldn't run. Even if I left this planet, he would find me. He would always find me.

But the blood magic wasn't so simple as to give him everything with nothing in return.

To form the bond, all barriers between us would become non-existent. I would feel what he feels…and in return, he would endure my pain should I run or resist.

The intense burning that filled my chest also filled his. The pain he felt was now mine.

He'd all but chained me to him, and in doing so, chained himself to me too.

All to keep me safe…well, not quite, but mostly. His desires were thick and raw and filled with such sweet agony. He wanted to do things to me, things he tried to protect me from.

None of the Horsemen were good men, Julian especially, and I'd broken whatever control he had when I left them.

The worry ate at him. The fury clawed. It shattered all pretenses that he held that kept him from crawling to my bed and led him to making a bargain with the girl who could do blood magic.

To get me and to keep me, he all but opened his soul.

I should be furious. I should fight him, and the beast, with every ounce of my being because of the kind of male Julian was. Because the type of possessive behaviors I'd run from my whole life ran deep in him.

But he wasn't just Death.

He was Julian.

My Julian. The one who would do anything to protect me, even come to terms with himself and the truth he already knew.

I was his greatest weakness, and yet, staying away from me—even *for* me—was never an option. The beast and I chose him as a mate and he accepted it. I was his, in every sense of the word.

But he was also mine, and that kind of surrender didn't come naturally to Death. He forced my hand, but in doing so, he finally made up his goddamn mind.

Was it strange that I was almost happy he had done this? Desire may be its own demon that demands you feed it, but so was love—even the twisted kind. I wondered if this was a bit of both because he and I were finally on the same page.

I ran my fingers through his hair and it was softer than I expected. I tugged his head so that I could pull him up and he acquiesced, resettling his weight by moving both arms above my head.

"I understand," I whispered.

He stared down, his eyes so dark they didn't even look green. I wanted to say more, but another pain lanced through my chest. This one worse than the others before. I let out an awful throat-straining scream. My back arched off the bed as I simultaneously tried to get closer to him and crawl out of my skin. I understood why he had done it, but the pain he put me in —the pain he put us both in—was immeasurable. I don't know how he was bearing it without cringing. Tears blotted the corners of my eyes as my body twisted, trying to break away from the torment even though I knew I couldn't.

"Make it stop," I begged. "Please make it stop."

There was only one way it would. He and I both knew that now.

Julian pulled back off the bed causing it to worsen. I clawed at my chest and he snatched my hands, pulling them away.

"Sit and don't move," he commanded.

I did as I was told, sitting on the edge of the bed. He released my hands and knocked my legs apart with his knee. I trembled with anticipation, widening my legs without needing further instruction as he kneeled in front of me. He leaned forward and softly kissed the brand between my breasts, the bone-splintering pain lessening, dulling. I brought my hands around to rest on his shoulders. Contact was helping.

His lips trailed down my naked chest, over my abdomen, straight to the aching heat between my legs. He grasped one of my thighs and pulled it over his shoulder, lightly blowing on my clit. A ragged gasp escaped my lips as he leaned forward and continued blowing as he buried two fingers inside me. I rubbed my hands over his shoulders and down his back, scratching him with my nails. He growled against me and my hips surged forward, but he held me still as he ran his tongue over me.

The oddest sensation filled me as the beast internally guided my hands to the back of his neck. A burning sensation rippled through me, and once again, I was too late to realize it was happening. Julian knew, and he stopped as the fire burned between us.

Where I should have been crying out in release, I nearly sobbed in desperation as I branded him. I was so fucking close when the burning receded, but a small part of me had the good sense to not scream at him. He was going to fuck me, of that I was certain.

"You branded me," he murmured.

Was that awe in his voice? Couldn't be…I tried to write it off, but it wasn't so easy when his emotions flooded me.

"Don't act so surprised," I snapped, not nearly as apologetic as I'd been when it happened with Laran or Allistair. Julian bound me without asking. He was already in this for life. His ass didn't get an apology. He laughed, pulling away.

"What are you doing?" I groaned, spreading my legs wider to show just how desperate I was.

"Turn around and get on your hands and knees," he ordered.

Whereas Laran and I had been interrupted, Julian had every intention of fucking me sore before the other Horsemen caught up to us. Wherever we were. That was a different question for after I came.

I pulled back onto the bed and did as he told me. The bed dipped as Julian got on behind me. He lifted the hair from my neck and pulled it taut.

"Lift yourself up. I want to feel you," his voice rumbled huskily.

My stomach muscles contracted as I pulled myself up, my back coming flush against his chest. He wrapped an arm around my waist, placing his hand over my stomach. I pushed my ass back, trying to rub against him. Clearly it wasn't as alluring as I thought when he let out a dark chuckle.

"What do you want, Ruby?" he asked, his voice no more than a whisper in my ear.

"You know what I want, asshole," I growled.

My breath hissed between my teeth as I felt a sharp smack on my sex. It stung, but this kind of pain felt good.

"You're being a brat. We'll need to work on that."

I shivered against his words, but not in fear. He may have been more savage when it came to pleasure, but I felt nothing but safe with him. So, I kept my mouth shut this time.

"Much better." I could hear the grin in his voice. "Now, what do you want?"

The pain in my chest ripped through me, shredding through any snarky retorts I had left.

"You!" I screamed.

Julian growled in approval and then he released me. My shaking limbs were barely holding me with all the tension coiled in my muscles. The lightest tap on my back was all it took for me to fall forward, landing on my elbows, face down. My legs shook with anticipation as his head touched my entrance. He thrust once, filling me in one go. I moaned into the sheets as I fisted them, biting down on the smooth fabric as my body nearly came apart.

What in Satan's name—how big was he? It's not like I was a virgin, but damn. I hadn't been fucked in years. May as well be. Still, when he pulled out, that familiar heat flared in me, still so close to the edge. He slammed back into me and I rocked forward.

I barely registered my hair being lifted as Julian wound it around his palm. He gripped it, pulling it taut, wrapping his arm around my torso, guiding my body up so that I was right where he wanted me.

And he thrust into me. Again, and again, and again.

With my back arched and his hand splayed across my abdomen, I lost myself to sensation as he pounded into me. I didn't even feel the climax creeping up before it tore through my system, making me clamp around him as I shuddered with relief and screamed his name.

He liked this. I could sense it as he continued to pump into me, chasing his own release. I pulled on the kama around me, inhaling deep breaths as I pushed my ass back, giving myself to him wholly. He thrust into me once more and roared. The wood panels above us shook under the force of his power. I thought he was going to level the house.

When the trembling stopped, and our breathing calmed, he let go of me. I fell forward on weak knees.

"You can't possibly think I'm done with you yet," his breath whispered over me.

The beast purred, and she wasn't the only one.

It was going to be a long night.

CHAPTER FOURTEEN

I STARTED to fall into a blanketed haze of lust and kama.

I don't know how long had passed or how many times he had taken me before I noticed the eyes watching us. The golden gaze that prowled from the corner of the room. Allistair stepped out of the shadows and the crisp cut of winter was joined by something sickly smooth as honey. It wrapped around my limbs, holding me in place while Julian fucked me from behind.

Not that I would have been able to move anyway with my face pressed into the mattress and him holding my arms behind my back. Julian had more of a fetish than Allistair when it came down to not letting me move. Demons and their kicks.

I felt it the moment Julian noticed who'd walked in on us. The slightly possessive tinge to him as he pounded me relentlessly. One hand held my wrists and the other gripped my hip, guiding me into him how he saw fit.

Allistair stood on the sidelines, his body relaxed, his gaze anything but.

Let it be known, I had never considered myself an exhibitionist. Until the transition, I'd never taken to watching others or letting them watch me. There was something so raw, but so intimate about it. Me watching him, while he watched Julian take me.

His hands moved to slip off his suit jacket, leaving it on the floor where he stood. My heart quickened.

Was he going to join us?

"Would you like me to join you?" he asked aloud.

I felt behind me, waiting for the intense jealousy that filled Julian before. While I was in no way his exclusively, I was theirs, and I needed to consider how they felt.

The beast reached forward tentatively, pushing me to encourage Allistair. While the blood magic Julian had done prevented her from coming forward until this was over, she was very much still there.

And she very much wanted him too.

Julian released his grip on my wrists, my arms falling to my sides, his hand reaching down and pressing against my hardened nub. He pinched the pinnacle nerve bundle, drawing a low moan from my lips. Golden particles wet my tongue, inciting another bout of sex driven cravings. I couldn't get enough of this stuff. I needed more.

"Ruby, do you want this?" Julian asked.

"Allistair..." I groaned, unable to reach for him or say more.

He raised his golden eyes to meet Julian's, asking his permission. He must have agreed, judging by the rip of fabric as Allistair tore his shirt away. The sound of a zipper caused another wave of euphoria to wash over me and I pushed myself up, supporting my weight while Julian's rhythm never ceased. My lips hung slightly ajar and my eyes closed when I felt him before me.

I didn't wait for his instructions. I knew what he wanted.

Opening my mouth wider, I tasted the white drop of liquid on his tip as he pushed it in. A groan reverberated from him as I skated my tongue along the underside of his shaft, sucking him deeper. Julian was pushing me closer to the edge, literally and figuratively, my body shifting forward, slowly inching into Allistair with the pounding I was taking from behind.

"Are you going to roar for me, Ruby?" Allistair asked.

The hair lifted off the back of my neck as Allistair wrapped it around his hand, using his grip to pull my head back and widen my mouth. I wasn't prepared for the brutal assault of him slamming to the hilt in one go. I gagged once, trying to breathe through my nose, the orgasm creeping up on me slipping through my grasp because of it. I growled around him and his cock twitched at the back of my throat.

Bastard.

"I want to hear you roar for me like you did for him," Allistair's voice infiltrated my mind. He wasn't backing off.

I sucked hard and it drew a low hiss from his lips. He was close. Enough so that I could push it. I felt it as the pressure within him began to build.

The fingers on my clit stopped and I felt another sharp smack on my ass.

I groaned at the heat that quickly followed in its place. My body was becoming rapidly addicted to the little bouts of pain Julian liked to inflict. The way it shattered all rational thought, forcing me to succumb.

"He asked you a question, Ruby," Death commanded behind me. He pulled out entirely, his tip just sitting at my entrance, waiting for me to comply.

"Fuck you," I snarled internally at Allistair for pushing, and Julian for pulling away.

The second blow that smacked my ass had me gagging and my abdominal muscles clenched. There was nothing hard or heavy inside me to tip me just over the edge into oblivion. I groaned in frustration, Allistair still in my mouth, his breaths becoming labored as a fine sheen of sweat trickled down his lower abs.

They were going to draw it out of me, one way or another.

Fire licked inside my veins, crackling to life around me.

"Put it away, Ruby," Julian demanded.

I swallowed hard as Allistair was pulled from my lips and the next smack reverberated through me. I could hear the air whoosh before another followed, hitting my upper thighs this time. So close to where I wanted to feel him. Heat blossomed in my skin as I tried to rein it in, to pull the fire back.

"I said, put it away Ruby. *Now.*"

His power slithered over me as he rained down blows on my ass. It hurt like hell, but I didn't want him to stop. In a backwards way, it wasn't him that held the power in this. But me. In pushing him, I was also pulling. I encouraged the slaps. I relished in the stinging bite of his palm, knowing that some depraved part of my soul had guided us both here, and in the fire within, I found silence.

I tentatively reached out towards the flames as if they were an extension of myself, similar to the beast in that way. The banter and thoughts flowed between us quite easily, maybe the flames could too. Far too exhausted to fight his command, I pulled on my link with the flames and the beast, urging them to retreat.

No one was more surprised than me when it worked.

The beast wore the slightest of grins, something akin to pride coming from her.

I blinked through the tear-stained haze, only just realizing that the blows had stopped. My ass was going to be so fucking sore—

The bed shifted as Julian moved away, leaving me rather deprived of attention. That was not what I wanted out of this.

I groaned as I pushed myself up to a sitting position, sweat and tears plastered my hair to my face, and I raked a hand through my tangled locks. Out of the corner of my eye, Julian moved around the bed, coming from behind me to stand off to the side. His body was massive and gleaming in the pale moonlight coming from the windows. On his chest, over his right peck, a silver skull glowed. His brand, I realized.

Was he going to—

"No, I am not the one who gets to brand you first," he responded.

From the shadows, another fair-haired demon stepped out, but this one gleamed like gold. Shirtless, in nothing but a pair of well-worn jeans, Rysten walked up to the edge of the bed.

"Hello, love," he whispered softly. Leaning forward, he gently took my face between his hands and kissed me. I reached out, wrapping my arms around his shoulders. The kiss deepened as our tongues intertwined. The beast growled in approval.

Behind me, the bed sank. I pulled back slightly, trying to see who it was, but Rysten held me firm. Strong hands and an aura like honey touched mine as Allistair's hands roamed down my bare back.

Was he going to—

"No," Rysten answered my silent question.

His lips left mine to trail down my neck, two sharp points dragging against it. *His fangs,* I realized with a startle. I'd never seen his fangs.

Rysten stepped aside and Allistair pushed between my shoulder blades, guiding me down to my hands and knees. He rubbed his palm over the warm red skin on my ass and his fingers deftly spread my cheeks. I tried to clench them shut from shock, but it was already too late for that. Something wet and slippery slathered over my rim as Allistair's breath fanned the sensitive patch of skin just below my ear.

"Laran got to be branded first," Allistair said.

My breath hitched as something pressed against me, sliding in and stretching me; too small to be his cock, but too insistent to leave even a shred of doubt about how this was going to go.

"Julian got to fuck you first, and repeatedly," he continued, pushing and twisting two fingers in and out of me. The feeling turned from uncomfortable to downright pleasurable just as Allistair stopped his ministrations and pulled away.

"Rysten will get to brand you first, after you accept him."

The smooth tip of him pressed against me, and that scream from earlier…the one I hadn't been willing to let loose…it was starting to form again as he slowly pushed his way in. I made no move to stop him as a burning sensation filled me, and it wasn't fire. Rysten's dexterous fingers grounded me as they trailed across my hips and slowly skated between my already wet folds.

"I get to claim your mouth and your ass before the others, just to keep it fair."

My lungs were going to be bloody shreds by the time they finished with me. Fuck, I might have loved and hated them at the same time in that very moment. Allistair grunted as he settled inside me. I scolded myself to not pass out as he began slowly moving.

Too full. I breathed heavy. In. Out. In. Out.

There was too much sensation. I wanted it all, but it brought me to the teetering edge of madness with how they touched me, and broke me, and pieced me back together again. A scream ripped from my throat as Allistair thrust into me once. Twice.

"There is my roar," he groaned in satisfaction.

His cock stilled inside me again, giving me a chance to adjust. I leaned forward wanting to pull away, but not wanting it to end. Allistair made the choice for me, pulling halfway out before thrusting back in. The painful feeling mingled with a sliver of pleasure.

I had been on the brink of release, and all the pent-up frustration from Julian's hand had been torn from me, so I was left behind a trembling mass of limbs that shook with exhaustion, and I had no choice but to want and take what they were giving me.

Allistair scooped his arm under my torso, lifting me to my knees, my hands coming to rest on Rysten's chest. My watering eyes met his while he silently pried apart my swollen flesh, filling me with his fingers just as Allistair picked up his pace. He placed one hand on the curve of my neck as he kissed me. I moaned deeply, pleasure sinking its claws into my body further.

He tasted of wine and blood, a strangely erotic combination. His tongue slipped past my lips, entwining with mine as he drew me deeper into the cloudy haze where words would no longer suffice. On my knees before them both, I gave myself over, arching my back for Allistair while leaning into Rysten. One hand went up to rest on the curve of his chest where it dipped just below his throat.

The beast nodded in approval, guiding me as fire kindled beneath my palm. Rysten wrapped his hand around my throat, applying pressure and his fingers twisted around my clit as my orgasm rapidly tore through me, Allistair cursing as my muscles spasmed and tightened around him. He slammed his cock into my ass once more, finding his own release.

Kama filled the air, pressing into my skin. I relished in the feeling of Allistair behind me and Rysten in front of me as I branded fire and magic into his skin, claiming him as my mate.

The hand on my throat tightened as an unfamiliar energy washed over me. It filled my blood with darkness and shadow, infusing my very soul with a raw energy that grounded me. It was the calm after the storm. The midnight breeze that called. Whereas I filled him with fire and life, he filled me with peace and darkness.

And deep within, the beast and the flames settled as she sighed happily. Truly content for the first time in twenty-three years, in the arms of our mates.

****ALLISTAIR****

She was truly insatiable.

I'd never met a succubus that could push me to my limits. She put out enough kama to keep me fed just by standing in the same room as her. After a week, I had to claw my way out of her bed, leaving her with Rysten and Laran just so I could get a word with Julian.

"Any word on Bandit or Moira?" I asked him.

I had to keep my voice down, even on the porch outside with several walls between us. One never knew what abilities might come out during the transition, and the last thing we needed was her sent into a rage this deep into it. How the beast had managed to keep it together without us spoke to that entity's power and control.

"None," Julian answered.

I nodded once, because I knew what that meant. Someone had likely seen them with Ruby and trapped them.

"Has Sin found anything?" I already knew the answer, but I needed it off my conscience. I needed to know that we were trying every avenue to find her familiars.

"Not that she's reported. She said the trail ran cold at the underground. She suspects Le Dan Bia have them now, but being what she is, she's unwilling to enter to find out." Julian was able to detach himself from this because of the blood magic that linked them for the duration of her transition. He had difficulty focusing on much else. That was not the case for the other three of us. We knew what we would face when she found out.

Transition or not. Beast or not. She was not going to take that information well.

"Ruby might try to kill one of us when she finds out," I replied, and Julian nodded.

"I'd expect nothing less. Good thing I cannot die."

The same could not be said for her familiars.

CHAPTER FIFTEEN

I FLOATED ON SMOKE. Or maybe I was flying.

It was hard to tell as I looked down at the world below. Blanketed by a moonlit sky, blue flames ravaged a forest. In that sky I sat, watching it all burn. Normal fire needed time to catch and grow into an all-consuming beast, but the flames of Hell were not normal. They did not operate that way. Instead, all that they touched instantly turned to ash as they swept across the land.

The beast felt a small thrill at the scene below, but I didn't share that with her this time. I did not wish that. Fire was life and light and cleansing, but it was also deadly and destructive. The winds blew warm air across my skin and layers of fabric drifted around my bare legs. Two long drapes of cloth hung over my shoulders and barely covered my breasts. It was cinched around my waist with a dainty gold belt. The onyx cloth wrapped around my calves, curving around my ankles. I was sitting on smoke, or a cloud more likely, given that the flames didn't give off smoke. Where I was or how I'd gotten up here was beyond me. I felt a steady unease that this wasn't right. Here, wherever I was, didn't deserve to burn.

I reached out to the flames below, calling them back to me. They stilled in their rampant destruction. A very clear line between all that had already burned and the world beyond that still could. I couldn't let that happen.

The same as they were mine to unleash, they were also mine to control. To prevent from destroying everything.

I held onto that thought as I pulled them in, only then noticing the beast's smile.

"You are ready," she whispered.

I blinked, and when I opened my eyes it was the midnight sky that greeted me. Millions of little white lights lit up in constellations that you couldn't possibly see in any city. I stared at them for a moment in awe.

"Ruby!" someone shouted.

I blinked again and looked to my side. Dark glitter covered the ground as far as my eyes could see. It sparkled beneath the night sky, reflecting the stars above.

What in Satan's name had I done this time?

I yawned deeply and stretched languidly like a cat before pushing up off the ground into a sitting position. The Four Horsemen stood in front of me, each of their expressions ranging from bad to worse. I knew I was in deep, deep shit, and I hadn't even consciously done anything this time.

I groaned against the stiffness in my legs as I moved to stand. I'd fallen asleep and set everything on fire again, that much was clear. I was also stark naked, and I felt sticky between my thighs. That probably had to do with the ungodly amounts of sex I'd been having for…well, I don't know how long. I just couldn't seem to get enough. After Rysten branded me, it all got a little wonky. I remembered skin, lots of skin, and the distinct taste of each of their kama—and lots of biting, maybe some blood…aw hell. I was a filthy slut and they totally just went with it.

What's the point in being a demon queen if you couldn't act a little sinful sometimes? My new position was beginning to grow on me and it had a lot more to do with the four in front of me than any crown.

"How are you feeling, love?" Rysten asked, walking forward. Also naked. They were all naked. Hmm… I swallowed hard, averting my eyes from skipping from one male's package to another.

"I'm—" I coughed like I smoked a pack a day for twenty years. "My throat's dry."

Rysten nodded like he expected this and leaned down. Instead of just offering me his hand like a normal person, he scooped me up in his arms. I flailed, not all that much a fan of being picked up. I get that lots of girls loved that shit, but I was tall. That saying about tall people? The bigger you are the harder you fall? For someone who spent a lot of time falling, I had found that to be quite true.

Rysten locked an arm beneath my knees and wrapped the other around my naked back, cuddling me to his chest even though cuddling was the last thing I felt like.

"Put me down! You big oaf—" I elbowed him in the chest and Rysten sighed.

"You think you can manage not to burn anything else down for now?" he asked lightly.

My brows furrowed as I narrowed my eyes.

"Maybe…" I trailed off, opening my mouth to continue when the air whooshed around us. Instead of standing—or being carried like a lazy fuck —in the middle of a burned down clearing, we were now standing in a familiar living room. Rysten carried me to the couch as Julian stepped out of the shadows behind him. A ring of fire appeared to our left and Laran came striding through with Allistair. Rysten laid me on the couch almost gingerly before pulling away. He flipped the light on in the kitchen and started rummaging through the fridge.

This was weird. So weird on so many levels.

Allistair moved to pour himself a glass of scotch and settled in the armchair across from me, his half-hard dick was more distracting than I think he realized as his eyes raked over my naked body. We were gross— disgustingly gross—and yet, I probably could have ridden him right then and there without a care. I must have officially lost it.

Julian came out of the kitchen carrying a glass of water and two little red pills. He handed them to me silently and walked away as I downed the water and what was probably ibuprofen in about three seconds flat. To top off the strange atmosphere, Laran picked me up despite my grumbling and repositioned himself next to me with my head resting on his chest.

Hmm…maybe losing it wasn't so bad.

One of his arms snaked around my waist and the other pushed my mass of hair aside. His fingers trailed down my neck to the muscle where the neck and shoulder meet, slowly massaging out the tension. My toes curled inward as I let out a small moan of relief, and the very odd, fairly normal atmosphere froze as one of the other three turned to look at us, and Julian shot him a death glare if there ever was one.

What happened to sharing? I mentally sighed, not really giving a damn.

"He only likes sharing if he's involved," a warm voice echoed.

I jumped in surprise, looking around before I realized it was Laran. The whole mind speak thing was going to take some getting used to.

"Telepathy," he answered aloud, still addressing something I clearly hadn't said but trying to freak me out a little less. I relaxed back into him, and he continued with the massage.

"So, you can hear my thoughts now?" I asked. Around the room, each of them nodded and I twisted my lips. "Then why can't I hear all of yours?"

"You shouldn't be able to hear ours unless we send them to you, but you seem to be projecting yours while also listening into ours."

Allistair seemed troubled by this. A thin tendril of wariness wrapped around him. Hesitation.

"This bothers you," I commented.

The scent of fresh coffee came over me as a sizzling sound filled the air. My eyes swept to the kitchen where Julian was filling a giant coffee mug while Rysten fried something that smelled suspiciously like bacon. I wondered if it was Saturday…

"You displayed a lot of abilities during the transition. While it's not expected that you will keep them all, you showed many to such a degree that it is unheard of…" His voice trailed off as Julian filled my vision. He silently handed me the cup of coffee, holding out his other hand to take the empty glass. I traded with him, muttering my thanks as I took my first sip of pure heaven in far too long.

"Why wouldn't I keep all of them?" My mind seemed to snag on this. *Did that mean I would lose the fire? If I lost that—*

"You won't lose the fire, Ruby. Any abilities you displayed before your transition will still be there, just stronger now. Some things you were able to do during should have also stayed, others probably not."

I nodded along even though that didn't make a lick of sense to me. Why would I keep some and not others? That seemed dumb. Allistair sighed and Laran let out a chuckle. Apparently, they thought that was funny.

"During the transition, a demon takes on every ability in their genetic pool. As your body starts to change to fit immortality, the weaker ones don't usually stick. Instead, that energy gets absorbed in the process and repurposed for other things. Like accelerated healing."

While his explanation made sense, my body was clearly not doing its damn job. The ache between my thighs, while not painful per se, was not exactly pleasant. Allistair cut me a ruthless grin and Laran's hand tightened around my waist.

"You're not completely through the transition yet," Allistair said by way of answer.

"Yet?" I asked. He nodded, and I took another swig of coffee.

"You went through the worst of it at the cabin. At this point, you shouldn't have more than a day left before you'll be feeling better than ever. Until then your body will need a lot of sleep and food—" His eyes flicked down to where I was licking my lips. Just the mention of—"Real food, not just kama," he inserted tightly.

The tension in the air thickened, his cock hardening to a thick column. Kama pulsed from behind me, as Laran's magic hands pulled the tension from my shoulders. It brushed over my skin, turning my brain to mush for a second.

In the kitchen, a bang and loud cursing pulled me out of it. I looked up to see Julian giving Laran another death glare, followed by a mental threat he probably thought I didn't hear. I grinned to myself, hiding it behind the lip of my coffee mug as I took a long sip. The bitter burn did just what I needed it to, clearing my head of more thoughts of sex.

"So…" I drawled out. "Why did you take me to the cabin and not back here?"

"We didn't have a structure strong enough to hold you," Julian answered from the kitchen. He came out holding a plate of bacon and lifted my feet to sit at the end of the couch. "We had hoped this one would be with the wards, but after you broke out the first time, I wasn't chancing it again."

Broke out? Ha! I whooped their asses and jumped three stories like a boss. Nice way to downplay it, Julian. Real nice.

Allistair choked on his scotch and coughed twice as Rysten grumbled in the kitchen. It was only Laran that sounded half as amused as I was when he let out a deep laugh.

"So you took me out in the middle of the woods, so I couldn't run? Or if I did, it's not like I had anywhere to go…"

Julian nodded, offering the plate of bacon. I happily took it and began munching away.

"You know that's creepy right? You literally took me to the middle of nowhere, so you could—"

"Fuck you?" Julian said, staring at me without remorse.

I shrugged. Fuck me. Smack me around. It wasn't all that different when I was doing it with him. The dark glimmer in his eyes told me he heard that and had plans for a lot more fucking and spanking. I shivered, and it was entirely out of desire. Not an ounce of fear.

"We also had to get you away from the city, love. There were too many people that would have died if you decided to go all supernova in your sleep," Rysten added, walking into the living room while scratching the back of his head.

On his chest, just below the dip in his throat, a dark blue pentagram swirled like smoke. On one hand, it looked kind of cool because brands never did that. On the other hand, my fire didn't have smoke, so I don't know why they kept manifesting that way. He took one look at the seating arrangement and moved to sit on the adjacent couch.

I knew that demons felt quite comfortable in the nude, but this group nudity thing was taking it to a new level. I would need some time to get used to this new dynamic.

"We have all the time in the world now, little succubus, once we—" Allistair cut off short, his eyes flipping to Julian. I frowned, tilting my head sideways.

Were they really trying to keep things from me again? What the shit—

"It's not what you think," Laran said. His hand drifted over the tops of my shoulders as he tried to massage the tension out. His chin sat just on top of my head, where he'd tucked me into him.

"That would be easier to believe if you four didn't continue to keep secrets and try to control every aspect of my life," I replied, more than a little salty.

Mates, we may be. Perfect, they were not. Or sane. Can't forget that one.

"We only do it to keep you safe, love—"

"Cut the shit, Rysten," I snapped. Something was missing here. Something so obvious, it was right in front of me... "Where's Moira?"

Silence.

Looks like I was getting to the crux of it on my own.

"Where. Is. Moira?" I repeated. She was my familiar, devil-damnit. If they won't tell me, I could find out myself. Opening my mind, I reached out, trying to feel—

"She's going to find out anyways."

"And heads are going to roll when she does."

"The banshee made her choice—"

"—Moira is her familiar, as is Bandit."

Laran was the only one that didn't think of my raccoon as vermin. Speaking of—

"Where are Moira and Bandit? Where are my familiars…" My voice trailed off as a scene appeared before my eyes.

Back in the underground, Julian had grabbed me. I remembered him grabbing me, I didn't realize Bandit had fallen off when he did. He scurried out from between our feet and dove into the mob. Where no one had seen him since…

…or Moira.

I blinked, my body lurching as I pulled away from Julian and the memory cut short. He was really going to regret binding me with blood magic, because the transition wasn't over, but they were missing—and now I knew it.

* * M O I R A * *

I picked through the remainder of the half-eaten turkey sandwich one of the guards had been eating last night. As unappetizing as it was, it was still food, potentially the only food I might see for forty-eight hours. Not that many people brought things down here from the world above, outside of strippers, booze, and bait for their barbaric ring.

I'd been trapped in a ring much like this as a child, time and time again. Now, no one knew I was here. I was free to walk and to wander and to watch, but they couldn't see or hear me, and I couldn't directly interact with them—me and the trash panda.

In the asshole's defense, his skills at finding trash to eat for both of us had been coming in handy down here, not that I ever expected to need it. I was just happy the little bugger seemed concerned enough with keeping us both alive that he thought to share instead of keeping his rump fat and happy. Although, he did make a better pillow when he was.

I tore the sandwich in half and handed one to him. Bandit wrapped his paws around it and started scarfing it down. At least my opposable thumbs were useful in taking water bottles from the bar and keeping us hydrated. Not that it stopped the guards from emptying out the water bowls I made for him because they thought they were trash. I was over this fucking curse two weeks ago. Lifting my wing, I glared at the rune on my back.

Fucking Fae. Fucking Seelie.

I swear, when I get out of here—and I will—someone was going to die.

"Take it from someone who knows, the Fae are not the easiest to kill."

My neck actually cracked from spinning around so fast and Bandit leapt to my defense.

"You can see me?" I was in complete disbelief. After two weeks of being nothing but a ghost, this had to be a hallucination. Only my imagination would come up with a woman that beautiful that could speak to me in my darkest hour.

"I can, but I'm actually here for him." She pointed a purple claw towards the trash panda and something about it jogged my memory.

"I've seen you before," I said to her. She smiled a little vixen-like and snapped her fingers. The clothes changed from dark fighting leathers to a pair of tight jeans and a cropped shirt that read 'Voodoo Doughnut' in Pepto-Bismol pink. "*You!*"

"Me," she agreed, nodding her head like this was amusing.

"What are you doing here? And how can you see me?" I asked, narrowing my eyes. After talking, and screaming enough, I'd finally figured out how to control the sound waves to some degree, but it was easier to ignore them entirely given I couldn't do a damn thing about my curse.

"The whys and hows aren't all that important." She swiped a clawed hand out and caught Bandit faster than he could react. The raccoon twisted to bite her, but she was already pulling away. "I'd perk up, though, if I were you. Ruby will be here soon."

She disappeared like she'd never been there to begin with, but even in the dark light I didn't miss what she'd taken from Bandit. Hairs. Five little blue and black hairs.

I pulled the raccoon to my chest, feeling protective over him. Because whatever she came for, she got it, and I had a bad feeling about what might bring Ruby running.

CHAPTER SIXTEEN

"You left them at the underground!" I screeched. It wasn't a question.

I jumped away from the couch, landing on my still wobbly feet. The plate of bacon tipped off the couch, falling to the floor where no one reached for it. All eyes were on me as I crossed my arms over my chest and glared daggers at Julian. Sure, they were all at fault, but it was Julian that had them call off the search.

Laran. Laran had been the last to come to me in my transition. He had stayed out the longest to search for Moira and Bandit, but it appeared they were gone. Except I knew that couldn't be true because they were my familiars, and if they were in pain at any point, I would have felt it…wouldn't I?

Shit. Shit. Ball-licking bastards—

"I can assure you I don't lick balls," Allistair inserted.

I rounded on him with my cup of coffee still in hand and did the only thing I could think of.

I threw it at him.

I threw my perfectly good, hot coffee at his face and stood my ground. I didn't even have the fucks to give to run like I probably should have.

"You bastards left them there!" I yelled.

Something flickered deep inside me; not the beast, and not the bonds with the Horsemen. Something else. Someone else.

I pushed it aside, almost positive it wasn't Bandit.

"We didn't want to leave them, Ruby, but you needed your other mates —" Julian tried to interject.

"We seemed to be getting along just fine without them," I snapped. Okay, maybe not the greatest insult ever, but I was so beyond angry. *Moira and Bandit were out there somewhere, probably scared and lonely and—*

"I highly doubt the raccoon is scared or lonely, love. He's a wild animal. He can survive outdoors." Rysten's words did nothing to calm me. I knew he didn't like Bandit, but I didn't give a shit. "And the banshee is a legion now. She can take care of herself—"

"You left my *familiars* in an underground fighting ring that takes pleasure in *killing*. Do you even understand the gravity of this situation?" I asked, true hysteria creeping into my voice.

"We didn't abandon them," Laran started. I turned to him, my hands clenched at my sides, not amused in the slightest if this was some kind of joke. Whatever he had to say, it better be good. "We called in a friend of ours to find them. If anyone can do it, she can."

She? Something ugly touched my chest. *Jealousy.*

Allistair chuckled under his breath, despite the coffee dripping down his body.

"What the hell is so funny to you?" I snapped at him.

"You. I can't believe you're feeling jealous after the two weeks we've just had," he continued laughing under his breath, but my insides furled at the horror in his statement.

"They've been trapped in the underground for *two weeks?*" My voice didn't rise this time. There was no hysteria. Only the bone chilling cold of what I'd done.

Moira, who had been so scared she could barely move when we went down there…she was trapped. I just knew it. Why else would they not be able to find them?

"We don't know they're down there." I heard the words but tasted the lie beneath them.

"Where else would they be?" I replied coldly, all but calling him on it.

"They could have escaped, love—" Rysten stopped talking when my dark gaze flicked to him.

"You don't believe that any more than I do."

"I'm sure they're fine—" Allistair started to say and I finally snapped.

"Don't tell me that!" My head spun as power gathered inside me. Fire licked at my skin, burning away all the unmentionable substances coating it. "Stop telling me what to think or how to feel because you guys fucked up. *Again.* You knew better than to leave them down there. I would rather transition and be in pain than have you abandon them down there. You fucking knew," my head swung around savagely to stare at Julian. He did know, but he also cared so little for most things outside of me, his brothers, and his duty, that it wasn't at the forefront of his mind during our time together. He had such an easy time making the call, he didn't even regret it.

"You left my best friend and Bandit in an unfamiliar city. The Gates of Hell, no less. You left them in one of the nastiest fighting rings on the continent, where either one or both could be…"

My throat closed up. I couldn't afford to think like that. I couldn't afford to let anger or jealousy or anything else cloud what I needed to do.

The atmosphere in the room quieted.

I stormed off down the hallway and into the first bedroom I saw.

My mind was racing through a million scenarios as I ripped open the drawers before me. I dressed without thinking or feeling…no, that was a lie. I couldn't not feel, but what I did…it hurt. The Horsemen had done a lot of crazy and stupid things. I had too, but this decision stung like betrayal.

It's not like they didn't know she was there, or Bandit. They knew, and they still chose to leave. No matter the reasoning, that was unacceptable. Moira wasn't just my familiar, she and Bandit were my goddamn family and if they couldn't learn what the hell that meant, then I wasn't going to waste my breath.

"Where are you going?"

I couldn't see them, but I knew which one asked. Only one of them would phrase it in such a way as to make me question myself. They knew what I was going to do, and somehow, he made it sound like a threat.

"I'm leaving, *Death*," I spat. "Someone has to go find Moira and Bandit."

Part of me felt like I was being a bit harsh. I mean, the beast was the one that brought them, and I was the one who wanted to go down there and deal with Le Dan Bia to begin with, but that didn't excuse the blatant disregard for their lives. It didn't excuse that Moira may be down there being tortured, or worse…

Someone rested a hand on my shoulder, but I shrugged them off, pulling a tank top over my head. On top of the dresser, a stack of hair ties sat. I stole two and pulled back my ratty hair. It could really do with a good wash, but that would have to wait. Moira was out there somewhere, and Bandit too.

"Ruby." Another hand grasped at my shoulder and I tried to shove them off. Once again, whatever strength I had before was gone. Maybe that was one of the powers I wouldn't get to keep. That kind of sucked if it was the case, but it's not like I got to pick and choose. That's life for you.

Rysten stepped directly in front of me as I moved to the doorway. I knew it was him by the pentagram on his chest and the white brand on his arm. It looked like some sort of biohazard symbol with rings encircling it. I stopped before running smack into his chest, but I didn't look at him. I didn't want to. Rysten was sweet and kind and…manipulative. He knew what it meant to be human. He knew how to play with my emotions better than any of them. Twenty minutes and enough self-doubt and they'd be trying to lock me away again, convincing me they could sort out this mess. I wasn't having it. Not now and not ever.

"Ruby, love, I'm not trying to manipulate you," he whispered. He lifted one hand to the side of my face in a sweet gesture, his thumb brushing over my cheek. I stupidly leaned into him before I could stop myself. Slapping his hand away, I shook him off and took a step back.

"Don't 'love' me, Pestilence. She's my best friend, and Bandit's…well, *pet* doesn't quite cover it, but he's important. They're family, and I'm not leaving them out there while I finish the transition."

Rysten sighed deeply and someone stepped up beside him. I lifted my chin just enough to see his honey-colored eyes.

"If you try to put me to sleep, I'm castrating you, Famine," I growled. A little bit of the beast crept through despite the blood binding. With my transition coming to an end, the spell must be weakening.

"I'm not going to put you to sleep—" He broke off abruptly and both he and Rysten turned around as one.

What were they doing?

Julian was gone first with the others hot on his heels. I stood there dumbfounded.

Was this all a joke to them? Did they think it was funny?

I followed after, prepared to give them a piece of my mind if—

I stopped dead in my tracks because standing in the living room was none other than the girl from Voodoo Doughnut. I say girl, but her eyes held a lifetime or sorrow with the hardness to withstand it. She wore dark fighting leathers splattered in blue. Demon blood. My thoughts went silent when I saw what she was carrying in her arms.

My heart stuttered once. Then twice.

It was a lump of fur, both blue and black. His head lolled to the side, and though his limbs were shaking, they were losing energy fast.

Water pricked at my eyes as I ran to him. Because I knew. I knew deep, deep down what this meant.

I stopped a few feet away and the Horsemen remained silent. Failure ripped at their hearts. It wrapped around them, squeezing so tight it—

I pulled away from them. I didn't want to hear it. To see it.

"Give him to me," I demanded. My voice shook with pain and loss and a sorrow that very soon would consume me. The silver-eyed woman walked forward and placed him in my arms.

A prickle of life flared inside him as she handed him over, but it wasn't enough. It wouldn't be. With him in my arms, I could see the deep gashes and red blood that his fur had hidden.

The woman spoke, but I didn't hear it.

I registered that the Horsemen were talking. Saying something.

But I didn't hear it.

Someone had hurt him.

Someone had killed him.

I looked at my familiar. My raccoon. My Bandit.

And my heart broke as the last sliver of life left his eyes.

I could heal a soul, but I couldn't save a body.

I could burn the earth, but I couldn't save him.

And in that moment, I knew that a part of me was going to be forever changed.

I readjusted him in my arms, unable to see much of anything past him through the blurry tears in my eyes. Placing one hand on his chest, I pushed forward whatever energy I could. Wishing his soul healing and peace as the light faded from him.

It was blue, the same color as my own.

And when it died…

Something inside my chest unfurled, dark and ugly.

Someone was going to pay for this.

Someone was going to die.

"Who did this?" The voice that came out of my mouth didn't sound human, but it wasn't the beast. This was fury that she would let me act on alone.

The woman stepped forward, her face unreadable. Impassive.

"I found him in the underground hosted by Le Dan Bia. They put him in the pit with a hellhound and…" The woman looked to the Horsemen behind me, not wanting to say what I had already put together. "Moira asked me to bring him back to you before he left this world."

Though grief and despair had me, my mind pulled apart the pieces of information I needed. I was correct that they had never escaped Le Dan Bia. How the Horsemen had never found them…I wasn't sure what to think of that. Only that there was more at stake than setting a precedent. They had killed him, and Moira hadn't come back.

Why?

"Why isn't she with you?" I asked.

Question. Information. The pounding in my chest told me I only had a small grasp on the fire itching to leap out at them.

The Horsemen had left him. I had left him.

The pounding quickened.

"She was trapped in a cage, but alive. I could not bring him back and save her. She asked me to bring him so that you could say goodbye." I grimaced. Moira had chosen to stay in her own nightmare, so I could see Bandit one last time.

A small light filled me at the selflessness of that act.

I would save her, and I would kill every single one of them doing it.

"Ruby, you need to think about this—" Julian placed a hand on my shoulder that I stepped away from, a cold resolve settling over me.

"We may be bonded, but you are *not* my keeper," I snapped. A tendril of something far from sanity was wrapping its way around me. Around my words. I didn't try to push away that sliver of darkness. That sliver of shadow and night that Rysten had branded onto my very soul.

"It's not safe," Julian insisted. He tried to take a step forward, but one dark look from me was all it took to stop him in his tracks.

"You do not get to decide what is safe or not anymore. You have failed." There was a hardness inside of me that would not break under him. Under any of them. "I am the heir. I am Lucifer's daughter. Not you." He flinched under my words like I'd struck him. In truth, that would have been kinder. "They took him from me. They killed him, and I am not going to stand by and just let that go. I'm not going to let them take Moira too."

There was something scratching and clawing and screaming inside of me now.

Vengeance.

"Le Dan Bia are going to learn what it means to cross the Queen of Hell, and you can stand with me as my mate or you can continue to sulk, but I've made my choice."

With that, I turned to the strange woman with silver eyes and white hair. The purple ends were flecked with blood. Blue and Red.

She stepped up holding out a hand. A silent gesture that she would take me where I wished to go. As far as the Horsemen were concerned, I had no idea who she was. Clearly, they knew more of her than they'd clued me into. So, I guess I wasn't the only one keeping secrets.

"Wait," Julian said. I paused and only half turned to him.

His jaw twitched with anger. I knew with great certainty he was itching to argue and then fuck me six ways to Hell. Now wasn't the moment, and he knew that.

He felt it. My grief. My rage. My despair.

He felt it all because of that damned blood bond he'd forced on me.

And it was coming back to bite him.

"Yes?" I asked, my voice as cold as the bite of death that clung to us. Him and I.

"We're coming with you." That's all he said. No apology. No groveling. No brave words or promises he couldn't keep.

He was coming with. Him and my other mates. I looked from one to the other, waiting for looks of affirmation from each of them.

Maybe they knew I didn't want words. That there was nothing any of them could say to make this better. Only actions. I wanted to see that they would stand by me. That they would fight with me. That in the end, they would not attempt to stop me.

Because even if they tried, they couldn't.

Not right now. Not when my emotions were so far gone, and a whisper of insanity was beginning to wrap around my pain-filled soul.

No. Right now there was only one thing that would make it better.

That was the blood of my enemies.

They moved quickly, dressing themselves much as I had. Dark jeans.

Strong boots. My flimsy tank top wasn't ideal for what was to come, but I was very much aware of the fire pulsing beneath my skin. These clothes likely wouldn't last long.

Neither would Le Dan Bia.

And very soon, the legions of Hell would know that their Queen was not simply a girl that ran, but a living, breathing woman who wasn't afraid to burn the rot of evil out from whatever cesspool it came from.

I was done running. I was done hiding.

I was done holding back.

CHAPTER SEVENTEEN

I STOOD in front of the darkened alley. Last time we were here I thought
the beast crazy. Sure, I had wanted to free the Fae, something I fully
planned on doing once Le Dan Bia were taken care of—but I hadn't had
the guts to really stomach what went down below the streets of New
Orleans. Monsters in the night. The things that made even demons afraid.

Yes, I hadn't been prepared before.

This time I was.

Julian held his hand out for mine, and Death and I walked into the
shadows like two old friends. The heat of my transition didn't burn within
me as sorrow weighed on my soul. Only ashes and darkness.

Desolation and destruction.

Rage…and desperation.

A scream split the air the moment we stepped back into existence.

A scream that hit me square in the chest. My heart thudded and a
sheen of sweat broke across my skin as I took her in. Demons of every kind
swarmed. They poured from the walls and the shadows. They sent spikes
of poison and souls of the dead. They mounted at every point of the room,
to attack.

And Moira, she wasn't locked up like some caged animal.

She stood at the center of it all. Wings of fire snapped from her back and the brand on her forehead glowed. A determined glint lit her brilliant blue eyes as she assessed the demons coming for her. There had to be hundreds, and the only thing keeping her alive was that there were so many —too many for them to effectively attempt to dispatch her.

Well, that and her scream.

They ran for her and from her, but none could touch her. Anything that came within ten feet found itself exploding in the weight of her sonic scream. The demons began crushing each other as the makings of a stampede began. Moira launched herself into the air, soaring straight to the ceiling.

How she had survived even a moment down here was beyond me, but I would make sure it wasn't for nothing.

Above us, a portal of fire licked at the ceiling. The flames burned a deep orange and red. The demons below shouted obscenities, but nothing they said could prevent Laran and Allistair from falling through.

They landed with a boom and the real fighting took off. That was our signal. Our time to move.

I willed the fire to life as an extension of myself and my hands lit up. The demon nearest us didn't have time to react until he was burning, and by then it was already too late. He dropped to the floor in agony that would continue until the flames ate every bit of him from inside out.

Did he play a part in Bandit's death?

I didn't know. I didn't care.

Acting without remorse, I flung the fire wide around me. It inched its way up my arms a little higher, a little hotter, as bodies exploded in clouds of black glitter.

One after another they met a horrible end by my hand, so fast that the air didn't even smell like burnt flesh. Only sweat and blood and agony. Because they'd put me in a blind rage that I could not and would not contain.

Someone grabbed me from behind and I sent an elbow back into their throat. The weight trying to pull me disappeared instantly as I turned and flung another wave of power.

In my dreams I had done this and more quite easily. I destroyed an entire cabin and parts of a forest without realizing it. But that kind of fire didn't come from this kind of raw pain. Every one of them was another slice to my chest that I could not seem to heal. Someone here had killed Bandit. Maybe more, but I'd never know who. I'd never be able to pick them out and make their pain last longer. Make them fear their death whilst they looked me in the eyes.

For all I knew, the person responsible died by War's wrath, a single swing of an axe and they would be beheaded for good. Or maybe it would be Rysten, who infected them from the inside out, festering deadly diseases that ate their bodies faster than any poison could. Allistair's methods better suited my tastes for revenge, the way he walked without lifting a finger and bodies dropped. He sucked the emotions from them like a leech. Stronger than any incubus, he left them with nothing. No sense of self. No cognizance of life. They simply fell to the ground with eyes wide open. It should have disturbed me, but it wasn't so different from what one does when their soul dies. They felt a pain and loss so deep that they often couldn't even scream, and then there was nothing. My fire eating at them was probably a relief and I hated that. I hated that no matter what I did, it didn't make it better.

Killing them didn't make it better. Letting them live wouldn't make it better.

Nothing could fix this broken hole inside of me where Bandit should have been.

With that thought, the fire inside died out. I turned with my heart only half in it, and maybe that's why I wasn't surprised by what came next. I wasn't shocked by the ripple of pain that spread through me, not so great that it could overrun the emotional state I was in, but strong enough to eat through the adrenaline.

From above, a banshee screamed, and I looked up, expecting the pain to not be mine, but hers. The thought filled me with true terror, until I saw that she was fine and well. She glided to a stop, her flaming wings flicking embers into the mob below. She was dressed in the same clothes she'd been in the night Julian took me. Blood flecked at her feet and shins, but her skin was unmarred. She was untouched.

So, what had caused her to scream in such anguish?

My eyes fluttered as I worked to draw my gaze up to her face.

Now I saw the absolute horror that had made her scream.

…it was me.

I stumbled forward, following her line of site—straight to the spike sticking out of my stomach.

I swallowed hard.

Not good. This was not good.

I had taken out demon upon demon this night, but a spike slipped through. One that undoubtedly belonged to a chupacabra. Their venom was poison to demons. Not enough to kill the immortal, but enough to seriously injure.

And me? Was I immortal yet?

I didn't know.

My head spun with the horrible truth, but I could not bring myself to simply stand here and wait to die. Despite the exhaustion creeping in, I willed the fire forward. More. Faster.

It burst forth from my chest in a wave of unprecedented power, spreading outward. It crawled up the walls and onto the floors as I used everything I had to incinerate the entire damn building.

One way or another, I was ending this. My knees shook disjointedly as I took another step forward. It seemed that my body no longer wanted to support me. In fact, I no longer seemed in control of it at all.

The world tilted on an axis. My vision faltered. My legs failed.

I only briefly registered the crack that rang in the air. Was that my head? My darkening vision led me to believe so.

Was this it? Was tearing apart Le Dan Bia all I accomplished as Hell's Heir?

Somehow that seemed like a crock of shit.

What was the point of being some precious heir if you couldn't ever do anything?

I swore to myself then and there, that if I lived, I was embracing this destiny. That if I survived…I would wipe out the evil in both worlds on my path to the throne.

And as the darkness closed, I prayed that if this was the end, I would find Bandit on the other side. That we would go wherever comes next together. And that the Horsemen—however misguided they were—found peace and happiness. That they didn't blame themselves. That Julian wouldn't succumb to guilt. That Rysten would hold onto his humanity. That Laran would trust again. That Allistair wouldn't try to drink himself into oblivion.

That Moira didn't blame herself.

The darkness wrapped around me, and that tendril of shadow and night held me close.

But even deep in the recesses of my mind, I heard it.

I heard a monster roar.

JULIAN

I'd lived what the human world would call a thousand lifetimes. I'd seen wars fought. Kings rise. Devils and empires fall. I'd endured more than my share of hardships. I've died a thousand deaths or more.

Never once in my life had I felt an all-consuming fear.

Until now.

A gnarled spike, two inches in diameter, protruded from her stomach. And even through the bodies of demons moving to run away from her, I could see every glorious inch as she lit up. The beast couldn't come out, but she didn't need to anymore. Now that Ruby knew how to control flames, even dying, she was going to make it count.

It started with a glow beneath her skin. Her eyes turned an iridescent blue, reflecting an unnatural light. There was determination and pain painted on her face. She clenched her fists together, and the shift in the atmosphere was sudden. Flames shot out from her, but unlike the fires that she started while sleeping, these flames took the form of animals—raccoons —as they chased after every demon attempting to flee. They traveled so swift and sudden that the concrete began to crack as the structural integrity became compromised. Her power blasted down the floors and up the walls and through the ceiling. It covered every inch of visible space so that in that moment, all I saw was her.

Then she fell.

I couldn't say what happened around her after that. I couldn't tell you if the roar that followed was me or one of her other mates, or even her familiar. I just ran, skidding to my knees in time to catch her before she cracked her head on the craggy concrete.

She blinked. Her eyes already glassy as she stared up at me unseeing.

"No-no-no-no-damn it, Ruby—you can't do this—" It wasn't even a choice in that moment for me to even consider grieving. She couldn't leave me. She couldn't leave *us*.

I couldn't allow that.

The spike in her stomach said otherwise as blood started to pour out, oozing to fester around the wound. Beneath the smeared blood, her skin began to turn black. Poison.

I swallowed hard because there was only one way she would survive this.

There was a reason I didn't brand her first. In fact, I intended to be last. To be branded by Death was more than by any of the other Horsemen. It was something I wanted to talk to her about. To let her have the choice, since I took her choice in everything else.

It was meant to be a gift, but now that was taken as well.

She had to live. That was where I drew the line.

Which meant she had to change.

I pulled the stake out and tossed it aside, placing the palm of my hand over the wound that now gushed blood and poison. I siphoned off a piece of my own soul with my magic and pushed it into her.

Branding with a mate was a special kind of process because you gave a part of yourself, and in doing so, you made a part of them like you. I was more than a necromancer, but there wasn't a word for what I could do. The way I could exist, both dead and alive. In the veil, but not.

No other necromancer could defy Death, but I was the exception. I earned my name. I made my name.

Her skin felt cool beneath my hand, but the black poison was starting to recede. While the wound still gushed blood and gore, the magic of my soul was now planted within her. A piece of me for the piece of fire she gave me.

That is what separated mates from other types of bonds. There was a give and take that did not come easily or naturally to demons. Even many harems in Hell consisted of one demon taking pieces from all of their partners, but never giving. With mating, it was a choice.

And I chose to make her immortal.

Truly immortal.

CHAPTER EIGHTEEN

A LOT of people tended to say something profound when they were dying, these calming strung together thoughts that really made no fucking sense to me. Things like 'Death was easy. Life was hard.' When really that couldn't be further from the truth. Death was the end. It was permanence. Beyond the veil where I wavered was an endless existence of drifting. Would I retain my mind? I had no fucking clue, but I didn't trust it. Not one bit.

Here in this place of existing and not, there was no pain. At least not physically. I walked, but there was no floor. There were no people. No voices. No whispers. Not even that all too famous bright light everyone liked to claim they saw.

There was nothing.

Nothing but me and endless darkness.

I lifted my right hand and called forth my fire. Against the murky black depths, it was bright. So bright that I winced before extinguishing it. As much as it sucked, the darkness was better. The beast agreed somberly, shifting inside me.

That seemed strange to me. That here I was, wherever this was, with a body I was certain wasn't actually real—that the beast would still exist within me. If this was some corporeal dream, surely she could have her own body? Or would she even be here at all?

Again, I wasn't sure, but I didn't trust it.

Something just seemed wrong.

Do dead people normally have this much presence of mind?

"You're not dead."

My head snapped up and I turned, looking in the direction the voice had come from.

Standing in the darkness, a glowing white figure dressed in blood and leather walked forward.

Voodoo Doughnut girl.

My would-be assassin-turned-savior.

"Where are we?" I asked, my voice echoing off of non-existent walls. This was weird…

The mercury-eyed woman crossed her arms over her chest and flicked her long, sleek ponytail over her shoulder. The ends were white, not purple as they had been only hours ago. Which meant—

"We're not real, you and I."

She smiled, not quite cold, but calculating nonetheless. In her eyes were secrets that many had died for, ancient truths I could only hope to learn. This woman was old and powerful. She was unlike any demon I'd ever known.

"Very good, Daughter of Hell. We aren't real. Not in the sense you are thinking, anyway. This place is the in-between. The veil."

Ice slithered through my veins. So I was that close to death—but what was she doing here? Wouldn't it be more fitting to find Julian? She cocked her head, examining me with a peculiar interest.

"It would be more fitting to find Death here—were you going to die. As it is, he's currently occupied with removing the spike from your stomach. Nasty poison, that is, but you'll be fine."

Okay, now this was really beginning to freak me out. The Horsemen had said I was picking up on their thoughts. That I was projecting my own. But if I didn't have a body, and we were in the veil—shouldn't I have been able to shield myself or something? Was that even a thing?

The woman continued to stare at me. Somehow calling her that didn't seem like enough. She was certainly not a girl, but nor was I sure she was a demon. Blood magic wasn't a gift that demon-kind held. Which made me think that, like me, she was something *other*.

Something…different.

"Who are you?" I asked. She considered me for a moment.

"My name is Sin, but that's not the question you want to ask." She spoke with more than confidence. It was an eerie wisdom. The distinct sense of knowing that the person before me was not all she seemed.

"*What* are you?" I corrected. She nodded; that was the question she expected.

"That's a secret. One you are not ready to know."

I frowned, blowing out a steady breath. Okay, back to the riddles, I guess. Her vagueness didn't bother me as much as it should have. She was supposed to be an assassin, after all, one that not so long ago was sent to kill me. Yet…neither the beast nor I sensed danger from her. While she was dangerous, that knife point wasn't currently aimed our way. That didn't mean I trusted her, but an ally didn't necessarily need trust to be worth listening to.

"I was stabbed. I'm pretty sure that's why I'm here. What it doesn't explain is why you are too. Which makes me think it has something to do with me. Why are you here?"

She inclined her head and rocked back and forth twice on her feet before coming forward. Closer.

"It's hard to explain, given that I don't understand it completely myself. Last time I saw you, we entered a blood oath, with you owing me a favor. I sealed the oath, closing a tiny sliver of my magic inside you. That sliver was supposed to stay there. Dormant. Waiting until I called upon you, where it would ultimately be released back to me."

"Okay," I drawled. "But I nearly died and you're the one I'm seeing. I'm not sure how a tiny sliver of magic does that."

"You entered the transition less than twenty-four hours later"—she paused when I opened my mouth to ask how she knew that, but then closed it as soon as I thought about who I was dealing with. Of course she knew.—"And proceeded to make your presence known all across New Orleans."

She shot me a less than amused look and I, unlike the beast—whose fault it was— at least had the good graces to blush and look away. It had not been the smartest of choices.

"I'm still not seeing the correlation here—"

"Sometime between when I left you and when the Horsemen called me in to find you, you started using magic you shouldn't hold. Magic that is very dangerous for you to possess, should my master find out." She raised both her eyebrows, prompting me to follow her train of thought. Willing me to come to...

I came up blank.

Sin sighed, uncrossing her arms to roll her shoulders back.

"You somehow took that tiny scrap of magic inside of you and synthe-sized it."

Oh...was she saying that I copied her magic? How was that even possible?

"Um...you do realize that I'm a demon, right? Demons can't use—"

"*Most* demons can't use blood magic. A select four that we both know of can. They were created that way so that they could bind you. As they tried. However, you were able to break it—not because of your sheer strength—but because you possessed an inkling of my magic and multi-plied it. The blood oath is still in place. You did not absorb it or break it. You simply...copied it, as you say." She frowned, and I got the feeling this woman did not show her emotions easily. Something about this troubled her.

"You said that it's dangerous for me to have it..." I started, a little unsure with how to phrase this.

"If my master learns what you possess, we are both dead. There is not a world where your guardians will be able to hide you that *she* will not find you," Sin replied swiftly, without sparing me anything. I grimaced at the implications. Clearly, I wasn't dead now but that could always change at the drop of a hat. Things tended to do that in my life.

"Then I hide it. That shouldn't be hard to—"

"You will not be able to hide it. The Horsemen already suspect, given how strong your telepathy is. The thing you call mind speak, where you are able to listen in, is something that I exclusively can do. Which only leaves one option..."

I took a step back, raising my hands in front of me. I seriously did not like the sound of that. Anytime someone used ultimatums, it tended to end with something about killing or torturing me. I didn't care who she was, or how real or not this body may be. If I wasn't dead yet, I was going to attempt to stay that way.

"Listen, you may have helped me out a few times, but I..." My voice trailed off when she lifted her hand and began to draw.

Was she—no.

No. That was not possible.

I know I said and thought that before, but this—her—I couldn't even finish that thought before the shapes she drew became indigo-colored symbols in the air. A moment later, I felt a pop in the space around me.

I shook my head, not liking the sudden onslaught of dizziness.

"What did you do…" I muttered, pressing my palm flat to my temple and rubbing it in circles.

"Silence. I ensured that neither your thoughts nor your bonds with the Horsemen would give you away. After you wake, they will no longer be able to hear your thoughts, nor will you hear theirs. Should you try to speak about it, you will find yourself unable to. It will be like this meeting never happened."

I backed away, trying to shake my head, but found myself getting more and more dizzy. How was that even possible? How was any of this possible?

"They cannot know, Ruby. No one can. You are the future of Hell, and I am not willing to sacrifice that or the future you will buy me by allowing you to get either of us killed."

My world spun in circles as the heavy fog in my brain dragged me down...down…under. It wrapped around me like a blanket, lulling me to sleep.

But I didn't want to go. I couldn't. Not without knowing one thing first.

"Are you a…" The final word never left my lips. It seemed the ability to talk was now one I also did not possess.

Sin stared at me with heavy resignation and a tinge of sadness in her eyes.

"Goodbye, Ruby. Until we meet again."

And with that, my eyes fell shut and my consciousness faded.

CHAPTER NINETEEN

What was that god-awful screaming?

I tried to roll on my side and burrow my head under my arms, but a sharp pain in my stomach, like something tearing, snapped me right awake. I blinked twice, using one hand to wipe at my eyes. The sheer amount of ash and grit was an assault to my senses, making my eyes itch and water. My throat was dry as the desert sands. What was it they said about Hell? Endless torture where you will beg God for just a single drop of water? While the sentiment held true, that wasn't what was going on here.

For one, I was pretty sure Hell didn't have ten-foot tall raccoon breathing fire…

My eyes flew wide open, trying to take in every detail of the scene above me. Standing next to me was a black and blue striped raccoon so large I could ride on him. His face was set in a fierce expression as he zeroed in on something just beyond my vision.

I groaned, having a bad feeling upon seeing pretty much the entirety of the room had exploded into ash. Few things were immune to the flames of Hell.

"Now listen here, vermin," I heard Rysten's voice carry. I could imagine his hands held up in surrender as he inched forward. "Ruby isn't doing well right now, and I need to get to her—"

"Bandit?" I murmured. The raccoon sat back on its haunches and turned to look at me. Unnaturally blue eyes with pentagrams in them stared back at me. His ears twitched in recognition and he lowered himself to the ground, nosing me gently.

I nearly sobbed in relief as I tried to pull myself up into a sitting position, but a strong hand on my shoulder held me down. I groaned from the strain and turned my head sideways, only then realizing I wasn't flat on the ground to begin with. My head was resting in Moira's lap while Julian kneeled at my side. Behind him, Laran and Allistair stood watching me with worried expressions. I didn't want to read into any of their faces or emotions. They were all too heavy for the elation that was growing in my chest.

Bandit was alive. He was—

Currently jumping to snap at Rysten again for trying to get too close.

"What in Satan's name did I do to deserve this treatment while the overgrown trash eater runs wild…" Rysten muttered.

I chuckled under my breath and my throat itched, causing me to descend into a fit of coughs that triggered a terrible pain to rip through my stomach. I moaned, cringing into Moira's lap while she brushed my hair back from my face.

"Hey, Rubes," she said softly. "I thought we'd lost you there…" Her voice trailed off instead of saying things that were better left for later when it was just the two of us, not that there was any guarantee I was getting alone time anytime soon.

"I imagine I'm a bit harder to kill now," I rasped, smiling wide despite the pain in my stomach. Moira grimaced while looking down at me, lifting a single delicate eyebrow. She knew exactly what I was feeling, whether I faked it or not. Blasted familiar bond.

"Not hard enough. I don't know what you were thinking coming here," she said. I frowned. What I was thinking?

"You were trapped. Of course I came for you."

The Horsemen stilled beside me. I inched forward, opening my mind to them…only to run into an invisible barrier.

Damnit!

Sin wasn't joking. I don't know what she did, but whatever spell she cast over me definitely wasn't letting me listen in. Just when I was getting used to it too. Ugh. She and I were going to have a chat next time we met, about what she did to me and why.

I got the distinct feeling she was leaving a lot of information out, but until I better understood my abilities and *how* I originally copied her magic, I wasn't getting any answers. Not like I could mention any of this to anyone, since she so conveniently made sure of that.

I needed to find out more about Hell and who might possibly be after me. Sin was powerful enough to get around the Horsemen entirely, and even she feared her master. That didn't bode well for me, and as much as I begrudged her for doing it without asking, if people knowing really would put an even bigger target on my back, I was probably better off with her blasted spell. Not that it would stop me from cursing her to Eve and back when we met again, because we would. I had no doubts about that.

"How did you know that?" Moira asked sharply, breaking my concentration.

"Do you remember that demon from Voodoo Doughnut?"

Her eyes darkened, and her mouth tightened. "She came to you?"

I nodded, and Moira turned away, hiding the troubled expression in her eyes. I reached out, opening my mouth to ask her what was up right as I heard footsteps. Suddenly, Bandit wasn't the only one growling. I turned, catching only a brief glimpse between my overgrown raccoon's legs.

"Eugene?" I asked. The air around us thickened, and while I couldn't hear their thoughts, I could sure as Hell feel their emotions.

Jealousy and possessiveness took over, and I knew without a doubt they would kill him. If not them, then Bandit or the growling banshee beside me.

Shit.

"Ruby?" Eugene called. He didn't take the time to explain why he was here or what he was doing. That was his first mistake. His second was not thinking before walking toward the snarling raccoon. Bandit reared back, a growl ripping from his throat. Next thing I knew, blue fire was shooting out, and despite the damn hole in my stomach, I'm sprang to my feet.

"Stop!" I shouted.

Everyone froze.

I took that split second of silence and inaction to inhale a deep breath, deeper than it appeared my body wanted to take. I bent at the waist wheezing, and a wiry arm wrapped around my midsection. She grasped my arm and tossed it over her massive wings, draping it around her shoulder. I gave her a painful grimace as thanks and hauled myself up to a semi-decent position. The Horsemen closed ranks around us, with the exception of Rysten who was now beside Bandit, as a united front against the very large —but not so smart—rubrum.

"What are you doing here, Eugene?" I called out in a rasp.

He blinked sheepishly and ducked his head, still awfully oblivious of the raccoon creeping forward to bite his head off. I reached out and placed a hand on his furry black and blue tail, patting him reassuringly. Bandit stopped his advance and sat back on his haunches. Again, my throat thickened as my eyes pricked with unshed tears.

He was alive. I didn't know how. I saw him die. I saw his soul die.

But he was alive, and I could only assume magic had something to do with it given his new size and the fire.

I turned my attention back to Eugene who was looking increasingly uncomfortable at this point.

"What is that *male* doing here, Ruby?" Julian asked like it was *my* fault.

"Can we kill him?" Laran asked in complete seriousness.

"What?" I stumbled forward to try to put myself between the idiot demon and my mates, temporarily forgetting that pesky hole in my stomach and a ripping pain tore through me. "Motherfucker—no you can't kill him! Bandit—don't you dare!"

Bandit stopped his creeping and gave me an annoyed grumble, except it was a hundred times louder now that he wasn't the size of a large cat. I rolled my eyes. Only my raccoon would almost die and come back freakishly large with fire and still have an attitude problem.

"Eugene, if you can't tell, this isn't the best time. Why are you here?" I asked, putting a hand to the shrinking hole in my stomach. It was closing. Slowly. That meant my transition was nearing the end, even if dark blue blood was still dripping down my fingers from where I was applying pressure to it. Getting stabbed with a poisonous spike was high on my list of things never to do again.

"Donnach sent me," Eugene said. His lips pressed into a sad almost kind of smile. "He wanted to remind you about your deal." The rubrum shifted uneasily, and it hit me that he wasn't as clueless as he seemed.

"I see..." I said slowly. "Well, it doesn't look like any demons survived, at least up here. I assume he must know that already if he's willing to send you all this way."

Eugene gave me a pained look and I got the impression that despite what I'd done for him, he didn't want to be here anymore than I wanted him to be. Donnach must've really wanted those Seelie freed.

"It shouldn't be too hard freeing them now…" I trailed off at the swell of emotions coming from not only Bandit and Moira, but the Horsemen as well.

"Your deal? What is he talking about?" Rysten asked without looking away from Eugene.

"The beast and I sort of made a deal with this guy named Donnach to free the…people they're holding here. That's why I was here the night you guys came for me."

No one called me out on my hesitation, but the smooth hands running along my bare hip bones wasn't just for the hell of it. Aged scotch, heated seduction, and something wholly sinful settled over me.

"Why can't this Donnach free them himself?" Allistair asked, his voice singing with the smallest hint of persuasion. I leaned into him, pulled by the power that lured me. He brushed my hair aside, letting out a low chuckle in my ear. Moira bristled beside me and Julian let out a grumble, snapping me from his spell.

Unfortunately, Eugene was not so lucky to escape Famine's charm.

"Donnach couldn't free them without risking a war with demon-kind," he answered, scowling deeply in confusion. I turned and whacked Allistair on the arm, but I may as well have hit concrete. The slap echoed in the dark and muggy underground.

"Why would there be a war?" Laran asked, a hint of a growl in his voice.

A sigh escaped my lips. I really should have known I couldn't keep it from them.

"Because Donnach is Seelie and the Le Dan Bia captured a number of his people to use in their fights. They're being held here underneath the pit and I have to free them." I paused at the indignant sighs and grunts from the Horsemen. No one outright told me I couldn't, but they weren't thrilled with this new development. "He swore under magic that his people wouldn't hurt me once I freed them, and as the future Queen of Hell, I felt like it was important not to start my time by blindly turning an eye to shit that demons aren't supposed to be doing to begin with. Maybe my father did, but I'm not that kind of demon, and I refuse to be that kind of Queen."

From in front of me Rysten's shoulders slumped a little. "I suppose that means the rubrum has to remain intact?" he asked under his breath, but I didn't miss the thinly veiled threat. Rysten, the sweetest of them, was not pleased about Eugene's presence. Even more strange, I couldn't tell if their possessive nature was grating my nerves or if I was beginning to kind of like it…nope. Definitely couldn't be that one. Grating, it must be.

"Yes, I would appreciate you guys not being assholes. The beast and I are not interested in mating him for devil's sake." I rolled my eyes and Eugene froze, his eyes going wide.

"You guys thought—" He broke off looking back and forth between me and the Horsemen, then to Bandit who had gone back to growling at the red demon. "No, no…I owe Ruby a debt. She saved my soul. I swear on the sixth ring where I was born that I have no interest in laying a claim on her…I'm also gay." He looked downward, no longer wanting to hold eye-contact now that he realized what all the puffed-up chests were about.

Not my almost dying, but his maleness.

Assholes.

"If we're all done asserting who is and isn't Ruby's mate, can we get on with freeing the damn Seelie so I can get some sleep. I'm fucking exhausted and I need a steak," Moira grumbled. I can't say I faulted her. All I wanted right now was a cup of tea, a hot bath, and a warm bed. In that order preferably.

"This way," Moira said, taking the lead. She led us to the door behind where the bar used to be. Now only piles of ash and concrete remained. As a group, we walked over to the dark hole in the wall.

"You've been through here." It was less a question than it was a sad statement.

"I wasn't in a cage," Moira assured me, and I frowned. "I'll explain it… later." Her eyes shifted towards Eugene. She didn't trust him. Rightfully so.

We followed her down the stairway to a deeper part of the under-ground. My breath came in short pants from the physical exertion it took to get down there. Because hobbling on flat ground was apparently too much to ask for.

"You okay, love?"

"I'll manage," I replied through clenched teeth, trying not to let the pain bleed through into my voice or my actions. Moira slowed her step, waiting for me to catch up at the bottom, and wrapped an arm around my waist to help brace my movements. "Thanks."

"Don't mention it," she muttered.

Laran touched my arm. I knew it was him by the warmth of his hand and scent of wildfire.

"Allow me." He moved by us, taking the lead. I didn't have the strength to keep them from 'accidentally' harming Eugene, free the Fae, and argue about coddling me. I'd been stabbed and had come close to death. So this time I suppose it wasn't really coddling. Not when I put it that way.

A ball of flame erupted in the air and he suspended it on his way down, lighting our way to the bottom. We followed after him with the rest of the Horsemen behind us.

At the bottom of the stairs, a rusty metal door blocked our path. Or it did until Laran kicked it down. The door itself didn't open, but the stone wall it was set in cracked at the force of his blow. The surrounding rock split and the entire frame as well as part of the wall came crashing down. A plume of dust kicked up and I hacked and coughed until it cleared, Moira holding me up through it all.

Fire shot out from his hands, massive glowing orbs of red and orange hovered several feet off the ground, illuminating the metal bars and causing screams of panic around us.

I gasped, but Moira didn't make a sound.

She knew what was coming. What awaited us in the dark.

Cages. So many cages. They lined the walls, stacked on top of each other from the floor to the ceiling. Most of them were empty. Most, but not all.

As Donnach had promised, four cages in the far corner on the right held grey figures. Their black hair was scraggly and matted, their slate skin covered by only filthy rags. Black bruises adorned them, covered in healing cuts and fading scars.

It was horrifying. Repulsive. I had to fight the urge to vomit just thinking about the mess Moira came to me in, and as it was, Moira was staring down at them with a grim expression and bleakness in her eyes. Her arm around my waist squeezed tightly, as if she were holding me together.

My steps trembled as we walked farther into the room, because in the back, something growled—low and deep—and with a purpose.

"We need to get them out and get out of here before that thing gets loose," Julian said.

No kidding. I squinted to see the far corner of the room, but metal bars and shadows masked it. Only the deep steady breathing of the monster gave any clue as to what was down here with us.

I stepped forward, examining the Fae in the first cage. She was a woman, not much older than me by the looks of it, but it was hard to tell when she was covered in so much grime.

I went to undo the lock on her cage, but there was only one problem with that.

It didn't have one.

No locks…and yet, the Seelie were very clearly trapped inside.

I stumbled forward with Moira at my side to better look at them. Laran followed, keeping close beside us. He reached forward trying to wrench the door open, but the metal didn't yield. It didn't bend. It didn't break.

That couldn't be good.

"Did the Seelie you made a deal with mention how you're supposed to get them out?" Allistair asked, coming up on my other side.

Two cages over, I saw Eugene attempt to phase, reaching through to rescue them. The floor dropped out from under him, but the metal bars stayed firm and didn't allow him access to the other side. He let out a grunt, holding onto the cage while lifting his legs out of the hole his power had created.

"No, he failed to disclose that information," I muttered.

Never mind the fact that if neither strength nor phasing would work, what chance did I really have? I could try to melt them with fire. It was unlikely to work and would probably injure or kill the creatures inside. I was pretty sure the cages were not only iron to weaken the Seelie, but they were somehow magically enhanced to prevent normal means of getting to them. Like phasing through shit was normal, but hey, for a demon it was.

"Do you know how?" I asked Moira.

She took a deep breath, her eyes as turbulent and troubled as a firestorm. "I'm not sure…"

That meant she had her suspicions. Moira stuck out her boot toeing the edge of one cage. "Hey, you," she said to the nearly catatonic girl. I would have thought she was dead if her pinky hadn't twitched. "Yeah, you. How do we open these cages?"

Another twitch. Her head slowly creaked to the side, and through cracked lips and a bruised face she responded.

"Blood magic," she spat the words with a venom I wouldn't believe possible since she was only moments from death's doorstep.

Moira sighed and pulled me away. Judging by the look on her face, she had suspected as much. Blood magic to open those cages could mean any number of things, and I didn't understand how to undo spells done by the Unseelie. Most demons didn't. The Unseelie were few and far between, almost as rare as the Seelie in that way. They kept their magic to themselves and so information about it was sold at a premium.

However, I'd met a woman who could do both kinds of magic. It made me wonder all the more.

We slowly backed away as her eyes fell shut again. The exhaustion was finally catching up with me. Between my dizziness and Moira's strange behavior, we moved further away.

"What are we going to do?" I asked, trying to block out the growling coming from the back corner. It was really creeping under my skin. "We can't just leave them here."

"Sure we can," Moira mumbled. I cast her a sidelong glare and she pursed her lips, sighing deeply. "I'm not saying we should, or even that I want to leave them here. This place is a graveyard. Souls linger here. The dead speak." She shook her head. "But blood magic is rare. The Unseelie don't just hand that shit out to anyone. I dunno. Something doesn't feel right here." Moira scratched the back of her neck, breathing slow. Watching everything. She was naturally more paranoid than most people, but I agreed with her. Le Dan Bia had been the largest clan on the North American continent for over a decade. They rose up from nothing and became the portal keepers, quickly amassing power. Now throw blood magic into the mix and…it was certainly enough to make one concerned.

I pressed my lips together and glanced over at Julian. I could ruminate on Le Dan Bia at another time. "Can you open the cages?"

Julian's jaw tensed as he took me in and he ran his thumb along the curve of his bottom lip. I shivered despite the sheen of sweat on my skin and heavy air, thick with swamp water and mosquitos. I sincerely hoped that Hell wasn't just a more extreme version of Australia.

I don't think I could handle the heat *and* everything trying to eat me.

"She said blood magic is what keeps them in?" he asked. I nodded once, and Moira's wing swept around the back of my body. "I can open the cages, but I want a promise from you first."

Of course he did, because what demon ever did anything for free? Just me. Ruby Morningstar, tattoo artist, Queen of Hell, and apparently, demon slayer if you have a good enough sob story. I could add that to the list of things I needed to work on.

"What kind of promise?" I asked him, stepping out of Moira's warm embrace. I had to pull my dirty locks of hair away from my face so that I could look up at him. Even with my tall stature, Julian was a giant.

"No more leaving us. No abandoning us for strange males," he said and cut his eyes sideways at Eugene. I held back the eyeroll. "No making deals without talking to us first." I leaned forward, both from dizziness and the uncontrollable pull I felt to him. "Yes, you're going to be Queen, and we will all need to learn how we're going to make this dynamic work…" His words trailed off as he took in the other Horsemen. I knew then he wasn't just talking about Moira or Bandit, but the four mates the beast and I had chosen. He drew his gaze back to me, a darkness smoldering the green in those dark depths. "But not for a second will that stop me from tying you up to my bed for three days."

I gasped… I couldn't tell if what I was feeling came from his words or the dark look in his eyes as he said them.

"Well, that's quite the list of requests."

"I'm not asking."

I swallowed hard and nodded. Yeah, we were getting there, but there was still a long way to go with him. With all of them, really…and we may never get there. But at least the sex would be great on the way.

"No, because that would be too normal for you," I sighed.

"If you want *normal*, you have Rysten," Julian replied. He reached out and brushed the back of his knuckles along my jaw before turning away without a word.

I swayed where I stood, watching Laran hand him his axe. Julian gripped the pommel with ease and then brought his hand down on it. A spray of fresh blood scattered over the row of cages. The metal glowed bright where the blood touched it. Julian handed the axe back and leaned over to wrench one of the cage doors open.

The girl inside lifted her head and looked up into the eyes of Death.

There was nothing fearful about her expression, nor was there any gratitude. Only a deep-seated hatred and loathing. He stepped aside to open the next cage and her eyes slid to me. Curiosity swept over her face as she assessed my presence. I inched forward around Laran, tilting my head to the side.

That's when I felt it.

Recognition.

"You're the Heir," she said. Her words were hardly more than a whisper, holding just the briefest hint of that strange lilt that the other demon hunters also had.

"Am I still the Heir if the King is dead?"

I don't know why I asked her that. Possibly because everyone referred to me that way, despite the fact that Lucifer was long gone. He'd died months ago now.

"Donnach was right about you. That you would be different." It was both an answer and not.

"How do you know I spoke with him?" I asked her.

She crawled out of the cage, rising to her feet. Shredded garments hung from her limbs, leaving her orange runes on display.

"Because I was sent here as a trial for you, and a punishment for me. I'm happy to see he was right, given that I would have been left here to rot had he been wrong." Her words sent me reeling and the gentle swaying of the room intensified.

When the moving stopped, and my vision cleared, I saw that the four Fae had been released and were grouped together. The woman raised her head again to look me in the eye. Never mind, the demon who had actually released her, or the giant raccoon I knew was prowling at my back.

"He wanted to test me. Why?"

She smiled, and it wasn't pretty. Her black teeth glinted in the low firelight, pointed and deadly.

"Because my brother wishes to return home."

She didn't give me more than that as she lifted her hand and began drawing. As with Donnach, the air thickened and the markings swirled together. A distinctive pop sounded, and magic exploded outwards. A small portal forming with only a light haze of orange between this dimension and the next.

"I don't even know what that means," I said. Each of the Seelie went before her until only she remained. She paused only inches from it.

"For now, it doesn't matter." The dark Fae woman lifted her hand and drew another rune. It floated before her, suspended in the air. "But when the time comes, I owe you a debt. Stay safe, Little Morningstar."

The flow of magic shot through the air, hitting me square on the shoulder. I gasped in pain, slapping my hand over it. It burned hot, hotter than the flames of Hell, that's for certain. I peeled my fingers away, flinching at the feel of the harsh air against it.

The skin was orange and glowing. A series of hash marks and interconnected lines that came together to form a rune.

Devil-damnit, how in Satan's name did this keep happening to me?

First the damned blood oath, and now this. I turned to demand she remove it, but the girl was already gone—and with Julian diving towards her disappearing figure, the portal snapped shut behind her.

"What the hell did she do to me?"

Allistair stepped in front of me and pushed my hand aside. His eyes crinkled in worry, but I knew it was more than that. Inside of him, a deep concern was starting to form the longer he looked at the rune.

"There's good news and bad news," he said eventually. I blanched and made an impatient grunt for him to get on with it. A smirk tugged at his lips, but his heart wasn't in it. "The bad news is I don't know what rune this is."

Well, that was just flippin' great.

"And the good news?" I asked him, my shoulders shaking with exhaustion.

"I know someone that can help us find out."

I nodded, reaching up to run my hand down my face, rubbing the grit from my eyes. They stung like a bitch after all of this.

"Well, I guess we can add that to the list of 'shit Ruby needs to figure out'," I muttered to myself. He slid a hand under my jaw, his fingers curling around my chin as he tugged it upwards.

"We'll figure it out together, alright?"

He didn't leave any room for brokering when he looked at me like that. I leaned in, unable to help myself and let my lips brush across his. Allistair let out a small groan, pulling my closer. One hand snaked around my waist while he switched his grip on my chin to grabbing the hair at the base of my neck.

My tongue slipped out, parting the seam of his lips—

"Ruby, babe, I love you to death, and you deserve some after almost dying today, but can this please wait until we are back at the apartment?" Moira interrupted.

I groaned, pulling away reluctantly. The world slid out from under me and I had to roughly grab at Allistair's shoulders as he supported me to stay upright. It seemed that both my head and my legs had decided they were done for the day.

The hands holding me changed from warm and butter smooth to delightfully chilly as Allistair passed me off to someone.

"She's still losing blood," Allistair said. I didn't like the worry I heard in his voice.

"Don't coddle me. I'll be okay…"

Still, even with my insistence, Julian hoisted me up, his arms gripping me under my knees and back. He cradled me to his chest carefully, a stern frown forming at his lips as he looked at the hole in my stomach. It was only the size of a dime now, but blue blood, black dirt, and all sorts of other substances were coating me. What I really needed was a damn shower with a fire hose.

"You're in pain," he said.

"I wasn't aware being stabbed was supposed to be pleasant," I responded dryly. Julian's frown deepened. Against my better judgement, I rested my head against his chest, fighting the wave of dizziness upon me.

"We're going to take care of everything, Ruby," Allistair said. His voice was low and sweet, but thick with a raw untamable power. I only realized what he was planning to do.

"If you put me to sleep, I swear to the devil I'm never sucking your cock again," I growled, snuggling closer to Julian. Like he would protect me.

"Darling, I don't have to do anything. You'll be asleep before we're even back at the apartment."

He wasn't wrong. Julian turned for my raccoon and the Horsemen began talking. Something about Bandit and not fitting in the apartment. Before I knew it, the darkness was fading in. Black swept up on me, but this time, there was a comfort in it. A solace. Instead of a desolation that crept through and left me isolated, it was a shadow that wrapped around me and comforted. A shadow that held a tendril of Rysten with his embrace, and a hint of something that hadn't been there before. Another kind of darkness that was strong enough to pull me into its depths and never let me go. A permanence of a sort. Almost like...death.

CHAPTER TWENTY

Fur tickled my nose. Bandit. Demon raccoon couldn't just let me sleep—

I bolted upright in bed, remembering a second too late that I had been stabbed. I cringed, waiting for the pain to follow, but after a moment of sitting there, it never did. I looked down, expecting to see my own naked flesh, but a crisp white t-shirt hung from my shoulders. The material was long and baggy, it must have been one of the guys'. I tilted my head forward to smell it. Crisp. Clean. Just a hint of—

"Are you smelling my shirt?"

I froze, looking over to my left where Julian was leaning back against the black ebony headboard. His hair was smooth and blonde, not a hint of dirt in sight. He wore a snug white t-shirt, much like the one I had on, and dark jeans. His feet were bare, and as crazy as it sounded, he actually had attractive feet. Was that even a thing? The bed we were sitting on had an ivory comforter. The walls were white. Startlingly so.

We were sitting like nothing had happened, clean as could be. I was confused as hell, but the first thing out of my mouth was, "Yup. Sue me."

Julian cracked one of those rare grins and shook his head. "I have better things in mind," he said huskily. My inner succubus purred and leaned toward him, but Bandit was having none of it. A disgruntled grumble sounded from behind my head and the air whistled past my hair as something just barely skimmed my scalp, and Bandit, now back to his normal size, was sitting on my lap.

"Bandit," I breathed happily. He looked up at me with those unnatural eyes. Blue with pentagrams, but past the blue and black fur, he was still my Bandit. Wiggling eyebrows and all. "He's small again," I said, having trouble asking the right question. My raccoon clawed at my shirt as he pushed himself closer and reached up to wrap his paws around my neck. I scooped him up in my arms, holding him there.

"Apparently the raccoon can now change his size, along with breathing fire," Allistair said. I looked up to see him standing in the doorway. "You must have imbued him with your magic, you or the beast."

"Mhmm," I drawled. "And coming back to life—did my magic do that to him too?" Bandit cuddled closer, letting out a purr.

"We're not sure," Julian answered. "I think it has something to do with him being your familiar." I scratched behind his ear while I thought about that.

"Does that mean Moira can't die either?"

If it did, that was one less thing to worry about in Hell. She was a banshee with the powers of the legion now, but she wasn't unkillable. Unless somehow the bond with me was what saved Bandit and could save her too.

"We're not sure," Julian repeated again. Firmer this time.

I rolled my eyes and filed that away under things we never test. Maybe it was. Maybe it wasn't. Somehow, I still came out of the transition with my soul and my familiars intact. That had to count for something.

"So…" I trailed off. "What happens now?"

Wasn't that the question of the day. What happens? Where do we go next? I suppose with both Moira and I having gone through the transition, the logical step was likely Hell. But what would we do there? And what about Sin and this mysterious master she keeps warning me about?

The question and uncertainty of it all made my head hurt.

Allistair cleared his throat in the doorway. "That's something we need to discuss, but first—hungry?"

He wore low-slung jeans that fit his hips well. This was the first time I'd seen him in anything so informal, without a shirt, no less. Not that I was complaining. He crossed his tan arms over his chest and the muscles swelled doing funny things to my libido. I licked my lips involuntarily when he tilted his head sideways and the curtain of dark hair moved with him. He arched an eyebrow in question.

Shit. He hadn't meant hungry as in sex. He meant food. Like, real food.

Of course, after a little group debauchery, my mind went totally to the gutter. Well, mine and the beast's. While I turned my face away to hide the scarlet that was no doubt creeping across my cheeks, *she* didn't give a damn at the forwardness of our assumption. In fact, she was more than a little eager for that, but we had things to discuss.

After that…well, I'm not a saint.

"I'll take some coffee, if that's alright." He nodded and turned to leave, giving me a nice view of his backside. Julian let out a small growl and I glared at him. Arrogant, possessive shit.

"Last I checked, you all agreed to this arrangement, and you really didn't seem to mind sharing back at the cabin," I grumbled.

Bandit started wheezing again as he let go of my neck and rolled backwards onto my lap. Damn raccoon. He *was* laughing. Was that a thing? Could raccoons laugh?

I guess he could, just like he could breathe fire and change size.

"I chose to be bound to you of my own free will, just as you have chosen the four of us as mates. Does that mean you will always do what we ask? Clearly not, or you wouldn't have almost died on me." I swallowed hard. How was it that he could take an offhand comment and make it something so deep and raw? "Just as that doesn't mean that we won't have our issues with possessiveness. Demons don't naturally share, Ruby. The most powerful of us form harems, yes, but most are for strength. Not…this."

Ahh, and we have now come to the heart of it.

"But you want this," I said.

He nodded. "I do. Just as Rysten, Laran, and Allistair do. We are males in our own right, and while they may be my brothers in guarding you, sharing your bed won't always be easy." He paused, running a hand across his jaw. "But most things in life aren't."

I took a deep breath and let it out, feeling my shoulders relax a little.

"We'll find a way to make it work," I said, sounding surer than I probably should be about this. "Make it…fair." I liked the sound of that. Apparently, Julian did too because he grunted in acceptance and moved to stand.

"That's all I ask. I'll leave you two to talk." With that, he walked out of the room, nearly plowing over Moira in the process as she came into my line of site. She side-stepped around him, drawing in her massive wings. It was an awkward motion, but leagues better than I would have expected from a girl who only had them a few weeks.

Being trapped in the underground may have forced her to learn. The thought settled over me like a grey cloud, leeching away the ease I had been feeling.

"How're you doing?" she asked. She wore a white tank top and her dark green hair was pulled into a messy top knot, two dark blue horns sticking out in front of it.

"Shouldn't I be asking you that?" I answered softly. She pressed her lips together and looked away. "I'm sorry, I—"

"Don't," Moira replied swiftly. She sighed and placed a small hand over my arm. "Please don't apologize. You didn't know that would happen. It's not your fault."

"We were down there because of me—"

"Ruby," she insisted. Her tone was stern but edged with weariness. "The demons didn't trap me. I wasn't kept in a cage. I was..." she paused, swallowing hard. "I thought I died at first. I could walk and talk and touch —but no one knew I was there. No one but Bandit and one of the Hellhounds they kept caged. I ate their food. Smashed their liquor. I even slapped one of them, but no one could interact with me. They thought I was a ghost." There were shadows in her eyes as she looked at everything but me. Her posture was too stiff as she rocked back and forward on her feet. Being down there may not have killed her, but there were walls around her mind now. Walls around her heart. Walls where there shouldn't have been, not with me.

"I don't know what to say," I told her truthfully. I had no idea what I was supposed to say if she wouldn't let me say I was sorry. "I feel like it's my fault for why you were down there, and while the Horsemen carted me off, you were stuck—"

"I wasn't stuck," Moira said. She turned to the side and lifted one flaming wing. I blinked once and swallowed.

"That's a rune."

"I think Donnach used his Fae mojo so that I couldn't leave. Bandit has one like it on the bottom of his back-left paw." She turned again, tucking her wing around herself.

Was it a subconscious act? Did she realize how her mannerisms had changed already?

I didn't know, but I sure as shit wasn't comfortable with the red-colored rune on her upper back. I didn't speak the language of the Fae, either race, but the mark that looked like a bird cage wasn't hard to understand.

"So, he spelled you to keep you and Bandit there. How? I was watching him the entire time—"

"I've thought a lot about that, and the only time I think he could have was when we were transported, before we came to our senses. If Bandit had been paralyzed as well, then we might not have noticed…"

Her logic wasn't bad, but if it were true…who knows what else he could have done. Where else there could be marks on our skin. I ran a hand over my shoulder, feeling violated even though it wasn't me he marked.

"It was premeditated. He planned to make sure I would enter the underground and save the Seelie one way or another. I don't see how he could know that, though," I sighed. A knock at the door drew my attention. Allistair extended a pale hand holding a steaming cup of black coffee. I took it and smiled gratefully.

"Everything alright in here?" he asked, far too casually. Moira picked a piece of lint off of her leggings, turning aloof. I nodded to him and he turned to leave. "I'll let you two catch up then…" He trailed off as he awkwardly left.

"What are you thinking?" I asked her, moving to take a seat on the giant white bed. Moira picked at her nails while she weighed her thoughts back and forth. Paranoia and distrust was eating at her.

"It's going to sound crazy," she said. I smiled at that.

"I'm sure I've done crazier." A slight grin tugged at her lips, but only for a second.

"I think Eugene was a plant. That the Seelie man somehow orchestrated this entire thing. You trusting the rubrum. Him transporting us to him. Appealing to your humanity to get you to go into Le Dan Bia and release his people…"

She was right. That did sound crazy, but that didn't mean it was wrong.

"I don't know how he could have done it. I know that by forcing us to stay there, it was his guarantee you would be forced to come back and deal with them. There's something missing…" She took a deep breath, gnawing on her lip thoughtfully. I trailed my hand over Bandit's fur and he rolled onto his back so I could rub his tummy. That red rune she told me about flashed into sight and my hand stilled. A thought clicking that hadn't been there before.

"You said Bandit was also with you right? That he couldn't get out?"

"Yeah," she nodded. "They couldn't see or interact with him anymore than me. When he thought you died, he lost his shit and grew, that was the first time they seemed to notice. They saw me when you crossed over the threshold, so I can only assume that's when the spell broke on both of us." She glared over her shoulder at the rune on her back, her arms tightening around herself.

"It's—"

I choked. Blinking rapidly, I doubled over and coughed hoarsely. Moira walked around the bed and took the cup of coffee out of my hand before I spilled it. She clapped me on the back, waiting until the hacking subsided.

"You alright?"

"Yeah, I was trying to tell you it's—"

I choked again. The coughing came harder as I struggled to breathe. My chest tightened, and a dread settled in me. I knew what happened. Or at least pieces of it. Enough that *she* knew I would figure it out. That I would piece together what happened with Donnach and her own uncanny timing as she delivered what I thought to be Bandit's body, moments after we returned from the cabin. We'd just been arguing about me going to find them when she showed up. Julian wasn't going to let me go. The others probably wouldn't have either, and then I thought Bandit died and I lost my fucking mind. But if Bandit was trapped there the entire time, she couldn't have brought me his body, which meant she somehow brought me something that looked and felt like him in every way—and made me think he had died. That Moira was following.

I don't know how, or why, but she did.

Tears blotted at the corners of my eyes and I stopped trying to fight it. The invisible silence that she'd forced upon me. I wondered if the rune was somewhere on my body. I'd have to look for it later.

"It's what?" Moira asked me after I'd been sitting in silence. There was no way to tell her the truth, but I didn't have to feed her lies.

"It's a mindfuck," I said. She nodded her head agreeing and handed my coffee over, falling back some into the conspiracies her own mind was spinning. It made my head hurt to think about it. To wonder how far back it started. To deduce where happenstance ended, and Sin's planning began —her and Donnach. I wasn't completely sure, but I had an inkling of what she might be, and if I was right—if she was helping Donnach—I took a long drag of coffee and swallowed hard.

"If Donnach did spell you," I paused as her eyes darkened, "why do you think he did it?"

Moira blinked, trying to follow my change of questioning. Or at least that's what I thought she was confused about as she squinted a little and furrowed her eyebrows.

"He wanted the Seelie released, obviously."

"Yes, but that's short term," I said, thinking out loud. "The Seelie girl made it sound like it was more. When I asked her why she said, *to go back home*. What do you think she meant by it?" Again, I had a suspicion, but I didn't want to be rash in my assumptions.

"Everyone knows the Seelie came from Hell, but what's that got to do with you saving his sister's sorry ass from the bait ring? It doesn't make sense, but I get the impression they don't want it too either."

I nodded. We were agreed then. It was Hell she was talking about. Where else could it be? They came from Hell. That was their world, and Lucifer and Lilith booted them out.

It's not really surprising that they would want back in, but I didn't see what we'd have to do with it and how me releasing the Seelie played into it. Or really, me having Julian release them since he gave the blood.

We fell into a nice sort of silence. The kind where I gave Bandit belly rubs and he purred so loud it filled the void that might have been awkward otherwise. Moira let out a tired breath and sank back onto the bed beside me.

"Do you want to talk about it?" I asked. She stared at her hands as she twisted them round and round.

"Not particularly. You feel guilty and I'm not in a place to comfort you and deal with my own stuff." She unclasped her hands as if she'd just real- ized she'd been fidgeting. "It's a shit situation no matter how we look at it."

"Yeah, it is," I agreed. She didn't want an apology, so I wouldn't give her one, and I wouldn't make her be the person to make me feel better after all of this. While I didn't choose to leave her there, it happened. It fucking sucked, but sometimes life happened that way. Sometimes there are no words. Nothing that can fix it or make it better.

But we can stop from making it worse.

"Do you want to watch a movie together, just me and you?"

She smiled, and for a second, there was light in her again. I knew it wouldn't last, but neither would the smothering claustrophobia and panic that was eating at her. Just like when we were kids, it would ease again, and while a part of her may change, my Moira was still there. She was stronger than this. Stronger than the shit life threw at us. We both were.

"Sure," she said.

We moved to the living room and settled in with a large plush throw blanket and grabbed some munchies. Bandit curled in my lap and Moira leaned against me. If someone asked me, I couldn't tell them what we ended up watching. I don't think either of us were actually into it, but we stayed that way, the three of us huddled together, because we'd been through the wringer and come out alive.

The guys didn't come looking for me, and while we never spoke of it later, I appreciated it more than words could say.

CHAPTER TWENTY-ONE

I RUBBED the sleep out of my eyes as I stumbled away from the couch and towards the bathroom. We'd fallen asleep there last night, bottle of wine, box of Oreos and all. Bandit grumbled as I moved away from him and pulled his lazy ass off the couch to trail after me. His paws scratched at my bare legs as he mewled.

"For fuck's sake," I muttered. Scooping him up, I made my way to the bathroom and redeposited him on the bathroom counter. Taking a piss with him on my lap wasn't happening, and it was too fucking early for me to deal with his crying if I left him in the hallway.

I made my way through my usual morning routine and started running a bath. Bandit decided that the shiny drawer knobs on the vanity were interesting enough to not wail about my ignoring him. I took care of my business while he spent two minutes opening and closing the drawer closest to him, absolutely fascinated by the way the light refracted off the metal knob. I was just rinsing my toothbrush when I saw something…

Why was there blue on my hand? I moved, turning my wrist to see a line of what looked like thin blue ivy-like vines running up my arm and disappearing under my shirt.

Holy Hell. What the fuck had happened to me?

I reached down and grasped the hem of the baggy white t-shirt. Did I want to see what was under this? I had been stabbed, after all. Well, it was there either way. May as well get it over with.

I lifted it over my head and flung it on the bathroom counter. Blue vines traveled up both my arms and across my chest, straight to where the pentagram sat snuggly between my breasts. It looked the same as before. Plain black. Unmoving. The vines swayed and crawled across my skin, down my belly and onto my legs. It was crazy that I hadn't noticed them before now and I was absolutely sure they weren't from the Horsemen.

A smoke-like skull was branded onto my belly. Its mouth was open at an odd angle. I squinted, moving closer to see. My fingers brushed over what looked like a textured edge and found it to be rough. The skin there was puckered with hardened scar tissue.

My stab wound, I realized. It was where I had been stabbed, and while I should have recognized that immediately, the scar was hardly noticeable between the brand and healing. Certainly, no longer a hole. Instead of something days or even weeks old, this could have been a scar from years ago. I wondered if that was my own natural healing now that I'd transitioned, or if Death's brand had done something. Altered me somehow.

I suppose only time would tell.

I brushed my hair behind both my shoulders to get a better look at the ivy creeping across my chest. It was kind of eerie, but also kind of sexy. Maybe these were from Lola?

I'd never heard of a demon with two brands, but what did I know? Not a whole hill of beans, apparently.

My eyes skipped over the rune left by the Unseelie woman and settled on something else. A discoloration of sorts around the curve of my neck where it attached to my jaw. I turned sideways and pulled my hair out of the way. Rysten's brand. It was white, so white that it actually stood out from my skin. His brand was a modified bio-hazard symbol with rings going through it. The whole thing couldn't be more than six or seven inches long, but it was really obvious once you knew it was there. While I didn't mind, I wondered if I should be having a talk with them about where I get branded. Otherwise Laran might try to brand his flaming Celtic knot on my forehead as a show of dominance.

If left to their own devices, they might start pissing on me to claim ownership, and the beast might come out and kick their asses again just to make it perfectly—and painfully—clear who was in charge.

Overall, it wasn't as bad as it could have been, and I didn't see a mark from Sin that could indicate it was the cause of my silence. That unsettled me even more, the lack of a mark despite her magic clearly being at play. I wasn't sure if it was better or worse that she hadn't left one. It was certainly well planned.

I turned away from the mirror and dipped one foot in the scalding hot water. Groaning in pleasure, I settled in. Just as my back hit the curved porcelain of the tub, a furry tail wrapped around my neck. I glanced over to see that Bandit had moved himself to act as my pillow. I sighed happily, content to sit here for the next hour until my skin was wrinkled and pruned.

Unfortunately, once again, fate had other plans.

Just as I started shaving my obscenely hairy legs, a doorbell rang. I didn't know we had a doorbell. Hell, I didn't even know where the front door was. The Horsemen had a knack for transporting me in and out by means of shadow walking, Pyroporting, or mirror walking. It seemed the one gift my transition hadn't given me was any form of teleporting, but if they had their way, they would carry me everywhere like I was some sort of invalid.

I continued shaving my legs, hoping, praying that whoever it was would go away, or that at the very least, I didn't need to get it.

The doorbell rang a second time.

"Ruby," Moira called. "Someone's at the door."

"No shit, Sherlock," I muttered as I finished my right leg. "Can't you get it?" I called back. A loud groan sounded from the living room.

"I can't move," Moira said. "I'm in a diabetic coma after all those Oreos." I rolled my eyes.

"It was only one bag," I griped. I'd seen her plow through two and a half before admitting defeat.

"But they were double stuffed," Moira mumbled, barely loud enough for me to hear.

"Oh, for Devil's sake." I set the razor aside and stood up, sloshing water all around the tub. Bandit leapt down and shook himself free of the water that doused him. I dried myself with a towel and pulled on the only bathrobe I saw. It was much slinkier than my own, and I grinned to myself in amusement. It was too large to be Moira's, and there was a price tag still on it. One of my mates had gone shopping and thought to buy me one. Judging by the slick, expensive material, I would guess Allistair.

I leaned down and scooped Bandit up, opening the bathroom door to wander back into the living room. The doorbell went off a third time.

In another room, I couldn't pinpoint which, someone rumbled a string of curses. A door opened and Laran appeared around the corner, wearing nothing but a pair of sweatpants. His golden skin shone in the morning light, and the fiery Celtic knot on his hip stood out against the black band of the sweats. His dark hair was pulled back to the base of his neck, the red tints flashing only briefly as he came to stand before me and angled his head.

"You don't usually wake until late morning," Laran said. His eyes roved to the "V" of my bathrobe where my brand sat. Those creeping blue vines moved beneath my skin, as if they sensed his presence and wanted to entangle him.

"Can you stop ogling each other and answer the fucking door," Moira grunted. She had one hand thrown across the back of the sofa haphazardly and her massive wings were spread at odd angles behind her.

"The others have it," Laran replied.

"What?"

Laran placed a hand on my lower back and led me around the kitchen to another hallway I hadn't noticed before. A stairway descended to a single entrance where I could only just make out a red bald head through the window above the door. The other three Horsemen crowded around the door as Julian pulled the knob to answer.

"Eugene?"

My rubrum friend looked up at me with a pained smile. He felt awkward. As usual, the guys were being assholes and didn't want him around because he had a dick. I rolled my eyes as I made my way down the stairs and weaved between them, *accidentally* brushing up against each of them as I went. I felt stares on my back as I stepped in front and looked up at Eugene.

"Hi Ruby," he mumbled as he blushed purple. "You're looking…well." His eyes purposely stayed on my face even though we both knew he wasn't interested in the lady bits beneath the robe. Finding some underwear beforehand might have been a better idea.

"Thanks, you too," I said kind of awkwardly.

Don't get me wrong. It was nice to see he made it out alive and all, but I wasn't sure why he'd shown up on my doorstep knowing how the

Horsemen felt. I also couldn't figure out how much of our 'friendship' was real, and how much had been him playing into Donnach's hand. Did he know what his lover was capable of? Was he aware of how we'd been played? Maybe, this too, was a ruse.

Suddenly, I didn't feel quite as welcoming. That same paranoia that ate at Moira was beginning to wrap around me.

"Is there a reason for you being here?" Laran asked behind me, his thick arm wrapped around my waist and I knew he was glowering at him over my head. Eugene swallowed hard and thrust out the box he was holding.

"Donnach wanted to send his thanks." He lowered his eyes and Laran took the box since I was occupied holding Bandit.

"For the deal he emotionally manipulated me into?" I asked dryly.

"I—I don't know what to say." Me neither. "He created a weapon to help you…in Hell. It will only work for you."

That got my attention.

"We can take this from here," Allistair said coldly, cozying up to my other side. I was going to die of testosterone poisoning long before someone stabbed me again. That was for damn sure.

"Of course." Eugene turned to back away and fuck me if I didn't feel bad because he was sorry. I stepped forward begrudgingly.

"Wait—" I stood there, kind of awkwardly holding my hand out for him. I wasn't the hugging type, but after saving his soul and him sticking with me for five days, planted or not, I felt like that warranted more than a snide comment and dirty look. "Thank you, Eugene. For everything."

Eugene laced his hand in mine and shook it kindly, his eyes crinkling at the corners when he smiled. "And thank you, Ruby. If you ever need me—"

And apparently that was where the end of the Horsemen's patience fell. Laran yanked me inside and slammed the door on him.

"You guys are assholes!"

But I wasn't the least bit upset by it.

Allistair just shrugged, wrapping his long fingers around my elbow to steer me back up the stairs. I shook my head and chuckled.

"What was that?" Moira asked at the top of the stairs. We gathered around the kitchen island and Allistair handed me a cup of black coffee while Laran set the box down in front of me.

"I'm not sure…"

Taking a sip of my coffee, I tapped on my shoulder to motion for Bandit to move and he readjusted himself around me, slumping around my shoulders like a scarf. I gripped the edge of the box and opened it up.

"What is that?" Moira asked, letting out a kind of squeak.

"A gift," I replied as a smile started to spread across my face. Donnach had made me something special. I wondered if it was asking for forgiveness after manipulating me, or if it truly was a sign of thanks.

I hoped I'd never find out.

It was a crossbow of some sort, but small with a leather harness to strap it onto my arm. The contraption itself was made of a dark metal that was speckled yellow. Bright red runes adorned the crossbow and a small white card sat on top.

To new beginnings, it read.

New beginnings, indeed.

I pulled it out and the beast smirked for the first time that day. She liked shiny things. She liked things that hurt. This was both, and it held all her attention.

"Do you even know how to use a crossbow?" Moira asked, raising a skeptically amused eyebrow. There were still shadows in her eyes, but not as pronounced. Last night had softened her some and hardened her in other ways.

We knew it wasn't going to be an easy journey.

"Nope, but I'm going to find out." My answer was met with several groans as I started to fidget with the small contraption. A large hand settled over mine and I looked up at Laran.

"We need to check this out before you can use it," he said in complete seriousness. Part of me wanted to be a child and ask why, but the adult in me told that bitch to shut up.

Yes, it was a cool toy. No, I could not afford to drop my guard just because Donnach hadn't tried to kill me directly. He was still responsible for some unforgivable shit, whether he knew I realized it or not.

I relinquished my hold on the crossbow to Laran, so he and Allistair could examine it.

"There's a card at the bottom," Moira said. She reached into the empty box to pull out a white envelope. "To Ruby Morningstar, you have returned. We look forward to meeting you," Moira read aloud.

Laran froze beside me and the rest of the Horsemen narrowed in on the letter in her hand. This didn't sound like it was from Donnach.

Ummmm… "Does it say who it's signed by?" I asked.

Moira turned the slip of paper over and her face paled. Fingers slightly twitching, she reached out and showed me the card.

The Six Sins.

Laran peered at it over my shoulder and let out a string of curses. "Damnit, Julian—they know—the Sins know." As soon as Laran said it, Julian went quiet and Allistair let out a deep, semi-dramatic sigh.

"We knew this was coming, Death. We can't hide her here forever. It was only a matter of time once word reached Hell and we had a deal," Allistair said.

"What are you talking about?" Moira asked, her voice rising with tension. She reached out for my hand, and I couldn't tell if she realized the glass wall had just warbled.

"The Six Sins have summoned her, and as the heir, she has to answer their call," Julian answered.

He had fallen into a resigned state over this like the flip of a switch, and with us no longer blood bound, he masked his features carefully. Not that his attempts kept it all from me. His emotions were bleeding out. Worry. Anxiety. Nothing so close as to make me think I was a dead woman, but certainly enough to know this wasn't great.

"Well, I guess that answers my next question. Looks like we're going to Hell," I said with a grim realization. It was true. This was actually happening. I would go to Hell and meet the Sins, even if they were members of my father's former harem. That wouldn't stop me from doing what I had to do.

Sure, I still had a lot to learn and not a lot of time. My enemies were out there, and if Moira and I were right—some were closer to us than anyone realized.

But. I was alive. I was breathing. I had both my familiars safe and sound, and the strength of my four mates behind me. I was about as close to ready as this heir to Hell was ever going to get.

And this time, I was playing for keeps.

This time…I was going for my crown, and no one, not even the Six Sins, would stop me.

EPILOGUE

SHE STEPPED ONTO THE LEDGE, nothing more than a shadow in the night. The wind had died down and the skies calmed for the time, but a storm was coming. A storm whose outcome would last many lifetimes.

She stared at the young girl, Lucifer's daughter. Her eyes were blue like his, but she looked like her mother. Every bit as beautiful as the Deadly Sin of Lust. If the girl proved to have half her cunning and none of her father's ego, they might actually win this game. *Might.*

"Having second thoughts, Sinumpa?" the voice said from behind her. A dark Seelie man with red runes upon his skin stepped up on the ledge. They watched the girl and her guardians from afar, just as Sin had always watched her.

"No. I will do what must be done," she said with a determined hush that whispered over the sleeping city.

"And compelling my lover; was that part of what had to be done?" the man asked, an edge of spite in his tone, but he knew better than to push it.

"Her mind was too strong for me to get her straight to you. The rubrum's was easier. More pliant. We've been over this. You know why I chose him. Don't tell me you are growing a heart now." She inclined her face toward him and raised a single white eyebrow. Her mercury eyes bore into his with secrets that even the old Fae did not and could not possibly know.

"No," he relented. "But you almost showed your hand. The green one is onto you, and she does not have the distraction of four lovers to stop her from seeking."

"The green one doesn't possess enough information. As it was, Ruby needed the push," Sin replied. Like a lone wolf, she had stalked this child for twenty-three years. Always waiting in the shadows. Always watching. Not even her master knew that she had followed Lola and the girl many years ago, that she had kept tabs long before Satan's fall.

Her master was powerful and cunning in her own right, but Sin had been planning her freedom for many years now. She had learned from the best.

Beside her, the Seelie man snorted. "You made her think her familiar was dead. She could have destroyed the city if you'd made that spell any stronger. She only felt an echo of the loss of losing a familiar. One of your riskier moves, that was. I don't disagree with it, but it was dangerous."

"She is not one to break easily. I needed something to unite them and spur her into action. Without that, your sister would still be trapped down there, need I remind you." She didn't look at him, but he cut his eyes sideways, pursing his lips in annoyance.

"They would have come for her familiars eventually, and Morvaen would have dealt. She was punished for her disobedience, and now I have four Seelie who are willing to attest to the girl's morals. It's a win-win, the way I see it. She will have allies to usurp her father's killer, and we will have the chance to return home."

He clenched his fist in strength, turning his attention back to the blue-haired woman. She had the gauntlet crossbow attached to her arm. It fit perfectly, but that was no surprise. He'd used her hair to craft her something that would be exclusively hers. It would never miss. It would never run out of arrows. She would never lose it.

The magic that went into its creation was a small price to pay for what the young queen would bring him. It was an apology, for what he and the white-haired woman had done to her. What they would do to her, to see their ends met.

"Return home…" Sin paused, drawing his attention back to her. "Do you still wish to return home after all this time? Hell is not what you once thought it."

The man went quiet as the night sat around them. The air stagnant, but not quite stifling. He truly hated this world and the limitations it brought.

"Anything is better than here, where I feel my immortality slowly leeching away. This land does not like magic…" he trailed off, examining the fine wrinkles that had begun to form on his hands. Five thousand years. That's how long he had walked this earth.

But age was catching up with him. After so long, one might think he was ready for what came next, but all the ancient Fae wished was to return home. It had been far too long.

"The time is coming. The Sins have called upon her, and even Death knows better than to resist their summons. She will be tested, and should she survive, they will back her. It won't be long now, Donnach." Sin clasped a hand on the elder Fae's shoulder and he did the same to her. It was a sign of respect; a parting of ways, similar to goodbye, but not so informal.

"She must survive. The fate of the worlds depends upon it." A sliver of his age and desperation leaked through into his voice. He had held on for thousands of years, just for this moment. He wouldn't lose it now because of the Sins and their games.

"Ready your people, friend. I will watch over her."

As she always had.

But she looked forward to the day the only back she had to watch was her own.

Freedom was so close. One wrong step would send it all up in flames.

She wouldn't allow that. She couldn't.

The Seelie man tipped his head to her and Sin disappeared into the night. In the blink of an eye, her white hair vanished, leaving nothing more than a flowery scent she could not rid herself of, although she had tried many times.

Donnach turned back and looked across the street through a glass wall while Ruby and her protectors remained oblivious to the Fae watching over them. She was young and inexperienced, but she was also his only hope.

Because in this deadly game of chess, everyone knew the most powerful piece on the board was the Queen.

To be continued…

BRIMSTONE NIGHTMARES

PART I
BRIMSTONE NIGHTMARES

CHAPTER ONE

WHO WOULD HAVE THOUGHT that Hell's gate was inside a donut shop?

Okay, not a donut shop, per se. The infamous French café was much classier than that. Still, the powdered sugar things on my plate were really deep-fried donuts if we were all being honest. While it wasn't Martha's, I wasn't turning down donuts and black coffee for my last meal on Earth.

"So, how's this going to work?" I bit into a sugary sweet piece of dough. "We just walk through the portal and bam—we're in?" Bandit reached over my shoulder and swiped a beignet off my plate, stuffing it in his mouth before I could try to steal it back. I gave him a sideways look that he pretended not to notice as he dove off of me, onto the table, and flung himself at Laran. I shook my head as Laran nuzzled him behind the ears. Sucker.

"Pretty much." Rysten nodded, picking at his own breakfast. "There's typically a queue to get through the portal, but you being who you are and us being the Horsemen, they're going to make an exception." I nodded along, trying to take it all in.

"Not to mention my badass wings," Moira piped up. She stroked the tip of her marbled blue wing and tucked them in tight. While she wasn't completely back to her usual self after being trapped in the underground of Le Ban Dia, she was better. It would take time for her to work through what happened. I would respect her choice if she chose to never say what went down in that dark place—as long as she got better.

"They can't see your wings," I reminded her, taking a sip of coffee. Hot and bitter. Just the way I liked it.

"Such a pity." Her dismissive tone had Rysten rolling his eyes and she left it at that. We lapsed into a comfortable silence for a few minutes, finishing off our breakfast while I decided how to phrase my next question.

"So, when we get to Hell…" I paused, nibbling on the edge of a beignet. The anxiety of it all had my stomach in knots. "How exactly is this going to go down?" Another sip. I cocked an eyebrow, looking around the table from Julian—who sat stoic at my left—all the way to Moira who placed herself on my right.

"Don't look at me." She raised her hands. "You know as much as I do."

Point taken. I switched to staring at Rysten. He sighed and became very interested in his donuts, as if grappling for words. It was Laran that spoke.

"When we left Hell, our mission was to retrieve you as fast as possible. Return, so that the Sins could judge you. It should have been less than a week."

I frowned. "But I had a life…" Laran nodded, understanding.

"You did," he agreed. "But you are Lucifer's heir. Neither the Sins nor your father took whatever life you would build in their absence into account while planning. They didn't take *you* into account. You were born to rule and it's as simple as that for them. Just as they are the chosen stewardesses, we all assumed that you would accept your role without too much…trouble." Bandit moved around his shoulder, perching perilously close to a tray a server was holding. One swipe of his paw as the server walked by and a beignet went missing without anyone else noticing. Bandit stuffed it in his mouth and turned around. His cheeks were comically packed when he looked at me.

"What are you saying exactly?"

"He's saying," Julian said, settling back, the dark green of his eyes weighing on me, "that we were supposed to return with you in under a week and it's been almost two months." I took another swig of coffee, swallowing hard.

"Well, yeah…but I had to transition and there was the whole thing with the imp—"

"The Sins aren't known for their patience," Allistair said. "One day on

Earth is a week in Hell. It's been over a year for them since Lucifer died. They probably think we either didn't want to bring you…."

"…or I didn't want to go," I finished for him. Allistair gave me a tight smile and nodded once. "Well, it could be worse. I could be dead." Laran choked on his beignet.

"That won't happen," Julian said with great assurance. I wanted to spout some nonsense about 'pride goeth before the fall,' but after all the near-death experiences it wasn't nearly as funny as it once might have been.

"Either way," Moira interrupted, running a hand through her dark green tresses, "she's not dead and we're here now. What was the original plan?"

"The Sins intend to test you. Test whether you are worthy to rule," Allistair answered. I didn't miss the way Julian fell pensive beside me, seeming to be out of it, but the nerve in his jaw twitched, giving me the impression it wasn't that simple. "When we cross through the portal, we'll land in Lust. Then you'll meet with the current Sin of Lust and be asked to complete a challenge to prove that you are capable of ruling her province should she fall, if another has not already taken her brand to replace her. Once you pass, we will move to the next Sin, and the next, until you pass every test."

"Honestly, love, you're half-succubus. You should be fine," Rysten said with a wink. Somehow that didn't ease the slow tightening creeping through my chest. Worry. That I wouldn't be up to par. That I would fail. That the beautiful illusion of what they've told me is just that. A dream that will never come to pass.

"Should be." I had to work to keep the bite out of my tone. "That doesn't mean I will. What happens if I fail?" I asked them. No one answered me. They were too busy mentally communicating with each other, and unfortunately—thanks to Sin and her rune of silence—I could no longer hear it.

"We have a backup plan," Julian eventually said. My eyes narrowed.

"What is that supposed to mean?"

"It means"—Rysten leaned back and dug through his pocket—"that we won't let anything happen to you." He pulled out something and extended his hand. When his fingers unfurled, I frowned.

In the center of his palm sat a silver ring flecked with gold.

"Um…" I was at a loss for words. "If that was meant to be some kind of proposal, you're a little late." Laran threw his head back and laughed. The sound was followed by the booming of thunder and the wind picked up outside. It would be strange to be an elemental, where something as simple as a laugh could trigger a change in the atmosphere. In New Orleans, so many of them gathered in one place and it didn't often make for sunny skies.

"It's not a proposal, love. It's our get out of jail free card." Rysten dropped the ring into my palm and dug through his pocket, pulling out another and handing it over to Moira. She slipped it on her right-hand ring finger, and we both watched as it shrunk to fit her perfectly. "Have you ever heard of *The Divine Comedy?*"

I snorted. "Is that a question?" Moira snickered into her coffee cup.

"So, you know all about the rings of Hell?" Allistair asked. *Well, now, I didn't say that…*

I slid my eyes sideways, chewing on my lip. I paused, and my lip slipped free of my teeth at the twinkling amusement in his eyes.

"There's nine of them," I replied, fairly certain of myself until the four of them all started laughing and I remembered that was the human version. "Um…seven?" Julian's large arm fell around my shoulders as his foot hooked around my chair and jerked it closer to his.

"First, there's six provinces," Julian said. "It's only because of that damned poem that everyone refers to them as rings." His free hand reached around and grabbed the small silver piece out of my hand, holding it up. I realized my own mistake just before he said it. "Second, the rings he referenced were *these*." I could feel his sharp green eyes on my face, and the proximity between us in public should be a lot larger if they wanted me to think clearly.

"I think she gets the point," Allistair said. The corner of Julian's lips turned up as he dropped the ring back in my hand but made no move to put more distance between us. "Dante was the only known human to be taken into Hell that also found his way back, but by then his mind was utterly broken. *The Divine Comedy* is closer to the hazy remnants after a vivid dream than it is to Hell itself. The rings are how you get from one province to another. Hell is so large, and only a very small percentage possess a form of teleportation, so the Unseelie created rings with blood magic and brimstone. For most demons their ring will take them to anywhere within the province they were born.

Yours will take you to any of the six provinces that the Deadly Sins watch over."

"Six? That doesn't make sense. But I thought there were sev—wait, did you just say that demons can't normally just go wherever they want in Hell?" Moira asked, and the tone of her voice clearly suggested how put off she was with that thought.

"No," Rysten answered after taking a sip of his café au lait. "Most demons are born and die in the same province. Unless they have the money or power to do otherwise."

"Harsh," Moira whistled.

"There are worse things," Rysten shrugged noncommittally.

"Such as?" she fired back.

"Being born on Earth," Allistair replied. A noise of spluttered disagreement.

"What's so bad about Earth? I'd rather be born here than be a born a slave," Moira said acidly.

"Earth robs you of your magic. While Hell is overflowing with it," Allistair said. "Only the strongest of demons or Fae can truly thrive here because the very ground itself leaches away your power."

"We are stronger in Hell," Laran said and nodded in agreement. They continued discussing the advantages of being in Hell compared to the barren planet that was the only home I'd ever known. I vaguely wondered if my own abilities would be stronger in Hell and shuddered at the thought. The flames were destructive enough as it was.

I turned the ring over between my fingers, feeling the slightest sliver of power emitting from it, not completely different than my own. Almost familiar in a way…

"How does it work?" I asked, angling the silver in the light so that the etchings on the inside revealed themselves.

"Think of where you want to go and twist the band once," Allistair rattled off. A knowing smirk lit up his lips as Moira twisted her ring and nothing happened.

"Mine's broken," she complained. Bandit let out a raucous laugh.

"No, it's not," Rysten said.

"Yes, it is."

"They don't work on Earth."

"That's a dumb design," Moira said sharply.

I rolled my eyes, thinking on what he'd said. Most demons were born and died in the same province, but I'd been born in Hell and came to a new world. I may as well be an entirely different kind of demon because I couldn't fathom a world where I didn't even have the choice of where to live.

These were my final moments on Earth, the place I grew up, the world I was raised in, and it struck me that I had very little clue of what truly waited for me on the other side. Sure, the Horsemen could tell me about it, but in the end, I wouldn't know until I got there. It was almost surreal to sit in this rickety wooden chair, simultaneously knowing and not knowing what was to come.

Not two months ago these four males walked into my life, and I knew then it would never be the same. If someone had told me I'd literally be sitting in front of Hell's Gates, drinking coffee and eating donuts with the Four Horsemen—who I'd branded as my mates—well, I'd have asked what they were smoking and where I could get some. Never in my wildest dreams had I imagined this would be what became of my life, but I wouldn't change it.

In these four that I still knew so little about, I found happiness. That's not to say I wasn't happy before, living with Moira and Bandit…but it was a different kind. This ache in my chest felt so wholly different from the kind of pure emotions I felt for my familiars. Where they were a gentle breeze on a summer day, my four mates were a disaster. A beautiful, natural, reckless disaster that left me gasping for air and wondering how I could possibly survive.

Maybe I wouldn't. I turned the ring over, letting my thoughts wander. They'd called this tiny piece of metal a get out of jail free card, like it would somehow save me from the wrath of the Sins should I fail. As I angled it under the light, something caught my attention.

"When did you have these made?" I asked. That strand of blue was too familiar to be anything other than my own hair. Moira's probably had her hair as well.

"How did you know we had them made?" Laran asked. I glanced up, only then noticing the way all five pairs of eyes were on me.

"Well there aren't exactly factories cranking these things out, and even if you made this when I was a baby"—I thrust my thumb in Moira's direction—"you didn't plan for her. So, you had to have these made after coming to Earth. Yes?"

Laran nodded slowly, watching me curiously.

"We had them made yesterday," Rysten answered. "After your transition. Once we knew that neither of you had any form of teleportation." The very mention of my transition had my blood heating a little. I plowed on, choosing to focus on the need to know instead of the need that was never sated with me.

"Blood magic," I mused, still trying to lock down on that niggling feeling inside. It was just a ring. Moira also had one…so why did I feel like there was something strange about mine? "I'm guessing you didn't make them yourselves?" I phrased it like a question, hoping for some sort of confirmation one way or the other. Allistair watched me closely.

"No. An old friend of mine made them," he said slowly. "Is there something wrong?" he asked, his gaze flicking between the ring I still hadn't put on my hand and the strange path my line of questioning had taken.

"Just curious is all," I answered with a smile.

"You should try it on," Julian said suddenly.

I swallowed hard, not sure why I was so nervous to begin with. None of them would do anything to harm me. Well, nothing to truly harm me. A little bruising or blood otherwise…I held up the ring with one hand, positioning it just over my right ring finger. Allistair's deep golden gaze drilled into me, watching me slowly slip it on.

It settled at the base of my finger and shrunk to size. Holding my breath, I waited, but nothing happened. The faintest trace of magic touched me, but it was so slight compared to what was already within me that I didn't even shudder. Both foreign and familiar, I knew the magic in this ring just as I knew who made it, but it seemed my fears—at least in this—were for nothing.

My response to it was the reason she had spelled me in the first place, and now they thought I was acting strange for nothing. I moved my hands to my lap, forcing myself to be at ease.

Julian rubbed my shoulder, softly kneading the tissue. I froze, forgetting myself for a moment because the gesture was so strange coming from him. Julian paused. "Something wrong?" His lips skimmed the hollow of my ear and my eyes fluttered. I fought the urge to sink into him. The only thing that stopped me was the narrowed eyes of my other three mates.

"No—"

"Ready?" The voice carried on a heavy note. A subtle thrum of the old south to it. Standing with his right arm crooked in a proper motion of a server, the demon had dark skin, long dreadlocks woven with gold, and bright purple Cheshire eyes.

Enigma. Chaos demons.

Their kind weren't common on Earth, partially because their inability to blend as well as most other species. Enigmas were incapable of glamoring themselves because of the chaos that lived within. It leaked out into the atmosphere causing misfortune wherever they went—usually in the form of breaking things. Two tables over, a waiter stumbled. Three cups of coffee tipped off the tray, straight into a rubrum's lap. It was only seconds before a fist went flying and the cafe descended into madness.

I swallowed hard and Julian's arm dropped away from my shoulders.

"We should be going while they are distracted," the enigma said. My eyes drifted over the scene as multiple demons had to move on the rubrum in an attempt to subdue him. Most other demons didn't even bat an eye at the outburst.

As if sensing my hesitation, cool fingers brushed across my cheek. I turned into Julian as he captured my chin between his forefinger and thumb. "We will keep you safe." His dark eyes trailed over my face for a fraction of a second longer before he dropped my chin and pushed back in his chair. He got to his feet and extended his hand, waiting for me to follow him and take it.

Ordinarily I would have gotten to my feet and stalked off, but I wasn't feeling all that sassy or brave today.

I took his hand and he pulled me to my feet. Without another word, the enigma turned and led the way through the cafe. My palms started to sweat as we came to pause before a black metal door that was scraped in spots. The paint had faded to leave a silver sheen beneath the claw marks. The enigma shot us a grin over his shoulder before pushing the door open.

My feet stalled as my mouth fell ajar.

I wasn't sure what I was expecting, but a ten-foot-wide hole that plunged straight down with no end in sight wasn't it. The weathered concrete floor gave way to some sort of craggy black stone as it neared the abyss.

"What the fuck are you doing here, Jax—"

"I'm on an assignment," the enigma cut in. His purple eyes flashed with something mischievous.

"No can do," the same guard who'd called at him stepped up. "We're under strict orders. No one is supposed to go through that portal." He thrust his chin towards the portal and came to stand toe-to-toe with Jax. The enigma smiled at the other demon, clearly not all that concerned.

"If that's the case, you can be the one that tells the Sins why I couldn't escort Lucifer's heir and the Four Horsemen back to Hell," Jax said. The pale demon raised his eyebrows and flicked his gaze towards me. The beast pushed forward to smile callously at the demon, and he flushed.

"See something you like?" she asked in a flat, dead voice. Rysten stepped in front of me, blocking the male's line of sight. A low growl reverberated from him. That seemed to please her. I shoved forward, rolling my eyes as she receded with a smirk on her face.

"That's his daughter?" the guard asked in a hushed voice. "I thought it was just a rumor that she'd been in NOLA…"

"Are you going to let us through or stand there ogling at my mate?" Rysten asked softly. It wasn't the caress that woke me from my nightmares, but the whisper of death and decay. "If it's the latter, you won't be standing long."

Moira snorted and the glamor around her dropped. The other guards surrounding the portal cast her wary glances as she smiled ruthlessly, flexing her wings like a proud stallion might strut. The very tip of one whacked into the back of Rysten's head, and she snapped them in tight, whistling to herself as he looked over at her. What I would've given to see his face.

"Who is she?" The same guard that had been staring at me only a moment before now watched Moira with interest. She lifted a dark green eyebrow and ran a hand through her hair, pushing it back so that the brand on her forehead glowed. The horned helmet with black wings.

"No one," Rysten growled.

"Out of your league," Moira said at the same time. She twisted her lips in a smirk at Rysten's expression, not even noticing the way the guards watched her.

"Doesn't matter," Jax answered, crossing his arms over his chest. He nodded toward the portal and said, "What'll it be, Levi?"

The guard looked over all of us, seeming to weigh his decision back and forth. The Horsemen seemed utterly at ease, and I got the feeling if he denied us entry it might not matter. He likely wouldn't live to see that decision through. Levi must have realized this as well because he took a few steps back and swept his arm towards the pit to motion us forward. An uneasy knot twisted in my stomach as we approached the chasm.

"Out of curiosity," Levi mused, "which Sin sent you?"

The enigma paused at the edge of the rock. His bright purple eyes shining faintly in the low light as he stared down into the seemingly never-ending hole. "Which one do you think?" He let out a dark chuckle. "The only one I was dumb enough to make a deal with."

He stepped off the ledge without a shred of fear. I wish I could say the same, but even the beast couldn't make me that brave. A warm hand wrapped around mine and I looked up at Moira.

"It's going to be okay, Rubes."

"You say that about everything," I scoffed. Inside me the panic was slowly rising. This was it. My last moment on Earth. And I was quickly becoming paralyzed with fear. Sharp claws pricked my leg as Bandit tried to get ahold on my jeans to pull himself up. I bent at the waist and scooped him up with one arm. He clung to me as his tiny paws wrapped around my neck, like he understood what was happening.

"I say that because I know it." She tapped her temple with her free hand and flicked her eyes towards the abyss. "We're going to get through this, and you're going to pass the trials and get your crown. It's what you were born for."

I shuddered. *If only it could be that simple.*

My arms broke out in goosebumps at the subtle heat emanating from the portal. The energy felt familiar. Almost like…home.

Without giving myself the chance to rethink it, I gripped Moira's hand and held Bandit tighter—and then I stepped over the ledge and into my future.

My life on Earth was done.

My life in Hell…it was only beginning.

CHAPTER TWO

THE RUSH of the wind rattled my bones as a scream ripped from my throat.

The time Allistair pushed me off a cliff felt like a lifetime ago, and I thought that was bad. Little did I realize how much worse it could get. At least the lake beneath had stars to look at as I thought I was hurdling towards my death. The abyss was simply nothing.

There was no light. No stars. No end.

We could be freefalling to our deaths for all I knew. Not that I believed that. Jax had stepped off without fear like he'd done this a hundred times, and while I couldn't turn to look, I did sense that the Horsemen were falling behind us.

A light touch to my back made me twitch as a warm hand grasped the back of my shirt. I craned my neck to the side as flames sparked in my hands. Golden blonde hair tinted blue shined in the low light, and my terror thawed just a smidge. Rysten's comforting darkness wrapped around me, settling like a security blanket. Moira squeezed the hand she held tight, her palm growing slick from the smothering heat of the portal.

Tiny beads of sweat flew behind her as whatever force pulled us downward grew hotter. Moira opened her mouth and yelled in carefree abandon like she was having the time of her life, oblivious to the power I sensed and ignoring the stifling temperature.

Pressure built, making my ears hurt. Rysten yelled something that was lost in the chamber as it echoed off the stony rockface around us. Bandit followed it up with a savage growl, his claws hooking into my back like devil-damned talons just as the swelter and strain became unbearable.

Like breaking through a sound barrier, a pop filled my ears and suddenly we weren't hurdling down anymore—but up. It started as a tiny flicker of blue in an endless darkness. A light where there wasn't. And that spot continued to grow. A hole appeared above us, one that was an impossible azure, almost like the sky, but somehow brighter. I squinted my eyes to discern what it was as droplets of water splattered against my face. My mouth fell ajar. Only as we were cresting the edge did I realize that the speck of blue was actually the other end of the portal. We shot twenty feet straight through a spray of rushing water and into the open air.

A cool breeze filled with the scent of smoke and ash hit me. I reached a peak in my ascent, becoming weightless for a split second before gravity rushed in. Rysten's fingers slipped from my loose t-shirt as a sudden force kept me from falling, and he was jerked away. I swung my gaze wildly, breathing out an uneasy sigh at the sight of flaming wings. Moira hovered above me, gripping my hand with a strength I didn't know she had while she pumped her wings to slow our descent.

Hell, I thought to myself. This is Hell.

The skies were a jewel tone of sapphire blue, intense amethysts, and the deepest of reds. Ruby. Grey wispy clouds hung overhead, luring my gaze to the mountain range and dark plumes of smoke in the distance. That was far off, though, and between here and there was a stretch of burning forest. Trees so tall they had to be a hundred feet from the ground, reaching their spindly branches for the sky. Ones that hadn't yet been eaten by the flames had lost any of their original color, glittering black ash dusting every inch from trunk to the furthest tip of a branch. Flames so dark and devastating flickered in patches where only those ashes remained, encroaching on the hauntingly beautiful trees.

My feet had only barely touched the ash covered stretch of beach when I asked, "What happened here?"

"You left," Jax answered before Rysten could. "Lucifer died, and without power to hold the barriers, our world started crumbling."

"It's not exactly like I had a choice in the matter," I said tersely. The beast's ire rose at what he implied. Like it was our fault. It was Lola,

Lucifer, and the Horsemen that took us from our home world. They were the ones that left us on Earth for twenty-three years.

"You asked what happened. If you don't like the truth, then change it."

"She can't go back in time, asshole," Moira snapped. Her wings spread wide as she stepped up beside me and bared her teeth at the chaos demon with a fierceness not even a hellhound could muster.

"That's not what I meant." He swept his hand all around, referencing the burning patches of Hell. If not on fire, I imagine it might have been beautiful. It still was, in a way. "She's the only one that can stop the borders from continuing to collapse inward on Hell itself. If she doesn't like how our world looks, then she's the one that can change that."

"What do you think I'm doing here?"

Jax eyed me shrewdly. "It takes balls to enter Hell when the Sins aren't happy with you. I'll give you that. Whether or not you fix this remains to be seen." I swallowed hard, biting back my words. There was no point in arguing with him when he wasn't the one I needed to convince. Jax was just an errand boy. The real people calling the shots were somewhere out there —in the fiery depths of Hell.

I turned my back on the burning landscape to look at the sandy shores we'd landed on. The beach stretched on for miles in the opposite direction. Sand mixed with ash, giving it a marbled effect of black on white. The tide reached for my boots as it pushed in and out, but never got closer than six inches away.

"What's that?" I pointed to a mass of rocks. Water crashed against them, giving off a misty spray that reflected rainbows a good thirty feet out at sea. This ocean had some of the clearest water I'd ever seen, which made it all the more troubling at the way it glittered in the sun as particles of ash danced within.

"The portal," Rysten answered as Julian appeared out of the rocks. A blowhole, I realized, as he shot into the sky looking like some god of legend. His white hair sparkled with the same ash that permeated the air and sea and every part of this devilforsaken land. As he crested mid-leap, his legs swept forward, and he hit the ground running, far more graceful than the tumble and roll Rysten took in the sand.

"Already forgotten how to stick the landing, brother?" Julian asked as he came to a stop. Rysten rolled his eyes as both Allistair and Laran burst from the portal, sending a shower of glittering water several tens of feet high and landing a few feet over from us. Bandit chose that moment to fling himself from my arms and into the crystalline waves, if you could call them that. This close to land the water didn't get higher than a few inches, but that didn't stop Bandit from rolling around in it, coating his fur with sand and salt.

"I'd be wary of letting your familiar get too far," Jax said behind us. Bandit waddled a few feet farther to where the tide came all the way up to his chest.

"Why is that?" I asked, debating taking my shoes off and joining him. No sooner did the thought occur did a dark tentacle snake around Bandit's entire body and pull him under. I lurched forward to grab him as Bandit let out a garbled cry of dismay that was abruptly cut off by the waves.

"The Kraken."

"What?" I screeched. "You mean to tell me a motherfucking kraken just—"

I didn't get through my sentence. A large mass rose up from the water, pouring gallon upon gallon of sea water off its sides. Tentacles—all eight of them—were as long as any bus and the undersides dotted with massive suckers the size of my head. And one of them held Bandit by the foot.

I grit my teeth against screaming for him and instead reached for the flames of Hell. That squid was about to become calamari.

A burning orb of blue appeared in my hand when Moira grabbed my wrist.

"What are you doing—"

"That thing is massive, and the waves are rough. If you kill it, it could land on Bandit and he could drown," Moira said.

"If I don't kill it, he could be its dinner!" Bandit let out a mewling wail as the sea monster's mouth opened and let out a roar. A tongue as fat and thick as any tentacle twisted crudely in the air, pointed teeth as large as my raccoon covered every inch of it. I tore my arm away from Moira, adrenaline making me desperate. Fire licked up my right arm as I hurled a ball of blue fire. It put a hole straight through the fleshy part of the tentacle holding Bandit. The monster thrashed in pain as the fire spread, eating away its skin. Bandit went falling. A gust of wind from the rapid thrust of Moira's wings slammed into me as she jumped into the sky and darted forward to catch him. Another tentacle took a swipe at her, and the split second it took for her to dive and recover her balance sent Bandit careening into the depths of the sparkling black ocean below.

"No!" I shouted, but just as my voice broke across the waves, something crazy happened.

A second mass rose from the water where Bandit had just fallen. One with teeth and claws of its own. He stood over thirty feet tall, water cascading over his body as his black and blue-ringed tail twitched side to side.

"What in Satan's name——" Rysten started to curse. The growl coming from Bandit's chest cut him off as my raccoon stood on two back legs and lifted his arms in the air, letting out a roar that pierced the fear coiled around my heart. Fire shot from his mouth, only missing Moira by inches as she dove to the side, the muscles in her wings strained against the battering winds as she tried to get out of the way of Bandit's raging as fast as possible. Fire rained down on the kraken, blasting it to pieces as claws slashed ferociously. The kraken tried to wrap a thick tentacle around Bandit's short snout in an attempt to close his mouth and stop the spewing flames he breathed.

It was a bad move for the monster. Bandit lunged, his jaws snapping shut over the meaty appendage. He bit clean through it and the flames ate at the moist flesh, leaving the air smelling fishy and charred as the tentacles dropped off the body, one by one.

Within moments, the only remains of the great sea monster were ashes in the waves.

Moira swooped around and landed on the beach beside me, looking as shocked as I felt.

"Remind me next time I call him a trash panda that he can eat me," she muttered. I took off at a dead sprint into the water.

"Wait, Ruby!" Rysten called.

"Damnit!" Julian growled.

Water splashed behind me, but I didn't pay it any mind as Bandit reached out and grabbed me. He let out a purr, setting me on his shoulder as he walked us back to land. Oh, how the tables have turned. I wrapped both my hands in his wet fur, clinging tightly as my body swayed back and forth from the wind and his scampering. He still lumbered around like he weighed thirty pounds and not thirty thousand.

"Now look what he's done—" Rysten started. Moira elbowed him hard and crossed her arms over her chest.

"You don't get to speak. He might never give her back just to spite you," she said pointedly. Rysten shut his mouth, glaring to the side at my best friend.

"Ruby, get him to put you down," Julian demanded.

"Why? I can just ride him to the first Deadly Sin like this." I wasn't being serious, but the dark look in his eyes made me snicker. Bandit's massive shoulders shook as he let out this booming noise and fell to the side. I realized too late that he was laughing and I lost my balance. Airborne for only a second, my butt smacked hard against the wet sand, six inches from the incoming tide. "Ugh," I groaned.

"You saw that! The vermin almost got her hurt," Rysten said. He reached out to help me up. I ignored the gesture, pushing myself up with my own hands and feet.

"Pussy," Moira said under her breath, making me choke on a laugh.

"You guys are ridiculous sometimes," I said, brushing my hands together to get the clumps of sand off. Bandit threw himself sideways and the ground shook for a second as he started rolling in the sand again, his thirty-foot form steadily shrinking. I shook my head, muttering, "Completely ridiculous."

"You would do well to heed the warnings of your mates, child," another voice carried from behind them. Jax came strolling up to the water's edge, hands in pockets with a bored expression.

"Bandit literally just killed the kraken. I think it's alright to say I'm safe with him," I replied rather pointedly. Bandit preened under my praise, sitting up nicely as he shrank the rest of the way to his regular size. I smiled and scooped him up in my arms while he chortled happily. "And if for some reason I wasn't, I can take care of myself. But thanks for the input."

"Careful of that pride, Baby Morningstar. The Sins aren't the biggest fans of that particular vice." My lips fell open and then my jaw snapped shut.

"Speaking of the Sins, aren't you supposed to be taking us to one of them?" Moira asked sharply. He smiled bitterly and motioned to the burning forest.

"You want to lead the way?" Judging by his expression, he didn't know Moira was immune to the flames.

Nevertheless, she said, "I don't like this guy's attitude. Can we get rid of him?"

Jax glanced over his shoulder and let out a raucous laugh.

"Why are you laughing?" I asked, completely exasperated and we'd only just arrived.

"You think I wanted to do this? I was sent by one of the Six Sins. It's not like I get a choice," Jax said. I looked over at the Horsemen who seemed to be weighing the enigma's worth.

"Which Sin sent you?" Allistair asked eventually.

"Lust."

My mother's sin.

"Fuck," Allistair said. Yeah, that about sums it up.

"You don't turn down a present from Lust. She's not one to take kindly to it," Rysten explained.

"Of course, not," Moira grumbled. "Because that'd be convenient or something."

"I owe Lust a debt and this is what she asked from me to pay it. Escorting you to Inferna is about as easy as it will get with her—"

"Inferna?" Laran asked with a frown.

"Did I stutter?" the enigma retorted, drawing a laugh from Moira.

"Lust may have sent you, demon, but you forget who you're speaking with," Laran growled.

"Inferna wasn't where we were supposed to start, was it?" I asked, a lead weight settling in my stomach.

"No," Julian said, brushing a hand over his jaw. "It wasn't. Then again, Hell shouldn't have started burning either."

"Then why did it?" I asked.

No one seemed to have an answer for that either.

"Is there a way to test the chaos demon and see if Lust really sent him?" Moira piped up.

"We could peel his fingernails one at a time—" Laran started, completely serious.

"Or we could not," I cut in, because I was clearly the only voice of reason around here.

Laran shrugged.

"I can hear you," Jax called loudly.

"Good!" Moira shouted back. "Maybe you'll be less of a dick since she's the only thing stopping them from peeling your nails." She turned away and let out a little huff. "Asshole." I ignored them entirely.

"Can we not just pyroport into Inferna and be done?" I asked, looking at Laran.

"No," Julian said. He faced the forest looking at something far away that none of us could see. "If Hell is on fire, it means the borders are destabilizing and the landscape itself is moving. From here on out we can't use teleportation to get around."

I wrapped my fingers in a tight fist and pressed my lips against it in frustration, the cold metal of the ring bit into my chin. "I'm assuming the rings also won't work?" It was a long shot, but one I needed to ask either way.

Rysten shook his head. "Those can't take you anywhere they haven't physically gone before, and since we had them made on Earth, they can't go anywhere here yet."

"Even if they did, we could be entering any number of places with the current state of things, including the belly of a monster," Laran answered.

"This is shit," Moira declared. She wasn't wrong. Any form of magical teleportation was off the table, which meant we were going to have to do this the old-fashioned way.

"Sounds like we're hiking to Inferna, then." I rolled my shoulders, rocking back on my heels and into the squishy sand. Julian continued to stare off into the distance, but the other three all exchanged various looks of unease. "Unless you guys have a better idea…" I trailed off, raising an eyebrow expectantly.

"It's not that," Allistair sighed. "Ignoring the many things we might come across traveling over land, the only way into Inferna is through the coliseum."

"Coliseum?" Moira stepped forward, sounding far too interested by this. Allistair nodded.

"Hela's idea of *population control*," Rysten said. His fingers curled into air quotes while his cheeks were pulled taut in distaste.

"Is there another option?" I asked.

No one spoke. No one wanted to say it, but the truth was—no—there wasn't. If we couldn't get there magically, we had to find other means, which meant trekking through the forest.

"Do you really think I'd be here if there was?" Jax asked us, his voice dripping with sarcasm.

"Not the point," I said, focusing on the Horsemen. A warm wind blew down the coast, whipping my hair away from my face. Bandit let out a squeal of delight, his tiny paws scrabbling to grab the strands as they danced in the air.

"I think…" Rysten started, "that we don't have another choice. Lust will have already evacuated her province if she sent him to escort you."

"I don't understand that," Moira said suddenly. "You four are like a bajillion years old. You should know how to get there just as well as this guy." She waved her hand in Jax's direction.

"Not if we're dead, we can't," Laran said quietly. My muscles locked up at the very idea. "Hell is very dangerous, and Lucifer had a great many enemies. The Sins won't want to take any chances on her making it back, with or without us." He looked away, and there was something hidden in that gaze of his. A worry he did not want me to see.

"No one is going to die," I said sternly. Not that my heart listened to me. My pulse quickened and my palms heated at the very thought of losing any of them…fire arced across the sky and I stilled. "What was that?"

Jax looked directly upward, narrowing his eyes. "If I had to guess: you."

"Me?" I pressed a hand to my chest as Bandit wrapped his tiny arms tightly around me.

"Likely," Allistair nodded. "If the fire is eating away at Hell it's because the magic that maintained the borders has failed, and it's the same magic that runs in your veins. I wouldn't be surprised if all of this was connected to you." He swept his arm wide, toward the forest.

"Do you think I could put the fire out?" I asked.

"Possibly. Though it would take a great amount of control to put it out and not spread it faster," he answered. I swallowed hard.

"If it's happening because I took too long coming, it's really my responsibility to at least try." Allistair cocked his head.

"It's worth an attempt," Laran said, his axe appearing out of nowhere. He swung it with ease.

"It's not like we actually have another choice," Rysten added. "The forest is burning and we have to go through it to get there."

"So, are we agreed? We're walking to Inferna?" The four of them busted out laughing.

"Walking?" Julian turned toward me, only a fraction of his expression visible. "You do know we are called the Horsemen for a reason, don't you?"

"Well, yeah," I laughed nervously. "I figured it's because, you know… never mind."

I broke off as four massive stallions appeared out of thin air. Moira let out a small shriek that had the forest quivering. "Are those what I think they are?" she asked, out of breath.

"You see them too?" She nodded. "Thank the devil it's not just me. The transition was enough crazy for one lifetime, thank you very much."

One of the horses, a dark chestnut red color, strutted forward, flicking its tail affectionately. Without waiting for me to put out my hand, it leaned in and bumped me with its nose.

"Well, hello there," I murmured, securing Bandit in one hand and patting the horse with my other. I expected my raccoon to lunge and bite, but he was being surprisingly docile for once.

"Oh, of course, it's War's familiar that approaches her and the trash panda without a bloody reservation," Rysten grumbled.

"Familiar?" I asked. Rysten nodded and Laran beamed like he was damn proud. "You four have horses for familiars?" I repeated. Allistair shrugged, but it was Julian that caught my eye. His horse was ginormous. The thing had to be standing over eight feet tall. With a dappled grey body and silver mane, it was beautiful. Julian patted its side affectionately, not saying a word while I watched the private exchange between them.

"Technically, they're manifested familiars," Rysten said.

"Huh?" I asked, swinging my gaze around to him. His was pure white with a mane that practically glowed. "What do you mean manifested familiars?"

"We were born with them," Allistair answered, patting his pure black beast. It lifted its head and snorted, proud as the man who'd bonded to it. "They're technically a part of us, which is how we can go into your world without them, and when we're here we can communicate with them across great distances."

"Can they teleport?" I asked, looking down at Bandit. Could he?

"Aye," Laran answered, sidling next to the red one still nosing me. "Ours can teleport to us, but yours are a different type of familiar. They won't be the same."

Bummer. That would have been cool if Bandit could have.

"What's your horse's name?" I asked him as it tried to munch on my hair. I jerked back.

"Epona," he answered warmly, running the back of his knuckles along her side.

"It's a girl?" War had a horse for a familiar and it was a chick? I had a raccoon. Who was I to judge?

"She is, as is Death's familiar, Rhiannon." Hearing her name, the silver mare walked forward and lowered her head. Instead of poking me like Laran's, she waited for me to pet her. Expectant and intense, just like Julian. I reached out and touched her face.

"I hate to break up this little reunion," Jax snapped and didn't sound like he was all that sad about it, "but we're wasting daylight if we plan to ride."

Laran let out a dark chuckle. "Who said anything about you riding, enigma?"

CHAPTER THREE

Turns out, he wasn't joking. While the Horsemen's familiars may have liked me and tolerated Moira, it wasn't happening for the enigma. Jax couldn't get within five feet of one without it snorting and rearing up to bash his head in.

"There has to be a way to do this," I groaned. We didn't make it all this way to be thwarted by an asshole and some reluctant horses .

"Anybody have a bottle?" Moira asked.

I cocked an eyebrow. "Why?"

"He's an enigma," Moira said, like that meant anything.

"So…" I drawled out, waiting for an explanation. Moira sighed, running her palm over one of her horns. Her flaming wings fluttered almost irritably.

"They can travel in hollow objects. Which means he can hitch a ride without the horses flipping their shit." She hiked her thumb over her shoulder, pointing at the large male with amethyst eyes.

"You can't be serious," Jax started.

"How else are we going to bring you with?" she snapped. Her stomach rumbled even though we'd just had breakfast. A hungry Moira was a dangerous one.

"No one has a bottle or lamp that I can 'hitch a ride in,' so—"

"Actually," Allistair paused. He rubbed his hands together, his lips twitching in a sensuous grin. "We have everything we need." He waved his hand wide again, and this time saddles appeared on the horses, and in Moira's hand was a small glass vial.

"You mean you could do that this entire time?" I asked him.

"When I'm in hell, I can."

"But not Earth?" I asked curiously.

"My magic isn't as strong on Earth. Here, I can make my glamors real." He waved a hand to the world around us dispassionately. "Rather convenient, if I do say so myself." He grinned.

"Can you change clothes?" I asked. His lips curved up.

"Yours, I can. What do you want me to take off?" My cheeks flamed under his golden stare.

"Can we *not* do this whole foreplay-not foreplay-dirty talk-thing when I can still hear you?" Moira groaned. "Her transition was bad enough and I wasn't even there."

That sobered me up instantly.

"I'm sorry, Rubes, I just—"

"No, it's alright," I said and waved her off. My slightly hurt feelings weren't her responsibility, and certainly not over that. I turned my attention to Allistair. The heat in his gaze hadn't cooled a fraction, though I was downright chilly in my wet clothes and squishy shoes. "Can you dry my clothes and give me better shoes if I'm going to be riding a horse?"

With a wave of his hand it was done. Not only were my clothes dry, but they smelled clean as well, and the boots fit me perfectly.

"Alright," I said, hiking farther up the beach. "We ready to go?" I turned back, putting my hands on my hips. Jax and Moira were staring each other down as she held out the bottle. "You two alright?"

"No," Jax answered.

"Yes," Moira said at the same time.

"Okay, then," I drawled. "The sooner you get in the bottle, the sooner we can be to Inferna and you can be done with us." That only made him glower more.

"You have to let me out as soon as we stop," he told her.

"Yeah, yeah, I won't keep you locked in the bottle like a sadistic bitch. I am one—but that's not my style." She continued telling him all the things she would do instead, and it really wasn't helping our case.

"Moira, just promise to let him out so we can get going. When that's done, we're out of here and we can find food." At that she obliged, and with her genie in a bottle we mounted the deadly steeds and set off for the forest like this was some sort of fairytale and not a fucking nightmare.

~

WHILE BETTER AND faster than walking, riding on horseback wasn't all it's cracked up to be when you've never ridden a horse and are suddenly sitting astride a moving creature while attempting to put out the flames of Hell. We started a slow walk to give Moira and I time to adjust on Nessus, Allistair's familiar. After several hours of gripping Moira's waist rather awkwardly—thanks to her wings—I was over the novelty of it. She steered us as smoothly as possible, occasionally adjusting her grip at Laran's quiet instruction. I focused on the forest, and more importantly, the flames.

While in New Orleans, the beast had taken to teaching me how to finally control the cursed fire that only answered my call. I hadn't thought this particular gift was a blessing apart from when I was in a stabbing mood. Fire was destruction. Death. The ultimate form of ending and becoming something else entirely.

But it also gave me the power to stop the destruction.

Hell was burning, but I could end it.

I reached for the flames, lifting my hand towards them to act as a guide. Pressing my lips together and closing my eyes, I sent out a lick of magic— simply tasting what power sat in the forest, drifting lazily through the undergrowth like a heady fog—and Hell answered.

My eyes flew open as magic shot from the very ground itself and fire erupted around us. The horses let out a sound of dismay and Nessus reared back. I clamped my thighs tighter to his sides, gripping Moira with all my strength as she held tight to the reins.

Black flames only glinting with blue towered around us as I looked every which way.

"Easy!" Allistair's voice cut across the six-foot gap between his familiar and Laran's. Nessus stilled under his person's command, his hooves dropping back to the ground.

"Uh, Ruby," Moira called over her shoulder. "I don't know if you've noticed this, but you made the fire worse—"

"I'm well aware, thanks," I ground out between clenched teeth. On

Earth, it had been difficult to control magic because there was none in the atmosphere around me. It taught me to draw it out and use it as an extension of myself, but here...here my power was already *everywhere.*

I didn't need to send even a sliver of myself out to find it.

"Hurry it up, babe," Moira breathed. Nessus, while not actively attempting to throw us off after Allistair's rebuke, wasn't exactly happy either. His dark head thrashed back and forth, making his body jerk and my concentration slipped.

"Almost there," I replied, not wanting to waste more time when the dark tendrils of flame were already nearing Rhiannon's beautiful hooves just ahead of us.

Instead of flinging my own power out to search, I pulled it in, and even when every drop of my own magic was locked so tight it was stifling—I continued pulling. My hands clenched as if gripping the slippery whips of flame in my bare fists and I drew them into myself, even when there was nowhere to put it.

"You good?" Moira asked as the horse lurched forward. His hooves hit the ground with a thud that rattled my bones and threatened to upend me despite the death grip I kept on Moira's waist.

"Fine," I answered, not wanting to say much more when the magic writhed just beneath my skin, still searching for a way out. They'd said I might be able to control it, and they were right, but the power that was now restless within me wasn't my own. Just familiar, like an imprint of a memory felt long ago.

Unlike my own power, it didn't settle and linger, but instead fought savagely like an animal trying to tear its way out of a cage, seeking out any weakness inside me. I grit my teeth against the intrusion, hoping, praying to an already dead devil that I'd taken enough out of the forest to get wherever we were going.

That prayer went unanswered when some time later we stumbled across more fire and I had to repeat the same trick. This time it came easier, but holding it was getting more difficult.

Instead of wrapping my arms around Moira's waist, I rested my hands on my knees, fists closed and nails digging into my palms hard enough to pierce the skin.

A copper tang hit my nose, making me grimace, but it was working.

Pain brought clarity. It eased the churning power in my veins that pushed against my skin and threatened to unleash the deadly force.

Taking slow, steady breaths, the muscle straining in my ribcage let up as the sun began to descend on the horizon.

"Hey, are we going to stop sometime soon? My thighs are killing me," I lied. Well, not completely. My thighs were killing me, but the pressure trapped just beneath the skin was far worse and I feared I couldn't take any more fire if we came across it before stopping for the night.

"Soon," Julian said from up ahead. I clenched my teeth shut and focused on breathing through my nose. It was getting better, but not fast enough. The constant jostling wasn't helping.

It felt like forever when I asked, "Are we there yet?"

Moira pulled Nessus to a stop and turned to look at me over her shoulder. "Are you alright?" she asked, point blank.

"Yeah, yeah, I'm fine..." My words trailed off as dark spots appeared in my vision.

Too much pressure...

"You don't look fine." She squinted in the setting sun as the horse gently rocked side to side. All the twisting and writhing in me had finally died down, leaving me heavy when the flames finally settled.

"Sure...I am," I said. My voice came out distorted, sounding far away. It echoed in the space between my words, widening the gaps of silence as it repeated over and over in my mind.

"Ruby?" a voice asked. I tried to place it. To connect it to the face before me.

To tell the green-skinned girl that I was *not* alright, because I didn't realize until too late why the darkness was swarming in.

But there it sat on the tip of my tongue as night finally took me and the sun slipped below the horizon.

CHAPTER FOUR

An uncomfortable crick in my side had me groaning. I rolled on my side and rubbed the sleep from my eyes, blinking hard to discern what happened. Then the thoughts came tumbling into my mind so fast and vivid that I lay there panting for a moment before asking, "Where am I?"

I blindly patted around me for something to get a grip on. Rough edges pricked my palms and my hands came away dirty. *Devil-damnit, what happened now?*

I placed my hands back on the rocks beneath me and pushed up, ignoring the pinching pain.

"Whoa there, Rubes—"

"What's going on?" I breathed. My head swam as gravity worked to pull me back again and strong hands grasped my upper arms.

"Easy, love," a voice murmured behind me. "You fainted. If Moira hadn't been watching you would have fallen right off Nessus."

I swallowed, tasting nothing but salty air and dirt. "I fainted?"

"Yup," Moira said, exaggerating the 'p.' She turned back for something and held up a bottle of water. I reached for it, nodding in thanks.

The top cracked as I roughly turned it and drained the bottle in several long gulps. The plastic crinkled when it hit the ground. I wiped my mouth with the back of my hand.

"I really gotta stop doing that," I said.

"Littering?" Moira asked pointedly with a twist of her lips.

"Fainting," I snorted. Moira scowled.

"My job would certainly be a lot easier if you did. As it is, I'm the one in charge of making sure the enigma doesn't get up to anything...shady." Two booms echoed behind her and Moira rolled her eyes.

"What was that?" Not sure I wanted to ask.

"Trouble."

Moira let out a small sigh as she looked at something over my shoulder. A silent conversation seemed to pass between her and the person on the other end of that gaze. The fingers at my forearms tightened, and I had a pretty good idea who that might be.

"I need to go check on Jax and make sure he's not asking for a death wish." I quirked an eyebrow and she smirked dubiously before getting to her feet and walking out of the—

"Are we in a cave?" I said, trying to turn so I could see behind me. Not that it would have mattered because it was all darkness. A cavern ceiling spanned one side to the other, not smooth, but rocky and uneven. Ahead of me, the low light of a fire lit the shadows under a moonlit sky.

"Not quite," said a second voice. Honey, seduction, and a hint of scotch permeated the air. I blinked up at Allistair. His dark hair seemed to absorb the night as it framed his pale skin with an unruly wildness that was unlike him. Instead of the standard suit that I'd come to know and love, he donned the same low-slung jeans and tight t-shirt I'd gotten a peak at just before we set off for Inferna.

"What's that supposed to mean?" My voice came out huskier than I intended. Hungrier than before.

"We're in a tunnel on the edge of Lust's province," Rysten answered behind me. His fingers loosened their hold around my forearms and slid across my shoulders. I leaned into him.

"Okay," I answered. "Why are we in a tunnel at the edge of Lust's province?"

"Because this is Hell," Allistair answered like that meant something. I raised my eyebrows and he inclined his head, his sensuous lips looming too close to be so far away. "Bad things happen at nighttime. Unless you're in a city, you don't want to be caught out in the open when the sun goes down."

My eyebrows drew together and I took a second appraising look of the tunnel because this didn't really seem that much better. "A Kraken tried to eat Bandit ten minutes after coming through the portal. I feel like bad things are implied in the name." My voice had more steel behind it than what I really felt. I was from here. Born here. And after only a single day, it struck me how incredibly out of my depth I was.

I wanted to hang my head in my hands and plead to go home. Tell them that I give up. Keeping Bandit and Moira safe were more important. We could go live on some remote island in the middle of nowhere while this apocalypse business worked itself out...but I didn't get that option. There was no 'working itself out' that didn't involve me and my beast.

And so, while it was scary as fuck and the first day here was more than a little disheartening—I was Ruby Morningstar—Satan's one and only child.

"Perhaps it is implied," Allistair nodded. His lips twisted in a wry grin that did bad things to my libido. "But there are many good things too...if you look for them."

"Uh huh," I said slowly, fighting the smirk threatening to break through. "What kind of good things are we talking about?" I asked, more than a little breathless. Allistair leaned forward, stealing a kiss with the briefest brush of his lips before pulling back with a chuckle.

"You'll see."

"What kind of answer is that?" I groaned, remembering the pressure in my head when it suddenly throbbed to life. I pulled away from Rysten and got to my feet. Oddly enough, I didn't feel very weak after that—all things considered. I stretched my arms high and my joints popped like a kid shooting a coke can with an air gun. I shook my limbs free and turned to wink at the two Horsemen standing behind me, clearly enjoying the show.

"See something you like?" I purred, not the least bit ashamed. I certainly liked the view from where I stood.

It wasn't Allistair's sexy smirk that did me in, though, but Rysten's soft eyes. "Always," he whispered with conviction. I smiled softly, emotion swelling in my chest.

Unnamable, just the way it would stay.

Behind them something stirred in the shadows. I froze, my eyes narrowing on the lumbering movements—not at all stealthy. Remembering Allistair's warning, my hand came up to summon fire...when I saw Laran.

"What were you doing back there? I almost set you on fire—"

"You can't burn me."

"Well, no…" I paused, running my thumb over my bottom lip before crossing my arms. "But I could set fire to the cavern, which would compromise the rock's structural integrity and weaken it enough that it could potentially collapse on you…" I trailed off when they started snickering. "What?"

"Well, it's just…" Rysten paused when I raised an eyebrow.

"We don't typically see your more…calculating side," Allistair said quickly. I snorted. "Sometimes I forget you're the girl that kept a tank of chloroform in her office."

"Ah." I smiled fondly at the memory of tattooing Kendall's face. "You really shouldn't forget that. If anything, I've evolved." I lifted a hand, letting a sliver of flame dance over my fingers.

"Where'd you learn that?" Laran asked as he slowly advanced toward me. His dark hair was pulled back into a low ponytail at the nape of his neck, revealing the slight scar that nicked the arch of his right eyebrow.

"Moira," I murmured, putting the fire away. "When she started college, she was going to school for civil engineering. She'd listen to her videos while I built a client base tattooing people in the studio apartment we shared before I bought the house that was blown up."

"And you learned that just from listening?" Laran asked. I nodded, scratching the back of my head.

"I wasn't much for school because I found the environment stifling. Some people can learn while being packed in a room and told to read from a textbook, but I'm not one of them." I shrugged and picked at a leaf that was stuck to my flannel. "I learned a lot while she was in school."

Ironic as it was, I probably learned more during her four years than I did the past eighteen, between her videos and my ex's. I'd seen a variety of men with very different professions while passing the time, some more helpful than others.

"Why'd she switch to business?" Allistair asked. His eyes flicked behind me to look at Moira. I felt her change in emotion the minute she walked in. The erratic excitement and swaggering bitchiness she wore with pride.

"Have you ever studied civil engineering?" she asked, her voice on the very brink of a screech. Ever since she'd transitioned, she seemed to stray the razor edge of screaming like a—well, banshee—and speaking like a normal person.

"She got bored," I answered in short. He blinked, reassessing Moira.

"Bored? Studying engineering?" he asked skeptically.

"Bored studying *civil* engineering. It's fucking droll. Also, the other students were all pricks that had a pine tree up their asses." I choked on a laugh as she sauntered up beside me.

"She did *very* well and the guys in her classes were intimidated," I explained as she flicked her dark green hair over one shoulder.

"I switched to business because I could start my own company with Ruby. I had it all laid out and we were just getting started. With my brain and her fingers, we'd retire as millionaires," Moira huffed. The three of them seemed more than a little surprised.

"I don't know why you're all shocked. I may have a birthright, but she's a fucking genius." I rested my arm on Moira's shoulder as she put one around my waist. Behind us a deep baritone let out a cough of derision.

"If you two are done talking about what you wasted your lives doing while Hell's been burning, I'd like to know what War found," the enigma jested. I tensed, debating between saying something and letting it go when Moira shrugged.

"He's kind of an asshole," I whispered to her.

"You have no idea."

Was that a blush creeping up her cheeks? No fucking way. I snapped my jaw shut just as it started to fall open, and I turned to Laran.

"What were you searching for?" I asked. Laran's closed fists drew my attention as he glanced between me and the asshole at the mouth of the tunnel. Anger wafted off him. Aggression and....possession. "Laran," I said lightly, pretending that I didn't notice how he might throttle Jax for talking to me like I was the reason his world was ending. I mean, I was...but it was only half my fault. I wasn't claiming responsibility for being shipped off as a baby no matter who tried to feed me that bullshit. "Laran," I repeated. His attention wasn't on me, and his feet were already moving. I made a split decision and the beast came forward.

"*War.*"

All it took was a single word and he stopped mid-step. Turning to look over his shoulder, the beast stared back at him expectantly. "Your mate has asked you a question. You'd do well to remember what she is capable of when you don't answer." Her words were chilled. Apathetic. The beast receded with ease and I stared up at him not even missing a beat with our shifting. I was getting the hang of this.

"Of course," he answered softly. Laran turned his back on the enigma, giving me his undivided attention. Out of the corner of my eye I didn't miss the assessing gaze of the chaos demon, or Julian standing behind him —Bandit riding on his shoulder. "Did they tell you why we came here?" he asked.

"Allistair said the boogeyman comes out at night—"

"I did not," he growled.

"I'm paraphrasing."

"Can we get on with this—" Jax started, and like that he went one step too far. Laran's eyes darkened, blotting out any white as his savage fury and territorial urges finally got the better of him. He lifted his hand without turning, and the enigma lifted off the ground.

He clawed at his throat but there was no one there.

"Dude, I already saved your ass once. You really don't learn, do you?" I started, crossing my arms over my chest.

"He's slow," Moira said, not sounding the least bit concerned as she toed a rock with her boot. In her nonchalance, she missed the way Jax's panicked gaze flicked to her.

I sighed. "Put him down, Laran. As much as he's an asshole, Jax isn't exactly here because he wants to be." There was once a time that such a show of brutality would have sent me running for the hills, but not anymore. While I didn't revel in the violence, I also didn't shy from it when need be. This just wasn't one of those cases.

"He doesn't treat you with respect," Laran answered.

"Yeah, he's not the first jackass to and he won't be the last. While rude, it doesn't warrant death, so let's dial it down. It's awfully dark outside and we're standing next to the entrance of the tunnel. I would like to know what the hell the next step is here." At this, he appeared to see reason. His fist unclenched as his hand dropped and with it, the enigma did too. Ignoring his spluttering coughs and furious gaze, I focused on Laran.

"I was searching to see where it let out. The vast majority of the tunnels in Hell lead to the Garden—Sloth's province. I was hoping that this one did, but it's collapsed," Laran said. "We'll have to find another way."

I frowned. "Another way?"

"Another way to Inferna," Julian answered.

"What's wrong with the way we're going? We'll get there eventually."
Utter silence.

Laran looked at the ceiling while Julian looked on with...pity? I whipped my head around to Moira who was picking at the dirt under her nails with a dagger. I didn't even bother to spin around on the two behind me, because they'd all come to a decision already. Without me.

And here I was letting them distract me because I didn't know any better—no, that's not right—because I expected better. I expected honesty.

Shame on me for holding these demons to the same standards they tried to hold me to.

"You fainted today," Julian said slowly. Softly. Hesitantly. "When you absorbed the fire, you were taking in too much power, weren't you?" I said nothing. They didn't get my answers when they withheld their own. "It's okay, Ruby. We're not mad at you because you took too much, but we didn't notice in time when you started to shut down."

Emotion clogged my throat making it hard to breath. I swallowed down the hardness and infused my spine with steel.

"We're looking for alternative route to Inferna so that you don't feel like you need to extinguish the fire. Once we get there—if the Sins have all truly gathered—then we can work to find a solution once you take the throne." He continued, but I wasn't listening. I brushed past Laran and strutted towards the mouth of the tunnel. I stepped around Jax, who finally had the good sense to not say shit, and I didn't even look at Julian as I walked by.

A hand snaked out to wrap around my wrist, pulling me up short.

"Let go of me," I snapped, rounding on him with a fierceness he didn't expect.

"No."

"Damnit, Julian," I growled. Fire started in my hands, burning dark and deadly.

"Put it out," he ordered.

"Fuck you," I spat back. "You don't get to order me around." I tensed, recalling my transition, though hazy as some parts were. "You have five seconds to let me go."

"You're not walking off into the woods—"

"One," I said simply. His eyes turned cold. Feral.

"I would listen to her, Julian," Moira warned.

"Two." Julian tightened his grip on me.

"She's going to get herself killed—" Laran started. He knew I would bolt if Julian didn't back down.

"Three," I said. My arms began to shake, my legs trembling with the urge to run.

"Damn you, Death. You do not want to see her temper—" Moira spoke faster now, trying to plead with him. Trying to reach me.

"Four," I snarled, baring my teeth.

Power was building. It flowed through me and clashed together with a thunderous crack. All of the pressure from before…I realized it didn't simply leave me while I slept. It *integrated.*

Somehow. Someway—I absorbed it and made myself *stronger.*

The same as I had done with Sin's blood magic.

I inhaled deeply, preparing myself for the line I did not want to cross when—

"Please."

I stilled. His grip dropped away.

Then he said the only thing that could make the power leave me cold.

"I'm sorry, but *please* don't walk away." His eyes still burned, and his breath tasted of winter. His emotions were an ice storm: turbulent and brutal.

But he was trying.

"Tonight, we camp here and tomorrow, we ride. Those are my conditions." I kept it simple. I wasn't in the business of playing games. We were mates, for fuck's sake. He wore my brand and I wore his. If he couldn't run decisions by me before taking it upon himself—if none of them could—I would find a way to rule Hell on my own.

He didn't have to be perfect. He had to realize who he fucking branded.

"Ruby…" He gritted his teeth.

"No, Julian. I'm not mad that you're concerned. I pushed it too hard today, I get that, and I'll work on it—but you don't get to make decisions for me." I turned to look at the rest of them pointedly. "None of you do. How can you expect anyone to take me seriously as a queen when the four of you can't even seem to do it?"

To that, they said nothing.

But that's okay. I didn't want pretty words. I wanted actions.

"Take it or I walk, Julian. Trust me or let me walk away now." His jaw ticked and I was completely aware of just how much this took from him, but I was going to win this particular battle before it started. All of them needed to nip this shit in the bud, especially him.

In the end, he did. "Tonight, we camp. Tomorrow, we ride," he agreed. "But that isn't the last of this conversation. Understood?"

I bit back the grin that wanted to break through. "Understood."

"Good," he growled. "Tonight, you're sleeping with *me*."

My toes curled in my boots with anticipation. This was a compromise I was more than willing to make.

CHAPTER FIVE

BLEARY-EYED and in desperate need of a shower, I climbed onto Rysten's familiar, Arion, and settled in for the journey. After riding a horse all day and Julian all night, it was only my immortality that kept me from not crying like a wimp every time my mount shifted impatiently.

He smacked my ass raw more times than I could count. I loved every second of it at the time. Now? Not so much.

"Can we get moving already?" I grumbled, only barely covering my wince as Rysten climbed up behind me. His large thighs pressed into mine as he settled his arms loosely around me, one hand resting on my stomach.

"Just waiting on your familiar and her genie, love," he rumbled in my ear, drawing a screeching from Moira in return.

"He is not *my genie!*" she yelled.

"I'm no one's genie, thank you very much," Jax muttered. She crossed her arms over her chest and glared at him.

"Get in the fucking bottle," she seethed.

"Not if you're keeping it between your tits again," he replied, standing firm.

"Oh, for fuck's sake," I groaned. "You're the one who's been complaining about us not getting a move on, enigma. Get in the devil-damned bottle." Moira lifted her chin to smirk at him. "He's not going between your tits. Put him in the fucking saddle bag. I have a headache and Bandit's being an asshole because I'm out of sardines."

We all turned and looked over at the raccoon-turned-hellcoon sitting proudly on Laran's shoulder. He looked more than a little hellish with the branded eyes and blue fur. He lifted his head and let out a loud chittering while grabbing at Laran's hair. The demon had to be a fucking saint because I would have walloped him for that shit, but War took it in stride.

"She has a point. The trash panda is being a little shit this morning. But I don't have to deal with it anymore. So, in the bottle you go." Moira uncapped the bottle, extending it to Jax.

"In the saddle bag?" he asked, waiting for her to say it. Moira rolled her eyes, but obliged.

"You'll go in my saddle bag, right next to the condo—" Before she could finish, he evaporated in a cloud of smoke that was instantly sucked into the bottle. When not a trace of his essence was left, Moira capped it and looked at me with a smirk.

"Saddle bag." I pointed to the one hanging off of Rhiannon. After my little fainting fiasco the day before, I would now be riding with Rysten and she'd be with Julian.

"Do I have to?" she groaned. I gave her the *don't fuck with me* look. I was without coffee and bacon. She sighed and slipped the bottle in the bag without any more shenanigans. I had to look away when Julian grasped her by the waist, albeit clinically, and helped her onto the saddle.

She's your familiar. Get it together! I chided myself. It was only because of that she could even be that close to him without me losing my shit. I knew that after Julian and I had fully mated, it would never be the same again. Being a shade, Rysten's magic was able to sense if I would faint again, so I had to ride with him. Which left Julian as the only other fully branded mate Moira could ride with, despite the beast's mild annoyance that a female— even our familiar—was riding with any of them. He was the only one she would allow as neither of the other two had given her their brands yet. As far as she was concerned, it was still an uneasy time until we were fully branded.

Which meant I was even bitchier.

Sore thighs...and other bits. No coffee. No bacon. My best friend was riding all pressed up against *my mate* and to make matter's even worse, I needed a shower.

Turning forward I forced myself to relax into the saddle as we started out for Greed's province.

We only made it twenty minutes before Moira started her own version of *are we there yet?*

"So..." she started. "We're still in Lust's province, yes?"

"Yes," Rysten answered behind me.

"That's ruled by the Deadly Sin of Lust?"

"Yes," he repeated, his lips brushing against my temple, drawing a small grin out of me despite my dour mood.

"That used to be Ruby's mom?"

"Yes..." Rysten was slower to answer her this time.

"Shouldn't that mean Ruby's the new Sin of Lust and this is her province now?" Moira asked, like it made perfect sense.

"No." Rysten shook his head and pulled on the reins making Arion sidle up to Rhiannon's side. "The Six Sins, while also Lucifer's harem, were *chosen* to rule within Hell. In the event that one of them were to fall, it was that Sin's duty to appoint someone beforehand. If she couldn't, the remaining Sins or the ruler of Hell would, but Lola chose someone," he explained.

"Alright," Moira said. "So, this new chick, did she just join the harem after the original Lust died?" If I had anything other than curiosity about my mom, this conversation might have hurt, but after thinking my egg donor gave me up because she didn't care only to find out she *died* hiding me was quite a change. I no longer hated the idea of her, but I also didn't know how to love someone I didn't know.

"Doubtful," Julian said. "Lucifer and the Sins formed their relationship at the dawn of Hell. By the time Ruby was born he was very committed to them, especially Lola. Even as her province had gone to another, I would have trouble believing he would mate with any other after her loss."

"You make it sound like he loved her," I found myself saying.

"He did," Julian answered in earnest. I glanced sideways at him, biting the inside of my cheek. "He had a child with her knowing it would mark the end of him. For him, I think there was no greater love than Lola." His eyes focused on me with such a deep connection that I blushed. It didn't take a rocket scientist to figure out who he related to in this story.

"What about Lola?" Moira asked.

"What about her?" I replied, somewhat defensively. Moira shrugged.

"Don't you want to know more about her? I mean, your dad may have been Satan, but your mom was a Deadly Sin—the only other Sin to have kids was Lilith, and she's not even a real demon," Moira said, almost a little envious.

"I mean, I don't know," I said, struggling with words. "She's a succubus and I'm a succubus. I don't know what else there is to really get to know there."

"She was more than just a succubus," Laran said, coming up closer.

"What do you mean?" I asked, more than a little skeptical.

"In many ways she was the strongest Sin. Certainly, the most compassionate. While her abilities weren't as flashy as Hela—or as terrifying as Saraphine—she held her own among them with her mind. Your mother was a brilliant woman." Laran paused before adding, "Just like you."

"What about the other Sins?" I asked, fully aware I was turning the conversation away from Lola. It was early in the morning and I didn't sign up for a conversation this deep.

"What about them?" Rysten asked.

"Who are they? What are they? Aren't these things I should know about them?" Until coming here it never occurred to me how little I truly knew about Hell, even when jumping through a portal.

"Well," Rysten started, rubbing his lips across my cheekbone. His stubble scraped my skin, making me shiver. "After Lola comes Saraphine, the Sin of Greed. She's a nightmare."

"As a demon or a person?" I asked.

"Both," Laran chuckled.

"It was part of why I was hoping to avoid Greed's province so early," Julian murmured. "She's not likely to be forgiving if her realm has burned as much as Lust's."

"Who's after Greed?" I continued without commenting on his assessment. I already had enough to worry about. No point in stressing over a she-demon I didn't know.

"Depends on how you look at it," Allistair answered. "Sloth's province runs under the whole of Hell. She'd be contesting with Saraphine over it if it weren't for the fact that it's underground and no one wants it."

"Why does no one want it?"

"Because it's underground," he replied like that made sense. I frowned, but didn't ask again. I figured I'd find out soon enough.

"If it's not Ahnika's province, it would be Gluttony. You'll like her," Allistair grinned. "It's nothing but booze, bacon, and blood with Lamia." I wasn't sure whether I should be smiling or grimacing.

"I want to go to her province," Moira muttered.

"Don't we all," Rysten replied, his hand on my stomach sliding lower. I turned to stare at him over my shoulder, calling him out on his brazenness when he started toying idly with the button on my jeans. My face flamed as I spun forward in my seat like nothing was going on. He certainly wasn't—

"Inferna is divided down the middle. Half of it is in Gluttony and half in Wrath—Hela's province," Allistair continued. "Don't let the name fool you, though. She's not as bad as she sounds."

If only I was paying attention to them and not the button that just slipped free and the finger that was slowly teasing at the edge of my panties—

Flickers of blue caught my attention up ahead as we approached the first fire we'd seen today. It wasn't quite as dense or as tall as yesterday's flames, which suited me just fine, but it did put a damper on whatever ideas Rysten had.

"Just when things were getting interesting, eh, love?" He grinned against my temple and I smirked to myself when Moira turned and shouted, "Aye, Ruby, you're up!"

I resisted the urge to groan when Rysten chuckled. "You're the one that asked for this."

"Don't remind me."

By the time Arion pulled to a stop, the sun had dipped to the jewel-toned horizon just above the mountains in the distance. I'd spent the better part of the last eight hours putting out fires, and while it was thinning more and more, the flames of Hell seemed to never end. At least I didn't pass out this time. Small blessings, I supposed; although, who in this world would grant them was beyond me. It's not like God gave a damn.

"How far to Greed's province?" I asked, trying to keep the strain out of my voice. Between the day of riding and impending exhaustion, I could have stripped right there and slept on a rock. Unfortunately, my Horsemen had other plans.

"We're right on the border, but the capitol of Greed is half a day's ride and we do not want to enter the City of Hoarders at night. If Saraphine has left for Inferna, the city will have descended into chaos by now," Julian said, by way of answer. There was a terseness to him that I really wasn't liking, especially with Moira's mood souring the longer they were in close proximity of each other.

"City of Hoarders?" Moira asked.

"The demons that thrive in Greed are collectors of sorts," Julian answered with a harsh twist of his lips.

"What do they collect?" Moira continued.

"Everything."

"What's that mean for us tonight?" I said, changing topic before a fight broke out. We were all running low on fucks to give at the moment.

"We camp," he replied with a grunt.

"Seriously?" Moira snapped. "After all the bitching and whining about being out in the open at night, we're stopping in the middle of the damn forest?" Julian grit his teeth, pulling Rhiannon to a sudden stop just ahead of us and slipped from the saddle, leaving Moira to figure out her own way down from the unnaturally tall horse.

"Do you see a cave?" He motioned around him. "How about a tunnel —or better yet, an actual building?" Moira pressed her lips together, glaring at him. "No?" If looks could kill, he'd be dead, but neither of those things were possible. "I guess we'll just have to fucking make do."

"Who shit in your coco puffs—" She didn't even get to finish her sentence before I hopped off Arion, hitting the ground hard on the balls of my feet and stumbling when my legs locked painfully.

"Guys. Both of you take a damn chill pill." To my utter surprise and satisfaction, they both shut their mouths and went separate ways.

"I'm going to scout the area," Julian said without looking at me. A sliver of hurt cut at my heart, but I turned the other way and brushed it off.

"Don't let his piss poor attitude get to you," Rysten said from behind me. That was easier said than done when it came to Julian, but I knew better than to force the topic until he was ready to talk.

"I'm going to deal with Jax," Moira said from across the clearing. She gripped a small glass vial with swirling smoke containing the enigma's essence. She thumbed the lid awkwardly for a moment before a large pop filled the clearing. Smoke drifted lazily out of the vial, reforming as a shadow that came to life as a demon. Violet eyes settled on Moira and a blush crept along her cheeks.

Laran was just slipping from his saddle when Bandit let out a chitter now that dinner was in sight. He rolled around on Epona's back, falling sideways and into the saddle bag when Laran opened it.

"You going for a walk soon?" I asked, wanting to focus on anything other than the headache forming at the base of my neck, the aching in my thighs, and the heated looks Moira and her new stud were giving each other. Tensions were running high.

"I was," Laran paused. "But you look like you could use more than a walk." I blinked, mostly out of surprise. He was always blunt with words, and while I appreciated it, the blush on my cheeks betrayed me. My Horseman of War let out a deep chuckle. "Not what I had in mind." Laran flashed me a wicked grin and pulled something from his saddle bag. I saw the sleek grey instrument with yellow speckles and realized what he was holding.

"Wait—you're going to let me practice?" I rubbed my hands together, shifting side to side so my stiff legs wouldn't go numb.

Laran nodded. I couldn't help bouncing a little as I followed him deeper into the woods and away from camp. "After the Kraken, I got to thinking that you may need more ways to protect yourself—beside the flames." At my frown, he explained, "The flames are very effective at killing, but sometimes you don't want to risk the collateral damage using them would cause. While a great last effort weapon, I want you to have other methods at your disposal."

"Starting with the crossbow?"

He nodded. "Need help strapping it on?"

"Please," I said, my cheeks aching with how wide my smile was. Laran quickly went through what each strap was for and how to put it on by myself.

"Make sure you curl your fingers over this one—there you go—just like that." I smiled faintly as he assessed my grip. His brows puckered slightly inward as his full lips pressed together while he turned my hand every which way to assess. "I think you have it," he finally said.

I lifted my arm slowly, twisting it both ways.

"How do I fire it?" I asked, careful of the bolt sitting cocked within the bow.

"You see that fig tree?" He motioned with a tilt of his chin. I nodded. "Point your arm towards a piece of fruit. Make sure the bolt is pointed directly at it—" He slapped my arm when I squinted and lost concentration. "Tighten your muscles. You don't need to squeeze so hard you cramp, but another demon shouldn't be able to slap your arm away without trying." At his instruction, I lifted my arm again and held steady. "That's it." He grinned when I grit my teeth, waiting to be told how to fire. "To shoot, all you have to do is flick your wrist."

"Well, why didn't you just say that?"

His only answer was a devilish smile as the last of the sunlight peeked through the branches, highlighting the red streaks in his hair. I blew out a breath and looked at the fig high up in the trees.

"Breath in and hold. As you release your breath, do it slowly, and try not to move your arm too much." I sucked in a quick breath and held it for three seconds before slowly letting it loose. Snapping my wrist down, the arrow went flying and...dropped.

I was so transfixed on the arrow I noticed the moment it stopped mid-air and gravity took over.

I opened my mouth to ask if that was supposed to happen and hesitated at the wicked gleam in his black eyes. My teeth clanked as my mouth snapped shut.

We stared at each other for a hard moment, my irritation and his amusement slowly transforming to something else.

"Try again," he said. The wind rustled, sweeping the edge of my flannel up to send a trail of gooseflesh across my bare midriff. Laran's eyes heated as they flicked to the pale stretch of skin.

I swallowed against the lump in my throat and lifted my arm again. Moving to grab the bolt, warm fingers wrapped around my upper arm as he stilled me.

"I need the bolt..." I trailed off at the gleam of silver already in position and cocked to fly.

Magic. Seelie magic. Taking it in stride, I stopped, took aim, and breathed. Hold. Release. With the snap of my wrist I watched the bolt fly and once again drop out of nowhere.

I frowned. That wasn't normal, but the only consistent part of it was me and the crossbow. So, either the damn thing was broken—or the much more likely option—it was me.

"What am I doing wrong?" My voice came out sultry. Huskier than I expected. I groaned into my hand, wishing for the umpteenth time that I didn't sound like a thirsty bitch. I'd rather be able to shoot a man instead of fucking one. That would show real talent.

One of these took effort.

"Not focusing hard enough," Laran answered. His eyes dipped to my lips and I instinctively ran my tongue along the edges of my teeth before remembering myself and biting down on my lip to hide that devilish tongue away. I swear, some days it had a mind of its own where the Horsemen were concerned.

"Not hard enough?" My voice was all purr as my gaze swept down to his jeans and back up. Laran let out a small growl.

"Focus, Ruby."

A smirk made its way to my lips as I slid my gaze back to my target. *Focus.* I inhaled deeply, closing my eyes. Holding my breath, I opened them again, and breathed—letting the bolt fly.

It soared and my smile split wide as I watched it close in on the target— only to fall. Again.

"Damnit," I swore under my breath.

"Focus on the target, not the arrow," Laran's breath fanned my ear. I gasped, turning my face to look at him. Strong fingers brushed down my jaw as Laran faced my head forward. "Focus," he murmured. My breath stuttered as I lifted my arm, aiming the bolt again.

Calloused fingertips pressed into my hip bones, pulsating warmth into my skin beneath the thick material. Sweat dotted my brow as those same fingers swept down, under my shirt and back up, skating along my ribs to my— "Focus," he growled.

"I'm trying," I snapped back. "Hard to do that when you can't keep your hands to yourself."

The warmth disappeared instantly as he removed his hands and stepped away. Sweeping towards the fruit I was aiming for, he waited expectantly. Pissed at him for moving away and pissed with myself for telling him to, I aimed at the fig and snapped my wrist, but my attention was all on Laran.

The bolt released, shooting through the air in a wide arc and whipping around. It defied all physics as it shot at Laran and landed in the thick muscle of his arm. A strangled noise slipped from my lips as I dropped my hand away and stepped towards him. Laran didn't blink or bat an eyelash as he held my gaze and reached over to grasp the bolt sticking out, ripping it free.

"Laran!" I crowed, diving forward. I whipped my shirt off to press against the bleeding gash in his arm. Meanwhile, War just smiled as if this was all very amusing.

"I'll be fine, Ruby," he said quietly. "It'll heal."

"You don't know that," I replied stubbornly.

"Oh, but I do," he grinned again. "Lift up the shirt."

"No."

"Suit yourself," he growled. Grasping my hips, he pulled me to him as his lips came down on mine. Laran kissed with a wildness that was all fire. His lips parted mine with ease, his tongue tasting me. Not hesitant or challenging, Laran's kiss didn't demand—it gave. Everything and all that he was, he poured into that kiss. Into me.

I arched my back into him, holding the shirt tight to his wound as I reached up to wrap my other arm around the crook of his neck. Laran pulled back with a groan, sucking my bottom lip as he did. With a pop, he released my lip, his hands reaching down to slide over the sides of my breasts that already ached for his touch, across my abdomen, all the way to the 'v' of my hips. His knuckles brushed the sensitive skin, just underneath the hem of my flannel, and I jumped, letting out a gasp.

"What are you doing?" I asked with a shaky breath. My hooded eyes looked both ways, but no one appeared to be around.

"Motivating you." With one arm, Laran held me tight to his chest, my head resting on the curve where his neck met his shoulder. He leaned into me, his lips skimming the column of my throat while his teeth left nibbling bites that sent jolts of pleasure shooting through me. Strong fingers slid between our bodies, pressing into the seam of my jeans. He ran them back and forth, finding my clit through the thick material and twisting his arm to press his palm into me. It only took seconds and I was panting.

"Oh, good god—"

"There's no god here, baby. Only me and you," he rumbled as I rocked into him. A low moan slipped from my lips.

"This is so wrong," I groaned. "You're hurt." Even as I said it, I pressed the shirt harder, but didn't stop. Laran pressed his other hand into my back, urging my rocking as all the tension of the trip settled on me looking for a way out. I chased my release, tilting my head back to part my lips in a plea.

"Laran I'm going to—" He stepped away before I could finish, his bloody t-shirt slipping from my fingers. With his heat gone I was too cold, but also too hot. Needy. I'd have dropped my jeans and bent over right there if he asked me, but he didn't. He stopped, despite the slight taste of his kama on my lips and the red particles floating in the air.

"Focus, baby girl." His eyes blazed despite his steady words and my body ached for him.

"I want you," I breathed.

"Prove to me you can hit your target and I'll take you however you want."

A challenge? Oh man, I hadn't hit a damn thing except his arm.

"And if I don't?" I asked.

"Then you have to find your own release," he answered. His eyes filled with fire. Light and shadows flickered there, existing side by side. I took a deep, steady breath and aimed.

My eyes zeroed in on the fruit and this time when I snapped my wrist, the bolt flew true.

The fig fell from the tree limb, but my attention was on the glorious male kneeling at my feet as he undid the buttons on my jeans with a wolfish grin on his lips.

My pants didn't even hit the floor before his mouth was on me.

Laran spread my folds and pressed his tongue flat against the bundle of nerves. My legs quaked as he licked me, slipping two fingers into the wetness between my thighs. Laran sucked my clit between his lips and bit roughly, a rugged chuckle escaping him as my knees went weak.

"Mmm, I knew you could hit it. I was getting hungry."

He wasn't talking about the fruit.

CHAPTER SIX

H$_E$ BROUGHT me to climax twice with his wicked tongue before I straddled him in the grass. I rode him again, relishing in the way he worked me over his cock until we both collapsed in a tangle of sweat-slicked limbs. We finished target practice completely naked before putting clothes on and gathering up the figs for dinner. While Allistair seemed to be able to glamor anything we needed, food and water included, there was something thrilling about sharing the fruits of my labor, quite literally.

We walked back to the campsite, arms full and smiling like a couple of high schoolers and not a Queen and her consort. With Laran it was easy, simple. Our relationship wasn't as disruptive as Julian, or a balance of control like Allistair's, or even a guessing game like Rysten's—because while Pestilence certainly cared for me, he was just as bad as the others when it came to my safety. They were all possessive with me, but more than that, we were still working on building trust. Laran and I were already beyond that. He had proved it to me from the beginning, loving me enough to treat me as an equal and never pulling punches when it came to the truth; in return, I was pretty sure I loved him first.

The thought made me go still.

I…loved them.

Like the echo of thunder, my heart almost cracked with the immense realization, because as soon as you loved something it became a weakness. I already had two that my enemies used against me, and now...I swallowed hard and lifted my head. Laran's coal black eyes met mine, silently asking if I was alright.

I smiled despite the lead weight in my stomach, and it poisoned me. The feeling running in my veins, while strong and deep and *sure*—also scared the shit out of me.

So, I stayed silent and fell into step beside him like nothing was wrong and my heart wasn't aching with the sting of resentment against my father's enemies for forcing me to be so cold with my mate. They protected and cared for me. They gave me everything that was them.

But I wouldn't say those words until it was safe.

I wouldn't let my heart bleed all the more, because if they said them back and then something happened...it just might kill me.

So, I tucked those words in close and stuffed them down inside until we were safe. One day, and one day soon, I would say them.

But today wasn't that day.

"What took you so long?" Moira snapped. Her light green arms were crossed over her chest while she leaned back against a log. One of them had already made a log cabin out of wood and started a fire, even though it was hotter than—well, Hell.

A small chuckle slid between my lips as I amused myself, but no one besides Laran seemed to find it all that amusing.

"Is she delirious?" Jax asked, and I couldn't be sure, but I thought he was being serious.

"Do you have a death wish?" Moira asked, turning her ire on him. "Everyone knows only I get to be bitchy and get away with it. Get with the program, genie."

The enigma's lips thinned and his eyes turned luminescent. If I didn't know Moira could hand him his ass, the beast and I might have felt protective where she was concerned. But Moira was a legion now. One who clearly wasn't all that worried about a pissed off enigma with how she liked to goad him.

"I'm not a genie," he growled. His hands clenched into fists at his sides. "I'm an enigma, one of the most powerful of my kind, and you'd do well to remember it." Moira just kept her back turned to him and flipped her hair. No one did condescending quite like her. She exuded this vibe that she was above everyone, especially the one she seemed to delight in taunting. With her back to him, though, I was privy to the smirk on her face as he glowered at her. "Are you listening to me?"

Suddenly, his voice went all rumbly as he started to grow larger, his skin shifting.

"What in the Devil's name is going on here—" I asked, the figs tumbling from my arms as several things happened simultaneously. Frozen to my spot, I watched it all as if it were slow motion.

The trees shifted as soft footsteps surrounded us. Out of nowhere, people—demons—wearing masks made out of wood, carved and crudely painted, stepped out of the forest. They carried long wooden sticks with arrowheads attached to the ends, an archaic form of a spear. Tension rippled across the clearing as they moved swiftly, closing in around us.

Jax bared his teeth at the masked demons. His skin trembled, blurring as it shifted and molded into something else before my eyes. Four legs with clawed feet jutted forward, and hair as dark as his skin sprouted. His teeth grew larger, more pointed, as his face became that of a predator. The transformation complete, a hellhound stood in his place, and it was only those glowing purple eyes that made him recognizable. He gave Moira a pointed look—as if telling her to stay—as he turned, *protecting* her against the unknown demons now boxing us in.

"Drop the weapon!" someone yelled. It wasn't a voice I recognized.

A blunt force connected with my back.

Wrong. Fucking. Move.

I stumbled a step forward and only Laran's hand grasping my arm kept me from falling. Lightning flashed across the sky. A warning from the Horseman of War.

"Aw, fuck," Moira drawled standing up. "You've really done it now."

"Drop it!" the same voice commanded from behind me. Laran's eyes darkened as he pulled me closer. I stopped him with a pat of my hand against his rough fingers.

"I got this," I murmured. He stepped back a fraction giving me room to react without bearing down on me. I winked at him, and in that blink of an eye, the beast came out to play.

Fire came to life at her call, racing up her arms as she turned on a dime and grabbed the end of the blunted walking stick that had been used to prod me like fucking cattle.

"Now, now," she trilled with a husky laugh that was both seductive and terrifying. "Is that any way to treat your Queen?"

The end of the stick caught fire under her grip and the masked man holding it shuddered. His fingers trembled as the fire slowly ate its way towards him. She reared back, striking him in the head once with the not-yet-flaming end of the stick. He crumpled to the ground easily and she let out a tsk, sending the spear up in flames while she was at it. Black ashes blew in the wind within seconds. They quieted.

"I warned you!" Moira called from behind me. Through our bond I could tell she wasn't all that worried. Not when Jax-turned-hellhound was guarding her hide while the beast was out. No one fucked with our familiars and lived.

"Queen?" one of the faceless demons asked. The new spokesperson for the group walked forward, stepping over the crumbled body of their friend without hesitation.

This she-demon wore brown leather pants and moccasin style shoes with a loose shirt made of a dark indiscernible cloth. Her spear was larger than the others and decorated with a swatch of fabric on the end that swished lightly as she moved.

"Did she fucking stutter?" Moira snapped from behind her. The beast didn't bat an eyelash at the outburst. She preferred to watch the strange woman.

"Who are you?" The voice behind the mask was muffled, making it deeper. More animalistic in its tone than human.

If the she-demon meant to intimidate, the beast wasn't impressed.

"I go by many names," the beast mused. "Take your pick."

Silence extended between them as the masked demons seemed to weigh this. I could almost hear their telepathic conversations, but thanks to Sin, that was no longer one of my abilities.

"I think she's lying!" a voice in the crowd called out. There was a chorus of cheers, both for and against, but they all fell quiet when the strange girl before me lifted two fingers beneath her mask and let out a shrill whistle.

"Her fire is blue. Its ashes are black. If she really is Satan's spawn come to return and put an end to the fire, I—for one—do not wish to die this day." Another chorus both for and against rang out, but this time it seemed in my favor.

"Um, I hate to be the bearer of bad news," Moira piped up behind me, "but you guys kind of lost the power to say what happens here." All heads apart from ours whipped towards the girl now sidling up beside me. "This guy here," she hooked her thumb to the right, "he's War, and he's a lot nicer than your Queen when she's cranky." I would have chuckled, but the beast only stared apathetically, seeing them all as objects in the way instead of living and breathing creatures. Pieces on a board she would take out if needed. "Assuming you somehow could take War out, there's no way you'd get past her other three mates." She swept her hand wide, motioning just behind the crowd where Rysten, Allistair, and Julian now stood. "Also known as the Horsemen: Pestilence, Famine—and the big motherfucker in the middle—that's Death. He really doesn't like other people poking her with sticks."

If they weren't afraid before, they should have been then.

We'd faced worse odds. I'd killed more demons with far less skill than I now possessed. In a fight to the death, they wouldn't win.

Which is why it came as quite the shock when the masked she-demon threw back her head and cackled.

She withdrew the mask, showing off a mane of golden hair that would have been enviable if I were insecure. As it was, the beast withheld all judgement…until she turned and walked right up to Rysten. He stared and stared until she said, "Long time no see, golden boy. It's been a while for us."

Then she kissed him.

CHAPTER SEVEN

I've been through a lot of things in my life. Seen a lot of things. Done a lot of things. Set a lot of things on fire... and my fingers twitched for her to be next.

Never once have I considered cold-blooded murder when it came to something as simple as kissing, but when she strolled up to Rysten and wrapped her arms around his neck, pulling him to her...red. My vision went red.

A dull roar filled my ears as the world slowed down to the beat of my heart. The only sound was that of the pounding in my head. I longed to move and pull her away, but the smallest thread of sanity kept me grounded to my spot and told me to watch. To listen.

I stared at the back of her head. Waiting for him to respond. Waiting for him to refute what I just saw. To correct her. To push her away. To do something.

I wasn't the girl that stood for this, and after everything we'd been through, he should know that. I also wasn't the woman that let jealousy eat at her like poison. I cared about myself far too much for that, and with his brand on my neck, I'd think he'd know that too.

But still, I waited.

Rysten's silence must have shocked her as well, because she pulled back, just enough for me to see his face. To the see his furrowed brows and his eyes squinting as he looked down at her.

"Iona?" he asked. The confusion in his tone was clear. A cool hand wrapped around my elbow, drawing me closer. I knew it was Moira. That she was pulling me to her, hoping that her touch would soothe me as it often did. I was as numb to her as I was to the vision before me. I simply stood there—and I waited.

Assumptions make an ass out of everyone.

Isn't that what people always say?

It seems that no one thought to mention how much this hurt; how much giving a shit *hurt*. His silence was hard, but his first word? That was harder.

And I was trying really fucking hard not to assume what the fuck this all meant—because his first words weren't a correction. They weren't an apology. They weren't even addressed to me.

They were for her.

A blade twisting through my chest would have been kinder.

My hands curled into fists at my sides, nails biting into the palms. The world seemed to be at a standstill, waiting for them to say something. No one more so than me.

Because I wouldn't believe it. I couldn't. After everything we'd been through...

"Iona, I thought you were dead. I watched you die," he uttered and then he backed away. His golden hair lit up like the dying sun. His eyes sparkled like gems, but there was a dangerous undercurrent within. That dark power he kept locked up tight was straining. The veins beneath his tanned face turned black as he struggled for control over his emotions.

"I'm sorry—" She reached for him again and he recoiled.

"No, I watched you die," he repeated. His head shook. He sounded very sure of this.

"I almost did," she murmured, swallowing hard. I wanted to tear my eyes away because it felt like watching a lover's quarrel. One that didn't involve me.

"Clearly." Rysten's mask snapped into place, hiding his emotion from all except me. Even with the added touch of glamor to keep his true feelings concealed, the bond allowed me to see and feel through it. Inside, he was hurting.

"Aren't you happy to see me, Rys?" she asked, a slight whine to her voice that had me closing my eyes and turning away. I didn't know what I was watching unfold, but I was sure I didn't want to be a part of it.

"See that you're alive after thousands of years?" I felt her reaction. The way her heart echoed mine from moments ago. "I looked for you. I mourned for you, and you've been doing what all this time? Hiding? Working?"

"It's not that simple, baby—"

And that was when I started walking.

"Don't call me that!" he roared. "I'm not your anything anymore. You left me."

A bundle of fur at my feet made me stop. Bandit pulled on my jeans and I bent at the waist to scoop him up. Water pricked my eyes, but I'd be damned if I let myself cry over this. Rysten already owned a piece of my heart. He didn't get my tears too.

"I *lived* because of you," she snapped. "When my body was broken and bleeding out, I thought of you. He tossed what was left of me into the lake, but I survived because of *you*." I clung to Bandit as I walked away. All eyes seemed to be on the arguing couple. All except mine.

I had no desire to see where this was going.

Storming past the makings of another campfire and a snarling enigma in hellhound form, I pushed between the few demons in masks standing at the other side of camp and continued on.

On to where I could no longer hear Rysten's accusations and that woman's excuses. On to where the bond wasn't so sharp between us, and his pain didn't bleed over into me so acutely that it felt as if she'd betrayed me and not him. On to where the last of the setting sun dipped below the horizon and that jewel-toned skyline went grey.

Focusing on the colorless sky was easier than sorting through the pains in my chest and the ache in my heart. A sharp wind rustled the trees around me. Branches whipped, trees swayed, and an unsettling cold slapped me in the face. I touched my cheek and my fingers came away wet from tears I didn't even know I'd shed.

I glared at the liquid on my fingers. Tears mixed with sweat and dirt and heartbreak.

"For fuck's sake," I cursed, wiping my hand on the tight pants I wore. Bandit nestled closer as I lifted the edge of my shirt to clean my face.

What happened back there looked pretty bad, and I reacted on that, but at least I hadn't burned her alive. I was a lot of things, a murderer included, but that didn't mean I had to act like it. Inside me the beast writhed with anger and dark promise. She wanted to punish the blonde for touching Rysten, but the way I saw it—it wasn't the blonde's fault. Iona. That was her name.

She wasn't the one bonded to me. She probably had no idea.

It was on Rysten to set her straight, and while he'd been pretty shocked to see her—reasonably so from what I heard—that didn't excuse him. That didn't place the blame on her.

The beast didn't really fault that logic, but she was far more forgiving towards him if the other she-demon was dead. Something about that snapped me from my own stupor and made me roll my eyes. How very...beast-like of her.

Our bond connected us in ways I wished to escape at this moment. I could feel his emotions spike. Betrayal was prominent. Guilt. I couldn't figure where the emotions came from or why, only that they were there and for some reason, they had hit a staggering frequency despite the greater distance.

Their argument must be cresting just as my head was clearing and the rising bloodlust cooling.

Bandit curled around me tighter and he bared his teeth at the outer forest, but nothing was there. Just dirt and trees and grey. Turning from the far-off horizon still very much out of our reach, I looked back towards the direction of camp.

I sighed. "We should probably get back," I told Bandit. His ears twitched, but other than that he didn't respond. Not that I really expected him to.

As I started walking the strangest feeling crept up on me. Almost...no, that can't be right. I brushed my hands over my arms and against the goosebumps that were rising on my skin beneath my flannel. Then the hairs on my neck stood on end.

It was silent. Far too silent.

My footsteps slowed to a crawl as I approached the tree line. On the other side would be the clearing where the Horsemen, Moira, Jax, the four steeds, and the many masked demons should be.

Why was it that I felt eyes on me then?

I stared straight ahead as the wind whispered across the forest floor. A twig snapped.

I spun around, but it was the wrong move. A hand clamped over my mouth. I panicked.

Reacting on nothing but instinct and adrenaline, I brought my foot back and down on the foot of my would-be subduer. They held strong, though, and the scent of flowers washed over me.

"Listen carefully because I won't repeat myself," a female voice whispered in my ear. Deep and husky. The scent of blood and lilies settled around me. "You're in great danger here. My master is watching both of us." A chill skittered down my back, leaving me cold. Sin was nearly as tall as I and her slender fingers as calloused as the Horsemen's. The rough pads pressed against the column of my throat as if in warning. "I am trying to help you, but my hands are tied in how much I can do. Your path is set. All that's left is for you to follow it."

The second her hand dropped from my mouth I whirled on her. Mercury eyes watched me with a carefully crafted sort of stillness that wasn't natural. This woman was every bit the predator my beast was, except one of these was born out of nature and the other...I could only guess.

I tampered down the rising anger by reminding myself who I was talking to. Sin wasn't one to fuck around when she wanted something. She didn't understand shit like boundaries. Hell, she stripped my telepathy with a twirl of her fingers. That alone should give the beast pause, though it didn't. It was good the beast wasn't the one in charge here, or Sin might already be burning.

The corner of her lips curved up in a crude sort of smile.

"You're a smart girl. So was your mother."

"What the hell are you talking about, Sin? The path is set? What fucking path?" I threw my head back and closed my eyes, pressing the palm of my hand to my forehead. I took a deep breath and said, "Is it even possible for you to speak plainly? I'm getting tired of the games here."

Her lips twisted into a grimace. "We all are. This world is dying, and we're being forced to leave it in the hands of a child. If I could speak plainly and tell you exactly what to do, I would—but there are things in motion you don't know or understand yet."

I shook my head and my hand fell away. "Why are you here, Sin? You seem to only come when I'm either going to die or already dying. Since I am currently neither, your sudden appearance makes me think those demons in the woods might change that." I raised my eyes to the treetops looking for any sign of eyes watching, but we were alone. As alone as one could possibly be in a forest filled with monsters.

"They are not who they appear." She looked over my shoulder as if seeing something faraway. "They've been…changed by time and desperation."

I rocked back on my heels and wiped my thumb across my bottom lip.

"Great. So, they *are* trying to kill us," I said. My voice was oddly steady for the panic I should be feeling. There was once a time that one full demon would make me scared, but that time was no more. I'd killed men, dozens of men, in the name of destroying evil and avenging my familiars. I'd lit them up without a thought and watched their corpses burn until only black ash remained, all without a single grimace.

The masked demons, while problematic, were not my biggest concern.

"Who isn't?" Sin scoffed, looking to the treetops above us.

"That's the real question," I murmured, more to myself than anything. Sin cocked an eyebrow in my direction and I sighed. "What changed them?"

Sin didn't react, but that in and of itself was a reaction. Her unfettered response was too cool. Too...practiced. The way her eyes didn't avoid me but also didn't drill into my soul. She never shifted or otherwise fidgeted when we met. Sin was far too confident for that sort of thing. That didn't mean she didn't have tells, though.

"Magic." Her eyes flashed, the only warning I'd get about straying too close to questions she can't answer. Her half-answers wouldn't work forever.

"*Who* changed them?" I rephrased.

That cruel smile—the one that danced on the edge of chaos—sat on her lips again.

"I can't tell you."

"Can't or won't?" I pushed. The silver of her eyes darkened a fraction.

"Both," she answered with the slightest growl to the word. I narrowed my gaze, flicking my eyes between her and the tree line.

"Do they have a master?" I asked so quietly I almost wondered if she didn't hear it.

But then came her response, and it wasn't even a sound. Just a silent word on her lips. "Yes."

I nodded slowly, taking that in.

"You know," I said, "your master may prevent you from saying a lot. The rune of silence you placed on me prevents me from doing the same. I can't say anything to the Horsemen. I can't talk to Moira. This whole thing would be a lot easier if I could speak with *someone*, though. Maybe they could help me—"

"No." Her tone was sharp. Short. She didn't leave room for arguing.

"I understand very little about this world and now I'm having to rely solely on you to handle whichever of Lucifer's enemies is after me." I'd been playing this game with her for a little while now, but my patience was running thin after what went down in New Orleans. Now after trekking through Hell, my temper was even thinner. "I know that your hands are tied, but you're giving me breadcrumbs here. One of these times someone is going to be one step ahead of you and it's going to be me that dies because of it."

The silver of her eyes seemed to transform and glow as she watched me, jaw tight and body stiff. She didn't like that I was pushing back, but I didn't have a lot of fucks to give at this point.

"Devil-damnit, Sin," I whispered a curse. "You owe me after all the shit I went through."

Sin continued to watch me as I let out a sigh and moved to step around her. Cool fingers touched my forearm.

"She is going to invite you to the Garden tonight. Go with her. You and your mates will be in great danger, but you will find the answers you seek." Her words were punctuated with strain and inundated with weariness. She was struggling with something. If only I knew what.

"Thank you," I whispered.

"Don't thank me just yet."

I glanced sideways, but her eyelids were shuttered, keeping the hidden truths in her eyes concealed. "I don't understand everything you've done or why. At times it has infuriated me because I wish that this were simple. My life will never be simple again, though, and I have to learn to live with that." I paused, sucking in a deep breath. "I'm going to choose to overlook what happened in New Orleans. Without you I have very few allies. That doesn't mean I trust you. It means that I trust you had a damn good reason for what you did to me and mine." Her eyes opened, zeroing in on me. "I trust that you meant what you said that night, that you want to see me on the throne. Which is why I'm not going to let the beast do what it really wants to you. *This time.* Next time, I make no promises. Your master clearly holds a lot of power here, and I need to find out who they are, with or without you."

"You're threatening me?" she chuckled, not sounding even the slightest bit scared.

"No, I'm warning you that this is your last chance before the beast overrides my forgiveness." She paused, tilting her head to the side. "I'd like us to be true allies. Friends, even, when this is all over. Friends don't stab each other in the back to meet their own needs. Remember that."

Her hand dropped away from my arm, and I didn't need to look to know that she was already gone.

Sin came to deliver a warning and I gave her one instead.

Perhaps if we both listened to each other we'd all make it out of this alive.

ALLISTAIR

Where the fuck had she gone?

I'd been scanning the clearing while Iona and Rysten were at each other's neck, hashing out the details of a history I'd rather forget. While everyone was watching them, I had been watching her. The shock on her face. The flush that crept up her neck and over her cheeks. The bitter tang of betrayal when Rysten made the mistake of letting Iona kiss him and not correcting her. She was like an open book when I could read her body and emotions, and Rysten had hurt her greatly.

But then something happened.

Her eyes went cold and she disappeared, along with any trace of the bond. If I hadn't watched it with my own eyes, I might have thought it was one of the fuckers in a mask toying with us, but that sort of power...no, none of them could have done it. She glamored herself so efficiently that I, nor any of the other Horsemen, could not find her.

"Where is she?" I telepathically shot towards Moira. Her familiar seemed none too troubled in the slightest and was more concerned with analyzing Rysten's every move than helping us find Ruby.

"She needs space," came the chilled reply. It was the same she'd given the last five times and I was losing my patience, but no matter which of us asked, she was unwilling to comply. Her loyalty was to Ruby, and Ruby alone.

"She could be in danger," I thought, changing tactics. The corner of her dark green lips curved up in a cruel sort of smile.

"I pity the idiot that tries her right now."

I clenched my teeth and turned away. She wasn't wrong, and that made this all the more dangerous. The last thing we needed was an all-out fight with Iona's faction before reaching Inferna, which is what it very well could turn into if they were here for her and noticed she was gone. Except fucking Moira was stonewalling me and the damn raccoon had gone with Ruby, which left me with no way to find her until she decided to show herself.

Stretching my fingers to keep from curling them into fists, I headed towards the edge of the forest, opposite from Rysten and Iona. If she was looking to get away from them, it made more sense for her to go that way.

"You're threatening me?" came the hushed chuckle of amusement I knew all too well. I peered out into the trees as I glamored myself to blend in with them.

"No, I'm warning you that this is your last chance before the beast over-rides my forgiveness," a second voice said. I squinted my eyes. "I'd like us to be true allies. Friends, even, when this is all over. Friends don't stab each other in the back to meet their own needs. Remember that."

A shadow appeared where I now knew Ruby to be standing. The faint outline of two women and a raccoon. Sin's fingers slipped from Ruby's forearm as she took a step away. In the blink of an eye the white-haired woman was gone and Ruby stood alone.

While my eyes roved over her for signs of distress, my mind was more occupied with what exactly those two were doing with each other. Sin had only met Ruby once in passing…or had she?

I wanted to believe that my little succubus wasn't keeping secrets from us, but the hard edge to her expression as she stared toward the clearing didn't leave me so certain. Half my instincts told me I should go to her now and try to pull the truth from her lips, but the other half told me to wait. Watch. Ruby was loyal to those she considered hers, even if she didn't say everything. Devil knows there are things that we've been reluctant to tell her. After all she's given up for us and for this, the last thing anyone wanted was to bring her more pain. In doing so, though…she may have sought out other answers from people with less reservations. Like Sin.

Torn by indecision, I hesitated as a banshee's screech split the air.

Ruby's eyes flashed obsidian and then back to blue as she pulled her shoulders back and walked towards the clearing. Walked, not ran. Which meant either Moira wasn't in trouble, or Ruby trusted her to handle it on her own. I doubled back, instantly assessing the scene before me, just as Ruby did.

What I didn't expect to find was Iona sprawled out on the forest floor, Moira's boot planted on her sternum.

CHAPTER EIGHT

"WHAT PART of *mated male* did you not understand the first time, blondie?" Moira snapped. Iona tried to sit up and Moira's boot pressed down harder. Fire swirled in the depths of her blue pentagram eyes.

"Rys—what is she—" Iona only rasped half her sentence when Moira stomped again, forcing the air from her lungs as she ground her boot into the flimsy homemade shirt.

"Do not look at him. Do not speak to him. He is your *nothing*," she growled in a voice that made the beast proud. "I don't give a shit who you are, but you will not come between my girl and her men—"

"Moira." My voice cut through the crowd like blades against paper. "Get. Off. Her."

"She disrespects you knowing that he's mated—"

"It is not her place to respect that bond. It's *his*, and that is something he and I will deal with later."

I could feel Rysten's eyes on me. Sense his panic as I purposely didn't spare him a glance. They'd turned my life upside down and inside out, but I didn't grovel. I didn't beg. If he wanted me, then it was on him to fix this. That didn't mean I needed to ream him in public. This was no one's business but our own.

Moira lifted her boot from the demon's sternum and crossed her arms over her chest with a huff. Iona scrambled to her feet and dusted off her basic clothing, eyeing me with apprehension. "You have his brand…"

She was confused. Hurt. There was more than a little spite in her voice to cover it up. Envy too. I chose to ignore it.

"And he has mine, but that is neither here nor there." I kept my voice clipped and my expression detached. After all, they weren't here by happenstance. I had to play along, but that didn't mean I had to be friendly. "Who are you and what do you want?" Her lips fell ajar as if surprised by my straightforwardness.

With a heavy sigh she readjusted her stance to a slightly more defensive posture. Her chin lifted and the self-importance of it all had me…bored and annoyed. I was so over the mean girl shit.

"I am Iona LeGrase, the Deadly Sin of Envy's niece."

I blinked as she extended a claw-tipped hand that had Moira stepping in front of me with a growl.

"If you so much as scratch her, goldilocks—"

"I think she gets the point." I squeezed her shoulder causing Moira to turn her chin up. I shook my head once, and she furrowed her brows but stepped away. My best friend's instincts were right not to trust her, but I couldn't tell her that. Not if I wanted to find out the truth about who was after me.

"I'm Ruby Morningstar, and this is my familiar, Moira."

"I'm also a legion and a banshee. I wouldn't try anything if I were you," she said with a purse of her lips.

Iona appraised her distastefully, a tendril of apprehension running through her before she said, "Welcome to the family."

Swallowing down the painful emotions riding me, I lifted my hand to hers and clasped it. She was stronger than me, but for what she had in strength I made up for in fire. My palm grew warm as I let the flames play just beneath my skin. Not enough to burn her, but enough to feel the heat as she tried to crush my fingers.

A bead of sweat dotted her brow when she released me. I kept my expression cool. Civil.

"She's only speaking metaphorically," Rysten said with a piercing look in her direction. I lifted an eyebrow without looking at him and a slight blush darkened his skin. "The Sins, apart from you mother, never had children. Merula formed a very close relationship with Iona's mother."

"They were practically sisters before she died," Iona added bitterly.

"I see…" The words hung there, not hostile, but not exactly friendly. I ignored Rysten's eyes that pleaded with me to understand their complicated histories, just as much as I ignored Iona's calculated gaze. At the end of the day I didn't particularly care if we shared blood or not. Moira and Bandit were my family. The Horsemen were. This girl—she was a stranger trying to kill me. I needed to get closer to her, but I didn't particularly want to understand her. It was easier that way.

"This is all fine and well," Allistair interrupted, "but what are you doing all the way outside Rieka?" His eyes narrowed slightly as he took her in. I didn't miss the way his posture remained stiff.

"Hunting," the girl answered, giving him only half her attention. The other half was on my Horseman. Rysten. The beast growled, warning me that if Iona didn't keep her hands and eyes to herself that the not-so-friendly alter-ego of mine was going to deliver the warning in person. With a punch to the cunt.

"What do you mean by *hunting*?" Moira asked before someone else could cut in. Iona regarded her with enough animosity that I felt the need to step a little closer to my best friend.

"I mean that Hell is on fire and half the planet is in chaos, Rieka included. Lust crumbled first, and Greed wasn't far behind it once the borders destabilized. The Sins went into hiding, leaving the rest of us to fend for ourselves." Iona waved to the group of demons around her. "This is all that's left of Sector Forty-Nine."

I swallowed and refused to look away even as the guilt leaked in. She could be a liar about everything, but I knew first-hand how destructive the flames were when I lost control and destroyed my own tattoo parlor.

"Why didn't you go to Inferna?" Allistair asked.

"It's full," she answered. "Lust was given the order to evacuate first and by the time the fire reached Rieka, it was too late."

"Surely your *aunt* would have made room for you. Since you're close enough to be family," Moira commented. Iona looked like she just drank piss the way her lips twisted, and eyes brightened.

"She's the leader of a province," Iona snapped. "She doesn't get to play favorites. Something you might know if you were from here."

Funny how she didn't seem this snappy about me being Satan's kid until Moira threw her on the ground for kissing Rysten. I wondered how much of her being here was for me and how much was for him. I supposed we'd find out soon enough.

"I didn't grow up with a silver spoon up my ass. Sorry if I don't understand how it works." Moira threw her hands in the air and I groaned.

"Moira, why don't you go sit with Jax and see if you can get him to change back. I don't think they're going to attack us now..." I turned to Iona. "Are you?"

She gave me a flippant look but spoke clearly. "No. We never intended to hurt you. We just needed to make sure you weren't here to mean harm."

"Interesting way of showing it..." Moira muttered. I cleared my throat and she blew out a breath, stalking off towards the shaking enigma-hellhound.

"She's got a point," Laran said. "Holding weapons to us is not the best way to show peace. Even I know that." The corners of my lips turned up as War slipped an arm over my shoulders. Iona looked anything but peaceful in the way she watched Moira leave.

"When Rieka burned, neighbors turned on each other," she said slowly, her voice far calmer than the look in her eyes. "You were just as likely to be stabbed for the shirt on your back while walking down the street as you were to find someone that would help you. I won't apologize for being vigilant when you're this close to one of the two ways in and out of the Garden."

"It's still open?" Julian asked.

"It is. Only path not on fire that leads through to Inferna," she answered, baiting us.

"Funny that, we're headed there right now," I said before anyone else could answer. If she was going to try to lure us, I may as well let her think I was naïve and didn't see through the subterfuge. I'd been feeling out of my depth to a certain extent ever since we arrived in Hell, but bitches certainly made it feel like home.

I wondered how much of this was personal for her and how much was the unknown face that's been following me since Portland, trying to kill me at every turn.

"I can't guarantee you passage through the Garden, but if you're here to fix this mess, the least I can let you do is stay through the night." The creeping sensation along my spine had me on edge. I already knew not to trust her. I was walking into the viper's nest with eyes wide open.

So why did it feel like there was something I was still missing?

"That would be great," I said before I took the time to reconsider the decision. Sin said if I went along, I'd find my answers. No matter how much I hated the looks she continued to give Rysten, nothing was stopping me from searching for the truth.

Not fear. Not Rysten. Not even love itself.

"If we stay with you, do we have your word that you mean no harm?" Laran asked.

"You do." Her voice resonated with a truth, but as we moved to pack up our camp, a sliver of emotion escaped through her nonchalance. I tilted my head to the side. It felt like...regret?

It was gone so fast I almost thought I imagined it.

Almost.

CHAPTER NINE

Epona's side brushed against me reassuringly. On her back sat Bandit, gnawing his way through the straps. He wasn't the biggest fan of the other demons and given that he wore the devil's mark, they weren't fans of him either.

Not that it stopped him from snapping at anyone that stepped a little too close to me or the horse. He seemed to be growing an attachment to her, one that I hadn't expected given her massive size. She was a gentle soul, though, which was strange given whose familiar she was.

A cool hand pressed against my elbow as a slim arm hooked around it. The scent of peppermint floated over me as Moira leaned in to whisper, "I don't trust her."

"Me neither," I muttered, trying not to pay too much attention to how closely Iona walked beside Rysten. Jealousy. Territorialism. Call it what you want, but the green-eyed monster was not a pleasant feeling when it chose to visit.

It helped that every time Iona got close to touching him, Rysten stepped a good three feet to the side to dodge her.

"Something's off about that one," Moira continued. "She didn't lie earlier, but I don't think she was telling the full truth." I stumbled when my boot hit a rock and Moira caught me easily. I grinned at the way her small frame held the brunt of my weight without breaking a sweat. She'd always been strong-willed, but now she had the body to match it.

"What makes you say she wasn't lying?"

"I can tell," Moira said evasively. My eyebrows inched up my forehead and she chuckled under her breath. "Ever since I transitioned, things have been...different. There's power in words, and I can taste it. Lies taste bad."

"You never talk about what happened," I said. It was my way of prodding, but just a little. If she wanted to talk, that was her choice; the same as if she chose to be silent.

"It's still happening," she murmured. I paused, the eerie tone of her voice had my skin prickling.

"What do you mean?" I said slowly. Moira stopped, and because we were at the back of the group, no one minded one bit. She looked up at the night sky. On Earth it would have been a hazy blue-grey that was too murky to discern much of anything. Here, it was more saturated, and the sky shone like navy paint splashed across a canvas. The stars popped like glittering gems against the darkened atmosphere.

"Our lives changed the day Allistair paid your bail. We've had a lot of ups and some pretty low downs. I've been kidnapped, drugged, tortured, imprisoned, and starved to a certain extent when Bandit and I had to share any food we found." My mouth went dry and I wished I'd never asked now, but I opened up the door for her to speak. I needed to hear what she had to say. "I think if we only looked at the bad things, people would wonder why I'm still with you. Why I chose to stand by you all these years. Why I chose to follow you into Hell. But you know what? The same thing could be said about you with me.

"I remember the day you stood up to Brayden Patterson for me. He wouldn't stop throwing rocks and you slugged him in the face so hard his nose was never straight again. Neither was your right index finger." My hands flexed as I remembered the impact. "You've fought people for me. You've risked yourself time and time again. You've been teased and tormented, and if we're both being honest, that night in Pandora's Box never would have happened if I hadn't insisted on taking you out alone because I don't like to share." I opened my mouth to refute it, but a slight finger rested on my lips telling me to shush. "We've hurt each other by association, but we've also completed each other in ways that no one else understands. You wanted to know why I don't talk about what happened?

About my time with Le Dan Bia, about my transition, about being branded
—the thing is, I'm still living it. Every day with you, I am preparing for the
next horror I might face. I'm terrified that one day these close calls will be
just a little too close, and I'll lose you like *that*." She snapped her fingers,
and it reverberated in my bones. "So, I don't talk about it. I prepare. I practice when no one is watching. I listen to the things people don't say. I watch
the world around us. Because our lives are still changing, and until it stops,
I have no intention of pausing to think about what has happened and
letting it distract me. The second I do might be the second someone strikes
and then all the talking in the world won't matter if you're gone. Being
angry won't matter if you're gone, because all I'll have is myself and my
own resentments. And that's the worst place to be."

I stared at her and couldn't find words.

Certainly not one's like hers. Moira didn't talk because she existed in an
eternal state of fight or flight. Our lives were dangerous, and she was absolutely right that we hurt each other by association, but she was also right in
that I wouldn't change the pain if it meant not knowing her. She didn't talk
about it or let herself feel it because we were still living it.

And to her, not feeling it meant that she was better equipped to keep it
that way.

Bottling emotions was never my thing. I was the kind that let it all out
and got over it, but not Moira. She held it close and locked it up tight,
turning it into fuel to do and be better, and in the end…she exploded.

Today wasn't that explosion, but the building of it.

She gave herself a foundation built on spite and hope and guilt and
love. She crafted herself into the perfect disaster. Wild. Passionate.
Disruptive.

I wrapped my arms around her shoulders and pulled her close,
knowing that one day soon, in the right collision of events, she would go
bang—and nothing would hold her together then.

"I love you, Moira," I muttered into her shoulder.

"I love you too. That's why I don't like this." It didn't take a genius to
know what she was talking about. "Her timing is too convenient. Rysten
thought she died like three thousand years ago, and now all of a sudden she
makes an appearance?" Moira scoffed. "Puh-lease. This bitch is here to
drive a wedge. Which is why I lost my shit when she tried to kiss him,
again."

I froze and both my eyebrows shot to my hairline. "Again?"

"He pushed her away the second time," Moira said. "But the fact that he told her he was mated and she still tried that shit...I just couldn't stop myself. I'm tired of all these petty bitches. You won't go beast mode on them, but there's nothing stopping me. I'm no one." She shrugged her shoulders with a wicked smile on her lips.

"You're not no one—" I argued. She threw her head back and let out a loud, obnoxious laugh that had half the masked demons turning to look at us.

"Oh, babe, I'm no one, but that's fine by me. Being your familiar is more than enough responsibility." She patted my back. "Means I get to do all the fun things, like pick on the Horsemen because they can't do shit about it."

I snorted. Of course, that would be a perk to her.

"They're not the only ones you've been picking on lately..." I started, letting my voice trail off while tilting my chin towards Jax.

"That's because he's a dick." Her forehead went tense as she purposely stared straight ahead.

"Uh huh." I threw my arm around her shoulder. "So are you. Your point?"

She spluttered for a second, grasping for a response. I cocked an eyebrow, fighting a smile and her cheeks blushed pistachio. "I choose to be a dick, thank you very much. He wouldn't know how to be nice if it bit him in the ass."

I snorted. "You keep telling yourself that."

"I'm serious—" Moira said loudly, elbowing me in the ribs for cracking up so hard. A heavy arm landed around my shoulder, edging between us. "What the hell?" She jumped away from the intrusion. "Famine, I'm not all about your incubus cooties, man. Save that shit for Ruby and a closed door."

"Mind if I cut in here?" Allistair asked, his lips brushing over the tip of my ear as he leaned into me.

"Just help yourself." Moira rolled her eyes and he flashed her a wink as she moved up ahead to give us room to talk.

"You handled yourself better than I expected," he said quietly, the overt flirtatiousness slipping from his tone.

"Oh?" I asked. "And how did you think I would handle myself?"

"I wasn't completely sure Iona was going to make it out of that alive."

Was that a ghost of a smile?

"I'm not that petty," I snorted, blowing a sweaty strand of hair away from my face. "Besides, I meant what I said. This is between me and Rysten. How Iona acts isn't my business."

He nodded silently, watching them up ahead of us, the same as I did.

"You're wise for one so young."

"She's not the first bitchy ex I've dealt with. I doubt she'll be the last." But I wished she was. I wished it more than anything. Ever since puberty I'd been dealing with women like this. It's a devil-damned miracle that I had Moira.

"She's not an ex," Allistair said. I frowned.

"But she kissed him. Moira said she tried to again—"

"When you are close with someone it's not uncommon to kiss them here. She took it a step too far, though, and I didn't see the second time. I was too busy looking for you." My breath hitched and I tried to smother it with a cough, but the look in his eyes said it all.

"How much did you see?" He seamlessly missed the roots and under-brush as we walked, even while watching every expression that crossed my face.

"I saw you threaten Sin. Care to tell me how long you've known her?" My teeth sank into my bottom lip as I looked away. Two fingers grasped my chin turning my face back to him.

"A while," I found myself saying. "She came to me in Portland."

His lips slipped ajar as an understanding settled over him. "She's the one that saved you from the Seelie." It wasn't a question, so I didn't treat it as one.

"Amongst other things." I wasn't trying to be purposely evasive, but I wasn't sure where the rune would come into play and prevent me from speaking. It was better to be vague than have him stumble upon something I couldn't tell him about and have another one of those damn coughing spells.

"She's dangerous, Ruby—"

"You think I don't know that?" I snapped, harsher than I intended. My mouth closed as his fingers slipped from my chin. Running a hand down my face, I sighed deeply. "I'm sorry. I'm not trying to be an asshole here."

"You're under a lot of pressure. I get it, and I even get why you might have kept this to yourself. Julian is prone to jumping the gun when it comes to you." We both looked to where the Horseman of Death rode atop Rhiannon. "Just be careful with Sinumpa. Nothing with her is easy, or free."

"Speaking from personal experience?" I asked him.

"Yes," he answered, turning his gaze to the ground in front of us. Avoiding mine.

"She was the girl, wasn't she?" I asked softly. His muscles went tense. "The one you loved?"

"*Thought* I loved. It wasn't the same." I wanted to ask him the same as what, but I wasn't ready for the answer to that yet. If he said what I thought he was implying, it would be awkward when I didn't say it back. Not until this was all over.

"But that was her?"

"Yes."

We fell silent as I thought about that. Sin was the only woman in all of his life that he felt anything for besides me. I suppose that was when I ought to feel jealous, or at least territorial. But unlike Iona—who was playing with fire—Sin wasn't driving wedges. On the contrary, I wouldn't have known at all if he hadn't seen us together.

When it came to whatever happened between them, I didn't really feel any which way about it. They'd both clearly moved on and his straight forwardness left me at ease.

"I'll be careful. I promise."

He nodded. "I trust you, Ruby. I just don't trust her."

"Will you keep this between me and you?" I rolled my shoulder back and slipped one arm around his waist as we walked.

"For now." His knuckles brushed softly down my side in an intimate gesture. My blood heated, and not because of the exertion. "Julian would lose his shit if he knew you two were in contact, but there's not exactly anything we can do. You're your own person, and even if we wanted to keep you from Sin, she would find a way." He sighed, sounding far closer to his age than usual. "Just know that if you get in too deep with her that I'm here."

My eyes closed as I turned and placed a soft kiss against his chest. "Thank you."

"Always, little succubus."

I smiled, feeling truly content despite where we were headed.

Even going into Hell could be a pleasant experience if you had your people with you.

Then the excited cries rang out into the night as Moira came doubling back into view. "We're here," she said as she projected her voice to me through the crowd.

I looked beyond her and the thin slip of trees to the mouth of the tunnel that led underground. The warm fuzzy feeling in my chest dissipated.

This was it.

"Ready to find out why no one wants to live in the Garden?" Allistair chuckled.

No, I couldn't say that I did. But unfortunately for me, Iona had the answers I needed. "Let's go," I said with more enthusiasm than I felt.

My gut had kept me alive this long, maybe it would keep us alive a little longer.

CHAPTER TEN

NEVER HAD I been so wrong.

The very rockface itself seemed to be acting as an oven trying to broil me alive. While Allistair insisted it was always this way, Laran and Julian were speculating that it was worse than usual, but at least underground no one had to fear that they'd burn from the flames. In some ways, it was similar to the portal since it was made of the same stone, and like the portal —it was downright uncomfortable. With millions of pounds of rock surrounding me, not even the slightest breeze giving relief, and Bandit's god-awful whining—I understood why no one wanted to live here and no Sin contended for this province. It sucked. No two ways about it.

After walking for what felt like hours, I was ready to faint or cry when the tunnel finally opened up into what everyone had been calling the Garden. A sprawling underground city filled with a million tiny flickering lights that centered around a clear luminescent lake. Towers of black stone rose up from the water, each individual floor appeared like a pavilion with columns instead of true walls acting as the structure. Within them demons laughed and dined, they fucked, they fought, just as they would anywhere else.

Children high above us, on the upmost floors, ran out to the edge and looked down ten stories without fear. One of them, a boy not so far out, reached up and wrapped his hand around a gleaming cable—the place was filled with them. They spanned from one tower to the next, going up and down and straight across. Some even led off into the rock wall, seeming to disappear, which made me think they were actually caves.

The boy's cable led straight to the rock beach where I stood. I frowned as he whipped up a length of rope dangling from his belt; on the end, a metal hook reflected the water's low fluorescence. He slipped that end over the cable and without any hesitation, he jumped.

My mouth fell ajar from shock, but before I could even say anything the boy rocked himself forward and detached his clip, somersaulting in midair to land like an Olympic gymnast. No one around me took notice as he went to work helping load people onto the boats and then pushing them off the edge of the lake. "Did you see that?" I asked the Horsemen around me, pointedly focusing on everything else but how Iona continued trying to use her persuasion to get Rysten to join her boat—like she was strong enough for that to work on him. A look of disgust came over his features as he regarded her once before storming off to the side of the shore.

"See what?" Laran asked, coming to stand beside me. I pulled my attention back and pointed to the boy in a half-mask, wearing cinched baggy pants with layers of fabric and rope around his waist. Only a single white brand spanned half his back.

It gave off the same light as the water.

"That kid. He just rode one of those cables from across the lake." Laran nodded, brushing a hand over his stubbled jaw.

"Ahnika came up with those. It's the fastest and easiest way to get around here."

For the Sin of Sloth, I imagined her to be a little less…ingenious. Guess that's what I got for assuming. "It's a clever idea," I said.

"And it sure as Hell beats the climb up." Allistair pointed to the tower and motioned vertically. I squinted, trying to pick out how you got from one floor to the next when I saw— "Are those ladders?" My voice sounded a little breathy and shrill at the mild panic of having to climb hundreds of feet after already being this exhausted…

"Yes, but we won't be staying in a tower while we're here," Allistair answered, guiding me towards the shore.

"We won't?" I breathed out a sigh of relief and muttered, "Thank the Devil." Laran and Allistair chuckled, both offering me a hand to help me into the surprisingly stable boat.

"We'll be staying in a cave closer to the other side of the lake," Allistair said. I moved to the far end and waited patiently as they loaded Rhiannon. Epona followed, carrying Bandit as he slept and snored obnoxiously loud. "I'm surprised the boat can hold their weight," I said as Allistair and Julian joined me.

"These boats can't sink, flip, or otherwise be destroyed," Allistair said by way of answer. He reached out and clasped a paddle before War pushed us off. A pang of sadness hit me as I realized Laran was staying with Rysten. I saw him gather up Moira, Jax, and the final two familiars before loading themselves on a boat that trailed behind us.

"Must be magic," I breathed, taking the chance to absorb my reality.

I was in Hell—underground—sharing a boat with two horses and two of my mates.

Shit didn't get any crazier than this. It really didn't.

In such a short period of time, my life had changed so drastically, I don't even know if the old me would recognize what I'd become. Sure, on the outside we looked the same, but inside I was different. Changed in ways I couldn't even fathom then. I had powers. Dangerous. Deadly powers. I had brands. I had familiars. I had enemies that weren't just jealous women anymore— and more than anything—I had responsibilities.

To myself. To my family. To my mates. To an entire world.

If I wasn't still riding the wave of shock and incredulity, suffering a caffeine withdrawal induced headache accompanied by mild exhaustion … well, I'd probably have either fainted or panicked by now, but I didn't have time for that anymore.

In a matter of months, life as I had known it crumbled around me and served as kindling. Up in flames it went and where the glittering black ash settled, my new life grew. I'd reoriented my entire spectrum of being, and here underneath a caverned ceiling that glittered like the ash of my flames, I'd never felt more afraid, but I'd also never felt stronger.

The stalactites loomed hundreds of feet in the air, glowing water dripping like rain from the ends of them. I thought of the old Bible verse about a man in Hell begging God for only a drop of water. It never came.

Maybe he'd have had better luck begging Satan.

"Penny for your thoughts?" Allistair asked, sidling up beside me as he guided the boat.

I wasn't exactly in the mood for a heart-to-heart before I talked to

Rysten, so I settled for something a little simpler. "It's beautiful," I whispered, waving my hand to the ceiling high above us.

Allistair chuckled. "Until one falls and kills someone."

"That happens?" I asked, unable to judge how truly large they were without much light.

"Yeah, about once a century or so. It's Ahnika's preferred execution method." I blinked slowly, thinking about that.

Not only was she a genius, she was also vicious.

Yet another reason for me to *stop assuming.* Even as I thought it, I kept my eyes and attention glued to the ceiling instead of turning to the darker thoughts and feelings that settled in the back of my mind.

"I'm sorry—hold up for a second—did you just say *execution method?*"

He grinned up at the cavern canopy. "Yeah. Even in Sloth there is the occasional execution, although, it's far better here than Greed. Saraphine is a sadist that makes even Julian look like a choir boy at times."

I blew out a low whistle. "Damn. How do you even use a stalactite to execute someone? That's gotta be over three hundred feet high..."

"Six hundred," a gravelly voice said behind me. I could feel a blush creeping up on my cheeks after Allistair's sadist comment, but what did I have to be embarrassed about? They all knew each other even better than they knew me.

"Like I said, I don't see how that's even possible."

"Sound waves, believe it or not," Allistair said, dropping his hand to my lower back to guide me forward. "Ahnika is the strongest banshee in the world. One scream from her and she can direct it to split one of those straight from the ceiling."

"That's insane."

"Moira could probably do the same if she tried," Julian said. He was trying to be nonchalant, but I didn't miss the very calculated way he glanced behind him and up at the stalactites. I only needed to think about that for half a second to know how much of a bad idea it was.

"Don't give her any ideas," I muttered. She would practice trying to drop them on Rysten just to see him dodging out of the way, all the while cackling something about whack-a-mole.

"Wouldn't dream of it. She's already a big enough pain in the ass," Allistair replied, but Julian stayed silent. I turned my slight frown to the front of the boat just as we hit land. The stop jolted me, and it took all my balance and Allistair's fingers gripping the material of my shirt to keep me from being tossed out of the boat.

What it didn't do was keep Bandit sleeping. My raccoon woke with a damn vengeance, jumping to his feet with a growl and reaching for me.

"You good?" Allistair asked. I nodded and he released me, stepping out to offer his hand as I wrapped one arm around Bandit and gave him the other.

Something cool and wet whacked against my arm. I dropped my gaze to glance over my shoulder at Rhiannon as she tried to nudge me along. Pushy horse. She was definitely Julian's familiar.

"I think she's giving you a hint," Allistair smirked. I pursed my lips at him but held his hand tightly, more out of necessity than anything. These rocks were slippery, and I was just as likely to bust my ass as I was to fall out of the boat and drown. While my pride didn't like it, my body was sore and shaking.

Fingers trembling, I gripped him as I stepped onto dry land. The second he released me my body swayed, but a sturdy side was there to catch me as I stumbled. Epona turned her head to nuzzle Bandit and I smiled faintly, petting her forehead while I waited for the dizziness to fade.

Winter and pine invaded my space as a cool arm wrapped around my ribcage, pulling me back into a hard chest. "You're dehydrated from riding and walking. Let's go find you somewhere you can rest for a little bit." Those wicked fingers toyed with the hem of my shirt, briefly brushing against the skin of my stomach, and just like that, resting was the last thing I wanted. But Julian—like his horse—was stubborn as a damn mule.

Without asking, he swept me up in his arms and walked farther into the cave while the others were busy unloading. Bathed in the red and yellow firelight of torches placed in rungs bolted to the craggy rock side, the cave was…homier than I expected. Chaise lounges lined the walls with plush cushions and a fur rug that had enough room for ten people.

"This place looks like the get-up for some ancient king out of a history book," I said, my eyes trailing over every lush fabric and vibrant hue. The blue and green pillows had swaths of purple material pinned and sewn in beautiful designs with beads hanging from threads on the corners.

"It was," he grinned. I frowned, noting the smaller things then. The things that weren't immediately obvious. Like the lack of boats apart from ours, the lack of footprints, and even the thin layer of dust on the otherwise gleaming pleasure chamber.

"Lucifer?" I asked softly, already knowing but needing to hear it anyway. He nodded.

Once upon a time Lucifer shared this place, probably with Ahnika—the Sin of Sloth—but possibly with others too. Maybe even my own mother.

Laying on these pillows was a lot less appealing all the sudden.

"Iona thought you deserved to have your father's chamber…" Julian said quietly, trailing off at something he saw on my face.

"I feel disgusting after the last few days. Is there anywhere I can wash off first?" I was stalling and we both knew it, but it also didn't hurt anyone. Part of me wondered if Iona had planned this or if it was the master pulling her strings. If they knew just how out of place I felt sleeping in a king's nest while crowds of people holed up in the towers, sleeping in hammocks stacked on one another…

The rest of me was selfish and didn't mind the distance from Iona one bit. It gave me a chance to get my bearings without her sly smile and tanned hands trying to worm their way around Rysten. He could handle himself, but I wasn't comfortable putting him in the position to begin with when I knew there was something there and still, I agreed to come down here.

I needed answers, though. We all did.

"There are some pools around the back of the cave where you could bathe…" he trailed off, lifting an eyebrow in a silent question. My cheeks heated because that sounded like a great way to get my mind off whatever Iona was planning.

Until someone cleared their throat. Instead of desire, a cloud of dark emotions that weren't mine fell over me.

"I can take her," Rysten said. His usual playfulness was non-existent today. Where my Horseman of Pestilence loved to tease and get under his brother's skin, today there was nothing. Only loneliness and a well of betrayal so deep he was using every fiber of his being to not feel it.

The snarky asshole in me wanted to brush him off, but I couldn't do that. He wasn't Josh—who I caught pants down stumbling out of a broom closet. He was Rysten: the demon that made Josh bleed from the eyes for touching me without consent after slipping me a demonic roofie. He was the man that watched *How to Get Away with Murder* with me and brought me pad Thai when I was upset. He came to Earth for me and learned our customs, just so he could be there for me in ways the others couldn't when the day came for me to be called home.

Rysten wasn't like any other man that came before him, or even like my other three mates. He was sweet and sensitive. He was the guy that let Moira throw an eggplant at his dick, and if that wasn't caring I didn't know what was.

"I can walk," I said to Julian. He looked between the two of us, his gaze oscillating back and forth before he put me down, sliding me across his body in a seductive manner. Part of me thought he might be trying to get a rise out of Rysten, but with a quick peck to my lips and a warning look over his shoulder, Julian went back to the mouth of the cave, leaving the two of us alone.

"Thank you," Rysten said in a hoarse whisper.

"For what?" I folded my arms over my chest, drawing on that core of strength that fueled both me and the beast. She sat back, looking on with approval at how I chose to handle him.

"Not berating me in the middle of a crowd. Not tossing my ass aside when I deserved it. Not..." He swallowed and the well of hurt coming from him pulsed like a throbbing injury. "...Not dismissing me right now."

I nodded, a little bit of the tension slipping from my shoulders. Angry as I was, I wouldn't kick him when he was already down.

"Let's go find these pools Julian was telling me about," I said, motioning for him to lead the way. He stepped ahead of me and around the love nest that had bile coming up the back of my throat. I screwed my eyes ahead and tried not to think about who Satan did or did not fuck on the pillows I was supposed to sleep on. Most kids thought the idea of their parents having sex was gross, but both parents being deceased put a true somber spin on it.

We kept walking, the silence between us somehow both easier and harder to accept. The farther we went from those pillows, the easier my breathing grew, but the bleakness leaking from Rysten was stifling when I had fewer emotions surrounding me to counteract it.

One thing I never told anyone was how much other's emotions always bled into me, making me love them or hate them before a word left their mouth. In Moira's case it was easy— she was easy—both her and Bandit in terms of being around them. They both were what I liked to call emotionally safe. I knew what to expect from them and it rarely overran my own sense of self. But with the Horsemen, I was only really coming to realize how deep each of their own emotional pools reached. I'd always considered Rysten the easy one because we could sit and watch Netflix while drinking tea on my old faded couch. He indulged me in dates and food while letting me have the emotional distance I physically couldn't keep with the others.

Rysten was supposed to be easy, and maybe that was on me for not seeing past the shields and the masks and the many layers of him. Maybe he held off this part of himself because I wasn't ready for it, or maybe he simply needed time before showing me.

Because in that moment, Rysten wasn't easy. He was anything but. And being so close— yet, so far away—was killing me. But I respected myself too much to give even an inch until we spoke.

"I'm sorry I let her kiss me," he said, and it was hardly a breath.

"Then why did you?" I replied, both aware of what Allistair told me about Iona and their past and wanting to let Rysten explain it for himself.

"I was in shock. And I know that sounds like a terrible excuse, but I hadn't seen Iona in over three thousand years because I thought she was dead. Then she was standing before me, looking like not a day's gone by. I —" He broke off, his hand curling into a fist that he put to his mouth. "I didn't know what to do or say or how I was supposed to respond—and because of that, I disrespected you by letting her kiss me like we were something that we weren't."

I let out a heavy sigh, searching for the words that would help us both.

"Before I comment about that kiss, I need you to know something." I paused, wanting to look at the ceiling, the walls, the floor—really anything except him. But in the same way he owed me an explanation, I owed him my attention. "Whatever you did before me, that's okay. You are thousands of years old, and I'm only twenty-three. I have a past at twenty-three and while the beast is a jealous entity by nature, it would be naïve and unfair for me to expect that nothing ever happened with anyone." He blinked in surprise, the glazed sheen I saw there slowly leaving. "I don't care what kind of relationship you and Iona had. You're with me now, and what you do now is what matters to me. Not who or what you were then. Alright?"

His lips parted, and he stared at me, the flicker of hope in him growing.

"I never loved her," he blurted out. The beast preened at that. Inside me a warm fuzzy feeling spread before cooling rapidly. There was the L-word again. It seemed to be popping up all over the place now that we were in Hell, and I wasn't sure I was ready to face the confession I suspected was coming next. "Not like I lo—" I lifted a single finger to his lips, keeping those words safe between them.

"It's okay. I'm not just saying that." I paused at the flash of hurt that went through him. No one told me how much more difficult my simpler gifts would be with four partners. The Horsemen experienced emotions on a spectrum that human boys I'd been with didn't seem capable of. I found it incredibly attractive, but it also scared me.

I had everything to lose in this moment, including those words—which is why I couldn't have them. Not yet.

"You stopped me," he murmured against my finger.

I nodded. "For now." Licking my lips, I pressed them together and then continued. "I don't want to remember here and now, with her between us, as the moment you first told me that. I want it to be without pressure or the trials to come looming over us. I want to look back in another thousand years and have it been a moment to remember. Can you give that to me?" I asked him, a subtle purr entering my voice. Inwardly I lifted an eyebrow at the beast and she shrugged flippantly. When had she ever given a shit what I thought?

"I can," he said in slight growl.

The truth of his words resonated in me, and I didn't need Moira's gift to know that he meant it.

"Good. I'm not your owner or your keeper. We're in a partnership, and just like you trust me—I trust you—and that includes making it clear to other females who you're with." My tone wasn't demanding, but there was no room for negotiations or protest. "If you're going to be with me, then you're with me and that's it. If you wouldn't like seeing another male do it to me, don't let someone else do it with you. Understand?"

He nodded slowly, not out of hesitation, but the growing desire inside. Where the empty hole of pain and misery consumed him, that bitterness fueled an underlying need for me. A need to feel something as bright as that blossoming hope and burning fire.

He'd given me a piece of his darkness in his brand and I found it comforting. Maybe he could find peace in my fire.

Rysten lifted his hand to my face, slowly pushing my hair back so he could curl his fingers around my jaw possessively. "You're the only one I want, Ruby. You're the only one I've ever wanted and seeing you here, something just feels so...right. Like it was meant to be. I don't believe in fate or destiny, because I knew your old man. At the end of the day, he was just a man. But you"—he swallowed hard but didn't look away —"you're different, Ruby. Special. And I don't mean because of the brands you wear or the power you hold. You're like fire, and you're going to light up this entire world." A blush crept up my cheeks in the low light of the cave, but with any luck I didn't look like a blueberry. "I'll protect the brand I put on your skin with every breath I have, from now until the very end."

Beneath the warm skin of his palm the brand pulsed with a dark magic that filled me with a very different kind of burning. Desire thickened the air with a headiness that had me swaying for reasons other than exhaustion.

I pulled away abruptly and took a few steps deeper into the cave, flashing him a coy smile over my shoulder. "Are you joining me or standing there waiting for an invitation?"

A smile with just a hint of darkness crept up on his lips, making my heart clench in my chest. I turned back and continued deeper into the cave without waiting. He would follow. Just as he followed me into Pandora's box, and through New Orleans, and even straight to the throne.

A trickling sound pulled my attention to the four-foot gap between one rock and the next, a faint blue light shimmered within. I stepped through the gap and stood two feet from the edge of the first body of water. It was no bigger than a hot tub and heavy steam floated like fog above its surface. Multiple pools in various sizes surrounded the first, staggering in levels and overflowing from one to the next. Overhead a rocky shelf acted as a waterfall that rained down a heavier stream of glowing liquid into the highest pool.

I grasped the edge of my shirt, feeling eyes on my back. With a quick yank outward, the buttons popped and the flannel fell open. I let it slip off my shoulders, falling to my feet in a pile of dirty fabric and torn threads. Fingers ghosted my back, silently asking permission. I swept my hair over one shoulder and glanced back at Rysten, lifting a single eyebrow. Daring him.

He undid my bra in a single motion and it fell to the ground as a slight groan escaped his lips. He wrapped his arms around me from behind, coarse hands trailing up and down my naked sides, squeezing the flesh at my hips as he pulled me flush against him.

I ground my ass back into his erection, feeling the thickness as he ground into me in return.

"Too many clothes," he whispered around my neck. Lips trailed down the column of my throat, triggering an adrenaline rush like a hit of ecstasy straight to my bloodstream.

"Take my jeans off me," I said softly.

His cock twitched before he pulled away, following my command without even a flicker of hesitation. Sometimes I wanted someone else to take the reins—to let go and feel the release of power— and sometimes I wanted to dominate—to give the orders and feel the power I held over them. Regardless, I was always in control. With my four mates that was possible. They were comfortable with sharing and with each of them I took on a different role that suited our relationship.

With Rysten, our lives were complicated and messy, but our sex didn't have to be. Neither of us were shy without clothes on, and in my transition, I'd learned every inch of him. I looked forward to exploring it again and again.

I turned around to make it easier for him to undress me and was greeted by the sight of Rysten on his knees. He undid the laces on both of my boots, taking the time to take off my shoes, then my socks, before gliding his hands over my pants. I loved the way he made every act something both sensual and caring.

I reached for his hair, running both my hands through his honey-blonde strands without reservation. He groaned again, resting both his own hands at my hips while I pulled hard enough on his hair to force his head back.

"How does it feel when I touch you?" I whispered. I was well aware that the touch of a fully transitioned succubus was like an aphrodisiac, and while the Horsemen had greater self-control than most...I was their equal and they weren't unaffected.

"Like Heaven," he bit out as I dug my nails into his scalp. "Like Hell," he amended, drawing a chuckle from me. I eased my grip, letting his head fall forward. He looked up at me with a devilish glint in his eyes that set my blood to a boil.

"Undo my jeans," I whispered. Biting into the plump flesh of my bottom lip as his fingers skimmed the sensitive skin around the edge of the fabric, popping the button so that it echoed in the cave. Our breathing was hard and heavy, and he hadn't even really touched me yet.

"Lower the zipper," I ground out as his breath fanned over my skin, driving me crazy. He took an agonizingly long time to follow my command, the tips of his fingers running over my thin panties while he did so.

"Now hook your thumbs in the sides of my jeans"—I sucked in a tight breath at the way his nails skimmed straight down my skin—"like that," I groaned.

He looked up at me with an amused smile that said far more than words. While he followed every instruction without refute, it was very much his choice—just the same as I followed Allistair and Julian in the bedroom. The soft scrape of his nails kept me grounded in the moment, here with him and only him.

"And now?" he asked, knowing damn well what his slight touches did to me.

"Take them off."

Rysten had a way of making tenderness sexy. He didn't dive in for the kill or hurriedly rip my clothes off me. He savored me. Slowly, achingly slow, he peeled my jeans and underwear down my legs. Lifting one foot at a time, he placed a gentle kiss on each of my toes, pulling the rough material off me entirely until I stood there naked while he was clothed.

I dropped my hands from his hair to either side of his face, guiding it upward as I leaned down and placed a brazen kiss on his lips, purposely cutting my tongue on his fang.

Rysten took a stuttered breath as the taste of my blood coated both our lips.

When I pulled away, his eyes dilated locking onto the smear of blue. I'd noticed his fascination with my blood over the months, though he never said a word. Now was as great a time as ever to see if my shade had a secret fetish he'd kept from me. Given his reaction and the rumors about blood and sex, I was more than a little curious to see how far I could push before he tried to bite me.

Rysten watched as I walked around the side of the water and slipped one of my feet in, letting out a content sigh. I sat down on the edge of the pool, letting the rocky surface bite into the flesh of my ass as I placed both legs in.

"Do you like this?" I asked him, our eyes locking from across the water.

"Or this?" I asked with a husky tenor as I opened my legs wide for him to see just how wet I was. Rysten swallowed, rocking forward as his eyes traveled the length of my body. I dipped my hand in the water and left a trickle of liquid as I ran it up my thigh, two of my fingers dipping down to rub myself. His eyes flashed, the veins darkening to black like they did when strong emotions were at play. "That's what you like, isn't it?" I willed the words from his mouth.

"Yes," he answered and no more. I pinched my clit between two fingers and pulled, drawing a low moan from him.

"Undress for me," I commanded. My fingers stayed, stroking the wetness between my legs while he whipped his shirt off and undid his own shoes. I was writhing against my hand by the time he pulled his jeans and boxers off, standing naked and glorious before me.

He didn't take a single step towards me. He was waiting for me to tell him to.

I smiled knowingly and pointed towards him with the same hand I had just been using to pleasure myself. Crooking two fingers, I breathed, "Come." He slipped into the water before me with far more grace than I possessed. His feet touched the bottom, the water resting just above his waist, completely transparent.

Only when he stood before me, between my legs but still no contact, did I find the physical distance unbearable. "Touch me."

It was all he needed to hear.

Rysten reached forward, cupping my face in both his hands and then he kissed me. Licking and sucking and biting my lips, he slipped his tongue in my mouth and tasted me. I moaned into him, my hips jumping forward, closer to the edge of the pool so the I could wrap my legs around his waist.

"How'd you know?" he said against my lips.

"Know what?" I asked, the question punctuated with a moan as his fangs scraped over my bottom lip.

"Blood. How did you know I'd be into the blood?" He left my mouth, trailing his lips over my jaws and down my neck leaving tiny nibbling bites, although nothing like the bites I felt like he wanted to give.

"First time," I breathed as his hands wrapped around my hips, lifting me clean off the edge to place me as close as I could possibly get to him, the tip of his cock brushing over the wet opening between my thighs. Close, but not close enough.

"Explain," he demanded, biting a little harder at my collarbone. I gasped and he pulled back, his eyes wide. "I didn't mean to—"

"Shhh," I whispered, putting a finger to his lips. "The first time we kissed you cut my lip and licked the blood away. It didn't take a genius to figure out you might have a thing for it." I gave him a smile and tilted my head.

"I don't like hurting you, though." A very pained look came over him and I wrapped my arms around his neck, trying to pull him closer again. He didn't budge.

"You're not hurting me," I sighed. "And even if you were, I wouldn't mind it. I like pain, Rysten. I *like* biting and scratching—but I *love* having it done to me."

His frown fell away, but he was still hesitant when he leaned back in. I ran my fingers through his hair, letting my nails bite into the skin at the base of his neck.

"I'm not my brother," he growled.

"I don't want your brother right now. I want you," I growled back. "I want you to show me how good this can feel without the transition coloring what's between us," I whispered, slightly less aggressive.

He placed his lips to my throat in a gentle kiss. "You promise to tell me if it hurts?"

Out of all my lovers, Rysten had the most will power when it came to me, but like he said himself, at the end of the day he was just a man— powerful though he may be. A man I could bring to his knees and savor all the same.

"I promise," I whispered back, loving the pressure of his wet fingers gripping my ass as he moved us through the water. My back hit an uneven edge and one of his hands came around to rub up and down my slit. I arched my back off the rocky edge, throwing my head back in abandon as two fingers entered me and started moving in and out. His thumb pressed against my clit making me squirm, and his other hand roughly gripped my backside.

"I've wanted to do this ever since that night I accidentally tasted you," he whispered against me. A hazy blanket of lust came over me as his teeth tested that tender bit of flesh at the crook of my throat. I pressed closer and his teeth came down hard, breaking the skin as he bit me. The pain, if I could even call it that, was fleeting as my orgasm ripped through me. His fingers twisted inside my seeping flesh and curled to hit my G-spot, while his lips—warm on my neck—drank all that I gave.

Just as I drank all that he gave. Kama gathered on his pores and stirred in the air around us like fallen snow. I breathed it in, reveling in the power this gave me. He gave me.

"I want to be inside you," he groaned. Not quite a question, but still seeking permission.

"Sit on the edge of the pool. I want to ride you."

He wasted no time, lifting me onto the rock and then pulling himself out. Water dripped from his body and onto the warm floor as he took a seat on the ledge, reaching for me as I reached for him. With my legs straddled on either side his hips, I reached between us and guided myself down onto him. My mouth fell open as pure pleasure invaded my senses.

"Oh, fuck yes," I moaned, lifting up and then dipping down. His hands gripped my thighs, slick and soaking from the pool as we both climbed higher and higher.

He leaned forward, pressing his mouth to my nipple and sucking while I chased my release. He rolled the puckered flesh between his teeth, and I knew he was going to bite me a moment before he did. I arched my back, pushing my breast more fully into his mouth. His fangs latched into me—sending me right over the edge.

My mouth fell open in a silent scream as my second orgasm ripped through me, harder and far more brutal than the first. My thighs quaked as I rocked against him, my inner walls clinging to every inch of hardness as his body fed mine. Kama rained down in a torrent as his own release followed on the heels of mine. Thrusting upwards he pumped into me, gripping my hips so that I couldn't move. My knees burned and water pricked the corners of my eyes from the intensity as the last of my shudders died out and we went limp in each other's arms.

CHAPTER ELEVEN

"Everybody decent back here?" Moira hollered from behind the chunk of rock that kept the pools hidden from anyone walking by.

"Ummmm," I drawled, looking over at our piles of discarded clothing. The last thing I wanted was to put on all those dirty, sweaty layers. We didn't have soap, but I felt as close to clean as I was going to get until we reached Inferna. "Is there any chance you have some clean clothes with you?"

Moira let out a harrumph and I could imagine how she was rolling her eyes. "As it so happens, I do." She tossed a stack of clothing through the gap that landed in a heap about six inches from us. "Because you are so unbelievably predictable. I hope you at least made him crawl before you got the D—"

"Okay, thanks, we'll be out in a few," I replied, falsely chipper.

"I've been told to tell you that you have five minutes before Julian comes back here. So, when I say get dressed, I mean—"

"We're coming, greenie," Rysten called back lazily.

A stream of expletives was the only reply she gave as she walked away.

I shook my head at him, lips pursed as I climbed out of the water and reached for the only towel she brought. "Dibs?" I asked, sheepishly holding up the corner of it.

He grinned. "Go ahead. I can use it when you're done."

"Well, in that case, don't mind if I do." I quickly dried off and wrung my hair out three times before handing the towel over.

I dressed in the undergarments Moira brought me, groaning at the insanely tiny jean shorts. Her version of revenge for leaving her so I could have it out with Rysten. I shook my head but donned the booty shorts. We were low on clothes down here, so unless Allistair wanted to magically conjure me a pair of jeans, beggars couldn't be choosers.

Rysten leaned against the cave wall, arms crossed over his chest and a pensive expression on his face as he watched me.

"What?" I asked as I tugged down my favorite Portland State shirt with the green Viking on it. His eyes flicked down my body but then seemed to think better of it.

"Nothing," he replied with a wink. I eyed him skeptically but took his hand as we walked back to the front of the cave.

"Finally!" Moira exclaimed, throwing her hands up in the air. "I was beginning to worry you guys were back to doing the horizontal tango again and I'd have to come get you." She threw an arm over her face dramatically, acting completely oblivious to the shade of robin's egg blue my face was probably turning.

"Moira," I hissed. "Are you really giving me shit after that time I caught you spread-eagle on the dining room table while your girlfriend—" I broke off mid-sentence as a blonde-haired, blue-eyed fiend stepped out from behind the Horsemen. The beast hissed and I plastered a brittle smile on my face. "Iona."

It was the only greeting she was getting from me, if not for the kissing thing, then for the sudden cuts running through my chest from emotions that weren't mine. I squeezed Rysten's hand trying to comfort him as best I could. The darkness dissipated to a low fog that I could mostly ignore as he squeezed my hand back.

"Ruby," she replied. Her own expression was arranged in a pleasant smile, though not genuine, and her eyes were hard as cut sapphires. She'd cut me open and bleed me dry with them if she could. I didn't need to be an empath to know that.

"Is there something I can do for you?" I asked, not trying to be rude, but not exactly kissing ass either. The tension was palpable.

"Actually, there is." Her eyes flashed for a second, flicking to Rysten then back. "There is a feast being held tonight in your honor. I came to ask if you would all attend. It would mean a great deal to the people down here, particularly those of us who are looking forward to returning home once you complete your task." Her words were saying everything right, but her eyes, the set of her lips, the eerie darkness in her heart, and the white brand snaking up the bare flesh of her neck—all said otherwise.

"We're busy," Rysten said in a cold voice beside me.

"We'd love to," I replied at the same time, internally cringing. I didn't want to. I'd actually prefer sleeping on my father's musty sex pillows over putting Rysten in the line of fire and spending any kind of time around her. I deferred from extinguishing the flames for this, though. I changed our entire course of action and put everyone at risk knowing this she-bitch was working for someone that wanted us dead. I needed to find out what she knew for this sacrifice to be worth it.

"Which is it?" Iona asked, looking between the two of us.

"We'll attend," I said firmly, giving Rysten's hand a squeeze.

"Excellent. I've taken the liberty of having an extra boat brought so that all of you and your familiars can attend. We wouldn't want you to roast down here before you could do what you need to." I nodded slowly while lifting an eyebrow in Moira's direction.

Was it just me or was she talking kind of strange? Moira nodded once, scowling at Iona. I still hadn't pieced together what kind of demon she was and that alone was unsettling.

I nodded without saying a thing and she turned for the boats.

I couldn't help feeling like I wouldn't be returning here tonight. Maybe it was paranoia or maybe it was intuition, but something in the back of my mind told me we were being led like lambs to a slaughter. I looked around at our group, from Death to the enigma, and found that they'd chosen a piss poor sacrifice.

I chuckled under my breath and Iona turned at the boats to give me a look before climbing in. I chose to get in a separate one with Rysten, along with Moira and Jax, who was being oddly silent given that we deviated from the original plan. I kept that to myself as Epona followed behind me carrying a very dramatic Bandit. He flopped down on her saddle, lounging back as if this was all very trying for him. I rolled my eyes as he threw a furry arm across his face, then peeked over the edge to see if I was looking. He rolled over and began pulling on her russet colored mane. "That's not going to make her go faster, bud." I shook my head at him, and he chortled ruefully in protest as the boat was pushed off the rocky shore. Bandit switched to gripping the edge of her saddle like a boogie board and started making clicking noises, similar to how Laran did when trying to get her to speed up. Epona and I both looked at him with varying levels of *are you shitting me?*

Jax took the duty of steering us through the Garden while Rysten dropped my hand and wrapped an arm around my shoulders, pulling me close. He placed a tender kiss on my forehead and the tension in my shoulders melted.

"I hope you know what you're doing, love," he whispered.

"Trust me," I whispered back.

"Always."

A steady beat filled the cavern, a deep bass thumping to a lyrical tune. Music called to us, different from the overly machine-edited music on Earth. There was something more primal to this. Almost animalistic in a way. As it drew our attention, flickers of yellow and orange danced against shadows as we approached a cave on the other side of the river. It was so large that I wasn't sure if cave was the right word. The entrance was a hundred feet wide, and tall enough for even Rhiannon to wander inside without a problem. On the rocky beach, a smoldering bonfire roared while masked demons danced erotically and intimately with each other. Where I came from this sort of thing had been looked down upon, considered taboo even. Not in Hell, it seemed.

Our boat came to a halt so abrupt it pulled me from my stupor, but Rysten kept a firm grip on my waist to keep me from tumbling over. Bandit, the devil-damned raccoon, threw his hands in the air and fell to the side. Moira's wing shot out, catching him just before he could hit the water and the little bugger had the actual nerve to hiss and pout at her for stopping his fun. I wasn't taking any chances after the ordeal with the Kraken, even if the water was crystal clear.

She lifted her cradled wing and deposited him into the bottom of the boat. Bandit jumped to his feet and let out a mewling cry as he palmed at my bare leg to be helped up.

"He's worse than a child," Moira groaned.

"At least he doesn't talk back," I muttered, scooping him up.

"No, instead he grows to be thirty-feet tall and picks you up like he's goddamned King Kong," Moira griped.

"She's got a point," Rysten said, eyeing Bandit distrustfully. I stepped out of his warmth to climb onto the shore, taking a deep breath before I turned to face the demons gathered.

"This isn't so bad, yet," I said. We moved closer to the writhing group of dancers. They were covered in paint and adorned with flowers, while wearing their exquisite and terrifying masks. I could admire the beauty in it, if the magic pulsing through the air hadn't been so constricting. Thick and heady; the closer I came to them, the more it invaded me.

"*Yet*. That's the key word there," Rysten murmured, staying close to me. I didn't fault him with the way I could feel eyes on us, and Iona sidled up beside me.

"They're celebrating the rise of their new queen," she said. I nodded, my eyes darting around for the catch but seeing only smiling faces.

Were they all in on this? Was it just Iona? What about the kids that ran through the groups of people throwing flowers in the air and chanting in a language I didn't understand?

I swallowed hard.

"All of this is for me?" I asked, more than a little skeptical.

"It is," she smiled, waving to the children that approached us.

They wore slipper-like shoes and bright swaths of clothing. Their faces and arms were painted, but also smudged with dirt. A little girl with green skin held up a flower lei. It was made of lilies.

"For me?" I asked. She nodded. I took the lei and slipped it over my head, a distant feeling of ease slowly setting in.

"Lady Iona said you're going to stop the fire. Are you going to stop it?" Her curly green hair framed her paint-smudged face. The imprint of flower petals plastered against her glistening, sweaty skin. Large green eyes the color of spring grass looked up at me with hope, and fear—and more than anything—desperation.

I took both of her trembling hands in mine and sank to my knees, wincing from the bite of the gravel.

"What's your name?" I asked her.

"Elissa," she said in her high-pitched voice.

"That's a beautiful name," I said, a faint upturn to my lips, though I couldn't bring myself to really smile.

"My daddy picked it, but he's gone now."

It took every fiber of my being not to turn away under the weight of the young girl's gaze. There was an accusation in her green eyes that left me with guilt, whether or not it was rightfully mine.

"I'm sorry about your dad. I'm going to do everything I can to stop the flames."

My words rang hollow and the girl backed away. I let her hands drop between us, not understanding what she muttered. It sounded foreign. Melodic. I glanced up at Rysten, but he looked away. A deep frown marred his face and his eyebrows were drawn together in concern. Whatever worries I had about this being a terrible idea, that didn't soothe them.

Slowly, I rose to my feet.

"There's a lot like her, aren't there?" I asked quietly.

Iona nodded. "Unfortunately, yes. Very few are immune to the flames, as I'm sure you know." She cast me a sideways glance that almost seemed like...pity.

"You know," I started, not entirely sure where I was going to go with this but following my gut, "I never knew that I was Lucifer's kid and had this grand destiny laid out for me. When the Horsemen found me, I didn't even think I was a full demon." I smiled at the memory, remembering the way I'd ordered them out of my house. Back then I thought I could close my eyes to it. That if I ignored it long enough, this thing called fate would pick someone else.

Iona glanced sideways like she didn't believe it. "How did you *not know* you were a full demon?" Her voice was incredulous, but I nodded anyway, pretending not to notice it.

"I'm twenty-three and I only just finished my transition four days ago." Her eyes widened almost comically, the reality that was my life seeming to set in. "Before that I just had minor powers. Persuasion. Immunity to fire. Succubus *charm*." I very pointedly left off soul-shredding because she really didn't need to know that. It was a power I was going to save in my back pocket. A just-in-case for when everything else failed.

"The flames?" she asked, her eyes slowly trailing down me like she was only just seeing me for the first time.

"Came to me after the Horsemen showed up, shortly before my transition." I snorted, thinking back at it. "I accidentally started a fire in my living room the morning after they manifested. The Horsemen wanted to whisk me away then…" and just like that, the humor dissipated.

"But they didn't."

I nodded. "But they didn't." She silently looked ahead still, listening to me but not outwardly giving me her attention. Her expression was neutral, indifferent, but as she watched these people something inside her softened. Something that couldn't be seen with eyes, only felt with emotions. "I wasn't ready," I said, admitting the very thing aloud that she would probably hate me for. Part of me felt compelled to speak; to tell her this even though I knew it would likely not win me any favors. "I had no idea how to control the flames. My life was falling apart around me and I hadn't even transitioned yet. At the time I was very…mortal. It was a weakness that I knew would cost me my life if I set foot in Hell before I was ready for it."

"So, you put your life before everyone else's because you weren't *ready?*"

"Iona," Rysten snapped, choosing to step forward. I placed a hand on his arm and gave him the look. The one that told him to stay out of it.

"No, she's right." He opened his mouth to dispute that and come to my aid, but I didn't want or need to be saved. Not from this. "I did put everyone in danger because I wasn't ready. I did, and I can own that." I turned to her and found the blue of her eyes so similar to the color of my flame it was piercing. "But I also had no idea what would happen to Hell. I don't know how much you know about Earth, but I was raised there with humans and without the knowledge of who or what I am. I had no idea what I was capable of. I didn't know that I should try to prepare myself for my new life so many people, like Elissa, wouldn't suffer."

"And if you had?"

"I can't say whether I would have come sooner," I answered honestly. "I think I would have tried, but if I hadn't learned to control the flames, I likely would have only made things worse."

"How do you figure that?" She raised her eyebrows and still I smiled.

"Ever since I got here, I've been working to put out the flames. I can't do anything about the borders until the Sins confirm, but I've been trying to stop it as best I can." She narrowed her eyes a fraction, but didn't dispute it. "If I hadn't learned to control them before I came, I likely wouldn't be able to put anything out and would have lost control, killing everyone instead."

"That's rather prideful of you to assume."

"It's also true."

She gazed at the people around us, but this time it wasn't like she was really seeing them, she just didn't want to see me. "You are not what I expected you would be," she said eventually. "Your youth and ignorance make you both ideal and not for the position you wish to hold. So far you have fallen from your father, but I am unable to forgive or forget the monster he was. While much of Hell mourned, there were many of us that also celebrated."

"I have no idea what kind of person my father was," I said quietly.

"I know," she answered. "That's why I'm telling you." While the echoes and shouts of excitement played, and the shadows danced with their demon counterparts, Iona, Rysten, and I stood apart from it all.

"While many regarded him as the savior of this world, he was also the destroyer. I know, because I was alive when the first true Queen of Hell ruled." I blinked. *First? There was a first?* I wanted to turn to Rysten but Iona's knowing smile kept me watching her. "Her name was Genesis, and this was known as the Garden of Eden. Few remember because most that were there died in the war between immortals. I was only a child myself when Satan bridged the gap between this world and Heaven. His arrival was the beginning of the true fall for this realm."

"What happened to Genesis?" I blurted out. "How did she die and Lucifer become King?"

"No one knows what truly happened to her. Only that she fell madly in love with your father and he didn't return her affections. Genesis died and the entire world shook from her loss. Storms raged. The seas revolted. Genesis was a being of *life*, a creator, who wanted nothing more than to have children of her own. In her death, that's exactly what happened."

My heart beat like the clapping of hooves as the blood pounded in my ears. I could tell this was it. I was on the precipice of what I needed to know.

"While she had made what you now know as demons long before your father's arrival, her death created two beings from the essence of her. Two young girls that much of the world believed held the true claim to the throne."

"Lilith and Eve," I murmured.

She nodded once. "Lilith and Eve. The Fae were born from Genesis's demise, but they were only babies when your father took power."

Suddenly things were beginning to make sense and I could understand why the people in this world might wish that I didn't exist. Lucifer wasn't from Hell either, but nothing stopped him from coming in and claiming it, meanwhile their true ruler died and left behind children that had been denied a birthright. "But now he's dead…" I said hoarsely, my voice hardly more than a whisper.

"Now he's dead," Iona agreed. "And I can't say that I'm sad, but I do pity you." She fingered the flower lei around her neck and mine suddenly felt like a vice. Not just any flowers. *Lilies…*

Deep in my bones I knew it then. It was something I couldn't explain because I only had pieces. Parts. They ran together in my memories. Every flash of a flowered white tattoo that was branded on someone meant to kill me. The imp. The blood magic. The silent *she* that lurked in the back, just waiting for the day to return to her throne.

Eve had come to Earth and died. She created a race of children to hunt demons. The stories of that were clear.

But her sister…

"Do you believe she deserves to rule?" I asked Iona. Emotions collided within me as I struggled to focus on what to think of this. What to feel. Was I truly Queen? Or was I an imposter?

Either way, the flash of surprise in Iona's face couldn't be masked.

She knew what and who I was referencing, still she said, "I don't know who you mean."

"Lilith," I spat her name, causing several around us to look in our direction. Rysten's hand appeared on my lower back and I knew he had moved closer. "Do you believe she deserves to rule?"

Her eyes were conflicted. "I…" She looked away from me, like my gaze was suddenly too much to handle. Guilt swam within in her, followed by regret. Whatever they had planned to do was already in motion, except it wasn't demon magic I needed to truly watch for. No, it wasn't demons at all —but Fae. "I don't think it matters who or what I want anymore. It's not going to change anything."

The words had barely left her lips when a banshee's scream made the ground shudder. My head split in two as Moira's pain flooded me and whatever kindness I felt for the she-demon beside me dissipated.

CHAPTER TWELVE

BLUE FLAMES RUSHED up my arms as I glared at Iona.

"Was this all just a distraction?" I asked, even though I already knew. How foolish I'd been thinking it was Iona I needed to watch. She'd lured me into a den of demons and I'd sang and skipped alongside her, all the while telling myself my eyes were wide open.

I was a fool, but a fool with power.

"There's that Morningstar temper that your father was known for," she murmured. I shook my head and took off through the crowd. Iona would have to deal. First, I needed to find—

"Ruby!" Rysten yelled, his fingers wrapping around my wrist and pulling me to a halt. I looked back at him and a sense of dread filled my stomach. Was he going to try to stop me? "Laran just disappeared. No one can get ahold of him."

Fuck. I was really beginning to wish that I had just lit her ass on fire and been done with it.

"Find him." We locked eyes and silently I was hoping—praying to the beast, to Lucifer, to the Sins, and the monster I knew—I prayed that someone was listening and we would all make it out of here alive.

Rysten nodded and then disappeared into the shadows.

Alone with only my fire and my wits, I ran, following that wisp of a string that tied Moira and I together as people. That bond that would forever keep her by my side.

"Moira!" I yelled, crashing through the crowd. My feet slipped on something liquid and I fell to my knees before her. The crowd jumped back as I waved my arms wide, shooing them away.

She convulsed sporadically, her head whipping side to side. Her eyes squeezed shut and teeth clenched together, I looked her over but could find nothing wrong.

Across from me, Jax kneeled with his eyes closed and hands resting flat over her.

He would be the picture of serenity if I didn't know that inside him a storm was brewing.

Like me, he was trying to figure out what was wrong. His hands clenched into fists as he pulled away.

"It makes no sense," he mumbled, more to himself than anything.

"What doesn't make sense?" I snapped, clutching her thrashing head in my hands. I moved to place it on my lap, scared she might crack her own skull if this kept up. "What are you talking about?"

"Her!" he yelled. "She told me she wasn't feeling well, then she collapsed. I assumed it was magic, but..." His words trailed off as the brand on her forehead began to glow. I had no idea what that meant, but I bet we were about to find out. "There's no trace of magic on her. If there were, I could stop it. Whatever she's fighting..." he swallowed and looked up at me. "I have no idea what it is."

"Fuck," I growled, wanting to smash my fists in the ground and set it all alight. The beast was already gnashing her teeth, begging to be let out, but I wanted to handle this—I needed to handle this—to show myself that I could.

With no Horsemen, no Bandit, and no fucking clue what I was facing, I had to come to terms with that fact that I was severely outnumbered, outmaneuvered, and out of my depth.

"Moira," I rocked her head side to side. "I need you to wake up, babe." Desperation wasn't leaking into me anymore. It was pouring out of me profusely. "Wake up, Moira. Come on." The fire from my hands engulfed her and the thrashing stopped. I had no idea what I was doing, only that last time my fire saved her and maybe it could again.

But nothing happened.

She burned. She breathed.

And yet, she didn't wake.

I pulled away, letting out a frustrated growl. Jax remained silent, watching as I turned to the masked onlookers. "What did you do?" I asked them.

No one answered.

"What. Did. You. Do?" I repeated again, slower. Deadlier. Terror was eating at me. Terror over Moira's unconscious body. Terror over Laran's disappearance. I came down here to find answers and felt like I was going to find an early grave instead.

"They did nothing, Lucifer's Daughter," came a voice.

It was sweet and innocent and all things good in the world. Deception at its finest. Evil at its worst. Darkness that hides under a mask of light and beauty.

"Lilith," I whispered.

"My, my, what a clever girl."

"What did you do to her?" I asked, hating how weak I sounded. Wishing I was half as strong as the world seemed to believe.

She let out a trilling laugh, reminiscent of windchimes. "Much like your mother, not clever enough," she replied sweetly, ignoring my question entirely. My blood boiled.

Moira's head slid from my lap as I laid it on the ground and rose to my feet. Her footsteps were soundless, but the swaths of fabric from her dress brushed the stone. The pounding of my blood filled my ears as she came into view. The woman of my nightmares.

Was it a strange twist of fate that I was the Devil's daughter and she looked like an angel?

Golden eyes blinked down at me and lips that were the palest shade of pink turned at the corners to form a smile. Her gown was made of the whitest gossamer I'd ever seen. So wholesome. So pure. Her hair blended into the billowy fabric as it swayed around her.

"You even look like her." She nodded with the slightest purse to her lips. Disdain, I realized. "But your eyes, those are all your *father's*," she said with a breathy sigh, moving closer to place two fingers under my chin so she could see them clearly

I shuddered against her cool fingers as her nails grew sharp.

The beast decided right then and there that she'd had enough, shoving forward long enough to light her ass on fire. Lilith's grip didn't falter as the flames licked up her fingers, over her hand, halfway up her arm, and the skin beneath remained unearthly pale and smooth.

I'd expected her to burn and this to all be over. I expected my gifts that made me powerful to not fail me. With a cold realization I came to the crux of this. I expected to always and forever be more powerful. To be invincible.

And in thinking that I forgot the very lessons that kept me alive all the years before I had any power to my name.

She cocked an eyebrow, a smirk forming on her face as I scrambled to hide the stricken expression on my own. The flames didn't burn her, which meant I wasn't just in trouble. This time, I was utterly screwed.

The white of her dress turned as black as the essence of her soul. Stripped of her ethereal beauty and cast in only glittering ashes, Lilith stood before me as the last of the fire winked out, and with it, my only hope.

Sin had stripped me of my telepathy. Lilith had taken the fire. Moira was down and Bandit was nowhere to be found. While the Horsemen weren't accounted for, something told me they wouldn't be showing up to save my ass just in time.

I was on my own and my enemy was literally the Queen of the Unseelie. She was about as ancient as it gets.

"Such fire, young one. Your father had that too." She smiled fondly for a moment, her expression nostalgic as she disappeared into a memory. Whatever she was thinking, her heart beat for it. Before I could draw any conclusions her eyes sharpened again, and that same smile turned brittle. Disparaging. "And now that fire will be mine."

"I hate to break it to you"—I paused, turning my cheek to wrench my face away from her grasp—"but that's not possible."

I'd never seen anything so beautiful or wicked like the look she gave me. I swallowed hard against the dryness in my throat. "There was a time when I thought so too, but then you were born and it changed everything."

"What?" To my credit, my voice never wavered, but inside...the beast was silent. Watching. That worried me.

"Well, Lucifer's Daughter, that story started a very long time ago. Back when I was just a girl and your father was just the King—the one who stole my title." Her teeth were pointed and her nails were claw-tipped, but in that brief flash of a second, I saw a woman with mercury eyes and not gold. That realization came too little too late. Still, I kept her talking.

"You see, your father was not a demon as many believed, but a primordial. Just like Genesis. Just like God. One of the fun little quirks of their species is that they can bind themselves to a planet, and by extension its power. But when that being dies…well, so does the planet. Unless, there's another primordial to bond to it." That sense of dread was now magnified. It settled in my stomach and clawed its way up my throat, taking hold of my heart like a parasite—one intent on never letting go.

"Hell started to implode, just as it is doing now—except last time Lucifer bonded to it. He saved the planet and the people made him King. *Not you.*" Those last words were whispered like a goodbye.

If she was suggesting what I thought she might be…the muscles of my empty stomach spasmed as I fought the urge to gag up bile.

"You are clever," she said and clapped happily, but it was all a farce. Did her followers see it too? "Yes. The original Six that Genesis made struck a deal with your dear daddy, and it was only after I got rid of my sister, Eve, that he even found me competent enough to become the Sin of Pride, reducing me to one of his whores instead of giving me my rightful place as Queen." Her hand clenched into a fist and I wondered if she saw the way her pride truly did eat at her. If I had to guess, my father was probably not a good man, but I couldn't see him being worse than this. Worse than her. "I spent centuries trying to convince him to get rid of the other Six, but your daddy—he just had too much *love*, as he would say. I waited, biding my time until he eventually knocked one of them up. In hindsight, I should have known it would be Lola. He always did want what he couldn't have."

There were so many things about this story that struck me as wrong, but I didn't interrupt because I needed every second to try and find a way out of this situation. Chances were if she was immune to the flames, she was immune to other things too, and even if I could get her down, there were still *hundreds* of demons I'd have to fight off as well. I needed to think.

*Think…think…*a slight numbing settled over my skin. A fuzziness entered my brain as I tried to puzzle my way out of this one.

"Are you feeling alright, dear?" she asked, pulling me from my stupor. My pores clogged with sweat as the heat truly pressed down on me. "I must say, I was worried it wouldn't work. But your father fell for the same trick."

I tried to open my mouth but couldn't form the words. My tongue lolled and my head felt too heavy. I squinted as the lights behind her flashed. My feet stumbled even though I was standing up… then my knees hit the cave floor and my heart began hammering into overdrive.

"Lilies grown in the soil of crushed pure black lotus on the Brimstone City will take on the same qualities, except it's far more potent. One touch to the skin or inhaling its scent is enough to kill the average demon within minutes, which is why no one *dares* grow them. As it is, this will likely only incapacitate you for half an hour at most." She paused to laugh…and laugh and laugh. There was a true madness to it and my stomach turned sour. I thought of the children who'd brought them to us. Their hands were bare.

"The children…" In my heart I knew my search would come up empty if I scanned the crowd for that small child called Elissa. My revulsion for this woman that wanted to crown herself a queen only deepened.

"Were orphans. Lower demons with no parents to care for them and no purpose of their own. I gave them a purpose. They were carriers of my crown." Even as she said it, several faces in the crowd turned away. Iona was among them, her eyes glued to the ground. She'd so shamelessly scorned me for a father I never knew, and yet…

I gagged, but no bile would come up. Lilith scrunched her nose with disgust, rolling her golden eyes as she flicked a lock of white hair away from her face.

"You're a monster," I spat as best I could.

"I am," Lilith admitted. "But aren't we all?" She motioned to the demons beyond.

I shook my head and the very ground itself seemed to move. I gritted my teeth, panting hard through the wave of nausea that flooded me. The world had slowed to a crawl.

"Not like…you," I rasped, struggling to make my lips work. Spit flew as I spluttered and shook.

"It's almost time," she said and smiled. "And here you thought I was talking because I wanted to entertain your childish notions. Pathetic girl." She squatted down and put her face eye level to mine. "Unlike Eve and I, you were born with the beast. Your father knew that, so he bound your powers and the monster in a bid to hide you from me so that I would focus on him. It worked for a time, until I realized something. Why wait to control you when I could have the beast all the same?" In my steadily worsening state I saw the monster beneath her skin. The true Lilith—and it was a terrible sight to behold. "Well, I tried and I failed—killing both him and the beast in the process—but you, Ruby, are my second chance. I learned from him where I went wrong and brought you out of hiding at the same time." She breathed in deeply, inhaling my scent before releasing it like a sigh of relief. "Now, I will have the power of the primordial and reclaim my throne, and you, dear girl, are the one who will help me."

She pressed a chaste kiss to my lips that made me squirm. Her tongue slid over my teeth and she bit down sharply on my bottom lip, pulling back to smear my blood all over her bottom lip like it was the greatest of delicacies. I'd done something not so different with Rysten only hours ago, but the perverted way she went about it made my stomach turn again.

"Mmmm, you even taste like him too," she mused.

Crazy. I didn't know if Lilith was always nuts or —if like Eve—time had turned her, but I needed to find a way out of here right now. A gurgled cry of outrage slid from my lips as she stood to walk away.

In that moment it was do or die, and just like with Danny and the imp, I turned to my last gift.

Blinking once, I opened my eyes and sought out for her soul. It may work. It may not. I was out of options and the Horsemen clearly weren't coming.

I focused on that swirling pit of black in her chest and reached for it—
Only to be blocked.

Impossible.

At least I thought it was. It seemed the more I learned, the more I realized how little I knew. Or how deep the bonds of betrayal could go. Out of the corner of my eye a second figure strode forth, and whatever hope I had of escaping fizzled out completely.

"Siiiin," I moaned. Allistair had warned me. He said that Sin looked out for no one but Sin, and I'd foolishly believed her instead of him. I'd stupidly listened to the emotions I felt instead of the words I heard.

And now it was going to cost me *everything*.

She walked by without sparing me a glance and dropped to one knee. Her head bowed as she uttered, "Mother."

Lilith smiled and it all became so clear. "My dearest one," she purred. Her claw-tipped hands stroked Sin's hair with undeniable fondness. "I knew when you were born that you would be the one to liberate me, and now, I will liberate you. Sinumpa, Heir of the Unseelie, Daughter of Cain, Child of Mine—you are released from your blood oath of service."

Lilith sliced a cut from the corner of Sin's eye to her cheek, leaving a scarlet tear. Blood welled on the tip of her claw as she cut her palm. The wound on Sin's cheek glowed red and then hardened. A scar.

"You are free, Sinumpa, by the rules of our oath. However, this day saddens me so, and you will wear that upon your face henceforth, daughter." My lips trembled out of control from trying to speak but having no control over my body.

"Thank you, mother," Sin murmured. She leaned forward to kiss Lilith's feet and nausea rolled. This is her master. The woman behind the mask. The evil that hid in plain sight. The harbinger of my own destruction.

The beast growled, thrashing about in my mind. Any control that I held was long gone, but whatever affected my body held us both prisoners, here in my mind. My consciousness was waning, even as the crowd of demons began parting to reveal...*them*. My Horsemen.

They were here, but there would be no saving me.

They couldn't even save themselves.

RYSTEN

All our lives we'd been told that our purpose was to serve the next Queen of Hell. To serve. To kneel. To fight for. To defend. To lay down our lives, and before we'd even met her, we were prepared for this day. For the day that we might not survive.

We were prepared to do anything that ensured her survival, even at the cost of our own lives.

But no one prepared us for the soul crushing desperation that would sit on our backs if failure became imminent. No one told us that the sole reason for our existence could be snuffed out with the snap of one's fingers.

No one realized that we would come to love this woman so much it hurt. So deep that it burned.

They didn't tell us those things. Protect. Serve. Defend. That was our duty, and we were happy to do it at the expense of all...until now.

I wished we'd never come back to Hell.

I wished we had let it burn and kept her far away.

I wished we had more time.

I wished for a lot of things that would never come to pass, and I knew that now. I had been smart enough to cherish those moments with her like they would never happen again. Because a small part of me had known that the duty tasked upon us would be our downfall.

And now we kneeled on the cold stone floor with poison-laced flowers around our necks, meant to kill even the strongest of demons. Even a primordial.

If Ruby was down, the truth of it was that we never had a chance.

"My boys," Lilith cooed. We weren't her anything and the vile old woman knew it. While she may have helped make us, she was no mother of ours.

Her claws patted my cheek gently, curling around my chin. She wrenched my face upward, but I kept my eyes on Ruby. On the light. No matter what happened now she needed to survive.

"You'll look at me when I speak to you, Pestilence." The prick of her nails was nothing compared to the overwhelming panic of what was to come.

We were the ones that found Lucifer's body last time she'd tried this. Or what was left of it.

I spat and a glob of iridescent blue smacked against her skin. I didn't need to look to know her features contorted with rage; the slap of her hand that sent me reeling was enough.

"The truth is, Lilith, that you're not a queen and stealing the power of the primordial won't make you one." Her foot swung out and Ruby's scream pierced the air as my head slammed into the stone floors again and again. Bone crunched, but I still only felt an inkling of what she was doing thanks to her damned poisons.

"Stop! Get your hands off him!" Ruby screamed, but the words were only barely intelligible.

Lilith stilled, pulling away from me.

"What did you say to me?" she replied in a singsong voice that rang true to madness. She was taking it as a challenge and Ruby didn't know better than to challenge the Unseelie Queen.

"Get your devil-damned hands off my Horseman," Ruby growled. Her hands curled into fists and her nails scraped at the rock beneath her, turning bloody and blue as she let out the most unholy of shrieks. It would have given Moira a run for her money.

"Well, well. You're just full of surprises, aren't you, Little Morningstar?" Lilith grinned. That only incited Ruby further. Her back bowed off the concrete as flames completely consumed her, growing brighter and brighter. I wouldn't look away, even as she grew too bright to truly see.

Her form blurred as the flames wound around her like a living, breathing entity. She didn't scream this time. She bended and bowed and contorted, but through it all she fought, and the flames raged. She forced her arms to lift her and her knees to hold. She rose with a vengeance and she walked with a purpose. "Did you really think that I would lie down and watch you do this?" she growled.

And then…she exploded.

Fire unlike anything I'd ever seen poured from her, burning out and into the cavern. It raced over the stone shores and the glowing water, snaking up the spires of every tower, crawling over every crook of the cavern walls until it was all that existed—and still she burned.

She burned more than Lucifer ever had, even in his deepest rages.

And she burned for me.

It continued for a suspended frame of time where I wasn't sure if seconds or minutes or even hours had passed. Black and blue and every color in between consumed my vision in the most glorious of blazes, but despite her raw power… despite that immense strength that was buried within her…

Despite it all, she couldn't go on forever—and Lilith still stood.

"You are strong, child," she called out, licking her lips. "I'll give you that." The fire grew thin, showing just how much Ruby had laid waste to. Lilith took an appreciative glance as stalactites fell from the ceiling into the clear waters below. The towers were blackened and crumbling. Every piece of cloth, fabric, or otherwise burned to a crisp and yet…the people were unharmed.

There was only one thing that makes a demon immune to the flames.

"Brimstone," Laran murmured beside me. He must have come to the same conclusion.

"Why won't you die?" Ruby growled in a voice that was half her and half the beast. Her eyes had gone dark, but not truly black. She was fighting for control in a battle she would not win.

"I've spent *centuries* planning, child. Did you really think I wouldn't take into account your primordial power?" Lilith laughed a slight cackle. "No, girl, I thought of everything. Including the possibility that you might be blessed with your mother's gifts."

Lilith snapped her fingers and a silver dagger appeared in her palm. Ruby's legs shook as she took another step forward. Her outpouring of power had left her weak as Lilith circled the four of us.

"What are you doing?" the beast snapped. Ruby's body jerked back and forth as they vied for power. Lilith watched with a slight smile on her lips as she came to a stop before Laran.

She reached down and grabbed a fistful of hair, wrapping it tight around her palm as she wrenched him upwards and moved to stand behind him, the silver edge of her dagger at his throat. We both knew that dagger was imbued with blood magic. "Don't let her break you. You must survive, baby girl. *For me,*" Laran called out to her.

"Teaching a lesson," Lilith said chipperly. "I only need two of them."

Ruby's eyes ran black and the beast took two trembling steps. She knew what was coming. We all did.

And it was too late.

A flick of her wrist was all it took. Laran let out a strangled noise and Ruby's legs collapsed entirely as his blood flowed straight from the vein onto the glittering ashes at her feet.

"Laran," she choked. "Laran, please don't go—" Shudders racked her shoulders as she caved in on herself. "Please don't." She pleaded with the dying demon as she crawled to him. "Laran, please…please!" she begged as tears rolled down her cheeks. She repeated his name over and over again until the gurgling stopped and the light faded from his eyes. "LARAN!" she roared in a voice that could have woken the dead.

Lilith walked to Allistair, dagger in hand, and any fight Ruby had in her was gone by the time Lilith said, "Now, then. You're not going to struggle, are you?"

She shook her head as the pieces inside her well and truly came apart. I saw it in her eyes that she knew she would die, and Lilith knew that. She knew that Ruby would give anything for us.

Including the very heart that beat in her chest.

"Take them to the water's edge, but don't let them touch it," Lilith ordered. Demons burst into action to follow her every command, and trembling fingers grasped me by the sides. I recognized them, even after three thousand years.

"I'm so sorry," Iona whispered. I didn't have the strength left to spit at her. I didn't have the will power to tell her I'd rather die than touch her. There was only one thing I wanted more in this world than to see Iona burn in that moment.

"S-save h-h-her," I whispered through my broken jaw, through the seeping blood and foggy haze. Lilith's flowers were impeding the healing.

"I can't," she murmured back. "This was the price I paid for life."

"Saaaaa—" The rest of the words never came out. I managed to keep my eyes open as Lilith approached Ruby.

My girl. Her eyes were glazed over when Lilith lifted her up like a child. She didn't struggle. She didn't speak. The spark in her eyes...it was gone.

"Ruby," Allistair wheezed beside me. "Keep… fighting… little… succubus," he groaned. She didn't respond. I felt my body being moved, partially lifted and partially dragged. After the beating to the face Lilith had given me, I should feel every shift, but it seemed that her poisonous flowers had numbed the pain, at least physically.

Iona settled me on the rocky edge of the shore, giving me a front row view of Ruby being lowered into the water. She was naked and her brands glowed faintly, the blue vines limp.

"Gather, my loyal followers, for tonight is the beginning. With this sacrifice we will create a new world. One built on the bones of our enemies." Lilith's words rang in the cavern as all stared on in silence.

"Ruby," Julian growled. "You fight her, Ruby! You don't stop—you understand me—" His words were pointless. She wouldn't lift a finger again. Not if it meant the death of one of us.

Lilith began chanting. Softly at first as she lifted the dagger over her head.

There wasn't a flash of fear in Ruby's eyes when Lilith struck her. Straight in the sternum.

A sickening snap filled the air.

Then again.

Then again.

Then again.

Lilith stabbed her until the water turned bloody and both their skin turned blue.

She stabbed her until Ruby no longer jerked with each strike of the knife.

She stabbed her until the outline of the pentagram on her chest had been cut away, and Ruby…she was only holding on by a thread. There was screaming. So much screaming. Not of Ruby herself, but the three of us bound and unable to stop this. The outcry of a pain so deep that the mind could not grasp it.

My life had been so long. So very long. Never had it felt so long as it did now. I didn't want to exist in a world where she didn't. She was my light. My soul. My whole fucking universe.

And she couldn't die.

Something snapped inside of me as Lilith began carving away at her own chest, never missing a beat in her chant. Dark magic filled the air. So vile and wicked that it threatened to put her light out, but I gave it all to her.

My magic. My strength. My will to live. I was the strongest shade ever created and I used that power to hold her together. To hold her body together. To try to heal whatever damage I could.

Even as shadows encroached on us, I gave. As a dark void rose from Ruby, I gave.

As the waters ran black, I gave.

It was only when Lilith stood before me that I knew the truth. That hopelessness finally consumed me.

She painted my chest in my mate's blood...and there was no more to give.

I had given right until the final shudder of Ruby's heart...when the world went dark. Truly dark.

And in the blackness, a voice spoke to me. A darkness I knew.

A beast of ancient power filled with so much rage that it could not be soothed after the wrong done to it. It had been stripped of the other half of its soul.

We both had.

CHAPTER THIRTEEN

Existence was such an odd thing.

One moment you are there and then you are not. Most believe that the worlds of Heaven and Hell are where you went after— the next plane of existence—but the truth is that no one really knows. Not even Death, who both lived and died on that precarious line in-between.

The veil was a place of existence, less like Hell and more like a state of mind. One that you never wake up from. And I didn't want to wake up. Not now. Not ever.

She took him from me, but what she didn't know was that I followed him well before the last breath left my body. I used that tiny sliver of magic that Death bequeathed upon me to go to the veil and hold onto him. Here we existed together. But on the other side, past the veil…I didn't know. I didn't want to know.

"You can't keep me, baby," he murmured in my ear. "You have to go on. You have to survive."

"I'm not letting you go," I said, clinging to him tighter.

"She killed me, Ruby. You can't change that," he said gently, pressing the pads of his fingers into my jaw as he cupped my face. "It's okay. We were all prepared for this." I swallowed hard and dug my nails into the hair at the base of his neck.

"I. Am. Not. Leaving. You," I whispered in a harsh voice. "It's not happening. I refuse. Do you understand me?" My bottom lip quivered as the tears threatened to fall. His eyes softened as he leaned forward and placed a kiss against my forehead. I leaned in, fighting the emotion swelling in my throat when I realized that I couldn't smell his scent; that tinge of firewood and smoke. That I never would again.

"If you stay with me, you're leaving them behind. You know that, right?" he asked me.

"They have each other. I won't leave you here alone."

"You're leaving Moira and Bandit behind. They won't survive without you." His tone was soft, sweet even. I hated it.

"Stop it," I snapped. "Stop trying to get me to leave you. You can't! I won't!" I pulled harder on his hair and it only drew a chuckle from his lips.

"I'm not making you do anything, babe. I couldn't even if I tried," he whispered against my hair. It put me at ease, but only for a moment. "I'm just telling you what you already know, and you don't want to hear it because the truth is you might be able to survive this if you leave me, but every minute you spend here is another one your body dies more." My hands shook as I held him close, afraid that if I gave any slack, for even a second, he might slip away into the great abyss beyond.

"I don't want to do this without you," I blurted out, taking an unsteady breath. "I don't want to fight Lilith. I don't want to fight for Hell. I don't want to do any of it if it means doing it without you. I don't want to be alone." Tears were falling now. Big. Fat. Ugly tears. They ran down my face and onto his chest.

"You'll never be alone, baby. You know that." But he was so wrong. I didn't know that. I didn't know what came next or when. I never knew when the next time may come that someone I loved died.

Love. Not loved. He was still here. Still with me.

"I'm not going anywhere, Laran. Not without you."

"Actually," another voice interjected. My blood ran cold. "You are."

"Sin," I spat. Laran froze as I spun around using both my hands to grip his arm behind me. "You fucked me over, Sin. This is your fault," I hissed. She narrowed her mercury eyes and cocked her head.

"I warned you. Do not blame me because you made a choice and did not like the outcome." There was a hint of caution in her tone, but I didn't care anymore. She thought this was a game and she was the one moving the pieces, but it wasn't a game for me. It was my life, and it was over, and there were no do-overs for any of us.

"You betrayed me, Sin. I don't care how you twist this. You led me here, feeding me just enough to make me think you were on my side. Laran is dead because of you!" I screamed, finally finding the fury inside. "We both are!"

Sin took a deep breath and released it in a heavy sigh. "I'm sorry for what this war has already cost you, Ruby. I truly am. I told you from the beginning to trust no one. Not even me." Her eyes…they were so old and filled with so much pain. Under different circumstances I might have pitied her. I might have understood.

But I was dead. She said it herself.

"You won't be dead for long, Little Morningstar," she said so softly I almost missed it.

"Don't call me that," I growled, and it was one hundred percent me. No inkling of the beast resided inside my soul anymore. Sin nodded.

"Say your goodbye's, Ruby. We have much to do if we're going to save Hell."

"What? No—"

"I call on the blood oath for the favor owed. You will live, Ruby, and we will fight another day."

The skin on my breast stung as the sliver of blood magic activated on her command. A pressure filled me, pushing and pulling. It disoriented my mind and pressed down on my body. If I had bones here, they might have shattered upon the weight of the blood oath as it forced me to obey its call.

"Laran," I gasped, turning into him. I wrapped my arms around his shoulders and refused to let go.

"Shhh," he whispered. "It'll be okay, baby. Go to the Sins. They'll know what to do." Then the thrashing began. I felt my body again. Every muscle spasmed, attempting to split as if the very atoms that were me could not be contained. Still, I clung to him as the magic began to pull me back.

It could take me, but I wasn't letting go. I would keep him. I didn't come this far just to lose him forever.

I couldn't do it. I wouldn't do it.

I was stronger than this. I was stronger than it all.

And somehow, I would save him too.

"I love you," he whispered. It sounded like a goodbye.

"You're not doing that, Laran. You're not leaving me. I'm right—"

A sudden dull ache filled me, like I had been dropped a hundred stories and then dragged through the street. My back was against something solid and sticky. I clenched my fingers but only found the scratch of my nails against stone.

No. No. No. Where was he? I never let go. Where was Laran?

My eyes flew open as I bent up at the waist and an onset of nausea and dizziness filled me.

"Whoa there—"

"Take it easy, Rubes—"

"Where is he?" I whispered. Broken. Splintered. I turned on Moira and her eyes shuttered. "Where is he, Moira?" I growled, louder this time. Stronger. The muscles in my chest were knitting themselves back together the more I spoke. The bones and cartilage were bending and reshaping and reconnecting the longer I was here. But it was him, the loss of him that filled me so deeply, so acutely, that every single ache and pain and slice and break was *nothing*.

"I'm sorry," she said. Her pentagram eyes swirled with emotion when she opened them to look at me. "I'm so sorry, Ruby. Laran… he's…gone."

Gone.

Gone.

Gone.

It rang in my ears like the last nail in a coffin and I screamed. My head whipped back and forth as I searched for his body on the charred shores of the Garden. Lilith was gone, and so were my other Horsemen.

But Laran, he was dead.

I crawled on all fours, wading through the congealing blood. His beautiful tanned skin was no more. His body pale and void of warmth, his eyes stared, wide open and unflinching even in the face of death. A raw sound erupted from my throat as I started pounding on his chest. "I told you not to leave me," I screamed. "I told you not to go!"

"Ruby—"

"Let her be," Jax whispered to her. "She just lost her mate, the others were taken, and Lilith has the beast. Give her a moment to grieve."

What they were saying didn't register. They sounded far away and cloudy. A vague feeling swimming through the haze that was consuming me as I beat his chest and screamed and cried. "Please don't be dead…I'm sorry…please don't. Please don't. I'm so sorry…"

My tears ran down my face and onto his body, mixing with his blood. I begged and pleaded with him, and when that didn't work, I begged and pleaded for someone else. Anyone else. Save him. It was all I wanted.

"If there is anyone out there in this world or the next that can hear me"—I gasped for breath as the hyperventilating began and I choked on my words—"save him," I sobbed. "It's all I ask. Bring him…back to…me." Tears and snot ran down my face as my throat clogged from too much emotion. I don't know what prompted me to say the words, but in that moment, I would pray to God herself if she would save him.

"You summoned me?" a woman said. Her voice sounded strange here. Too light for the gravity of loss I was experiencing. I wheeled around, covering as much of him as I could with my own body.

The person I saw…

"You're—"

"Morvaen. You freed me, Daughter of Hell."

Holy shit. Had I actually called a Seelie *into* Hell? I tried to see through the tears, but my puffy eyelids blurred my vision. The cavern went silent, as if they just realized the being in our midst was not one that had walked in this world for a very long time.

"Why are you here?" my voice cracked and the features of her face softened.

"You summoned me, my lady. The rune upon your arm was activated. What is it you ask?"

My breath hitched in my throat. Was there really a chance…was this the universe's way of telling me it wasn't over? That this wasn't the end…

"Save him," I choked out. "I don't care what you have to do. Just save him."

A murmur rippled through the room as Morvaen got to her knees beside me. Compassion was there in her silver eyes as she reached for the man I protected even in death. I scrambled to the side, watching her every movement as she began to draw.

Symbols. So many symbols she placed on his chest. His face. His arms.

Magic filled the air, but this time it was not dark or violent.

Like a warm breeze at the end of winter, I felt the first ray of hope.

Morvaen reached for me and I didn't hesitate to stop her as she started placing the same symbols on my skin. She drew orange runes over every inch of my back, a heaviness building in the space around me. The gravity of it weighing me down.

The very instant her hands lifted from my skin I felt the pressure that had shaped around me snap. The air stood still. My throat constricted each time I tried to take a breath, and as the edges of my vision started to go dark, I heard it.

The beating of a heart.

CHAPTER FOURTEEN

Laran let out a choking rasp and the vice around my throat released. An influx of oxygen flooded me and I collapsed forward onto him. The coppery tang of blood laced with his scent of firewood and smoke filled me with…peace. I had feared it would never return. That he would never return. That this soul-crushing loss would be so deep that I might never overcome it because a piece of me had gone to the veil and beyond.

But that piece came back when his arms tightened around me.

"I told you I wasn't letting you go," I breathed.

"I never doubted you," he whispered.

All wasn't right in the world. Three of my mates were missing. Lilith was gone, and she took the beast with her.

I came here for my crown and lost my life.

Now…I was coming for it all, and this time…

I looked to my best friend and the enigma that watched over her carefully—to my raccoon and the way he sat at Laran's feet—to the four horses that now watched over us—to the crowd of demons staying as far away as they possibly could—and finally, to the dark-skinned Fae sitting across from me

"Thank you," I told her.

"I owed you a debt, Ruby Morningstar. Now it is paid." Her eyes searched as she took in our surroundings. "But I must ask, where are we?"

The brush with death one too many times had left me exhausted to the bone and a weary grimace was all I managed.

"You can't tell?" She eyed me warily and I took that as a no. "We're in Hell."

Her mouth fell open and she said, "You summoned me…to *Hell?*"

"It appears so."

She went quiet, then, "How?"

I groaned, pressing my cheek against the steadily heating skin of Laran's chest. "I'm not entirely sure." Rough hands clung to my side, his fingernails biting into the skin as he held me, almost as if he feared letting me go.

"I see," she said eventually. Her dark lips curved downward before she turned and started to assess the demons cowering in the corner. "Should we be worrying about them?" she asked.

"Probably," I grit my teeth against the soreness in my muscles as I tried to pull myself up. Laran was there helping me even as his own limbs shook with exertion. The clacking of hooves and a wet nose pressed against my face had me pausing to look over at the ridiculously large mare. Her soulful eyes looked deep into mine as she pressed her muzzle against me and then brushed up against Laran.

"Hey girl," he murmured to Epona. His gentle hands brushed over her side as he muttered sweet things under his breath. It filled me with a sort of bittersweetness. I was so grateful that he was here and alive to soothe his familiar, but as I looked over at the other three horses…my heart broke all over again.

Tears threatened to fall from my eyes, but I couldn't wallow in my grief. I took a deep breath and scooped up Bandit, letting his claws prick my bare skin as he climbed up to my shoulder. The light flashes of pain grounded me, reminding me of Julian and what I stood to lose should I fail. Emotion swelled in my throat, making me swallow hard.

A shuffling of feet drew my attention to the crowd as it parted and a hollow-eyed Iona stepped forward. In an instant something shifted inside of me. I growled, waiting for the beast's snide remarks about skinning her alive while fire danced just beneath the skin of my fingers. But there was no beast and there was no fire. Only glittering ashes and memories.

That pissed me off even more. I strode forward as a snarl ripped from my lips and Iona, she had enough wherewithal to flinch, but made no move to block me as I swung a wild right hook that landed true. Her breath stuttered as her neck whipped around. A crunch echoed across the cavern. She fell to her knees before me and wept.

I grit my teeth against the urge to wrap my hand in her hair and see just how many times I had to smash her face into the stone for her head to crack open. Violence wasn't my first choice. It had never been, until the beast.

And now it seemed that she had changed me inexplicably. The call for restitution rode me hard, even as she let out the most awful sobs, blood and snot and tears smearing her face. "I'm so sorry," she cried. I wanted to kill her, but deep down I knew she wasn't the one at fault. Not truly.

"She stabbed me in the chest six times. She killed me. She killed Laran. Now she has the beast and took my Horsemen for Devil knows what," I spat harshly. "It's a bit late for sorry, Iona."

I turned my back on her. There would be no forgiveness for what she had done. Not now. Not in a hundred years. I may not kill her, but she could live with the guilt.

Feeble fingers grasped for my ankle. I stilled. "Rysten and I were raised together. I love him, not as a mate—as a brother—and he loved me."

"You have a fine way of showing it," I replied scathingly. She winced, but didn't contradict me.

"Your father saw that he cared and threw me into the burning lake of Inferna. I would have died…I did die…but Lilith saved me. She gave me life in return for my soul and that debt was only paid by bringing you here." She shuddered again, her teeth clanking as the adrenaline in her system crashed. "I didn't know he would love you," she whispered. "I-I didn't know s-s-she would take him t-too."

"If you're telling me this because you hope you'll get sympathy from me, you're shit out of luck. You didn't just bring this on yourself. You brought this down on me and mine, and for that…" For the shaking mess that she was, I was the picture of indifference. It was that or fall apart, and I couldn't do that again. Not here. Not in this moment. "I could have understood your hate for me after what my father did to you, but you sold your fucking soul. What did you think would come of it?"

"I didn't know," she sobbed.

I smiled coldly because that was a lie. I no longer had my empath powers, but I didn't need them to know what she felt. "You knew. You just didn't care. You thought you'd have Rysten in the end and I'd be the spawn of Satan Lilith told you I would be." I turned and strode away, not even flinching as her wailing echoed through the cavern. The sound of despair cemented me in that moment. Her pain kept me from coming unhinged. It calmed me. Even though my hands shook with the need to break something. The need to burn something.

I no longer had even a trace of power. I could feel that as steadily as the bond between Laran and I. She'd taken everything, and while I might be immortal...I was useless.

I was weaker than I'd ever been in my life. I'd lost three pieces of my heart. I'd lost a part of my soul in the beast. I'd lost my powers, and the next time I came face-to-face with Lilith I would fucking roar.

But first I needed to find my way out of here.

"We need to leave. It's not safe here," I began, pausing when I registered Jax was still here.

After I'd burned every inch of the cavern... he should be ashes right now. But he wasn't.

"We need to get to Inferna," Laran said.

"Find the Sins," Moira agreed. I continued watching Jax while she spoke, analyzing his every move. "Ruby, why do you look like you're about to stab someone?" Her voice was weary.

"You should have died," I said to Jax. His eyes narrowed on me, but I couldn't tell if it was confusion or something darker.

"What do you mean?" Moira asked, looking between us.

"I mean I let it all out. The beast and I used every trace of fire I had in me to try and take Lilith out, but she and her minions didn't die and the fire kills everything it touches." Moira's eyes widened, and she took a step away from him. "How are all of you alive?"

"Brimstone," he answered as Moira started to circle around him. "The punch they were drinking was laced with brimstone. It's the only substance that is immune to the flames, but it's also a poison." He looked pointedly at Moira. "Unlike the demons down here that I'm sure have been working up a tolerance for centuries, Moira hasn't."

"That doesn't explain anything, enigma," I replied. "She didn't need brimstone. She's immune to my flames and that has nothing to do with you."

"She's a legion," he said, as if that explained it all. "Pain can be delivered unto her, but she will return it sevenfold. Moira woke with a vengeance and when she touched me, the brimstone she consumed passed." I frowned as understanding flashed on Moira's expression.

"What do you mean *it passed?*" I asked.

"The mark of Cain," she said slowly. "I didn't know if it was true. That it could return pain sevenfold. All I had to do was touch him, though…" She gnawed on her lip, looking between us. "I don't know what to say when I barely understand it myself. The brimstone moved from me to him, and then you went supernova."

"It saved me," Jax replied. "If you hadn't woken when you did, I would have died from the flames." He didn't have any tell-tale signs of a liar, but after what I'd just gone through, I wasn't taking any chances.

"When we leave, you're going back in the bottle until we get to Inferna." It wasn't a question or a request, and I could tell he knew it by the set of his jaw.

"I'm not your enemy here." His eyes strayed to Moira with concern.

"You're not my friend, either. And right now I can't afford that." I crossed my arms over my chest and stared blankly at the underground lake that was no longer glowing or clear. Dark blue waters stained the shore where blood covered the rocks.

"And if you're attacked getting to Inferna?" the enigma asked.

My tone was flat when I replied, "Well, you'll be about as much help as you were this time."

"That's completely—"

"It won't be an issue," Laran cut in. He settled one arm around my shoulders and pulled me close. "Lilith took the beast and bonded to Hell in the waters of the Garden. That means the landscape will no longer be shifting and the fires should be out." I blinked, looking up at him.

"Are you saying we can pyroport straight there now?" I asked in a breath.

"I am."

We could get to Inferna in minutes. I could be seeing the Sins in mere minutes. The thought no longer terrified me, but in my current state it was difficult to feel much of anything. Instead of taking out my rage on Iona, I'd given in to the apathy so I could function. The pain was still there, the grief and the anger and the twisted feelings that I didn't even understand were still with me.

Later, I promised myself. *I'd deal with it later.*

I turned away from those thoughts and focused on the people. On the pricks of Bandit's claws as he protectively wrapped around me, purring softly under his breath. Laran's warm arm around me that held fast. On Moira's blue pentagram eyes, watching me with such open sadness that I flinched away. Laran looked at me with that same worry and I just said, "Open the portal. There's nothing left for us here."

He watched me for a heavy moment. I was torn between wishing I knew how he felt and embracing the solitude that may very well be the rest of my existence—if I couldn't get my powers back—however short it may be if Lilith learned I was alive. "As you wish," he nodded, holding out his hand to conjure forth a ring of flame.

It burned bright from the crimson tendrils to the sunburst heart. I looked at the colors and felt heat, but for once the warmth didn't soothe me.

Morvaen crouched on the floor, looking very unsure of all this.

"You can't just portal home, can you?" I couldn't bring myself to feel bad for calling her when she saved Laran, but I could understand how she was out of her element. I knew that feeling all too well.

"I don't think so," she answered. "It is not my magic that brought me into this world, but yours." Her fingers traced a rune in the air, but no matter how much magic she summoned, a portal would not form. Her hands contorted as she fisted them in frustration, her head hung low. "The door won't open," she whispered. Anxiety colored her tone as her dark grey skin blanched.

I held out my hand and she looked up at me. Her lips parted as she followed the tilt of my head to the flaming ring. For a brief second, indecision warred with the sorrow of being trapped before she reached out and her fingers grasped mine.

"Hell does not like my kind," she said as we faced the portal.

"It seems it doesn't like mine either," I spoke without turning. "Maybe together we can manage to stay alive."

Laran stepped up to my other side and gripped my hand tightly. The four horses walked in first. Then Moira and Jax, and finally it was our turn.

The first time I walked through a portal of flame I thought I was a girl on fire.

While I was no longer that girl and there was no fire in me, I found that

I still burned. Even in the depths of grief. The deepest parts of my soul still held embers, but this time when I ignited, it would be pyres of reprisal that I lit.

A reckoning was coming after what Lilith did here tonight, and when I was done Hell would never be the same again.

CHAPTER FIFTEEN

I HAD STEPPED into a portal of fire and I didn't know what I had been expecting, but it wasn't the dull roar of a crowd assaulting my senses. Light poured down on us, blinding me as a gust of warm air wrapped around my body. The glittering ashes of my past drifted in the wind, settling on the baked earth around me. I pressed my toes into it, curling them inward. My hands shook at my sides as I took in what I was looking at.

"Where are we?" Moira yelled.

The reddish-brown earth spanned out before me, shifting to rocks of various heights and then past those, farther up, were stands…seating. I turned in both directions, both awed and terrified at the rows upon rows of demons. They surrounded me so fully and their cheers were deafening.

I thought back to what the Horsemen had told me, about what exactly the gate to Inferna was. It was only when Bandit let out some horrible screech in warning that I knew where we were.

"The coliseum," I muttered. "We're in the coliseum!"

"Run!" Laran yelled. Morvaen took off at a dead sprint. I only got a glimpse of something large and dark as my feet stumbled and she half-dragged, half-carried me. Bandit held fast to my chest just as I clutched her, trying desperately to pull my knees up, only to feel the burn of skin being shredded by friction against the rocky ground. I let out a grunt and put everything I had into hooking my feet under me and putting on a burst of speed.

I found traction, just as a massive rock loomed before us.

"We need to get on top of it," I panted, gripping the Seelie woman's hand for dear life and praying that Laran could handle whatever that thing was. In a fight between demons and monsters, I was no longer the biggest one of all. I was the weak link, and I hated it.

"We must jump." Morvaen sounded like this was a mere walk in the park to her and it occurred to me she was going slower so that I wouldn't fall behind. I was going to owe her a damn debt before this all was over.

"I'm not…a great…jumper," I panted, completely out of breath. Her plum-colored lips curved upwards in a feral grin.

"No worries, my lady," she called out. Her hand tightened around mine as she sped up. I was just starting to stall out when she bent her legs and launched into the air, dragging me with her. My arm felt like it was being torn from my body as we went airborne. I dangled helplessly beside her and Bandit let out a cry of dismay as the flat top of the rock was closing in too fast.

Morvaen landed lightly on the balls of her feet as my own body hit the stone in a heap. Bandit, for all his strength, was flung from my chest and into the low layer of dust that filled the coliseum below us.

I couldn't see him, but I could sense that his presence was there. Given that Bandit was better equipped to protect himself than I was, it shouldn't have worried me as much as it did.

I scrabbled to my feet despite the bone-deep exhaustion. Pain prickled over my fresh wounds, but even without my powers they were healing incredibly fast. Small blessings, I supposed. Weak or strong, at least I was hard to kill.

I pulled myself up so that my knee wasn't bent at an odd angle, flinching when it popped loudly. A slight burn spread around it telling me that whatever my crash landing had fucked up would be fixed soon.

"Your mate is strong," Morvaen commented as the dust settled enough to see Laran. Naked and covered from head to toe in both his blood and my own, he stood alone against a hellhound of epic proportions. This thing made the one in New Orleans look downright small as it towered over him, drool dripping from its jowls. Crimson eyes watched him with malicious intent as it stalked around him in circles. The hellhound made no move to attack, but its raised hackles gave notice that it could at any given moment.

"That thing could swallow him whole," I answered in a voice that sounded far calmer than I felt.

"He is War, is he not?" Morvaen asked. She didn't sound worried, but we were far enough back from the fight now that we were as close to safe as you could get in an arena of hell beasts.

I swallowed hard and nodded. I had to trust him, just as he trusted me. "He is War."

Storm clouds swirled overhead as the skies darkened and the first hint of rain misted. The winds grew rough, sweeping away the dust to reveal Moira and Jax fighting their own battles on the other side of him. Morvaen gasped as the creature they were backing into a corner became visible.

"Is that a—"

"Cerberus," I answered with a grave nod.

Hellhounds were one thing. The damn things were vicious to the bone and only obeyed the call of its master. A Cerberus was in a whole other category of its own. Unlike the savage Hellhounds, taming a Cerberus was near impossible. Legend had it that each head possessed a different ability and a mind of its own. Getting all three minds to agree on a master was not easy. That had led to their near extinction.

Or so I'd thought.

By the looks of it this one was in rough shape. Blood dripped from its side where claw marks had slashed through the skin. Moira stood before it, hands on her hips. I couldn't see her expression from here, but I got the distinct impression she didn't want to kill it. Hellbeast or not, she had a soft spot for dogs…even the ones with three heads.

A rumbled whine drew me back to the hellhound. The beast no longer looked like it wanted to kill Laran, rather like it wanted to…play. The great giant sat back on its haunches and lowered its head. He reached forward and pet its snout. I couldn't hear him from where I stood, but I wouldn't be surprised to find that he was speaking to it much like he had Epona.

"Where are the horses?" I asked with a jolt. They'd gone first. Was there a chance that it ate them? I shuddered in horror right as Morvaen pointed to another peak to the right of us.

"They fled behind there." I let out an exhale and nodded, but that still left one.

Bandit.

I looked behind us but there was no flat ground, only jagged rocks, and none of them held a black and blue raccoon or any sign of blood and fur. My pulse quickened as I turned back towards the rest of the arena. He wasn't known for staying out of trouble. The hellhound's ears perked up suddenly, glancing to a spot on the left side of us.

*Oh no…*a ball of fur and fury launched itself across the coliseum.

"No!" I shouted as the dog took off like a hound on a hunt. Bandit was fast, though, diving between its legs—narrowly missing the paws that could kill him with a single step as he went straight for Moira. No. Not Moira… the blood drained from my face as he went for the Cerberus.

Three sets of large green eyes swiveled to Bandit as he ran full speed, stopping right before it. Dread filled me as I judged the distance. We were a good twenty feet up and several hundred out. Powers or no powers, I needed to get off this damn rock. Sinking to my butt and never taking my eyes off Bandit, I slid forward. The sharper edges of the rock sliced through my naked skin with ease, but the drop was harder. The impact jolted straight through me as my feet hit the ground. Still I ran.

Hobbled. Broken. Bleeding. I ran.

And then Bandit did the most peculiar thing of all.

He rounded on Moira and Jax, snapping his teeth. Jax took a step forward and blue fire shot out from Bandit's mouth as he started to grow in size. Five feet. Ten feet. Twenty. He kept growing. His body becoming so large it surpassed the Cerberus that was huddled behind him. From this angle I could see his tail, the way it flicked back to wrap around the three-headed beastie.

He was protecting it.

But Moira was not the greatest threat here.

The hellhound watching him was.

A pounding started in my head, combatting the dizziness from blood loss and over exertion as I ran as hard as I could. My fists clenched so tightly the nails dug into my palms. I only barely felt the prick of skin breaking. My single focus was to get to him. To reach him in time. I didn't know what I could do, but I just couldn't be useless again. I couldn't. I wouldn't.

A whisper of something foreign raced through my veins. The pounding continued, growing so loud it was all I could hear. It was all I knew. A flash of pain raced through me, starting at my palms and spreading through my entire being. I grit my teeth, sprinting as fast as a I could. It happened in the blink of an eye. The impossible.

I went from over a hundred feet away to standing inches from a snarling hellhound.

Each of its teeth were as large as my face. I swallowed hard against the urge to run as I took a step back. It let out a loud harrumph, its rancid breath blowing the stringy, blood-caked pieces of my hair away.

It took a step forward and I took a step back. Fur brushed against my naked body and I recognized the scent of Bandit immediately. I didn't know what just happened. I couldn't wrap my mind around it, but somehow—someway—

"Ruby?" Moira asked, her head whipped around to where I had been just a moment before. "How did you—"

"I don't know, but we've got bigger problems at the moment."

Moira nodded, raising two fingers to her lips. I frowned right as Jax clapped his hands over his ears. Her whistle sliced through the crowd like a knife through butter. The crowd fell silent. The hellhound stopped. Everything in the arena seemingly froze.

A slow clapping began. I looked around, trying to find where it was coming from as the clouds overhead cleared. A single beam of light shined down into the center of the coliseum and that's when I saw her. Dressed in battle leathers, an oversized battle-axe strapped to her back, wearing that strange half-smile I hadn't seen in two years.

"*Dina?*" I asked, squinting in disbelief.

"Hello, Ruby. It's been a blink since I last saw you."

CHAPTER SIXTEEN

LARAN GROANED, running his hand over the stubble on his face. "You know her?"

I nodded. "That's Dina. She was my mentor. She taught me everything about tattooing…"

"No, babe." He shook his head, looking at her as he said, "That's Hela, the Deadly Sin of Wrath."

I looked back and forth between the two, my mouth hanging open as slow realization set in. My lips pressed together as my feet began to move. I wasn't exactly sure what I was going to do when I came to stand before the woman who'd been my teacher and friend. The woman who'd bought oranges by the dozen because they were the closest thing to human skin a novice could tattoo on. The woman who spent countless hours shaping me as a person and an artist.

No. I had no idea what I would do, but the rage inside me did.

A crack split the air and I looked from my hand that I hadn't noticed moved, to the darkening blue palm print on her cheek. I couldn't find it in me to be sorry or feel scared.

"That was for lying to me about *everything*," I said.

The coliseum was quiet. A dead sort of silence filling it. I'd already died twice. The veil didn't scare me. A second crack snapped me from my own controlling anger as a second bright blue palm print appeared on her other cheek. Dina—or Hela—didn't look quite so happy now. "That was for leaving without saying goodbye."

Her eyes softened as tears gathered in them. "I deserve that," she whispered as she wrapped her arms around my shoulders and pulled me close. I let her, not because I forgave her, but because I needed to feel something—anything other than this anger and grief and despair so sharp and deep that I feared I'd bleed out from the inside before I could ever recover.

So, I let her hug me and I embraced her fiercely in return—but I didn't cry. The time for tears was over. I'd lost it all, and in the depths of rock bottom I was regaining it piece by piece. I needed to hold together, and if I cried, I would come apart at the seams.

"I've missed you, Blue," Hela murmured softly against my hair.

"Why did you lie to me?" I asked in a scathing tone. She pulled away and took any semblance of peace with her. The blue of her eyes shined so bright, far more vivid than it ever did on Earth.

"I had no choice. None of us did." She smiled even as a single tear slid down her cheek. She brushed it away and turned to wrap an arm around my shoulders. With her other hand she lazily drew a circle with two fingers and a ring of fire appeared. I tensed. "It leads to my home," she said, answering my unspoken question. I eyed her warily and then turned to look for the others. Laran watched Hela with a neutral expression. Moira looked downright pissed and that probably had to do with the same reason I was. Morvaen was slowly making her way to us, eyeing the hellhound that hadn't moved a single inch since Hela had appeared.

"Does your house have clothes and a bath available without anyone trying to kill us?" Moira asked. Hela eyed her with fading amusement as she really took in the state of us. Something like guilt flashed in her eyes, but I couldn't be certain.

"Of course," she said before looking back at me. "The other Sins would like to see you, though. If you're up for it?"

"Do I get an actual choice?" I asked, already knowing what I was going to do but needing to ask it anyways.

"Yes." The tightness around her eyes showed me how much that question pained her, but there was understanding there too. "You have always had a choice. Just as we have always been watching."

I frowned. "What do you mean by that?"

She smiled but it was filled with trepidation. I didn't get the same feeling I did in the Garden; an unknown sense of impending doom I never had any chance to prevent. Instead I felt...anxiousness. "You'll see," she answered, stepping forward into the flames. She left me there to decide for myself, the hellhound following after her. I looked back at Bandit and motioned for him to come to me. Usually it only took once, but he looked uncertain, glancing around us before eventually shrinking down to his usual size. The Cerberus whined as he brushed against her before coming to me.

I arched a brow, glancing between the two of them as Bandit bounded up to me.

"Of course, you choose a damn hellbeast to get cozy with." Bandit waggled his eyebrows, casting a last look of longing over his shoulder. I scooped him up and turned for the portal. If he wanted a girlfriend, he'd have to wait.

Moira came over beside me and squeezed my shoulder. "It's been a long day, Rubes. You just gotta last a little longer," she murmured under her breath for my ears only. I nodded, staring into the bright yellow flames.

"It's not me I'm worried about."

We all followed after her and into the portal as one. When we stepped out there were no crowds or coliseums. The sudden hush of silence apart from bare feet slapping against the sleek surface was uncomfortable. The towering pillars only served as a reminder as to how small I was. Hela stood before us holding out several thin robes. I took one without speaking, not that it stopped her from looping her arm through mine and guiding me down the hall. I kept my head slightly turned making sure no one appeared behind us.

"Time has changed you, Blue." It was a simple statement, but it cracked through my armor, if only for a moment.

"You have no idea," I snapped, trying to shrug her arm off. Hela didn't let go. She was assertive. She always had been. "I've been fighting my ass off for months just to survive while you've been doing what? Hiding here? Playing gladiator in a devil-damned coliseum? What the fuck?"

Her skin grew hot against mine as her eyes flashed with streaks of lightning. The hellhound trailing behind us let out a growl and Bandit returned the sentiment. "There are many things you do not understand, Ruby. I cannot blame you for that when we are the ones who chose to keep you in the dark, but I can ask you to at least hear us out."

"You left," I said harshly. "Walked out. Poof." I snapped my fingers. "I needed you and you disappeared overnight without even a note or a good-bye. Do you know how much that hurt?" I yanked my arm roughly and she finally dropped it. "You don't get to make demands of me."

Hela stalked ahead of me, lithe and graceful even in armor. "You don't want to listen to me?" she called over her shoulder. "Fine." She stopped in front of a pair of doors that were ten feet tall and black as onyx, a silver pentagram adorned the center, divided by the seam. She grasped the handles and flung them open, breaking the star. "Maybe you'll listen to them."

My heart skipped a beat, suspending for the moment it took me to look at the four women standing around the longest dining table I'd ever seen.

"No fucking way," Moira blurted out. "*Sadie?*"

"You two have gotten into far too much trouble ever since you moved out of my house," the green-eyed shade said with a smile. The tips of her fangs toyed with her plump bottom lip. She'd been the house mother at the orphanage where Moira and I had met.

Another woman scoffed. This one I didn't recognize. "They got in too much trouble *in* your house. There's a reason it was me Ruby came to every week." She smiled, and it was a cruel thing. Her beauty was too much to be real. Her white-blonde hair and pale skin made it difficult to tell what she might be.

"That's only because I wasn't there anymore," another woman smarted off. I took her in. Her black hair was striking against her pale skin and ruby red lips. I knew this wraith. Mere. She was one of the orphanage mothers I'd spent the majority of my formative years with until I'd gone to Portland.

"Oh, please," the cruel beauty smirked. "Hela and I are the only ones she actually missed." Her sharp brown eyes landed on me. "Aren't we, Ruby?"

"Uh…"—I stifled a yawn—"I don't know who you are."

"A nightmare," not-Mere said flippantly.

"I'd rather be a nightmare than a wraith," the beauty snapped. The Horsemen had said that the Sin of Greed was a nightmare. Her true name was Saraphine. "At least I'm not haunted by the souls I send to the veil."

"That you know of," not-Mere muttered under her breath.

The fourth woman, a banshee sitting in the corner, let out a cackle as she leaned back in her chair to kick her feet up. Heavy boots hit the long wooden table with a thunk, mud and grass falling in clumps while she leaned over and grabbed a handful of grapes, plopping them in her mouth. "You're all jealous, yet *I'm* the one that's green. Oh, the irony," she smirked. The blonde nightmare rolled her eyes and slowly her form changed...

"*Martha?*" I asked.

Speechless.

The sharp-eyed owner of my beloved diner back in Portland blinked and flashed me a smile as she crossed her arms over her chest. "You must be having a mighty hard time without bacon or coffee in these parts," she drawled. Her voice changing to that of the woman I'd known for over a decade. My throat constricted.

"I left you everything," I whispered, stumbling back. The form of the old woman disappeared in an instant and it was again the blonde...Saraphine standing before me. This time her eyes weren't quite so striking as a softness formed in them.

"You're a kind girl and you take care of your own," she said. "Let it be known I never doubted you would make it this far. I knew from the very first day you walked into my diner."

"Me neither," Hela agreed, though the expression on her face made it clear she didn't often agree with this woman about much of anything.

"She's always been destined for greatness," not-Mere concurred.

"She was destined for something, I'll agree with you there," the banshee said around a mouthful of grapes. I lifted an eyebrow and she grinned fiercely, her form shifting before my eyes into...Joe...

"You gotta be fucking kidding me," I said, mostly to myself. The middle-aged cop with the receding hairline and beer gut smiled tepidly.

"Did you really think we would let our sister's daughter grow up alone?" he asked, shaking his head the way he used to. In a blink, the banshee reappeared with a rueful grin. "You're smarter than that, Morningstar," she said, mockingly using my last name the way Joe had during our frequent encounters.

I looked around the room at each of the women that had been involved without me knowing it throughout the span of my life. "I don't know what to say to this," I said honestly.

"Thank you, perhaps?" the banshee suggested, making Saraphine— Greed—roll her eyes.

"She's in shock," said not-Sadie.

I turned to Laran, not sure if it was anger or just surprise riding me when I said," Did you know?"

"Who they were?" he asked, looking around them in shock. I nodded. "No," he shook his head. "Never."

"Of course not," the banshee said and yawned. "We had to keep it from the likes of Lilith. You four really had no chance." She examined her nails, looking quite proud of herself and reminding me a little too much of a certain other banshee. I swiveled to glance at Moira who was watching the she-demon at the table with narrowed eyes.

"You lot have been following her this entire time?" Moira asked all the sudden. The Sins looked her way and nodded. Not-Sadie's lips thinned as if she knew where this was going. "Then you either suck at your job more than the four fuckers who brought us here, or you purposely turned the other way all those years because not a single goddamn time that she's needed someone have any of you been there."

Hela looked like she swallowed something sour, but the banshee—not-Joe who's name I didn't know—just dropped her legs to the floor with a heavy thump and rose to her feet, arms crossed over her. "You really think that she kept herself out of trouble with the law all those years? Possession? Assault? Arson, really? No charges ever pressed against her and she never saw a judge? And yet you came and paid a bail. And she always dealt with me. That's not how any of that works. Don't be so obtuse," she chastised Moira, rolling her eyes before my best friend could respond. "Turned the other way? Please. If she'd kept her nose clean it would have made my job all that easier. I could have been sitting on my ass all day eating donuts while I glamored myself doing shit, but no. I was constantly overriding the damn files to get her off with nothing more than a slap on the wrist," she groaned and leaned back against the table. "It was exhausting. I'm fucking glad to be back here."

Well, at the very least that answered who she was. Only sloth would bitch about me causing more work for her when she had the least hands-on role of them all.

"Lazy," not-Mere griped.

"Jealous," the banshee smiled.

"Can we get to the fucking point?" Moira asked bluntly.

"The point," the Sin of Sloth said, "is that we've been in the background all these years. Raising you without you knowing it was us. We watched over you, keeping away the worst of the monsters so that you would live long enough to one day be able to do it yourself."

"But who are you?" I asked, an anger beginning to form inside the more I thought about it. They seemed taken aback, but how could they not realize that this wasn't just a shock. No…it was a betrayal. I needed to know who they were—who exactly I was dealing with all those years.

"We're the same people we've always been, Blue—"

"Who are you *really*?" I interrupted.

Hela sighed. "You already know I am the Sin of Wrath."

"And you?" I asked the banshee.

"Sloth," she answered. "But you can call me Ahnika."

I looked at the nightmare. "Greed?" I asked.

Sadness emanated from her as she took me in and nodded once. "Call me Saraphine." Her lips were pressed to hide a frown and the pinched corners of her cheeks showed her strain.

"And you?" I asked not-Sadie.

"Lamia," the sweet-faced woman said. "Sin of Revelry." She stroked the dark blue sapphire that hung from her neck with an admiration.

"Not Gluttony?" Moira asked.

"I am a glutton by nature, but my taste is for the finer things in life," Lamia said. "You would like my realm," she added. "I throw the best parties."

"Like Satan you do," not-Mere griped.

"No need to be a jealous ninny, Merula—"

"Envy?" I asked, cutting Lamia off entirely without apology. I didn't have time for their bickering.

"In the flesh," the woman who had raised me in my formative years answered.

I mentally counted down the Sins…

"There's only five of you," I said. Six sins. Everything had been very specific about this before. Not seven. Not five. Six. "Who is missing?"

They all seemed to share a look with each other without moving an inch, and regardless of who these women were to me, I froze. *More fucking secrets?*

I opened my mouth to say as much when a voice spoke and ice spread through my veins.

"I see you all started the party without me."

Standing behind me was one of the last people I ever wanted to see again. In the blink of an eye I reacted, turning on my heel to slam my palm into her temple. She sidestepped easily, blocking my rebound and the following three blows I let loose after that. It was only when the shiny metal crossbow materialized on my arm with the bolt already cocked that her hand came up to grab my wrist, stopping me from letting it fly.

I let out a growl, but it was Laran that said, "What the fuck are you doing here?"

"Great question," she said offhandedly. I moved to punch her with my other hand and she was forced to let go of the crossbow to sidestep the swing. I wasn't a bad fighter by any means but going up against a several thousand-year-old opponent wasn't exactly a recipe for winning if you played fair. I concentrated on her with all I had and snapped my wrist to fire. The rest was left to chance.

The bolt flew true, striking her chest cavity with enough force to break the bone. Sin took a step back and glowered. "Feel better yet?"

"Hmm," I drawled sarcastically. "Three of my mates are missing and my soul was ripped in half, so I'm going to go with a solid no." She sighed, wrenching the bolt from her chest. The site of her blood cooled my own some.

"At least they're not dead," she scoffed.

"No thanks to you!" I roared.

My fingers twitched and I felt it again, the makings of something stirring within me. Like an ember of power that if only I could grasp it, it might grow to an all-out flame. I reached for it, but the ember evaded me.

"Guys?" She cleared her throat, looking over my shoulder. "Can I get a little help here?"

"You're lucky she doesn't have more Hela in her," Merula replied. Sin gave her a flat look and snapped her fingers. The bloody clothes were instantly replaced with clean ones.

"What is she doing here?" I demanded angrily. A growing unease was beginning to fill me.

There were five...now there are six.

"Ruby," Hela sighed. "Meet your mother's replacement. Sinumpa—the Deadly Sin of Lust."

CHAPTER SEVENTEEN

I OPENED my mouth and closed it three times, trying to find the right words to say. That's the thing, though—there weren't any.

"Replacement?" I said softly, but my voice sounded hollow. Cold. "You mean to tell me that you replaced her with the bitch who got me and Laran killed?"

Again, the Sins looked between each other, but Sinumpa—she just watched me. Her eyes were slightly narrowed as they skated over me from the top of my head to my bare, dirty feet. "*They* didn't replace anything," she said.

"Oh?" I lifted both eyebrows. "They didn't?" I scoffed callously. Bandit wound himself around me tightly. "Please tell me who exactly made you the Sin of Lust, then?"

Sinumpa let out a sigh and her shoulders dropped a fraction. "Your mother."

"Bullshit."

"Is it?" she asked, daring me to contradict her. "You were just a little babe when I found you both in Atlanta. Your mother knew the score. She still begged for me to spare you. Not her. *You.*" I swallowed hard because I hadn't wanted to hear about my mother days ago and I didn't want to hear it now. "She passed on her title to me so that I had the power to keep you hidden until it was time for you to be found. Did you know that?" She unbuttoned the top four buttons on her blouse and pushed the material aside. "Did you know that she branded me before she ordered me to kill her and mutilate her body so that my mother would believe she had been thoroughly interrogated and died during torture while refusing to give up where she hid you?" There on her skin was a deep magenta brand made up of swirling lines that overlapped each other. "Did you know that, Ruby? Did you—"

"I get the point," I spat, biting the inside of my cheek. Bandit braced himself on my shoulder, baring his teeth at the Fae woman.

"No," Sin continued. "I don't think you do. The only way you can become the Sin of anything is if the last Sin passes on her brand and title to you. Lola gave me hers when I found you in Atlanta. *I* was the one that hid you before the rest of Lilith's children came looking. *I* was the one that hunted down every monster that got too close so that the other five could watch over you without blowing their glamor. *I* was the one that kept you alive for twenty-three years, so don't tell me you *get the point.*" At the end of her little speech I wasn't left with an immense gratitude I assumed she expected I should be feeling.

My entire life had been a lie, but that wasn't enough. Raising me to never know the truth was not sufficient. They had to lie to me about who they were as well. It made the time on Earth and the experiences I cherished feel cheap.

Deceived was not a strong enough word.

More like the ultimate betrayal.

"Was any of it real?" I asked. This time my tone was not cold. Nor was it burning. It was empty. Like the hole in my chest where my mates had been carved out from. "Or was it all just preparation to keep the heir alive, only for me to fail because no one told me a fucking thing?"

"We didn't want to keep you in the dark," Saraphine said. I didn't want to call her Martha. She wasn't. She never had been in the first place. Saraphine was a stranger—just like the face that looked back at me—and I preferred it that way. "But we all had our roles to play. Roles that were agreed upon before Lola died. Not even Lucifer knew that we had left and gone to you."

"Why though? Why bother being there at all when you could have just brought me back to Hell, or sent the Horsemen sooner, or any number of things that wouldn't have ended the way today did." I lowered my head.

"You didn't fail," Hela said. "Today went exactly the way we'd expected it to go—with the exception of War almost being killed." My neck cracked with how fast my head lifted to look her in the eye.

"You knew that was going to happen to me?"

"We planned for a great many things," the banshee—Ahnika—said. She lifted the grapes high over her head, dropping them into her mouth one by one. "If you'd all take a seat, we might even be able to start at the beginning," she continued lazily. She quirked an eyebrow as another grape fell, her teeth clanked together as she bit it in half mid-fall, the other slice toppling to the ground. She didn't seem to notice.

I took a deep breath, glancing at Moira and how she had her arms crossed over her chest. Beside her, Jax looked torn between remaining there and splitting. He'd done his job after all. He'd gotten me to Inferna alive. Past him, Morvaen idled by the door, watching everything around her with narrowed eyes. She didn't trust this place, and she was right for that. I still hadn't figured out what we were going to do with her, but at the moment getting some answers and getting my Horsemen back were the top priority.

Laran came up beside me and squeezed my side gently, placing a scratchy kiss on my temple. It steadied me for what was to come, and I went to sit at the opposite end of the table from Ahnika.

I crossed my legs as I leaned into the soft cushioning. My right arm rested on the arm of the chair, curling upwards so that I could brace my chin on my closed fist. The crossbow remained cocked, jutting just far enough out that if I were to fire, the bolt should miss me and still fly true. I didn't expect to need it. Hell, I didn't think it would do much more than anger whoever I hit. I was without power, though, and this metal contraption gave me a piece of that back. I clung to it even as my fingers grew so cold, they felt numb. "You wanted to talk, so talk. From the beginning."

Ahnika's eyebrows bunched together for a moment before her feet dropped away and she leaned forward on her elbows, steepling her fingers. I had her attention now. "Alright, Baby Morningstar. From the beginning."

She nodded once, and the other Sins took their seats. A calm settled over me as I tilted my head. Inside there was a Ruby that hurt. A Ruby that bled. I couldn't afford to be her right now. I couldn't afford to lose my head.

There was no beast to balance me anymore, and for that I had to balance myself. Right now, that meant putting aside all my feelings, because feelings wouldn't save anyone.

But the truth might.

And so, I listened.

CHAPTER EIGHTEEN

"IN THE BEGINNING when Eden was new, a primordial of great power came into being. Her name was Genesis," Ahnika began.

"I've already heard this story," I sighed.

"You've heard Lilith's version of this story, but she was barely a babe when Eden came to an end and Hell was born," Hela answered. I closed my mouth and inclined my head for them to continue.

"Genesis was the primordial of creation. She created us first, Lola included, as the original six. We each held an aspect of her, and that feature became what we were known for as she created others. She divided our world into provinces and gave us each a piece, tasking us to watch it while she watched over us all, and for a time it was good." Ahnika leaned forward and dropped the empty grapevine on the plate in front of her.

"And then Lucifer came," Merula said. She pushed her silky black hair over one shoulder, her cherry red lips twisting in a grimace. "In a blaze of fire, the primordial of the flames tore a rift in the boundaries between the worlds. Genesis was smitten the very moment she'd seen him because Lucifer was the first being she hadn't created. The attraction only grew the longer he remained, until it reached the point of obsession." She curled her fingers, showing the blood red shade of her nails. "After his falling out with God, Lucifer would not find himself tied to one woman—"

"Why?" Moira asked. Merula sent her a chiding glare, but the question was a valid one.

"Because he had already done so for God," Ahnika answered. "He gave her everything. His heart. His soul. They'd been created as equals—him the primordial of fire and her the primordial of light. A perfect harmonious pair..."

"She wanted more," Hela said, taking over. "God wasn't fulfilled by Lucifer's love alone and decided that she would no longer be bound to one. She would be worshipped by many. A being above him," she said. "A God."

"Lucifer would not be tied down again after that," Merula said. "This drove Genesis mad, and in her madness, she revolted in one final act of creation. She'd wanted real children so desperately she split herself in two—creating the Fae—while dooming her world." She shook her head of dark hair with disapproval.

"The world started to break apart at the seams because Genesis had bonded to it," Merula explained. "Primordials do not *have* to bond with a world, but if they do it vastly increases their power. And that planet, that realm they've bonded to, becomes dependent on the primordial to sustain life. If that primordial dies, the only true way to stop it from imploding was for another primordial to now do the same. Lucifer was our only option, contrary to what Lilith might have told you. Without him, Hell as we came to know it never would have existed because Eden—the world—would have died. Us along with it."

"That's not to say that your father was a saint," Lamia chimed in. "He quite enjoyed the indulgences that being bonded to Hell earned him and he grew to be known as King. Lilith was only a baby when he bonded to the planet and your father took it upon himself to raise her and Eve. She grew up a selfish little twat thinking that she deserved to rule simply because she and Eve were born out of Genesis's death. Much like her creator, she focused on the wrong things. Obsessing over her lack of primordial power instead of the very people that Lucifer gave her by making her one of us. She abused it. Dabbling in dark magic at terrible costs, all the while he refused to see her as anything but the sweet little girl that looked just like Genesis." She rolled her eyes to the crystalline chandeliers above us. Her lips pursed as she looked directly at me. "Then Ragnarök came. A banshee of such great power that he didn't just herald the death of those around him, but the end of the world. He foretold of a future where Hell would burn like it never had before. The borders between this world and any other's Lucifer bridged would be set aflame. Billions of humans, demons, and even angels would die."

"Heaven would burn too?" I asked.

"Yes," Hela answered. "Your father was the purest form of fire forged into the body of a man. He would pyroport between not just distances in Hell, but worlds themselves. It was how he came here, and how inevitably everything he touched would die—if not for you."

"But I did die," I interrupted.

"You did," she nodded. "But you came back. Ragnarök foretold of a daughter that would be born unto fire. That she would wield this great power and ultimately be the key to stopping the apocalypse. This girl would be brought back to her people by four horsemen and put an end to the burning."

"But I don't understand—" I began.

"You will," Merula stopped me. "By the time Ragnarök revealed his prophecy, Lilith was already as mad as the woman she called mother, but ten times more ruthless. Genesis was a selfish deity, not unlike us. We were created in her image after all. But the child she created was a true monster." She shook her head. "I was with her when the prophecy was spoken. I saw that gleam in her eye. I know jealousy when I see it and the moment Ragnarök foretold of you, Lilith began making plans."

"And my father never saw this?" I asked, skeptical. They all shook their heads, solemn but angry. They had every reason to be.

"She was once a master of deception," Sinumpa began, taking over the story. "But over time she began believing the lies she told. She became delusional, falling into her own web. Ragnarök's prophecy made her desperate, because she knew that one day Lucifer would fall, and when he did there would be someone that could take his throne—the throne she viewed as rightfully hers from the beginning." She lifted both eyebrows as she stared down the table at me. Her nails tapped the long wooden table with enough strength to rip a heart from a man's chest. "She got the idea in her mind that if your father could sire a primordial, then she could give birth to one, if she had the right child with the right bloodline." I swallowed the bile in my throat. Revulsion eating at my insides. Sinumpa smiled coldly. "I see my title and lineage didn't escape you in the cavern. Sinumpa, Child of Lilith, Daughter of Cain." She spat her mother's name like it was venom. "Right around the time Lilith got the idea that she needed a male Seelie, one of Eve's spawn came tearing through Hell with the mark of Cain on his head. She trapped him and then she raped him. Again. And again—until she became pregnant with me."

A child born of blood and pain. A girl raised by a monster dressed as an angel. I pitied her, even if only for a moment.

"My fath—Lucifer allowed this?" Her lips tightened at my change mid-sentence.

"Lucifer didn't know about it. Nor did he find out about the hundreds of other males she held at different points across the years. And while I'm quite unique, I'm not a primordial—unlike you." There wasn't a hint of jealousy in her tone, only bone-deep weariness. The kind of tired that wasn't brought on by a bad day or week. It settled in you day after day. Growing. Eating away at who and what you are until only a numb sense of emptiness remains. "Each one raped until they were able to sire a female child."

"Why female?" Moira asked.

"Males are inferior in the Brimstone City. Used as slaves and breeding studs by the women of Pride. She considered them too primal. Prone to giving into base urges instead of capable thought," Sinumpa answered without having to even think about it.

"Harsh," Moira mumbled. Sinumpa only shrugged.

"She was building an army out of children that would live for eternity. Some having children of their own that would also be enslaved from birth. It was only this very night that I earned my freedom."

"How was she able to hide this if she was the one pregnant?" I asked. Demon women carried their children to term for two years before giving birth. Were the Fae the same?

"She didn't," Ahnika answered. "Hide her pregnancy, that is. Your father didn't take issue with her having children. They were never...romantic. He raised her, after all. He never thought it strange that she would want children given Genesis was her mother. It wasn't until the Horsemen came about that he started to realize what she really was." All of the Sins nodded and once again the conversation passed onto another.

"Like me, Lilith shares an affinity for Greed," Saraphine said.

"She really shares an affinity with each of us, if we're being honest," Ahnika sniped. Greed nodded her head, clearly not disagreeing.

"She does, but her Greed became prevalent the day Lucifer came to her with a proposition." She didn't smile as her gaze slid to Laran. He froze under those sharp brown eyes that in this light held the reddish tint of a nightmare. "He believed in the prophecy that Ragnarök spoke, that you would be returned by four horsemen. But they were not demons that existed yet. So, he made them. Made you, that is." I reached out to grasp Laran's hand, clinging to his warmth. "He wanted you to be the perfect guards for his little girl when she came into existence, so he bargained with the monster he raised. Four women volunteered to be the mothers of the Four Horsemen, knowing they would not survive the process. Four sterile women, I should add. Lilith impregnated them with her own blood magic and Lucifer's power. Just enough fire that they would be immune, just enough strength that they could contain you. No more."

"What did he give her in return?" I asked, dreading the truth.

I waited as Laran took a deep breath and then answered me.

"Our childhood," he said. "She already had free reign in her domain and he couldn't give anything that actually belonged to any of the Sins, so he bargained with us."

"This was before she killed one of the she-demons carrying a child," Sinumpa inserted.

"What?" Moira and I said simultaneously.

"I was closing in on a millennium at the time, so the details from my adolescence are a bit fuzzy," she said, turning to Hela beside her. That she considered a thousand years adolescence said a great deal about the woman I was coming to see more clearly.

"She poisoned one of the she-demons and Lucifer found out. He was enraged by it, given that he was supposed to hand over the babes once they were born. Forced to strike a new deal now that so much was at stake, he swore on a blood oath that as long as she did not physically harm the Horsemen, or allow them to be harmed, then as long as he lived no one could kill her without meeting the same fate—including himself." Her lips pinched, telling me what exactly she thought of that blood oath.

"It was a desperate move that he never should have made," Ahnika stated.

"But he did," Hela sighed "And when the three she-demons gave birth, one was carrying twins. Even at the time he felt that this was his best move for you and for Hell. The odds of one mother dying and then one having twins was too much to be a coincidence. In his mind, the Four Horsemen meant that Ragnarök's prophecy was inevitable."

"It was a self-fulfilling prophecy that might never have come to pass were the Horsemen not created," Ahnika snapped.

"A prophecy that has come to pass, nonetheless" Merula sternly.

"A prophecy that kept us from taking out the bitch before she massed enough power and support to actually become a problem," Ahnika replied.

"Can we cut the arguing and get back to the story?" I cut in, leaning forward onto the table. I grabbed an apple off the platter in front of me and took a bite.

"For many years we continued with this uneven truce. As promised, the Horsemen were raised by her and passed into the transition, at which point they were free to do as they pleased. Years passed. Millennia went by. Then Lola became pregnant. It changed everything." Hela looked at the wooden table in front of her and the expression on her face made me think she was seeing something the rest of us couldn't. "You changed everything. Before you, primordials were never *born*. They came into existence when they were needed. Your arrival meant change was coming, and with it the new age." I held up my free hand to stop her and Hela paused, inclining her head forward for me to speak.

"I hear what you're saying, but I'm not a primordial. I'm only half. My other half is succubus." I was fairly certain of that given that I drank kama like an addict in need of a fix.

"That's only partially accurate," Hela said hesitantly. "You require the sustenance a succubus might, but your power is primordial. We sensed it when you were born. It was the reason Lucifer bound your beast. He'd hoped that would keep the power confined until the Horsemen came for you."

"I've had low-ranging abilities my entire life," I said. Moira scoffed and I ignored it.

"You did," Merula agreed. "But that is because your power is not the flames as we thought it would be."

"What are you talking about?"

"Oh, Little Morningstar, you have much to learn about your kind," Ahnika said with a cackle. "There is no such thing as a half-primordial being. Just as the abilities that you've exhibited were no accident. Genesis held the power of creation in her fingers. Your father held fire. God held light. Others have come, both on Earth and in other worlds, before and after Genesis's death. Yet you sit before us, completely ignorant to the fact that you are the most powerful primordial ever known to date. I would wonder if you were faking the humble behavior had I not interrogated you before. You're not exactly what I would call a great liar." Several of the Sins snickered, no doubt recalling memories of me with fondness that I now thought of with a sense of betrayal.

"What are you talking about, Ahnika?" I asked.

"Until your father died no one could lay a hand on Lilith. She was unstoppable by the time he crossed the veil. She took your beast thinking that it would give her the power of the primordial—your power—but your power doesn't lie solely with the beast."

"You're speaking in riddles I don't understand. Of course, my power lies solely with the beast."

"No, Ruby," Hela said. "It doesn't."

"Lilith is currently operating on the assumption that you are dead, but if she had killed you, the beast would have died as well. It's a symbiotic relationship," Sinumpa said. I couldn't call her Lust. That was Lola's Sin and that just felt too odd. I couldn't call her Sin because we weren't friends. We were simply allies until the greater purpose had been achieved. "She thought you were a half-primordial—something that doesn't exist—and because she hails from Genesis, she thought she knew all there was to know about your kind. She didn't realize that you, dear girl, are not a primordial of flame like your father. You're a primordial of *magic*. You absorb the powers you come into contact with, making them your own." Her mercury eyes glowed eerily, reminding me of the day she stole my telepathy…that I sort of stole from her. She'd said something similar at the time, before making me unable to talk to my Horsemen or anyone else about this. She smiled, like she knew that's where my mind had gone.

"You did this with your father's power as a baby," Merula said.

"And your mother's powers," Saraphine said.

"And when you killed that boy in my house at sixteen," Lamia added. I spluttered for a moment.

"You knew about Danny?" I asked.

"Child," she smiled. "You think that you could kill someone and I wouldn't notice? Who did you think cleaned it up with the authorities?" I felt Moira's hand snake under the table to wrap around my knee, squeezing gently. I didn't like to think about Danny. What I did that night. The way Moira and I became blood sisters.

"After I entered a blood oath with you, you showed signs of my magic," Sinumpa chimed in, nicely leaving out that she also blocked me from showing anything once she figured it out.

I stared around the table from one person to another and I realized this was it. They really, truly believed that I could stop Lilith because I was some ultra-powerful primordial.

The thought was…I couldn't contain the snigger that started under my breath and built to a full-on cackle. I laughed so hard that tears formed in my eyes and slid down my cheeks. Until there was a cramp in my side and even when it hurt, I still laughed…and when it finally died out into the heavy silence, I spoke.

"You guys put your hopes and dreams in the wrong girl." Another chuckle slid from my lips that bordered on insanity. "Lilith killed me. She stole the beast and my power. I have nothing."

And I truly believed that.

Hela said, "You're wrong, Blue. You have your blood."

"What?" I shook my head a little, not sure they were really listening if we were back to this. I came here hoping for answers so I could fix what happened. Not be told I'm the messiah they've been waiting for. Weren't they listening?

"Your power is in your blood, Little Morningstar," Ahnika said. "It is the reason we tested you the way we did. You had to go to Lilith. Sinumpa had to be freed of her oath. All of this had to happen. It was the *only* way."

The back of my legs hit the chair as I stood in an instant, thankful they couldn't see my shaking limbs below the table. "The only way for who?" I demanded.

"For any of us," she whispered.

"Why?" I pushed. Her answers weren't good enough. The pounding in my skull from dehydration and blood loss aiding the righteous anger.

"Because you now possess the power you need to win this once and for all," Sinumpa said. I opened my mouth when Moira spoke.

"Blood magic," she whispered. Her blue pentagram eyes turned up to me, swirling as the always did. "In killing you, Lilith used *her* magic on you."

I froze. My breath hitched in my chest as all of what they'd told me came together and I finally understood.

Lilith was powerful enough that even the Sins couldn't take her on. If I had her power and the Sins at my disposal…

"That's not all you have," Sinumpa said suddenly. She motioned to my hand. No, she motioned to the…ring. My 'get out of jail free card' as Allistair called it. I don't think he meant it this way. "I locked a tiny sliver of your magic inside of it. Everything that was your mother's and father's is there, when you're ready to take it."

Take it. I played those words over in my mind.

Lilith had taken everything from me. She'd taken everything from every person around her. My Horsemen. The Sins. My father. Her own children.

She bit the Devil. It's time she learned this Devil bites back.

CHAPTER NINETEEN

DRIP.

Drip.

Drip.

I pulled my knees in close and tucked them under my chin. Bloods and scabs and dirt and leaves swirled around the cobbled shower floor. The rounded pebbles were uncomfortable against my skin as I leaned back into the wall behind me, vaguely listening to falling water. The cold droplets splattered against my body. Images of Laran's severed neck flashed through my mind. I tilted my head forward onto my knees, trying to calm the storm inside.

They were gone. Not dead, but gone.

Stolen.

Yes. That's what they were. Stolen, along with my beast.

I hadn't even known that was possible until this night. Then again, I didn't know what I really was either—or what I was really capable of. They said I still have magic, that my blood itself is magic, that Lilith will never be able to take my true power.

I was thankful for it. Now more than ever. Losing everything had been a wake-up call. Never in my life had I been so cocky, so overconfident that I thought my powers would save me. I wanted to say that if I'd been smart enough this never would have come to pass, but I didn't really believe that.

The Sins had set me up, and at the end of the day I didn't have a choice. They set the stage, and like the puppet I was—I danced.

Last time I took my powers for granted. I took my safety for granted. I took it all, hoping like a child that it would all be alright.

That hope almost broke me.

My hand closed around the iron handle. It screeched in protest as I turned it. The water slowed.

Drip.

Drip.

Drip.

I wasn't going to hide in here and hope. I wasn't going to sit on the floor and cry or scream or pray. They all had the same result.

Nothing. They would do nothing.

They would save no one.

I sucked in a breath as my arms fell to my sides. I pushed my splayed palms into the ground. I let my hands feel every uncomfortable inch of it as I pushed myself off the bathroom floor and rose on my own two legs. They weren't shaking anymore.

And if I had my way they would never shake again.

I went to stand before the mirror.

Drip.

Drip.

Drip.

Water splattered the floor behind me as my wet hair plastered itself to my face. I stood cold and naked in front of the mirror as I took in every scar she left, every brand she stole, every bare flawless inch…and I hated it.

I hated the scars, not because they were ugly, but because it was every cut and stab of the knife that took my beast. Every bare inch of skin where the Horsemen's brands should have been were an empty chasm in my heart as I realized that even with my magic, I could no longer feel them.

They were gone.

But not dead.

I had to remind myself of that. That there was still a chance to save them. That I could still take back everything I'd lost and more, because if I didn't remind myself, if I didn't focus on that…I may have had the power of a primordial, but I still had the heart of a woman. A woman who was rapidly losing the battle inside herself. Before, the beast had threatened to burn the world. I was scared to admit that without her I very well might, and not a soul could stop me. I was terrified that the Sins could see the truth in my eyes, that I'd lost more than my mates tonight. Lilith had stolen the beast, half of my soul, and it was changing me. I wanted to save Hell… but if I lost them all, I may very well be what destroys it.

Drip.

Drip.

Drip.

My lips pinched together in a severe scowl as I traced my fingers over the hardened scar tissue on my chest. It formed a pentagram of its own, the skin slightly raised and uneven in its healing. The blue vines that had once danced all over my body now curled tight around that wound. I swallowed hard, my eyes drifting upwards in the mirror to where Laran stood. He leaned against the stone wall, shirtless and stoic. The runes Morvaen had given him to save his life had faded from his skin over the last hours. The ones on my back still remained—bright and glowing—an iridescent orange that had not faded.

If I wore them for an eternity I would still get on my knees and thank her. Those marks on my skin were such a small price to pay for what she returned to me. I would never forget it.

Drip.

Drip.

Drip.

We didn't say anything to each other. Both of us had been lost in our own minds when Hela had shown us to our room with the promise to return in the morning. We had to prepare, she'd said. For Lilith, is what she didn't say. Even with all the power in the world, I'd had my ass handed to me once. I couldn't let it happen again. I would not get a third chance.

Again, my eyes drifted back to my body. So bare by comparison to what it had been before. They had made me a work of art, but Lilith had laid my canvas bare.

I didn't like it. The lack of brands made me feel more naked than the lack of clothes ever could. It wasn't so long ago that just the idea of brands scared me. What they meant. The commitment involved. That certainly wasn't the case anymore.

Drip.

Drip.

I shuddered.

Laran pushed off the wall. Something in his gaze changing, morphing in time, and not so very different than the darkness I felt settling around my own heart. There was a fire there tonight, one that I knew would consume me if I let it. I wondered if he saw the same thing in my eyes. If he saw the same shadows that danced.

Warm hands settled on my shoulders as he swept my hair to one side. His fingers traced over the very runes of power that saved his life and mine. I trembled.

He didn't stop.

He traced every line and when there were no more, he continued tracing. His fingers greedy as he caressed my skin, pressing to every nick, feeling every cut. His nails bit into my hips with a sudden fierceness, and through it all his eyes blazed with a dark fire. I wasn't the only one who had lost things tonight.

"I'm so sorry," he whispered hoarsely. I refused to close my eyes and shy away from the intimacy I saw.

"This was not your fault," I said back, my voice just as rough.

"I never should have agreed to let Lola take you to Earth," he said suddenly, surprising me. "I never should have let you leave my sight. I should have fought hard, done more—"

"There was nothing you could have done," I said softly. "The Sins decided my fate before you all were born. They picked and chose what to tell you. They hid things from the Devil himself. There was nothing you or anyone could have done to prevent what happened tonight."

Except perhaps me. Maybe.

My thoughts were only that, just thoughts, and yet they seemed so very loud in the confines of the bathroom. Laran's gaze grew steadily darker.

"You're doing it again," he whispered. I could see my own eyebrows draw together in the mirror, just slightly. A pucker forming in confusion. "You're projecting your thoughts."

The breath hissed between my teeth.

That only meant one thing.

My silence had been broken.

Something hardened inside of me that reflected in his eyes. I didn't ask what it was, because I knew. He was finally hearing all of the things none of them had been privy to. The dirty little secrets I held against my own will. The bargains I struck. The choices I made. The inevitable vice of crushing failure that weighed on me, and the bitter taste of loss that ate at my heart. He was hearing the things I wasn't saying, and I made no move to hide them from him.

Splayed out like the pages of a book, I let him listen and I let myself feel.

My breath hitched as he leaned forward and pressed a soft kiss to my naked shoulder.

"I hear you," the voice of his thoughts whispered through my mind. *"I hear you, and I want you to know something."* His lips skated across my skin as he ran them over my collarbone and up the crook of my neck. His breath fanned the hollow shell of my ear as he stared at me in the mirror. I put my hands on the counter in front of me as he said, *"I love you, Ruby. I love every broken and damaged piece of you. I love the ugly parts. I love the beautiful ones. I love your strength, and above all, baby, I love your fire."* His teeth bit down on the lobe of my ear, drawing a low gasp from me. My fingers curled, wrapping around the edge of the counter.

"You're going to set this world on fire, Ruby, and we're going to burn for you." The front of his body pressed firmly against my back as one of his hands came forward and parted the delicate flesh between my legs. My eyes stayed on his as he started circling my clit with two fingers. A low groan slid between his lips and my pupils dilated. *"Tell me what you want."* His silent words wormed their way into my mind, far more intimate than anything before. I pushed my hips back into his erection as one of his fingers slid inside me.

Everything. I wanted everything. I didn't want to be numb or unfeeling because I'd lost. I wanted to feel it all and remember what it was like to live. I wanted to hold onto that, to this, because when you're dying in a lake of your own blood and fighting for every breath, this is what you fight for.

I wanted this, because next time I faced her it was all or nothing.

Either we were all walking away together, or no one was.

His fingers slipped out of me and slid forward to press on the bundle of nerves. My own wetness made it easy for his fingers to glide, pulling my body tighter and tighter. I grit my teeth, arching my back. I wanted him, and I wanted him now.

Laran didn't waste time toying with me. There were no power games between us. There was no restraint. Only pure, unbridled passion as he thrust inside me and I moaned. My head tilted back into his shoulder and Laran stilled.

"Look at me," he said. *"I want to see your eyes."* He rocked back before slamming into me again. My head lolled forward as he gripped my hip with one hand and rubbed my clit with the other. Flesh met flesh as his hips slapped against me. Losing himself to this thing between us. This beautiful and savage thing called love.

My legs quickened, going straight as a rod. I watched the black of his eyes as sweat beaded on his temple. Right as I approached that mind-numbing bliss, his fingers slipped away and with it, my release. I bit back the growl of frustration as his hand slid along the length of my body, settling over my heart.

What was he doing?

As soon as I thought it, I felt it. *"You asked for everything. I am giving all that I am. Whatever you need, I will be with you to the end because you are mine…"* The embers of power in my chest caught fire as the sizzling heat beneath his palm poured into me. I breathed in the faint wash of his kama as the pulsating length beneath my legs slid in and out of me, driving me higher and higher.

A scream built in my throat, not of pain, not of power, but of an emotion far greater.

All-consuming, the blazing inferno ripped through me, and still I gave him my eyes, watching him as he watched me. *"…and I am yours,"* his mind whispered.

I shattered into a million pieces as he let out a groan and several shallow thrusts. His cock twitched inside me as my inner walls clamped around him, pulling more and more. Fire glowed beneath my skin as my veins lit up in a blaze of red and blue.

We continued like that, giving and taking from each other all night until it didn't feel as if we were two people at all, but one.

It wasn't until the next morning that I saw the scorch marks on the stone counter.

Two blackened handprints, glittering like stardust.

JULIAN

Our bodies were puppets. Prisoners in our minds.

Lilith stole us to use as instruments against the very she-demon I loved.

She took us from her. She took her from me.

I saw her soul wavering in the space in-between. Well, half of her soul. The other half now resided within us. The beast.

Lilith had ripped her in half and still they both clung to life. Clung to each other.

The beast was enraged. She was vengeful and murderous and dark and twisted. It was a wonder to me how Ruby held up against the immense power of the beast when I could barely hold a fraction.

Time stood still in this suspended state of being alive but not living.

I had no idea how long had passed, only that I had to hold on—for her —because if we gave in, the beast would well and truly destroy us all.

Even me. I'd never thought about dying because I didn't think it possible.

If we failed them, though, I had a feeling I might just find out.

I didn't fear the veil. I feared losing her. If we lost, the beast was kind to end my misery.

I would help her tear this world apart myself, piece by piece.

And so, I held on.

We all did.

CHAPTER TWENTY

I growled under my breath. My fingers curled into fists, biting into the skin. "I already told you I don't know how," I snapped. The white-haired Fae only tsked, her fingers weaving violet runes mid-air. Whatever she was casting I wanted no part in it.

"You did it once, Lucifer's Daughter." Sinumpa smiled and it was a treacherous thing. "Yesterday you had the audacity to pull it on me because you thought I meant you harm. Have you forgotten so soon what I did to you?" she taunted me. Toyed with me.

I wanted to shoot her in the devil-damned face just so she'd stop smiling like a jack-o-lantern on Halloween. The problem was that I truly did not know how I summoned the crossbow. One minute I had nothing and the next it was there, already strapped to me. Cocked and loaded.

With a flick of her fingers the rune spiraled high above me. It pulled together and then broke apart with a bang, a light sheen of purple descending around me .

"What is this?" I demanded. From the sidelines Bandit let out a rumble and it took both Moira and Laran to calm him down enough so that he didn't launch straight into this fight with me. The Sins each sat on their thrones looking down at us with varying levels of calculated interest.

"A trap," Sinumpa said. Her voice pure with malicious intent as her

672

mercury eyes darkened. My blood quickened as I looked around wildly. Trying to find a way out.

The magical barrier touched the ground and began shrinking inward. A real and true panic started to hit me. I couldn't be confined. Not again. Not ever again.

"Summon the crossbow, Ruby. It's the only thing that can break it," the Fae woman called. I took slow, measured breaths.

"*You can do this, Ruby. I believe in you,*" Laran's voice whispered into my mind. I found solace in that. Not peace, but drive. A burning motivation to get myself out of this. One way or another.

Think, Ruby. Come on.

I grit my teeth focusing on the crossbow with all my might, but the impending shield was getting closer. Shrinking faster. I was out of time and the damned crossbow wasn't coming. Which meant I needed to find another way out of this.

I rubbed my hands together, feeling a true calm wash over me.

It was moments like this the beast usually took over. She got me through the hard things with a detachment I'd never felt until now. A forced stillness that spread inside me, twisting and warping my mind. The eerie silence filled me.

I lifted my hand and pointed.

Burn. The word echoed in my mind.

Fire ignited, a mass of swirling red and blue. My father's flame and Laran's. It built at the tip of my finger, compressing in on itself, like a star preparing to explode. Sinumpa tilted her head curiously as the fire snapped free.

It hurdled towards her barrier at a breakneck speed, tearing a hole through it, sailing straight for its true target.

The breath hissed between her teeth as she realized my intent. Shouts rang out as something dark and ugly swirled inside me. This wasn't the beast.

Oh, no. This was me.

Every ounce of rage I held came forward. She dropped to the ground, narrowly missing the swirling ball of flames. I snapped my fingers and it swung around, returning to me. The room fell silent as I walked forward, my boots thudding softly against the polished stone floors.

Sinumpa tilted her head, looking up from the ground. I held the

swirling orb of chaos in one hand and nothing but a closed fist in my right
as I leaned down beside her.

"I will never forget what you did to me. I don't even know if I'm
capable of forgiving it, though it would certainly be easier on me if I did,"
I said softly. "You didn't just help her take my life away. You brought me
back to use as a tool in a war I shouldn't have to finish." Something like
regret flashed in the depths of her silver eyes. I ignored it. "I will never be
the same girl I was in Portland because of what you've done. I had to
change in order to survive this, and I will. I wasn't the one to start this war,
but I will finish it. And when all is said and done, and your mother is
nothing more than ash on the ground—I will still remember what you did,
and you had better hope"—I paused closing my hand around the orb. The
power extinguished in a flash of light—"no, you'd better pray that when I
get them back, they can piece me together again. That they can quench
this rage, because anything that I perceive as a threat to them is where I'll
be setting my sights next, *little Fae*," I whispered so softly. You could have
heard a pen drop half a mile away with how quiet the palace had gone. It
was as if time itself stood still and took note of what I was and who I was
becoming. "You took everything from me and if I have to build my own
throne on the bones of my enemies, then so be it. Remember this next time
you think of taunting me. "

I stood and walked away.

Laran and Moira stood with me, letting Bandit loose. His feet echoed
on the cold stone floors as he launched himself up and into my arms. I
caught him squarely against my chest and paused.

When I looked up to the Sins, these women that I'd known all my life, I
think they saw it. That whatever their hopes had been, whatever they had
been striving for—no matter how things had to happen—the way they
chose to go about it was wrong.

"You asked me to train and I will," I told them. "But not with her." My
fingers tightened in Bandit's fur as he curled around me.

I thought I could do this. That I could train with her as they'd asked.

I would not be a puppet any longer.

In their betrayal I'd become someone else entirely.

Heaven help the next person that crosses me after what they've done,
because nothing in Hell will. I was done playing their games, and as I
walked out of the throne room, I think they realized it too.

This time we were going to play my way.

CHAPTER TWENTY-ONE

Wind whispered over my face. A gentle caress as I leaned against the balcony. Several hours later and my temper had only marginally cooled. With a night's rest and enough food, the magic was coming back at an alarming pace. Fire roared to life like it had in the old days, except this time I knew how to control it. All of my other gifts the beast had taught me how to control were there too, just waiting to be used.

My chest constricted. A pang of emptiness hit me.

I missed her. I missed our conversations. I missed the presence that sat by me in the fire, guiding me through my nightmares and urging me to take my destiny by the horns. I'd never truly wished her gone, but it was only in losing her that I realized how much I'd come to rely on her. We were two halves of the same whole. Or we used to be.

She had been my darkness and I had been her light.

Something told me we both had fallen in this. That I wasn't the only one suffering.

My hands tightened on the railing as my skin began to glow again. The sky overhead darkened, and lightning flashed. I swallowed hard, pushing down those emotions. I couldn't afford to lose it here.

I heard the door in my room being opened. A faint whispered conversation. A rustling of feet. The curtains to the balcony drifted lazily to the side and I felt her. The burning fire of Wrath as she plopped down beside me and pushed her legs between the rails.

"Mighty fine weather you've conjured here," she said, squinting at the brewing clouds. I let out a steady breath, trying to will them away. War's power over the elements was strange still, and not something I had expected to need to learn so quickly after he branded me.

Maybe Hell itself was responsible for this as well.

"I didn't ask for this," I said quietly, waving my hand at the clouds. Hela smiled kindly, lifting her own hand. The clouds broke apart and sunlight seeped in. It bathed the sprawling city before us. Lighting up every alley, every home, every demon that dared walk in the streets when a somberness had stolen us all. Lilith hadn't come yet, but it was only a matter of time and we all felt it.

"None of us did," Hela said. Her fiery hair swayed in the breeze as her lightning eyes flashed, not with fury but something else. I didn't want to feel it, but I did. I suppose I had Lola to thank for this. "Our paths were set from the moment Genesis brought us into creation."

"You chose how to handle me. You chose to keep me in the dark, Hela. That is not something Genesis, or Lilith, or anyone else chose."

She nodded. "We did choose that. Do you want to know why?" she asked me.

No, I thought. Her lips curved up. She must have heard it.

"Well, I'm going to tell you anyways," she said, patting the ground beside her. I pressed my lips together but took a seat all the same. Pushing my legs through the railing reminded me of better times. Of the late nights we shared in her flat, sitting on a balcony grate that was far more uncomfortable than this. We used to talk for hours, watching the sun die in the sky and the moon be born. I bit my cheek because that wasn't who I was anymore, and neither was she. Those memories wouldn't do me any good in the coming battle. "I can sense your internal struggle, you know. While I was not an empath like your mother, your telepathy is so strong that you project your thoughts. I know you don't want to hear it, but Sinumpa was right to mute it. If Lilith had realized what it is you truly do, she would have drained your body dry, and that very well may have taken your magic, even if Sinumpa could save you. As much as you hate us for what we have done, remember that we did not ask to be the rulers of Hell. We, like you, never chose this." She waved to the people below us. "We were created and given a purpose. Similar to you in many ways, except we wanted more for you.

"The six of us made a pact when you were born. Your mother included, being the Sin of Lust at the time. We decided that while you were destined to save Hell, you were also only a child. A baby. We could not change your destiny, but we could alter the path towards it, so to speak." She nodded to herself, her eyes staring down unseeing. "In Hell, you would never have had anything resembling a normal childhood, even for a demon. So, we chose a different path for you. One that gave you time to learn and to grow and to experience all that life had to offer. We gave you as long as we could on Earth, because time was all that we ever truly could buy you. It was our gift to you, though you may not see it that way."

I sighed, leaning forward to rest my head on the rails. I didn't want to feel sorry for her; for any of them. I didn't want to feel anything for the Sins, but I did.

"Will I die?" I asked.

It was one thing the prophecy didn't really cover. There were a lot of vague notions about me saving Hell. About the flames. About the Horsemen.

None of it ever said what happened at the very end.

"I don't know," Hela answered. I appreciated her honesty, but damn— it stung. "For a primordial to bond to a planet, a great sacrifice must be made. Sinumpa said that Lilith stabbed herself as many times as she did you, effectively bringing herself to the edge of death before bonding to the Horsemen so that they could act as an anchor for the beast."

"Haven't I sacrificed enough?" I asked, more to myself than her. That didn't stop her from answering.

"You have sacrificed more than anyone should have to. Should you truly defeat her and survive the encounter, you will be worthy of so much more than the broken world you've inherited."

"And the trials?" I asked. A light mist blew through the valley, spraying us on the elevated balcony.

"You've already passed them," she said with a twinkle in her eye. "We were going to tell you today, but then, well…" she trailed off, but the implication was clear. Then I stormed out of my first "training" session with Sinumpa.

"I meant what I said. I'm not training with her." My hands fell away from the rails, crossing over my chest.

"I'm well aware," Hela said. "But you still have much to learn and very little time. While the flames can handle many things, Lilith will have had her army consuming brimstone long enough now that they will be all but useless. Laran's gifts now run in your veins, but I should know well enough that the power of the elements won't be enough to bring Lilith down. The crossbow given to you is a Seelie weapon. Their magic is one of the only things left in this world that can still harm her."

"I don't want to rely solely on a weapon when she's already proven to think ahead," I said. The Sins were convinced the power Donnach had put in the little gauntlet crossbow was enough to kill her, but after what went down in the Garden…I wasn't so sure.

She will plan for this. She had to. And I had to be ready for that.

"It's better than relying on the flames as you do now," Hela said reproachfully.

"That won't be the only thing I plan to use when the time comes," I snapped. I didn't want to disclose everything to her. At this point I didn't really know who I could trust, past those that were bonded to me.

"What do you mean?" Hela asked, sounding more curious than angered by my tone. Odd for the Sin of Wrath, but then again, our years spent together may have at least earned me some patience.

"I mean"—I paused, exhaling a breath—"there are other ways. Things that haven't been considered. Lilith came out of nowhere last time. She already proved to be powerful and now I'll have my own gifts to contend with as well. I have very limited time until she hears I'm still alive, and that's assuming she hasn't already. How long do you think it will take her to arrive?"

Hela grimaced, her head leaning side to side as she internally weighed the numbers. "Weeks at most. A few days, more likely."

"Exactly," I murmured. "That's not enough time to train me on anything really. After months I've only just mastered the flames. It really makes no sense to put it all on me because ultimately, if I were facing her alone, I would fail. Lilith has been planning for thousands of years just how she might destroy me. I would be a fool to think I could train hard and that any one thing could save me and end this."

The wheels had been turning since last night. The makings of a plan.

"What are you talking about?" Hela asked me.

I looked out over the city again. To the children that clasped their parents' hands. To the people that stuck to the shadows. To the shiny lake of flame. All the way to the volcano that sat at the mouth of the valley, acting as an entrance. I could hear the roar of the coliseum if I tried hard enough.

"Lilith has been planning this for an eternity. I plan to throw something else at her. Something she doesn't see coming," I paused, looking over at Hela. I wouldn't tell her everything. Hell, I wasn't telling *anyone* everything. Not even Laran. In my spiraling anger, I found the part of myself that survived so long, not on power, but something far simpler. "I was raised in the human world thinking that I was a demon with very little power, but surviving, nonetheless. I may never be that person again. But being her for twenty-three years taught me enough to know there's a better way and I plan to find it."

Hela went silent, her eyebrows slowly inching up her forehead. A laugh rang out and lightning arced across the sky.

"Ah, Blue," she smiled. "You and Sinumpa are far more alike than you realize."

I didn't say anything as I looked over Inferna. I had no idea what she was talking about, but in that moment, I didn't really want to know.

ALLISTAIR

The bitch's cackle made me flinch internally, though my muscles no longer moved at my command. I was chained to the feet of her throne. It was a chair built from the bones of her own children.

Failures, she called them. Disappointments put to better use.

She was fucking crazy.

"Did you hear that, my sweet Famine?" she chimed. I wished I could stiffen. I knew what was coming.

"Yes, my love," I answered, though not of my own accord. The beast thrashed, wanting to rip and slice and tear and *kill*. I had no doubts if she ever got free that she would end her for what she had subjected us to.

It would not be slow if the beast had her way.

It would be savage. Bloody. Ruthless. Brutal.

She would fucking destroy her.

As it was, she was caged. We all were. I prayed to Ruby for the thousandth time. I prayed that she hurried. I prayed that she was safe. I prayed that no matter what happened she got through this.

"Oh, how I just *love* you like this," Lilith purred. I wish I could gouge my own eyeballs out when she let the thin fabric of her white dress slip from her shoulders and fall to the floor.

I tried to stop myself. To resist. But I wasn't in control anymore. I was a prisoner in my own mind as she had me sit upon her throne.

I was unable to stop her from grasping my length and squeezing. Her hand jerked up and down and my revulsion reached an all-time high. This was not the first time she'd done this. It wouldn't be the last.

My dick hardened against my will and she gripped the base, straddling me on her throne of pain and lies.

"Tell me you love me," she breathed, placing herself directly over me. She slid herself down my cock, her wet cunt dripping with poison.

I'd never hated what I was until this moment.

I'd never wished to die.

I loved Ruby. I loved her so very much, but I didn't know how much more I could take of this.

My lips parted and said the words she wanted to hear. "I love you, Lilith."

She moaned, her breasts bouncing up and down as she clenched around me.

I hated myself when my hips jerked, and I emptied inside of her.

She cried out, climaxing around me and a small part of me died as she leaned forward, breathing in my scent. Her kama stank, invading my pores as she licked up the column of my throat and hummed merrily.

"Go back to your place, Famine. I want to play with Pestilence." Internally I flinched as she pulled away and lifted her naked body from mine. The mess of her release and mine pooled into my lap.

"Yes, my love." My legs stood, the liquid falling and smacking against the concrete surface, echoing in the silence of her throne room.

I couldn't control a damn thing as I took my place beside Julian, watching Rysten as he was forced to sit upon the same chair.

I had no choice but to see and feel my brother's despair as she climbed on top of him, her cunt still wet from Julian's release…from mine…

If I ever got free…

I would rip her limb from limb and feed the pieces to Bandit. I would carve the Devil's mark in her chest and pull out her still beating heart just to crush it with my bare hands.

I would let the beast flay the skin from her body, layer by layer until the damaged husk of that monster matched the person she was inside.

As it was, I waited.

I waited for Ruby.

I waited for freedom.
I waited for this to end.
The beast roared in fury.
But I could do nothing.
So, I held on to that small sliver of hope, and I waited.

****MOIRA****

He closed the door softly behind him, turning into what he thought was an empty hallway. I crossed my arms over my chest and tilted my head.

"Going somewhere, genie?"

"Moira." It was all he said; my name coming out in an exasperated sigh.

"My question still stands, Jax. You're wearing a jacket which means you're headed outside, and the backpack leads me to think you might be leaving entirely. So…" I drawled out. "Are you?"

His purple eyes settled on me as I lifted my eyebrows.

"Don't give me that look," he groaned.

"What look?" I said sweetly, batting my eyelashes. He rolled his eyes to the clouds.

"*That* look…" he muttered. "Like you're disappointed in me or something."

"On the contrary"—I wagged my finger back and forth—"I expected you to leave much sooner than this." He narrowed his eyes slightly.

"You're not mad?" he asked, genuinely confused.

"Mad?" I asked. "We fucked. It's not a proposal, big boy. I had an itch and you scratched it. Don't make this awkward." He scratched the back of his head, looking perplexed. Like he wasn't quite sure what to do with me.

"Alright, so, why are you here?" he asked, crossing his arms over his chest. I tilted my head to the side, listening to my surroundings. The howling wind and occasional errant breeze caught my attention, but it was otherwise quiet. Excellent.

"I needed to ask you a couple of questions before you left," I said. "Like, where are you going?"

His eyes widened for a moment at my straight-forwardness and then he coughed. "Typically, girls don't ask that if—"

"I'm not looking for a hookup," I rolled me eyes. His cheeks darkened from a blush. "Don't get me wrong; you were good and all. I'm just not looking for any sort of relationship—not even a casual one. The world is ending and I've got enough people to keep an eye on as it is." He nodded as if he understood, but there was something in his eyes that I pretended not to see.

"I see," he muttered. "If you must know, I'm meeting up with someone."

"Sin?" I asked. He blinked twice.

"Possibly."

"She was the Sin that called in a favor to escort us to Inferna, right?" I brushed a hand over my sleek green braid, flicking the tail over my shoulder.

"She was."

"And your debt is paid now, yes?"

"It is."

"Good," I smiled, clapping my hands together once. "You see—the thing is—I hear things. Lots of things. And a little birdie told me the most *interesting* thing about Sinumpa, but it seems that every time I manage to track her down, she simply disappears. Why is that?"

"I'm not sure," Jax said, blowing out a rough breath. "You'd need to ask her."

"I plan to," I nodded.

Well," he started as he went to sidestep me, "if that's all—" The words caught in his throat.

Jax started coughing. "Not…possible…" His eyes bulged in alarm, shocked by what was happening. I sighed, taking my time to stroll to a stop in front of him. I leaned down, putting us at eye level.

"Enigmas are only immune to magic from those *beneath* them in power, Jax. I'm a legion; the familiar to the strongest primordial to ever come into being. You heard it yourself. So, let's make this easy." I blinked, and the pressure fizzled out as he found himself able to breath. "I want to know where Sin is and where you are going."

"Can't…tell…you…" he managed to choke out between coughs and heavy panting.

"There, there," I patted him on the back. "You know how rough I can be in bed, enigma. And I know you like it. Do you *really* want to push this—"

"Blood…oath…"

I sighed and clenched a fist, choking him again. It didn't escape my notice that he was hard, and I couldn't help but find it rather amusing.

"You were looking for me," a voice whispered through the shadows. I smiled, letting Jax have another couple of seconds to sweat it before loosening my grip. He collapsed onto his knees, leaning into my right thigh.

"You're…going…to be…"—he coughed hard and cleared his throat—"the death of me." I winked at him and patted his dreads for a moment before turning to spare Sinumpa a glance.

"You're leaving with the enigma," I said. "Where are you going?"

Her silver eyes glowed like the light of a dying star. She was the most beautiful being—male or female—I'd ever seen, and she was appraising me with interest.

"I get the impression you already know," she answered.

"Earth," I whispered.

Sin nodded.

"The borders are closed." I swallowed hard and looked down the corridor at nothing in particular. "How is it possible that you can portal between worlds?"

"How did you know where I would go?" she asked, ignoring my question entirely.

"You're splitting town and nowhere in Hell is safe. That doesn't leave many places…" I trailed off, but it was only a partial truth.

"Tell me." Sin strolled forward, her leather boots silent on the stone floors—even to my ears. "Do the dead talk, green one?"

I looked to the ceiling, the corner of my lips turned up. Yes. Yes, they did. Incessantly, really. But just as I could shush the living, so too could I silence the dead if I so chose. Usually I just let them chatter away. Never knew what stories you might hear.

"Sometimes," I admitted. "But this did not come from the dead."

"Then who?" she asked. There was a sharp edge to her tone and I didn't like it.

"I'll make you a deal, Sin," I said boldly. "I want to know why you're leaving Ruby to face your mother alone. If you can tell me that—and tell me the truth—I'll tell you how I found out."

Sinumpa grinned as she stepped right up to me with a swagger, starlight shining in her eyes. She extended a hand, and I swear my heart damn near jumped out of my chest.

I didn't hesitate for even a second. Our hands joined, and I saw it. In my mind, I saw the truth…

If Sin stayed, we would all die. Lilith had bound her so tightly in blood oaths that her presence would end us all. The Sins. Bandit. Me.

The *only* one who could end this was Ruby.

Sin was leaving because there was no other way for Hell's humanity to recover should she stay. It was a risk—the largest one of all—because it left the weight of the world on one woman's shoulders. But it was also a gift.

The only gift she could give for what she had already done.

CHAPTER TWENTY-TWO

My footsteps were silent as I padded from one room to another. I'd left my boots next to the door so that I could be as quiet as possible and not disturb the sleeping raccoon. He was sprawled on Laran's chest, drooling everywhere. Laran had conked out as well, but I wasn't as worried about waking that one. He was sleeping like the dead since we'd returned here. Said it was something about the land returning him to full strength. I didn't dwell on it, or his reasons. He needed his energy for what was to come, and I needed to be ready.

Stepping past Moira's door, I ignored the inkling of guilt that niggled at me for not talking to her about this first. The less each person knew, the better.

In a world where even your thoughts weren't private, I needed to be wary of how much I let anyone know. Then again, that's why I was here.

My closed fist came up to knock on the door, hovering mid-air when it swung open before me. I blinked as Morvaen leaned out and looked from side to side before motioning for me to come in. I swallowed once and nodded, lowering my arm as I stepped over the threshold.

"You knew I was coming?" I asked, slowly striding forward into the suite. Two armchairs were arranged to face each other with a small table between them.

"I suspected," the Seelie woman said. She took a seat in one of the chairs, waiting for me to sit in the other.

"Why is that?" I continued, plopping down across from her. The leather pants I'd been given stretched to the max as I crossed my legs. While tough and durable, they weren't exactly the most comfortable. The movies never mentioned that. Then again, they didn't mention a lot of things.

"You're fighting an enemy that has already beaten you once. An enemy that demons no longer remember how to beat because they've been in her clutches for far too long. A smart individual would speak to one of the two creatures in this palace that have an understanding of the Fae." She leaned forward, lifting the teapot from the table and pouring two cups. I leaned forward and accepted mine gratefully while she continued. "You cannot be in a room with one of us without trying to kill her. So, it is no surprise that you came to me as the lesser evil."

I took a sip of the steaming herbal brew. "You know what I am, yes?"

"A primordial of magic."

I nodded. "And you know how I gain new magic?"

"By coming into direct contact with it," she answered. "Much like you have with mine," she added. I pressed my lips together in a tight smile.

"I haven't seen traces of your magic yet, but after everything I've been told, I do believe it is there." I took another sip, settling deeper into the armchair. A contentedness filled me.

"I do as well," Morvaen said. "Is this why you have come to me?"

"Yes." The word bubbled up and spilled out of me before I could think. I swallowed another sip of tea and frowned. "I came because I want to understand the difference between blood magic and rune magic."

"It's really quite simple. When Genesis split herself in two, half of her essence created Lilith and half created Eve. Lilith received the magic of the body and all that is tangible. It relies on blood sacrifices in return for power," Morvaen said.

"And Eve?" I prompted.

"The magic of the mind. Rune magic is far more nuanced in that it works with what cannot be seen. Its power comes from inside us." She motioned to a spot on her chest, over her heart. "The soul."

"Donnach made me a crossbow with Seelie magic," I said. The words came to my tongue without thought or effort. "The Sins are convinced the crossbow is the way to kill Lilith, but the truth is I'm not very good with it even though it is spelled to hit whatever I'm aiming for. Nor do we have the time to fix that," I continued. "And I believe relying on something so simple is foolish, really. I need to find a way to beat Lilith so that she doesn't see it coming." I frowned again, looking at my cup.

Morvaen nodded, setting her tea in front of her. "You'll have to forgive me for spelling the tea with truth. We Fae cannot lie, but your kind can. In this world I need to know who you truly are, Ruby Morningstar, if I am to give you what you seek."

"And what is that?" I asked her, deliberately taking another sip of tea. I had nothing to hide from this woman. All the better that she sees it.

"The power of the Seelie. The reason Lilith feared our kind enough to send her own sister onto another plane of existence knowing that it would ultimately kill her." I nodded, tipping the cup and drinking the last of my tea. The rim hid my smile as I let out a breath.

"Right," I drawled. "I want to know it all. I want to understand, but most of all—I want to save this world from her. I need my Horsemen and the beast back. The people need peace. The land needs time to heal. I don't want a war, Morvaen. I want an execution."

She nodded, and in her silver eyes I saw understanding. She leaned back, crossing her hands on her lap as she watched me. Long hair so black it looked like liquid tar hung over one shoulder, showcasing her runes along the other. "You're a curious woman. Do you know how many times in the thousand years I've lived that I have given another my rune of protection— the same one I placed on you—so that it may call on me for a favor owed?" I shook my head. "Twice. Once for a lover that betrayed me. The second time was for a girl I thought to be my enemy. You could have ordered me to do anything with that rune once called upon, and all you asked for was to save your mate."

"I will never be able to show you my gratitude for what you did," I found myself saying. She blinked and I could tell that surprised her. "I am only holding onto my humanity by the barest of threads. I want to save this world, but I don't want to live without them. The rage will consume me until I will either destroy them all or wish I were dead myself. Maybe both. You saved a piece of me from dying that day, and for that, words will never be enough to show how I feel."

This rage was a terrible thing. It made me strong enough to live through what I had, but not so strong that I might overcome it if things don't go my way when this is all over.

Was this the price of such power?

Or was I simply not strong enough to begin with?

"Spelled tea or not, your honesty comes out easily for a demon," Morvaen said simply. "You are humble for a primordial being, but more than that, you have lost all there is to lose and still you cling to humanity. You are worthy of the knowledge you seek." She stood from her arm chair, offering me a hand. I took it, setting my empty cup aside. "Many of the Seelie lost their magic in those early days on Earth. They feared losing their story with each passing generation, and so my father devised a spell unlike anything we had seen before."

Her fingers began to twirl and orange strokes of power came to life. I watched, transfixed as always. "What does it do?" I asked.

"It is the holder of all knowledge," she said. "Every Seelie child performs this spell at least once in their life upon reaching the age of maturity. Once it is cast, that Fae is bestowed with the knowledge of Seth and every Seelie that has performed it after him." One by one the runes began to float in a loose circle, and the more she added, the more they started to lock together like pieces of a puzzle.

"Did you say Seth? As in Eve's son?" I asked.

"Aye," she nodded. "He was my father. Cain, his brother, came to Hell for glory. Abel died as a sacrifice. My father wanted the Seelie to live on. He settled in New Orleans and after many generations of children, I came to be. Some of us are born with more magic than others. Not all Seelie can withstand time and settle into immortality. He created this spell because of it." I stared at her, near speechless.

"Why would you do something like this for me?" I asked her as the runes started to move faster. They locked together forming a mandala of light.

"You are the future of this world. A future I would like to be a part of," she answered. Her fingers stilled and the intricate circle of light stopped. "Which is why I offer this not as a gift, but as a bargain. I will give you the knowledge of all that we were and are so that you have the power to put the Blood Queen down, but in return—when all is said and done—my people get to return home."

I stilled. That wasn't what I had been expecting. Answers? Maybe. A trade? I had considered brokering one, but I hadn't expected this.

"Will this truly give me what I seek?" I asked her.

"You will know our history. You will understand our power. You will know what my magic is—the magic that now runs in your veins—and you will know how to use it. I have never offered this to another soul, but then again, there has never been one with the power to complete the ritual and survive. Only the power of the Seelie will do." As she spoke, goosebumps formed over my arms. There was something in the air that whispered of ancient power and forbidden secrets.

I'd come here to bargain for something else entirely, but what she offered…it could change everything.

"And what if I asked for something more?"

"I have nothing more to give," she answered steadily.

"Could you bring your people here?" I asked. Soldiers. That's what I'd come to ask for. Seelie soldiers that could fight blood with magic. The hunters of all demon kind.

Morvaen shook her head. "As you already saw, I am unable to open a portal directly to Earth, not even to bring someone in. That power lies with a being who is bonded to this planet and the only way to surpass it would be both blood and rune magic. Neither of which you are proficient in." I cursed because she was right. I hadn't the faintest clue how to use the blood magic. It was the reason I wanted the Seelie on my side to begin with. "And even if I could open such a portal," Morvaen added, "I am not at liberty to offer my people for your war. Seth's Wisdom is the most I can give."

I took a deep breath, looking between the glowing mandala, the Fae, and the greater world beyond. I had no idea what this would do to me, or who I might become. I could never go back, though. Only forward. If this knowledge gave me the power to defeat Lilith, then so be it.

I held my hand out to her, well aware this may come back to bite me in the ass, but I was out of options.

Morvaen took my hand in both of hers, turning it palm upward. She scrawled a symbol into the flesh before pressing her own palm against mine. A searing ripped through my skin, fading to a stinging ache before I could even react. Morvaen smiled and I had the distinct feeling it was genuine, despite the way it looked like a sharp grimace.

"Let's get started."

CHAPTER TWENTY-THREE

It FELT like my flesh was being peeled from my body, but I drew every damn line of that spell.

Seth's Wisdom, they called it.

It was a rune that exacted so much from you that only those with a purpose greater than themselves could survive the crushing weight of the knowledge it held. Morvaen could have warned me, but she didn't. I'd be more pissed about it if it would have made a difference. I was getting everything it had to offer, no matter the costs. So even when my bones seemed to break, and my blood began to boil, and the pressure in my mind became so strong I thought my skull had been split in two—I kept drawing.

The very moment my fingers completed the final flourish, a darkness consumed me. Pain racked my body to the point that all I could do was separate myself from it and focus on reaching for the only light. The spinning rune. Seth's Wisdom.

Their faces flashed before me.

Bandit.

Moira.

Laran.

Allistair.

Rysten.

Julian.

Me.
I was doing this for us.
I would not fail.
A doorway appeared and I didn't hesitate.
I didn't falter.
My fingers wrapped around the handle and I felt it.
Knowledge.
Power.
Everything.

＊LARAN＊

Three days.

She'd been comatose for three days. All the while Lilith drew closer.

I tried entering her mind, but my telepathy was not strong enough.

I sent Moira, but she could not breach whatever place held her.

Bandit curled himself around her feet as we waited.

I'd fallen asleep when she was on the balcony. I'd woken to her in bed beside me. No one knew what had happened. No one knew how to fix her.

I held her hand in mine. The pale skin stretched taut over blue veins. Moira paced at the foot of the bed, snarling at anyone who dared enter.

She couldn't last much longer like this, and the war would not wait for her.

I needed her to come back to me.

I needed to know she was alright.

I just needed…her.

"Soon," a voice whispered. I blinked and looked to Moira. She had stopped and was looking at Ruby like she'd seen a ghost.

"Did you hear that?" she asked.

"I did."

"Soon," the voice repeated.

Nothing about her changed. The blue strands of hair stayed limp on her pillow. Her breathing never faltered. Her pulse never jumped.

But Ruby would be waking up.
Soon.
I just hoped it wasn't too late.

CHAPTER TWENTY-FOUR

My eyes opened after an eternity of pain.

I'd lived every nightmare.

I'd suffered every torture.

I'd felt every single death that the Seelie had endured.

I saw their plight.

I saw their struggle.

I saw their persecution.

And in the end…I understood them.

Seth's Wisdom had aged me centuries. At the end of it—when I had lived their lives and known their sorrows—when the bitterness and resentment of all that had been done to them subsided, I got what I came for.

Every single rune that had been created since the dawn of time now sat on my fingertips.

Every single event that led us here sat in my mind.

A choking noise pulled my attention. I blinked, turning my head. The soft fabric of a pillowcase brushed against my cheek. A cold wind blasted the baby blue curtains in the air like streamers, chilling me to the bone as I took in Laran's face.

"Wh-what's wrong?" My voice was scratchy. My throat dry. I felt like I'd swallowed sand and then tried to speak, and the craggy sound that came out was pitiful. *How long had I been asleep?*

"Three days. Almost four," Laran murmured. Black eyes so dark they reminded me of ashes from my flames looked at me with sadness. "What happened? Where have you been?"

There was no easy answer.

The body and mind were two different things. While I had taken a journey that felt closer to a millennium in my mind, my body had been lying in bed. I'd lived a thousand lives and died a thousand deaths in the span of days. I'd hunted demons and had been the hunted. I'd seen rape and torture and cruelty that could turn an iron stomach. All at the hands of Lilith.

I now knew Morvaen and every other Seelie that had crossed through Seth's Wisdom and come out alive. I knew them as well as I knew myself.

Where had I been? The question turned over in my mind.

"Everywhere," I answered. Knowing that wouldn't appease or makes sense, I sat up. Stretching my arms high over my head, I reveled in the series of pops as my stiff body came to life again. "I'm not able to disclose what you want to hear. I'm sorry," I added. "It's not my secret to share. I went looking for a way to beat Lilith."

He opened his mouth—paused—then asked, "Did you find it?"

Did I find it?

"I found…" I hesitated, a breath exhaling from my chest. My fingers fisted in the black satin sheets. The ornate tapestries that hung on the wall drew my attention as I struggled for the right words to say. "Answers."

"You're not going to tell me, are you?" He didn't sound upset, but I still felt the need to explain.

"No," I sighed. "Lilith has my power. She can get into anyone's mind. Now more than ever I need to hold the truth close." I unclenched my fingers from the slick fabric and slid my legs over the edge of the bed. The dark stone floor felt warm beneath my feet as I stood, still leaning back onto the bed while I faced him.

"I know. It's better this way," he said. His mouth moved to form a smile, but it fell short. The corners of his eyes were strained. I blinked, taking in the dark circles from lack of sleep and the sallowness of his skin. My heart clenched.

"Is everything alright?" The uneasy look in his eye said no, it wasn't alright. In fact, something was very wrong.

"You were…*asleep*…for a few days," he started slowly. My pulse quickened. It hammered unnaturally as he looked toward the ceiling and his hands clenched tight around nothing. "During that time, we got word Lilith is on her way."

Pounding turned into an all-out gallop, but I didn't move an inch.

I simply asked, "How long?"

He lowered his head, and in the early afternoon light I could see several days of growth on his beard. I didn't say anything as he looked me up and down. A pleading entered his eyes, and I knew what was coming.

"How long?" I asked again.

"Not long enough."

"How long?" I repeated, harsher.

"Damnit, Ruby." He clasped my jaw in his hands, holding me like I was the most precious thing in this world. And I knew I was. "I'm scared, alright? I trust you that whatever happened you truly believe you've found the way to end this, but I am scared. You've already given so much…" Desperation leaked out of him. I closed my eyes as he leaned his forehead against mine.

"It's okay to be scared," I whispered. "I'm scared too."

"I don't want to lose you. Not again."

"You won't." I opened my eyes and leaned back, ignoring the gut-wrenching pain as his hands dropped away from me. "Just as I won't leave this world to her. She has the beast, she has my mates, and she holds the people of Hell prisoner to satisfy her every whim. That is unacceptable."

"You've changed, baby," he whispered. I pressed my lips together to keep from flinching.

"My soul was ripped in half and I survived. Everything has a price, Laran. You know this," I said, fighting my own desperation to comfort him as I stood strong.

"I do, which is why I won't ask you to run. We've already lost too much. I just wish we had more time."

"How long?" I asked softly. He must have sensed this was the last time I would ask. My next move was to walk out the door and find out for myself. A darkness passed over the balcony, casting the room in shade.

He swallowed hard. "It's already begun."

CHAPTER TWENTY-FIVE

I RAN TO THE BALCONY, ignoring the loose swaths of fabric as they twisted around my limbs, trapping me in their confines as I looked up. A mass loomed over us, a hundred times greater in size than the enormous palace I stood in, blocking the sun and blanketing Inferna in a bleak shadow.

"What is that?" I breathed.

"The Brimstone City," he answered gravely. "It was once known as the province of Pride. Lilith's domain."

"It's *floating*. Why is it floating?" I asked, unable to stop the panic from coloring my tone.

"Lilith wanted a city that no one could enter without her knowing; a city that transcended the barriers of magic. She sacrificed one hundred of her children to create the spell that keeps the city airborne."

Horror washed through me. I clenched my teeth together as the world turned dark, seemingly bleached of color as the sun disappeared entirely. It was only the torches lit below us that kept the city visible in any way. In the span of minutes, Inferna had gone from a sprawling wonder to looking like a hellscape straight out of the Bible.

"People are warring in the streets." I wouldn't have believed it would happen that way if I hadn't seen it myself. The way two friends turned on each other mid-stride and began trading blows with torches. Parents turned on children. Brother on sister. Wife on husband. Inferna descended into chaos as the floating city sat directly overhead, crushing the atmosphere with its very presence.

"That's the power of Famine at work," Laran said behind me. "He toys with their emotions. Makes them feel what he wants them to feel."

"He can't be doing this by choice." There was no way. Allistair was many things…but not this.

"She took your bonds with them," Laran muttered. "There's no telling what she's truly done in the days they've been gone."

"No," I contradicted him. Frowning, I tapped my chin. "She took the magic of those bonds that held us together. She didn't take the feelings behind them. They chose to be my mates, which lends the question—how much awareness of this do they truly have?" I murmured.

"Her magic helped create us," he said. "It's hard to say." The wind howled through the valley and the biblical references weren't lost on me. I was about to walk through the valley of the shadow of death, but I wasn't praying to any god. I was prepared to finally be one.

"We'll get them back, Laran. I promise."

"Don't make promises here, Ruby." He let out a rough exhale, the knuckles of his fists turning white. "Just…be safe. Be careful. Don't over-play your hand. I have fought so many battles and won many a war. The loser doesn't always lose because they were not good enough, or strong enough. It's because they made a mistake." He shook his head slightly as he remembered things that I'd never lived through, but some of the Seelie had. "A single mistake could cost your life and I don't want to lose you. The first time you faced her, we both died. You barely survived, and haven't trained with the Sins but once. I don't know how you're going to pull this one off, baby, but…"

I stared at him—knowing the mighty Horseman I saw but only now truly seeing the man. Even demons, powerful as they might be, had weaknesses. I was his.

"Trust me," I whispered, taking his hands in mine. "Trust that I know what I am doing. Trust that I am strong enough. Trust that…" I grasped at the fire in his eyes. "Trust that I will not fail—that I can put this world back together again."

He brushed the hair away from my eyes, placing a kiss on my forehead. I leaned in, but I did not yield.

I wouldn't. Not now. Not ever. Not for anyone.

"I love you," he whispered.

"I know you do," I said with a sad smile. This was the only goodbye I would get with him, with any of them, if I fucked this up. "But I need more than your love this time. I need your complete trust to not try to stop me. No matter what."

He leaned away as I took his hands in mine. "Ruby, you are the only woman—demon or otherwise—that I will bow to ever again. I trust you and that you know what you're doing…even if I don't understand. I will stand by you until the day I die. I've done it once already and I will do it again. If that day is today, so be it."

We kissed and it was everything. It was fire and passion and desperation—that connection that all people sought. Human. Demon. Fae. Mortals and immortals alike spent entire lives looking for this thing between us. Some called it soulmates, but I refused to believe there was only one person in the world you're meant to be with. It's an awfully big universe, after all.

I found my match in four exceedingly possessive, sometimes devious, and always devoted mates. They couldn't be more different from each other if they were born centuries and worlds apart. They weren't perfect, but they were mine. I'd experienced the love that some people never found in all their searching, and I'd felt it four times greater.

With it had come this loss so crushing that I was left with nothing but scraps of a soul and wisps of power when they had been ripped from me. I'd loved so fiercely that when I lost them all, it was the most devastating experience in the universe. To have a love so consuming that it burned, and you burned with it. Bright. Fierce. True.

That was what we had. That was what *we all* had.

A love that changed the worlds.

A love that could and would overcome anything.

I sucked in a breath as a harsh wind whipped at my skin, rattling my bones. My teeth grit as I stormed back into the bedroom and readied myself—not for battle—but for war. We dressed silently, clothing ourselves in the fighting leathers of Hell before we stormed the palace halls. Our footsteps echoed in the empty silence as we made our way down to the throne room. My footing slipped on the bottom step of the quartz stairs and Laran steadied me with a single hand—not missing a beat.

I mumbled my thanks as we approached the onyx doors with a silver pentagram engraved on them. The wood panels hung ajar, the metal hinges melted or broken.

Backs to us—I saw them.

My Horsemen.

Pestilence stood to the right wearing armor made of gold. His blonde hair appeared honeyed, his cheek bones strong and sharp. My Rysten had always seemed so carefree, but this man in metal was merely a phantom apparition of his previous radiance. I turned to Death, standing regal and glistening in the starkest of whites. He'd always been a stoic sort that straddled the edge of cruelty. Now, not even a hint of warmth resided inside him. Even with his back to me, I could sense the swirling abyss eating him alive. The darkness that swallowed all light.

I couldn't say that the last one I saw was the one that hit me the hardest, but it was a blow to my gut, nonetheless. Allistair did not carry the light that Rysten did. Nor did he harbor the demons of Death. Allistair was a man who wore a mask. A fiend that walked into your life and stole your heart before you even knew he was reaching for it. To see him dressed in onyx, painted a dark knight…I saw the duties that confined him. The rules that bound him. The lecherous chains of submission that buried the man I knew so deep underneath…I had no doubt he wasn't truly in control as he brought about anarchy.

They stood, soldiers of pain.

Bringers of destruction.

The apocalypse.

And I wondered…I wondered if it wasn't the flames I was meant to stop. If it wasn't the barriers between the worlds—I wondered for the first time…if it was *them*. If they, the Horsemen who brought me here under the guise of a savior, were the very apocalypse that I was destined to be the savior of—or to fall myself and bring both the worlds with me.

A cackle pulled at my attention.

And I knew who stood there—the woman in white that stole them.

A crown of lilies adorned her head, their color tainted in comparison. Her dress, if it could truly be called that, was two panels of fabric hung over both shoulders and bound around the waist by a golden chain.

"I heard your rumors. That the girl lived…" her voice carried as she stared down the Sins—all of them but one. Sinumpa was absent, but she'd already betrayed me one too many times for me to think she'd stick around.

I don't know what my mother was thinking, but she chose a coward. Both her and Jax were gone, but not the others. The Sins and Moira were armed and ready to defend without even knowing if I would make it in time. Bandit stood tall on her shoulder, teeth bared and eyes blazing. Pride swelled within me. "How pathetic."

"Pathetic?" Hela asked, her voice carried as well, fueled by an errant wind. Her flaming hair lifted as lightning's wrath filled her gaze. "You killed the very man you claimed to love after killing the mother of his child. You've sought vengeance for a throne that was never yours. You've tried to steal the power of the primordial, and committed war crimes against our people and yours—all in the name of a throne that doesn't belong to you." Power radiated in every word as that rage she was known for came to life. She stood like a beacon light against the darkness. "Your end is now, Lilith. Lucifer is gone, and we will not allow this madness to reign in our domain any longer."

"My, my," Lilith mocked. "You have grown rather big for your britches, Hela. Tell me, is there any bite behind that bark." She flicked her fingers and the flames leapt at *her* command. My flames. That rage I'd kept so close to my heart came bubbling up as they incinerated Hela's clothing. It seemed she had been smart enough to consume brimstone before this fight.

"Is that the best you've got?" Hela taunted, throwing her hand in the air. Thunder roared as a bolt of lightning came down on her. The hairs on my arms rose when she pointed to Lilith and the electricity at her fingertips struck her with enough force it rattled the building. I held my breath as she stilled, neither falling nor retaliating.

"You should know by now that these childish abilities you have won't work on me," Lilith spat. The sweetness of her tone had dried up. "You were merely a *flaw* created by Genesis. I am of her blood. Her very *soul*," she said, her tone dripping with disdain.

Hela's fingers balled into fists, and while she'd never show it, there was very real fear there. It was palpable.

Lilith lifted her hands as if in a gesture to say, *my turn*. Demons did not play fair, though. The moment she moved, both Moira and Ahnika stepped forward and let out a scream.

As a child, she was strong enough to shatter an eardrum. As a transitioned banshee-legion, Moira held the power to bring down buildings. That was by herself.

When the Sin of Sloth let loose her own scream, they had the strength to cause an earthquake.

The ground began to rumble as the earth protested against the mighty power being thrown at it. Lilith clapped her hands over her ears as all three Horsemen before us fell to their knees under the strain.

Lamia stepped forward and the veins around her eyes turned black as she extended her hands toward the fallen woman and whispered a word I didn't have a prayer of hearing, if not for her thoughts.

"Bleed."

At her command, Lilith's skin split. The arteries of her neck exploded, raining blood upon the dark navy floors. Her legs collapsed, her white dress stained red as her blood seeped into the fabric. Lying in a pool of her own blood, the earth split and opened its gaping mouth.

Her body tumbled into the chasm.

Lost to the darkness within.

The screams died away, drowned by a sea of silence and apprehension.

No one rejoiced or applauded. I did not dare to even speak as the gaping mouth closed shut.

Because deep down—knowing what I did now—I knew that even I could survive that.

Which meant Lilith could as well.

The moments spanned in time, but the Horsemen never rose. Behind me, Laran had grabbed a handful of my shirt to steady me as something thick and pungent began to clog the air.

Dark magic. Blood magic. Only it wasn't Sinumpa or me using it.

The ground shook as a great power built beneath it. Chunks of stone the size of baseballs rattled. Poison burned at my nostrils.

No one had even a moment to dive for cover. One second the ground quaked as a whining sound resonated deep inside. The next, it didn't just split. Oh, no. The stone itself fractured and caved in.

A figure cloaked in red and black rose, floating upwards as if suspended in water. The lilies in her hair were crushed into nothing more than bloody petals and broken stems.

"Did you really think that would work?" she asked them. I heard it in her voice in that moment. She meant death; if left to her own devices, she would destroy the very world she wished to rule if it meant obliterating the Sins.

Her hands raised and a phantom darkness wrapped around her. It took only a second to realize what was happening. I'd never been on the outside when I used that particular ability.

I never saw the way one's own soul poised to strike.

She intended to rip every soul in that room from its body.

But she hadn't planned on one thing.

Me.

My fingers twirled as the depraved soul of a mad woman sought its victims. If you blinked, you would miss it. The glow of a rune so bright and blue it hurt to look at. My rune. My power. My protection.

A barrier snapped into place around her, trapping that hideous soul within. I squinted, searching the blackness for even a spec of blue, but there was none.

Lilith looked every which way, spinning around.

The Sins faces were set in shock. Moira's in a smirk, despite the odds as she knew them.

But Lilith's—her lips were set in a grim smile.

"Well, well, well," she purred. "The bitch wasn't lying after all. Little Morningstar came to play."

There was a time when her taunting set fear in my heart, but when I smiled over the head of my enslaved mates, it was all teeth and no fear.

She thought she was the biggest, baddest bitch on the playground.

But I was the Devil now, and you don't steal from the Devil without paying your pound of flesh.

CHAPTER TWENTY-SIX

Rage was a dangerous thing.

It was all consuming as fire itself. It was as vast and expansive as the sea. It settled deep within, festering and rotting if you let it. But more than anything, the reason rage was so powerful was because you couldn't simply choose to lift it.

It came and went as it willed. Sitting on your chest like a demon in the night until it decided to leave you and afflict another.

I could not change it. I could not calm it. I could simply live with it, and in that I found power among the powerless.

Most people stricken lost themselves in the grips of passion, but I honed mine into a strength of its own.

My rage guided me. It fueled me so that I had no reservation when the end came.

She'd stripped me of everything, and for that she was going to lose it all.

"I must say, you look better than when I left you," she noted. Her eyes carefully straying towards my chest. My brand. "Tell me," she murmured. "How'd you do it?"

I smiled even though I wanted to rip her limb from limb. Her clawed hands formed fists. It bothered her that I'd survived. She was unsure of herself now. Unsure of her power. Unsure of mine. I reveled in it.

"Well," I started. My boots thudded against the floor as I slowly started for her. "It was really a number of things. As it was, my body was slowly trying to stitch itself back together, but with so little blood I would have died and stayed dead, were it not for Sinumpa."

Her eyes flashed with a fury, and if for some reason I did not succeed, I had no doubt that she would hunt down her daughter to the ends of this world or the next. I pitied her, Sinumpa, in that moment. She was a cursed child who grew into an imprisoned woman.

"Sinumpa?" she said, attempting and failing to hide her surprise. I flashed a Cheshire grin that only served to piss her off more.

"Oh, yes," I nodded. "You see, while you've been planning my destruction, she was planning yours. Her actions are what set all of this into motion, after all." I waved a hand at the palace around us. "She found me when I was a baby, made a deal with my mother, then convinced you she became the Sin of Lust because she "took" it. You were so desperate to believe that someone truly wanted to see you on the throne that you didn't see her for the double agent she has always been. Not that I blame you there," I added. "I'm an empath and I didn't see her for what she was until that moment in the Garden. She led me to be slaughtered only to bring me back with a blood oath."

Rage. It was a dangerous thing. Lilith loved to toy, but if there was one thing I realized in all those Seelie memories I'd lived through, it's that she was a slave to her own emotions and too prideful to see. It was going to make for the sweetest of endings.

"So, you lived." Her eyes slid to Laran. "And you somehow managed to save the spare. You're insistent. I'll give you that." Between us, the three Horsemen rose and closed ranks around her.

"They can't save you," I said. Her expression froze.

"You may have lived but you have no power. The beast lies within *them*," she growled.

"The beast wasn't the holder of my true power," I replied steadily. Her pupils thinned to slits, making the gold of her eyes that much brighter.

"You're lying!"

"No," I smirked. "But you wish I was."

My taunting pushed her over the edge. Flames raced to greet me and I greeted them as my own. They licked at my skin and burned away my clothes until I stood nude for all to see.

"Impossible," she whispered as I cut the flames out with a snap of my fingers. She stared at the brand on my chest. Over the hardened scar tissue, blue vines curled protectively in the form of a pentagram.

"Clearly not if I'm standing before you," I said, reveling in the way her pale cheeks darkened to a pink. "You see, for all the great time you've spent plotting my death and your eventual rise—you never took the time to properly realize what I am." I gazed at the apathetic faces of Pestilence, Death, and Famine. On the outside, they appeared so empty, but inside they were drowning in such darkness. Such pain.

"What…you…*are*?" She let out a cackle that would give Moira a run for her money. "You're *nothing*. No one. You think because you survived me once that you will again?" she smirked, but I sensed her growing unease just as she could feel my calm.

The blackened soul in her chest roused a second time, aiming for me. I thought it so very telling that while she might look like a saint, inside she was a monster of the worst kind. An animal bound to its instincts. A madman with no control.

Lilith moved to strike, and this time I didn't block her. I met her head on.

Our phantom forms met in a collision of great power, but try as both might, there was no harming one another. She could not hurt me, just as I could not hurt her. It was an impasse.

"You see, Lilith—the thing is—you stole my magic without understanding what it could really do. I don't blame you. I myself didn't truly understand until now." I shrugged with a faked nonchalance. Our souls continued to twist and twine, but there was not a thing she could do. "In stealing it, though, you put us on a level playing field. You can't hurt me, because all you have to throw at me—is me. You understand?" She gnashed her teeth as her soul continually attacked but made no ground. "We are so evenly matched that I knew I couldn't defeat you like this. It would never work, and given enough time, you'd probably outsmart me because you're far older and more experienced. I never had a hope if that's how I planned to beat you."

She switched tactics, using her nails to slit her own wrists. Fresh blood slicked her fingers as she began to chant.

Still I smiled. Desperation was eating at her.

"That worked on me once," I nodded, gesturing to the magic gathering around us. Without an outlet, it would inevitably fizzle out. "The only problem is that you've already used that trick. You stole the beast and ripped my soul in half. It was the most painful experience in all of my life. It will probably be the worst thing I endure until the end of times." As I predicted, the magic flared and like a firework on display, it burned out.

"How are you doing that?" she snapped. The angelic mask she so loved to wear fell away as the cold-hearted murderer beneath finally looked out and realized that something was very wrong.

Or very right, depending on your perspective.

"I've already told you"—I paused to wag my finger—"I'm not a demon. Just as you are still only a blood Fae."

"That's preposterous—"

"Is it?" I purred. She was seeing red, but her bag of tricks was running empty. "I think you're only just realizing that I'm telling you the truth. I am the same as I've always been. A primordial of magic." I waited, letting that sink in, continuing only when she opened her mouth to speak. "And by using your blood magic to kill me, I also hold that power now too. Which would make us truly equal, if not for one *little* thing." Her features had gone stark white. Her pulse was through the roof and anxiety was clawing its way up her throat. She was well and truly scared.

She was right to be.

"You killed my mate, and to bring him back I accidentally called on a favor from the Seelie. Do you know what happened then? Do you know what she did?" Her lips moved, but no sound came out. Her mind was working a million miles an hour to keep up. "She tied my body to his using rune magic. Directly on my skin." I turned a fraction for her to see the runes and she began shaking. "Yes, you're a clever girl, aren't you?" I mocked coldly. "Figured out that I now have the one and only thing that can beat you?"

"You won't do it," she said, barely attempting to taunt me, though it fell short on her breathless lips.

"Oh?" I asked. "And why is that?"

"Because I tied the Horsemen's lives to mine. If anything kills me, they'll die too." She was so smug that it infuriated me.

"You think that only just occurred to me?" I asked her. She blinked, not saying a word. "I'm not the fool you take me for. You're selfish. Rotten. As much as you think yourself above all others, you build in safety precautions, just in case," I said. "But this time they won't save you."

The Sins took in a collective gasp. No one had seen it coming. That was the beauty of it. The unpredictability.

"You wouldn't do anything that would kill your mates."

"Who said anything about killing them?" Both my eyebrows rose as she tried to control her expression and manage the emotions riding her. She was as much a slave to herself as Josh had been, and in the end, what goes around comes around.

"You look confused, so I'm going to spell it out for you," I told her. "Rune magic is so very special. It's both the one magic that can stop you and the one magic you don't possess. I can deflect you. I can cage you. I can do a great number of things around you—even to you—but you won't pick up the magic that way." I lifted my hand and began to draw. A blue luminescence followed my finger. It was the essence of my soul, and I painted the symbol of an upside-down lotus with it. "When they grant a rune of protection for a favor owed, it is the receiver's magic that is used when it is time to call upon it. I learned this in New Orleans after the tangle I had with La Dan Bia. I saved a Seelie woman's life and she granted me a favor. When I called upon it, it was my magic that pulled her into Hell. Hers wasn't strong enough to get in or out." Next, I drew a skull shrouded in shadow. She still hadn't figured it out yet. "I made a deal with that same woman. She gave me Seth's Wisdom. Do you know what that is?" The last symbol was a modified biohazard sign. She recognized them, but she still hadn't figured out what I was doing with them. No one did.

"It allows me to relive every Seelie ancestor's life that has ever cast it. In the span of four days I lived through thousands of years, and for what you have done to the Seelie alone you deserve to pay, but I don't have the patience to extend this out much longer," I said. Then I began drawing one last symbol. This one was important because it wasn't Seth's Wisdom that gave me this idea.

It was Sinumpa.

At a certain point I had to wonder if she knew what this would bring about—if she knew that is was this rune that changed everything.

I poured everything I had into that rune. Every hope. Every fear. Every bit of me that I could. I gave it my all, and when my fingers lifted, the three Horsemen dropped.

It all happened so quickly after that.

"What have you done?" Lilith screeched. It pained me to do it to them, but that pain would be temporary. I appeased myself with that knowledge as a slow realization dawned on her.

"The very first life I lived was Eve's, your sister." I paused. The power to silence three of the Horsemen was immense and keeping it up this long wasn't easy, but I needed to get this out. Not just for me. But for Eve too. "I saw what you told her. I lived the horror through her eyes when you said you were going to take the beast from Lucifer, and I lived every gory detail thereafter. I know exactly how you planned to use the Sins, but they were too strong, and you were too weak. You improvised with Lucifer originally, and because of it you learned you couldn't hold the power of the primordial yourself. You needed someone to hold it for you. To bear the brunt of the darkness." The rune of silence became downright crushing, but I was reaching the end of this sorry tale. "Eve was a kind girl, a bit of a pushover with you, but even she wasn't willing to let Lucifer die for your delusions. She threatened to tell him, and you had her framed for opening the portal *you* used to talk to God. She was cast out of Hell and went mad, but not before she gave her memories to Seth—and his children gave them to me."

This was it. The end. The moment that I didn't just kill her.

Oh, no. I did something worse.

"I've silenced the Horsemen, which I'm sure by now you've realized also cuts off your connection to the beast. Which means you can no longer protect yourself with my magic. I'd ask if you had any last words, but I don't care even if you did."

I let go. She screamed. Oh, she screamed.

I listened to every single note as I tore her soul straight from her chest and consumed it whole.

And after thousands of years, Lilith's reign in Hell finally ended.

CHAPTER TWENTY-SEVEN

SHE SPENT SO LONG TERRORIZING the world that when it ended there was only silence. It dripped from the ceiling and spanned the length between her body and me.

Lilith was not dead. She was gone.

Her soul didn't go beyond the veil because there was not a soul to be had. She was destroyed indefinitely, but her body remained, because her body is what kept them alive.

Without a soul, the body itself would wither and die rapidly.

It would, if not for one thing.

The beast.

Her soul was never taken into Lilith. She couldn't have held the beast if she tried. Now she was an empty vessel still tied to the Horsemen. I didn't have to lift a finger to prompt it—I simply had to lift the silence.

And as the runes I'd drawn began fading into the distance, the heavy smothering of that power dwindled too. I eased my grips on the last of it, sucking in a heavy breath as my knees shook and collapsed. The shuddering crack that ran through me echoed in the empty hall.

Then she spoke.

"Ruby?" a neutral voice said. It no longer sounded anything like the voice of the monster it belonged to before.

"Hello, Beast," I replied softly with a true smile. Free of the rage and pain and destruction. "This must be very strange for you."

"She took me," the beast said. There was confusion in her voice. "I lost my light. I lost *you*."

My throat closed up and I began to crawl. No one moved an inch as I pushed against the straining exhaustion in me and dragged myself to her.

Curled inward, she tilted her chin to look up at me. It was Lilith's face —undeniably—but it was not her eyes that stared out. It was not her soul that now dwelled there.

It was not her body anymore.

It was the beast's.

"I'm so sorry I wasn't strong enough the first time," I told her. Those pale lips pinched together. Displeasure. I knew her emotions as well as my own.

"Do not apologize for wrongs that you did not commit," she told me. That brought a faint grin to my lips. "You have freed *us* of her black magic. You did what no other before you could. Do not apologize, for you are a true Queen worthy of me."

I nodded slowly, a single piece of me healing with her words. I wrapped my arms tight around the shoulders of my other half, and the tears began to flow. She did not cry. She was not capable of such emotion, and I understood that. Slim pale arms wrapped around me in return, though, clutching me to her just as I held her to me.

There were other arms then. Other hands. Other bodies.

I smelled seduction and sin as whiskery lips placed a short kiss to my lips, promising of so much more. Allistair tasted of scotch and honey and my own salty tears. I cried even harder as a fair head leaned down over my shoulder, Rysten's sunshine hair tickling my face as it stuck to my wet skin. Laran's warm hands grasped my waist, holding me as close as he could while huddled on the floor with me at an awkward angle—and then there was Julian. My white knight. He kneeled behind the beast and reached past her to grab my chin, tilting my head. We worked in perfect sync as I parted my lips, kissing him with abandon. A wild war cry sounded as Bandit ran at full speed, leaping to land right in the thick of things with a clash of fur and nails. The beast let out a huff but didn't make a move to stop him from clawing his way between us and settling on our chests with a purr of contentment.

A mighty groan from far above us had me pausing. I looked from each of the Horsemen, to the beast, to the ceiling—where a series of booms blasted from the rafters like thunder.

"What is going on?" I asked, my weak legs protesting as I attempted to stand. Julian reached down and plucked me from the ground, clasping one arm around my back and one under my knees.

"It's the Brimstone City," Moira said. The ceiling cracked and pieces began dropping. "It's falling."

"Devil-damned bitch," I cursed. I couldn't have one fucking moment of peace, could I? "She put in a fail-safe, didn't she?"

It was the beast that nodded once and said, "If you killed her body, you would have killed the Horsemen. She didn't think she would die, but she planned for it. The Brimstone City is indeed falling."

"Can you stop it?" I asked her.

"Can you?" she replied.

Shit. No. No, I couldn't. My powers had been completely exhausted. I was unable to stand on my own two feet. There was no way I'd be able to hold a falling city.

"What options do we have?" I asked, looking between the Sins. Their faces were grave.

"There is no time to evacuate all of Inferna," Lamia said. "It is simply too large." Abandoning the hundreds of thousands of people that lived here wasn't an option to me. There had to be another way.

"Could you blast the city apart?" I asked Moira. Her eyes widened.

"Are you crazy?" she demanded.

"Sometimes," I answered. "Can you?"

"No!" She looked at the ceiling as if judging the possibilities. "If I managed to somehow break it apart, we all would be crushed beneath the rubble, as would the rest of Inferna."

My head landed against Julian's chest as I scrambled and searched my brain for something—anything inside all of Seth's Wisdom. But the problem was that this was blood magic; a blood spell. Something I didn't know how to use yet.

"There's got to be something we can—"

A crackle of light. A flair of color. An ember guided by a phantom hand.

An ancient rune to open a portal between worlds appeared in violet.

Sinumpa.

She hadn't abandoned us after all. My heart pounded and my palms grew slick. The incandescent rune exploded in a bang, tearing a hole between the realms. I put a hand over my eyes to shield them against the blinding light.

A pair of boots clicked. I parted my fingers, glimpsing between them.

Backlit by the shimmering glow, Sinumpa came striding in. She took one look and flashed a Cheshire grin. "It seems I've arrived just in time."

"You came back…" Moira murmured. Stunned. "Can you stop the Brimstone City from falling?"

"No," Sinumpa said. She hooked her thumb over her shoulder, pointing to the portal behind her. "But they can."

Behind her, people started pouring out of the portal one by one.

Morvaen came first, followed by Donnach and many more. I didn't know what to say as the Seelie came into Hell, leaving the safety of Earth to come to a land that was going to be crushed in a matter of minutes. Dozens. Hundreds. They came, and when the portal finally closed…they kneeled as one. Every single man, woman, and child that crossed through dropped on all fours in front of me.

I squeezed Julian's bicep, our silent communication for him to let me down. I approached Morvaen on shaking feet. I got on my knees and touched her shoulder, concern leaking through my voice. "What have you done?"

"You and I made a deal…Ruby," she said, testing my name on her tongue. "I gave you Seth's Wisdom and you promised to let us come home."

"But the Brimstone City is falling," I told her. "You've doomed your people."

"We have not." It was not her who answered, but Donnach. He got to his feet and the hundreds of Seelie followed in his stead. "You and my sister were not the only ones with an agreement." He glanced at Sinumpa who stood to the side watching the ceiling crumble away.

"You made a deal with Morvaen to gain the ancient knowledge of the Seelie," the white-haired Fae said. "I struck a deal with Donnach. In return for my ceding the province of Lust, he would stop the falling city. We have to live here, after all."

"You…I…how…what the fuck, Sin?" I stammered, looking for words. "You didn't have any guarantees I would beat Lilith, but you bet on it all the same?"

I wasn't sure if I should be flattered. She'd already proven to be a gambler of fate. Who's to say she wasn't on her way to being as crazy as Lilith had gone.

I'd never seen her look so young or carefree; a lightness dancing in her eyes for the first time. Looking at her, you'd never guess a city was falling above us. "I knew you had it in you, but I couldn't tell you anything. So long as Lilith was alive, I was bound by so many blood oaths that would have not only taken my life, but the lives of all my siblings. I couldn't do that to them anymore than you could kill your Horsemen. We all made sacrifices, girl, and once we fix this you are going to do what you've said you would all along."

My lips parted as I breathed, "And what is that?"

Sinumpa stared. Measuring. Weighing my worth. Judging the girl I once was and the woman I had become.

"Make the world a better place, and if you have to, burn out the rot with your own hands."

I stared back and then I nodded. For all she had done, I didn't know if I could forgive her—it was still fresh and raw and much too soon. But that didn't mean that I didn't understand her. Why she had done it. Why she was willing to sacrifice so much for me to become the woman she knew I could be. I was a child born to not just flame, but magic. Shaped and molded by the Six Sins, honed to be a queen; in creating me, they lost the girl I was. She had kept much hidden from me, I sensed her regret in that —if only for a second.

Sinumpa was a proud woman that would not apologize.

I was aged by the things I had survived through, and I would not forgive. Not *yet*.

But we reached an understanding.

And for that, Hell would go on.

She lifted her hands and began to draw. They all did. Every single Seelie. They drew in shades of violet and crimson and navy and every color that existed. They wielded their magic with such unity that demons could never manage.

And as they put the floating city back in the sky, I realized that they had something all of demon kind could learn from.

A unity born not only of loyalty and purpose, but of strength.

The strength to survive.

****JULIAN****

She'd changed. I could see it in her eyes. As she paced before the bed, I noticed a grace in her movements that hadn't been there before. There was a worry that troubled her despite winning the war. A weariness that only age and time could give you.

My woman was not the twenty-three years her body was anymore.

She had become something far older in a span of days—doing the unthinkable to save us.

I didn't have words to convey how freedom tasted after being reduced to a prisoner in my own mind. I was simply content to watch her and to know that no matter what happened from here, no matter how much damage had been done…we would find our way through it.

Together.

"Killing her was too kind for what she did to you," she spat. It wasn't just fire in her anymore. If you watched closely you could see the shadow too. The darkness that had settled next to the flame. That wasn't going away anytime soon.

"You made her pay…" Allistair murmured softly.

"It wasn't enough," she whispered. "It wasn't—"

"Stop," the beast ordered. Ruby looked over to where she sat upon a chaise in the Queen's Suite. The dresses Lilith loved had been replaced by leather trousers and long shirts. She wore fur-lined boots to go with the discarded jacket on the floor. The white hair of the woman I'd hated had been shaved from her head, leaving her bald.

The beast was more content for it.

She didn't like being without Ruby, but if she had to reside in this body for now, she planned to make it her own.

Ruby stared at her and something silent passed between the two. The beast's flat expression softened for a moment. "You saved us," she said to Ruby. "You ended what so many before you could not. Do not dwell on what you could have done. Focus on what you will do now."

"I will never forgive myself for the things she did to them," Ruby said softly. Tears stained her cheeks as she cried utterly silent. These were not the racking sobs of loss, but the cold feeling of shame and regret.

"You did not do those things to them," the beast growled.

"But they happened," Ruby snapped. "They happened and I wish they hadn't. I wish I could have done something sooner. I wish…"

I rose from the corner of the bed and pulled her to me. "Listen to me." I leaned forward and brushed a lock of her hair away from her face as she leaned into me, resting her cheek on my chest. "The beast is right. What was done, was done. You cannot change it. You could not prevent it. You gave everything you could, Ruby…" I swallowed, searching for the words to help her. To help us. "And in the end, you saved us all. You made sure that she can never hurt anyone again. That gives us closure." It was the truth, every word. "You did that."

She looked up at me, her cheeks colored a light blue from the flush of tears.

"Will it ever stop?" she asked me. "The rage. The despair. This feeling of powerlessness. Will they ever go away?"

I opened my mouth, but I didn't know what to say. I didn't know what to tell her. She couldn't just get over it. That wasn't an option. She'd lived through too much. Seen too much for that to ever be possible.

So, I gave her the only thing I could, even knowing it might hurt her.

"No, my girl, I don't think they will." The look in her eyes…it was crushing. Truly soul-crushing. "But with time, it will lessen. They say that time heals all wounds and that's not quite true. It softens the intensity of them. Until it's only a memory of the pain, but as you've learned, memories can still be quite painful." She nodded and I knew she was thinking of the Seelie then. Of the thousands of lives she'd lived. "It will get better, though. For all of us."

Both Rysten and Allistair nodded. Laran was battling a different sort of turmoil. Much like Ruby, he blamed himself because he was spared from Lilith's touch. He was not the type to grieve as Ruby did, but he had his own way. We all did.

"Do you promise?" she asked, her voice thin from exhaustion.

"I promise."

And I meant it. It would get better, for all of us.

Her eyelids fluttered as the day started to take its toll. Allistair stepped in front of us and held out his arms. *"May I?"* he asked silently. I picked her up and handed her over to him.

He held her with a reverence, whispering words meant only for her ears as he carried her to bed. As he placed her in the center and moved the blankets to cover her, her hand snapped out, grabbing his wrist faster than the blink of an eye.

"Stay," she pleaded. "I don't want to be alone right now."

We looked at each other and I knew it then. After this there would be no separating again. Not for safety, or protection, or worry over her life.

Simply because we needed her, and she needed us.

To heal and to live—truly live.

And in my mind I whispered to them all, even the beast. *"You will never be alone again."*

MOIRA

"You're leaving again, aren't you?" I asked into the darkness. Below me, Inferna was celebrating with a party that took over the streets and raged into the early morning hours. But above—on the rooftop where I stood— there was only me, my thoughts, and *her.*

"I've done what I set out to do," Sinumpa replied. "The Brimstone City will not fall again. Hell is free. There is nothing more for me here."

"You know," I said, turning away from the railing, "you kept that whole bit about the city falling to yourself when you left the first time." Her eyes were shadowed, but a weary smile sat on her lips.

"Another oath," she answered vaguely. I nodded.

"And telling Ruby that your siblings were the reason you left?" I asked her, more curious than anything.

A single sigh. It said everything she didn't.

"They were part of it," she settled on. "Not all, but part. Ruby didn't need to know what my being there would have cost her. She's angry—rightfully so—and I don't need her approval to move on."

"Another gift?" I turned my cheek a fraction, grinning at her. A cool breeze whistled around us. This high up it was a world away from the festivities below.

"Maybe," Sin conceded. "She doesn't blame me. Not truly. But having somewhere to aim it now that Lilith is gone…it will help."

I nodded because she wasn't wrong. "Thank you." Her right eyebrow twitched and I elaborated. "Thank you for all that you did. For her…and for me."

Sinumpa stood there and it was like she saw the sun for the first time in a very long time.

"You're welcome…Moira," she spoke softly. Intimately. I liked the sound of my name on her lips.

"Enjoy your freedom, Sinumpa," I told her. It was a goodbye, but not forever. Something told me our paths would cross again. One day.

She turned and then paused. Over her shoulder, she said, "Until we meet again."

No, not forever. Just for now.

I stayed on those rafters until the break of dawn. A thunderous applause broke out over Inferna at the start of a new day, and I knew it was time.

Time to finally answer that voice that had been speaking to me.

Time to answer the Cerberus's call.

CHAPTER TWENTY-EIGHT

Those early days of settling were not easy. Many long and hard meetings had to be held about the fate of Hell, the Seelie, the Brimstone City—and where I fit into all of this. Tempers were short and nights were long. I savored every moment of it because you never knew when the end would come. We were immortal, but not infallible. Lilith had proven that.

The Sins themselves were as divided in opinions as the divisive lines that were drawn between their provinces. Sinumpa had stepped down and vanished into the night, leaving Lust without a representative. Donnach filled that space upon my own suggestion and tensions were smoother for it. He appreciated my willingness to give them their own seat of power and it went a long way in easing the Fae's worries. The Seelie were given one of the most ravaged parts of this world, and because of that I was going with them when they journeyed there to help with the restoration. I wanted to truly see my mother's land and make this as painless a transition as I could.

My Horsemen were coming with me, but Moira was not. As much as it hurt us to part from one another, she felt a call to go to the Brimstone City and oversee that rehabilitation as an ambassador on my behalf. Without a true successor to that province, the Sins and I saw it best to hand over the task to the only person who was up for the job. Lilith had kept her children and people as slaves. The physical damage to the city during the falling was sparse compared to the damage to their minds. As a survivor of abuse, like called to like. It didn't hurt that the Library of Pride had the most in-depth knowledge on legions in all of Hell.

It saddened me, but she had a familiar of her own now who would keep her more than safe. I smiled over at the Cerberus who stood smartly beside my best friend. They'd tied a blue bow around its neck to make it look less frightening for the ceremony. Not that it lasted long. Bandit had taken a liking to the three-headed female Moira named Fate.

The dog was scared of its own shadow, but if she thought you were trying to harm Moira…familiars don't fuck around.

Yeah, Moira would be in good hands.

I smoothed my dress nervously, running my hands over the feathery soft fabric. After all I'd been through, I refused to wear white this day. It was no longer the color of purity in my mind, and there was nothing pure about me anyway. Instead, I'd opted for a deep blue floor-length gown, the same color as the jewel-toned sky and sea.

My feet were bare as I padded down the long aisle. All around me the demons and Fae of Inferna looked on with respect and happiness. I felt their joy, and while it was fucking nerve-racking to take this last step, they gave me my strength. I stared straight ahead. On the left side of the aisle stood Laran, Allistair, Julian, and Rysten. None of them had truly recovered from these last months of being hunted. We were still seeing shadows when there were none, but after all that had happened, it would take time to get better. The pressure of the beast had changed each of them inextricably those last days.

Julian was gentler. Rysten was rugged. Allistair was…struggling. We all were, but he—more so than the others—was struggling with what had happened to them during their time with Lilith. Struggling with having his choices taken from him. Struggling with what he was as a demon and what he thought I needed him to be as a man. He lost himself in me every night, trying to forget what was done, but there was no forgetting…

Immortality was a blessing and a curse. We would never forget what brought us here, but we would cherish every moment we had. Every image. Every touch. Every sound. Every feeling. We cherished them more.

"Ruby?" Moira asked, drawing my attention. I'd stopped in the center of the aisle. Taking a deep breath, I continued to walk the rest of the way, turning my head and my thoughts to the Sins.

While there was still much to be done—and it would not come easy—

the one thing they'd all agreed on was my right to become Queen. I'd earned it, or so they said. It was a bittersweet day for me; I would ascend, but the beast would not be with me. Much as we tried to find a way to free her from Lilith's body, we still hadn't discovered a way to free the Horsemen if we did. Neither the beast nor I were willing to risk their lives on anything short of a guarantee, no matter how much it pained both of us to be apart.

She stood at the top of the stairs, watching me. A secret smile twisting her lips that the rest of the world would mistake for a grimace. Not me. For a jealous being by nature, she held no qualms with this arrangement. In her mind we would find a way to reunite us, eventually. It was an oddly optimistic view, truth be told. Not that I told her that.

"Focus, Ruby. This day is important," she chastised in my mind.

I pressed my lips together to hide my own smile as I started up the stairs. At the top of the dais stood the Sins. The women who had raised me.

Hela was the first to step forward. Her flaming red gown was the same shade as her hair. Lightning struck high above us. The throne room still hadn't been fixed and most of the ceiling was missing. I didn't mind the open air one bit.

"A week ago, I watched the young woman before me triumph over our greatest fear. Today, she stands before us to receive the blessing of the Sins and become the next Queen. Ahnika, what say you?"

The Sin of Sloth stepped forward, her light green skin beautiful against the black floor-length number she wore. She came to stand before me and pass her judgement. "I was the last Sin to meet you, Ruby. The last to leave my mark. I have watched you grow from a petulant young girl to a true leader. You are many things, girl, but indolent isn't one of them."

I nodded my thanks to her and we hugged. This was a slight deviation to the ceremony I was supposed to have. Tradition said they would brand me, but me being what I was, I didn't want it. I already had enough power at my fingertips that I needed to master, and unlike my Seelie magic, nothing else came with an ancient rune that could teach me every aspect in a matter of days.

Ahnika stepped back and said, "Saraphine, what say you?"

I'd known this she-demon as an old woman named Martha in my time on Earth, but here in Hell she was known as the fiercest of the Sins. Her long blonde hair trailed in the breeze as she stepped forward. "You are the daughter I always wanted. Those years I got to watch you grow in the plastic seat of a dingy diner have been the greatest of my very long life, child. You are kind, but you don't let people walk all over you. You stand up for what is right, even when it is not easy. You've given up everything to become what we needed you to be. My girl, you are many wonderful things, and you hold no greed in your heart."

When I hugged her, it felt like home. Black coffee and bacon, the scent of fresh asphalt and baked apple pie. I clutched her slim shoulders tight as tears pricked the corners of my eyes. Saraphine was crying when she stepped away and said with a heavy voice, "Merula, what say you?"

Merula had been like a mother to me once upon a time. She was as strict as they come, but in her heart she truly loved children. I had always believed she truly loved me in her own way. "I was the first Sin to be allowed the privilege of raising you, and for ten years I did just that. I watched you grow from a babe to a scruffy-faced tomboy, into the beautiful woman you are today." She smiled and there was a sadness there. "Envy is not something we could easily test you on, but I watched you with Iona when you first came to Hell. I watched how she envied and pushed and took from you. But you never succumbed to the same jealousy I myself cannot always control, just as you never coveted what others had on Earth. You are many things, my child, but envious is not one of them."

I hugged her and I meant it, even though she'd sent Iona to me. While my heart was hardened and the darkness within had not abated, I'd found ways to not let it control me. To not let the ways I'd changed dictate my own happiness. Some days were better than others—but I was trying—and that's what mattered.

She stepped away and said, "Lamia, what say you?"

I'd known her as Sadie in my old life. She had been the house mother at the orphanage I spent most of my teen years in, and while she hadn't been nearly as hands-on as Merula or Hela, she'd let me grow from afar. I met her toe-to-toe. "I watched you experience many hardships while you were with me. Both of you," she said and glanced to Moira. "Neither of you believed you had any power, and you were content. You did not covet your neighbor. You did not take more than you needed of anything in life. Even here today, you reject the ceremony to take our brands because you do not want the power it would bring you. Ruby Morningstar, you are many things, but you are not a glutton."

I hugged Lamia knowing without a shadow of doubt that she saw more than she ever said back then. Our connection was brief before she was stepping away and said in a steady voice, "Hela, what say you?"

My blood fizzled with nerves as she stepped forward to stand in front of me. "Blue, I wish I could say that wrath was not a sin you are afflicted with, but it would be a lie." I inhaled sharply and half the room took a collective gasp before she smiled. "You have a fire inside you that burns. I saw it when you were younger, and over the past few months it has only grown. If you let it, this fire would consume you—and us." She paused, her index finger guided my chin upwards to look her straight in the eyes. "But, as you well know, it is not the great power itself that matters, but what you *do* with it. You've used that strength to become a woman that I myself wish I could be. Ruby, my friend, you have wrath, but you are not a slave to it."

I couldn't hold in the tears as they dotted the corner of my eyes. My heart had split apart in pain and been forged back together by fire, but never had I wept from happiness. I let her go and wiped my tears with the palm of my hand, turning to face the beast. She was the final decider.

Without being told, she stepped up and took the spot Hela had vacated. In her hands was a crown of glittering black metal with sapphire gemstones. She held it between us and I placed my hands over hers. "I made this crown for you myself, in the hope that I might one day wear it with you." There was a sadness in her voice that was unmistakable, but there was hope too. She was becoming more…human. I wondered if she realized it. "We will be united again. Our soul will heal, but in the mean-time, you rise, and you will rule. There is no other as worthy as you." She lifted the crown and I took the cue to drop to my knees before her. The crown was heavy on my head, but not crushing. I no longer felt constricted or confined. I chose this.

"Rise, Ruby Morningstar, Queen of Hell," she declared.

I pushed back on the balls of my feet and turned to face the people— my people. Sinumpa's words came to mind as I looked out to them, and I knew deep down that I'd found what and who I was always meant to be. A queen that would serve first and rule second. A leader that would change this world.

"Long live the Queen!" the beast projected. Every voice in the room and the hallway beyond and the streets below heard her as a rallying cry rang out so loud that even Heaven might have heard it.

"Long live the Queen!"

In my heart of hearts, I knew then that this wasn't just the end of an age. It was the beginning. My beginning, and theirs.

Life was a gift and I had no intention of wasting it.

As I looked down at each of my Horsemen, I whispered those three little words in their minds. When I said them now, it was because I wanted to—because I meant it—because the best was yet to come.

**** M O I R A ****

Three months later…

I let out a yawn that ruffled the pages of the ancient text. I'd already read
the damn thing three times, but whatever answers the Sins had claimed it
held didn't seem to be there.

My hand slammed the book shut and I pushed back in my chair,
standing to head for the door. I strode down the aisle and out of the library,
the heavy doors closing behind me. The night air was cool, almost chilled.
This high in the clouds it was always that way, though. I stuffed my hands
in the pockets of my leather jacket and took a walk.

I wandered aimlessly for a bit, nodding to the blood Fae and demons
that also inhabited this city with me. In my time here, I'd grown to have
quite the name. I rather liked it, if I was being honest.

But the loneliness could be crushing at times.

I'd seen Ruby only just last week for spring equinox. We'd celebrated in
Inferna but stayed in Lamia's mansion this time instead. Months had
passed and the reconstruction was still underway at Hela's palace. Which
was fine by us since Lamia did indeed host the best parties. Ruby and the
Horsemen had come out in full glory, looking far better than when I'd last
seen her. I knew she was happy. I felt it, even though phantom whispers of

destruction still dwelled within her. The beast and those mates of hers balanced my best friend well, as did the bloody raccoon.

I scrubbed a hand over my face and let out a whistle into the wind.

The people of the floating city heard my call and moved as the giant three-headed dog barreled down the streets. Behind her, three little monsters squealed in delight.

They had three heads like my Fate, but their faces were fucking raccoons. It wasn't enough that he'd impregnated my damn dog. No, he'd given her three mutant trash pandas that never left me the fuck alone. Ruby thought they were so adorable with their little faces and blue fur.

Terrors. They were devil-damned terrors.

Fate came rolling up to me and planted a slobbering kiss on my face, her three brats nipping at her heels. I was looking forward to the day I could pass them onto Ruby. As it was, Fate still had to feed them, and they were doing wonders for the kids here. Lilith's youngest daughter was a three-year-old half-banshee who was fearful of most things—except three-headed dogs, apparently. Having the monster-babies around was helping her and some of the other kids. Enough so that I let Ruby talk me into keeping them a little longer…but at twelve weeks, these bad boys were going to her.

I grasped a handful of Fate's fur and swung myself onto her back. I could just fly if I felt like it, but this was more comfortable for both the Cerberus and me. Here on a floating city, thousands of feet above with nothing but wind, we took all the comfort in each other we could.

She let out a howl and took off down the steps, her spawn trailed behind us as we traveled half the city before Fate came to a stop. One her heads lolled, giving me the biggest puppy eyes. I groaned, pinching the bridge of my nose.

"Fine." I threw my hands up in the air. "You can come, but the ugly trash pandas gotta stay outside. Got it?" The middle head let out a whine and I groaned, looking to the night sky above me. I would pray, but given my best friend was the very deity these people prayed to, that wasn't going to do me much good. Her other familiar was the reason I had this problem to begin with. "Ugh, whatever. Just keep them quiet, will ya?" The third head nodded while she wagged her tail. I leaned in to scratch her between the shoulder blades, then turned to walk into the bar. The swinging shutters hit the walls with a wild bang. Fate and the three stooges came in behind me and went to curl up in the corner of the lounge.

Demon bars on Earth had been downright normal compared to the ones in Hell. They let literally anything in, because you never knew who or what was a familiar. Mine were regulars and well acquainted with the massive dog bed in the corner. A generous contribution from an "anonymous" donor, i.e. Ruby. She was worried I spent too much time alone and thought having dog beds put in wherever I frequented most was the best way to encourage me to get out.

I didn't have the heart to tell her that I had no desire to enter a relationship just yet. While it was lonely at times, I still hadn't left that place of fight or flight. I wasn't ready for anything serious right now. That's alright, though. I had Burt the bartender, and for tonight he would be enough.

"Evening, Moira. What'll it be?"

"The usual," I said, pushing the sound waves forward for my voice to carry. He smiled as I sat down at the counter and slid an oversized frosted mug of amber liquid to me. This shit was brewed from fermented white lotus and tasted like perfection. I inhaled deeply and took a long sip, exhaling on a happier note.

Sometimes it was good being me. A cold night in a pub with an open tab and Fae beer to drink was always one of those times.

My immortality had only just begun and I planned to enjoy every second of it.

EPILOGUE

"Alright, everybody," the green one said. "Tonight is the night we crown the King of Fools!" Then the other ones with opposable thumbs began grunting and stomping their feet.

"*Pffft. And they say I'm the animal,*" Bandit huffed. He rolled his eyes, settling against Fate while the banshee went on. Not far, Ruby sat with their pups.

"*Moira doesn't care for the babes,*" Fate said.

Bandit knew from his time with her that the green one was prickly. She would need to be persuaded. While Fate adored her familiar, Ruby was a far better bond mate. She enjoyed feeding him sardines and thought it was adorable when the little ones had flaming burps. Yes, she was a better bond mate.

"*Have you tried having them groom her?*" Even the green one shouldn't be able to resist that affection.

"*She complains about 'spit'.*"

"*What is spit?*" he asked. She licked him behind the ear and he let out a purr.

"*I'm not sure. It comes from licking.*"

Bandit narrowed his eyes at the green one. Ruby's four mates were standing on chairs, along with other demons. They were all covered in food.

"My person likes to be licked," Bandit said, recalling all the times her mates seemed to groom her. It was a bit excessive, though, even for him.

"Maybe she'd like it more if they were cleaning her all together," Fate mused. Bandit lifted an eyebrow and listened as Fate told him her idea. Bandit liked it. He liked it very much.

Rising up on all four paws, he stretched languidly before shrinking. He needed to blend in for this. Weaving through the crowd of drunken persons wasn't hard. Neither was finding a bucket of delicious vegetables. He was very tempted to eat some of them…maybe just a nibble.

Bandit snatched an orange off the top, stuffing it into his mouth before anyone noticed. A sly glance at Ruby said she was still preoccupied by the triplets. Good.

He grew a little in size, just enough to snatch the handle of the pail with his teeth and disappear before anyone saw him. Sneakily, Bandit dashed up the stairs to the second floor. His bucket clanked against the wooden steps, but no one paid any mind with all the cheering going on.

It only took him a moment to climb over the railing and heave the bucket onto the rafter right above the green one. Perfect. He clapped his paws together and let out a chitter. Taking great care, he grabbed a giant tomato that squished in his paws. Balancing right over her, he held the tomato out and dropped.

"What the—" she said. He grabbed an egg and tossed it.

"RUBY!" she roared. The rafters swayed a little with her annoyance. Bandit wasn't worried though. He dug through the fruits and veggies to find the litters' favorite.

Kiwi.

He threw the little green fruits off the rafters, cackling as they pelted the fuming demon. The babes followed the scent of food and left Ruby to chase the green one. They quickly caught up, despite her running, and pounced. Licking at all the delicious fruit splattered on her.

"What in the world…" Ruby frowned, looking up to where the food had come from. She spotted him and Bandit backed away slowly, hoping she wouldn't notice… "Bandit! Get down here," she called.

Welp. Fate's rumbly laugh hit his ears as he quickly scaled down the rafters and bolted through the crowd, outside and onto the street beyond. Fate came after him, followed by the triplets, and they ran through the alleys under the pale moonlit in a land that was finally at peace.

"Moira's not happy with you," Fate told him as one of the young ones hopped on her back, grabbing at the first head's ears.

Bandit let out a raucous laugh that lit the sky with blue flame while the green one's cries about *that devil-damned trash panda* followed him.

It seemed that the more things changed, the more they stayed the same.

At least where Bandit was concerned.

He was but a simple raccoon, after all. One that now had an eternity of trouble to look forward to—and with Rysten and Moira to terrorize for many years to come…

Bandit grinned into the dark shadows of the night, ready for wherever life might take him, so long as he had Ruby.

And sardines. He couldn't forget those.

The End.

—This is the end of Ruby's story. If you loved this series and want to check out more from me, going my reader's group Kel's Krew to check out the latest news on all things Kel Carpenter.—

ABOUT THE AUTHOR

Kel Carpenter is a master of werdz. When she's not reading or writing, she's traveling the world, lovingly pestering her editor, and spending time with her husband and fur-babies. She is always on the search for good tacos and the best pizza. She resides in Bethesda, MD and desperately tries to avoid the traffic.

Facebook Group
Newsletter

ACKNOWLEDGMENTS

I have so many thoughts—but not many words—for all the things I feel about finishing this series and leaving this world. A little over a year ago, an idea came to me while I was in the shower. A story about a dark queen and her four horsemen, and since then, Ruby has taken such a radically different journey than I first foresaw. I loved writing these characters and this world. It's a bittersweet moment to say goodbye to something that's eaten up every spare moment of your life for over a year, but here we are, and there's a lot of thanks I need to give to some pretty awesome people for helping me get here.

~To Analisa Denny, thank you for being my editor, for all the long conversations that you didn't need to have—but still did—for caring about my characters as much as I do. Thank you, more than anything, for being my friend. I look forward to your red pen, and whatever comes next for us.

~To Courtney Lummus, for reading every book and making it better. Thank you for supporting me and always being there.

~To my tribe of author friends: There are so many of you that I want to thank for always inspiring me and being there when I needed to talk books. Special shout-outs to Amanda Pillar, Alex Lidell, Meg Anne, and Rita Stradling. I love you guys.

~To the members of Kel's Krew: you guys have no idea how much your support has meant to me. Thank you for all the crazy gifs and raccoon posts these last months. Caitlin Thom, Sandra Portillo, Aaricka Swanson— you ladies inspired some very interesting characters that made their way into this final book. Thank you.

~To my fiancé, Matt…I love you, babe. Thank you for standing by me and helping out with all of the tedious, boring things around the house so that I have as much time as possible to write. I wouldn't have been able to do all this without you.

~To my friends and family and readers that have supported me along the way, to you I give the most thanks. I was told being an author was a pipe dream. That I would never be able to get by as a writer. But I am, because of you guys. Thank you for coming on this journey with Ruby, Moira, Julian, Rysten, Allistair, Laran, and of course—everyone's favorite —Bandit.

Thank you from the bottom of my heart.